**Maxim Jakubowski** is a Lon
born in the UK and educated
publishing, he opened the world-famous Murder One bookshop in London. He now writes full-time. He has edited over twenty-five bestselling erotic anthologies and books on erotic photography, as well as many acclaimed crime collections. His novels include *It's You That I Want to Kiss*, *Because She Thought She Loved Me* and *On Tenderness Express*, all three collected and reprinted in the USA as *Skin in Darkness*. Other books include *Life in the World of Women*, *The State of Montana*, *Kiss Me Sadly*, *Confessions of a Romantic Pornographer*, *Fools For Lust*, *I Was Waiting For You* and *Ekaterina and the Night*. In 2006 he published *American Casanova*, a major erotic novel which he edited and on which fifteen of the top erotic writers in the world have collaborated. He compiles two annual acclaimed series for the Mammoth list: *Best New Erotica* and *Best British Crime*. He is a winner of the Anthony and the Karel Awards, a frequent TV and radio broadcaster, a past crime columnist for the *Guardian* newspaper and Literary Director of London's Crime Scene Festival.

*Recent Mammoth titles*

The Mammoth Book of Irish Romance
The Mammoth Book of Alternate Histories
The Mammoth Book of Bizarre Crimes
The Mammoth Book of Special Ops Romance
The Mammoth Book of Best British Crime 8
The Mammoth Book of Sex, Drugs & Rock 'n' Roll
The Mammoth Book of Travel in Dangerous Places
The Mammoth Book of Apocalyptic SF
The Mammoth Book of Casino Games
The Mammoth Book of Sudoku
The Mammoth Book of Zombie Comics
The Mammoth Book of Men O'War
The Mammoth Book of Mindblowing SF
The Mammoth Book of New Sherlock Holmes Adventures
The Mammoth Book of The Beatles
The Mammoth Book of the Best Short SF Novels
The Mammoth Book of New IQ Puzzles
The Mammoth Book of Alternate Histories
The Mammoth Book of Regency Romance
The Mammoth Book of Paranormal Romance 2
The Mammoth Book of the World's Greatest Chess Games
The Mammoth Book of Tasteless Jokes
The Mammoth Book of New Erotic Photography
The Mammoth Book of Best New SF 23
The Mammoth Book of Best New Horror 21
The Mammoth Book of Great British Humour
The Mammoth Book of Drug Barons
The Mammoth Book of Scottish Romance
The Mammoth Book of Women's Erotic Fantasies
The Mammoth Book of Tattoo Art

THE MAMMOTH BOOK OF

# The Best of Best New Erotica

Edited by Maxim Jakubowski

RUNNING PRESS
PHILADELPHIA · LONDON

Constable & Robinson Ltd
55–56 Russell Square
London WC1B 4HP
www.constablerobinson.com

First published in the UK by Robinson,
an imprint of Constable & Robinson Ltd., 2012



A copy of the British Library Cataloguing in Publication data is available from the British Library

UK ISBN: 978-1-78033-092-1 (paperback)
UK ISBN: 978-1-78033-093-8 (ebook)

1 3 5 7 9 10 8 6 4 2

First published in the United States in 2012 by Running Press Book Publishers,
A Member of the Perseus Books Group



US ISBN: 978-0-7624-4435-9
US Library of Congress number: 2011930507

9 8 7 6 5 4 3 2 1
Digit on the right indicates the number of this printing

Running Press Book Publishers
2300 Chestnut Street
Philadelphia, PA 19103-4371

Visit us on the web!
www.runningpress.com

Printed and bound in the UK

# Contents

# Acknowledgements

CHAPTERS IN A PAST LIFE © 1993 by Marilyn Jaye-Lewis

L'ENFER © 1992 by Alice Joanou

EROTOPHOBIA © 1998 by O'Neil De Noux

ENTERTAINING MR ORTON © 1998 by Poppy Z. Brite

WORTH MORE THAN A THOUSAND WORDS © 1998 by Lawrence Schimel

MRS FOX © 1996 by Michael Crawley

SWEATING PROFUSELY IN MÉRIDA: A MEMOIR © 1994 by Carol Queen

TAROT © 1998 by Florence Dugas

BLACK LILY © 1996 by Thomas S. Roche

THE PRESCRIPTION © 1998 by Carol Anne Davis

PLAGUE LOVERS © 1998 by Lucy Taylor

NIGHT MOVES © 2000 by Michael Perkins

MOVEMENTS © 2000 by Michael Hemmingson

DO WHAT YOU LOVE © 2000 by Susannah Indigo

ONLY CONNECT © 2000 by Lauren Henderson

BOTTOMLESS ON BOURBON © 2000 by Maxim Jakubowski

PAYING MY FRIENDS FOR SEX © 2001 by Matt Thorne

GATORS © 2001 by Vicki Hendricks

THE COLOUR OF LUST © 2002 by M. Christian

THE END OF DAPHNE GREENWOOD'S TRAVEL CAREER © 2003 by Tara Alton

EYE OF THE BEHOLDER © 2003 by Mark Timlin

AMERICAN HOLIDAYS © 2003 by Mike Kimera

SCREEN PLAY © 2004 by A. F. Waddell

SECRETLY WISHING FOR RAIN © 2004 by Claude Lalumière

WHAT HAPPENED TO THAT GIRL © 2005 by Marie Lyn Bernard

BLINDED © 2005 by Donna George Storey

THE PENIS OF MY BELOVED © 2006 by Ian Watson and Roberto Quaglia

NOTHING BUT THIS © 2006 by Kristina Lloyd

DON'T LOOK BACK © 2006 by Alison Tyler

THE EROTICA WRITER'S HUSBAND © 2007 by Jennifer D. Munro

# Introduction

Maxim Jakubowski

Back in 1991 I approached Nick Robinson with a view to convince him to add a volume of erotica to the then fledgling but already successful Mammoth line. It took a couple of years of repeated insistence to overcome his initial resistance to the idea. If crime and mystery, science fiction and fantasy, thrillers, spy tales and horror were the obvious genres to include in the Mammoth list, I pleaded, why not erotica? A literary genre which was similarly looked down at by the establishment but had good commercial prospects and, I argued, a ready-made public and intrinsically had as much quality as other fields of popular writing, together with a prestigious heritage which had been in recent decades muddied by the more down-market and exploitative side of most publishers' production.

Although he and his team were at first reluctant, they finally gave me the go ahead and *The Mammoth Book of Erotica* first appeared in 1994, with Carroll & Graf in the USA enthusiastically taking on the reins of the American edition. The book was a surprising success from the outset, going into several reprints and being taken up by a variety of book clubs. Having the field to myself, I was in the privileged situation of being able to select stories and extracts from some of my favourite contemporary writers who had not shied away from writing about sex in an explicit manner in their work. I included Clive Barker, Leonard Cohen, Anne Rice, Samuel R. Delany, Marco Vassi, Ramsey Campbell, Kathy Acker and many others. I wanted to validate my contention that erotica was not just sex scenes but could feature plot, solid characterization and emotions alongside the expected hydraulics. Sex was and always will be an integral part of the human make-up and I do strongly feel it is essentially dishonest to censor it out of our writings for the sake of propriety or social convenience. Further, I was of the opinion that we were going through a Golden Age of erotica that was as good as many of the classics from the 1930s or the 1950s, after which the field had seemingly taken a step back. The only problem was that it remained hidden within publishers' general lists and was most often not highlighted as such. In all fairness this was not the case in France, for example, where major authors like Apollinaire, André Pieyre de Mandiargues, Aragon, Bernard Noël, Pierre Louys suffered no critical backlash for their outstanding erotic tales and had been succeeded by more modern practitioners like Alicia Reyes, Françoise Rey, Vanessa Duriès and others. Not surprisingly I had spent many years in France and my outlook had no doubt been influenced by this healthy state of affairs.

But in the English language, since the heyday of Henry Miller and Anaïs Nin, erotic writing had remained in the shadows, with the sole efforts of Brian Kirby's Essex House imprint and authors like Marco Vassi, Michael Perkins and David Meltzer toiling with little critical feedback in a faraway forest, away from the throng.

By highlighting what had been happening for many years in one place, I hoped erotica would again be taken seriously.

It was.

It is now over a decade and a half later, and the Mammoth Erotica series has reached fifteen volumes. Robinson Publishing has now become Constable & Robinson, merging successfully with one of Britain's most respected and oldest imprints, while in the USA, Carroll & Graf was integrated into the Perseus Group and the series now appears there under the Running Press imprint.

Last year we celebrated the tenth anniversary volume of the series, although technically it has actually featured fifteen volumes, as the first five (*The Mammoth Book of Erotica*, *The Mammoth Book of New Erotica*, *The Mammoth Book of International Erotica*, *The Mammoth Book of Historical Erotica* and *The Mammoth Book of Short Erotic Novels*) were not numbered. Sales are now into the hundreds of thousands worldwide and I believe erotica is now held in higher esteem in the world of letters and books as a result.

It is now, of course, a much more crowded area as success naturally attracts imitations. But, on the other hand, the added publishing opportunities have allowed new editors and dozens of writers to make a name for themselves in the field and new talent is emerging on a yearly basis, which personally delights me.

The only drawback, and this is very much a personal bee in the bonnet of mine, is that this profusion of erotica has also diluted the impact of the writing and too many of the new writers see the genre as an excuse for minor sexual fantasies or wish-fulfilment scenarios, which they affectionately treat jokingly as mere smut, with little of the psychological depth or naked emotions I, for one, expect in good writing. Both the plethora of publishing opportunities and the lack of quality control on the expanding internet scene and in self-published ebooks is much to blame for this sorry state of affairs.

But enough of criticism. This is a celebration of what is good about erotica.

The present volume features some of my favourite stories from our first thirteen volumes (the last two are still readily available in stores and online). When I made my initial selection, I ended up with a 1,200-page volume, which I then had to painfully shrink down to acceptable size, such was the embarrassment of choices available to me. I had to restrict myself to one story per author, even though some have contributed several outstanding stories to the series over the years; stories I absolutely adored could not be reprinted because they were just too long; writers who deserved to be here have been left out because of lack of space – the choices were heartbreaking.

At any rate, here are thirty wonderful tales of sex, life, hotness, passion, of erotica at its best.

If you have not been converted to the sensual and intellectual pleasures of our genre already, this is your chance.

Jump aboard.

Maxim Jakubowski
April 2011

# Chapters in a Past Life

Marilyn Jaye-Lewis

## 1. Anal

I knew a woman who had a virgin asshole until she was in her early thirties. I never understood that kind of woman, she's not at all like me. I'd read about *Last Tango in Paris* in my mother's *Cosmo* when I was only thirteen, for God's sake – and the accompanying article, too, all about how to do it through the back door and, more importantly, why: because a *Cosmo* girl is an American girl and American girls love pressure.

I don't know if it was related to that distant article or not, but I dropped out of college in a real hurry, after only about six weeks. Something about wanting to feel alive instead, and that's how I ended up in New York; at the tail end of the disco era, pre-AIDS, a time when any self-respecting underpaid New York office worker drank heavily on his or her lunch hour and didn't have to be choosy about who he or she wanted to fuck when the work day was over because eventually you fucked everybody. And there were so many exciting cross-purposes going on! For instance, drugs. Did you fuck somebody sheerly because s/he had the good drugs? Or did you use the good drugs as bait to get somebody to fuck you? Of course, if you hung in there long enough, the inevitable descent into hell finally occurred. That's right, you remember it: you fell hopelessly in love with a completely *insane* person, a dangerously paranoid schizophrenic perhaps, but you were too fucked-up on the good drugs to even notice it. Maybe for a couple of years.

When it happened to me, it was with a woman. Back then, she wa already twenty years older than me, so *God knows*, if she's stil now she's using a cane to get around. But she was in fi 1980, thin as a rail of course. All bone, no muscle, h rigueur in 1980. We didn't lift free weights. Every ounce of energy was reserved for lifting cocktail glasses off the wet bar (a long distance endurance process) and for raising those teeny-weeny silver spoons, over and over – all right, I won't go on. I guess your memory's a little better than I'd thought . . .

So I'll call her Giselle. Not that her name was anything close to that, but it *was* similarly unpronounceable and she possessed that quick, nervous energy sometimes, reminiscent of the leaping gazelle. And on our first date – or more succinctly – when we hit on each other in that 10th Avenue after-hours meat rack and went home together to fuck like dogs, she was in fine, lithe, energetic form. I know we were kissing in the back seat of that cab, but I don't remember how we got from the cab to her sparsely furnished living room in that huge penthouse apartment in midtown, with the vaulted ceilings and all that glass. That part's a complete blank, but what happened from that point on is clear and that's the sex part and all that matters anyway.

Giselle's husband was apparently loaded. And not one of those cash-poor types, either. He seemed to travel on business constantly – or so he said. At any rate, he was away an awful lot and Giselle had nothing but time and money to take his place. You'd think those two things – time and money – would have been enough, but when you're remarkably thin and nearly forty, and beautiful and sharp and hopelessly underutilized like my dear Giselle, it takes a lot more than time and money to get your rocks completely *off*. Hence, Giselle's insatiable drive towards the strange.

I'd agreed willingly from the outset, I just want that part to be clear. I had my clothes off in a hurry and was letting Giselle douche my ass, simply because she wanted it so much. I was happy to let her do it. I was on my knees and elbows in her half-bath, right off the living room, there. Completely stripped with my ass in the air, a bulb syringe squeezing warm water into my rectum while I had a lit cigarette in one hand and a nice glass of Merlot in the other.

When the water had done its trick and we were through making a mess in the half-bath, Giselle led me back to the living room and she showed me the huge leather ottoman, how it lifted open for storing magazines and stuff. But she kept her bag of toys in there. It was a pretty big bag. That leather ottoman was sort of like a Playskool Busy Box for the seriously grown up. When she'd emptied out the ottoman, Giselle encouraged me to bend over it, so she could fasten my wrists securely to the wooden casters underneath. She even had specially made rubber wedges she'd shove under the casters to keep them from rolling all over the carpeting. Right away it occurred to me, when I saw the specially made rubber wedges, that it wasn't likely I was the first girl Giselle had stripped and douched and put over the leather ottoman. But I was OK with that. I drank like a fish and took a lot of drugs back then, so I was usually feeling pretty self-confident.

Once Giselle had secured my wrists, she inserted a steel thigh-spreader between my legs and buckled each padded end snugly around each of my thighs. And even though the thigh-spreader worked fine – it kept me from being able to close my legs – Giselle attached a padded ankle-spreader between my ankles, too. I guess she just wanted to be sure. And then she came around the front of the ottoman, gave me a hit off her cigarette and a couple of slugs of that great Merlot.

My head was buzzing. I loved the feeling of being exposed – in fact, forcibly so. Giselle leaned over and kissed my mouth for a while. It made me feel hot. It made my naked backside squirm. When her tongue pushed around inside my mouth, it made my ass arch up and it made me want to have her tongue poking into my hole.

"Look at this," she said.

She pulled a colour Polaroid from a leather envelope and placed it on the floor under my face and went away.

I studied the Polaroid curiously. It was a picture of a girl much like myself. Well, it was impossible to tell if her face looked anything like mine, but she was totally naked and kneeling over the same ottoman, her legs forcibly spread in the same way, and she was tied down in the same provocatively helpless position. It could have *easily* been a Polaroid of me.

That's when I saw the familiar bright flash coming from behind me and heard the quick grinding sound of the inner workings of the camera. In a mere sixty seconds, the colour Polaroid in front of me was replaced by a colour Polaroid of myself. It was uncanny, you know; the similarities and all.

We didn't talk any more after that. Giselle gave me a couple quick swigs from my glass of Merlot and gave me one last drag off the cigarette, then she slipped the gag into my mouth. Tied it pretty tightly, I must say. One of those knots where you just know your hair's in a big gnarly mess in back.

Giselle got undressed somewhere, out of my field of vision. I couldn't see her. But when she straddled my back her slippery pussy was sliding all over my skin. It was obvious she was naked. She leaned down and spoke in my ear confidentially, as she replaced the picture in front of me with yet another one. Of the other girl again.

"She's awfully pretty, honey, don't you think? Her asshole's so tight, would you look at that? Incredible, isn't it?"

I grunted, *uh-huh*, and nodded my gnarly head in agreement.

"Not even a hint of a haemorrhoid, see? This girl's in great shape."

I have to admit, I was a little transfixed; *I'd* never owned a Polaroid camera that took such vivid close-ups! Giselle had obviously invested a fortune in her camera lens.

"She was very well behaved, if I remember correctly," Giselle went on. "She took it like a champ, that one did. You think you're going to be a good girl, too? Huh? You've been awfully accommodating so far." Giselle began to kiss my neck slowly and she rubbed her wet pussy all over my lower back. "What do you think," she repeated. "You think you're going to be a good girl?"

*Uh-huh*, I grunted through my gag. I was going to be a very good girl. I was going to be stellar.

"You like things in your ass? You've had things in your ass before, right?"

I nodded my head, yes, but I confess I felt a little tripped up; what did she mean by *things?*

Then a different Polaroid was put in front of my face, a slightly more startling one. "Same girl," Giselle whispered, "but do you notice anything different about her hole?"

It's a huge *gaping* hole, I thought nervously.

"This is how her asshole looked when I was through appreciating her. Pretty remarkable, isn't it?"

Giselle brushed some stray hairs affectionately from my forehead, I guess to make sure my vision wasn't obscured in any way. I was riveted to that Polaroid, the crystal clear close-up of that well-appreciated sphincter.

"Of course, this sort of appreciation takes a few hours," Giselle explained. "You don't have to be anywhere for a while, do you?"

I don't think I really responded to that, I was a little too transfixed. She left the gaping-hole Polaroid on the floor in front of my face and then disappeared somewhere behind me.

The anticipation is always the greatest part, isn't it? Man, you're just waiting and you don't even know what the hell *for*. But you feel real certain that you're going to get it, that it's eventually going to come. And that's the sort of excitement I was feeling; like some mad ferret had chewed his paw free from a steel leghold trap inside me and now he tore wildly around in the darkness of my intestines, wanting very much to find his way out. But that was 1980. *You know* I was young. I was still excited by things like suspense and fear, and the chance to get my asshole reamed by a seriously grown-up girl.

It started with a simple strawberry. A bright red one with a long stem. Giselle had straddled my back again and lowered the long stem down in front of my face. She twirled it gently, holding the stem between her thumb and forefinger. "What do you think?" she asked. "Can you take it? It's not too big but it's awfully fragile."

In an instant the bright red berry was gone and Giselle slid her slippery pussy slowly down my back, until I imagined she must have been on her knees between my spread thighs. The tip of the berry was icy cold when she pressed it against my tight hole, but I could feel my asshole clench even tighter. It was an involuntary reaction to the icy intrusion.

"I can see I have my work cut out for me," Giselle announced solemnly. "We could be at this a *long* time."

I felt something sticky dribble down the crease in my ass. It oozed slow, like honey. And I think that's just what it was. When the slowly dribbling drop inched towards my clenching asshole, Giselle's tongue was there to meet it. She pushed the sticky substance around and around, all over my anus. The stickiness felt strange. It was lightly pulling at my hole. But the warmth of her tongue, pushing into the tight opening now and then, felt good. My hole definitely liked that. When Giselle had licked the surface of my asshole clean, she dripped another trail of honey down the crack of my ass. Again, it oozed so slowly down I felt that this alone, this waiting on the honey business, could in itself take hours. My ass wriggled and squirmed impatiently, perhaps trying to assist the honey in its journey down, but when the honey finally reached its destination, and when Giselle's warm tongue was once again there to greet it, the honey felt even more appealing than it had the first time. I felt my sphincter muscle relax a little. I felt it eagerly anticipate her poking tongue. I moaned into my gag. And I arched my ass open for her.

"This is definitely progress," Giselle announced quietly. "But let's not rush it. You're not really ready for the berry yet."

Giselle came around in front of me and I watched her polish off my glass of wine. She sat naked where I could see her and she lit a cigarette.

"I know how to remedy this, though, so don't lose heart," she said.

"It takes patience and then you'll be able to get anything you want in there. Even something like a strawberry."

I watched her as she thoughtfully smoked and even though I didn't have some long list of things I'd been trying to get *in there*, I suddenly felt like I desperately wanted to please Giselle. I wanted anything in my ass that she wanted to put in there. My hips were rotating restlessly against the ottoman while I watched her smoke. I could feel the wetness in my vagina beginning to drool down into a puddle on the carpeting. I didn't know what she had in mind for me, but I had a pretty good inkling that my ass was going to get fucked good by this gorgeous skinny woman who, let's face it, was technically old enough to be my mother.

When she finally stubbed out her cigarette, I watched her snap on a latex glove. I'd never been with anybody who'd worn gloves like that before, except the doctor in the examining room and it made my stomach a little queasy watching her snap it on. I wanted to ask her where she got gloves like that, but I had that gag stuck in my mouth and couldn't say a word. But when she disappeared again behind me and, without much fuss, slid a lubed finger up my ass, I wasn't thinking about buying gloves. I just gasped. Well, I moaned a little bit, too. She worked that latexed finger into me deep. And it was so slick with lube my tiny hole couldn't put up any kind of resistance. It tried to push against the intrusion, but Giselle was insistent. She worked against the pushing hole. She slid two fingers in, in fact, and pumped them vigorously in and out while I grunted a little and tried to figure out whether or not I liked it.

But I didn't have a lot of options. I was spread open for her either way. She paused for a moment and squirted the lube directly into my hole. It was an icy and unpleasant feeling, but the sensation didn't last long. It was replaced by the less subtle intrusion of three greasy fingers this time. Three greasy fingers shoved into my lubed hole. Giselle was exerting herself, I could tell; she was grunting from the effort of pumping her three fingers against the muscle that was trying to expel her.

"Jesus," I gasped into my gag. And my eyes were riveted to the picture on the floor in front of me. That gaping hole. It was going to be mine before morning came and I was sickly curious about how we were going to achieve this.

"Are you ready to pick up the pace?" she panted. "Are you ready for some action?"

Of course I couldn't answer her and I guess she didn't really expect me to, but Giselle came around the front of me then and let me watch her strap on the dildo.

"What do you think?" she asked urgently. "Can you handle this guy?"

She was referring to the dildo, to its overall *size.* But I was too caught up in looking at her. I'd been with girls before, and girls with dildos, too, but I'd never been with a woman yet who had actually strapped one on. Giselle looked hot. I was eager again.

"What do you think?" she persisted, as if she'd forgotten about the gag. "You think you can take him?"

I grunted my urgent approval as I watched her lube it up. *Uh-huh,* I grunted several times, and I even nodded my head.

And when she climbed onto me, mounted me, pressing the greased-up head against my asshole, easing the dildo into my rectum, it was like I was fourteen again and I was with that boy. We'd skipped school and we were hiding in his father's den. It was dark and very quiet in there. Their maid was home, but she didn't know we'd skipped school and snuck back into the house. She didn't know we were hiding in the den. But we had decided we were going to do this thing, we were going to try it out. We were determined. And I'd brought my torn-out article from my mother's old *Cosmo* and my plastic jar of Vaseline in my shoulder bag. We didn't get undressed because we were afraid of needing to leave in a hurry. So we just unzipped his fly and took his hard dick out. We smeared Vaseline all over that thing. And then I leaned into one of his father's big leather club chairs, I laid with my face pressed against the cool leather, while the boy shoved up my skirt and pulled my panties down to my knees. Vaseline makes everything a greasy mess, especially nice leather club chairs, but it sure helped that boy's hard-on slide right into me, right into my asshole. It was like we'd talked about over the phone, he was actually fucking my ass. I wasn't sure I really liked it, but I wasn't sure I didn't like it either. The pressure felt exciting, I liked the feeling of being filled up. But what I liked most was his fully clothed weight on top of me while my panties were around my knees, and the way he smelled while he grunted and pumped away at my virgin asshole, the way all boys smelled back then; like mown grass and sweat and tobacco and spearmint gum.

That was how it felt with Giselle, like I wasn't really sure I liked it, but I wasn't sure I didn't like it either. The dildo felt huge in my ass and I was grunting into my gag. But her naked weight was on top of me. Her breasts were pressed flat against my back and she was sweating from the effort of pounding my hole. I loved all that sweat. And I didn't mind it when she pulled the dildo out and reminded me I wasn't fourteen any more and that it was 1980. She shoved a glob of Crisco up my ass and proceeded to pump me with a dildo too huge, too heavy to even attempt to fit into the harness. Giselle didn't strap it on, she held it with two hands and shoved it clear down to its base, stretching me completely open.

I groaned like some drugged animal giving birth in a public zoo, but I was loving every minute of it. The Crisco made it easy on my hole. I opened right up and accepted every round fat rubbery inch of the fake dick that Giselle pounded so mercilessly into me.

And my eyes were glued to the photo in front of me, I was transfixed by that gaping hole. I was suddenly in love with the mystery girl in the Polaroid. I knew now what had stretched her open, I knew now how she must have felt – spread wide and securely battened down. A gag probably shoved into her mouth, too, so she could grunt over and over in it as her rectum was filled to capacity, her ears filled with the sounds of Giselle's own grunting, from all the strenuous effort . . .

When Giselle had worn herself out she disappeared briefly into the half-bath then re-emerged with a soaking towel. The towel was hot and felt great against my tired hole. And when Giselle had wiped away most of the grease, there was the familiar bright flash again behind me and the sound of the grinding inner workings of the camera. By the time she'd untied my gag, the new photo was ready.

"What do you think?" she asked softly, as she laid the Polaroid of my seriously opened hole on the floor in front of me. "You think you can handle that berry now?"

I'd forgotten about the strawberry. "I suppose so," I panted, although I wasn't entirely sure.

"I'll wedge it in with a little honey and then I'll eat it out of you. But I want to get a picture of it first. My husband loves these pictures," Giselle explained, "the ones with the food in the girls' asses. He carries them in his overnight case and takes them all over the world."

I wasn't sure I was particularly pleased with that idea, but I couldn't keep Giselle from wedging that sticky strawberry into my gaping hole. It took it easily this time, the berry perched right there in my puckered anus. Then the camera flashed away. I wondered what her husband looked like; would I ever recognize him on the street? Would it haunt me that somewhere in the world a man was flying from place to place with a picture in his overnight bag of me with a strawberry in my ass? And what about the mystery girl in the other Polaroid? What kind of food had ended up in her stretched hole?

But my worries melted away when Giselle's mouth found the berry. True to her word, she nibbled it out. She plucked the stem clean and then sucked the berry and gnawed it and licked it until it was gone.

"Come on," she said, as she undid all the hardware, the buckles and the restraints, "let's go to bed. Let's make a little love."

She refilled my wine glass but I didn't want it any more. I just wanted to be flat on my back underneath her on her big bed. The sun was just coming up in all those enormous penthouse windows, so when she straddled my face for some sixty-nine I could see her bung hole clearly. It was stretched like mine, but hers was permanent. She lowered it right onto my tongue while she shoved my thighs apart wide and buried her face between my legs. Her hot tongue licked at my tender aching worn-out hole, while her fingertips deftly massaged my clit. I tried to rub her clitoris, too, but she didn't seem to want that. She seemed content to just ride my tongue with her open hole.

I licked her asshole with all the earnest attention I could give her, but after a while, I must confess I couldn't help it; the way her mouth was making me feel between my legs absorbed more and more of my concentration. I couldn't give Giselle the amount of attention I should have. While her fingertips slipped all over my swollen clit, and while her tongue licked eagerly at my played-out asshole, I couldn't help myself, I came. I dug my fingers into Giselle's gorgeous ass and clamped my thighs tight around her head and came.

And since it was 1980 I didn't sleep with her. I stumbled into my clothes and left. I kissed her goodbye and all, but then I went out alone for breakfast.

A couple nights later she called me. "My husband's in Thailand," she said. "What do you say we go at it again? Are you up for it? You're not still sore, are you?"

My bung hole quivered. "No, I'm not sore," I said into the receiver.

"I have some new things that we could try putting up there. Are you game?"

And I realized I was. It was the beginning of my inevitable descent into hell with a completely insane person. "I'm game," I confessed.

"Good," she exclaimed quietly. "Be a doll and pick up some film. Now how do you feel about root vegetables?"

## 2. Swingers

Friday night I went home with some married people. I wish I could tell you they were those vibrantly tan, Hollywood fast-lane types but they weren't. They were just married people. Intellectuals. Two married couples clearly pushing something like their mid-fifties. I have to say they weren't even very attractive. They certainly weren't fans of cosmetic surgery or fad diets.

You're probably wondering why I went home with them, then. I'll tell you. They asked me to.

I was hanging out in one of those book bars. You know the one, the really well-lit place. Small and stuffy with the built-in bookcases lining the walls, a teeny-weeny fire in the equally microscopic hearth. I was there being stood-up. Nothing serious, though, no *tragedie l'amour*. It was just my intensely hyper garment-industry-worker girlfriend who had stood me up. She'd obviously got snagged into working more overtime.

So I was alone in a surprisingly comfy chair, nursing a glass of red wine tentatively since I wasn't sure if I was just going to turn around and go home. That's when they walked in. Two unattractive married couples in their mid-fifties. They made an instant commotion, dragging a tiny table around and scooting a bunch of comfy chairs together so they could all sit down in high spirits, practically on top of me, and proceeded to order an incredibly expensive bottle of wine. I loved watching that; the waiter trying to find a spot to stand in that was anywhere near them while they ordered, and then having to set up an elaborate pedestal wine bucket somewhere in reach of them, too. Thank God they smoked. They really needed some more stuff on that tiny table.

They couldn't help but notice me right away since they were practically sitting in my lap, and they kept trying to engage me in their small talk. I resisted their stabs at friendliness until they offered to share their wine, which necessitated their ordering another bottle. The waiter was really glad to see a fifth party, me, push into the already unmanoeuvrable fray. So physically we got close in a hurry. We couldn't help it. Still, one of the women, Fran, seemed to impinge on more of my personal space than I thought was really necessary. Right away I figured she was hitting on me. It took a couple glasses of that expensive wine before I realized they were all hitting on me.

I went home with them mostly because I couldn't believe they'd had the balls to ask me. They were so matter of fact about it, too, like they always came on to younger, much more attractive single women and got affirmative results. I was swept off my feet by their sheer blind optimism. Well, no. Actually I was swept off my feet by them, literally. I think they wanted to rush me into the nearest cab before I could change my mind.

We wound up in the home of the couple who lived closest to the bar. It was a really nice apartment. That couple, Cy and Ruthie, had never had any kids. Every extra penny had been available for them to spend on themselves. They favoured upholstery, too. Everything was upholstered, in every conceivable pattern. I could tell an interior decorator had been paid handsomely to have his or her way with Cy and Ruthie. But I ceased noticing the decor when Fran started to undress me.

At first I felt alarmingly uncomfortable because no one else was undressing. I shy away from being the only one naked in a crowd of strangers and I was wondering what I'd got myself into. But after she'd stripped me naked, Fran pushed me gently down on the sofa and began to massage my feet. I began to relax. I sank deep into the upholstered sofa while Fran sat on the coffee table in front of me with both my feet in her considerable lap. Her hands were unexpectedly soft and steady. She worked each and every one of my toes and the balls of my feet with just the right amount of pressure.

She smiled encouragingly at me while the others just watched. I wondered if I was being lured into some exhibitionistic *pas de deux* with Fran. As I sunk deeper into the couch in an increasing state of bliss, I wondered how a group of people arrived at that sort of arrangement. "Hey, I know," I imagined them saying, "let's all go out together, find a girl half our age and watch her get frisky with Fran." There would be general agreement all around.

Then Fran broke my reverie. She lifted my foot to her mouth and sucked in my big toe. I was ready for it. Fran's mouth was so warm and wet, I moaned. And slowly but surely things started to move around me.

Cy got out of his chair. He came over and stood by Fran, his crotch level with her face. He unzipped his fly, but when he took out his dick it was flaccid. Completely limp. Fran didn't seem at all perturbed but I felt a little indignant. I was thinking, Hey, I'm naked here! The least you could do is worship me, have a raging hard-on! But, alas, Cy was no longer nineteen and Fran appeared to be used to it. She went right to work with her mouth, alternating between my big toe and Cy's flaccid dick until remarkable things began to happen. It turned out Cy was hung.

Ruthie came over to join us then. She undid her husband's trousers completely, letting them fall rather dramatically to his ankles. Then, while Cy went to work on Fran's mouth with his stiff dick, getting her complete attention now as my feet lay limply in her lap, Ruthie kneeled behind Cy and seemed to be tonguing his ass. Her face was way in there and I figured if I was Cy, as I watched his huge erection pumping in and out of Fran's mouth while his wife, fully dressed and on her knees, tongued his asshole . . . well, I figured I'd probably be liking that an awful lot. I got wet between my legs watching those three carry on like that.

Kenneth, Fran's husband, was the last to take the plunge, but suddenly he was sitting on the couch next to me and he was naked. He had a lot of hair. A touch more than I would have preferred. He didn't seem to notice that he didn't appeal to me, though. He lifted my arms and held my wrists together behind my head, then proceeded to lick my armpits. It was an unusual move but it made my nipples shiver and get erect. As Kenneth licked his way down to my breasts and when his mouth closed around my erect nipple, I moaned again. Hairy or not, he was good with his mouth. My nipple swelled from the perfect pressure of Kenneth's sucking and I decided, at that moment, that I ought to have sex with older people more often, they understood pressure.

The coffee-table gang was starting to get rambunctious. Fran was flat on her back now as Cy straddled her on the low table, completely humping her face. She was making these eager but smothered little sounds that made it seem like she was liking it a whole lot. And Ruthie had removed Fran's panties. She'd pushed apart Fran's legs and buried her face between Fran's fleshy thighs.

Kenneth's mouth was still working expertly on my nipples, moving from one to the other, tugging tugging tugging, but now one of his hands was between my legs, rubbing my slippery clit.

I didn't think I'd be able to take much more of it; the free show on the coffee table and the prefect pressure on each of my three most responsive spots. I thought I was going to come.

That's when Cy startled all of us. He stopped humping Fran's face and went for her hole in a hurry. Ruthie had to get out of the way fast. She plopped down next to me on the sofa. She was the only one still dressed. She began to unbutton her blouse while Kenneth was rolling a rubber onto his erection. I felt a little overwhelmed. I didn't know who to focus on. It was obvious Ruthie wanted me to suck her fat little tits, but I was kind of hoping Kenneth was wanting his dick in me because I was definitely ready for it. That's when it occurred to me to quit sitting like a blob on the sofa and get a little assertive; get into the rhythm of being a swinger. Nothing was preventing me from having them both.

I turned over and raised my ass in Kenneth's direction while I let Ruthie guide my mouth to one of her jiggly tits. "Would you look at that tight tush," Kenneth declared as he slapped my ass hard. "Fran had a tush like that when I married her. Thirty years ago."

Then he mounted me. He slid his substantial hard-on into my soaking hole without needing any help from me. He slammed into my hole hard, making me cry out right away. He had a firm grip on my tush and was going to town.

Ruthie lifted my face from her breasts and started kissing me. Deep. Her tongue was crammed into my mouth while I grunted from the force of Kenneth's cock pounding into my pussy from behind.

I had never been with more than one person at a time before. It was kind of a scary feeling. I felt myself becoming insatiable. It wasn't long before I was flat on my back on the carpeting. Ruthie had stripped completely and was straddling my face. She had a tight grasp on each of my ankles as she kept my legs spread wide, giving Kenneth's hard cock free rein on my helpless hole, pound pound pound.

Ruthie's snatch was completely shaved. Her mound was smooth from the tip of her clit to the cleft in her ass. It had to be a wax job, I thought, she was that smooth. And I wondered: who waxes a fiftyish woman's pussy completely bald? I figured her husband, Cy, had something to do with it.

Cy was sitting in a chair now, sucking on a cigar, taking a breather, but his dick was still rock hard. It was poking straight up like the Chrysler Building. Not that I could see him too well with Ruthie's ass in my face, but I could tell that Cy was watching me get nailed. I was curious what he was thinking.

"I have to pee!" I suddenly announced as the urge came unmistakably over me. Rather than cause a chorus of disappointment and regret among my fellow swingers, the news didn't cause them to miss a beat. They'd switched partners before I'd even stood up.

When I came back into the living room (and I hadn't been gone long, mind you), Fran was down on all fours with Kenneth's hard-on seriously down her throat and Cy was fucking her ass. The incessant pounding she was getting at both ends was making Fran's boobs bounce around like crazy. The whole thing was mesmerizing;

what the men were doing to her and the way Fran seemed to be wildly into it.

Ruthie came in from the kitchen with a tray of decaf espressos. She had that look on her face, like she'd had her orgasm and was feeling completely contented. She sat down next to me with her cup of espresso and we both watched Fran go the distance with Cy and Kenneth. And right when Fran started to jerk around and squeal, an indication that Fran was probably coming, Kenneth pulled his dick out of her mouth and shot his load in her face.

She seemed a little peeved by that, but she didn't do much about it because Cy was still going hog wild on her ass. I wondered if Kenneth was going to hear about it later, though, when he and Fran were home alone: "How could you come in my face like that?" I could hear Fran saying. I knew she'd be capable of some serious chiding. "In front of everybody," she'd probably continue. "You know I hate it when you do that."

But for now everyone was amicable. Everyone was drinking decaf espresso except me. I hadn't come yet. I felt fidgety and distracted. Since I'd never been a swinger before, I didn't know the proper etiquette. Was it up to me to let everyone know I wasn't through yet, that I hadn't come?

I felt so ignorant, so ill equipped to swing. I toyed with the idea of slipping off to the bathroom again, to take care of myself alone. No one had to know what I'd be doing in there. I could come quick, I felt certain of that. Still I felt a little let down. I'd been having too much fun with everybody to suddenly resort to climaxing alone, in some stranger's bathroom.

After only a few moments, it seemed as though coming alone in Cy and Ruthie's bathroom wasn't even going to pan out. Fran and Kenneth were dressing. It was late, they said. They had a babysitter running up a fortune.

Then I wondered how old Fran really was if she had a child at home still young enough to need a sitter.

I figured I'd better get dressed, too. I didn't want to overstay my welcome. I helped Ruthie clear up the remnants of the espressos while Fran and Kenneth left.

"I'll get your coat," Cy said to me. "I'll walk you down to the street."

"That's okay," I protested half-heartedly. My head was pounding. This swinging business had left my now sober nerves a little raw.

"Nonsense. It's late. I'll walk you down."

Cy helped me into my coat and we got on the elevator. He pressed the button for the basement. I saw him do it. Maybe he was going to show me out the back way.

When the elevator doors opened, Cy led me down a narrow hallway and then out a door that led to the tenants' parking garage. It was dimly lit, with only a couple of naked bulbs burning.

"Look, you don't have to drive me," I insisted uncomfortably. "I don't live far. I'll get a cab."

"Why don't we get in my car anyway? I didn't come yet either."

I couldn't believe I'd heard him correctly. "What did you say?"

He looked at me and smiled engagingly. "I didn't come yet, either. I thought maybe I could persuade you to fuck around with me in my car."

I was stunned. I tried to feel affronted, but actually it kind of appealed to me. The parking garage was deserted.

Cy unlocked his car door and we slipped into the back seat. "We'd better not undress all the way," he said, "just in case anybody sees us."

I agreed.

I climbed onto his lap and started kissing him. On the mouth. My tongue was shoving in deep. Cy's breath tasted like wine and espressos and cigars and he suddenly seemed like he was seriously grown up. I felt incredibly attracted to him. "How old are you?" I challenged him. "Are you old enough to be my father?"

"Probably, why? Did you want to do a little role playing?"

"Excuse me?" I didn't know what he was talking about.

"You know, I could pretend to be your irate father and slap your fanny really hard until we're both really hot. Then we could cross over that line together."

I didn't reply. I felt a little overwhelmed by how instantly appealing his idea sounded.

I let him manoeuvre me until I was across his lap. He methodically lifted my coat, lifted my dress and, with minimal effort but a nice long lecture, he tugged down my tights, then my panties, and left them halfway down my thighs.

When my ass was completely bare and smack dab over his knee, he let loose with a good old-fashioned spanking. The stinging, smarting kind.

"Shit!" I cried, trying to shield my ass.

But he wasn't at all deterred by my screams. He lectured me sternly on the perils of going home with perfect strangers, and behaving rather wantonly to boot.

I squirmed around in Cy's lap as my bottom heated up and I tried to dodge the steady, stinging slaps, but Cy kept them coming. He clamped my waist tight against his thigh and aimed directly for my helpless behind.

I could feel Cy's erection growing underneath me. He was really laying into me, spanking me hard, making me squeal out promises that I'd never do it again.

When my ass was completely on fire and I didn't think I could stand any more, Cy released me. He turned me over in his lap and unbuttoned the top of my dress. Slipping his hand inside, he worked my bra up over my tits and fondled my nipples. They were instantly erect.

I was still naked from my waist to my knees. The feeling of being so awkwardly exposed, my bare ass burning, while Cy fondled my breasts and tugged on my nipples made me want to get irredeemably dirty with him. But that was going to be difficult to do while keeping our clothes on.

I turned over and undid Cy's trousers. I unbuckled his belt, unzipped his fly and his dick sprang out. I was happy to see it looking so lively. I buried my face in his lap, taking as much of his shaft down my throat as I could. I kneeled on the back seat with my naked ass in the air and I didn't care if anyone could see me. I was feeling unabashedly aroused. I sucked Cy's dick more fervently when I heard him begin to gasp and moan.

"Turn over," he said insistently. "Lie down on your belly." My bra was still up over my tits and the leather car seat was icy cold against my nipples. It felt great.

Cy unrolled a rubber onto his erection and told me to raise my ass up a little.

I did.

He mounted me with my tights and panties still around my thighs. I felt his dick poking into my asshole. At first I thought he didn't realize he had the wrong hole, but he knew what he was doing.

The lubricated condom slid into my ass without too much effort but the pressure was intense.

"God," I groaned. Then I cried out uncontrollably while his huge tool went to work on my pitiful little hole.

"I hate to have to do this," he grunted, "you know that. But maybe this'll teach you not to go home with people you don't know."

"God," I was panting as he pounded into my stretching hole. "Jesus, God."

"Are you going to be a good girl now?" he continued, lifting my hips off the back seat and deflty sliding his hand down to my swollen clit.

"Yes," I whimpered, "yes," while he rubbed my clit hard.

"Yes what?"

"I'm going to be a good girl," I cried, as his cock seemed to swell in me even more, filling me to capacity with every thrust.

"And what happens if you're naughty again? What is Daddy going to do?"

"Spank me," I sputtered. "Daddy's going to spank me!"

"And what else?"

"Fuck my ass!"

"That's right," he concluded. "Daddy is going to fuck your ass."

These last words he enunciated with amazing diction because he was coming at the sound of his own words. He slammed deep into my hole then and mashed me down on the seat. "Jesus!" he exclaimed with one last powerful thrust. "Jesus!"

And I was saying it, too: "Jesus!" Partly because I was coming underneath him, shuddering and squirming against the leather seat, but mostly because I was testifying. I wanted my joy to be heard.

# L'Enfer

Alice Joanou

We had a magnificent passion for dark alleys, expensive champagne, and each other. She was very rich and unhappily married. Happily, I was neither.

She was generous or silly enough to pay my way during the length of our affair, and I had the wit to make no objection. Her husband was an old man – yes, it was one of *those* marriages. She was an ornament, a gesture of diffidence towards his ageing, and a symbol of his wealth: having her on his arm meant virility, especially in the public eye. The old man didn't seem to mind that she was out nearly every night cavorting in the underworlds of Paris. She adored the cabarets and the most sordid cafés in Montmartre. He was glad to have her as his companion once or twice a month for the opera or some business function. Certainly, she was one of the most exquisite women in Paris.

She wore her sleek hair bobbed and was always dressed in the height of fashion. She never wore corsets or other restraining undergarments, not even knickers. When I asked her why she chose not to wear what other women considered such finery, she replied blithely that she liked the freedom it afforded her body. Her body. Her fine body. It was true that it would have been an insult to nature had she strapped it in or belted it down. Her body mirrored her soul. Her body was wild, animalistic. Her breasts were small and sat high on her slim torso. Her nipples' areolae were a deep-brown colour, and her torso, her hips, were virtually without curve. She had a dangerous body, and whenever I came near her I could smell that fire and needed to possess her. I could hardly keep my hands from tearing away the sheer silken dresses she wore. I could hardly stop myself from falling on my knees and taking her in my mouth, beginning with her feet. I needed to genuflect before her and taste her sex.

She almost always wore low-cut dresses with subtle slits in the sides of the skirt that rose perilously high on her long, slender legs. She decorated terrifying eyes with make-up, swearing, as she applied the make-up, that it served a protective device. She never went out without kohl smudged heavily around her eyes, the eyes of a corpse, blue-black and empty. Only now and again would they light when I took her in a violent way. Her eyes haunt me still. As if to compensate for such iciness, her full lips she painted with a flaming red tint she called "Madder Crimson". Her mouth was her vitality, and her smile was eccentric and not really beautiful. But it was human. Her painted red lips matched her luxuriant cinnabar hair. I loved watching her stand in front of the mirror, methodically making up her face. I watched her go through this preening ritual, and never did I grow tired of it.

One evening, I lay on my bed. The sheets were a sea of sweat and semen. We had been making love all day, and she said it was time to go out. To go out and see what kind of hell we could release upon a city like Paris. She wanted to go up to Sacré-Coeur and look out upon the city that loved her best. Paris was a city that looked good on her. It matched her lips and eyes. I was unable to move from the bed, half-mesmerized as she put the make-up around her eyes. Her back was to me, and she was naked, yet I could see her face and breasts in the mirror.

"Come here," I said to her quietly, almost unwilling to disturb her in her ministrations. But the sight of her body naked and pale and her face dressed for the evening gave me the strangest sensation. She looked nearly like a boy from behind, yet her face was clearly a woman's.

"You must come *here* if there is something you want," she said, her mouth smiling, her eyes dead.

"Please come here."

She ignored me and continued to put the finishing touches of light-pink rouge on her cheeks. And then she did something she didn't ordinarily do as she prepared herself for Paris: she took the powder puff and began to make slow circles around the tips of her breasts. Then she dipped the white puff in another powder that was a deeper red and began to rouge her nipples. My cock was already stiff. I had begun to imagine she was a young boy from the back and a gorgeous woman from the front. The idea of taking her from behind overwhelmed me. I had never entered her there. She had not permitted it. Her uncanny eyes were following my hand as it went involuntarily to my sex. She continued to slowly decorate her nipples, never turning.

Edith Piaf sang out defiantly and permanently damaged, her song wafting out in a thin line from the radio in the next room. It was summer and slightly humid. The flowers next to the bed violently perfumed the air. She was looking at me still. At last, I stood and went to her, taking the powder puff from her hand. Rather than put it on the vanity, as she suspected I would do, rather than take her immediately, I surprised her by dipping the make-up puff into the pot of rouge and reaching down to rouge her sex. She smiled and allowed herself a low sound of pleasure, realizing I had only just started.

"You look like a boy from behind. Are you my boy?"

"Yes," she answered, "I am your boy."

"I want to fuck you, boy. I am going to take you."

She made no reply, but raised her eyebrow at me in the mirror. She had a quizzical look on her face that was mixed with pleasure as I continued to lightly tease her pussy with the powder, making her blush between her legs. I set down the puff.

"Of course, from the front, you are the most exquisite woman I have ever seen." As I said this, I was dipping my fingers into a jar of pomade. My desire for him was unimaginable. My need for her was desperate.

"I am going to fuck you in the ass, my boy, my love. You'd like that, you little queer, wouldn't you?" He nodded . . . while she managed a wan, almost frightened, smile.

I rubbed my finger, lubricated with the pomade slowly up and down the crack of his ass. She sang with "La Vie en Rose". She opened her mouth. Edith Piaf opened her mouth and a flower scent came out. My love opened the lips of her crimson sex. I was to christen her a man. I wasted no time, though the heat in the flat made me feel as though I were moving exceedingly slowly, moving through an erotic heat that was material, that weighed down my caresses, and I noticed how heavy my hands were on his slim hips. I touched her breast, and the tip of my sex entered him slightly. She winced and moved backward in shock; he moved over me with delighted pain.

"Oh, my love. I've only just started. Does it hurt . . . ? Don't speak . . ." I whispered, suddenly afraid.

If he opened his mouth, I would know it was her. It had been so long since I had made love to a boy. She had distracted me from such need. She inhaled deeply, her eyes expressing nothing, the corners of her lips a mocking sneer. But within her strange smile she was urging me to take her. Without hesitation, I thrust my cock deep into his virgin asshole, violently needing to tear into her body, to enter a place I had not been before. She screamed. I put my hand over his mouth, while I took her nipple between my fingers and pinched. She fell towards the mirror, his cheek rested against the glass, and I reached down between her thighs and found her pussy wet. His body was perfect and delicious, and I took hold of his boyish hips with my free hand while I licked her clitoris with my fingers, expanding the possibilities of our bodies with every thrust of my hips, with every movement of my fingers into her soft, pink psyche. He fell hard against me. She fell hard against me. I could feel her breathing through her sex while I made a man of her. I crashed against her and she continued to look at me with that serene indifference. Once in a while her eyes lifted towards the ceiling. A diamond bead of sweat cut a path through the white powder on her high forehead.

His asshole was announcing her pleasure as it fit around my cock like a diabolical mouth, sucking me into a dark place of moral indistinction. I wanted to tear him apart, I wanted to drink the blood that was coming from between her legs. I wanted to consume her. I wanted to consume him. I could feel the white heat bloom from the back of my neck and cut a blazing trail down my chest. I thrust my fingers inside her terrifying depth. My cock was buried to the end of its capacity. She cried out and I came, pulling her hips over me, covering me. I looked in the mirror and saw her face instead of mine. Her eyes open, her mouth open. Edith Piaf sang.

"You make quite a lovely boy," I told her as we walked up the steep steps of Sacré-Coeur later that evening.

"May God forgive you," she said, laughing. "I hope we burn in hell together. I should hate to be there alone. Of course my husband will be there too, you know."

We walked up the stairs of Sacré-Coeur and surveyed the city that was nothing more than our fashionable accessory. We were perfectly happy that night, knowing that we shared one another's insatiable taste for the bizarre. That night we inaugurated, acknowledged, our mutual hungers.

I suppose I was a concession her husband could make in order to keep her by his side. It was the dead of morning, and we were stumbling down the street, intoxicated from an evening at Les Bals Nègres. Josephine Baker had been dancing that night, and the magnificent sight of her body, her immaculate breasts and legs, ah, Josephine Baker's legs . . . Watching her had fueled fantastic images of pleasure as she had moved wildly, mimicking, at times satirizing, the drama of the bed. It was all there, all of her to be seen, moving as though created to be desired.

As we tripped down a dimly lit street, we drank the remaining champagne of our last bottle. In the warm mist of the early summer dawn, an extraordinarily thin man stepped out from a dark doorway. His presence was abrupt and he stood in front of us, unmoving, his head cocked slightly to one side. She began to giggle at his appearance; I believe she laughed mostly out of fear. I could only make out his face when we got very close, an extremely bizarre visage that made me draw back for a moment. His prominent cheekbones created sunken hollows in his face, the effect heightened by the dreary gaslights of the alley. He wore all black, including a silk dress hat and opera cape, which she thought wildly funny, so dramatic a costume on a hot summer morning. His teeth and eyes shone in a peculiar way in the strange half-light.

She gasped when she got closer and looked into his unnerving face, and then, being drunk, she laughed and asked the man if he wouldn't like some champagne, holding up the bottle. He held out his hand, but only to beckon her closer. His ominous figure alarmed me, but, being young and stupid, I rushed forward. My mistress held my arm and quieted me. She moved cautiously, leaning her ear to his mouth to hear what he had to say. I couldn't help desiring her just then. Watching her neck tilt in that weird light, slightly terrorized, slightly mesmerized by the danger he presented. I wanted to possess her. I loved her so drunkenly that my thirst for her body could never really be quenched. I stared at her neck, at the lines of her collarbone, as she listened to what the stranger had to say.

He leaned in, his lips hovering dangerously near the nape of her neck. I almost yelled out. He began to whisper in her ear, and, as he spoke, I could see her become slowly breathless. Her back began to arch the way it did when I stroked her breasts. Her mouth fell open, and her lids half-closed over her eyes. It seemed as though the man were making love to her, but of course I could see that his hands were not touching her at all. I moved closer, moved by the tableau the man and my mistress formed in the grey morning light that was trying to get into that alley. And then I suddenly heard her beginning to making low moaning noises, her breasts falling out of the low-cut dress. And then quite suddenly she drew back, tossing her head back defiantly, and she began to laugh. It was inexplicable, whatever was occurring between her and this stranger, and there was a part of me that found a hollow solace in the fact that she had moved away from him. I also found that I was aroused in a way that was extraordinary. My feelings of desire were tinted with a bleakness, a sense of real danger that exceeded the games that she and I had indulged in at my flat.

She was moving towards me, beckoning me to come closer. I hesitated, still overwhelmed by a finishing sadness, a vague anxiety mingled with a potent desire to have her. Finally, I moved. The stranger leered in the background.

"He's asked us to come with him. He wants to show us a very exclusive cabaret. It sounds absolutely perverted. We really must go!" She paused and then whispered breathlessly, "He says it's called 'L'Enfer'. Isn't that superb! Come." And she took my hand.

I meant to ask her who the man was, and how did she know we were not stepping into some sort of terrible trap, but when I saw her slip the man a number of francs it was clear she had decided against reason. Of course I could not leave her alone and so began to follow their dark shadows down the narrow alley.

Remembering the silhouette of her breast, and her tongue flicking over her full lips as he had whispered in her ear, I wanted to take her, I wanted to push her against one of the doorways, lift her sheer dress, and take her. I still had the pounding rhythm of Les Bals Nègres in my ears. I wanted to fuck her to the cadence of Josephine Baker's feet. I wanted to rape her, gently, and then more and more forcefully. I could feel the familiar ache of desire, the pain she caused in my groin, but my mistress was already falling into the darkness of the alley, following her compelling stranger.

"What did he say to you, my love? What did he whisper in your ear?" I asked as I moved up behind her, holding her tightly around the waist. There was, perhaps, some ill-concealed jealousy creeping into my voice.

She said nothing but answered me with a devious smile that came when she was aroused, an expression that was made more corrupt by the lusterlessness, the obsolescence in her eyes.

After winding down a series of unfamiliar and narrow streets, we stopped in front of a nondescript door. Our "guide", as I had come to think of him, knocked lightly, paused, and then rapped in loud and quick succession. I felt something extraordinary on the other side, but part of me hoped there was nothing, that our guide was nothing more than a petty crook who had taken her money. Part of my body was ready for the confusion of an unforeseen adventure, and another portion of my being wanted nothing more than to drag her away, get home to the creamy eiderdown, the cotton of our sheets.

The door slowly creaked open. Humid air coloured with various scents of smoke came out. I thought I smelled the pungent, sticky smell of opium. We were greeted by a man who who had the colouring of a Gypsy, but no trace of an accent. His French was impeccable. For some reason this unnerved me. He had green-yellow eyes and luxuriant black hair in curls to his shoulders. He was well dressed. The door closed behind us, and I turned, startled. Our guide had left us.

Her mouth turned up like sensual question marks as she observed the Gypsy man's beautifully sculptured ass while he led us down a narrow corridor papered in dark-red velvet and lit with gaudy gilt candelabra. There seemed to be heat emanating from the walls and a muffled sound, not quite far away, vibrating them as if they were breathing and sweating like giant sheets of sex-blushed flesh. It was grotesque and nauseating. I felt the familiar tug of my cock, and was surprised at my arousal in this strange atmosphere. She was moving forward as if in another element beyond her. I watched carefully as she walked down the narrow hallway in front of me, her hand involuntarily caressing the red walls.

Quite suddenly we found ourselves in front of another door, and the vague music I thought I had recognized could be heard more clearly on the other side. The Gypsy swung open the door with ceremony and with a sweep of his arm motioned us inside. After she had handed over more money, of course.

What we beheld behind that door made us both gasp.

A gale of hot opium air and jazz exploded on our faces. There were beautiful young girls and young men. There were old men, bald and dying in the arms of prepubescent nymphs. Old whores danced with wealthy young students. But something else had made us gasp.

There were young boys and girls hanging hairless and well muscled, suspended from leather harnesses connected to the ceiling. There were four or five of them, and all the hanging men were naked, utterly exposed. Some hung from their arms and ankles, others from the centres of their torsos. I don't know how many of them were suspended thus in the centre of what seemed to be a large underground theatre. Their bodies nearly receded into the vast subterranean darkness, a sea of swaying, glowing flesh in the pale-red light of this very queer theatre of sex. The force of the music was lost in the face of these beauties hung low enough to touch in any way in which the patrons of this select cabaret could wish.

Imagine. Human beings, fresh young human beings, suspended in apparatus resembling something dangerously close to an item from the Inquisition. There were black girls with smooth, dark flesh, their nipples nearly purple in the orange light. I could see the ripples and dark hair of a Gypsy boy, or perhaps he was an Italian, the smooth flesh of his ass and hairless chest evoking that day, not long ago, when I had taken my mistress from behind. I was frightened by so much available flesh. There was an Asian girl with long, silky black hair that swept the floor, and near her a European girl with pink skin contrasting viciously with the black straps of her harnesses.

She clutched my arm, her mouth moved to make tiny O's. I did not know whether this unreal spectacle was seizing her with desire or disgust. Her eyes were without expression.

I could see men, clearly well bred, standing two at a time, taking a girl from front and back. A Japanese girl floating like an angel from the underworld, legs opened, sex exposed, was held aloft in murky opium clouds. Her cunt was being treated to a kiss by what appeared to be a woman of means, judging by the clothes she wore. I could see that her nipples were erect against the silk of her evening gown and I have to admit that the erection that had plagued me in the alley had not subsided; my balls were suffering with passion and need. The cold desire I felt disturbed me, for I wanted to possess not only my mistress but all those bodies suspended before me like so much provocative fruit.

Before I could lend words to my actions, I took my mistress roughly by her hair and began to bite her neck. The need to have her delicate flesh between my teeth was an absolute necessity. If I didn't take action, if I didn't claim her body in some way, however small, I would be lost. It is not something that I can, even now, rationally explain. I was satisfied only when I could taste the metallic copper and iron of her body across my tongue. It was only then that I could release my mouth from the nape of her neck. In this place, in this strange place far beyond even the darkest secrets of Paris, I had to mark her in some way. I had to know, *she* had to know, that in this flesh jungle where anything might happen she was still my mistress. I could hear her on my lips. The ruby colour of her pain and the rumbles of her acute desire played symphonically on my fingertips and tongue. She turned to me, to my lips, where there was a droplet of her blood. She gingerly put her finger to it and her eyebrows slanted as if to say she was shocked at my bestial need to be so possessive. But then her mouth softened and she raised her bloodied finger to her lips and drank of her own body. Then, while keeping her finger in her mouth, she parted her lips slightly, suggesting something with her teeth and tongue.

I had to tear her dress away from her breasts, I had to free them from the constraining fabric of the bodice. Never taking my hand from her breasts, I lifted the skirt of her dress and reached roughly between her silky legs for her sex. Then I grabbed hold of her slender hips and she pressed her body against me, moving slowly to the music. She was moving more and more forcefully against me now, her sex a warm invitation, her body tugging me in. I opened my trousers and did not hesitate to climb inside her secrets. I drove deeper and deeper until I felt her contracting in low, sing-song sounds of pleasure.

She was holding my wrists, her long fingernails digging deeply into my flesh, drawing blood, and the pain lit hidden fires of violence within me. I started fucking her with thoughts of killing her with my cock. I wanted to fuck her to death. Quite literally. She was screaming, and I imagined that I had been successful. I opened my eyes and saw traces of blood on my hands and then I fell forward, pushing into her last breath.

After we had recovered from our tryst in the corner, we began to move through the peculiar space. I held my mistress's wrist for some time, but everywhere I turned I was confronted with so many bodies. As my mistress had paid the required fee, I had nothing to distract me. Except my mistress. But as soon as I thought I might have some trouble tasting the fruits of hell, she silently demanded I release my grasp on her wrist. Then she disappeared into the darkness, drawn by some single-minded purpose.

I walked through the labyrinth of bodies until I found the Japanese woman, whose hair was so long that it dragged on the ground. Her skin was soft and white and her legs were spread wide to reveal her pussy shaved of any hair. Her naked sex was a queer sight and it aroused me immediately. She would have looked a child were it not for the decoration of her cunt. The lips of her sex were ornamented with two rings pierced through and, crowning that, her clitoris had been pierced and there was embedded a pearl. I had never seen such a beauty, and my body went before my mind and my hands found her before I could know the word for desire. I wanted to taste her jewellery. I had to kiss her pearl. There were no others near her and I was glad. I wanted to devour her alone. I wanted to take her with my tongue and my fingers and my cock, slowly and with singularity. I wanted to have the luxury of hurting her or pleasing her. Whichever demon, lust or violence, I wanted to act without intervention.

She was a beautiful young woman whose eyes betrayed a liking for opium. Her full lips were parted and she was humming a strange song in a very low voice. I put my hands to her small breasts and took her nipples between my fingers. I pinched them hard and watched her face. She smiled and continued to hum. She parted her eyes wider to look at me, and, as much as her restraints would allow, she rippled her body in response to my attentions. I leaned forward and slowly tasted of her skin. It was salty with sweat, and there was a lingering scent of lavender powder. I let my tongue play lightly over the flat of her belly. I turned my head, resting my cheek on her stomach, and found the sight of her breasts stretched tightly from bondage very pleasing. I fell into her. I moved my mouth slowly over the full, clean lips of her labia. When the tip of my tongue touched one of her rings, I tugged it and she thrust her body lightly against my mouth. I let my tongue enter her flesh, I could hear her pleasure, I could feel it on my mouth. Her body twitched, making her sway gently from the leather straps which held her wrists, ankles, and torso. As I teased the outside of her cunt with my tongue, I found her imposed submission utterly exciting and I slid my tongue inside her once again. I drank there and returned to her outer shell. I wanted to kiss her pearl. As my lips found the cool stone pierced through her clit, I could hear the buzzing of her body. I sucked the pearl and she began to writhe. I stopped. Her moans reverberated through my mouth as I undid my trousers, readying myself to take her.

As I stood, I noticed that two women had found the Japanese woman appealing and had attached themselves to the lovely girl's nipples, touching one another as they sucked her. The sight only irritated my cock more. I stood between her legs and, taking her hips in my hands, I forced her body over my cock, letting my member slide in slowly so I could completely enjoy the strange new feeling of the golden hoops and cool sea pearl against the heat and sensitivity of my skin as it moved in deeper towards her fiery core. She cried out when I finally fell forward with all my weight, not caring for her comfort or discomfort. I made love to her with more and more force, suddenly feeling the overwhelming need to ravage the girl's tighter orifice. When I removed my sex and started to push into her from behind, I found she was generously lubricated from the residue of my own kisses. And as much as I wanted to shamelessly brutalize her, I was pleased to find that she was wet with desire and she moved her hips in a slow, swaying motion.

I responded to her mute invitation by shoving my cock into her anus without hesitation. With one finger I began to roll the pearl in her clit. And then, as if a dream, my mistress appeared from some darker place. Her beautiful face was covered in sweat, and I could see her lips were swollen. She smiled a smile that had a hint of malice and without saying a word, without touching me at all, she leaned over the Japanese girl's exposed sex, putting her perfect mouth on the girl's cunt, where I kept my finger so my mistress's tongue licked both my hand and the girl's pussy.

A fierce bewildering pleasure was welling up from within me and the force of it nearly frightened me. I imagined it was coming from some bilious and evil place, for, as I watched my lover kissing the girl's sex, as I continued to take the woman from behind, I wanted to put my hands to my mistress's neck. I wanted to put my fingers into the flesh of her back, or her cheek, and with all my strength to tear into her, to be inside her in a different, an immediate manner. The simplicity with which I could achieve this horrible feat fed my lust and rage and I continued to push my body more forcefully against the girl. I began to know that there was nothing but trust stopping me from tearing the flesh away from my mistress's body. I realized that nothing could stop me if I wanted to kill her. I considered with cold precision how simple and fragile is flesh.

As though my lover sensed the maniacal rage in my pleasure, she stood and put her lips to mine. I shot my semen into the Japanese woman, as though relieving myself of the hideously dark thoughts that had only moments before nearly overwhelmed me to commit murder. My mistress gently pulled me from the girl. I was walking in a sleeping state, and the sound of my mistress's haunting and persistent humming chilled me.

My mistress led me to a dark corner of large, soft cushions to recline upon. Someone appeared and gave us champagne. I did not bother to pour the wine into a glass because suddenly I was taken with a thirst so great I thought I might damn near die if I didn't drink immediately. I felt out of control and at the same time in great command of my body, my life. In fact, I felt more in control at that moment than I ever had, the hollowed-out darkness in my heart seemed to be the very reason for my sense of grace. A vague tingling told me this was perhaps not the first time I had ever felt this way. I stole a sideways glance at my mistress for I did not want to encourage conversation. I wanted to be isolated in this queer and violent loneliness, this satiation. We rested in darkness for a while, then wearily we stole into the early morning light to make our way home.

* * *

She went home to her greying husband that morning, while I went to the flat she paid for with his money. It was a nice bohemian hideaway in the *troisième arrondissement*, the top floor with a large skylight that filled the place with sun when it made its rare appearances in Paris.

I fell onto the generous quilts of the iron bed. The furnishings of this lovely little nest were also compliments of my mistress's husband. And my clothing, and my food. I felt a moment of great bitterness and envy towards my mistress's husband. I was infuriated that I could not provide the things for my lover that I knew she needed. I felt irrationally murderous towards him, towards her, my situation, a situation I had been content with until now. It seemed that the visit to that infernal place had started my mind on a dangerous tread that I could not stop at will. At last I found myself sleepy from all the rage threatening to exhaust me, overwhelm me.

I fell into fantastic and violent visions. I dreamed I had bound my mistress to a thick post in the centre of the theatre of L'Enfer. The air around us swirled in orange narcotic clouds, and her beautiful boyish figure, the fine skin of her legs, shone as though she were drenched in exotic oils. Or perhaps it was a terror sweat. In my satanic dreams, I did things to her that I cannot even write. I attacked her helpless body with such a violent grace and ease that when it was over I scarcely thought about the strength it took to tear her limb from limb, and in fact was more concerned about the mess on my clothing . . . ah, but I must cease. Even the thought of that gruesome, dream, and, worse, the intensity of pleasure as I dreamed it – it is too, too strange.

The sun was warming my aroused flesh, now turning clammy in an unfamiliar orgasmic sweat. I lay there thinking about my mistress, and the nightclub called L'Enfer.

Two days later I received a note and a package from my beloved. The note read:

WE SHALL MEET IN THE DARKNESS AT
MIDNIGHT, MY LOVE.
A.

Just reading her note, seeing her handwriting, sent an electric thrill through my body. And then my mind turned instantly, without hesitation, to my unspeakable dream. I stood for a moment reading the sky in front of my eyes that held the terrible, bloody images of my mistress's demise. At last, and with a great deal of will, I shook my head and body and tore open the elegant wrapping on the box. Inside was a beautiful, black-silk tuxedo, complete with an opera cape with red lining. It was sinister, and I feared suddenly that my mistress sensed my more detestable motivations.

"Folly!" I shouted out loud, to disrupt my own mind from its obsessive wanderings. I shook the cloak free of the box and held it up to the light. It was so black it seemed to absorb the sun, and, when I turned it, the red silk was a great slick of beautiful, pure, fresh blood.

The early edition of the morning paper reported that an unidentified young woman who *appeared* to be Japanese had been found dead, her head floating in a small valise down the Seine. The police had not yet found the remaining portion of her body. She had lipstick kisses on her white cheeks and a small white pearl in her mouth.

All during the day I was seized with erotic frenzy. Vague pictures appeared and disappeared in my heated imagination. Suspended, naked bodies swayed under my fingers, the memory of L'Enfer a palpable reality. I wandered across the Pont Neuf and stared at the murky, mysterious water of the Seine. I found myself laughing quite uncontrollably as I thought I saw her shoe rolling and bobbing on the filthy surface. As I laughed, emptying my horrible sound into the wind, I envisioned the girl, her head upon the glorious body of my mistress, and the visage of my mistress sewn to the missing body of the dead girl.

I saw her red lips slightly parted, perhaps grimacing in pain or smiling with languorous pleasure. I remembered seeing her mouth open, the pearl tumbling about . . . though I can't be sure. I cannot remember if she was screaming, but I recall her terror combining rather elegantly with her ancient Asian complexion. I don't know whether I *thought* I saw that pearl in her mouth, or if I wished it there. And then I realized I was confusing my lover with the Japanese girl and, then again, I wondered if I hadn't confused the Japanese woman's lips for those of my mistress.

When it was time to dress, I was covered with a light sweat of desire and irritated by a persistent guilt. And, worse still, an erection that would not fade. I contemplated abating my need with my own hand, then thought better of it, waiting to see what mysteries the night had to offer me.

She came for me that evening, a vision of carnal appetites. Every detail of her body, her dress, her perfumed hair, exuded a need to be ravished. I tempered my own need, savouring the romantic pain of wanting her, wanting to take her immediately and forget the enticing nightmares awaiting us at L'Enfer. I held myself back, mostly because around the edges of her mouth I could discern a strangeness that worried me. I could tell she wanted desperately to say something about the article in the newspaper, but I put my finger to her mouth. There was a terrible silence inside me that suggested to her that she should not pursue the subject of the dead girl. I told her, while my hand still rested on her mouth, that I had read it too. And yes. It was dreadful. But I felt the corners of my mouth turn upward in an uncontrollable moment of pleasure. My queer expression was met with a questioning look from my mistress.

There was a new tension between us as we made our way to the alley, where we were to meet the tall stranger. I have to admit that I quite liked this new thrill. She was a little afraid of me and this pleased me greatly. I thought it fair for all the humiliations I had suffered. The embarrassment of being so frightfully over-educated and so dreadfully poor. She had given me money and she had debased me with her generosity. So if she feared me that night as we walked silently towards our destiny, it enhanced my contentment.

Oh, how I could hear the bells of Sacré-Coeur ringing for the souls of the dead, how vital, how omnipotent and wild I felt as those bells ran through my body. When we arrived at the narrow, foul-smelling alley our guide was not there. I was in despair, yet my heart still raced. We stood in grim, tense silence as the final tolling of the bells tore through the darkness. And then suddenly on the breeze a subtle caress of my mistress's perfume.

I stood perfectly still without turning to look at her. She moved close to me, breathing heated kisses on the back of my neck. Her hands wrapped around my waist and immediately she began to unclasp the buttons of my trousers. She squeezed my balls and erect sex firmly, and the sight of her long, elegant white fingers tipped with blood-red enamel stirred me beyond measure.

"I need you," she whispered into my hair.

I turned to kiss her. She looked supernaturally beautiful. The translucent powder on her face made her eyes and lips glow like fire in the dark. She wore a simple silk shift the colour of champagne and over that a luxurious fur coat. Between the sheer pleats of fabric, I could see her nipples and the full shape of her perfect breasts. She wore an extra-long strand of pearls around her long, white neck, fatalistic tears all the way to her sex, which I could see framed with the dark triangle of hair covering, no, framing, her perfection. I wanted to possess her, give her pleasure suddenly as a form of absolution for all the horror and violence to which I had given rein.

The night was cold and I swung the enormous cape around both of our bodies. I bowed my head without hesitation and I began to taste her breasts through the paper-thin material of her shift. Her nipples responded immediately to my touch. I raised my head and kissed her delicious lips, thrusting my tongue deep into her mouth. I avoided looking at her eyes for fear that some expression of doubt or fear might still linger there. Besides, taking her lips between mine, her tongue in my own mouth was far more telling, for my mistress's eyes rarely betrayed her state of mind. It was her mouth that told all without speaking, her lips that would betray her. Her tongue greeted my kisses and I was compelled to bite her tongue hard. I took that organ between my teeth and crushed it. How tender, how delicate the tongue really is, how easily I could have bitten it clean off. Her knees bent slightly under the pain I was affording her. Her moan was a sound beyond pleasure. I stopped just after the luxury of drinking a few droplets of her thick, warm blood. She tried to pull away but my hands reassured her of impending pleasures. I slipped my fingers under her dress between her thighs to find her secret anatomy alive and betraying her passion for mingling pleasure with a little bit of terror. Her sex was hot and inviting. I imagined her juices to be warm blood and I was hungry to taste of her. I kneeled.

The flesh of her labia seemed to coil round my lips. I had never felt the terror with another woman as the terror I now felt of tasting her thus. I was overwhelmed with a primordial fear that had no words. All my anticipation of the evening's events, all my desire for my mistress paled in the light of this new terror. But as quickly as it came upon me, it left, and I let the lips of her sex consume me. I drew my tongue along the outer rim of her soft, hot flesh and let her juices fall on my lips, on my ready tongue. Her body wrapped around me like a bloody mantle. I felt her hair on my lips, I was suffocated in the involuntary thrusts of her body in paroxysms of pleasure. I was filled with a hunger. I wanted to mangle her with my tongue. I stabbed it inside her as though it were my cock. As my tongue went inside her I felt as though I were tasting a great and powerful light, a wonderful and horrible sensation, cannibalistic, wondrous. I had to stop before something dreadful happened.

I abandoned her on the edge of a catastrophic orgasm. She was moaning, crazed, tearing at my clothing. I stood and watched her with a dispassionate stare. I loved the way she was pleading and begging. I was pleased by the fact that she was a helpless victim of her own needs.

I reached down to my trousers, willing to take her there in the alley, but she pulled my hand away. She kneeled in the dank passageway and, pulling the fabric of my trousers away with her teeth, she released my raging cock unto her kisses. She took my member into her mouth, letting it slide sensuously into her open throat. Her lips sucked lightly at first round the tip of my sex, and, as she raised and lowered her head in a steady rhythm, she pulled with her lips more powerfully. She ran her tongue like a feather over the tip of my cock, and with her hands she teased the rim of my anus, gently squeezing my aching sac. I felt more and more helpless as my desire grew. She was a great cat sucking with feline prowess on my throbbing sex. I felt like a child and this made me angry though I felt that could not stop the locomotion of my veins, pressed her head down on me hard and without relent until my seed fell into her throat. It was an awful moment: fleeting images of the Japanese woman, pictures of bleeding and screams more like memories than fantasy.

"Come along, my darling," she said in a voice husky with pleasure, "we don't want to miss the show."

The sound of her voice took me out of my misery for a moment. I helped her to her feet and brushed her hair from her face, an awkward attempt at apology. She smiled at me as if to say she too was sorry.

We linked arms and made our way more deeply into darkness as we moved unguided towards L'Enfer. The last chimes of Sacré-Coeur sounded off the damp sides of the crumbling buildings of Montmartre. We stopped in front of the same nondescript door. My mistress boldly stood forward and knocked three times, waited, and then five more times. The tiny wooden-hinged window inset swung open and the grey eye of the Gypsy could be seen clearly. He closed the small window and opened the door just wide enough for us to slip inside.

Tonight the Gypsy doorman wore a black leather mask over his entire head. It was a sort I had never seen at any masquerade and resembled a medieval executioner's mask. His beautiful black hair and handsome face were hidden and all that appeared were his eyes. There were holes in the leather for his nostrils and an aperture for his mouth, but this was sewn shut, a feature both violent and alluring. His chest was exposed, assuring both my mistress and me that it was indeed the same man who had greeted us two nights before. His body was unmistakably magnificent, even more enticing with the sinister black mask. Without hesitation, my mistress reached into her small beaded purse and withdrew a bundle of francs. I noted that her hand trembled slightly and I thought that unusual. She was ordinarily so calm. The doorman had enough manners not to count it, but he seemed to know by the sheer weight of it that it was not enough and he bowed discreetly and urged my mistress to give him more. She did, and she trembled more at this. We both seemed to know that more money meant something more rare, and probably more terrifying. The doorman seemed satisfied and bowed again at the waist then turned to lead us down the narrow red corridor, towards the theatre of L'Enfer.

We were prepared to witness something at least as bizarre and exciting as we had seen on our previous visit yet, in retrospect, I don't believe either of us was prepared for the excesses we were to witness on the eve of All Saints.

The dark space appeared to have changed so radically that for a moment I thought we had entered another place altogether. We faced a circular stage surrounded with heavy velvet curtains in the centre of the large underground room. The place was filled with the smell of opium and tobacco, and the queer scent of marijuana clung in languid clouds in the humid air. Groups of people sat at elegant little tables clustered towards the stage. In front of the stage was a pit just large enough for a small band, which was playing blue jazz that made the room hotter and my heart bitter. The darkness to the left and right of the tables held voices and the shimmer of expensive beaded dresses. The dark offered up a jeweled hand here and there and now and again I caught a glimpse of rouged lips and cigarette holders. As my eyes grew accustomed to the dark I realized that it was from erotically disembodied hands and mouths that the smoke came, and after a time I could see the languorous forms of opium smokers stretched out on tapestried pillows, the long stems of the pipes in their hands. It seemed that their bodies were dilating en masse, and all the smokers caressed one another in lingering, slow motions.

At last my mistress said, "I am going to try some opium. I really must – have you ever, darling?"

I just shook my head. I was not afraid of the drug, but afraid of myself. I wanted to stay lucid, yet I knew it was impossible in the hallucination that was this nightclub. But I knew that if she wanted to try something, she would. I thought perhaps if she tasted the opium she would lose the anxiety and fear she was feeling towards me and, in a moment of compassion, I wanted her to be less afraid.

But I knew her fear eroticized my violent motivations and suddenly I didn't want her to smoke the drug. But it was too late. Not wanting to cause a disturbance, I let her go. She moved hypnotically towards the dark figures on the pillows. I thought to follow but turned away, thinking that I would return for her before the show started.

I walked towards the tables, each lit with magnificent candelabra. In the dim light I could make out women's elegant fingers decked in jewels, and I could smell the fashionable scents of Chanel in the air. People talked secretively with one another, their heads tipped towards each other's lips to listen or to steal a kiss. I felt suddenly alone and excluded and was about to turn and find my mistress. Just then I felt a hand at my elbow attempting to lead me somewhere.

I looked to my right and found a woman standing by my side. She was absolutely beautiful. She wore her sleek hair long, as young girls do before they ritualize their entrance into womanhood by, regrettably, cutting their locks. Behind her ear she wore a rose. She had the colouring of a Gypsy, her eyes black and her skin a lustrous olive. She wore nothing to cover her breasts, and around her hips a silken shawl with a fringe. She pulled me to an empty table further away from the opium than I wanted to be, for I did not want to lose my mistress in this strange crowd, especially not tonight. But I was captivated by the dark woman's breasts, the tiny rings of gold pierced through her perfect nipples. The piercings looked beautifully strange and violently erotic, so much so that I followed the wordless motions of the woman without looking back towards my mistress. I wanted to touch this woman's breasts. I wanted to taste the metal on my lips as I had done with the Japanese girl days before. I wanted to – my thoughts were giving way to more violence and it was getting increasingly difficult to stop the powerful surges that came over me.

As though the dark beauty had read my mind, she brought my eager hand to her breast, and I reached out to take the tiny ring between my forefinger and thumb. I pulled a little, and the corners of her sensuous lips turned up in a wincing smile. I pulled at the ring a little harder and she half-closed her eyes, her long lashes brushing her cheek. I imagined that the little moaning sound that she made came from the contact of my lashes on her skin. I let my eyes wander down the front of her figure, her long, flat belly, her secret parts barely hidden by the silken shawl. I ran my hand along the flat of her stomach as I reached around her neck to pull her generous lips towards my own, because it seemed she was offering herself to me.

She tilted her head towards mine willingly and I tasted to my fill of her lips and neck. She bit my lips with a single-mindedness that matched my mood, and her fingernails dug into the nape of my neck. As we kissed, she unhooked the cape from my neck. Once she had removed the cloak, she surprised me by putting it about her own shoulders, which made her look magnificently sinister, her bare breasts surrounded by the black fabric of the opera cape, the contours of her body trickling with red silk. The small orchestra had started to play music that filled my head with the rhythm of sex, the music of fucking. My blood was responding to the beat of the music, and my sex was responding to the cloaked image of the tall woman, who was leaning towards me over the small candlelit table.

I knew I was about to commit an infidelity. And I wished that my mistress were closer to watch. I was going to ravish this woman, and I knew my pleasure would be that much greater if my mistress were forced to watch as I took and gave pleasure to an equally beautiful creature as she.

The dark woman and I sat together without uttering a single word. Her black hair was falling over one shoulder, nearly covering her breasts. I reached out and touched those tempting breasts again, brushing the hair away so that I could admire them throughout the seduction. I wondered if the piercing had given her great pain, and if she had enjoyed the sensation. I began to wonder if she had willingly put those strange rings through her breasts, or if someone had forced her. This last thought enflamed my desire and gave way to more brutal thoughts. I found her right nipple with my lips and began to tease her by pulling the golden ring with my teeth. She arched her graceful back to meet my mouth. She was beautiful in the candlelight, and I was aroused beyond compare, the public nature of our caresses making me all the more excited. I reached down and unwrapped the shawl which covered her lower body. She tipped her pelvis up to meet my hungering stare.

I nearly fell back in my chair, gasping when I saw what rested between my dark beauty's legs. Tucked in the dark thicket of her pubic hair was a fully formed male member. Since I never suspected for a moment that this mesmerizing beauty was endowed with such equipment, you can imagine my surprise. When I finally looked up to her face, I was met with the shine of perfect white teeth in the glow of the candles.

At first I thought his smile was mocking and the humiliation I felt turned my thoughts immediately vile. But then I saw the softness of her breasts, the inviting tilt of her body and I wanted to possess her.

Unsure as to what to do next, yet still aroused by her beauty, I found it difficult to fall into her caresses again for I had yet to have relations with another man and I had been taught to find the act repugnant. And that made me want him more, because he was forbidden. I kept thinking of my lover, who had disappeared into an opium cloud, and wishing she could see this anomaly of nature, this beauty with perfectly formed breasts and as perfect a member as I had ever seen. I could feel the Gypsy pulling me towards her. She began to kiss me passionately with his full lips, her dark nipples long and perfect to the touch. I couldn't resist taking them into my hands. He slowly began to open the front of my dress shirt with her long, feminine fingers, the puzzling, maddening smile never leaving his face. I felt as though he were challenging me to make love to him, to take her in my arms and possess her. Her smile was pressing me to accept what I wanted, what I desired. I was utterly perplexed, repulsed and simultaneously wishing nothing more than to possess this man/woman. She was wrapping her arms around me and, as he did, I could feel her cock against my leg. She began kissing my chest and unbuttoning my pants, his hand having found the profound evidence of my passion within the folds of my trousers. The intoxicating sensation was not entirely unfamiliar, and as she took hold of my sex I saw the fleeting image of the day I insisted on making a man of my mistress.

Before I could protest, he fell gracefully to her knees, her mouth over my cock. Her tongue flicked over the head and then he took the whole length into her mouth. I could feel her hair brushing my bare chest as his head fell lightly against my stomach, her cheek moving up and down against the tender flesh of my lower abdomen. I lifted my hips to thrust the full length of my member down her throat and he took it hungrily into her willing mouth. I started to press her head hard over my throbbing sex as I felt an orgasm filling every nerve of my body. I looked down to see my own hands pushing her hard, then harder over me, and I could feel the low masculine sound of his pleasure as he tasted me. She was touching her own cock and turned her body so that I might see what I was engaged with. Suddenly my mistress appeared from the dark, her eyelids drooping sensuously, obviously under the spell of the magical pipe.

The corners of my mistress's mouth turned up in a drugged smile as she saw the woman from behind, her dark-haired head moving languorously up and down against my belly. I opened my mouth to explain, then thought better of it. The pleasurable sensations running through my body were also making it impossible for me to utter intelligible words. My mistress moved towards me. In the hazy light she looked fantastically gorgeous. She came up beside me and began to kiss me passionately on the mouth as the Gypsy he/she continued to suck my cock. I pulled my mistress's face away from mine and said to her in a commanding voice, "Get under him. Let him have you."

"Who, my darling, who?" she answered, intoxicated and compliant.

"Her," I said, and pushed my lover towards the dark woman, who stroked her male member slowly as he licked my own member. She gasped and tried to move away.

"No," she said quietly, "no . . . I—"

I put my lips over her mouth and kissed her. Then I took her lower lip between my teeth and I bit until I drew blood as I pressed her languid body downward. I had to see this sight, two beautiful women together, one of them penetrating the other. I wanted to watch my mistress take her inside herself, I wanted to watch their breasts touch.

"Do it," I moaned and then let myself fall over into the blinding sensuality that had been threatening to overcome me. I pushed her down to the floor and she seemed to spill to the ground in her soft skin, her opium flesh, and her champagne-coloured dress.

The Gypsy moved magically when he saw my mistress presented to him, there at my feet. Through the dazed comfort of the after-effects of my pleasure, I watched my mistress struggle hopelessly for a moment under his feminine touch. He stroked her breasts with his, she fell upon my mistress, her dark hair spilling like wine, her narrow hips coming down hard upon my mistress, lifting her dress as he licked her nipples, the movement of his narrow hips flowering, slightly more feminine finally than masculine as she pushed her cock inside my mistress. And when my mistress lifted her body to greet the sensation, I let my head fall back. I closed my eyes and let the violent nausea overtake my senses. The sickness I was feeling was only a symptom of what I was coming to know as my true being. I was sick and delighted with the monster I was discovering within, the hideous malformed personality that had lain dormant, waiting for the opportunity to arise and overtake the superficial in my soul. The bestial. That is what I truly am. It took an evening at L'Enfer to allow for the inevitable release.

I heard my mistress crying out. It was a strange sound of grudging pleasure mingled with humiliation and rage. It was a sound that satisfied me. I felt more alert. I leaned towards the ground to find my mistress's lips and chin covered with what was presumably *my* sperm. The freakish man/woman heaved into her one last time, releasing a masculine groan of sexual release. Then the creature's cry turned to a roar of frustration, a keening sound of anger. She lifted herself away from my mistress and disappeared into the dark. My lover fell to one side, rolling slightly back and forth, her body not quite recovered from the trauma of such a pleasure. I realized that the dark-haired creature most probably took no real pleasure in possessing my mistress, but had done it for my pleasure. For when the thing had looked up towards me as he arched her back, we met eyes, and the calculated cruelty she found there was most telling, I am sure. She had therefore run. He was a wise woman, that poor forgotten creature. He was a very lucky girl. If she had stayed, I am afraid of what I would have done to him . . .

At last my lover opened her eyes and I found that the opium had not worn off in the least, yet a new expression was clinging to the sides of her mouth. It was a confused turn of her lips and I realized that the effects of the opium and the dark-haired creature that had possessed my lover were a trifle horrifying. I laughed as she half-stood and fell into my arms. Many eyes were looking upon us with great appreciation. I turned to find that the mysterious Gypsy had vanished into the opium darkness, leaving my lover to our private kisses. I pretended to give her comfort. But inwardly I laughed, and my hysterics, had they had a colour, would have been scarlet and shameless. I stroked my lover's hair. My affection for her had turned to hate, to resentment. I kissed her neck and put my arms around the fragility of her body. Again I was consumed with thoughts of the simplicity of murder.

My mistress was overcome with the seductive languor that opium induces, and she rested in my arms as I ordered a bottle of champagne. She fell in and out of her opium stupor, made worse by the champagne that I plied her with. She lay her cheek against the tabletop and I noticed how lovely she looked, her lips swollen from my kisses, her eyes mellowed and half-aware of the nightmare she had stepped into unknowingly. The nightmare she had in fact paid for.

After some time, the little orchestra began to play a low soulful tune. The guests at the tables readied themselves to watch the show. Slowly all light, aside from the candles on the tables, was doused. The lamps at the foot of the stage were lit, and at long last the curtain that surrounded the little stage in the centre of the club began to part.

The tableau was fantastic.

In the centre of the stage was an extraordinarily large chair. The back of it rose up at least six feet. Seated on it was a woman whose face was hidden by a black leather mask similar to the one the doorman had been wearing. In this instance, the only part of her face that was exposed was her mouth, a hole showing her lips painted bright red. Her hands were held with leather thongs threaded over her head and pinioned to an iron eyebolt in the centre of the back of the chair. Her legs were also bound, her sex shaved and widely exposed, her ankles tied to the front legs of this throne of sorts. The stage-lights caught a golden flash from between her legs and I realized that this woman wore rings of gold pierced through her labia, just as the Japanese girl had. A thorny shiver of recognition, of memory, rasped through my body. I studied the little chain that ran through the rings on the outer lips of her sex and then encircled her waist.

There was nothing more on the stage. Except a sleek black panther. The magnificent beast lounged alongside the girl's chair, its black fur gleaming in the theatrical lighting. It was an extraordinary animal. It lay with its mouth open, panting. It was chained to the massive arms of the chair, and, though the chain kept the animal at a safe distance from the audience, the beast was not going to be kept from the girl. The tension in the air matched my mood. It was a murderous perfume and every nerve of my body waited. I wanted to watch that creature tear into the flesh of that young girl. I wanted to put my hands round my lover's throat. I wanted to hear screams of shock mingled with my own delighted cries.

"Let's go home, darling," my mistress managed to whisper. She sat staring at the potentially gruesome tableau, unable to move. She was waiting for me to motivate the action of fleeing this scene. She was going to have to wait a long time. Or so I thought.

The panther stood up lazily, but her movements became more agitated, more predatory, as she heard and felt the sound of human fear. For some of the guests this bestial passion play was a bit too realistic.

"I only came here to realize fantasy!" I heard one woman exclaim indignantly as she and her escort stood to leave.

Good, I thought. It is good and right that all those unable to endure the instinctive realities of our bloodthirst, all those who would deny a chance to witness the feral, the barbaric savagery that sat within every heart, should well leave. L'Enfer was no place for merciful.

"Please, I'm begging you. Take me from this place," she said. For the first time I saw in her eyes real terror. I was so disappointed in her. Her eyes, her wonderfully sharkish eyes, were the feature of her

I most adored, most admired. And now in the face of this she wanted to run. She had shown her humanity and I couldn't forgive her.

The panther tried to lunge into the tables and chairs. She tried to swipe at the conductor in the small pit. But her chain kept her from making fatal contact. I ignored my mistress.

Finally, as though the panther had had the dignity not to attempt the obvious first, she at last turned towards the prey meant for her. The girl bound in the chair had already started screaming. But when the panther got closer, she stopped and began pleading. The girl beseeched the audience she could only hear. She begged certain people by first names, perhaps her abductors, her masters, her lovers . . . I watched as the panther circled in slowly. I could not pull my starving eyes from the scene.

"I must . . . I must . . . go . . . I must . . ." My mistress stood and stumbled to the floor.

I started to laugh when, through spraying blood, the poor girl on the stage began to actually pray to God.

I yanked my mistress to her feet. She fell against me. We started to move through the thick, sanguine air of L'Enfer. There were very few guests remaining seated. I thought the whole tableau brilliant and knew that I would certainly be back for more. The next morning, as I drank my chocolate in the sunny little flat, the newspaper was delivered. On the first page was a story concerning the murder of a beautiful young society woman found floating in the Seine. Her body had been torn to shreds and the police could only believe it was the work of a beast, a maniac, yet the tears on her body resembled *claw* marks. Her husband, an elderly gentleman, offered what I thought to be a minor reward to anyone giving reliable clues or information to the police.

I wake sometimes, plagued by a recurring nightmare. I have finally persuaded my new mistress, a wealthy girl rebelling against her family, to accompany me to L'Enfer. I know that only a visit to that place will sate my appetite.

I have become so hungry.

She is to be here any moment, at the flat she has recently rented for me.

# Erotophobia

O'Neil De Noux

*This story is for Debb*

She shook out her long brown hair, turned her cobalt-blue eyes towards me and winked as the slim Negro named Sammy began to unbutton her blouse. She was trying her best not to act nervous. Sammy's fingers shook as he moved from the top button of her green silk blouse to the second button.

I leaned my left shoulder against the brick wall of the makeshift photo studio and watched. The second floor of a defunct shoe factory, the studio was little more than an open room with a hardwood floor, worn brick walls lined with windows overlooking Claiborne Avenue and two large glass skylights above. It smelled musty and faintly of varnish.

The photographer, Sammy's older cousin Joe Cairo, snapped a picture with his 35mm Leica. Joe was thin and light-skinned and about twenty-five. Shirtless, he wore blue jeans and no shoes. His skin was already shiny with sweat. Sammy was also shirtless and shoeless, wearing only a pair of baggy white shorts. His skin was so black it looked like varnished mahogany against Brigid's pale flesh.

Yeah, her name was Brigid. Brigid de Loup, white female, twenty-seven, five feet three inches with pouty lips and a gorgeous face. Gorgeous. With her green blouse, she wore a tight black skirt and a pair of open-toe black high heels.

She bit her lower lip as Sammy's fingers moved to the third button, the one between her breasts. She looked at him and raised her arms and put her hands behind her head. Sammy let out a high-pitched noise and moved his fingers down to the fourth button.

My name? Lucien Caye, white male, thirty, six feet even, with brown eyes and wavy brown hair in need of a haircut. I stood there with my arms folded and watched, my snub-nosed .38 Smith and Wesson in a leather holster on my right hip. I'm a private eye.

"You're going to have to pull my blouse out," Brigid told Sammy.

Sammy nodded, his gaze focused on her chest as he pulled her blouse out of her skirt and unbuttoned the final two buttons. He pushed the blouse off her shoulders and dropped it to the floor.

I loosened my black and gold tie and unbuttoned the top button of my white dress shirt, then stuck my hands in the pockets of my pleated black suit pants to straighten out my rising dick.

Brigid looked at me as she turned her back to Sammy, who fumbled with the button at the back of her skirt. Her white bra was lacy and low cut. Jesus, her breasts looked luscious.

I moved to one of the windows and opened it and flapped my shirt as the air filtered through the high branches of the oaks lining Claiborne. The spring of '48 was already a scorcher, yet the air was surprisingly cool and smelled of rain. A typical afternoon New Orleans rainstorm was coming. I could feel it.

Brigid had come to me two weeks earlier, in a Cadillac, with diamonds on her fingers and pearls around her neck, and told me she needed a bodyguard.

Yeah. Right.

"I suffer from erotophobia," she said, crossing her legs as she sat in the soft-back chair next to my desk.

"What?"

"It's the fear of erotic experiences."

Yeah. Right.

If someone had told me back when I was a cop that a stunning dish would tell me *that* one day, I'd have looked at them as if they were retarded.

She told me her doctor prescribed "shock therapy", and she needed a bodyguard.

"I want to feel erotic. But I also want to be safe."

She told me she was married and her husband approved of what she had in mind.

"What's that?" I asked.

"Sexy pictures."

Sammy finally got the button undone and unzipped her skirt.

"Go down on your knees," Joe the photographer told Sammy, repositioning himself to their side. I kept behind Joe, to keep out of the pictures.

"Now," Joe said. "Pull her skirt down."

Brigid looked back at Sammy and wiggled her ass. Sammy's hands grabbed the sides of the skirt and pulled it down over her hips, his face about four inches from the white panties covering her ass. Brigid turned, put her left hand on his shoulder and stepped out of her skirt.

"Take her stockings off next," Joe said.

Brigid lifted her left leg and told Sammy he'd need to take her shoes off first. He did, then reached up to unsnap her stockings from her lacy garter belt.

He rolled each stocking down, his sinewy fingers roaming down her legs. Brigid put her arms behind her head again and spread her feet wide for him. She bit her lower lip again.

Sammy, on his haunches now, wiped sweat from his forehead and looked back at his cousin who told him the bra was next. I felt perspiration working its way down my back. My temples were already damp with sweat.

Brigid started to turn and Joe told her to do it face to face. He switched to his second Leica. Brigid gave Joe a look, a knowing look, and something passed between them. I was sure.

"If you don't mind," Joe added in a shaky voice. "It'll be sexier."

Brigid smiled shyly. "That's what I want." Her voice was husky.

Her chest rose as she took in a deep breath. Sammy stood up and reached around her. It only took him a second to unhook the bra and pull it off, freeing Brigid's nice round breasts.

Oh, God . . .

Her small nipples were pointed. Her breasts rose with her breathing. Sammy stared at them from less than a foot away. He blinked and said, "Wow."

Brigid looked at me and smiled and I could see a nervous tic in her cheek. She took in another deep breath, her breasts rising again.

Joe stepped up and tapped Sammy on the shoulder and told him to go down on his knees again. "Now," Joe said, "take her panties off."

Joe hurriedly set up for more shots.

Sammy tucked his fingers into the top of her panties. Brigid leaned her head back to face the skylights and closed her eyes. Joe snapped away and my dick was a diamond-cutter now. Sammy pulled her panties down, his nose right in front of her bush. She stepped out of them, and he leaned back and stared at her thick pubic hair, a shade darker than the long hair on her pretty head. Brigid turned slowly and pointed her ass at Sammy who reached up and unhooked her garter belt and pulled it away.

"OK. Stop," Joe said, sitting on the floor. He pulled his camera bag to him and unloaded both Leicas before loading them again.

Brigid slowly turned to face me. Her face was serious now and flushed. I moved my gaze down her body and almost came just looking at her. She winked at me when I looked back at her face, she rolled her shoulders slightly, her breasts swaying with her movement.

Joe told Sammy to stand up when the cameras were loaded. He took several pictures of them standing face to face, looking at one another and then asked them to stand side by side.

"No touching," Brigid said, reminding Joe of the ground rules. He nodded and had them sit next, side by side with their legs straight out. Brigid leaned back on her hands and Sammy leered at her bush.

Then Joe had them sit cross-legged facing one another. I felt my dick stir again when she leaned back and shook out her hair and the light from the skylight seemed to illuminate her body. God, she looked so sexy with her breasts pointing and her legs open and all her bush exposed.

Joe asked Brigid to stand and put her hands on her hips and move her feet apart as Sammy remained sitting, staring at her pussy, which was at eye-level now. Brigid looked at Joe when he moved her, his hand on her hip. They exchanged brief, warm smiles as he moved her.

Sammy let out a deep breath and Brigid laughed. I was breathing pretty heavy myself. Jesus, what a scene. Joe moved them around in different positions and snapped furiously and switched cameras again.

He had them sit again and entwined their legs. Sammy's dark skin was in stark contrast with Brigid's fair skin. Joe moved in for close-ups of Brigid's chest and moved down to snap her bush. She looked at him and moved her knees apart as she sat.

"Yeah. Yeah," Joe said, snapping away. "Don't stop."

Joe pulled Brigid up by the hand and had her stand over Sammy, straddling his outstretched legs as he sat. Then Joe had her sit on Sammy's legs, her legs open as she faced Sammy.

"Now lean back on your hands," Joe said.

Brigid leaned back, her legs open, her pussy wide open to Sammy and Joe behind him snapping away, and me peeking at her pink slit. She was hairy. I like that in a woman. I especially liked the delicate hairs just outside her pussy.

Jesus. What a sight . . .

She looked at Joe for a long second, staring at him the way a woman does when she's getting screwed. She wasn't looking at the camera, and Sammy was just a prop. She looked at Joe. The look on her face was for him. It was a subtle move, but I caught it. Joe snapped at a furious pace.

Brigid finally climbed off Sammy, turned and walked to the bathroom and closed the door behind her. She walked purposefully, as if she had trouble moving her legs.

Sammy lay all the way down and panted, his chest slick with sweat now. Joe picked up his cameras and hurriedly reloaded both. I opened another window. The air was misty now and felt damp and cool on my face. I looked down on the avenue at the tops of the passing cars and then looked straight out at the dark branches and green leaves of the oaks. I wondered what the passers-by would think if they knew what was going on up here.

The bathroom door opened and Brigid came out, walking more steadily. She stepped over to her purse and took out her compact, then touched up her face with powder, re-applied dark red lipstick.

She smiled at Joe and said, "No pictures right now. OK?"

He nodded.

Brigid moved over to Sammy and said, "Stand up and put your hands on your head."

"Huh?"

She bent over and grabbed his right hand and pulled him up. Then she lifted his hands and put them on his head, the way we did the Krauts we took prisoner outside Rome. She yanked Sammy's shorts down, pulled them off his feet and tossed them aside. He wore no underwear. His long thin dick stood straight up like a flag pole. Brigid smiled and looked Sammy in the eyes.

She reached down and grabbed Sammy's dick. He jumped. Slowly, she worked her hand up and down his long dick. Sammy moaned.

Brigid looked at me and said, "I don't want y'all to think I'm just a tease."

Jesus, a white woman giving a Negro a hand job. Unbefuckinlievable. I figured she knew it wouldn't bother me in the way it would bother most white boys. She had me pegged from day one, I guess, from the way I treated Joe and the Negroes we'd come across during her posing sessions.

Brigid looked at Joe and it was there again, that come-hither sexy look, but only for a moment. She bent over, her legs stiff, her ass straight up, and leaned over and kissed the tip of Sammy's cock. He rocked on his feet and she increased her jerking motion until he came. She caught it with her free hand and wiped Sammy's come on his chest when he finished. Then she turned to Joe and asked if he wanted a hand job. He shook his head.

She looked at me and said, "Need some help with those blue balls?"

I shook my head slowly and watched her go back into the bathroom. She left the door open this time and washed her hands. She towelled off, left the towel and walked straight back to me. She put her hands on my chest, leaned up and gave me a fluttery kiss on my lips.

Then she went over to Joe and gave him the same fluttery kiss. I could see him squirm and then close his eyes. He smiled warmly at her when she pulled away.

"Come on," she said. "Let's finish these rolls."

Joe told Sammy to go wash off. When he returned, Joe posed them together naked. The climax of the shooting had Brigid straddling Sammy's legs again as they sat, her pussy wide open and Sammy's dick up and hard again.

When Joe ran out of film again, Brigid got up and told me, "Time to get the film, big boy. I hope you counted the rolls."

I had.

Joe unloaded both cameras and gave me the six rolls of film. We watched Brigid dress. Sammy went into the bathroom. He was still there when Brigid and I left.

Sitting in my pre-war 1940 DeSoto, her legs crossed and her skirt riding high on her naked thighs, Brigid smiled at me and said, "Next time we'll shoot in a cemetery."

"Yeah?" I could smell her perfume again in the confines of the car.

"Joe knows some gravediggers at Cypress Grove. Posing naked among the crypts, in front of a captive audience . . . alive and dead, will be so delicious."

It didn't take a fuckin' genius to figure the one thing this woman didn't have – was erotophobia. I still hadn't figured her angle.

"When did Joe tell you about the gravediggers?"

She winked at me. "When I called him yesterday. That was when he told me he had his cousin lined up for today's session."

The rain came down hard now and the windshield was fogging as I tooled the DeSoto up Claiborne, away from the Negro section called Treme towards uptown where the rich lily-whites lived in their Victorian and Neo-Classical and Greek Revival homes. I cracked my window and felt the rain flutter my hair.

Brigid leaned against the passenger door and watched me. Her dress was so high I could almost see her ass the way she rolled her hips. She eye-fucked me all the way home, ogling me every time I looked her way.

Jesus, she was so fuckin' pretty and so fuckin' sexy and so fuckin' nasty. She hired me to make sure no one raped her. That was the last thing a man would do with a woman like her. At least, that was the last thing I'd do. I'd want her to come to me, wrap those legs around me and fuck me back.

"Want to come in and meet my husband?" she asked when I pulled up in front of her white Greek Revival home on Audubon Boulevard.

"No, that's OK."

"He's waiting for me to tell him what it was like." She raised her purse and added, "And to develop the film." Her husband had a built-in darkroom.

She pulled a white envelope from her purse and handed it to me. Cash. She always paid me in small bills. I actually got paid to watch her get naked and pose with her legs open. Tell me America isn't a great country.

Brigid opened the door, stopped, moved across the seat and kissed me. I felt her tongue as she French kissed me in front of her big house and I thought I would come right there. I watched her hips as she walked away, barefoot up her front walk to the large front gallery with its nine white columns. Her high-heel dangling from her left hand, she turned back and waved at me and went in the front cut-glass door of her big house.

The rain came down in torrents that evening. I stood inside the French doors of my apartment balcony and watched it roll in sheets across Cabrini Playground here on Barracks Street. The oak branches waved in the torrent. The wind shook the thick rubbery leaves and white petals of the large magnolias. I looked beyond the playground at the slick, tilted roofs and red brick chimneys of the French Quarter. The old part of town always looked older in the rain.

I leaned against the glass door and looked down at my DeSoto parked against the curb. The glass felt cool against my cheek. The street wasn't flooded yet at least. I took a sip of Scotch, felt it burn its way down to my empty belly, and closed the drapes.

I sat back on my sofa, in front of the revolving fan, and closed my eyes and remembered the first time we'd gone out to shoot pictures.

It was in Cabrini Playground. It was a real turn-on watching Brigid sit in a tight red skirt, sit so Joe could see up her dress and take pictures of her white panties.

The second time was in City Park where she stripped down to her bra and panties to pose beneath an umbrella of oak branches. Two workers came across us and Brigid liked that. She liked an audience. Joe moved us to the back lagoon for some topless pictures, only some fishermen saw us and got pissed at the half-naked white girl with the black boy, so we had to bail out. My dick was a diamond-cutter again as I sat on my sofa. I finished my Scotch, readjusted my hard-on, knowing the only relief I could feel would be in a hot wash rag.

I closed my eyes and remembered the two brunette whores we came across just outside Rome, the day before I was wounded, Monte Cassino, 1944. The girls were about twenty, a little on the plump side with pale white skin. They fucked the entire platoon and got up to wave goodbye to us early the next morning, when we moved out.

My doorbell rang. I stood slowly and walked down the stairs to the door. Through the transom above the louvered front door, I saw the top of a yellow cab. I peeked out the door and Brigid was there, her hair dripping in the rain. I opened the door and she turned and waved to the cabby who drove off up Barracks.

Brigid stepped past me and stood dripping in the foyer. Wearing the same clothes she had for the photo session, she shivered and cupped her hands against her chest, her head bent forward. I closed the door. I put my hand under her chin and lifted her face and she blinked those cobalt eyes at me. They were red now with a blue semicircle bruise under her left eye.

"Pipi hit me," she said, her lower lip quivering. "Can I come up?"

I took her right hand and brought her up and straight into my bathroom. I grabbed the box of kitchen matches from the medicine cabinet and lit the gas wall heater. Standing, I turned as Brigid dropped her bra.

"Don't leave," she said, bending over to run a bath. "You've seen it all."

I put the lid down on the commode and sat and watched her take her clothes off. She smiled weakly at me, her lips still shaking as she climbed into the tub. The water continued running as she sank back.

"How about some coffee?"

"You have any Scotch?"

I stood and looked down at her. Her eyes were closed and the water moved dreamily over her naked body and she looked so damn sexy. I poured us each a double Johnnie Walker Red and went back in.

A silent hour and two drinks later, as well as two hard-ons, she stood up in the tub and asked me to pass her a towel. In the bright light of the bathroom, her skin looked white-pink. She dried herself and wrapped a fresh towel around her chest just above her breasts, and took my hand and led me out to the sofa where we sat.

She poured us both another Scotch, left hers on the coffee table next to the bottle and turned her back to me to lie across my lap as I sat straight up. I had to adjust my dick again and she knew and smiled at me.

"I'll take care of that," she said softly and closed her eyes.

With no make-up, with her hair still damp and getting frizzy, with the mouse under her eye – she was still gorgeous. Some women are like that, plain-knockdown-gorgeous.

After a while she told me that Pipi, that's her husband, couldn't get it up when she came in and told him about what she'd done. She even dug out the previous pictures and went down on him, but he was as limp as a Republican's brain.

Then he hit her, punched her actually, and kicked her out, shoved her into the rain.

"At least he called a cab for me." She opened her cobalt blues and blinked up at me. "Guess you figured he's the one with erotophobia. Pipi's the one afraid of erotic experiences."

No shit.

She sat up, reached over and grabbed her drink and downed it with one gulp. I got up a second and moved to the balcony doors. I didn't hear the rain any more, so I cracked them. It was still drizzling so I left them open and went back to the sofa. I felt the coolness immediately. It was nice.

She settled her head back in my lap and closed her eyes again. The towel had risen and I could see a hint of her bush now. I reached over and picked up my drink and finished it, then put the glass back on the coffee table. A while later, she sighed and turned her face towards me and I could see by her even breathing she was asleep. The towel opened when she turned and I looked at her body again.

I wanted to fuck her so badly. I climbed out from under her head, stood and stretched. I reached down and scooped Brigid into my arms. I took her into my bedroom and laid her on the bed. She sighed again and I leaned over and kissed her lips gently. I grabbed the second pillow and went back out to the sofa and poured myself another stiff one. I was feeling kinda woozy by then anyway so I lay back on the sofa and tried some deep breathing with my eyes closed.

There was a movie I saw where a private eye turned Veronica Lake down because it ain't good business to sleep with clients. Fuck that shit. Brigid wouldn't have to ask me again. I pulled off my socks and gulped down the rest of my drink and lay back on the pillow and closed my eyes. I tried deep breathing and letting my mind float. And just as I was drifting I realized it wasn't Veronica Lake. It was Ann Sheridan. Or was it Barbara Stanwyck in a blonde wig?

The banging of the French doors woke me. I sat up too quickly and felt dizzy and had to lean back on the sofa. It was pitch outside and nearly as dark inside. Lightning flashed and the rainy wind raised the drapes like floating ghosts. A roll of thunder made the old building shiver.

The wind felt cool on my face. I started to rise and saw her standing next to the sofa. I sank back as lightning flashed again, illuminating her naked body in white light. I felt her move up to me and felt her arms on my shoulders as she climbed on me. She said something, but the thunder drowned it.

I felt the weight of her body on my lap as she ripped at my shirt. I tried to help, but she tore it and we both pulled it off. She grabbed my belt and slapped my hand when I tried to help. Rising, she shoved my pants and underwear down and then sank back on me. I felt her bush up against my dick, her mouth searching my face for my lips. Our tongues worked against each other as I raised my hands for those breasts.

She moved her hips up and down slowly as we kissed. I felt the wetness between her legs. She rose high and reached down to guide my dick into her. She sank on it and shivered and then fucked me like I've never been fucked before.

And she talked nasty. "Oh, fuck me. Come on. Fuck me. Oh, God I love your dick. I love it. Fuck me. Yes. Yes. Oh, God."

I like it when women call me God, even if it's just for a little while.

She bounced on me. "More," she said. "More!"

Hell, there was no more. She had it all.

She screamed and I came in her in long spurts and she cried out and held on to my neck. Then she collapsed on me and it took a while for our breathing to return to normal.

I looked over her shoulder as lightning flashed again and saw the wet floor next to the open balcony doors. The wind whipped up again and felt so damn good on our hot bodies. The thunder rolled once more and sounded further away. When I could gather enough strength, I kicked off my pants and shorts. I lifted her and carried her back into the bedroom. I climbed on her and fucked her nice and long the way second fucks should be, deep and time-consuming.

She wrapped her legs around my waist and her arms around my neck and kissed me and kissed me. She was one great, loving kisser. She made noises, sexy noises, but didn't talk nasty. She just fucked me back in long hip-grinding pumps.

After I came I stayed in her until her gyrating hips slipped my dick out. I rolled on my back and pulled her to me and she snuggled her face in the crook of my neck, her hot body pressed against me.

Every once in a while I felt the breeze come in and try to cool us.

She was still pressed against me when the daylight woke me. I slipped out of bed, relieved myself and pulled on a fresh pair of boxers before brushing my teeth. She lay on her stomach, the sheet wrapped around her right leg, her long hair covering her face.

I went to the kitchen and started up a pot of coffee and chicory, bacon and eggs. She came in just as I was putting the bacon next to the eggs on the two plates on my small white Formica table. Naked, she walked up and planted a wet one on my lips. She leaned back and brushed her hair out of her face and said, "I used your toothbrush."

"Sit down." I went back and put the bacon pan in the sink and poured us two cups of strong coffee.

"You don't have a barrette, do you?" She moved around the table and sat.

"Huh?"

"Left over from a previous fuck?"

"Yeah. Right." I put her coffee in front of her and sat across the table and ate my bacon and eggs and watched her breasts as she lifted her fork to eat. OK, I looked at her face too and stared into those turquoise eyes that glittered back at me as she ate. But mostly I looked at her tits. Round and perfectly symmetrical, they were so fuckin' pretty. I can't explain it. Tits have a power over men. Women will never understand. We have no fuckin' idea ourselves.

The eggs and bacon weren't bad. The coffee was nice and strong. After, we took a bath together. Soaping each other and rinsing off, we stayed in the tub until the water cooled and that felt even better than the warm water.

"Will you take me home? I don't want to go alone."

Brigid stood in the bathroom, her belly against the sink as she applied make-up to her face. In her bra and panties, she had her butt out. I told her I'd bring her home.

"I want to pick up some things. Will you take me to my mother's after?"

"Sure."

I finished my coffee, put the cup on the nightstand and then dressed myself. She came out and ran her hand across my shoulders as she passed behind me to pick up her skirt.

I finished tying my sky-blue tie, the one with the palm tree on it, and ran my fingers down the crease of my pleated blue suit pants.

"Nice shoes," she said when I slipped on my two-tone black and white wing tips. Women always noticed shoes.

I finished in time to watch Brigid finish. I liked watching women dress, nearly as much as watching them undress. I grabbed my suit coat on the way out.

"You're not bringing a gun?"

"You gonna get naked in front of any strange men on the way home?"

"No."

"Then I don't need to shoot anybody, do I?"

Pipi's black Packard was in the driveway. I parked behind it and followed Brigid in. I waited in the marble-floored foyer and watched Brigid's hips as she moved up the large spiral staircase. Figured I was about to meet old Pipi, the fuckin' wife-beater himself. I hate men that hit women. Hate 'em.

Just as I peeked in at the Audubon prints on the walls of the study, Brigid screamed upstairs. I took the stairs three at a time and followed the screams up to a large bedroom with giant flamingo lamps, blond furniture and a huge round bed with the body of a man on it. The man's head lay in a pool of blood. Brigid had her back pressed up against a large chifforobe in the right corner of the room, next to the drapes. She covered her face with her hands and screamed again.

The man lay on his side. I leaned over to look at his face. I recognized Pipi de Loup from the society page, even with the unmistakable dull look of death on his waxen face and his eyes blackened from the concussion of the bullet. The back of his head was a mass of dyed black hair and brain tissue. Brigid turned around and started crying.

I looked at the mirror above the long dresser, looked into my own eyes and felt my stomach bottom out. I saw the word "sap" written across my face.

I moved over and grabbed Brigid's hand and led her out of the bedroom and down the stairs and out to my car. I opened the passenger door and told her to sit. Then I went next door and called the police.

Brigid was still crying when I got back to the DeSoto. I leaned against the rear fender and waited. Two patrolmen arrived first. I knew neither. I pointed at the house. The taller went in, the other took out his notebook and asked my name.

A half-hour and fifty questions later, Lieutenant Frenchy Capdeville pulled his black prowl car behind my car. He stepped out and shook his head at me, took off his brown suit coat and tossed it back in the prowl car.

Short and wiry, with curly black hair and a pencil-thin moustache, Capdeville looked like Zorro – with a flat Cajun nose. He waltzed past me and stood next to the open door of my car and looked at Brigid's crossed legs. He pulled the ever-present cigarette from his mouth, flicked ashes on the driveway and told me, "You stay put."

He reached his hand in and asked Brigid to step into the house with him. He left a rookie patrolman with an Irish name to guard me while other detectives arrived, one with a camera case. I looked up at the magnolia tree and tried counting the white blossoms, but lost count after twenty. At least the big tree, along with the two even larger oaks, kept the sun off me as I waited. I looked around at the neighbours who came out periodically to sneak a peek at the sideshow.

A detective arrived and waved at me on the way in. He was in my class at the academy. He was the only white boy I ever knew named Spade.

Willie Spade came out of the house an hour later and offered me a cigarette.

"I don't smoke."

"I forgot." He shrugged and lit up with his Zippo. About an inch smaller than me with short carrot-red hair and too many freckles to count, Spade had deep-set brown eyes.

"I need to search your car. OK?"

He meant do I have your consent. I told him sure, go ahead, but didn't expect him to pat me down first. No offense he said. No problem I said.

While he was digging in my back seat he said we needed to go to the office for my statement.

"I'd like to drive," I said. "I'd rather not leave my car here."

Spade turned and wiped sweat from his brow. "You can drive us both."

"No," I said. "I didn't touch a fuckin' thing in the house. She opened the door and I didn't touch the railing on the way up the stairs. The only thing I touched was her arm, when I dragged her out."

Spade narrowed his deep-set eyes. "You touched more of her than her arm."

I nodded and leaned back in the hardwood folding chair in the small interview room. I looked out the lone window at the old wooden buildings across South White Street from the Detective Bureau Office on the second floor of the concrete Criminal Courts Building at Tulane and Broad. A grey pigeon landed on the window ledge and blinked at me.

"We found the murder weapon on the floor next to the bed."

"Yeah?"

"A Colt .38. The misses says it's Pipi's gun. He kept it in the nightstand next to the bed. The drawer was open."

"I didn't notice." I picked up the cup of coffee on the small table and took a sip. Cold.

"The doors and windows were all locked," Spade said, watching me carefully for a reaction.

"What time did the doctor say he died?"

"Between 2 and 4 a.m. Give or take an hour."

I nodded.

Spade leaned back in his chair and put his arms behind his head and I saw perspiration marks on his yellow shirt. His brown tie was loosened. "So you're her alibi and she's yours," he said.

I nodded again and felt that hollow kick in my stomach.

There was a knock on the door and a hand reached in and waved Spade out. A couple minutes later Spade returned with a fresh cup of java, along with my wing tips. He dropped my shoes on the floor and put the coffee in front of me. He pulled my keys out and put them on the table before sitting himself.

"Find anything?" I said as I leaned down and pulled my shoes on.

"Nope." Spade didn't sound disappointed. He sounded a little relieved. He put his elbows up on the table and told me how they knew the killer came in the kitchen door. It rained last night. The killer came in through the back with muddy shoes, wiped them on the kitchen mat and still tracked mud all the way up to the bedroom, then tracked mud right back out.

"That's why we had to search your pad and office," he explained the obvious. They had to check out all my shoes, and everything else in my fuckin' life.

"Let himself in with a key?" I asked when I sat up.

"Or," Spade shrugged, "the door was unlocked and the killer flipped the latch on his way out, locking it. We have some prints, but smudges mostly."

I nodded.

Spade let out a tired sigh and said, "You know the score. Whoever finds the body is automatically the first suspect."

"Until you prove they didn't do it. I know."

I didn't say – especially when it's the wife and the man who's fuckin' the wife.

"I'll be right back," Spade said and left me with my fresh coffee and my view of South White Street.

A while later, just as I was thinking how an interview room would be better for the police without a window, the door opened and Frenchy Capdeville walked in with Spade. Capdeville took the chair. Spade leaned against the wall.

Capdeville smiled at me and asked if I knew anything about the pictures they found in Mr de Loup's darkroom. I told them everything. Fuck, they knew it anyway.

I ended with a question. "Did your men sniff my sheets?"

Capdeville smiled again. "Who found the photographer?"

I waited.

"You come up with a nigger photographer for her, or did she?"

"She told me Pipi found him."

Capdeville blew smoke in my face and gave me a speech, the usual one. I could leave for now, but they weren't finished with me yet. They'd be back with more questions, he said, flicking ashes on the dirty floor. He made a point to tell me they weren't finished with Mrs de Loup by a long shot. Her lawyer was on his way and they expected an extended interview.

"One more thing," Capdeville said, looking me in the eyes. "You have any idea who did it?"

"Nope," I lied, looking back at him with no expression in my eyes.

They let me go.

* * *

I drove around until dark, checking to see if I was followed so many times, I got a neck ache. I meandered through the narrow streets of the Quarter, through the twisting streets of the Faubourg Marigny and over to Treme where I parked the DeSoto on Dumaine Street.

I jumped a fence and moved through backyards, leaping two more fences to come up on Joe Cairo's studio from the rear. As I moved up the back stairs, I thought how much this reminded me of a bad detective movie. Easy to figure and hard to forget.

I knocked on the back door. A yellow light came on and Joe's face appeared behind the glass top of the wooden door. His jaw dropped. It actually dropped.

"Come on, open up," I told him. "You don't have much time."

He opened the door and gave me a real innocent look, and I knew for sure he did it. I breezed past him, telling him to lock the door. I followed the lights to a back room bed with a suitcase and camera case on it.

"Going somewhere?" I sat in the only chair in the room, a worn green sofa.

Joe stood in the doorway. He looked around the room but not at me.

I put my hands behind my head and watched him carefully as I said, "She's gonna roll over on you."

Joe looked around the room again, his fingers twitching.

"If I figured it out, you know Homicide will. They're a lot better at this."

Joe started bouncing on his toes, his hands at his sides.

"They found the pictures. She'll bat those big blue eyes at them, roll a tear down those pretty cheeks and tell them, 'Look at the evil things my husband made me do . . . with a nigger.' "

Joe stopped bouncing and glared at me.

"Don't be a sap," I told him. "She'll tie you up in a neat package. Cops like neat packages, cases tied up in a bow. Get out now. Leave. Go to California or Mexico. Just leave, or you'll be in the electric chair before you know it."

Joe leaned his left shoulder against the door frame. "There's nothing for her to tell."

"OK." I stood up. "Wait here. They'll be here soon." I looked at the half-packed suitcase and said, "Don't tell me you thought she was gonna run off with you."

Joe puffed out his cheeks.

"Look around. Look how you live. You saw how she lived." I stepped up to his face. "She used you, just like she used me."

Joe squinted at me. "What you mean, she used you?"

"She came over last night."

Joe shook his head. "She went to her mama's."

"Come on, wise up. She fucked us both. Only you're gonna take the hot squat."

Joe balled his hands into fists.

I looked him hard in the eyes. "What's the matter with you? You killed a fuckin' white man. You're history."

He blinked.

"Forget her, man."

I could see the wheels turning behind his eyes. He opened his mouth, shut it, then said, "He beat his wife."

"I know." That was the thing that tipped the scales, that brought me to Treme, instead of just going home. I hate wife-beaters. I lowered my voice. "You killed a white man. You're in a world of shit, man."

"How . . . how did you . . . know?"

How? It was a gut feeling. It was the way Brigid looked at him, the way he looked back. It was that look of intimacy. Joe was the obvious killer, so obvious it was obscene.

"It had to be you," I told him, "because it wasn't me."

Joe blinked and I could see his eyes were wet.

"You willing to turn her in? You willing to tell the cops she was in on it?"

He looked at me and shook his head. "I'd never do that."

"Then you better beat feet. Go to California. Change your name. But get out now."

Joe looked hesitatingly at his suitcase.

"Forget her," I said forcefully.

"Forget her?"

"Like a bad dream."

I stepped past him. I knew if I was caught here, I'd be in a world of shit too.

Joe grabbed my arm, but let go as soon as I turned. He looked down at my feet said, "Why you helpin' me?"

"Because I'm more like you than I'm like them."

I'm not sure it registered, not completely.

"You're not getting rid of me to keep her for yourself," he said in a voice that told me he didn't believe that.

"She's done with both of us, man."

I went out the way I came, my heart pounding in my chest as I jumped the fences. I slipped behind the wheel of the DeSoto and looked around before starting it. I took the long way home.

It's night again. The French doors of my balcony are open, but there is no breeze. I'm on my fourth Scotch, or is it my fifth? I'm waiting for Capdeville and Spade. They'll be here soon, asking about Joe Cairo, wondering where the fuck he went.

I'll tell them I drove around and went to Cairo's on a hunch. Figuring someone must have seen a white man jumping fences, I'll tell them I tried to sneak up on Cairo, but he was gone.

They'll do a lot of yelling, a lot of guessing, but won't be able to pin anything on me. After all, I didn't do it. I was too busy fucking the wife at the time of the murder. I close my eyes for a moment and the Scotch has me thinking that maybe, just maybe she'll come. But I know better.

Rising from the sofa, I take my drink into the bedroom and look at the messed-up bed.

God, she was so fuckin' beautiful it hurt.

I sit on the edge of my bed. It still smells like sex. I'm sure, if I look hard, I'll find some of her pubic hair scattered in the sheets. That's all I have left – the debris of sex, the memories, and the fuckin' heartache.

# Entertaining Mr Orton

Poppy Z. Brite

*London, 1 August 1967*

"Have you been reading my diary?"

Kenneth looks up from the baboon's head he is pasting onto the madonna's body. He is standing on the bed to reach the upper part of his collage, which covers most of the wall, and the top of his bald cranium nearly brushes the pink and yellow tiles of the flat's low ceiling. They have lived together in this tiny space in Islington for eight years.

"No, I have not been reading your diary," Kenneth lies.

"Why not?"

"Because it would drive me to suicide."

"Right," says Joe with an edge of impatience in his voice. He has heard this threat many times before, in one form or another, and Kenneth realizes dimly that his lover either doesn't believe it or just doesn't care. That doesn't mean Kenneth can make himself stop saying it, though.

"But if you won't read my diary and you won't talk to me," Joe continues, "what's the point of remaining in this relationship? You're always telling everyone how I make your life miserable. What keeps you hanging about?"

Kenneth wipes glue from his fingers onto his pants, then turns and sits heavily on the bed. He took a number of Valium earlier in the day, but something in Joe's voice pulls his brain out of its pleasant half-numb fog. They can still listen to each other, and even talk seriously when they really try.

Of course, most of the serious talk these days is about writing. Writing Joe's plays, to be precise. The very same brilliant and successful plays that have made Joe's name synonymous with decadence, black wit, and tawdry glamour as far as London was concerned. If the talk isn't about Joe's plays, it is about what they should do with all the money Joe's plays are making. Joe spends most of it on toys: clothes, Polaroid cameras, holidays in Morocco.

"What surprises me," Joe continues, "is that you haven't killed me. I think you don't leave or top yourself because you can't stand the thought of anyone else having me."

"Rubbish. All sorts of people have you."

"Ah! You *have* been reading my diary."

Kenneth rises up suddenly in one of his outbursts. "When you come home reeking of cheap aftershave, I don't need your diary to tell me where you've been!"

Joe waves this away. "I mean, of anyone else having me permanently. And I can't conceive of it either, honestly. It's as if we've become inextricable."

Suspicion flares in Kenneth's mind. "Why are you talking about me killing you? Are you setting me up for something?"

Joe throws back his head and brays laughter, a sound which usually lessens Kenneth's tension but now induces a smouldering rage. "What did you have in mind? Me setting you up for murder and slipping back off to Tangier? My family gets your fat arse thrown in prison and you do your *De Profundis* bit again? Oh, Ken . . ." Tears are spilling out of Joe's eyes now, tears of laughter, the kind he used to cry in bed after a joyous orgasm. Kenneth remembers how they tasted, salt and copper on his tongue like blood.

"I think I *could* kill you," he says, but Joe doesn't hear him.

*Tangier, 25 May 1967*

Five English queens stoned on hash and Valium and Moroccan boy-flesh, sipping red wine on a café terrace against a blood-orange sky. Two American tourists, an older married couple, sitting nearby eavesdropping on the conversation and making their disapproval evident. Joe Orton lets his voice rise gradually until he is not so much shouting as *projecting*, trained Shakespearian actor that he is.

"He took me right up the arse, and afterwards he thanked me for giving him such a good fucking. They're a most polite people. We've got a leopard-skin rug in the flat and he wanted me to fuck him on that, only I'm afraid of the spunk. You see, it might adversely affect the spots of the leopard."

"Those tourists can hear what you're saying," one of the entourage advises. (Not Kenneth Halliwell; though he is present, he wouldn't bother trying to curb Joe even if he wanted to.)

"I mean for them to hear," Joe booms. "They have no right to be occupying chairs reserved for decent sex perverts . . . He might bite a hole in the rug. It's the writhing he does, you see, when my prick is up him, that might grievously damage the rug, and I can't ask him to control his excitement. It wouldn't be natural when you're six inches up the bum, would it?"

The Americans pay for their coffee and move away, looking as if they've had it considerably more than six inches up the bum – dry.

"You shouldn't drive people like that away," says the sensitive queen. "The town needs tourists."

Joe sneers. He has practised it in the mirror. "Not that kind, it doesn't. This is *our* country, *our* town, *our* civilization. I want nothing to do with the civilization they made. Fuck them! They'll sit and listen to buggers' talk from me and drink their coffee and piss off."

"It seems rather a strange joke," offers another member of the entourage timidly.

"It isn't a joke. There's no such thing as a joke," says the author of the most successful comedy now playing in London's West End.

*Leicester, 2 August 1967*

Joe leaves his father's small threadbare house and walks two miles up the road to an abandoned barn, where a man he met in town earlier that day is waiting for him. He is in his home town, which he mostly loathes, to see a production of his play *Entertaining Mr Sloane* and fulfil family obligations. Just now he has some obligations of his own to fulfil.

Joe often likes to have one-off trysts with ugly men, men he finds physically appalling, but this one is a beauty: tall and smoothly muscled, with brown curly hair that tumbles into bright blue eyes, a thick Scottish accent, an exceedingly clever pair of hands, and a big-headed, heavily veined cock.

In the late afternoon shafts of sunlight that filter through the barn's patched roof, they take turns kneeling on the dusty floor and sucking each other to a fever pitch. Then Joe braces himself against the wall and lets that fat textured cock slide deep into his arse, opening himself to this stranger in a way that he never can to Kenneth – not any more, not ever again.

*London, 8 August 1967*

Conversation after the lights are out:

"Joe?"

". . ."

"Joe?"

"What?"

"Why did you ask me if I'd kill you?"

"I don't know what you're on about."

"Do you want to die, Joe?"

"Do I . . . ?" A sudden bray of laughter. "Hell, no! You twit, why would I want to die?"

"Then why did you bring it up?"

"Hm . . ." Joe is already falling back asleep. "I suppose I just wondered whether you were that far gone."

His breathing deepens, slows. Joe is lying on his left side, his face to the wall. The collage spreads above him like a fungus, its components indistinguishable in the street-lit dark. Kenneth sits up, slips out of bed, maybe planning to take a Nembutal, maybe just going to have a pee.

But he freezes at the sight on the bedside table: Joe's open diary and, balanced atop it carelessly, as if flung there by accident, a claw hammer. Joe hung some pictures earlier in the day, so the hammer has every reason to be there. But the juxtaposition of objects hypnotizes Kenneth, draws him.

He extends his hand cautiously, as if he is afraid the hammer will disappear. Then it is in his palm, heavy, smooth wooden handle, a comfortable fit. He raises it.

"Joe?"

Slow breathing.

"Joe?"

*I suppose I just wondered whether you were that far gone . . .*

And the knowledge that he *is* that far gone, that Joe must know that or be blind, sweeps over Kenneth like a dark sea. All the years he has invested, his work, his talent, his whole existence subsumed by Joe. The infidelities lovingly recorded in the diaries, literally under Kenneth's nose (the flat is only sixteen by eighteen feet). In that moment the dam overflows, the camel's back breaks, the shit hits the fan, and life as Kenneth Halliwell knows it becomes intolerable.

Without allowing himself to think about it further, he lets the hammer fall.

Nine times.

The amount of blood on his collage is staggering. Even in the dark Kenneth can see that most of the cutout figures are spattered if not obscured entirely. The thing on the pillow is no longer Joe; it is like a physician's model, an example of a ruined cranium. And yet he still imagines he can hear that slow breathing.

After undressing (Joe's blood is sticky on his pajama top) and scrawling a brief, unremarkable note, Kenneth goes for the bottle of Nembutal and swallows twenty-two, washing them down with a tin of grapefruit juice. He is dead before his considerable bulk hits the floor.

Joe's sheets, however, are still warm when the bodies are found the next morning.

*London, 8 August 1996*

"Harder! It's not going in! *Lean* on it . . . Oh bloody fuck, Willem, get out of the way and let me do it!"

Clive shoulders his way up the narrow staircase and pushes Willem away from one end of a large sofa upholstered in royal purple velvet. The other end of this venerable piece is stuck fast in the doorway of the tiny flat. Clive leans against it and gives a mighty shove. Wiry muscles stand out on his neck and shoulders. Willem mutters something in Dutch.

"What?"

Willem points at a spot just below his navel. "What do you call it when the intestines come out?"

"Hernia? No, look, you push with your knees bent. Like *this* . . . Ugh!" The paint on the door frame surrenders several layers, and the sofa is in the flat.

Back outside, they struggle to get an antique steamer trunk full of Clive's photography equipment up the granite steps of the stoop. The staircase looms above them. Everything seemed much lighter in Amsterdam, probably because they had two friends helping. Now that they are here, their possessions appear enormous and unmanageable.

A young man passing on the street stops to watch their efforts. Clive is annoyed until the man, who is distinctly rough-trade, says, "Need a bit o' help wi' that there?"

They accept too gratefully, and he asks for forty pounds. They bargain him down to thirty-five. A bargain it is, for they could not have done it alone. By the time their things are in the flat, they feel sufficiently comfortable with the young man to ask if he knows where to get weed in Islington. The young man exclaims that he lives right around the corner and knows a guy who had some good stuff coming in today. They pay him the thirty-five pounds, give him an additional twenty towards the weed, and say goodbye, half-expecting never to see him again.

Of course, they never do.

"Fucking London," Clive grumbles over Indian takeaway that night. "Fucking welcome home. Forgot why I left, I did."

On the verge of thirty, Clive has received glowing reviews for his art photography, but couldn't get the lucrative portrait work he needed to live well in Amsterdam. He has decided that Dutch people don't care for having their pictures taken nearly as much as the English do. Even Willem, in all his scruffy blond loveliness, is a lousy model, always fidgeting, wanting a cigarette, wanting a joint, saying he is cold. Willem is a writer (some of the time) and can work anywhere (or not), so they have decided to relocate to Clive's home city. Willem is excited about the move; he is twenty-five and has never lived outside the Netherlands. Clive hopes it will be temporary.

"We'll get it somewhere else," Willem consoles.

"You're in England now, luvvie dear. You can't just wander down to the corner coffee shop and ask to see the menu. Anyway, I don't care about the weed." Clive makes an expansive gesture ceilingward. "It's the attitude of this place I loathe."

"The flat?" Willem looks around in alarm. He selected their new home, and particularly likes the pink and yellow tiles on the ceiling, though he wondered at the wisdom of bringing the purple sofa.

"No, no . . . London. Filthy place, innit? Always somebody ready to rip you off, from the drug dealer on the street to the poshest restaurant in the city." He looks up at Willem. "Don't you think so?"

They have visited London twice in their three years together, and Willem has been coming here on his own since his teens. He loves the grand spaces and vistas, the whirl of traffic, the diversity and dazzle. "No. I find it glamourous."

Clive smirks. "Wait 'till you've lived here a while."

Willem finishes his rice, sops up the last of the lamb vindaloo with half a chapati, and begins to clear away the containers. "Shall we do some unpacking tonight," he asks, "or are you too tired?"

"I think I'm too tired for unpacking."

Willem stops on his way to the kitchenette and looks at Clive. Clive is still smirking, but in a wholly different way.

"Only for unpacking?" Willem inquires.

"Well, the bed's already unpacked, innit?"

The first sex in a new home is unique, preserved somehow in the watching walls that have already seen so much. It marks the space as your own, and you are conscious of this during the act. It also awakens things in the space that may have lain dormant for years – currents, if you will, or points of energy, or electromagnetic impulses. Or ghosts.

Clive and Willem don't know anyone has been murdered here. Clive has heard of Joe Orton and his famous death, though he would be hazy on the details if asked. Willem has seen two of Orton's plays produced in Rotterdam, but knows little of the author's life in London. He found the plays very clever, had admired their facile wit. Now here he is, all unknowing, sucking his lover's cock on the spot where that wit met its end.

Admittedly, it is the obvious place for a bed, against one of the longer walls under the big window. Thirty years' worth of paint, the latest coat a semenesque oyster-white, covers the bloodstains and nightmare collages. Clive lies sprawled on the bed, his back arched, his fingers tangled in Willem's hair. Willem's mouth is hot and smooth on his cock, tongue teasing the head, lips slipping down the shaft. The soreness and tension of moving day begin to drain away, and Clive lets himself relax into a stupor of equal parts bliss and exhaustion.

*What the FUCK . . .*

This is Joe's first thought, and he suspects that it is not particularly original. But the feeling is too much to describe: the memory of the hammer blows, the sensation of leaving his body slowly, so slowly, trying to wrench himself free of the mangled meat like an animal chewing off its paw in a trap. Kenneth nearby, but maddeningly cold and dead, having taken the easy way out. Having got the last word. Kenneth was not bound to this place; he could have died anywhere.

After that, nothing. It might have been a second or a century since the first blow fell. There was no heaven, no hell, absolutely nothing at all. Just as Joe had always expected. Until now. Until he finds himself not only sentient, but in the middle of an orgasm.

"Willem!" he hears himself gasping. The name is unknown to him, but the sensations are deliciously familiar.

The young man who has just finished sucking his cock looks up, smiling. His face is square, honest, and beautiful, his eyes china-blue, his full lips still glistening with traces of come.

"Please, will you fuck me now?" he says.

"Well – well, all right."

"You're not too tired?" Willem has a charming little accent, German or Dutch; could be Hottentot, for all Joe cares.

"Absolutely not." As he gets up onto his knees, he takes stock of this blessed body he has found himself in. Its build is much like his own, smallish but solid. It has a big uncircumcised cock already swelling back to half-mast as Willem kisses his mouth, strokes his chest, bites his nipples. It feels young, healthy, glorious.

He turns Willem around and rubs his cock between the younger man's ass-cheeks. The crack of Willem's ass is lightly furred with gold. He groans as Willem pushes back against him. Willem passes him a tube of lubricant and a condom. Joe applies the lube to his erect cock and Willem's pretty ass, gently sliding a finger in, then two. He tosses the condom away, having no idea what else he is supposed to do with it.

Willem feels Clive entering him unsheathed, which is strange but not entirely without precedent; each of them has tested negative three times, and since the third time they've gone condomless once or twice. It feels so good that he doesn't protest now. Clive's naked cock slides way up inside him, faster and harder than Clive usually puts it in. Clive's hands are clamped on Willem's hips, pulling Willem onto him. Clive has always been a wonderful fuck, but Willem cannot remember the last time he felt so thoroughly penetrated.

It seems to go on for hours. Just when he's sure Clive is going to come, *must* come, Clive stops and catches his breath and kisses the back of Willem's neck for a bit, then starts fucking him again. At one point he pulls out, flips Willem over with no apparent effort, pushes Willem's legs up to his chest, and re-enters him. They settle into a slow, deep rhythm. Clive is nuzzling at Willem's mouth, not just kissing him but inhaling his breath, sucking hungrily at his lips and tongue. Hungrily. That's how Clive is making love to him, like a man starved for it.

At last Clive whispers, "I'm going to come now." His cock seems to go deeper yet, and Willem feels it pulsing inside. Then Clive is holding him ever so tightly, pushing his face into Willem's neck and

(Willem could almost swear) sobbing. His sperm sears Willem's insides, hot and effervescent, melting into Willem's tissues and suffusing them with something Willem has never felt before. It is a little like an acid trip, if all the hectic colour and strange splendour of an acid trip could be folded into the space of two sweating, shuddering bodies.

"Thank you," says Clive, kissing him. Willem sees that Clive *is* crying, and when he kisses back, the tears taste of salt and copper on his tongue.

Clive knows *something* happened while Willem was sucking his cock, but he can't say just what. It was the sex of his life (both his cock and Willem's ass are satisfyingly sore for days), but there was something detached about it, almost as if he'd been watching himself fuck Willem instead of actually doing it.

Never mind, he tells himself. They were both exhausted from moving; that's why it was a bit odd. Not bad, though. He wouldn't actually mind if it happened again.

Within days of their arrival, Clive's entire Amsterdam portfolio is taken on by a posh London gallery for a handsome commission. He won't be doing any portrait work for a while. On the way home to give Willem the good news, Clive buys a Polaroid camera.

When he enters the flat, he is surprised to see Willem banging away on his old electric typewriter. As far as Clive knows, Willem hasn't done a lick of writing since the move. But now a sheaf of pages has accumulated on the desk beside him.

"I wasn't thinking of anything in particular," Willem explains, "and then suddenly I had an idea for a play."

"A play?"

"Yes, I've never written one before. Never even liked the idea." Willem shrugged. "I don't know what's got into me, but I hope it stays."

# Worth More Than a Thousand Words

Lawrence Schimel

I have never been good at keeping a diary. It presupposes an audience, supposedly one's self, but I have never been comfortable with the idea. I am afraid someone will find it, and read it, and I will have bared my soul to a stranger, or worse, someone I'm close to. I am afraid because I have done this to others. Friends of mine. My sister. I have always been a voyeur.

Reading someone's diary is the thrill of the forbidden. The knot of worry in the stomach, the fear of being discovered. When I was younger, I read porn that way. I didn't need to. My grandfather kept stacks of porn magazines on top of the toilet in the bathroom of his apartment; I could have read them at leisure, in that small locked room, poring over the pictures. But I would go to a bookstore and sneak porn magazines from the rack, hiding them inside a copy of something innocuous like *Cats Magazine*. I would walk back to the middle of the store and stand in an empty section to flip through the pictorials. I hardly even looked at the pictures, glancing down for a second and taking a mental photograph, my heart racing as I quickly glanced back up to make sure no one was coming down the aisle where I stood, to make sure no one ever saw what I was doing. As soon as someone came near, or if I even thought they would, I closed the magazine and moved from Gardening to Humour, to wherever there wasn't anyone else.

My heart pounds the same way when I read someone's diary, even if there's no chance of my being discovered – they're away for the weekend and I have the only key to the apartment, whatever. It is forbidden, and I feel there is someone watching me as I reach for the slim, clothbound book that's hidden beneath the bed. I flip through the pages, scanning for any mention of myself, or anything else that catches my eye. I look for moments where the handwriting changes, clues to highly emotional scenes. I'm like a vampire, thirsting not for blood, but vicarious emotion. Thirsting furtively, at night, when no one else is around, lest I be discovered.

I am always careful to replace the diary exactly as I found it. If it were my own, I would notice if it had been moved, even if anything around it had been moved. I guess that's why I've never been able to keep a diary before. I'm too paranoid. Afraid of exposing myself. I've broken the trust of too many friends who left me alone in their rooms while they went to class or work, while they went on vacation for a week, trusting me to water their plants. Trusting me not to read their diary.

So I know someone else will read this. I can't help being aware of you. I feel as if I'm writing for you, not for myself. But I have something I want to write down, need to write down, so I don't lose it. So I don't forget. I know you're reading over my shoulder, so I'm going to fill in the background for you. After all, who knows what will happen? Fifteen, twenty years from now, the stranger who finds this book again, buried in an attic at the bottom of a box of books, might be myself. And my heart will begin pounding as I realize it is a diary, and I open it and read all the details I'd long since forgotten.

There are some who consider thirteen an unlucky number. Not I. But I've got reason; I have a lover thirteen years older than myself.

Not unlucky, but still witchy. She's definitely a witchy-woman. Enchanting seductress. It's almost impossible not to be drawn in by her. When we go out together I watch it happen to the men around her. And I, I was drawn in, as well, although it's harder for me to know what happened, trapped in her glamour.

I've wondered sometimes if it was a potion she made, something she wore. She's an aromatherapist, always using subtle essences of plants to influence mood. Lavender. Ginger. Scents I've never been able to identify. Her home is suffused with a rich aroma of comfort and warmth, an amnesiac to anxiety.

Yet each time a man is ensnared by her spell she is taken by surprise. It is perhaps that very aspect which is so appealing: she does not wield her sexuality like a weapon or tool, but is so familiar with it, so intimate, that it sits upon her as an integral part of her being, as simply as the features of her face. If you saw her, you would understand what I meant. If you saw her, you would be drawn in by her spell.

While she may not understand the effect she has, she is now aware of it. We met at a poetry reading in Boston, and exchanged business cards. Later that week, a story showed up in my mail, a piece entitled, "Desire". It was our first flirtation. I know not to assume that a first person narrator is the author, but I could not help noticing similarities, how men seemed drawn to the protagonist like moths to a porchlight on a summer's evening. The writing was infused with that same sensuality which surrounds her presence. Though the story wasn't full of explicit sex, it played a strong role, tantalizingly alluded to or glimpsed. And the writing itself was lush, like a flurry of caresses moving up one's thigh and across belly and chest.

A writer myself, I appreciated the sumptuousness of her prose. I was also very turned on by it. Words have always held strong sway over me. Perhaps she'd sensed this about me, and thus chose to make her first move in print. Subtly, yet relentlessly, working my weakness.

Perhaps because she understood this power words held over me, I was able to persuade her to let me read an erotic fantasy she had written for another lover of hers. Showering after the first night we spent together, I'd found her aromatherapy jars in the medicine cabinet. Later, I asked her if she ever used them in lovemaking. She said she had, and also mentioned this fantasy she had written. The moment she realized what she had confessed she said, "I can't believe I just told you that."

I begged her to let me read it.

I was curious. I wondered who he was, what he looked like, why she had chosen to write something for him. I wondered what it would reveal about her, her own desires, her fantasies.

And the idea of reading something meant for someone else thrilled me. I've always been a voyeur. In college, I would lie atop the window seat for hours, warmth on my stomach from the radiator underneath as I stared across the courtyard. I could never see much – the buildings were too far apart – but what I saw was never really the issue. It was the looking. Often I would spend an entire night staring at the yellow squares of light across the way, waiting for the brief shadows to cross their frame, unaware of how time was passing, lost in the act of watching.

Reading a fantasy for someone else held the same appeal. Already I could feel myself begin to grow hard with anticipation.

She relented. I'm still not sure why. She'd never shown it to anyone but the man it was written for. But for some reason I convinced her to let me read it. Maybe because she had realized how powerful words were to me, and wanted to help me change, to grow.

I remember almost everything I read. It's as if I had a photographic memory, which I don't, since I only remember words. But eventually I will forget, or not be able to remember exactly. I'm sure that already I must have changed things, remembering what I would have found more erotic rather than what she actually wrote.

He was an actor who starred in horror films. Naturally, he lived in LA, across the country from her. Most of their relationship therefore took place in words, on the page or the phone. Once, it took place like this:

For Paul
I woke up this morning with the most luscious fantasy in my mind. Here, let me share it with you. Then we can both enjoy it.

We are in a luxury hotel; it is night. You sit on the bed in a white silk robe, gazing through the window at the panorama below: a city bejewelled with light. A muffled whisper of traffic filters through to your ears, almost as soothing as the surf.

Your back is to me. I can see from your reflection in the window that your eyes are closed in quiet contemplation, listening to the city sounds below. I ease onto the bed and move towards you, circle your chest with my arms from behind, rest my head against yours. Your hand lifts to caress mine; you smile, sigh, eyes still closed. A gentle squeeze, and I pull my arms away, letting my hands glide beneath the collar of your robe and slide the silk away like milk pouring from your skin. I knead your shoulders for a moment and am pleased to find you already so relaxed. My fingers wind through your hair, soft, like a spider sorting threads for her web. Your moan is barely audible until it evolves into another sigh. I am so happy to please you.

Knowing how much you enjoy it, I let my fingertips sneak down to your neck and feather your back with caresses. They play at your shoulder blades, tease your spine, explore your sides as you wriggle against them. I switch to a calmer touch, flat hands soothing nerve endings, then tickle once more, enough to bring delight, no more.

You turn to kiss me. Once, softly, then again. Our mouths open and we feel the warm moistness of each other's desire. I hear a tiny sound of surprise from you and you move away, smiling.

"What's that scent?" you ask, leaning forward to sniff and kiss again.

"Can you guess?" I ask.

"Let me smell that again." You turn yourself fully around to embrace me and kiss me deeply. "Flower, I think."

"Yes, flower. A special flower."

Another kiss. Another sniff. "Not roses. Not lilacs; not so sweet." Another kiss. "Ah! Lavender."

"Yes!" I smile. "Do you like it?"

"Love it. Did you put it on your entire body?"

"Nothing so dull as that, sweetie."

You are intrigued, guessing that there is more. I know the notion of impending discoveries excites you. I can feel your erection against my thigh as you guide me down onto my back. Your hands are delightfully warm; I feel heat through the wine-coloured silk of my robe as they find my breasts. You whisper my name as your mouth reaches my neck. You kiss, and then you lick. "Lemon. That one's easy!"

I turn to bare more of my scented neck to you . . . take it. My fingers find your hair again as you clasp your hungry mouth to my neck. My turn to sigh now. A wave of passion crests inside me and I press you away and onto your back so I can devour you with hot, wet kisses on your neck and face. The fingers of one hand are still entwined in your hair. The other dances across your chest, down your stomach, finds you hard and holds as your hips push against me, a promise of delights to come.

Both hands move now to your face, learning the features with my fingers as a blind woman might. I close my eyes to enhance the sensation, resculpting the lines of your face. Your hands grab my wrists. You press them to your lips.

"Peppermint," you say. "Peppermint wrists."

"You're very good at this," I answer, kissing your hands. My tongue presses along the inside of your palm, spreads your fingers as it dances between them. "Have you done this before?"

"Never," you declare, tugging at me until I rest on top of you. You suck at my wrists like a child with a candy cane until the scent is gone. "But I sure hope to again." Straddling you in this way, I notice how very wet I am by the way you nearly slide into me without effort. But, ah, not yet, no.

I move forward, kiss the top of your head, rub my body along yours until my breasts are at your lips. Your lips part automatically and my right nipple stiffens in response to your tongue. You taste the left nipple before making your guess. They are both the same, but you are not sure you've got this one right. "Smells like . . . gin? Even tastes like gin." Determined to make your guess conclusive you taste once more, moving between my nipples, licking, sucking, thrilling me!

When I can find my voice, I tell you, "Yes. It's juniper berry. What they make gin from."

You release my breast long enough to grin and say, "Hmm, educational as well as nutritional," then return to sucking. Your right hand nudges between our bodies and finds me wet and wanting. One finger slips inside me and I press against it, moaning softly. Two on the next gentle thrust . . . oh, I could almost come right now! But, no, there are still discoveries to make.

Playfully, I push away, sitting up and pulling you with me. Our skin is flushed with passion, our breath quick, eyes sparkling. "I just want to make it last," I explain, "savour it."

"Savour it," you repeat, "I get it." You pass back through the familiar lavender garden, the lemon of my neck, and I lean back to let you revisit the juniper of my nipples. You brace me at the waist as I lean back further, resting on my hands as your tongue circles my navel. It's ticklish, and I giggle and squirm as you make up your mind what it is.

"Spicy. Hot."

"Like you," I say through my giggles.

You taste again, then declare, "Cinnamon!" triumphant.

"Go to the head of the class!"

With a raised eyebrow and a boyish grin you say, "I thought you'd never ask," and move lower still, to the final scented spot. This is the challenge, since you have to get past my own musk to find the herbal aroma.

The moment I feel your tongue probe the soft, moist folds between my legs I no longer care about herbs or slowness or anything except that you don't ever stop! How wonderful you are with your mouth; tongue tentative, yet firm. You move your head away, to make a guess at the aroma, I imagine, but I gently push you right back, moving my legs out from beneath me and letting you settle in. The heat and the wetness release the herbal scent into the air around us; amazing what a single drop can do. The earthy scent envelops us as your tongue carries me to an excruciatingly pleasant plateau, then coaxes me over the edge into the warm rolling ocean of orgasm.

As I begin to float back to the coherent world, I find my voice and say, "Paul, I want you inside me." I feel your weight and then I feel you push into me, a delicious feeling with the area so highly sensitized and flushed. My legs encircle your waist as your hips move, grinding against me in the realization of that earlier tantalizing promise. My arms come up under yours to hold on to your shoulders, bracing me for the thrill of each thrust. With one hand I grasp your hair, baring your neck where I smother my moans. I arch to let you reach further into me and orgasm again overtakes me. You move slowly, helping to prolong the delight. When I have settled back to earth once more, you let your passion have control, pounding against me with increasing lust.

"I'm so close," you whisper, your voice hoarse with pleasure.

I quickly turn you over so that I can be on top of you, sitting up. "Lay back and enjoy this," I tell you, as I match the rhythm we had a moment ago. You manage to smile broadly through your sighs, encouraging me with a word or two until eloquence deserts you altogether and your back arches and you buck and grunt and grasp my hips and hold me against you until you are spent. Keeping you inside of me, I bend forward to hold you and let you hold me as we catch out breaths.

After a moment of quiet, you ask, "Are you going to tell me what the final aroma was?"

"Won't you guess?"

"Something earthy, like the woods. Like you."

"It's patchouli," I say. "From India."

"It's magical," you reply.

"You're magical, my dear."

We fall asleep there, in each other's arms, the moist fairies between us and the aromatic fairies watching over us.

With Love,

Laura

Writing it down, I found myself aroused again. Often, I paused and put down my pen, rereading the passage I just wrote as I took off my shirt and ran my hands across my chest and back, along the line of hair that runs down my chest. With my left hand, I undid my jeans and stroked myself through my underwear as I wrote. Slipping my hand underneath the brim, I avoided my cock, teasing myself, running my hand along the inside of my thigh and letting the backs of my fingers tickle my balls. And as I write this now I hold my balls in my hand, gently squeezing and rolling them, pressing deeply against the muscle underneath, the root of my cock, so hard. Enough of writing for now—

The afternoon I first read that piece stays firm in my mind. We woke at two in the afternoon. The house was quiet. Outside, the neighbours could be heard in the yard, as could the trills of birds in the dogwood which bloomed outside her bedroom. It felt like a lazy Sunday afternoon in spring as we revelled in the indolence of rising so late. Laura had called in sick earlier that morning, at dawn, when we decided finally to go to sleep.

The night had been spent in touch, a revelry of physical sensation. I'd had no idea what to expect, when she'd offered to put me up for the night after a poetry reading in New York. I'd figured it was likely I'd wind up on a couch in her living room. Instead she'd given me a massage, by candlelight, on her bed, since my back was sore from lying on floor cushions at the reading. I had injured my wrist, which was in a splint, and thus could only lean on one arm during the entire performance, cradling my injured hand in my lap.

She rubbed scented oils into the muscles, a soothing sensation I had never before experienced. The combination of smells, from the oils and candles, the lighting, the lingering sensation of her fingers along my back – it just seemed natural as we were lying next to each other, to reach out and pet her stomach over the satin of her chemise. Though my hand was in a splint, the fingers were still free and danced across the fabric, thrilling the skin beneath with the light friction. Later, our clothes off, we rubbed our bodies together simply for the exhilarating sensation of skin moving against skin. Crouching over her like a wildcat, I ran my torso over her body, pressing down on her breasts to knead them gently with my own, dragging my body down across her belly, her waist, her legs, then back again. I dropped my head down to let my hair, which I'd been growing out for more than a year now, dangle lightly against her skin.

That night was touch for its own sake. We explored each other's bodies until dawn, kissed once, briefly, and slept. We stayed in bed until mid-afternoon. At last, I got up and showered, where I found the oils in her medicine cabinet. Wrapped in a towel, I went back into the bedroom and asked her about them, thus discovering the erotica she'd written for Paul. She made tea while I read the piece, understandably nervous about being in the same room with me as

I was reading, and soon returned to the bedroom with two steaming mugs.

"Tea?" she asked innocently, ignoring the fact that I'd been reading.

"Come here," I said, getting to my feet. I let my towel fall to the floor around my feet. I was very excited from her story; my erection throbbed, flushed with blood. I took the mugs from her hands and placed them on the nightstand, enfolding her in my arms. We kissed, and I drew her back onto the bed with me, running my hands along her back through the fabric of her robe. The neck of the robe hung wide, and I nuzzled her skin, running my tongue up to her chin, then back down to slide between her breasts. We rolled over, and she opened the belt of her robe, pulling the dark red fabric back slowly as if she were peeling an artichoke. I wanted to devour her. I leaned over her, bracing myself on my hands, when suddenly my right wrist gave out in a searing wrench of pain. I did not have the splint on, and the pressure of supporting myself had been too much. I bit back a cry, and collapsed on the bed next to her, cradling my injured hand under me, against my chest.

"I'm sorry," I said, "but I'm not up to this, it seems."

"Shhh," she said, rolling me over and sliding on top of me. "I don't want you to do anything that will cause you pain." She took my injured hand in hers and gently kissed it. She licked the palm, then ran her tongue down to my wrist, and slowly along my arm. When she reached my shoulder, she moved across to my nipple, teasing it with circles of her tongue and gentle bites. But she quickly slid backwards, dragging her body along mine as she kissed down my chest and stomach. The loose folds of the robe billowed about her like a butterfly's wings. Her breath was warm, exhilarating, as she explored my pubic area, rubbing her face against my hard cock as she tickled around my balls with her tongue. At last, her tongue met my shaft – a quick lick, a tentative probe. With her hands, she lifted my cock until it was perpendicular from my body, and slowly lowered her mouth over it, surrounding it, but not touching, not yet, only her warm breath. She held for a moment, and I burned with anticipation. Then her lips closed, and suddenly her tongue pressed against the length of my shaft, sliding up and down.

My breathing grew heavy as she drew her lips along the length of my shaft, teasing my balls with one hand as the other grasped the base of my cock and squeezed gently. I was so excited that it did not take long before her touch pushed me into orgasm. "I'm so close," I warned her, holding back to prolong the blissful sensation, and give her a chance to pull back if she did not want me to come in her mouth. She kept her lips firmly clamped, her head bobbing up and down furiously, and I could not hold back any longer. I let out a cry, which slowly faded into a sigh as I recovered from my orgasm. My lips and hands were tingling with bliss, and I held them against her body, whispering, once I got my voice, "Look what you do to me."

"How do your hands feel?" she asked, concerned.

"In ecstasy," I answered, with a smile. They tingled with pleasure.

Laura smiled as well. "I've found a new form of therapy for them, then. Something your doctor would never think to prescribe."

"They should make you a practising physician," I said, hugging her close to me and kissing her. My fingertips reflexively began to caress her thigh, but she stopped me.

"I don't want you to do anything that will injure your wrists. Just lay there and enjoy yourself."

I was frustrated with my body's betrayal of me, but succumbed to the bliss it was currently feeling. I lay in the afterglow, feeling incredibly self-indulgent, and enjoying it. The phone rang. I tilted my head to look at her and smiled as she turned to looked back. Neither of us wanted to get up to answer it. After the fourth ring, the answering machine picked up. It was her lawyer, saying that at last he'd submitted the final papers for her divorce, and that soon, hopefully, everything would clear.

I'd known she had been married, but had not realized the divorce was not finalized. Suddenly a gulf loomed large between us as I thought of where she was in her life with regards to where I stood in mine. But curiously, despite the vast differences in our lives, the closeness between us as we lay entwined, her hand gently squeezing my leg, my fingers still caressing despite her protests, did not dissolve.

"Ah, adultery," I said with a grin as I turned onto my side to look at her.

"A new experience?" she asked, also with a smile. I hesitated, and knew she was suddenly wondering, having noticed. But she did not ask. "Don't worry," she continued, "we've been separated for over a year now."

I deliberated whether to tell her, wondering what would happen to our relationship once she knew. "It's not new," I say. "For the past two years, up until September when he moved back with his wife in Syracuse, I've been seeing Brian Coney."

I waited for a response, hardly daring to breathe, unsure whether to expect outrage, incredulity, or calm acceptance. She smiled, and after a moment said, "Well, at last I get to sleep with him, if only vicariously through you!"

I smiled, pleased that she was so accepting. I knew that I could share how special that relationship had been to me. "Only you and he have ever made me feel an orgasm like that," I said. "Make me tingle. Too often it's just an ejaculation." I looked at her, and said, "Thank you."

She ran her hands across my chest and said, "I'm glad. You deserve it."

I chuckled and asked her, "Remember when Jo Ann said I looked like a young Brian Coney at the reading in Boston? Right before you said he was so sexy that you couldn't talk in his presence? Oh, how I was biting my tongue!"

She was curious about everything, then, asking questions about him, and my relationships with men in general. The questions were never accusatory, rather pure curiosity. I believe the notion may have even excited her, especially when I spoke of Brian. She did not ask me which I preferred, making love to a man or a woman, but rather what I thought were the best things one could do with either sex, and what I enjoyed most from each.

I spoke of finally learning to receive pleasure with Brian, of how before I had simply been going through the motions of sex, with either men or women, without enjoying it. How sometimes a need for physical intimacy will well up inside me until it's unbearable. How I need to touch and be touched, the feel of skin and skin. How sometimes I have to go through other things I don't want, or enjoy, to get those. When it builds up inside me like that, I almost don't have a choice. And there's almost always a man who wants to get me into bed, and I go with him, for the brief moments of foreplay – before he has my pants off, and his own, his large erection pressing against me – and afterwards, as we lie together, our bodies touching.

I think what I like most is lying in a lover's arms afterwards. I can never fall asleep like that – I'm too sensitized to the feel of warm skin against my own – but I relish it for as long as I can. But one has to go through sex to get there. Even if I don't enjoy the sex along the way, I'll go through with it, for that luxurious sensation afterwards.

If you haven't noticed, I've been avoiding writing about the event which made me need to write this account. It's so much easier to wallow in the background, spewing forth endless, easy details.

There's no emotional stake involved. Even talking about sex is easy, although revealing my desires and fantasies starts to get slightly uncomfortable. That's why I just realized, as I was writing the above, how much I'd been avoiding the issue.

Enough of cold feet.

Laura is a portrait photographer, by profession, and we began taking photos of me, to try and reveal my inner self. I've never been terribly aware of what I look like, and a comment to this effect made Laura decide on this project. I readily agreed. I was curious what she could show me. I'd produced a body of work as a writer that was much more familiar to me than my own body.

I hadn't been photographed in a long time, and was very nervous as we began. For one thing, I truly had no idea what I looked like now. Until I had begun to grow my hair out a year ago, my image had not changed in the last seven, eight years. I'd shown Laura two photographs of me, one taken when I was thirteen, the other at twenty, and both looked identical. Now, with shoulder-length hair, and the start of a beard, I had no idea who I was. I'd still been using those photographs of my younger self as my mental image of myself. It's how I'd always defined myself. That's how I imagined I looked to other people, since I had no other way of seeing myself. Laura was going to show me who I was now.

The first session went awfully. I'd taken the train out to her place after work Friday, and after a quick dinner, we went upstairs to her home studio, on the second floor of the house. I was so tense that it made Laura nervous as well, and seeing that she was now nervous only made me more so. It fed on itself in a vicious cycle, until the air was thick with uncomfortable frustration, and we finally called it quits. We went downstairs, leaving the studio set up in hopes that tomorrow we'd manage a better session. We made love that night, tension dissolving as slow caresses gave way to deeper passion.

Waking the next morning, I felt contented as a cat as I stretched in her bed as she moved around me. "I wish you'd been this comfortable last night," Laura remarked.

"You should run get your camera," I teased. "Or rather, you can walk. I'm not going anywhere."

"Yes, you are, dear," she said, tugging me upright and kissing me on the lips. She dropped a white terry-cloth robe in my lap. I smiled as I noticed the Hilton insignia embroidered onto it, and wondered if it had been stolen after a tempestuous weekend with one of her previous lovers, like something from the story she'd let me read. I put the robe on and followed her upstairs.

She positioned me in front of a large free-standing oval mirror in her studio, and stood behind me. Reaching around my waist, she undid the sash of my robe, letting it fall open. "I want you to look at yourself, touch yourself, until you know what it feels like from the inside," she said. "Until there are no boundaries between the you in the mirror, and the you inside here." She tapped her knuckles against my chest, and squeezed me gently from behind. Then, taking my hand in her own, she began guiding my fingers across my chest, pushing the robe from my shoulders until it fell to the floor. She released my hand and stepped back as I continued exploring, running my fingers over my arms and torso. I watched myself in the mirror, studying my body as my hands passed over each area. I felt the double sensation of touch, in my fingers and skin, not trying to analyse but simply feeling it.

I explored every inch of myself, running my hands along the muscles of my neck, even exploring my scalp, the fingers running through my own long hair as they felt their way along the curves of my skull. I ran my hands down my chest and back, onto my legs, crouching down to reach all the way to my feet. I stood again, my hands always in motion, exploring new areas – my thighs, my buttocks. I caught sight of Laura in the mirror, noticing that both she and the camera were watching me. I smiled, and did not stop my exploration. I grew hard, reveling in the multiple voyeurism: looking at myself in the mirror, looking at Laura looking at me. I could tell she was turned on by our voyeurisms as well, and began tantalizing her, staring into her eyes through the lens as I moved my hands over my body, grabbing my erection with one hand as the other circled a nipple or explored elsewhere.

And suddenly, I turned and looked at her over my shoulder, directly, no longer through the mirror. The camera clicked, the shutter winking open and shut like the lips of her labia moving apart and together again in fast motion. She put the camera down and I went to her, almost giddy with desire. We kissed fiercely. I undid the sash of her robe, and she shrugged out of it so quickly, like from one of those tales sailors tell of seals who shed their skins and become women. As her hands explored all the areas where my own had just been, I thrilled at the difference in the feelings. I remembered the mirror and looked up, to see my hands running up and down her back. I snorted with amusement, and pointed to the mirror. Laura turned towards it, and in that moment I leaned down to kiss her neck, her breasts, the entire time watching myself perform these actions in the mirror.

I took the café chair she used for portraits and positioned it in front of the mirror. I sat down on it and held my arms for Laura to come to me. She eased my knees apart with her hips and kissed her way down my neck, her breasts surrounding my erection. She licked my nipples, sucked on them, then began to drop lower, towards my cock. I stopped her, pulling her to her feet. "I want to be inside you," I said.

She looked at me for a moment, and I could sense what was going on inside her mind, her wondering, marvelling. I ran my fingers over her nipples, pinching them slightly, and desire overrode any lingering concerns she held. I pulled her towards me and she climbed onto the chair with me, slowly lowering herself onto me. I moaned as I slid into her, watching in the mirror as she rocked her hips backwards and forwards. I threw my head back, reveling in the sensation, and no longer cared about the mirror or watching us. I no longer needed it. I could feel my entire body from the inside, knew it exactly, perfectly. I wrapped my arms around her waist, and stood from the chair, slowly lowering us to the carpet. I kissed her fiercely, and then, supporting myself on my elbows since my wrist would give out, began rocking my hips, pushing deeper into her. She moaned with pleasure, her fingers grasping my shoulders tightly. I began to build speed, exploring deeper inside her with each thrust, reaching for those spots which would thrill her most. I was quickly hurtling towards orgasm, but held back, an almost painful sensation as each thrust brought me closer and closer. And finally, just when I could not restrain myself any longer, she arched her back and cried out as we pushed over the edge into orgasm at the same time. We laughed, kissed once, and collapsed in each other's arms, spent.

It's somewhat ironic that now, after she's pushed me from defining myself by words to showing me what I truly look like, I am writing about it. But in a way, it's exactly what I should do. It shows how I have grown so far. My body of work was much more familiar to me than my own body. Now, having explored my body by sight, by touch, to the point where I truly know it, from the inside, the only thing remaining was to explore it once again, in words, to make the two bodies one.

# Mrs Fox

Michael Crawley

Eleven days after I broke up with Angie I ran into Jeff, sitting in a booth at Sombrero Jack's. He was with a woman, so I tried to make it "Hi and Bye", but he insisted I join them.

"Paul, this is Mrs Fox – Cynthia Fox. Cynthia – Paul. We worked at Blackstock's together, years ago."

I half-stood and reached across to squeeze limp fingers.

"Call me 'Cyn'." Did her fingertips drag on my palm for a fraction of a second? I wasn't sure.

I knew straight away why Jeff wanted me there long enough to get a good look at her. He'd always been joking-jealous of me. I was bigger, and had all my hair. Some of the women in the old office had hung around my desk during coffee breaks, playing at flirting. It hadn't meant anything, but they hadn't done the same at his desk. He'd resented that.

Now he was with this woman – an older woman who was quite lovely – and I was alone. He wanted to make the most of it. I could live with that.

He said, "Cynthia and I live together."

I said, "You're a lucky man," and meant it. Her age showed in the laugh-lines around her big dark eyes, but her black hair was crisp and short and her body looked lithe, with hard, high breasts, half exposed by the shawl neckline of a sweater in clinging black jersey. She wasn't wearing a bra. She didn't need one.

Jeff ordered a round and poked the gold card he'd left on the table from side to side, to make sure I saw it. I resolved that when the time came for me to pay my shot I'd use cash. It'd spoil it for him if I used *my* gold card.

Jeff did the talking. It was impressive stuff – big deals with Chile and so on. He was selling prefabricated buildings or something. Maybe he *was* working hard. He had dark bags under bloodshot eyes. I half-listened and kept my eyes on "Cyn", which was what he wanted me to do.

When she excused herself to go the ladies' room I watched her hips slink away into crowded darkness.

"What do you think of her?" he asked.

"Very nice. A sexy lady." I couldn't comment on her personality because she'd hardly said a word.

"You don't know the half of it."

I was supposed to ask for details. I didn't. I'm no prude, but some things should be kept private.

Cyn seemed jittery when she came back. Her arm stretched halfway across the table to fiddle with the little glass ball that held the candle, to adjust the condiments, to take a napkin from the holder and shred it. She had nice hands – longish fingernails – very pointed – painted deep pink. Her fingers were slender. Tiny blue veins showed inside her wrists. Higher on her pale arms I noticed some bruising and broken skin, as if a bracelet had caught in something and yanked off, or like a rope-burn maybe.

It was none of my business.

Her collar seemed to gape more now, or perhaps it was just her leaning towards me. There was a purplish mark above her collarbone and another mark, the size of a thumbprint, on the slope of her right breast.

It was still none of my business.

It wasn't any of my business when Jeff's hand dropped out of sight and she winced, still looking straight into my eyes.

They stood to leave, with Jeff leering, "Bed time, Cynthia."

She took my hand in a proper shake, not that "fingertip" thing. Something pressed into my palm.

I gave them five minutes before I looked. It was a note, written on that tan paper they use for towels in washrooms, and a key. The note read, "I must see you. I need your help. Midnight." There was an address and a lipstick kiss. The paper was damp. Tears, or moist palms?

They were supposed to live together, but maybe Jeff had lied about that, or perhaps he was flying to Peru to do another of his multi-million dollar deals.

I thought for a while, but it had been eleven days since Angie, and I've always been a sucker for a "damsel in distress", even when I'm not horny.

I knocked on her apartment door, but too lightly for anyone inside to hear unless they were listening for it. I still could have turned around, but I didn't.

I used the key.

The hallway was dark. I said, "Cynthia? Mrs Fox? Cyn?"

There was a line of light under a door at the end. Something swished and cracked. A soft voice yelped. I strode on the balls of my feet and cracked the door. The bedroom was lit by candles. Cyn was on the bed, on her face, spreadeagled and naked. Her wrists and ankles were tied to the four corners of a scrolled brass frame. Jeff was stripped to his waist, his belt doubled in his hand, raised high. It came down hard, across her bottom.

When I see abuse something cold takes over. I did things to his wrist and his face and then he was whimpering on the floor. I prodded his thigh with the toe of my shoe and told him, "You have five minutes to get your things and go."

It took him three, with me watching him. Cyn needed me but I wasn't going to turn my back on him.

As soon as the front door closed I bent to the cords around Cyn's ankle.

"Please? There's some salve in the bathroom?"

It seemed obscene to leave her tied like that, but she knew what she needed first better than I did.

"It's awkward for me," she said. "Would you mind very much if you did it for me?"

I was as gentle as I could be. Thank goodness I'd got there on time, for there were only four weals, one high across the backs of her slender thighs, one crossing her bottom at an angle, and two, close together and parallel, blooming into darkness across her cheeks where they were fullest. There were other welts, faded to just pink lines under the translucent pallor of her skin. I smoothed ointment over those as well, though it was too late for it to do much good.

"Could you rub it in?" she asked. "It'll sting, but it does more good if it's worked in."

So I smeared the stuff all over and massaged.

She said, "Harder, please. Harder than that. Don't be afraid to hurt me."

I felt muscles twitch and writhe under my hands. It should have been very sexy, rubbing the naked bottom of a beautiful woman, but my concern for her pain blocked any erotic response on my part.

I wiped my hands and untied her. She rolled over and sat up but she didn't grab the bedclothes to cover herself so I found a satin robe hanging behind the door and draped it over her.

"Don't leave me," she said. "He might come back." Her fingers found my hand and drew it between her breasts. "I need to have you around, for tonight."

"I'll sleep on your couch."

"If that's what you want."

It wasn't. Now she was untied and partly covered, my body was reacting to her body, but if I'd made a move on her I'd have been exploiting the situation, and how do you embrace a woman whose rear is so tender?

She woke me with coffee, naked under that satin robe. "Do you have to go somewhere?"

"My office, sorry."

"Could you do my bottom again before you go?"

She lay flat on her tummy and tucked the robe up to her waist. The marks had faded to a pattern of bruises. In the daylight I could see that her skin wasn't broken, thank goodness. The salve must have been cool and soothing on her burning flesh, because when she squirmed under my hands it wasn't from wincing, but from pleasure. She purred once, when my fingers accidentally trailed into the crease between her buttocks.

"You'll come back?" she asked.

"After work. About six."

"Not for lunch?"

"I can't. Sorry."

When I got back she had a place set for one and a T-bone with a baked potato and mushrooms waiting. There was red wine and two full glasses. She was still naked under her robe, but dewy, as if fresh from a bath. Eartha Kitt was on the stereo, husking something about needing someone to bind her.

"Aren't you eating?" I asked.

"I ate earlier. I'll just watch you."

I ate and she looked at me. "You saved me, you know."

"It was nothing."

"You know what the Chinese say about when you save someone?"

"What?"

"You're responsible for them. You *own* them, but you have to take care of them."

I said, "We aren't Chinese," but her words stirred me. The idea of "owning" her appealed to something in my libido.

"You are my knight in shining armour," she said.

I shrugged.

"I *owe* you."

"No – not really."

"I owe you *this*, at least."

She came round and wriggled onto my lap. I just had time to swallow before her head tilted up and the prickle of her nails on the back of my neck urged my mouth down to hers.

It was a nice kiss, but not a "normal" one, if any kiss can be normal. She held her face away from mine by half an inch and slavered her wine-wet tongue across my lips, from corner to corner. I went to bend lower, but she held my head in place. Her tongue lapped backwards and forwards, as if my steak had left grease on my lips and that was what she was after. With me still held in position, her tongue centred and slithered between my lips. It withdrew, and slithered in once more, making slow sensuous love to my mouth.

As her tongue soft-raped my lips, she writhed on my lap, pressing down hard. It was as if her mouth was under perfect control but her bottom was passionate. I was concerned about her soreness but my cock wasn't. It was enjoying every urgent squirm.

She turned away at last, and took a mouthful of wine. Her lips covered mine. Wine flowed from her mouth to mine, sweet and warm with her saliva.

"Give *me* some wine," she said. "Squirt it into my mouth."

Her mouth opened like a hungry chick, giving me no choice but to jet wine in a long stream, straight onto her tongue. The more wine she swallowed, the more frantically her bottom twisted on my lap.

"Aren't you sore?" I asked.

She jumped up. With her back to me, looking back over her shoulder, she shot a hip and pulled the skirts of her robe to one side. "See? Almost better? All it needs is . . ."

"Is?"

"A 'kiss-better'."

What could I do? I planted a peck on one cheek, but she flexed it at me, so I licked from the crease where her thigh met her bottom to the small of her back.

"Oh yes! Being a bit tender makes me so much more sensitive. More, please?"

I'd known a number of women, and no two are alike, but this was the strangest seduction I'd ever experienced. I'd licked a few women's bums before, but never before I'd even touched their breasts, or made love to them in a more conventional fashion. The weirdness of it – the out-of-order of it – made it incredibly exciting.

I nibbled at the base of her spine.

She bent forward, hands on knees. "That's nice. Touch me, please?"

Where? Wherever I liked, I guessed. After you've kissed a woman's bottom, what caress is forbidden?

I reached around her and pulled her sash loose. My left hand smoothed up over her ribcage, enjoying the ridged smoothness, to cup her pendant breast. My right hand did spider-fingers up the inside of her thigh, touched springy hairs, fumbled, and found moist heat. I rotated three fingers on her, pressing gently. My teeth nipped at the pad of muscle just above her bottom's cleft. My left hand spread into a fan and strummed across the tip of a springy nipple.

Cyn said, "I could get off on what you're doing, Paul. You won't be shocked, will you? When I blow, I blow very wet."

I wasn't sure which of my caresses was getting to her, so I continued with all three. My left hand flickered faster. Two fingers of my right folded up into slick softness while a third found the head of her clit, and rubbed over it. My tongue traced an inch lower, to her tailbone – her coccyx.

She said, "Harder."

She hadn't been specific, so I plucked at her nipple, pinching its tip, substituted my thumb for the fingers that were inside her pussy so that I could use them to manipulate her clit, and rubbed the flat of my tongue in tight circles.

In a totally calm voice, she said, "I'm going to blow now. Don't worry. I can do it again, and again, for a long time."

She juddered on my palm, and hot-flooded into it. She'd been right. She did "blow wet". She soaked me to the wrist. Her spending smelled like fresh-baked bread.

"Now like this." Her two hands took my one and slapped it up against the soft saturated lips of her sex. "Do it hard," she said. "I'll keep blowing."

It made splashy sounds. I bit into her left buttock, forgetting how sore it had to be, and kept slapping up at her until she groaned and toppled forward onto her hands and knees.

She rolled onto her back, looked at me from under hooded lids, and said, "I blew three times. Now it's your turn."

"I can wait a while."

"No – I'm on the boil. Keep me boiling. I'm hot for you, Paul. Hot, hot, hot."

I stood and tossed my jacket aside.

"No time for that," she said. "Get it out and get it in me. Is it big? Is it a nice big one?"

How do you answer that? I didn't try. I didn't have to. She was up on her feet, the dishes pushed aside, and bent over the table, legs spread. That was something I knew how to respond to. Her squishy-wet pussy was poking back at me between her thighs. Its lips were spread, stuck by their own juice. I unzipped, pulled myself out, and entered her.

I didn't have to do much more. She went crazy from her hips down, rotating, bucking, flicking her bum from side to side, jerking back at me as if it was a battle. I just held on, pressing against her hard enough not to be twisted out.

I'm not usually quick, but I was then. My cock was like a water pistol with a blocked muzzle. Her gyrations pumped the trigger until the blockage had to burst, and then I gushed and gushed until my come was squirting back at me between her sex's lips and my shaft.

I took a step back, plopping out. "I'm sorry . . ."

"It's always quick the first time, isn't it? With someone new? Have some more wine. I'll be right back."

I made myself decent and sprawled in her recliner armchair. When she came back the tightly curled hairs of her pubes were glistening but the rest of her was dry. I assumed she'd used a douche or something.

She asked me, "How do you feel about oral sex?"

"I'm for it. Did you want me to . . . While I recover my strength?"

"No. Sit up."

She undressed me. All I had to do was lift up at the right times. It was sexy, being taken care of by a naked woman. My cock thickened along my thigh, but it didn't lift. It was too soon after a really spectacular orgasm.

She kneeled, took me in a cool palm, and addressed the head of my cock. "We'll soon have you up again," she told it.

"Give it a few more minutes," I said.

Cyn glared at me. "When I say you'll have an erection," she spat, "you'll have an erection. I'll be gentle this time."

It sounded like a threat.

Cyn squatted, naked, between my bare feet. The light was behind her. Her delta was black shadow. I had a silhouette to look at – a long shallow curve under one thigh, an outline like the cleft blunt end of an egg, bulging down, and then the swoop of another long curve.

The cleft wasn't regular. One side had a slightly out-turned lip. There was a spiked fuzziness on the other side of the egg-shape, as if water had matted her pubic hair.

I'd been *inside* that fleshy egg. My *cock* had split it, and beyond, deep beyond, past the hot mushiness into the throttling slick channel.

The thought brought a pulse.

Cyn lifted the base of the recliner, tilting me back and lifting my feet to the level of her breasts. She took hold of my right foot and her left breast. Her nipple dragged up over the sole of my foot, from the hardness of my heel to beneath where my toes curled over. It's sensitive in there, at the bases of your toes. I could feel the tantalizing spike there as well as with my fingertips. She folded my toes down with her palm, gripping her nipple with my toes, and writhed, prodding rigid flesh between my big toe and the next one.

"You're growing," she said. She was right. My cock was thickening and lifting.

Cyn plucked her nipple from my toes. Her head bent, mouth wide. She engulfed three toes, wet and hot. Her tongue squirmed over, and between, and under. She put her nipple back and flickered it from side to side, frotting its tip on my soaking toes.

My cock lifted higher.

"Keep perfectly still!" Cyn ordered.

She stood and bridged me, her arms straight and her hands on the chair's arms. My fingers wanted me to reach out to her dangling breasts but she'd said I had to keep still. I didn't want to spoil whatever she had planned.

My cock was straight up by then, not fully erect, but close.

Her arms bent, lowering her face towards my cock. Cyn's mouth stretched. She paused, my naked glans an inch from her gaping lips, pointed directly into her mouth.

She swooped. My cock passed between her lips, past her teeth, over her tongue, all without touching, and butted the back of her throat. With her mouth still open too wide to make contact, she made a deep gargling sound, *and pushed.*

Little bubbles from her throat burst against the glossy-tight skin of my glans. There was vibration, vibration so *intimate* that it seemed my cock's head had to be pressed against her larynx.

She nodded, once, twice, three times, and then withdrew slowly, closing her mouth on me as she dragged it off my stem. By the time my cock flipped out from between her lips it was hard enough to burst.

Cyn scrambled up the chair. Brief slithers of fevered skin electrified me as she climbed over me. Her knees bracketed my waist. She reached down between us, took my cock in one hand and her pussy in her other, and slammed her hips down.

I froze, letting her impale herself. She looked down at me, wild, almost hating. "Don't move! Don't you dare move! I'm going to have a big one. I can feel it building. Keep still!"

Her hips juddered. She glared into my eyes. Her lips twisted. Her face contorted. Her sex was slapping at me, mashing down. She wasn't focused on the feel of my cock inside her, just on rubbing her clit's head against my pubic bone. She wasn't making love to me. She was *using* me to masturbate with.

There was froth on her lips. Her eyes were insane. She reared up, made two tiny fists, and punched down. I flinched, but she didn't hit me. She pounded the chair's back to either side of my head.

"Drag me down harder. Pull down on my shoulders!"

I got a grip and pressed down through her entire body, to where we were united. She bore down with all of her might, trying to squirm her way through me, not riding my cock, just frictioning her squishy pubes and stiff clit, grinding and grinding.

Cyn screamed and toppled sideways, over the chair's arm, to plop to the floor, sprawling, limp, lifeless.

I hadn't come. It'd been an incredible experience. I'd never known a woman so totally *consumed* by her passion, but I hadn't come. She looked to be absolutely sated, but I hadn't come and my cock was nagging at me. I gave myself a stroke.

Cyn sat up. "Don't you *dare*! That's *mine*."

"I thought . . ."

"I *told* you I was multi-orgasmic. Be patient, damn you!"

She crawled around in front of the chair again, put both hands flat on the foot-piece, and pushed it down. I was lifted up. She leaned over my thighs, dragging the points of her nipples over their hairiness and took me into her mouth again. Her two hands lifted the edge, pulling me back, drawing me almost out of her mouth and then pushed down, driving me back into the steamy soft cavern. Up and down. In and out. I just lay there, letting her rock me towards . . .

My cock's head exploded inside her mouth. She sucked and sucked until I was dry.

"I didn't spill a single drop," she said.

"No – you didn't."

"I never will. If I do, you must punish me."

That was the first time she'd mentioned my punishing her. I didn't take much notice. It was just a figure of speech, wasn't it?

It was dawn before she let me rest. That was OK. It was Saturday morning. I could sleep in.

I woke at noon to the smell of bacon and eggs. After breakfast she suggested I might like to go get some wine and vodka because we'd drunk the last of her booze. When I got back she was made-up and wearing that jersey sweater and nothing else but a pair of metallic black stay-up hose.

I'd been contemplating maybe another session that evening, not at two in the afternoon, but my cock took one look at that tiny triangle of curls, black on white and framed by black jersey above and black nylon below, and made my decision for me. I took her in my arms for a long kiss with my hands checking out how well the weals on her bottom were healing.

They were doing well, but still tender. Whenever my fingertip grazed a ridge she shivered and gasped into my mouth. Her pubes bumped at me as well, which didn't discourage me.

"I wasn't nice to you, when you were on the recliner," she said. "I plan to make that up to you."

"You were fine – more than fine – fantastic," I said.

"No – I forgot your pleasure. I feel guilty. Let me do it right, please?"

It'd been a while since a woman had asked me to let her screw me, "please". I let her undress me and sit me back on the chair. She poured two half-tumblers of straight vodka over ice, set them on a side table, and climbed up astride me.

"I'm not ready," I apologized.

"You will be."

She did that shared-drink thing again, with vodka. That, and the heat that was radiating down from her pussy onto my cock, started to take effect. She chewed at my bottom lip for a while, tickle-touching my ribs and chest, brushing her fingertips across my nipples, and then she swooped down and bit one, quite hard.

"Ouch!"

She grinned at me. "Did that hurt?"

I rubbed my chest. "Some."

She tugged her sweater up into a roll above her breasts and said, "So – take your revenge."

I nipped.

"I bit you harder than that."

"Harder."

I clamped my teeth as hard as I could short of drawing blood. Cyn sucked air, arched at me, and clawed one hand down my chest.

I jerked back. *She'd* drawn blood. There were four parallel furrows with little curls of skin at the ends.

Cyn said, "Kiss better."

Her tongue-tip traced them, one at a time. When all four had been tingled she sat back and said, "And antiseptic." She poured icy vodka over my chest. It stung the scratches but then she put her tongue to work again, lapping and sucking it out of my wounds.

"More?"

I nodded.

"Watch closely. Don't be chicken."

I watched. She rested the heel of her hand on my sternum. Her fingers curled. Four nail-points prickled. I stared down as they made tiny dents.

"Say when."

The tension was unbearable, so I said, "When."

I reared from the searing, but it was *good*. Her nails had cut deeper this time, but that just left wider wounds to be tongue-lapped and vodka-stung. She was still licking at me when her hand groped to wrap around my shaft and she lowered herself onto it and I sunk right up into her sponginess.

Then she went berserk. By the time I came my face was soaked with the sweat she'd flicked with her flailing hair and my shoulders were sore from the gouges, but it was worth the pain. It was worth every delirious moment of it.

Then we had to have a shower together. I was sure I wasn't up to any more but she turned away from me and had me soap her long back and her round bottom and all the time she was reaching behind and slithering her soapy palm up and down on my cock, rubbing its head over her firm smooth slippery buttock, and I found that I *could* get another erection, and have another orgasm. I came thick and foamy, dribbling obscenely down the back of her glossy thigh.

When you come *on* a woman, instead of *in* her, it's like you mark her as your territory. It defiles her the way a brand defiles the haunch of a cow, making her more precious because she's *yours*.

We called out for fried chicken and she licked my fingers for me and then finger-painted her own breasts with chicken grease, so it was early in the morning before we slept again.

Sunday was the same, from noon till four in the morning. I was glad to go to my office on Monday.

She phoned at three. "What time do I expect you, and what would you like for supper?"

"Six. Whatever. Should I bring something in?"

"Lamb chops. What are you going to do to me tonight, Paul?"

"Do to you?"

"In bed, on the chair, on the floor?"

"Make long passionate love to you, Cyn."

"Give me the details. I want to be thinking about it till you get here."

"I'll call you back."

When I'd thought, and I called her, all she said was, "Is that all? You can do better than that, darling. Leave it to me tonight then."

I came home and found her on the bed, naked except for one stocking. The other was wrapped around her wrists and tied to the bedrail.

She said, "You bastard! You've got me in your power now, haven't you. I'm helpless and you can do anything you like to me."

I can play games. I sat on the bed beside her and rested my palm on her pubes. Leering, I said, "Do anything I like to *this*," and gave her a squeeze.

Her thighs spread wide under my hand. "I bet you plan to oil your hand—" she nodded sideways towards the bottle of baby oil that stood ready open "—and work it right up into me, no matter what I say."

I took off my jacket and rolled my shirt sleeve up. The oil was cool in my palm. I smoothed it over her pubes and her pussy's pulpy lips.

"I might scream," she said. "I might beg you to stop, but you'll be merciless, won't you."

"Merciless," I agreed. I folded three fingers together and worked them into her.

"I thought you were going to be cruel."

I straightened my hand into a blade and forced all four fingers and half of my palm between her lips.

"You were going to use your whole hand."

I added my thumb and wriggled, pushing as hard as I dared. Cyn set her feet flat on the bed and lifted her hips at me.

"Deeper. I can take it."

Women have babies, don't they? And don't necessarily split? I pushed harder, against slippery convoluted resistance. My hand sank in, deeper, to the heel of my palm. She was incredibly strong in there. Her vaginal muscles clamped. I struggled against the pressure. I pushed. Her constriction folded my hand into a fist. It was like my hand was in a hot wet rubber sack that was shrinking, slowly crushing my fingers.

"I have to take it out," I told her. "I'm getting a cramp."

"No! Revolve it first. Twist your fist in me."

I turned it left and then right and then started to withdraw, slowly, gingerly, unfolding my fingers as soon as I was able, and finally I was free.

"I'll be loose for about an hour," she said. "Better turn me over."

It took me a moment to understand, but then I did, and flipped her, and shucked my clothes. She was kneeling rump up, ready. I oiled my cock and poured more oil over her sphincter. Two thumbs pressed her open. I got my cock's head in place and then pushed down on it with the ball of one thumb. It slowly sank into her, and disappeared.

"Am I tight, back there?" she asked.

"Damned tight. Wonderfully tight."

"Cocks like 'tight', don't they?"

"Yes."

"You know how I'd be tighter?"

"How?"

"If there were two of you, one buggering me while the other one screwed me."

I stopped in mid-thrust. "I'm not into that – sharing."

She twisted her hips, plucking herself off me. "How *dare* you! I'm a one-man woman. You should know that. I was just thinking of something special to make you happy. Now you've spoiled it."

I apologized, but it was no good. She didn't speak to me for the rest of the night. I felt bad, but at least I got some sleep.

We made up the next morning. I moved in on the weekend. On the Monday I found she'd thrown out my robe and bought me a new one. I understood. Women always do that when a man moves in. They think they can smell the previous woman on it.

"It was a horrible disgusting thing. I don't know how you could have worn it."

That wasn't necessary. Perhaps my anger at her rudeness showed, because she instantly begged my forgiveness and suggested I might feel better if I punished her.

In the brief interludes between sex, she sometimes talked about her past. She'd been raped by a friend of the family when she was thirteen. She'd been raped again when she was twenty and working as a model. A guy she'd lived with, Bill something, had brought three friends home once and gang-banged her.

If I'd kept track right, she'd been raped on a total of seven different occasions and abused in other ways by every man she'd ever known.

We watched TV once in a while. I counted five celebrities that she told me she'd either had affairs with or fought off, including two women.

I found out what she'd been getting at when she'd suggested she'd be tighter if there were two men. She liked it if there was a vibrator deep in her rectum when I took her vaginally, and in her pussy when I buggered her. When I couldn't get it up, two vibrators were fine. It was best for her if I tied her up before going to work with the twin dildos, then "she couldn't stop me, no matter what I did to her".

Once she told me, "I wouldn't need this if you were as big as Jeff was."

Later she apologized again – and suggested I punish her again. That time I did. She complained that I didn't spank like I meant it and my hand was too soft. Mr Fox had done a lot of woodwork so his palms were hard. When *he* spanked a woman she knew she'd been spanked by a *real* man.

One night when I was seeing to her pleasure she made a pencil mark on a pad. When I asked why, she told me I'd given her eleven orgasms so far that night and she wanted to keep score. I really worked that night. By morning the score-pad read "twenty-seven". I remarked, hopefully, that it had to be some kind of record. "Not by a long way. Bill got me up to fifty, once."

We didn't go out much. When we did, she flirted with the waiter or someone at the next table and we ended up fighting.

I took her swimming in the pool in her building. That was fun until a couple of young guys came in. Somehow or another she lost the top of her bikini and that made her squeal loud enough to turn the lads' heads. I left her chatting to them, clutching her bra-top to her breasts.

When she finally came up she woke me to tell me I'd misunderstood her natural friendliness.

"I suppose you expect another spanking," I said.

"With your soft hands? Anyway, you aren't man enough, you hear me? You're a wimp, Paul, with a puny little cock. Those boys down in the pool, though, they were real men. You should have seen the size of the erections they got from looking at me."

I grabbed her and got her over my lap but even mad as I was I had to take care not to break her arms so she managed to wriggle off me. I pushed her down flat on the bed. The cords were there, tied to the four corners, ready for "play". I used them.

I slapped her bum four times, almost hard.

She said, "Wimp."

I grabbed my belt off the chair, lifted it high . . . and tossed it aside.

She twisted her face towards me as I pulled my underpants up. "What are you doing?"

"I'm going. This is where I came in."

# Sweating Profusely in Mérida: A Memoir

Carol Queen

The boyfriend and I met at a sex party. I was in a back room trying to help facilitate an erection for a gentleman brought to the party by a woman who would have nothing to do with him once they got there. She had charged him a pretty penny to get in, and I actually felt that I should have got every cent, but I suppose it was my own fault that I was playing Mother Teresa and didn't know when to let go of the man's dick. Boyfriend was hiding behind a potted palm eyeing me and this guy's uncooperative, uncut dick, and it seemed Boyfriend had a thing for pretty girls *and* uncut men, especially the latter. So he decided to help me out and replaced my hand with his mouth. That was when it got interesting. The uncut straight guy finally left and I stayed.

In the few months our relationship lasted, we shared many more straight men, most of them – Boyfriend's radar was incredible – uncircumcised and willing to do almost anything with a man as long as there was a woman in the room. I often acted as sort of a hook to hang a guy's heterosexuality on while Boyfriend sucked his dick or even fucked him. My favourite was the hitchhiker wearing pink lace panties under his grungy jeans – but that's another story. Long before we met him, Boyfriend had invited me to go to Mexico.

This was the plan. Almost all the guys in Mexico are uncut, right? And lots will play with me, too, Boyfriend assured me, especially if there's a woman there. (I guessed they resembled American men in this respect.) Besides, it would be a romantic vacation.

That was how we wound up in Room 201 of the Hotel Reforma in sleepy Mérida, capital of the Yucatán. Mérida's popularity as a tourist town had been eclipsed by the growth of Cancún, the nearest Americanized resort. That meant the boys would be hornier,

Boyfriend reasoned. The Hotel Reforma had been recommended by a fellow foreskin fancier. Its chief advantages were the price – about $14 a night – and the fact that the management didn't charge extra for extra guests. I liked it because it was old, airy, and cool, with wrought-iron railings and floor tiles worn thin from all the people who'd come before. Boyfriend liked it because it had a pool, always a good place to cruise, and a disco across the street. That's where we headed as soon as we got in from the airport, showered, and changed into skimpy clothes suitable for turning tropical boys' heads.

There were hardly any tropical boys there, as it turned out, because this was where the Ft Lauderdale college students who couldn't afford spring break in Cancún went to spend their more meagre allowances, and not only did it look like a Mexican restaurant-with-disco in Ft Lauderdale, the management took care to keep all but the most dapper Méridans out lest the coeds be frightened by scruffy street boys. Scruffy street boys, of course, is just what Boyfriend had his eye out for, and at first the pickings looked slim; but we found one who had slipped past security, out to hustle nothing more spicy than a gig showing tourists around the warren of narrow streets near the town's central plaza, stumbling instead onto us. Ten minutes later Boyfriend had his mouth wrapped around a meaty little bundle, *with* foreskin. Luis stuck close to us for several days, probably eating more regularly than usual, and wondering out loud whether all the women in America were like me, and would we take him back with us? Or at least send him a Mötley Crüe T-shirt when we went home?

Boyfriend had brought Bob Damron's gay travel guide, which listed for Mérida: a cruisy restaurant (it wasn't) and a cruisy park bench in the Zocalo (it was, and one night Boyfriend stayed out most of the night looking for gay men, who, he said, would run the other way if they saw me coming, and found one, a slender boy who had to pull down the pantyhose he wore under his jeans so Boyfriend could get to his cock, and who expressed wonder because he had never seen anyone with so many condoms; in fact most people never had condoms at all. Boyfriend gave him his night's supply and some little brochures, about *el SIDA* he'd brought from the AIDS Foundation, *en español* so even if our limited Spanish didn't get through to our tricks, a pamphlet might).

Damron's also indicated that Mérida had a bathhouse.

I had always wanted to go to a bathhouse, and of course there was not much chance it would ever happen back home. For one thing, they were all closed before I ever moved to San Francisco. For another, even if I dressed enough like a boy to pass, I wouldn't look old enough to be let in. But in Mérida perhaps things were different.

It was away from the town's centre, but within walking distance of the Hotel Reforma. Through the tiny front window, grimy from the town's blowing dust, I saw a huge papier-mâché figure of Pan, painted brightly and hung with jewellery, phallus high. It looked like something the Radical Faeries would carry in the Gay Day parade. Everything else about the lobby looked dingy, like the waiting room of a used-car dealership.

Los Baños de Vapour would open at eight that evening. They had a central tub and rooms to rent; massage boys could be rented, too. I would be welcome.

The papier-mâché Pan was at least seven feet tall and was indeed the only bright thing in the lobby. Passing through the courtyard, an overgrown jumble of vines pushing through cracked tiles, a slight smell of sulfur, a stagnant fountain, we were shown up a flight of concrete stairs to our room by Carlos, a solid, round-faced man in his mid-twenties, wrapped in a frayed white towel. The room was small and completely tiled, grout black from a losing fight with the wet tropical air. At one end was a shower and at the other a bench, a low, vinyl-covered bed and a massage table. There was a switch that, when flipped, filled the room with steam. Boyfriend flipped it and we shucked our clothes; as the pipes hissed and clanked, Carlos gestured to the massage table and then to me.

Boyfriend answered for me, in Spanish, that I'd love to. I got on the table and Carlos set to work. Boyfriend danced around the table gleefully, sometimes stroking me, sometimes Carlos's butt. "Hey, man, I'm working!" Carlos protested, not very insistently, and Boyfriend went for his cock, stroking it hard, then urged him up onto the table, and Carlos's hands, still slick from the massage oil and warm from the friction of my skin, covered my breasts as Boyfriend rolled a condom onto Carlos's cock and rubbed it up and down my labia a few times and finally let go, letting it sink in. He rode me slow and then hard while the table rocked dangerously and Boyfriend stood at my head, letting me tongue his cock while he played with Carlos's tits. When Boyfriend was sure that we were having a good time, he put on a towel and slipped out the door. Carlos looked surprised. I had to figure out how to say, in Spanish "He's going hunting," and get him to go back to fucking me, solid body slick from oil and steam; if he kept it up, he would make me come, clutching his slippery back, legs in the air.

That was just happening when Boyfriend came back with David. He was pulling him in the door by his already stiff penis, and I suspected Boyfriend had wasted as little time getting him by the dick as he usually did. He had found David in the tub room, he announced, and he had a beautiful, long *uncut* cock. (Boyfriend always enunciated clearly when he said "uncut".) David *did* have a beautiful cock, and he spoke English and was long and slim with startling blue eyes. It turned out he was Chicano, second generation, a senior Riverside High who spent school breaks with his grandmother in Mérida and worked at Los Baños de Vapour as a secret summer job. We found out all this about him as I was showering the sweat and oil off from my fuck with Carlos, and by the time I heard that he'd been working at the Baños since he turned sixteen, I was ready to start fucking again. David was the most quintessentially eighteen-year-old fuck I ever had, except Boyfriend's presence made it unusual; he held David's cock and balls and controlled the speed of the thrusting, until his mouth got preoccupied with Carlos's dick. David told me, ardently, that I was beautiful, though at that point I didn't care if I was beautiful or not, since I was finally in a bathhouse doing what I'd always wanted to do and I felt more like a faggot than a beautiful *gringa*. But David was saying he wished he had a girlfriend like me, even though I was thirty, shockingly old – this actually was what almost all of Boyfriend's conquests said to me, though I suspected not every man could keep up with a girlfriend who was really a faggot, or a boyfriend who was really a woman, or whatever kind of fabulous anomaly I was.

Then someone knocked on the door and we untangled for a minute to answer it, and there were José and Gaspar, laughing and saying we were the most popular room in the Baños at the moment and would we like some more company? At least that's how David translated the torrent of Spanish, for they were both speaking at once. Naturally we invited them in, and lo and behold, Gaspar was actually *gay*, and so while I lay sideways on the massage table with my head off the edge and my legs in the air so I could suck David while José fucked me, I could watch Boyfriend finally getting *his* cock sucked by Gaspar, whose black, glittering Mayan eyes closed in concentration, and I howled with not simply orgasm but the *excitement*, the splendid excitement of being in Mexico in a bathhouse with four uncut men and a maniac, a place no woman I knew had gone before. Steam swirled in the saturated air like superheated fog, beading like pearls in the web of a huge Yucatán spider in the corner;

David's cock, or was it José's or Carlos's again, I didn't care, pounded my fully opened cunt rhythmically and I wished I had her view.

You know if you have ever been to a bathhouse that time stands still in the steamy, throbbing air, and so I had no idea how long it went on, only that sometimes I was on my back and sometimes on my knees, and once for a minute I was standing facing the wall, and when Boyfriend wasn't sucking them or fucking me, he was taking snapshots of us, just like a tourist. The floor of the room was completely littered with condoms, which made us all laugh hysterically. Rubber-kneed, Gaspar and David held me up with Carlos and José flanking them so Boyfriend could snap one last picture. Then he divided all the rest of the condoms among them – we had more at the hotel, I think that week we went through ten dozen – and got out his brochures. He was trying to explain in Spanish the little condoms he used for giving head – how great they were to use with uncut guys 'cause they disappeared under the foreskin – and I was asking David what it was like to live a double life, Riverside High to Los Baños, and who else came there – "Oh, everybody does," he said – and did they ever want to fuck him – of course they *wanted* to – and did he ever fuck them – well, sure – and how was that? He shrugged and said, as if there were only one possible response to my question, "It's *fucking*."

When we left, the moon was high, the Baños deserted, the warm night air almost cool after the steamy room. The place looked like a courtyard motel, the kind I used to stay in with my parents when we traveled in the early sixties, but overgrown and haunted. The Pan figure glittered in the low lobby light, and the man at the desk charged us $35 – seven for each massage boy, four each to get in, and six for the room. Hundreds of thousands of pesos – he looked anxious, as though he feared we'd think it was too much. We paid him, laughing. I wondered if this was how a Japanese businessman in Thailand felt. Was I contributing to the imperialist decline of the third world? Boyfriend didn't give a shit about things like that, so I didn't mention it. In my hand was a crumpled note from David: "Can I come visit you in your hotel room? No money."

# Tarot

## Florence Dugas

Noon was gently moving towards two o'clock. As it was already summertime, no one could tell: somewhere in the world it's always noon. It was as if the sun had given her a sign, and she didn't return to work.

The sound of her heels against the stone of the road and the sidewalk is like a clamour of victory. She supplies a rhythm to the city, and her long, thin legs move, map, and order its topography, like a defiant army marching ahead under the newfound sun, celebrating the coming of spring. It is good to feel the heat spread across her skin, caressing her knees like two warm hands, even moving up between her thighs now no longer under the protection of nylon. The sun almost draws a crown of gold around her head, as if she were a chosen being. From time to time she even swings her head from side to side, like a racehorse in heat. Saying yes and no to her invisible mount while her heavy stream of hair undulates across her back. She straightens her back, holding her stomach in, and the flow of her hair swims gloriously in motion.

She walks as if she were leading a victory parade. The very word echoes across her brain, to the rhythm of her heels, and it amuses her to invent more meanings for it. To parade is more than just to walk at random, no mere promenade where you never know where the next step leads. "To parade is to move like God across his garden," Brisset used to say. It even makes her look a little drunk, dizzy from her newfound freedom. Walking along, parading, as if she were about to become the heroine of some medieval ballad sung by a troubadour beneath the window of a captive king. So much sun is unusual. Walking as she is, head high, she can no longer hear Paris surrounding her, just the sound of her heels clicking along; nor can she see the cars and passers-by, just the winged Génie of the Bastille, flying high up there close to Icarus. She is on parade: she's come out of her shell, the whole world is on offer, her steps are conquering space, taking her into a wholly new dimension.

The clock on the Gare de Lyon betrays an impossible hour, which even the sun denies.

"The next train? Well, you've got the Paris – Vintimille, in ten minutes. Seats? Oh, as many as you want. Non-smoking? Isn't the weather lovely? The sky is so blue. Yes, I understand."

The railways guy sitting behind the immediate departures window is actually not bad-looking at all.

It's true, there are few people on the train. In her compartment, just five men: four of them are playing cards, while the fifth, further down, appears to be sleeping already, with just his neck and short, greying hair visible from her vantage point.

With all those empty seats available, she chooses to sit on the right-hand side, so she can enjoy the sun for the rest of the afternoon.

She feels blandly happy, sunny, watching all the cows outside pass.

The train does not stop before Valence.

She walks out onto the platform to move her legs. A two-minute stop. Up in the sky, the sun hasn't moved at all, but the heat is now more oppressive, a sign they are further south, in the Midi. She can feel the sun rising ever so stealthily up her thighs, so much more aggressively than in Paris, and this metaphor first makes her smile, then makes her feel dreamy.

She shakes her head. I'm getting delirious, she thinks. But on the other hand she feels ever so free. She returns to the compartment from the other end and walks down the rows of seats as the train begins speeding up again. She sways dizzily between the wooden seats.

The man with grey hair is not sleeping. He is watching her navigate the passage, struggling against the train's increasing motion, as if he were looking through her. The thought that somehow between Paris and Valence, on this stolen afternoon, she has physically dematerialized amuses her. Is the man not really looking at her? He is quite handsome, in a prematurely greying way. His eyes are the same colour as his hair, pale grey veined with black – a man of marble. As she passes him, she gazes at his hands, laid out flat on the table. Quite beautiful hands that, in her imagination, she is already placing within her intimate theatre, the hands of a pianist, or perhaps a surgeon's hands ready to sew someone's wound up, or even a pair of warm and dry hands alighting on her knees, sliding up her skirt, moving into her underwear and grabbing her butt cheeks, hands capable of measuring her ass so much more than the sun outside.

She shakes her head, both amused and annoyed by her own cliché fantasy.

The four men are still busy with their card game. As she passes them, she sees it is a tarot deck, the same high numbers and cards, but something catches her attention: the images on the cards aren't the ones she knows, the turn-of-the-century scenes so familiar to the tarot. She slows down imperceptibly, still moving ahead, and turns back to look again, not quite brave enough to stand still. She's right: the characters on the cards are mostly naked, unlike the images she's familiar with. The man nearest to her, an ebony-coloured African man, still holds four cards in his hand – two small squares as well as an eleven and a twelve. On the first one, the characters are sitting around a picnic scene imitating *Le Déjeuner sur l'Herbe*; the seated woman is naked, but the man lying down is also, and another man, who is leaning towards her as if to bite her breasts, is getting undressed. She has difficulty seeing the other card, obscured as it is by the man's thick black thumb, but again the woman in the boat is nude. On the twelve, she can see only the upper half of the card: a ball somewhere in the background, but on the right-hand side the image of a man seemingly offering his cock deferentially to two sitting women whose clothes have been partly pulled open. One of the women is thrusting her peach glove-covered hand towards the imposing virile member. The man whose cock it is has grey hair, and it makes her think right away of the silent passenger in the seat a few rows back.

The black man throws the twelve down, and another of the men adds the twenty. She just has time to glimpse the image of four men sitting at a table playing cards, all in the buff, while a woman under the table is seemingly sucking off the player on the left. The illustrator had frozen the scene just as her mouth is about to devour his mushroom head and her cheeks are delicately deformed by the intrusion.

She shrugs. Scenes from a brothel, she reckons, no doubt a belle époque set of cards.

She walks back to her seat and distractedly watches the landscape roll by, sky moving between white and blue. The Rhône river flows heavily by, moving between nuclear power stations. At any rate, the stations do not affect the area's luminosity.

She senses a movement to her left and turns. The man with grey hair is there, looking over her shoulder. And like earlier, he has the same distant and detached look, as if his eyes are fixed on a point some ten centimetres behind her.

"May I?" he says, sitting next to her. He has a vaguely English accent. He calmly pulls up the arm separating their two seats, deliberately abolishing all distance between them, or any form of misunderstanding.

"May I . . ." These are the only words he says, and her quiet agreement, as she does not object, is all he needs for approval, as if those two words and the unspoken answer will justify all that will follow.

The man's right hand skims by her neck while his left hand takes hold of her knee. His skin is just as she expected: warm and dry.

He allows her just a few seconds to imagine what is about to happen. His fingers tread ever so lightly across her skin, as if he were caressing water without creating a stir across its surface.

His fragrance is both pleasant and discreet. She doesn't know why, but his smell reminds her of Louis XV furniture, burnished wood pieces.

For a while he doesn't move, his face just inches from hers, his hand almost motionless on her knee, his fingers delicately skimming her neck.

The dark clouds inside his grey eyes make him look like a phantom. And finally he bends slowly over towards her and kisses her. She holds on to him, slides her own hands under the fashionable grey jacket he is wearing, takes hold of his shirt, grabs his tie . . . The hand on her knee begins a slow and deliberate journey upward along her thigh and cups her cunt, forcing itself against the already wet silk. The man pulls the thin panties to one side of her gash, his fingers lingering against the soft and delicate lips with assurance. "With a sense of contained violence," she thinks aloud. And the mental image of her cunt in his grasp makes her smile and hold herself even more open. She allows her hand to slip under the man's belt, and through the thin material of his trousers grabs hold of his hardening virility, an initial contact that surprises her by its brazenness. She pulls on the zip of his fly and extricates the jutting cock now pulsing against her fingers, just as she leans her own body slightly backward so that the man's hands might have easier access to her stomach and, she hopes, her ass.

They caress each other for a few minutes. He inserts two fingers deep into the swamp of her cunt, two very long fingers with short, invisible nails, deep into the pit of her belly, exploring her with even more avidity than his cock could, seeking what she desires with an almost feminine science.

He has no need to change the pressure of his fingers against her neck. She leans over of her own accord towards the cock now surging through the folds of grey material and takes it into her mouth. It feels fresh, almost cold. First the thick, split apricot, which she surrounds with her tongue and bathes in her saliva, then the rest of his mast, as far as she can take it. Three-quarters of it almost, her mouth spreadeagled by this meat of desire, to the point of gagging against this dangerous weapon heading straight for her innards. She retreats to catch her breath and impales her mouth anew against the blood-engorged tip of his cock, torn between the need to suck him forever and forever, to fill herself with his wooden citrus flavour, and the sheer craving to feel him flow wildly inside her mouth, waves breaking against the back of her throat, and the freedom to drink all of him in.

The man then pulls his fingers out of her heaving cunt and, taking advantage of her position leaning back, moves them, still coated with her vaginal secretions, towards her ass and digs them both into her sphincter. She buckles, rears against the fingers now stretching her wide and, doing so, opens herself even more to his rough caress. And when the man's thumb at the front now starts applying pressure to her clitoris, she comes violently, feels her asshole spasm against the fingers now burrowing deep inside her, and only the cock now embedded in her mouth prevents her from screaming.

He allows her to enjoy the moment. His fingers are still digging deep into the very fundament of her ass. His thumb is held hard, unmoving, against her inflamed clitoris. He gently pulls her by her hair and allows her face to rest against his chest while she gasps for air.

Once the contractions slow down, he slides his fingers out of her and pulls her up against him as he moves onto the seat in front of her, between her splayed legs, and forcefully pulls her down onto him. Initially she fears she won't be able to accommodate him, that she's not open enough – he's so much bigger than anything she's had inside her before. His cock is still growing as he breaches her, his head brushing her labia aside as his shaft sinks deeply into her. Inside the hot furnace of her cunt, the man's cock feels as cold as ice. She bites her lips to keep from screaming when she feels the cock assault her back wall, and she takes hold of the top of the seat facing her and, seizing it desperately, allows herself to sway wildly, allowing his cock to plow every inch of her insides as she holds back her pain. The man, his hands gripping the sides of her ass, helps her rise and then again and again brings her down onto him, every time deeper and deeper, as if she were a cave with no end.

A few metres away from her, she can only glimpse the heads of the other four men every time she rises above the seat: they are still playing cards, oblivious to what is happening to her.

For a brief moment she realizes she would like to feel him flow inside her, mingling his sperm with all that is floating within her, then the thought is violently abolished because she comes again, ferociously, wantonly, literally screwed onto this cock that is splitting her apart, piercing her very heart.

She is gasping for breath when the man's hands let go of her butt and move under her shirt, partly freeing her breasts from the push-up bra, lengthily caressing her hard, sensitive nipples, enjoying himself, then pinching her breasts hard to bring her back to reality from her swoon. Through the waves of ecstasy she is also confusedly angry at him for having discovered she enjoys the combination of pain and pleasure. The man withdraws from her, settles to her left and folds his still-bulging cock so wet from her secretions into his trousers. Will she ever know the taste of his sperm, or just this lingering smell of wet rosewood? His smile is muted, almost affectionate, but distant again as he moves back to his seat, and the last thing she sees of him is his straight neck and his short grey hair.

She frees herself from the wet panties now cutting into her crotch and shudders, face against the windowpane. She watches the Rhône outside. An old piece of poetry by Victor Hugo comes into her mind: "The noisy river flows, a fast and yellow flow . . ."

The heat of the sun, the cool of the glass against her cheeks, and the dying vibrations inside her belly now peaceful, moving away, drying up . . .

She doesn't wake up in Avignon, nor in Marseilles. When she opens her eyes again, she can still hear the echo in the air of the voice that has just announced their arrival in Saint Raphaël. It is now evening, and only the sporadic lights of the approaching station puncture the darkness.

She had thought of going to Nice, but why not Saint Raphaël; she's never been here before.

She is now alone in the compartment. She rises, still unsteady on her legs – she fell asleep in an awkward position and her left foot has fallen asleep – and moves forward with a slight limp, gracelessly, towards the exit, and almost topples over as she walks down the train's steps. Blood flows back into her brain, the vertigo fades . . . she takes a few steps forward on solid ground and the dizziness returns.

I must be hungry, she thinks. And the act of thinking it makes her hungry. She walks towards the station's exit, figuring that, like all train stations, there must be a bar nearby, a bistro, some Arab grocery.

But all there is nearby is a Rolls-Royce parked close to the pavement, a very old model with the driver's seat open to the air and the back shrouded by dark opaque windows. The chauffeur, holding his cap in his hand, turns towards her. "Mademoiselle," he says, "we were waiting for you. Would you please . . ."

She is so surprised that she allows herself to be led, just two metres of pavement between freedom and the green English leather seats of the luxury car, and the door closes silently behind her.

Immediately, it's night behind the dark windows, which banish even the glow of the street lights, barely allowing pale haloes to survive, just like the mad stars in Van Gogh's skies.

The car is totally silent; it could be stationary, just a hint of vibration betraying its motion. They drive for a long time, and the young woman, who is hungry and thirsty and badly needs to pee, is now in a bad mood. They stop for a red light and she tries to get out, but the doors are locked from the outside. She raps her knuckles on the glass separating her from the driver. The man's neck doesn't budge.

The Rolls-Royce leaves Saint Raphaël and takes a small, winding road that rises above sea level and leads deep into the hinterlands. A long time. Hunger. Thirst . . .

At last, the car slows down as it runs parallel to a high wall that leads them to an intricate metal gate topped by a mess of white metal arrows. The door opens by itself, no doubt electronically controlled, unless there is an invisible caretaker in attendance . . .

Crunching across a gravel path, the car drives up to a small castle, one of the many modern-style monstrosities that the Côte d'Azur has given birth to over the past century, and comes to a halt in front of its steps. The stylish chauffeur gets out and ceremoniously opens the door.

In a rush, the sound of the early cicadas of spring invades the Rolls-Royce.

She alights, intrigued, worried, still angry. A man stands there, on the second step, and, astonished, she recognizes the grey-haired stranger from the train. How in the hell could he have reached this place before her?

"Please accept our apologies," he says. "You must be quite tired?" He ceremoniously takes her hand. He is now wearing a smoky grey lounge suit, the same colour as his eyes. "Come," he says. "We've prepared some food for you."

She agrees to enter the castle, although she also knows this might be a mistake, that maybe she shouldn't, now that the falling sun has retreated with all its elementary seduction and the menace of night is ready to take over.

Once inside, she glances back – intuition or ultimate temptation. The moon is full and shines over a freshly mowed lawn at the heart of which stands a white marble statue, maybe of Venus, or even Diana the huntress without her slings and arrows, the languorous shape of the goddess bathing in the moonlight.

The young woman turns back and, with quiet determination, enters the house.

"If you wish to freshen up," the man says, pointing to a door.

"Yes, I'd like to spray my warpaint on again," she jokes, repressing the anxiety quickly rising inside her throat.

As she washes her hands, she gazes at the reassuring image in the mirror: she is still pretty, still looks fresh despite all those hours on the train; some would even say the darker shade below her eyes was an added bonus. "What a face," she says nevertheless, almost out of habit.

A snack? On a small table at the centre of the art deco living room filled with delicate furniture, she can see all the things she likes: patisseries, fruit, finger-sized delicacies, lemonade – she is still at an age where you are allowed to enjoy sugary things. In the meantime, the stranger is busy starting a fire inside the big fireplace, kneeling in front of the first orange flames longer than he normally would, exposing his slim neck to her gaze, no doubt aware she is full of questions and in no hurry to supply answers.

He finally rises from his prone position while she finishes biting into a thin slice of an exquisite tart. "I will take you to your room," he says. "You'll find something you can wear for dinner. Take your time. If you want to take a bath, just tell Nora, and she will arrange it."

With his hand, he points to a corner of the room where a young coloured woman in a domestic's uniform is standing, straight and silent. She has pale grey eyes, shining in the light of the nearby flames like the eyes of a cat.

She hadn't even heard her enter the room. "We dine at eleven," he adds.

They walk up a wide, pink, marbled set of stairs, a bit too ostentatious for her taste. Then, after passing through a red vestibule, down a long corridor punctuated by doors numbered one to nine. At the other end, there is another set of stairs, probably leading up. They stop at number seven. The maid opens the door and stands back to let her go in.

The room is spacious, tastefully furnished. Not one piece of furniture is contemporary; every single piece, from the straight geometry of the dresser to the vanity table with its crystalline mirror to the bed shrouded with delicate linen, appears to be brand new, although they all obviously were made in the twenties.

On the wall, a Millet-style print: three farm laborers resting in a field, enjoying a drink, while a woman awaits them, sitting against a haystack; it's unclear what she might be waiting for, as, unlike any character in a picture by the Barbizon artist, she is totally naked, and when you take a closer look, her hands, though held against her knees, are tied with a thin piece of string.

This sets her thinking again of the four men playing cards on the train, the same sense of discontinuity between the image you expect and the more disturbing one . . .

"Do you wish to take a bath?" the maid asks. There is no trace of the Caribbean in her voice.

"Yes, please . . ."

The bathroom that connects to the room is huge, all green marble, all three walls covered by mirrors, as is, curiously enough, the ceiling. Exotic plants, suspended from shelves and metal stands, spread a delicate perfume of wet earth and heavy flowers throughout the room. The bathtub, carved out of a single piece of dark marble and held up by sphinx-like feet, is positively enormous.

The maid runs the water, pouring in perfumed oil that rises in bubbles, the strong fragrance of which blends easily with that of the green plants in the room. The perfume rising through the steam now obscuring the mirrors transports her back to that sense of dizziness she experienced on the train; it's like feeling slightly drunk on an empty stomach.

The maid comes towards her, unbuttons her shirt, unhooks her bra and then the skirt. She does not remark on the fact that she is wearing no panties. The young woman allows her to do so, suddenly assaulted by tiredness, or at any rate using the tiredness as an excuse to surrender to whatever is about to happen to her.

In the water, it feels to her as if she is swimming in the immensity of the tub. Above her, she sees the shrouded reflection of a young blonde woman in the misted-up mirror, her skin ever so pale, like a white mummy floating inside a green marble coffin, the blue-grey of her eyes lost in the distance. But the steam rises and finally wipes out this lazy landscape of curves.

The maid allows her to soak for a long time in all the fragrances the heat is now breaking up. Finally, she comes back and hands her a Japanese robe, pale green, embroidered with birds of paradise.

"Do you want me to give you a massage?" she asks. "The bath will wash the journey away, and the massage will wash the bath away. Afterwards, I shall apply your make-up. The commander has given me very precise instructions."

She lets herself go, agile fingers skimming across her skin with exquisite softness, slowly untwisting her nerves, polishing her muscles, effectively providing her with strength again after her energy has been sapped by the bath. The maid has her lie down on a folding table once she has slipped out of the robe. First, lying on her stomach, she is massaged from her neck down to her heels, unavoidably feeling something stirring inside her when the long, brown fingers knead her ass and thighs. But she'd rather believe it's just a feeling of comfort. She almost falls asleep anyway, listening to the gurgling sounds of the emptying bath.

She is then turned round. Above her, the mirror is clearing up.

The young Creole woman is working her shoulders, the beginning of her neck, grazing her breasts whose tips are hardening, not that she notices as her hands lower themselves towards her midriff, before moving back to polish her nipples from time to time. Her brown hands make the extreme winter pallor of her pale skin appear almost indecent.

The young woman looks at herself in the ceiling mirror, and from her perspective, the girl massaging her appears closer to her than she in fact is, as if it were her mouth, her lips massaging her, and not her fingers. But very soon, it is actually her darker lips that are now attaching themselves to her taut nipples, licking then sucking on her hard tips, racing across her tremulous skin, her pretty café au lait face soon ensconced between her thighs. All she can see is the back of her head, a mass of short, dense curls when the maid's mouth alights on her cunt, and the masseuse's tongue separating the delicate lips of her opening, skimming across her dilated clit. She feels as if she wants to come that very moment, if only to release all the tension building up inside her since she walked into the house. With her hands, she grasps the short dark curls and pulls the girl's face hard against her stomach – black against white – her lithe tongue butterflying over her clit now feeling more forceful, more incisive.

The young maid pulls her body down towards the edge of the table, both her legs now winging over the sides, the indefatigable tongue squirming around her red-hot button, plunging down into her wet vagina, tiptoeing across her anus and delicately forcing it open – she has never had the courage to tell any of her previous lovers how much she would like to be sodomized by a hard, burning tongue – all this while her long bronzed fingers keep on playing with her breasts. Finally she comes, no longer able to restrain her voice, flooding the girl's face with her juices. The maid rises, wiping her mouth, her chin, and her nose with a towel and, curiously enough, smiles not at her but towards the mirror on the ceiling. The thought that someone has just witnessed the whole scene through a one-way mirror dawns on her with absolute certainty. What other traps are to follow? She slides off the massage table, pulls the young maid by her hair as she had done earlier, forces her to kneel before her and presses her face against her cunt, the heavy-lipped and violent mouth against her small blonde bush.

"Drink," she says.

And she slowly pees into the open, willing mouth that doesn't miss a single drop, still watching the ceiling as she does so, now smiling at the mirror, pleased to be conveying in such a way to the master of the house that by defiling his slave, she is resisting his will.

She is then made up by the maid, slowly, a bit too gaudily for her taste. Then she is given a long evening dress, a glossy couture piece with classical lines that Madame Gray would have appreciated. Once inside the formal dress, she feels like a marble statue sandwiched inside a skin of blackness, the exquisite pallor of her skin enhanced by the nocturnal black of the material. No underwear or lingerie underneath the dramatic dress. The silk adheres to her breasts, her ass and her stomach; the sudden crispness of the wrap awakens her nipples.

"You are beautiful," says the young maid. "I'm happy the commander has brought you here."

Once again the stairs. The maid guides her from one door to another. She hears a bit of conversation; she knows that very soon she will be told where she is. She is both curious and worried and slows her steps.

The girl swings the door open and invites her in.

She is greeted by intense light. There are four or five men in dinner jackets and six or seven elegantly attired women; they all briefly fall silent and watch her walk towards them. Meanwhile the grey-haired stranger moves in her direction, takes her by the hand, and smiles, putting her at her ease.

"You are quite ravishing," he says. And he truly looks as if he believes it.

She smiles back, still cautiously, but holds on to him, surrounded as she is by all these unknown faces.

"Friends," he says, with a semicircular gesture of his hand. "All charming people, as you will see."

Why does he not introduce her to anyone? Why isn't she even provided with a name, a surname?

Just then a servant attired in quite incongruous Louis XV style calls out loudly that dinner is served, and they all march into the immense dining room, where a very long rectangular table dominates the proceedings. The plates are exquisitely sober; the silver knives and forks and crystal glasses shine wildly under the glow of the candelabras.

The grey-haired man is at the head of the table and indicates she should sit to his left. Facing her is a very beautiful woman whose splendour has however seen better days, a thousand wrinkles smiling, a thousand small pains betraying her long and cruel past.

On her left is the youngest man in the room; he is younger than her even, his face and skin barely out of teenage years, radiant, almost effeminate. He is all smiles and his conversation is artfully banal.

The meal offers all that Provence can supply, from the most refined to the most colourful dish. Her taste buds sing along. Stylish servants see that their glasses are never empty and provide the right wine for each course: a sublime Cassis white followed by a racy Gigondas from the Aix vineyards, and soon champagne, small bubbles adhering under her gaze to the shape of the cut glasses. Very soon, she experiences a new kind of drunkenness, like an aggravated echo of her dizziness on the train. The feeling surrounds her like a scarf; she feels she is burning up, her legs are like cotton wool, her breath is short. Her breasts rub anxiously against the silk of the dress, her nipples harden again under the black material, becoming quite visible. She has the impression that everyone present is watching her, evaluating her, judging her, as if the woman facing her, eating her strawberries and drinking her champagne, is already promising her a whole set of caresses and indulgences. She feels as if her stomach is incandescent, a combination of fire and water, and the wide smile of the woman across from her indicates she is aware of it, that she recognizes the torment inside her body, that behind the combined fragrance of the wines and the food spread across the now crumpled tablecloth, she has caught an early whiff of the purple taste of her inner juices. Right then, a foot deliberately brushes against hers, caressing her ankle, gliding across her leg and the silk sheathing her. She isn't sure if it is the smiling woman or her attentive host, or maybe the gauche young man on her left. The champagne bubbles float upward to the surface of the crystal glasses, and her eyes are transfixed by the thin rising columns, as if she were the one drowning inside the glass and her oxygen was running out . . .

When they all rise to make their way to the living room, she stumbles.

"Come," says the woman, holding her arm, "are you feeling unwell? You must lie down for a quarter of an hour, allow all that alcohol to settle . . ."

Together, they climb the monumental stairs. "I'm in number seven," she stammers.

"No need to go that far," the woman says. "I'm in one."

The room is predominantly green, with an array of heavy brown curtains; the bed is covered with a dark-green satin quilt, which feels so wonderfully cool when she settles her cheek against it and allows herself to relax. The woman helps her lie down, pulling her shoes off, caressing her thin ankles, taking them into her hands as if she were about to handcuff them.

But the girl is still overcome by dizziness and knows she will allow anything to happen.

She tries to overcome the feeling, she turns her head around, sees a painting on the wall, attempts to focus on its image, to capture some sense of reality from the shimmering fog in which the painting floats.

It's a small canvas, like the country scene in room seven, in which a court jester is offering a rose to a comedic maid – the very image of card one in the tarot – but the woman here has pulled her skirt up and is displaying a regal, sculptured ass to him. On closer inspection, it appears that the jester is actually not about to offer the rose to the young woman, but is preparing to pin the thorny flower straight into her satin globes. It even looks as if he has begun punishing her: a long, pink cut already criss-crosses her right ass cheek, petals lie on the ground following the first blow, and the girl's face reflects pain and submission.

This is when she realizes that the older woman has folded her dress back up all the way to her thighs, and is now twirling the blonde curls of her pubis with her fingers, even briefly inserting a finger into her gash, then smelling it with half a smile before licking the wet finger clean and returning her hand below to stroke her swollen cunt.

The woman suddenly stands and walks over to the wall, where she rings a call bell. Then she leans back over the prostrate young girl, lips grazing her mouth, skimming the breasts barely concealed by the crumpled silk of the dress, lingering over the uncovered stomach and the thighs that part automatically under her caress.

There is a discreet knock at the door. "Come in," the woman says, without looking up. It's one of the servants who had served at the dinner table; he has a peasant's wide and tawny features, which she had earlier found almost comical beneath the powdered wig he is now no longer wearing. But he is still attired in the Louis XV outfit meant to emphasize his thin waist. On him it has the contrary effect, highlighting his thick muscles, the incredibly wide shoulders and the lack of neck. He is a heavy-set man; his ferocious eyes remind her of a dog's.

"Come here," the older woman says. "Take your uniform off. That's good. Show us your cock, now. So, what do you think, my dear?"

The object emerging from the salmon-coloured silk pants is just like the man himself: short and massive. Sitting on the edge of the bed, the woman takes hold of the purple glans between two fingers, just as earlier she had been handling the strawberries. With her nail she gently pulls on the cock's crumpled surplus skin and the shaft begins to grow. Short but very thick, no more than fifteen centimetres long, but so thick she has to use both hands to circle it. The prone young girl sees it all as if in a cloud; the painting on the wall is the focus of her attention, but another part of her is also aware that she is about to be breached by this almost unreal object. The mushroom head is dark purple, the blue-black veins bulge, the hard brown shaft is pointing towards her, emerging from dirty pink boxer shorts – the whole thing seems more animal than human.

"Fuck her now," the older woman orders.

The domestic positions himself between the girl's thighs, spreads them wide, and places her feet high up on his shoulders, his thick shiny cock lurking at her entrance. He gradually forces himself in. Slowly, his cock plunges in, her diameter expanding obscenely as if it were literally sucking in this monstrous cock, and she finally feels its head butting her inner walls as the silk of his pants and the rough touch of his pubic hair rub against her thighs. She comes immediately – the tension was too strong, the expectation too intense.

Now the domestic methodically plows inside her with brute force, and she cries out repeatedly, the inebriation of her orgasm blending with the alcohol vapours, thrusting her ever higher on the scales of sheer pleasure. She can't help crying, throwing her body forward, impaling herself even deeper, opening herself wider. At the same time, she feels ashamed to be enjoying this weird cock so much, and the shame doubles her pleasure, as if her being whored in this improvised way gives her latitude to scream as no other man has made her scream before, to give herself like she has never given herself before.

Prompted by the woman, still sitting close to her, the domestic withdraws from her and, with two sharp movements of his wrist, jerks himself off, long, creamy jets streaming across the now for ever soiled black dress, thick snail trails of sperm jetting from his bursting cock and landing all the way up to her neck.

The woman dismisses him with a single gesture.

Once again, she leans over towards the still breathless girl, who is on the brink of tears as her orphaned cunt still gapes open, mumbling under her breath like a fish out of water, begging for the return of the cock that stretched her so, and she kisses her. The taste of her tongue is sharp, warm, and clever.

She then guides the girl to the nearby bathroom and undresses her. "Arms up," she says, as if to a child. Helping her out of the long, soiled sheath of the dress, pulling it over her head, and then the blissful feel of water running unendingly down her neck, her back, her breasts.

Then she brings her back to the large bed of crumpled satin, her body so deathly pale against the green surface, and dries her, methodically mapping every contour of her body, drying behind her ears even and between her splayed toes . . .

The woman indicates the silk dress, now all crumpled up at the foot of the bed. "Won't be much use again," she says.

From a dresser, she pulls out a maid's outfit, almost the same as . . . what was her name? Nora? was wearing earlier. A straight black skirt, a black shirt, and a white apron with an embroidered pocket. Before she is allowed to slip the uniform on, the older woman helps her roll on a pair of hold-up opaque black stockings and, finally, hands her a pair of small, dainty, zippered boots.

The woman quickly separates her hair into thick plaits and arranges a faultless chignon, with just three or four hairpins, almost a work of art.

Inside the apron's pocket, there is a key.

"It's a pass," the ageless woman explains. "It allows you access to every room on this floor or the next. Come, girl. It's all up to you now. You must prove to us that we can trust you." And with a gentle slap on her butt, she dismisses her from the room.

In the corridor, the young girl hesitates. Should she walk down again? With the pass, she opens the next door, number three.

It is empty.

On the wall there is a painting depicting a city scene with three young women wearing fancy hats, all holding each other by the arm, all totally naked. Somewhere behind them, another woman seen from the back is walking away, same hat, same nudity. She appears to be following a soldier whose silhouette can be glimpsed in the distance. The three women are aligned by height, from left to right. Curiously, the shortest one sports the heavier breasts, the next one's are pear shaped, well proportioned, and the tallest woman's are barely the size of two small apples, high on her chest, tiny.

"The tarots," she says to herself.

She leaves the room just as another identically dressed maid comes running.

"Ah, there you are, hurry. Number twenty has called again."

Off they go; she follows instinctively, entranced by the madness of the place, down the corridor, up a spiral staircase, then through another passageway where they come across two other maids, one of whom is Nora, the only one whose name she actually knows, standing outside the door marked twenty.

"What took you so long?" Nora asks.

She knocks on the door and turns the handle while doing so, just as a loud "Come in!" reaches their ears. Inside are four men playing cards, with a fifth man watching them – the grey-haired man from the train, the commander.

The girl barely has time to register the fact that these are the same four men, one of whom is black, the tarot players from the Paris–Nice TGV train – was it just this past afternoon? – when the grey-eyed man calls to them: "Come, girls, come!"

Flabbergasted, she watches as her three companions go to kneel before three of the men and, without even being asked, burrow inside their respective trousers and quickly gobble up the still soft cocks they discover there.

"Come here, young one," the man insists.

And now she finds herself on her knees by the black man, but the cock surging through his fly is already hard. It's like a long ebony stick, shining like polished wood under the light of the room's lamps, its skin taut like bark, an endless mast whose girth is fortunately moderate, so she doesn't have to dislocate her jaw to take it all into her mouth. However, the cock soon reaches the very back of her mouth and brings tears to her eyes, a sudden burst of nausea she represses as she moves her lips back down to the cock's head. But soon she finds the right rhythm, the adequate depth.

"Keep at it," says a voice.

The man exudes an animal smell, strong, tenacious. It occurs to her that she could well be sucking a horse or a wild beast. With the hand that is not holding on to his cards – none of the men has stopped playing – he occasionally applies pressure to her neck, precisely communicating the changes in rhythm he wants her to follow. He holds her by the chignon, forcing her to first slow down and savour every one of the centimetres she swallows and then relinquishes her; then he makes her speed up and suck faster and faster, as if he were about to ejaculate in ten seconds, each time assaulting the very back of her throat, fiercer every time.

All of a sudden, there is a clap of hands. The black man pulls her away and slides his cock out of her mouth. Fascinated, she looks at the glazed, obsidian member. He pulls her up, flips her round and throws her down on the table, pulling her skirt up at the same time. She is face down on the table, as are her three companions, heads aligned next to each other; her cheek touches Nora's. The black man bends over her and with no word forces himself inside her. His saliva-coated cock plunges deep into her asshole, quickly reaching the bottom, and never before has she felt so deeply impaled. Like an iron bar reaching for her heart, then retreating, before digging into her again. Never has she been fucked in the ass so hard, so deep as by this harder than hard ebony-coloured cock, this iron cock, this cock from hell.

On the table, right beneath her eyes, is the last hand of cards, and the courtly smile of the excuse card, and his mandolin.

Nora turns her head in her direction and kisses her, digging her tongue as far as she can into the girl's mouth, holding on to her tongue, both women grasping each other with the energy of despair as the continuous thrusts burrow through their asses, kissing and crying as the table shakes beneath them. There is a scream, a deep guttural roar, and the black man stops, still planted deep inside her ass, and she feels his come pouring out, burning her. She distractedly visualizes the powerful white jets irrigating her guts, like an unholy, boiling enema. Nora pulls herself away from her mouth and screams in turn, a shout of triumph as her flesh welcomes both pain and joy. But instead of withdrawing, the black man comes and goes a few more times inside her ass and she climaxes yet again, maybe because of the angle of the table pressing hard against her clit or the influence of the many orgasms occurring all around her. She swims in a sea of lust.

There is a pause. Then she hears hands clapping, slowly, in the background, ironic; the commander is smiling, complimenting them all.

"Excellent, ladies. Thank you. Now you may go." And specifically to the girl: "You're awaited in room four," he says.

She knocks on the door; there is no answer, but she enters anyway. There are two men in dressing gowns sitting on either side of a table, talking. The first thing she notices is that they are identical twins, although one already sports white hair, as if he has aged prematurely. She wonders what sudden emotion one day caused his hair to turn so white. He can't be much older than forty. She recognizes the two men, they were at dinner earlier, but they were seated at the other end of the table and she hadn't really noticed them.

The man with the white hair is handing a piece of paper to the other man. The heavy dressing gown's belt is loose and uncovers his right thigh, a heavy-set leg which she didn't expect from his cultured facial features.

The other man, not even acknowledging the presence of the visitor, is reading aloud: "They caress each other for a few minutes. He squeezes two fingers into the swamp of her sex, two very long fingers, nails cut short, into the deep of her belly, exploring her so much better than a penis could, his almost feminine scientific intuition aware of her innermost desires . . ."

He stops. "Not bad. But why 'sex'? Or 'penis'?"

"Why indeed? What would you have written?"

"I don't know . . . 'pussy' and 'dick'? A sex, it's so anonymous."

"What would a woman say when referring to her sex? 'Vagina' is too scientific, 'uterus' is too medical. In this present context, maybe 'pussy' is too vulgar. Or it might depend on the woman. Anyway, I'd definitely cut out the 'swamp'. Reminds me too much of the worst of Henry Miller. In *Quiet Days in Clichy*, doesn't he write of 'a drooling pussy that fitted me like a glove'? No, 'pussy' just won't do. So we're left with 'sex'."

"And 'penis'?"

"Still too generic. Its so-called exploration is no more than a continuous series of thrusts into the pit of her belly. Too prosaic for what the male member is capable of."

"Why not use a metaphor?"

"Which? A split apricot? A dick-shaped mussel? A mustachioed wallet? As it is I'm uneasy with the 'swamp', although I do enjoy its muddy, soaked-earth quality, a combination of liquid and hard matter."

"And her cunt? Just call it a cunt? Do women really think of their parts that way?"

"There's just a surfeit of metaphors. You can't just string too many of them together. 'Her cunt's swamp': it just feels wrong, too strong an image."

"The truth is you don't like metaphors."

"That's true. So, what would you suggest?"

" 'He slides two fingers into her divine gash, all the way down her magic walls, exploring her so much better than . . .'!"

"You're getting funnier all the time. But not very practical. Laughter and fucking, you know . . . Many years ago, when I was still fumbling among the amatory arts, at the beginning of my literary career, I was writing erotic stories with a friend; we were trying to use every expressive resource we could, we wanted to avoid all vulgarity, to retain a dash of poetry about it all. We tried everything: the subjective point of view, long sentences and little punctuation, like James Joyce in the midst of tits and ass, if you see what I mean, then more subtle metaphors – 'under his fingers the flower of her love garden blossomed . . . at the end of the path the labyrinth of Cytherea . . . exploring her so much better than all the previous arrows of desire had punctured her . . .' all rubbish of that kind, a compost heap of mythologies. But all it proves to us is that metaphors, however deceptive and clever they might be to the intellect, just pour cold water over any hard-on; a man who thinks too much just disconnects, if I can put it that way . . . But why don't we ask this girl . . ." He turns towards her.

She's been standing there silently, surprised that they hadn't even acknowledged her presence until now, seeing they had summoned her here.

"My dear, what do you think? How do you refer to your sexual organ?"

She is somewhat taken aback, but replies: "Actually I seldom refer to it by any sort of name."

"But if you had to?"

" 'Hole' or 'pussy', most often. No, not really. It sort of depends."

"On what?"

"On the situation. Sometimes I will enjoy shocking myself by using dirty words. Especially when it comes to the rear. I seldom use 'sodomy', too biblical in essence. 'Fucked in the ass', that's what I say, when it's about me. But that's mostly when referring to the act, not when it's actually happening."

"What do you mean?"

"Well, 'I'm being fucked in the ass' occurs so often figuratively speaking, that I can't really use the expression properly, if I think about it . . . But 'I want to be fucked in the ass' presents no ambiguity."

"And right now?"

"I've just been fucked in the ass," she says. "By a very well-endowed black man. His come is still inside my ass. See how useful the right words can be . . ."

She emphasizes this as the two robes both open like a theatre's curtains and two honourably sized cocks are standing to attention, like twins, ever so slightly curved, thick-veined helmets shining between the folds of the material.

She moves towards the men, gets on her knees, and caresses them both, although neither of her hands can grasp the full girth of the cocks. Slowly, delicately, she jerks them off; then, moving her head from side to side, she alternately sucks them both. They taste the same, smell the same . . .

But their reactions are different. Very soon, the man with the white hair lies down on the bed and pulls her onto him and positions himself deep inside her. As this happens, she feels the other man's hands spreading her ass cheeks and a cock, identical to the one fucking her, forces its way into her anal opening. She screams as he tears her apart, and realizes she has never been filled this way. Just a moment later, all three are motionless, she is impaled on their twin cocks, and feels they are surely about to breach the thin membrane that separates them and merge into one single hammer. One of the men is gently biting her breasts; the other scratches her shoulder. She flexes her whole body, offering her crotch even more fully, tightens her sphincter muscles and feels the cock's swollen ridge move deeper inside her, while the one in her cunt almost slips out. The invading cocks are burning her alive, but still manage to penetrate deeper within her, and as the one in her ass settles for a second, her cunt gapes open fully.

They all come almost at the same time. The ever so slight time delay allows her to experience the stream flooding her ass, and then the waves breaking inside her belly. Then the cocks lose some of their hardness, dilate and soften, and pleasure now takes a firm grip of her own body, she whimpers and squirms while still breached by the hot twin cocks and, in a moment of panic, she seeks the mouth of the man with the white hair.

They have not even undressed and, as soon as she leaves the bed, she is once again the image of a perfect, if somewhat crumpled, maid.

All of a sudden a telephone rings.

One of the brothers – they are both lying flat out on the bed, side by side, breathless – rises and picks up the antique set from the bedside table. "Yes?" he says.

She looks around her. Inevitably, on the wall, there is a painting. This one shows two men sitting, discussing literature, on either side of a small table, the man on the right-hand side holding a sheet of paper. Close to them, a naked woman, kneeling, visible only from the back, her long blonde hair reaching down to her waist, is seemingly sucking off the man on the left, the one with the white hair.

"You've been summoned," the brown-haired man says. "Room six."

As she leaves the room, they are already deep in conversation on either side of the table, with the sheet of paper held by one of them. She hears only the final words, read out by the white-haired man: "'She flexes her whole body, offering her crotch even more fully, tightens her sphincter muscles and feels the cock's swollen ridge move deeper inside her . . .'"

The other protests: "'Sphincter muscles'. What about Sybil's hole?" "The artist's entrance?" "The purple flower?" "Saint Luke's grotto?"

The door closes and she can no longer hear them. Room six? The sperm poured into her is running down her thighs.

The scene in the new room is almost symmetrical to that in the previous one. Two women, both naked, are sitting on either side of a table, their positions, their dark-red hair held up in chignons, not unlike creatures by Rossetti, the heaviness of their breasts, the exaggerated length of their nipples, the pale complexion of their pink skin and haughty, almost disdainful, facial expressions, all striking features including, as she moves closer to them, the colour of their eyes, grey changing into green.

However, this time around, they are not identical.

"Come, my dear," one says. "Come."

They ask her to stand still, between the two of them, and four hands quickly undress her, throwing the maid's outfit aside. They only allow her to retain the stockings, which emphasize the pallor of her thighs. The pale hands roam across her even paler skin.

"Look, she's just been fucked . . ."

"In front and behind," says the other. "There's a small stream of come emerging from her ass . . ."

"She's been well fucked," the first one says. "She is still very dilated."

"So it seems," the other calmly declares. "I could push my finger into her ass without even touching her edges."

The girl is momentarily shocked by the contrast between their poised appearance and the filth of their language, and particularly the clinical way in which they are describing her, as if they were conducting an autopsy.

She stands between them and, suddenly, the two women get down on their knees and without a word begin sucking her cunt and her ass, licking up the drops of come drying on her skin, biting the delicate flesh, digging their tongues into the still bruised openings.

The girl feels dizzy. The two women are so artful, even their violence has a touch of elegance, teeth assaulting her lips, fingers sliding deep inside her . . .

No man has ever sucked or penetrated her like this. The first one then the other, thrusting two then three fingers inside her cunt and her ass, withdrawing them and then occupying her again but this time with four digits, as if their hands were becoming slimmer, thinner, and soon she has a whole hand inside each of her openings. She moans when the hand forces her doors, but now her cunt and ass tighten around the invading wrists and she feels delirious.

Inside her, two hands are searching her, carving her innards apart, parallel hands as if in prayer, as if she were the object of a terribly ancient cult, being honoured and consumed by the members of her sect . . .

She has never experienced a vaginal orgasm this strong. Her sphincters are seizing up so hard they could cut the hands off at the wrists, to hold them captive inside her forever.

"She's really enjoying this, the bitch," the first one says.

"You're right," says the other. "It feels as if her ass is breathless."

"She'll never want to come any other way," says the first one.

They gently pull their hands out and the pain is atrocious, not just the initial one in reverse, but the very thought of losing them, to be confronted once again with the terrible void inside her, the emptiness of her life . . .

"Don't worry, my dear," says the first one. "We have many ideas where you're concerned."

"Do you want to take her to fifteen?" the other asks. "You were thinking of that, too, weren't you?"

Both women slip on almost transparent negligees, those spiderlike clouds a star of the silent cinema would wear, and move forward with the grace of goddesses. But as for her, they leave her naked; they just slip a dog collar around her neck and lead her all the way down the corridor and up to the next floor on a leash. She is surprised at how obedient she has become, so unlike herself. Or maybe they recognized this docile streak within her, the desire to submit to a master's orders, the repressed craving for slavery and the whip.

Had she known her tarot better, she would have realized that in room fifteen she would find a photographer, and one of those old-fashioned devices standing on a single leg and under the black cloth of which the operator must dive to ensure he is focused correctly on his subject.

The photographer is waiting for them. He is dressed in Second Empire attire, a short blouse and crumpled trousers, with a thin moustache and small Napoleon III-type beard. Next to him is the young man she had met at dinner: now undressed, she can see he is no more than sixteen years old at most. He sports the thin and curvy shape of a classical catamite, a lazy if gracious body spread over the bed, distractedly playing with his half-erect cock as they enter the room.

"Hello, darlings," says the tired adolescent.

"Hello, asshole," says the second woman. "How are you?"

"So-so," says the young man. "He's only fucked me twice since night fell. Do you think he no longer likes me?"

"Don't you like him any longer?" the first one asks the photographer.

"He bores me," says the photographer. "So what are you bringing me here?"

"Don't you think she's pretty?"

"Very," the photographer says. "I so enjoy such pale milklike skin." He examines the young girl all over. She blushes at being so exposed. "Her eyes are so shiny," the photographer says. "Have you just made her come?"

"Insanely," says the second woman.

"Sit down on the bed," the photographer tells the girl. "Take your stockings off, please. And you, little fag, come here."

She sits herself down on a short square of black silk, in the same pose as Rembrandt's Bathsheba. It all feels like a dream. The photographer moves his heavy apparatus and disappears under its black cloth. She hears the muted sound of his voice, commanding her: "No, thighs apart. Good, yes, like that. Lean backwards, steady your arms, breasts to the front, perfect."

He reappears briefly. "You," he says to the young boy, who is pretending to be terribly bored, "come and suck me off while I'm working, it'll keep you busy."

"Yes, uncle," says the young man with a touch of irony in his voice. "Right away, uncle."

The photographer again disappears under his cloth and, on his knees facing him, the boy, with obvious dexterity, pulls out a remarkable cock, disproportionate in places, whose fat and swollen helmet emerges triumphantly from a dry, nervous stem. The boy licks it quite methodically and witnesses the bulging fruit thicken even more under his ministrations.

"Swallow," says the voice under the black cloth.

Obediently, the young boy opens his mouth wide and, jaws wide apart, devours the strange and monstrous fruit.

All the while, the photographer is taking picture after picture, only making appearances to change the plates and sprinkle more magnesium into his flash, just his voice emerging from beneath the black sheet. "Yes . . . now each of you suck one of her breasts . . . like that . . . ah, a hand on her thigh . . . open wider, my pretty one . . . against that black silk background, you are just sublime. Throw her backward, now. One kissing her, the other licking her . . . yes . . . more profile, please, I can't see your tongue . . . no, don't look at the camera . . . very good, head thrown back . . . and you there, suck a bit better than that or I'll have you whipped right in front of these ladies . . ."

"Oh, yes," says the catamite, interrupting his labors.

Together with her two new friends, he has her adopt the most lubricious poses, ever on the lookout for the moment when she comes. Under their tongues and fingers, she experiences a whole series of orgasms, until she totally forgets where she is. Only the bright explosion of the flash, from time to time, reminds her that a man is taking photographs of her while . . .

Is it the caresses that are generating her pleasure or the fact she is being photographed? The orgasms, the flashes of light, one or the other or both are levitating her out of her body. Every time her mouth opens on a silent scream, the flash of the magnesium betrays the fact that the photographer has captured her moment of selflessness, stolen yet another parcel of her soul, her life . . . it's as if she was being emptied from the inside, as if her very substance was now flowing down her thighs, captured by the photograph, disfigured, transformed . . .

The sound of the door opening . . .

A bit later, a cock thrusting up her ass, another forcing its way down her throat, the room is now full of men and women, all the guests from dinner, each and every one fucking her in every way, and from orgasm to orgasm she feels herself grow wider, dilate until she is just a set of openings, of holes, deep abysses where cocks are ejaculating before being replaced by larger cocks or more numerous ones. Now they are penetrating her two at a time, in her cunt, in her ass, they come in twos to tease her mouth, and innumerable pairs of hands roam across her body, pinch her, sometimes spank her, and above it all the voice of the photographer encouraging them, and the brightness of the flash, and that anxious feeling that she is now no more than an empty space being furrowed, a nothingness full of come, devoured, eaten from the inside by a horde of vampires. Soon there will be nothing left of her, just some long blonde hair matted with sweat, a white expanse of flesh torn apart by caresses, a set of pale eyes she holds tightly closed while all of her is being impaled and only the violent flashes of light make their way through to her dead eyes.

Suddenly they all abandon her. From one moment to the next, it seems to her, there is no one left. She runs her hands in front of her eyes as if she were blind. The commander is standing in front of her and watching: the same cold marble eyes, the same early taste of the tomb. He gently applauds her, as he had earlier, but now there is no sign of irony on his face.

"Very good, my dear, very good indeed. I knew we could rely on you." He comes towards her, takes her hands, invites her to rise from the deeply soiled bed of black satin. "Come," he says. "There is one final thing for you to do."

Together they walk down the stairs. There are so many rooms, so many passages she will know nothing about, whose anonymous numbers will not be revealed. What masked ball or orgy in room twelve, what improvised concert in room eight? They find themselves on the steps outside the castle. The cicadas are now silent, the night is still far from morning, but she hesitates. The moon has moved across the roof and a wide geometrical shadow now covers a whole section of the lawn. All that emerges, on the frontier of darkness, is the statue of the goddess, even whiter in the light of the moon.

The commander leads her to the statue. The grass is mown short and feels hard against her bare feet. She shivers, not because she is cold, as spring down here already has a touch of summer, but because of the anxiety that always strikes towards the end of a night's party, when all is over and loneliness is about to knock on the door again and all you are left with is memories . . .

"Get up on the pedestal," he says. "Yes, like that, with your eyes facing the eyes of the goddess. Take her into your arms – very good, now your hands on her ass, yes. Now, don't move."

Methodically, he ties her to the statue with thin string. He ties her tightly, the rope biting into her flesh, her breasts crushed against the stone breasts of Venus – or is it Diana – and then her legs are pulled up against the legs of marble, ankle against ankle, until she can barely move an eyelash, her face pressed against the stone head.

"They're the same colour," says a female voice.

"That's true," says another man. "Maybe it's the statue that's actually tied to her."

"Predator and prey," jokes yet another. Are they all there?

"Let's begin," someone says. "It's time to end all of this."

The sharp whisper of the first lash precedes by a microsecond the blow that lands on her rump. She screams, or is it her tortured flesh that screams under the assault of the whip? But she is not surprised; she is already resigned, abandoned, punished because she is innocent. Innocent of what?

She screams, tries to wriggle out, but she is tied so tightly that the marble bites into her. She cries out as the whip keeps on finding her, with every new blow her skin opens up, like paper under a knife. Soon her ass, her back, her shoulders have become the mad canvas of a mad artist, blood spurting in lines and blotches, spreading, merging. The blood now turning her flesh dark, woman of bronze tied to woman of stone. Pain begins to anaesthetize pain, she is an open wound, furrowed, overtaken by heat, by fire irradiating from the very centre of her belly, and she is aware that this unbearable heat rising towards her heart will soon kill her as surely as the cold poison killed Socrates. She no longer screams, just feels the heat rising, the whip opening up new valleys, Venus watching her in silence, and when the time comes a ray of moonlight reaches out to seize her in its grasp, and she dies of unbelievable pleasure, part and parcel of the immense fire of the whip.

The moon finally moves behind the house, the darkness drowns the statue and its victim. They leave her tied there and walk back to the house in silence, satisfied.

There is but a bare sketch of dawn. A gentle breeze weaves across the park, though the wind is not strong enough to lift the bloodied strands of blonde hair now slowly drying.

In an hour or two, the cicadas will begin interrupting the silence again.

Noon, Gare de Lyon. The young woman with brown hair, captivated by the sun, has walked onto the first train. She will pay for her ticket on board, too bad about the likely supplement.

There is almost no one in the compartment. Further down the aisle sits a man with steel-grey hair, but she can only see his straight neck. Closer to her are four men playing cards, already well into their game. One is black, very black. When she walked past them, she noticed they were playing with tarot cards, and the black man was about to throw down a fifteen: a photographer, head buried under the cloth of an old-fashioned camera, is shooting an undressed model, a pale-skinned woman with long blonde hair. At his feet, an effeminate young boy is sucking him off with studious application.

# Black Lily

Thomas S. Roche

*(For Paul Bowles)*

The sun came up.

She might be asleep. It certainly seemed likely. If she wasn't then perhaps she had been, recently. She had stopped walking. Whether she was sitting or standing, it was impossible to be sure. She was conscious only of the newborn sun and of the infinite world of sand dunes stretching all about her. Even the hunger and thirst were immaterial. There existed only the sky and the sand.

"Amelia," she said, not knowing why she said it. It was a while later that she understood that it was her own name.

Her clothes hung destroyed on her body.

Things began to come back to her, in vague impressions, as if they were unimportant and without immediacy.

She could recall the shouts of the men at the fortress as she ran. There had been a few scattered shots. Half-heartedly, she wondered why no one had chased her, but it seemed that didn't matter. They had taken Jean; he had been the one they wanted, anyway. She was just along for the ride, and she didn't seem to make much difference in this world, where there was only the sky and the sand.

It seemed that the memories of the fortress dissolved into nothing and she was left without a past or a future. She supposed there were worse things.

Late in the morning, a caravan happened by. It took her a long time to become aware of it. By the time she noticed, the caravan was almost gone. There were many camels led by four or five men dressed in black. She leaped up and ran to the caravan, without knowing why she was doing it. The man was tall, swathed in garments of black, his face shrouded. He regarded her calmly.

"Is there room for me?" she asked in French, instinctively assuming the man would understand. She wasn't sure where she had learned the language. It came to her as out of a dream. Perhaps, then, she was French.

He made a gesture to indicate he didn't understand. She motioned at the caravan, trying to indicate movement. The man looked at her for a long time. Finally he shrugged and motioned towards one of the camels. She let him help her onto the animal. The foul smell of dung and animal sweat was somehow comforting. She felt the thick bundles behind her, covered by blankets. She was suddenly incredibly hungry. She reached beneath one of the blankets and found a bundled mass of twigs and flowers. A crumpled blossom came off in her hand. She brought it to her face to smell it.

The man was upon her, taking the flower away from her. He slapped her wrist and replaced the thing under the blanket. He shouted at her in a language she did not understand.

The woman looked down at him blankly. Perhaps the flower was valuable. The man seemed to be cursing at her again, and the woman looked down, sheepish.

"Amelia," she said, looking up, still not sure why she said it.

The man gestured dismissively at her and began to lead the camel forward. The woman closed her eyes.

A great weight came over her. Slowly, she drifted into a trance, until she slumped in the saddle. There under the sun she fell into nothing.

When she awoke, the sun slanted across her from a high window. She had no idea how long she had slept, nor did she care. She looked around, dazed. She was in a small room, stretched on a thin mat on a clean floor. The walls were hung with rich cloth, and a houkah as high as her waist sat in the corner. She had been placed in black clothing identical to that the people in the caravan had worn. Slipping her hand under the robe, she felt that she was still wearing her clothes, the cotton slacks and shirt from Bloomingdales. Outside the shirt she had a cloth tied around her breasts, cinched tight. It was uncomfortable, and puzzled her. But she was wearing her Western clothes. Thank God. Then even her concern dissolved and she wondered to herself what would have happened if the man from the caravan had disrobed her. It all seemed so immaterial. Possession of her body seemed such a nebulous concept. She relaxed into the mat and faded in and out of consciousness.

After a time, there was a knock on the door. Disinterested, she lay there without answering for a long time while the knocking continued. She stared blankly at the door. Finally there was nothing.

She was achingly hungry. Her needs were such that she could hardly feel anything outside of her hunger. But she could not bring herself to move, and even the pain of her hunger seemed irrelevant.

Amelia. She was called Amelia, she suddenly remembered. Her father called her "Amy", sometimes "A", pronounced like "Ay". For everyone else it was "Amelia". That was all she remembered clearly. Occasionally things would surface, and then drop out of sight into her mind, deeper than ever. The taste of birthday cake. The smell of leather inside a new car. The sound of President Truman's voice on the radio. Newsreels of the Bomb at Hiroshima. A harsh voice cursing her in French, foul breath in her face, sudden pain. Then it was all gone, and there was nothing that existed, except the sleep and the body she seemed to inhabit.

Once, when she reached under the black hood-and-mask to scratch the side of her head, something struck her as strange. Her hair had been cut. She felt sure it had been short before, but not this short. After the surge of panic, lasting half a second, she felt a vague curiosity. Why had she been shorn?

The knocking came again, and went. More time passed. Finally the door opened without a knock, and a girl came in bearing a tray of food. The girl was veiled, her eyes dark and intriguing. Amelia wondered if this was what the travel guides meant by "exotic". The woman looked down submissively as she kneeled beside the cloth mat. She waited there while Amelia struggled to sit up, then reached for the food. The hunger, long unnoticed or denied, came upon her like an avalanche.

She had to yank the mask down to eat, which pulled it across her eyes. So great was her sudden hunger that she didn't care or take time to readjust it. She ate blindly, stuffing her mouth full of the thick, heavy bread and then taking great handfuls of the smoky-tasting grey paste, and eating that with her fingers. She felt dizzy, sick. But she kept eating, and gulping down water from the metal cup. The water was foul and barely drinkable. There was also some tea, but she was unconcerned with that for now.

The girl kneeled, watching her through the whole thing. Amelia remembered suddenly that in her past life she had always been terrified to let people see her eat. That was one of the many reasons she was so skinny. The memory made no sense to her, as if it had happened to someone else, or she had seen it in a movie.

She finally lapsed, slipping back onto the mat, the mask still pulled down over her eyes. She lay, blinded, breathing hard from exhaustion.

Her orgy of consumption had left her spent. The girl immediately took a cloth and wet it from the carafe of water. She took hold of Amelia's hands and started wiping them, cleaning away the thick paste and the crumbs of bread. When Amelia's hands were clean, the woman moved to her face. She began to wipe Amelia's mouth, meticulously cleaning away the smears of food.

Amelia's mask was still down low, her mouth exposed, her eyes covered. Amelia didn't have the energy to pull the mask away so that she could see better. She could just barely see the woman's mouth and chin, lips slightly parted, as the woman cleaned Amelia's face. After a time the mask was tugged up a little and the woman looked into Amelia's eyes, just for a moment. Amelia felt a rush of stimulation and a sudden terror of seeing, which the woman seemed to sense. The woman pulled the mask down across Amelia's eyes again and moved back to cleaning her mouth and chin. She started on her upper throat.

Amelia felt a curious sort of comfort, her face being stroked with the cool water while she recalled the brief moment of looking into the mysterious eyes of the beautiful woman. Amelia felt a curious desire, all of a sudden. She felt quite sure it had been months. Except for that French soldier at the outpost . . .

Her mind refused to remember, and Amelia's need blotted out everything else. She found herself fascinated by the woman, seduced by her image. She remembered a moment a long time ago, before her last lover . . . but that woman had been a schoolteacher, and Amelia had been uninterested in pursuing an affair. She could not recall the woman's name.

Amelia wasn't sure what she was doing. She leaned forward and kissed the woman, through the veil, feeling the warmth of her lips and the softness of her tongue through the gauzy fabric. The woman responded, kissing Amelia back. The woman set down the cloth and pulled away her veil. Amelia still could not see, but that only heightened the taste of the woman's lips and the slick feel of her tongue sliding into Amelia's mouth. With her first demanding motion in days, Amelia squirmed against her, pulling the woman close. The woman melted into her arms.

Slowly, without passion, the woman began to open the laces of her garment. She took Amelia's hand and placed it on her breast. Amelia felt a curious sort of terror, but could not imagine what she could possibly be afraid of. She didn't remember there being anything dangerous about this behaviour. She took the woman's breast into her hand and caressed it, feeling acutely the hardness of the nipple against her palm. She lay in darkness as she touched the breast, drifting into confusion, as if she weren't quite sure what the breast was. Amelia felt the woman's slender fingers across the back of her head, felt herself being pulled forward as the woman leaned against her. The woman guided Amelia to her breast and Amelia's lips closed around the nipple.

She suckled there for a time, her lust having flared and subsided. She still desired the woman, wanted to touch her, devour her. But the intense need had settled into a faint ache deep inside her body, and it was enough to suckle on the woman's breast while the woman stroked Amelia's head.

After a time, the woman laid Amelia down again and began to kiss her, draping her breasts against Amelia's lips and then chest. The woman began to reach under Amelia's robe.

Amelia felt a wave of panic, not knowing why. She took the woman's wrist and started to shake her head, vehemently, saying, "No. No. I don't want to." But she knew that wasn't true.

The woman didn't understand. She kept trying to get under Amelia's robe, to unfasten it. The woman made a gesture with her mouth, as if trying to convince her. Amelia felt her stomach go weak, churning uncontrollably, her body aching for the woman to repeat the gesture against her. She remembered another person making that same gesture . . . Amelia shook her head vigorously and motioned the woman away.

Impassively, the woman adjusted her garments. She took the tray and left the room while Amelia lay there, unmoving. Tears had formed in her eyes.

She could not remember the mores, the social fabric of upper-crust New York society which had prevented her from making love to the girl. All she knew was that she could not do it.

Amelia drifted for ever. She had begun to forget the experience with the woman, but it came back in lush, sensuous morsels, making her squirm on the mat. She was fed and washed several times. She was much neater after the first time, requiring less cleaning afterwards. Amelia was vaguely aware, the third time she was served, that this was a different woman, as it had been the time before – three women, equally beautiful and equally different than Amelia. Each time, after she had been cleaned, Amelia would find herself kissing the woman, hungrily devouring her tongue, reaching out for her body. But she refused each woman in turn, prevented by some unknown force from making love with them, however much she wanted it.

After the third meal, Amelia slept for a time. She awoke to the scent of sandalwood and musk incense. It was dark outside, and there were no lights in the room.

She felt the mask being removed. Someone was kissing her – it was a man. She tasted his tongue and felt the surge of her need. With a curious enthusiasm, Amelia realized that she was going to be taken. She felt an aching hunger. While she suddenly knew that she could not remember the colour of her mother's eyes, or the address of her childhood home in Long Island, or the name of the man with whom she had travelled to this country, and that she should be able to remember these things, she knew, deeply, instinctively, that her giving herself to this man, or more accurately, being taken, did not spell decadence the way it would have to give herself to the women. That is why, she knew, she must succumb, dissolve, submit. That is why, she knew, she must be devoured by him.

That is why she became his.

Amelia's back arched, and she presented her lips for his consumption. She felt his rough hands on her robe, unfastening it, opening it up. He did not remove the mask yet. Amelia's head whirled in conscious surrender.

The robe came open, and he removed it from Amelia's body. He unfastened the sash around her breasts. She felt an explosive freedom. He had considerable trouble with her cotton slacks and shirt, as if he had never seen such garments before. But Amelia did not assist him. She lay passive, allowing him to take rather than giving herself to him, not wanting to break the spell of freedom that her inaction offered.

The pants and shirt joined the robe on the floor. Then her undergarments.

The smell of sandalwood filled her nostrils.

She moaned softly as she felt the man's hands on her breasts. His caress was strong, insistent, but there was an underlying gentleness, as if she were a profoundly important person, but belonged wholly to him. Amelia was still blind, but her mouth was exposed and he kissed her briefly before disrobing himself. Then he lay upon her, his naked form against her, as she presented herself for him. With his hands and his mouth and his body, he took her. He possessed each part of her body with sensuous fervour, starting with her breasts, continuing to her mouth, slowly working over her belly and back, then gently entering her with his fingers. Amelia remained passive, delighting in the sensation as his fingers slid smoothly into her. It was after that that he pulled her body against his. He guided her mouth to his shaft and, giving herself fully, her eyes still shrouded, enveloped by darkness, Amelia began to feed.

This was a transgression against her social code, but somehow its context was different than her other desired transgressions. Inexplicably, she pictured herself smoking in a bathroom somewhere; then the momentary image faded. The man guided Amelia onto her back, coaxing her legs open. She knew that the time had come. He laid himself fully on her, and she felt a sharp pain as he penetrated her. It had indeed been a very long time. She suddenly remembered the last time she had made love – it was in a hotel in Algiers with a man named Jean; then that memory dissolved and she only knew that she was making love now. A curious wave of fear went through her as she felt him settle down on top of her. Then her fear dissolved like the memory.

His lovemaking was gradual, as if he sensed that she had been slightly afraid. But Amelia's passivity gave way as his slow thrusting grew more deliberate. She pressed her thighs together around his body, feeling an astonishing sense of well-being. Perhaps it was that sense of well-being that caused the curious shaking in her belly and thighs. She began to moan, and it felt like she was having some sort of attack. But it felt curiously good. The curious feeling grew stronger and stronger, the pleasure blotting out all else. Her buttocks pressed against the mat as he made love to her, thrusting deep inside; then she lost all control of her body and it seemed that she passed into a world of sensation, her skin tingling. She felt a sudden shock of guilt and shame, which then dissolved to an oddly satisfied feeling. It was not unlike being extraordinarily drunk, as she could just barely remember having been once or twice, but the newness of the sensation fascinated her. After a time, she lost the feeling – it slipped away through her fingers like grains of sand scattering about her. When she did, she was aware that the man had finished inside her and was kissing her neck hungrily. He seemed very pleased.

The sensation had been unpredictable – like nothing she had ever heard about. As if she had passed into a new realm of the spirit. Perhaps she was dead, and this was heaven. Or hell?

Definitely hell, she thought, caressing his back as he kissed her, hard, nipping her lip so that she tasted blood with a frightened thrill.

The sensation returned to her, briefly, in a gentle spasm inside her.

It was most certainly a horrible transgression against the laws of her tribe. But she no longer remembered what those laws were, or who had made them.

Abdelsaid was unwilling to let them do it, at first. He had told his three wives that they were to provide the French visitor, Monsieur Breton, with food, to ensure that he was properly taken care of, and see to his physical needs if he would allow them to do so. They had offered, but each time the Frenchman had refused.

"You see," Abdelsaid told them. "As I told you. They have many of them in France. They fill the streets there, I heard it from the man who tends the camels. It is no surprise. Why not let me have my peace with him?" Abdelsaid smiled mischievously.

The three wives were like snakes, though, always possessive. Always acquisitive. The Frenchman had seemed so eager at first, they said. All three reported the same experience. He desperately sought their lips, their breasts, their bodies, wanting to touch them. But he had refused when they offered to provide for him.

"Monsieur Breton wants *me* to provide," said Abdelsaid angrily. "That is their way. Why else would there be such a thriving French market in the Black Lily, that would allow us to live with such finery?"

But his wives were insistent. "The Frenchman expressed such interest! Allow one of us to be present, in case such needs arise!"

"No! I forbid it!"

The voices of his three wives rose in cacophony, like a terrifying anti-song, something from Europe played on one of those portable boxes. Something horrible. Abdelsaid finally gave in, having known from the start that it was hopeless.

Abdelsaid was a stern man. But he could not stop the wind, nor hold the sun at one place in the sky.

Amelia continued to drift in and out of consciousness, floating in the curious pleasure of a life without memories. There was nothing before the man. Nothing before the harem. Nothing but the sensations of the sun streaming through the high window, the taste of the food the women brought, the sensations of Abdelsaid taking her. She knew only surrender.

Abdelsaid. He had wanted so much to know her name. She had known that from the way he had spoken to her, in Arabic, caressing her ear with his tongue. The way he had pointed to himself and said firmly, "Abdelsaid."

She had wanted very much to tell him her name, as well. She felt for a moment that something was there, that there was a place where she had had a name, that she had once been named. Perhaps she had known her name just yesterday, or only a minute ago. But it slipped away like it was nothing, and she just looked sheepishly up at Abdelsaid, wishing he would kiss her and caress her and enter her and make love to her once again. Abdelsaid waited patiently for the woman to tell him her name. But she did not. It was as if she did not know. He pointed at her and said over and over again, "French?" Amelia looked at him blankly, feeling that she did not know what the word meant. Finally she nodded and said, "French," pointing to herself. Abdelsaid shrugged and seemed to accept that.

He spoke for a time to her in the language she did not understand. The language was soothing, seductive, and she found that it was not important that she understand him. Her head came to rest in his lap and he stroked her hair gently while he spoke to her, his voice a rhythmic caress as if he were reciting poetry. She fell asleep with her head in Abdelsaid's lap, and soon he left her.

"Amelia," she said after he left; at first she wasn't sure why she said it, and then she understood that it was her name. Why couldn't she remember it before? She would have to tell Abdelsaid.

When Abdelsaid returned, he brought the women with him. All three. Identical, lush, beautiful. Their bodies rounded and full beneath the flowing clothes. So unlike Amelia, with her scrawny, underfed body. Amelia looked around blankly, not understanding. The three women set out a second mat in the middle of the room.

Abdelsaid kneeled beside the mat and began to kiss Amelia.

The women disrobed silently, setting their clothes just out of reach. They reclined on the mat, their bodies entwining, casually, their arms around each other. Amelia watched, overwhelmed. Abdelsaid was also watching them. But soon he was watching Amelia. Then his hands were upon her as he kissed her and gently coaxed her against him.

Amelia leaned on Abdelsaid and took him into her mouth. The three women caressed each other, their bodies seething, flowing together, becoming one. Amelia's lips slid deftly over Abdelsaid's shaft, as they had done before. Absent-mindedly, she rubbed her thighs together as she suckled on Abdelsaid's cock. She felt the curious sensation rising inside her again, though not quite coming to fruition.

After a time, the naked women filled and lit the houkah and Abdelsaid smoked. He gave the houkah to Amelia, who sucked the smoke into her lungs. It was harsh, bringing back vague memories of school gymnasiums and the back seats of cars, but those memories faded as quickly as they flared, and disappeared in the smoke.

After a time, Amelia felt very strange, as if she had fallen asleep but were still moving. Her body was enveloped with pleasant sensations. She watched Abdelsaid's three wives with hunger and curiosity. Their bodies were so different than hers, though very, very beautiful.

Then Abdelsaid bent down to kiss her, and she knew it was time. Amelia no longer wore the strange, impractical clothes under the robe, the ones she'd been wearing when Abdelsaid first came to her. Not even her underwear. Just the sash, holding her slight breasts flat against her body. Amelia went to take the robe off, but Abdelsaid motioned her not to do so.

He did not undress her this time. Instead, he simply lifted the robe, bunching it around her upper thighs and buttocks. Amelia felt him pulling the robe tight through her crotch. She felt Abdelsaid pouring oil between her buttocks, some spilling on the robe. Amelia watched the three women, who had begun to kiss each other, their limbs twined in a lush ménage.

Then Amelia felt a rush of fear and surrender as Abdelsaid mounted her from behind, but not in the fashion he had done before. The sensations were very different this time – stronger, perhaps because her need was so great. It was then that she became aware of the woman's smell. The third wife was against her, placing herself on the mat. Her thighs spread around Amelia, and Amelia, without thinking, began to work her tongue between the woman's legs, tasting something unfamiliar and oddly delicious.

The third wife moaned softly.

Abdelsaid was continuing to thrust gently inside her, silently moving in and out between her buttocks. The sensations were curious indeed, but not at all unpleasant. Amelia's whole body began to shake. And then suddenly Abdelsaid was finished. Amelia slumped, spent, against the mat.

Abdelsaid motioned towards the three women, speaking to them sternly. Amelia watched, without understanding. She heard the French word "Monsieur", perhaps it was the name "Monsieur Breton". She had known a Monsieur Breton briefly, in Nice. He had been a drifter, living nowhere, floating. But was a happy man. Amelia felt sure that she and Monsieur Breton had been lovers; fleetingly, she remembered a pleasant afternoon of sex in her hotel room. The three wives seemed to be arguing violently with Abdelsaid. The third wife was trying to open Amelia's robe. Abdelsaid grabbed Amelia, shouting, and held her against his body.

Sheepishly, the three women moved away from Amelia. They dressed in silence while Abdelsaid watched. Then the three women left the room. Abdelsaid followed them, and did not pause to kiss Amelia goodbye.

Abdelsaid cursed the women for trying to engage Monsieur Breton against his wishes. "He was plainly enjoying himself with me," said Abdelsaid cruelly. "He didn't need a trio of women devouring him. I already told you about the French!"

"You saw that thing the Frenchman did to Aouicha! He was enjoying it!"

Abdelsaid was losing his temper. "No! That's a French custom! It is not something they enjoy. It's considered a duty." He tried to change the subject.

The women argued with him late into the night. Finally Abdelsaid threw up his arms and forbade any of them to lay with Monsieur Breton. They were to satisfy his hunger, and that was it. But Abdelsaid knew that it would be impossible, that his secret would soon be discovered.

These moments with the French woman, then, were like succulent morsels for him to savour. Like the dried petals of the Black Lily. Their time together was to be brief. It made Abdelsaid very sad.

He made his way back to the French woman's room, his heart filled with longing.

Abdelsaid came to her again before the next mealtime, without his wives. His passion was incredible, his thrusting almost violent. Amelia was sure that he would break her in half as he possessed her, though there was a delicious thrill to his desire and at no point was she afraid. But she was left hungry and wanting, the aching need inside her. She wondered if it was possible to satisfy it some other way, to bring on that pleasurable sensation. Perhaps to cause it herself? She tried, but found it impossible. She grew lonely and afraid and began to weep in the darkness.

She had never had an identity, never known her name. It did not seem right that it should upset her. For she existed only in the present, only as a part of this elaborate ritual in the Sahara. She was nothing. Amelia had ceased to exist. Perhaps she never had existed. So why did non-existence torment this nameless woman?

She wept for a time. But when the weeping passed, it seemed that, too, was gone for ever and had never been. Perhaps as a dream.

What happened seemed natural, when the third wife came once again to feed. Once the meal was over, the wife undressed herself and began to kiss the Frenchman. The Frenchman's lips found the woman's breasts and he suckled for a long time while the woman stroked her hair. Then, eagerly, the third wife lay back on the mat, spreading her legs, presenting herself for the Frenchman's skilled kiss.

Amelia found that as she made love to the woman, her very being was subsumed into the woman's body. When the woman cried out, Amelia discovered that she had long ago forgotten who she was, or what she was doing.

She lay, in a curious, pleasant warmth, as the woman rolled her over and began to slip her hands under the robe. Amelia tasted the woman's tongue, and they kissed deeply as the woman's fingertips traced a path up her thigh.

The woman's fingers slipped between Amelia's legs, searching, seeking. The woman's eyes grew wide.

Flushing red, the woman drew back. It sounded as if she were cursing. She quickly gathered up her clothes, bursting into tears as she carried them away. Sadly, Amelia watched after her, confused, the ache of her desire unsatisfied. She wondered again if it was possible to bring the sensation upon herself, but it seemed as hopeless as before.

This was unacceptable. Abdelsaid knew it would be so. He had been flirting with disaster by bringing the woman here, even disguised as she was. He had become wealthy, by local standards, from the trade and export of the Black Lily. He could certainly afford a fourth wife. But the three existing would not stand for it.

"She will take away your affection!" they shrieked. "She will devour all of your love! They are like hungry beasts – especially their women! It is unfair – we cannot have a French girl here! It is improper! You must send her away!"

The three wives spoke in unison, overwhelming Abdelsaid. He would have fought with them, but he knew it was a fight he could not win. On the rare occasions where the women agreed on something, their collective will was unbreakable. Abdelsaid knew, sadly, that it was hopeless.

But he could not send the woman away. He had lost all sense of reality. He felt that he must make her his, for ever. Abdelsaid had fallen in love with the strange Frenchwoman without a name. With Monsieur Breton.

There was only one way that the Frenchwoman might be allowed to stay in Abdelsaid's house. Abdelsaid argued with his three wives for what seemed like hours. Finally, they agreed. Upon this condition, the French whore could live with them indefinitely. But Abdelsaid had to provide the Black Lily from his private stock. He assured his wives that there was more than enough Black Lily to accomplish the task.

The third wife returned to Amelia, bringing food. Amelia's memories of the incident were vague at best, but she felt an overwhelming sense of worry and of emotional need, and a desire to make love to the woman, to make everything all right. Amelia reached out, but the woman resisted. Finally, she gave in and allowed Amelia to kiss her, but her lips were stern and unmoving.

Amelia finally let the woman go, accepting the food. After the long hours of unknowing worry, she was famished. She ate greedily. In addition to the usual food, there were several large, dark flowers. The third wife plucked off the petals and encouraged Amelia to eat them. Amelia sniffed at them, unsure, but finally let the woman put the petals in her mouth. The taste was thick and sweet. It was some sort of dessert. But not a terribly exciting one. Amelia swallowed each of the petals, and the wife looked satisfied.

Amelia tried to kiss the woman again. But the woman pulled away and Amelia was left in the darkness, lonely and filled with a terrifying desire.

She slept more deeply that night than ever before.

In the morning, the first wife came to her with food and the black flowers. Amelia ate first the food and then the flower petals, wondering. It seemed more savoury to her this time. Again the woman refused to kiss Amelia after the flowers had been eaten. Amelia lapsed back into sleep. She did not know how many times she awakened and ate and drank. The taste and smell of the flower seemed to fill her consciousness.

When Abdelsaid came to her, many meals later, her need was intense. Abdelsaid kissed her, deeply, for a long time before he unfastened her robe and helped her out of it. He touched her chest, feeling the thin hair growing there between her breasts, toying with each of her nipples. Slowly he drew his other hand over Amelia's thigh. His hand came to rest in the hollow between her legs, seeking, more clinical than erotic. Amelia felt a curious absence of sensation, though her desire was still overwhelming, perhaps more than before. Abdelsaid seemed satisfied, and left Amelia with no more than a kiss.

Amelia was not disappointed, only curious. Why had he not wanted to make love this time?

The hair of her loins had begun to fall out, scattering across the mat like leaves in autumn.

He was aware of the woman, upon him. He could not recall how he came to be there, or what his name was, or even whether he had ever existed. Encompassed in her caresses, the insistent mouth and breasts of the woman, guided by her demanding movements, he came to want her. A curious sensation came over him as the woman sank down upon his body, pressing his cock deep inside her. Had he been here before, thrusting up into the woman's naked body while she whispered soothing luxuries to him? He found, after a time, that he could understand her words. When the sensations exploded inside him, he felt an intense pain, as if his body were being torn in half.

Later, much later, he became aware of another woman. But the first was still there. There was a warm touch upon his cock, the taste of her tongue, the texture of female flesh under his hands. There was the warmth, the muscled figure of the man behind him, penetrating him while the three women took their turns using their mouths and hands upon his shaft, their bodies sprawled underneath his kneeling form, pressed as it was against the man. He knew, somehow, that he belonged to these four people, the man and the women. They were as one being with five bodies.

He tried, shortly after the moment of his orgasm, to remember his name. It was only then that he understood. He did not have a name, and never had.

Abdelsaid was optimistic. The trade in Black Lily was increasing. The decadent palaces of the French, it seemed, couldn't get enough of the flower. And it was indeed rare. It grew only in the mirage oases in the southern part of the country, and the plants would not take root anywhere else. And Abdelsaid was one of the few traffickers who could find the flowers in the wild, and lead the caravans out again.

While the colonial government had declared an official crackdown on the sale of the substance, and promised brutal retribution against all traffickers, the soldiers and policemen preferred to line their pockets rather than interfere with the rights of free trade.

The locals mostly smoked the drug. The Europeans indulged alternately. It was only those who ate the drug who experienced its most extreme effects. Regardless, once the substance was taken out of the desert, it lost some of its secondary properties, and served primarily as a hallucinogenic. Certain of Abdelsaid's business partners were discussing the possibility of establishing an export trade through European shipping companies, of smuggling the substance to a country where it could be sold legally.

Now that he had Breton to lead the caravan, Abdelsaid was able to devote his attention to these more complex matters of business. Breton had learned the trade, had learned to speak and understand Arabic. He had proved an excellent guide. Breton's knowledge of French had suffered, however, as he learned Arabic. Abdelsaid supposed it had to be a heretofore unknown side effect of the Black Lily. There was nothing to be done about it.

And it was such a small price to pay. Any price was small, for Abdelsaid had kept the Frenchwoman he desired, albeit in a somewhat different form. But the love of the Black Lily knows no boundaries. Abdelsaid told himself this whenever he looked with pride at the Frenchman. Whenever he shared him with his wives.

It was enough, to have this small bit of luxury in this cruel world, thought Abdelsaid. For any amount of luxury is preferred to none, and some is preferred to very little. And no one can stop the wind, nor make the sun stand motionless in the sky.

Breton guided the caravan endlessly, from Abdelsaid's town to the oasis many miles across the phantom sand. He was one with the desert.

Breton knew he was from another place. But he also knew that place no longer existed.

Breton knew that he had been sent here, to guide the caravan through the endless desert. Perhaps he had been sent by the gods of his tribe, cast out. Perhaps to bring a blessing to Abdelsaid and his family, for Abdelsaid was infertile. Breton would be the father of Abdelsaid's children. Already Aouicha was with child, and Mimouna suspected also she might be pregnant. Breton imagined these children, in a sense, were a gift from a merciful deity, perhaps a gift from the Black Lily. Breton thought of the sons or daughters as a gift from the universe to Abdelsaid.

Perhaps these gifts were like the visions Breton saw as he slept or daydreamed. The sensations that flowed over him in his dreams. The intimate knowledge of a woman quite unlike Aouicha or Mimouna or Outka. She was more like a boy than a girl, and a mournful boy at that. She was English, he thought, or possibly French. He wondered if perhaps he had loved this woman at some point. He felt sure that he had not, that his union with her had been a matter of convenience.

Breton released his thoughts of the strange woman as he guided the camel train into the oasis, knowing he must turn his thoughts to practical matters of trade and the highest possible price for the blossoms of the Black Lily. He let his memories of the strange woman fly away on the wind, scattering like grains of sand through his fingers. He knew the woman was gone now. It was over.

# The Prescription

Carol Anne Davis

Dr Lorean had not long been in practice when it was rumoured that he was guilty of crimes against the person. Hearing these whispers, the city fathers were naturally vexed.

"But we cannot judge a man by some scurrilous words from the street," they agreed. "Especially when he has always seemed such an exemplary fellow. We must have proof positive of his venial ways."

And so it was arranged that Madam Gray, the most upright and responsible citizen in Victorian England, would visit with the thirty-three-year-old doctor. She would report back every movement of the physician's healing hands.

At the appointed hour, Madam Gray swept through Dr Lorean's cosy parlour and into his adjoining surgery. Such haughtiness was her usual mien. Dr Lorean rose gracefully to his full five foot ten, then he bowed low. "Welcome, Madam Gray. I am at your service," he said.

Lucinda Gray gave a half-hearted curtsey in return. The half-heartedness was partly due to her tightly lacing corsets. She glanced at the man's neatly trousered groin and suppressed a shudder. The city fathers had given her a little bell that she could ring if his attentions became too great.

Male attention was an unvisited land to Madam Gray. She had never been betrothed, had never known a suitor to take liberties. But she utilized her time by keeping house for her father (who had one of the largest estates in the country), so didn't feel the lack. It was her duty, however, she told herself as she gazed around Dr Lorean's dispensary, to save other gentlewomen from an unseemly fate . . .

The introductions over, Dr Lorean again seated himself behind his desk. He picked up his pen. "Are you well in yourself? What brings you here to me this August morning?"

"My last doctor has gone into retirement," Madam Gray said sagely. "And I'm brought low with a general malaise."

"I take it the two are in no way related," the physician said with a slight amused smile.

Was he suggesting an improper relationship? The twenty-five-year-old fingered the cameo brooch at her throat and felt a low pull of excitement. "He was an elderly gentleman, but he gave me sterling service," she said.

"As I profess to do too." So saying, the suave surgeon stood up and bowed again. "A full examination is called for," he announced.

How full did he mean? The virgin stilled into watchfulness. Outside the very birds quietened down. The silence was broken by a horse and cart clip-clopping and rattling along the road outside.

"We must shut out the world to safeguard your privacy, dear lady," the physician murmured, walking to the heavy Prussian velvet curtains and closing them fast.

Adult to adult, they faced each other in the centre of the room.

"Remove your outer garments for me," the doctor ordered.

Madam Gray stared into his eyes as she slid her crocheted ivory-coloured gloves from her wrists, then unpinned her jade green hat. "I shall be glad to rid myself of them. It is much warmer out than I anticipated," she said breathlessly. As she removed her headwear, a few tendrils of polished chestnut hair escaped their clasp.

"My dress?" she confirmed in a husky voice, her eyes darting around the oleographed walls as if in search of solace.

"Indeed, ma'am, for I have to examine every inch of you," the wide-eyed physician said.

Slowly Madam Gray undid the pretty glass buttons of her muslin bodice with its becoming drop shoulders. She undid the satin rosebud ribbons, then let the bias-cut garment fall to the floor. She forced herself to confront the fellow's unblinking gaze for a moment before turning her attention to the removal of her jade satin shoes.

"Now your petticoat," the physician bid.

Swallowing hard, Madam Gray removed the silken garment that covered her bustle. Then she removed the bustle itself.

"You can see more of me now," she said in a small voice. "Enough to examine?"

"It is my duty to see more yet."

"You mean me to remove my corset cover?" the younger woman clarified, her extremities tingling at this exceptional situation.

"Indeed, for how can I investigate your flesh when it is so covered?" the surgeon said.

The young woman took a sudden interest in the baroque design wallpaper as she removed the protective shroud.

"Now unlace the corset itself. Let me know if you require my assistance."

"I can manage," Lucinda Gray said firmly, though in truth it had taken two maidservants to lace her that very day. Now she glanced nervously at the impassive male observer, then looked down at the stem-waisted and overbust-style boned band.

With effort she unfastened and removed the constricting ties and unfastened the front, doing it as slowly as possible to stave off the moment of near-nakedness. At last she stood vulnerably, in her pantaloons and chemise.

"Your chemise, if you please," the physician said.

Madam Gray breathed in the scent of rosemary and geranium from the medicinal gardens outside and reminded herself that healing the sick was a rightly revered profession. The doctor might well be a wholly virtuous man.

She took off her chemise, then stood there, breathing heavily, clad only in her white cherub-embroidered pantaloons.

"You ladies wear so very many clothes that it is a wonder you ever become pregnant." Dr Lorean smiled.

Madam Gray glared at this retort. "I am not married, sir, so it is imprudent of you to discuss pregnancy."

The doctor stood up and walked towards her. "On the contrary, my dear, I have to determine that your female parts are all in good working order. After all, you shall one day want to give your father an heir."

"Perhaps," the younger woman replied. In truth, the young men of the parish found her somewhat imposing. And, far from being a generous dowry-bequeather, her father was a mean and unapproachable type.

"So remove your pantaloons forthwith, so that I may begin a full and thorough exploration of your womanly contours," the physician said.

"As you wish." But did he wish this for the good of her health – or the corruptedness of his appetite? Madam Gray pondered the ethics as she undid the ties which held her pantaloons firmly around her small waist. Truth to tell, she felt somewhat breathless at the thought of being naked before a man for the very first time.

Slowly she let her unmentionables slide down her smoothly rounded hips to the floor. She stepped out of them and stood with her arms by her sides, her bosom heaving. For the first time since early childhood she was in the presence of a clothed adult whilst she had on not a stitch. The exposedness of her situation was not lost on her – indeed, was uppermost in her imagination – but she consoled herself with the thought that she was a spy, who was really in charge.

"Now for your measurements," the good doctor said. He reached smoothly into his leather bag and brought out a tape measure. He proceeded to hold it against the back of her head, then run it all the way down to her unshod feet. On the way down his hand brushed her spine and her buttock cleft and her virgin thigh-backs. It was a featherlight sensation which nevertheless was felt by Lucinda as a very heavy rush. Surprised at the sudden exquisite sensation, the maiden swayed and let out a little moan.

"Be reassured – your height is fitting for the times and you carry yourself impressively erect," the physician murmured.

Madam coloured slightly at his choice of words and stared straight ahead.

"And now I will check your skelature," continued the man. He measured her shoulders from one silken arm-top to the next, his fingers soft and gentle. "And now your breasts."

The woman blushed more fully at this last word – a scandalous word. Why, even that part of the chicken was only referred to as "the white meat", lest it give offence! "You may want to loosen your stays each day to let your bosom move more freely," said the medical man, sliding his cold rule across both nipples before weighing the appendages in his smooth palms. "It will assist your body to breathe."

"I can breathe very well with my garments fastened," Madam Gray gasped in a strangely air-starved tone. Her breath faltered further as the physician thumbed the underside of her heavy round mammaries with his sensitive thumb-pads, and she gasped so harshly that the doctor asked if she were having an asthma attack.

"I take the air at Brighton and the waters at Bath. My constitution should be good," the naked young woman assured him.

"Then," said the doctor, "it only remains for me to examine your inner folds."

"Shall I lie down?" Madam Gray asked, for she was feeling quite light-headed.

"Not yet," said the man. "Just turn your back to me and lean your elbows on my examination couch. Then push your nether parts outwards, if you please."

"My nether parts?" the younger woman repeated haltingly.

"Yes. That reminds me – we must check your hearing at the end," the physician said. He walked forward and patted the surgical couch with his palm. "Just rest your head on your arms and part your legs a little for me that I may the better examine your buttock cleft."

"What could possibly go wrong in that region?" Madam Gray stalled. In answer, the doctor reeled off a string of Latin phrases. "Oh, I see," the baffled woman said. She looked at the couch, then looked back at the man. She must force herself to endure this new defilement. She'd have even more details to tell the city fathers at tomorrow's meet.

Slowly the Victorian matriarch assumed the buttock-exposing position. "Is that high enough?" she asked, thrusting her firm, small derrière back.

"A little higher yet," said the man, tapping at the top of each arse-cheek with his fingers. Madam Gray complied, wondering inside at the increasing sense of pleasure her interiors felt. There was nothing wrong with being as naked as Eve had been in the Garden, she told herself in a moral tone. She must just be glad to be free of her bustle and stays.

"You have excellent muscle tone," said the man, beginning to squeeze each proffered hemisphere. "Do you perhaps go riding, my dear?"

"No, but our house has many stairs and large gardens and I walk them every day," the lightly perspiring Lucinda said.

"Well, I recommend horse riding too," the surgeon prescribed. "A proper gallop, mind, and not side-saddle. It cures my other ladies of their sore heads."

"I have felt migrainous of a morning," Madam Gray admitted faintly, as he continued to explore her small bottom with his large, caressing hands.

"Evacuating fully is also important," Dr Lorean said, beginning to pull on a thin white rubber glove, one of those newfangled inventions. "We'll just make sure that there's no blockage there."

He reached for a small tub of gel and smeared it around the woman's most puckered parts. Madam Gray buried her head in her hands more fully as she felt his gloved and gelled fingers tracing their way around her secret pink entrance. She'd suffer in silence, she told herself stoically, then yelped with enjoyment as a digit was inserted into her rectum a little way.

"Relax," said the doctor as the poor woman almost shot over the couch. "We'll just widen you out ever so slightly. Easy voiding is of the essence, I always say."

Madam Gray shifted her weight from silken foot to foot, then tried to think of England as her backside was invaded a little further. But she ended up thinking of the strange sensation between her thighs instead. It was a sensation she'd known before, when she washed herself or woke up from disturbing night dreams. But now the sensations were much stronger, and growing all the time.

"Good, good."

Lucinda felt a sense of loss as the finger was withdrawn. Dr Lorean took off the glove and threw it into the bin, then washed his hands thoroughly. Madam Gray stood up and faced him without being told to and put her hands across her breasts.

"No need to be shy about your nakedness. You are like a fine horse to me, and I am a horse farrier," the man murmured.

Madam Gray snorted, then realized how equine she had sounded and changed it into, "As you say."

"Now, lie on your back on the couch and part your legs for me," said the man, "whilst I conduct the final parts of the exam."

"It will soon be over?" Madam Gray breathed.

The empty hours stretched out, out, out ahead of her. She wasn't due to report back to the city fathers till tomorrow, and had no further appointments for the full day.

"Oh, no, my dear, you must allow me to treat you fully," the surgeon said, fingering his cherrywood pipe without lighting it. "The internal examination takes a very long time."

"And do you enjoy your work?" Madam Gray asked archly as she clambered naked onto the low, long surgical examination table.

"Of course, for I make people better. It's a rare patient who doesn't leave my practice with a smile."

*With a loss of maidenhood, more likely,* the woman thought. She shivered at the thought of a man putting his . . . whatever it was that he put in to create a pregnancy. It sounded such an unseemly act, even if it was proper for the planet to survive. "How would a general malaise in myself manifest itself in my . . . in my female parts?" she asked as the doctor gently nudged her thighs apart with his scholarly hands.

"Well, you might have a psychic blockage, or indeed a physiological one," the doctor explained. He greased one hand, then placed the palm of the other on her lower tummy and palpated it gently. Then he slid his oiled fingers slowly inside her maidenly canal.

"Aah!" the young woman moaned, then turned it into a little cough.

"Are my hands too cold?" the physician enquired softly.

"They . . . they will suffice," Madam Gray said.

"If you prefer I could withdraw my digits and repair to the fireside . . ."

"No, don't! I mean, you must finish looking for any blockage and not mind my discomfort," Madam Gray said.

Clearly taking his work most seriously, Dr Lorean slid his fingers further up her heated conduit. "Everything is as elastic and wet as it should be, madam."

"It feels alternate," the younger woman admitted softly.

"The laying on of hands can make a real difference," the physician said.

Keeping one set of fingers inside her, he started to palpate her pudenda with his other adept palm.

"What are you doing now?" the would-be spy asked raggedly.

"I'm stimulating the gynaecological perineum. It discharges nervous excitement and leads to better sleep and a clearer head."

Only one thing was clear – the growing sense of awakening between her spread thighs and the parts usually covered by her unmentionables. Madam Gray closed her eyes and gave herself up to the response. It really was quite exquisite, and like nothing she had known before. Such rapture made her forget the lazy servants she had to chide, the too humid day, the nights that stretched so futilely. It made her think only of her most private flesh.

She whimpered as Dr Lorean continued to massage the triangle that made her tummy flutter so. The joy was journeying, striving. Madam Gray pushed her pudenda towards the ji

digital source of delight. "Easy," Dr Lorean whispered. "You can't rush the treatment." The young woman gasped as heaven on earth was almost realized. The sensations rose and rose and . . . as they peaked she cried out in guttural ecstasy, all thoughts of polite form deserting her. All she cared about was straining each sinew upwards in order to squeeze every last quiver of pleasure out.

"Indeed, there was a psychic blockage. I have cured it," Dr Lorean said quietly.

Madam Gray heard him dimly through her orgasmic yodelling and post-orgasmic gasping sighs. "Thank you, thank you, thank you," she eventually managed to cry.

She rested. She briefly slept. When she awoke Dr Lorean gave her an invigorating rosemary tea, then rubbed her down with a medicinal wet towel that had benefitted from an acquaintance with lavender.

As he brushed her nipples the maiden felt slightly tingly, and wondered if her blockage had returned again.

"Perhaps I should visit you once a month, sir, to repeat the treatment?" she asked girlishly.

"I shall look forward to fitting you in," the good doctor replied. He had left the room jerkily, just before she slept, holding a clipboard down low over his surgical coat. Now she noticed that he looked much more coordinated and relaxed. Perhaps he had rid himself of his own psychic blockage in his little parlour? He was obviously very good at it . . .

The next day Madam Gray made her report to the city fathers.

"Dr Lorean is an upright man," she said.

"Not a charlatan?"

The Victorian matriarch smiled. "On my oath, he gives excellent service."

"There was no impropriety?"

"I left his surgery well rid of the malaise that I had come about."

"In that case, the good doctor has no charge to answer. Let it be known that he is a man of stout reputation and conduct, who will not be investigated further," the city fathers said.

Madam Gray vacated the room, well pleased with her replies and the issue's outcome. But as she reached the street one of the flower puff ribbons fell from her dress. She bent to pick it up and her pantaloons rubbed against her body most beguilingly. In the interests of science she repeated the movement, and the exquisite pull happened again. Oh, dear, she said to herself, perhaps this is some sign of organic irritation. I must consult Dr Lorean forthwith.

Alighting at the doctor's rooms, she found a considerable queue. "He cures my head pains," one woman said.

"He makes my neurasthenia abate," offered another female.

"Since his treatment, I have been entirely free of nocturnal spasms," a third coy maiden chipped in.

After a very long wait – and oh, how fidgety was the queue, how overzealous! – Madam Gray reached the esteemed medical doctor, who was lying on a chaise longue and mopping his brow.

"Forgive me, madam," he murmured faintly. "My reputation has spread and I am quite in demand, quite overextended. I can see no other patients today."

"Tomorrow, then?" the affluent young lady said.

The doctor reached for his journal. "No, I fear that I—"

"I will pay double."

"I am indebted to you for the compliment, but . . ." The physician stared at the many-worded page.

"Make it triple," Madam Gray rejoined.

"Such largesse I can't refuse," said the doctor, who doubtless had many a bill to settle.

"Then your attentions are assured me," the largesse-bringer said.

An appealing notion then came to her, and left her smiling. "You shall have to tend to my malaise in my chambers," she said softly. "For I will have taken to my bed."

"You think bed rest is necessary?" A patch of nervous colour had crept into the physician's face.

"Indeed. It is a big four-poster bed, with lots of pillows, ideal for my comfort whilst you conduct your examinations," Madam Gray continued. She looked at him almost wolfishly as she stood up to leave. "Here is my calling card. The servants will admit you. I will expect your attendance on Wednesday at 11 a.m."

The doctor got slowly to his feet. His bow was distinctly shaky, as befitting a man who had spent the week exploring psychically blocked orifices. "Shall it . . . shall it be a brief visit, madam?" he said.

The healthy young woman stared at him – concentrating her gaze on his fingers for a lascivious moment. "Oh, no, sir. At triple rates I will expect exceptionally long and arduous service," she said.

# Plague Lovers

Lucy Taylor

Word spread quickly in the tiny, plague-ravaged town – the Flagellants were coming!

Gabrielle, sequestered in the house with her father and her dying mother, heard the news shouted out in the street beneath her window. She felt her blood quicken at the thought of witnessing such a spectacle – a band of penitents whose submission to the Lord was made manifest in deprivation and self-wounding. Despite her fear of mingling with the plague-infested crowds, she felt compelled to see them.

Snatching up her shawl and wrapping it around her thin shoulders, she crept down the wooden stairs, hoping that her father, exhausted by his day and night vigil at her mother's deathbed, would be dozing. She didn't want to have to speak to him, or witness the reproach and anguish in his eyes as she hurried past without so much as gazing at her mother.

Her father's back was turned to her, his head lowered into his big hands. Gabrielle took a breath and tiptoed towards the door.

*All I want*, she thought, *is to get out of here. Get away from the death and dying.*

The plague, or the Great Pestilence as some were calling it, had arrived in early summer. Word of a terrible illness sweeping the port cities of Pisa and Genoa had reached the town a year earlier, but here in this secluded Tuscan valley the villagers had felt secure and safe in their relative isolation. With spring, however, the plague had reached Orvieto, where a spiritual revival that added fifty new religious dates to the municipal calendar had failed to spare the city from devastation. Now death was everywhere – evidenced in the rattling of the carts that carried bodies for burial outside the village, the cloying, rotten-flowers scent of sickness that permeated the air, the moaning of the sick, the wailing of the bereaved.

Gabrielle had heard that, according to the priests, who divined such things by studying the book of Revelations, a third of the world had died.

And the plague had not yet run its course.

An idea, borne of terror and desperation, had been nudging its way into the back of her mind. Many people had already fled the town to take refuge in the countryside. No one really knew what caused the sickness, but escaping the "pestilential atmosphere" of more populated areas was thought to help. It was said the air was cleaner in the country, the food less apt to be contaminated.

When she was almost at the door, her father looked up.

"Where are you going?"

"Don't you hear the drumming? The Flagellants are on their way to the cathedral."

"Hah," her father snorted. "The Brethren of the Cross they call themselves. I call them the brethren of lunacy. Why expose yourself to the crowds to see a troop of madmen beat each other bloody?"

Her mother moaned and went into a coughing fit. Blood foamed around her mouth. Gabrielle's father dampened a cloth in a bowl of water and wiped her face. "There, there, my love," he whispered. "I'm here with you. I'm here."

The tiny woman, little more than bone and gristle, reached up and stroked her husband's face, a gesture rich with the tenderness and caring of devoted lovers after a long and passionate night. Gabrielle felt that she was witnessing something private and precious between her parents, something she could never hope to exprience herself.

"She hasn't long," her father said. "Can't you just sit with her?"

She shook her head. "I have to go."

"What kind of daughter are you? You feel no love for your own mother?"

But how could she? thought Gabrielle. Until the plague struck, until her midwife mother fell ill, neither of her parents had shown the slightest warmth or caring towards one another or, for that matter, towards her. Theirs was a union based on practicality and the running of a household, a way to satisfy the needs for sex, security, and mutual support. Love was a luxury for idle, wealthy ladies and lovestruck troubadours. The poor had no time for such frivolity.

Now Gabrielle observed the change in both her parents, a transformation that appeared wrought by suffering, and found herself both horrified and envious. For never had anyone shown her the kind of tenderness her parents now bestowed upon each other. It was as though, through suffering, they had paid some terrible price required for the giving and receiving of affection.

Looking at neither her father nor her mother, she hurried towards the door.

"Gabrielle!" The undercurrent of fear in her father's voice brought her up short. "You are coming back, aren't you? *Aren't* you?"

"I–I don't know."

"What if I fall ill? Your mother's taught you about herbs and medicines. You could make my dying easier."

Gabrielle stared at this man whose love she'd never managed to win, who'd never offered her a moment of affection. "I know nothing of my mother's skills," she said stubbornly.

"She taught you everything," her father insisted. "Please, girl, I don't want to be alone. Promise me you're coming back."

"I'm sorry," Gabrielle murmured.

Behind her, her father's voice rose in anger.

"You think you're safer in the outside world? The plague is everywhere. Only God can keep you alive."

Only God.

But God was nowhere to be found these days. The young abandoned the old, the healthy left the sick to expire in alleyways and filthy deathbeds, even priests refused to hear confession from the dying, lest they contract the sickness. Some people reacted to the danger by living lives of ascetic abstinence, while others, wanting to make the most of what time was left, indulged in every kind of excess and debauchery.

At the cathedral in the town square, Gabrielle stood at the edge of the crowd and held a handkerchief dipped in perfume to her face, for it was common knowledge that pleasant odours helped protect one from disease.

The Flagellants marched up the main street, men in the lead, women following. The men were stripped to the chest. Each carried a hard leather whip festooned with little iron spikes which he brought down, rhythmically and slowly, across the back of the one preceding him. Bent and bloody, the procession snaked towards the cathedral. They were silent and sweaty and a great stench rose from them – not the sickly sweet odour of sickness, but the musky tang of unwashed, bloodied bodies.

Gabrielle watched the blood streaming down their raw backs, saw how the sweat glistened and ran in the deep furrows that the pain had etched in their faces. Some appeared to be in agony, others simply exhausted. And some appeared to have gone beyond the pain and seemed entranced in what looked like ecstasy.

Gabrielle stared, transfixed by the bizarre spectacle, amazed by the stoic silence in which the Flagellants bore their pain. As one man passed by, she could not stop herself, but reached out to caress his mutilated back.

"What do you suppose it feels like?"

At first Gabrielle didn't realize the voice was speaking to her. Then fingers gripped her elbow. She whirled around, appalled and startled by the presumption of this stranger.

A young man with fair hair, tanned, pockmarked skin, and black eyes that glittered like a raven's regarded her. He was dressed in the rough, simple garments of the Flagellants, but his clothing had no rips or bloodstains, nor did his sturdy-looking arms bear signs of abuse. Something in the cunning, slyly mirthful way that he appraised her made her uneasy, as though he knew things about her she did not even know herself.

"What are you talking about?" she whispered, holding the scented handkerchief tighter to her face. "What *what* feels like?"

"The whip, of course."

"Pain beyond my ability to imagine it."

"At first, there's terrible pain," the young man said, "but still it seems bearable at first, or so you think. Then the lash keeps falling and the pain mounts. It fills your whole body, your whole being. At that moment, you'd sell your soul to make it stop. You think that you can't possibly bear it another moment, that you'll lose consciousness or die.

"Then it's as though the body becomes completely overwhelmed, and there's a giddiness. You laugh, you scream, you weep. At that point, you've gone beyond the pain – it's still there, but it's not your body any more, or you're not in it. That's when it begins to feel like a holy sacrament, like you've touched the face of God."

Gabrielle looked at the man's hand where it still rested on her elbow – large and heavy-knuckled, covered with fine wheat-coloured hair.

"How would you know about such things?"

"In the spring, I marched with the Brethren for thirty-three and a third days – to commemorate the life of Christ, as is the custom."

"And do you think your suffering will save you from the plague?"

"No. Only luck and my own wits will do that. But I learned a great deal about pain – and what lies on the other side of it."

He turned and pulled his shirt up to reveal his back, a gouged and furrowed tapestry of scar tissue and half-healed wounds. Gabrielle ran her hand across the scars. "You must be insane. Who in their right mind would choose pain when there's so much of it to be had without asking?"

"The Flagellants believe it brings them closer to God."

"I don't believe in such a God. No loving father would willingly send such misery on his children."

"Perhaps that's how He wins their love – by sending misery and then, according to his whim, providing minor comforts."

Gabrielle laughed. "Then you aren't talking about God. You're talking about Satan."

"Maybe he's the one in charge."

"That's blasphemy."

"That doesn't mean it's not the truth."

His hand, which up to then had rested lightly on her elbow, moved slowly up her arm. Heat spread through her belly as his fingers curled around the back of her neck and collected a great fistful of copper-coloured hair.

"My name's Gerard. You remind me of a woman I was once in love with."

"What happened to her?"

"She died of plague. That's when I joined the Flagellants. I thought the pain of the whip might take away the greater pain of losing her."

"And did it?"

"For a while. And then it made it worse. Now I think that only death will truly cure me. But I'm not ready to die yet." He released her hair, let it tumble in long glossy coils around her face. "I'm on my way now to the countryside. If I keep to myself, stay in abandoned houses, I figure there's a chance I'll survive. If you like, you could go with me."

She shook her head. "Nowhere is safe from plague."

"Perhaps not, but some places are better to die than others."

The crowd surged around them, pressing them close. So thick was the odour of blood, so sharp the cracking of the whips, that Gabrielle felt light-headed.

"Good luck to you, then," said Gerard, and began to elbow his way out of the mob.

Gabrielle thought about her mother, the foul-smelling boils that swelled along her armpits and groin, the dark blue spots that blotched her skin. Before long, she thought, her father would be dying, too, and it would fall her lot to tend to him, to comfort him in his death throes, press cool cloths to his brow, wipe up the waste that would gush from him. She knew she couldn't bear that.

But on her own, she also knew, she would be prey to the roving bands of looters and marauders that, emboldened by the almost complete absence of the law, terrorized the towns and countryside. That possibility terrified her, too.

"Wait," she called out, catching up to him. "Before you go – I want to know – I want . . ."

She hesitated, felt an unfamiliar heat creep up her cheekbones.

"I know exactly what you want," he said, and took her hand.

They traveled along narrow, rutted roads leading through the countryside of Tuscany, sometimes cutting through untilled fields and deserted orchards. Occasionally they passed through abandoned villages, where dogs and livestock roamed at will. Along the roadside, the corpses of those who had fallen while trying to escape lay bloated and putrescent.

The first night they camped in an open field with others fleeing the plague. The second night, after Gerard had led them on a circuitous route along the ridgetop of some hills, they came to an abandoned town where the only signs of life were feral dogs that roamed the dusty streets and wild-eyed rats that held their ground almost until the last instant, then skittered away as Gerard and Gabrielle approached.

Gerard picked out the most luxurious of the deserted houses. Like a lord and lady returning from an outing in the hills, he and Gabrielle made themselves at home.

"Who lives here?" asked Gabrielle, looking around the beautifully appointed rooms.

"We do, now."

"Whose house was it?"

Gerard shrugged. "Whoever it belonged to, they're gone now. Like everything else, the house belongs to whomever takes it."

That night, when Gerard moved on top of her, Gabrielle found herself aroused, but strangely distant. It was as if she watched herself from a corner of the room, moving beneath this man, arranging her body to accommodate his, but somehow profoundly absent. She let him penetrate her body, but knew that he could never touch her heart.

"You don't want me," he said finally.

"I *want* to want you. I want to feel something. I just – don't."

She turned away from him, finding no way to describe the sense that vines and briars encased her body and leaves of deadly nightbane numbed her heart.

"Have you ever loved anyone?"

The question seemed unfair, humiliating. "Of course I have."

But she saw he knew that she was lying.

Later that night, she dreamed of her mother. Saw her father bending down to wipe her mouth with a wet cloth and stroke her face. Her dead mother's eyes were open. Her father reached down and gently closed them, placed the cloth across her mother's face.

Something was wrong. She was awake now, but couldn't get her eyes open. A rag or cloth was tied around her head. When she tried to remove the blindfold, her wrists were seized. She was roughly shoved onto her belly and her arms bound behind her.

She knew about the bands of rogues and thieves who preyed upon those fleeing the cities. Surely it was such a miscreant who had her now.

"Gerard!" she cried out. "Help me."

"Silence," he hissed. "Not one word or cry or I'll gag you, too."

He pulled her up off the bed and dragged her into another room, where he shoved her up against a beam or column and bound her there face first.

"What are you doing?"

"Just because we've fled the plague doesn't mean we aren't going to die. I want to make the most of every moment. I want you to learn to love me. I'm going to *make* you love me."

So saying, he bent her over, kicked her legs apart, and entered her from behind. This time he made no effort to be gentle. His ramming hurt her, but when she squirmed and tried to pull away, he withdrew from her and forced his way into her other orifice, wringing forth screams of pain.

He gripped her hips and forced himself in deeper.

"You want this, don't you?"

"No!"

"Tell me you want it harder, deeper!"

"No, I hate it! Stop!"

"Tell me you want more!"

Finally, desperate to appease him and end the torture, she whimpered, "Yes, please, harder," her voice choked with tears.

When she said that, he thrust one more time, released his semen into her and then withdrew.

She sank to her knees, weeping.

Gerard grabbed her by the hair and yanked her head back.

"That was good," he said. "I'm proud of you. We're off to a good start."

Their next night in the deserted house, he again tied her to a beam, wrists secured over her head, and began to twist and squeeze her nipples. The pain was beyond anything she could have anticipated. She begged and pleaded, made promises of future acts of submission, but he increased the pressure. Then, because the pain was so unbearable and there was no escaping it, her body reacted by convulsing in a fit of laughter. She laughed and sobbed and, in between, implored Gerard to stop hurting her, but by the time he did her nipples had gone numb and, with the blood flowing again, the pain this time was greater than what she'd felt before.

He left her sobbing with fury at the pain and the futility of fighting it. When he returned, what seemed like hours later, he kissed her swollen nipples and fed her grapes he'd found growing in a nearby vineyard.

"Tell me how much you love me."

"I hate you. You're a monster."

"Tell me how much you love everything I do to you."

"Let me go. Please, just let me go."

"There is nowhere to go. The plague is everywhere. There's only death."

She spat the chewed grapes out at him, spattering his face with sticky pulp, then caught his finger in her mouth and bit it to the bone.

He cradled his bleeding hand and eyed her coldly.

"I'd thought that you were doing well. I see now I was wrong. I must be stricter with you."

He left her then, still tied, and came back brandishing a lit candle. At the first touch of the flame against her flesh, her courage failed her. She began to beg and weep, but Gerard was implacable. He moved the candle up and down her body, its shadow dancing across her flesh. Rarely did he let the fire make contact, but when he did, the agony elicited a howl. He singed a spot below her nipple, touched the flame to her thigh and the tender spot at the base of her spine, while she thrashed against her bindings.

"Tell me how much you like this! *Tell* me!"

The flame blazed in her face and burned her eyes. It filled her head with an unnatural light that grew brighter and brighter before exploding into darkness.

She dreamed she was a young child, ill with the fever that had swept through her village one winter, killing half a dozen babies and a few of the older children. Her mother had held her and sung her lullabies that had been handed down for centuries.

She had not got better right away. Instead, the fever had buoyed her along like a flooding stream, sweeping her far into the depths and byways and canyons of her mind, but, for the first time in her life, she had felt loved and safe, unafraid of the death the sickness seemed to be carrying her toward.

She opened her eyes.

He had cut her down from the beam and laid her on the bed. When she moved, the pain from her burns flared, making her gasp.

"Lie still," he told her.

"Why are you doing this?"

"Shhh."

He slid into the bed with her and spooned himself around her. His naked flesh was warm and comforting. When he cupped one hand around her breast and slid the other up between her legs, her sigh was both of pleasure and of resignation. His mouth roved over the back of her neck, his breath disturbed the tendrils of hair along her cheekbone, his tongue probed the delicate convolutions of her ear.

She turned and sobbed against his chest. "It's all right," he murmured. "The things I do may seem a strange way to win your love, but don't forget I marched with the Brethren of the Cross. I know the sorcery that pain and then the absence of pain can work upon the mind. I know that pain can penetrate a heart that can't be opened any other way."

He held her and she clung to him and sobbed harder.

Knowing how desperately she wanted closeness, comforting, appalled at the price she was willing to pay for it.

She had escaped the plague, thought Gabrielle, in order to endure something worse – the ever-increasing torments Gerard devised for her.

Sometimes it was merely being bound in humiliating positions and left alone to wonder when or if he would return. Sometimes it was being spanked until her buttocks burned as if she'd sat upon hot coals, or having the wax from a lit candle dripped onto her breasts and thighs.

When he wasn't using her, Gerard kept her bound much of the time and never let her move about freely without his supervision.

But sometimes, usually when the punishments had been most brutal, he would make love to her as though she were his heart's desire – indeed he swore she was exactly that – soothing her bruised flesh with tender caresses, moistening her sore and swollen places with his tongue. And this she found almost more difficult to tolerate than the punishment, for she both longed for his sweet comforting and despised herself for craving it.

It was after just such a time, when Gerard had followed up his punishments by making love to her slowly and in silence, each move deliberate and delicate, as if they were underwater, that he fell asleep without remembering to tie her.

Gerard was snoring deeply, and from outside came the snarling and yapping of feral dogs, but the only sound that Gabrielle heard was her own heart racing at the possibility of escape. Nothing else mattered.

Outside the night felt vast and unforgiving, stars pulsing coldly overhead. She picked up a stick to ward off wild animals and started across a field towards a stand of trees, thinking to hide there until the sun rose.

She had gone only a short distance, though, when the sky sank so low it pressed against her head and the earth seemed to undulate and roll beneath her feet. The shadows of trees became the outlines of marauders come to ravish her and kill her. The sighing of the wind became the hiss of air leaking out of bloated corpses that she, unable to see, might tread on in the dark.

Never had she felt so vulnerable and desperate for solace. The memory of Gerard's cruelties dissipated like fog. All she could think of was the softness of his kisses, the skilful pleasuring of his hands when he rewarded her endurance with some small kindness.

Near panic, she returned to the house, only to find Gerard waiting for her, brandishing a whip of the type used by the Flagellants.

"Ungrateful whore, is this how you show your love for me?" he said, but something in his voice made her believe it had all been a trick, that he had given her the chance to escape on purpose, either to test her or to seek an excuse for greater punishment.

How confident he'd been, if that were the case, she thought. How sure that she'd return.

No amount of begging could persuade him to forego the whip. He bound her wrists above her head and brought it down across her shoulders.

The pain devoured her, obliterating everything.

"Do you want more of this? *Tell* me you want more!"

"Yes!"

"Do you love me? Tell me how much you love me!"

"Yes, I love you, *yes*!"

The agony was terrible and breathtaking – it ripped the air out of her lungs and seared her flesh as though she were a witch burning at a pyre.

When it ended, her mind seemed to stop, to fog over with a pale, cool cloud of blissful nothingness.

Oh God, she thought, the pain has stopped. Oh God, oh God, oh GodohGodohGod . . .

Gerard pressed his mouth against her ear. "I'm here," he said. "Don't worry. Only a few more blows. I'll help you get through it."

Then the chorus of pain began again, the song of the whip mingling with that of her screams, carrying her down and down into a place beyond thought, beyond fear. Without dying, she had somehow ceased to exist. Her flesh did not belong to her, nor did her name – how could it when *she* no longer was – nor her past nor any thought at all. There was no room for name or past or thought in the brilliant, all-consuming clarity of her agony.

The god she called out to was no longer the God of the priests and penitents, but her private god – Gerard, who gave and took away her suffering.

"There, now, it's all right. It's over now. It's over."

He untied her. She pressed her face against his chest and sobbed with gratitude. He had caused the pain to stop. He was her saviour, her protector, how had she ever doubted him? When he began to kiss her, she kissed him back, then slid down his body, kissing every inch of him, anointing his skin with her tongue.

"I love you," she said. Then, when he gave no reply, she added, "Now you must love me, too."

To prove her devotion, Gabrielle worked diligently to please him. In bed, she acquiesced to every demand, and pleaded for new punishments. She prepared meals from whatever meagre food was available, combing the orchards around the house for fruits, making salads of wild grasses. In the fields she picked the pale purple-blue flowers that her mother had so often pointed out to her, gathering the luscious-looking berries in her skirt.

In performing these small domestic tasks, it seemed to Gabrielle that, indeed, she felt real love for him, even as she made a salad of wildflowers and grasses and crushed the purple berries to make a pie.

In the night, Gabrielle woke to hear Gerard arguing loudly with someone. Alarmed, she lit a candle. No one was there. Her lover was sitting up in bed, conversing with great animation. The pupils of his eyes were dilated; his skin felt hot and dry. For an instant, she fancied she could hear the distant drumming of the Flagellants, then realized it was his heartbeat, audible at several feet.

"Harder, I can't feel it!" he was shouting. "Harder! You must flog me harder!"

This went on for some time, before he fell into an exhausted, feverish sleep.

The hallucinations grew worse. Gerard imagined he saw whips descending and fires blazing at his feet. He cried out and flailed away at imaginary tormenters. So violent became his behaviour that she was forced to tie him to the bed with the same ropes that he had used to bind her.

He complained his mouth was dry and that he couldn't swallow, so she brought him water and put cool compresses across his brow. When she held and stroked his hand, she could feel his wildly beating pulse.

During a lucid phase, he said, "You could run away now. Why don't you?"

"You need me," she said, delicately licking the sweat from along his temple. "You wanted me to love you, and I do. If I can't take away your pain, at least I can help you bear it."

The days dragged on. Gerard was able to eat only a few spoonfuls of food, and his illness worsened. No spots disfigured his skin, no boils erupted along his groin, but still he grew ever weaker.

Gabrielle nursed him, fed him, kept him clean. At night she spooned herself around his back and stroked his chest and stomach, kissed his neck and outlined with her tongue the geography of scars that mapped his back.

When she had to leave him, if only for a moment, he would call out for her in fear.

"I'm sorry for what I did to you," he said. "I saw the emptiness in your eyes and wanted you to feel something. I wanted you to need me. To love me."

"I do love you," said Gabrielle.

He squeezed her hand. "I thought that I was different, that somehow I'd escape the plague when everyone else was dying of it. I don't know why, but I didn't think I'd die of plague."

"Nothing else I can promise you," she said, stroking his face, "but this I do. You will not die of plague."

Perhaps he even believed her, for he clutched her hand more tightly and kissed her fingers with desperation and desire.

He died later that night, holding tightly to her hand, voicing his undying love for her, even as his heartbeat grew so loud that the pounding filled the room. She had no energy for digging a grave, but dragged his body outside and left it for the dogs.

Some passers-by, headed east from Pisa, told her the plague still raged around her village, but Gabrielle no longer feared it. She had decided to return home to her father. She prayed he hadn't died. If he was only ill, then she would nurse him. If he was healthy still, then she would win his love the way she had Gerard's. She would crush more of the purple berries, the lovely, deadly nightbane berries that her mother'd always warned her of, and bake them in a pie. As with Gerard, she would feed him only small amounts, enough to provide a lingering and painful death, enough to give him time to well appreciate how lovingly she cared for him, how desperately he needed her, how exquisitely soothing was her touch.

She fantasized it as she began the journey home. How she would hold her father, stroke his brow, comfort him through his agony. How, at the end, he would pull her close and clutch her hand and tell her that he loved her.

# Night Moves

Michael Perkins

"Swing: to shift or fluctuate from one condition, form, position, or object of attention or favour to another."

*Webster's New Collegiate Dictionary*

## Midnight in the Garden

Bruise on her breast,
not my fingertips,
Gloss on her lips,
not licked from me.
Hair a tangled halo
I hadn't mussed,
Eyes swollen and wanton,
not turned my way,
Her smell of lust
stronger than
sharpest memory;
I could not swallow,
I could barely see.
This was what it meant:
This was being free.

## Part One

## East Hampton, 1976

### ONE

Mora and I had been in East Hampton for two days waiting for the sun to come out when we ran into Charles and Vy. It was July, the Bicentennial Summer, and we were on our first vacation as man and wife. We'd accepted a friend's invitation to spend a few days at his beach house, but the afternoon we arrived the rains came, and lasted through the following day. We were grumpy stuck inside. We wanted to lie naked in the sun.

The next morning, the sun made its appearance, and it was windy when we walked to the beach. We had the ocean to ourselves, but it was too rough to go in. Empty blue sky, empty white beach, empty green ocean. The freckled, lively children further down the beach who were our only neighbours had to be content with building sandcastles. Mora read a novel and wrote in her journal, frowning and chewing her lip. It was her way of arguing with me without saying anything, and also of arguing with herself instead of with me. I shrugged at her silence and went for a long run on the wet hard sand, where high rolling breakers left thick clumps of seaweed, but I couldn't outrace my frustration.

By evening, we were speaking only when spoken to and being scrupulously polite with each other. We brooded in marital silence over cold gin at Peaches, a restaurant in Bridgehampton where summer people went that year for a hamburger or a salad before rushing off to the parties that seemed to run around the clock, summer weekends on the South Fork. When there was a breeze from the ocean, the leaves of the giant maples on the sidewalk outside scratched softly at the window screens. On each small round table a slender mirrored vase held a single rose. It should have been romantic; couples all around us thought it was.

I reached for her hand and she put it quickly in her lap.

"What the hell is wrong with us?"

She sighed and I knew she was grateful that I'd spoken first. The answer was sitting on her tongue. "It's marriage. Holy wedlock."

"You want to expand on that?"

"I don't have to. We both know it's that – why it's that."

So we did. Jealousy. Possessiveness. Insecurity. Fights, screaming, threats, feeling trapped. And keeping score – that was the worst. That computerized reference file constantly added to of insult and injury, a never-to-be-erased tape of gritty misery.

"OK. What do we do now? Throw in the towel because the honeymoon isn't working out?"

"I don't know, Richard. I just think being unhappy is a waste of time."

"Agreed."

We stared at each other. Neither of us really *wanted* to be married. Not really. We were romantics, we weren't interested in snug harbours – when we spoke of love, we meant passion. Rub us together and you got fire.

From the time I first saw Mora I was under a spell. I know some magic was involved, because I was on the defensive after the break-up of a relationship I'd taken more seriously than I should have. The home truths I'd learned about my needs were so lacerating, I vowed eternal celibacy.

For six months I'd been living like a monk in a basement sublet in Brooklyn Heights. It had a single bed I used and a kitchen I didn't, and little else except for a colour television set and a well-equipped darkroom. No pictures on the walls, no plants to be watered, no cats to wrap themselves around my ankles when I came back late from my studio on West 17th Street.

It was a low, unhappy period in my life. I told myself I'd snap out of my funk any day, but the truth was I was drifting, getting by in a low key. I had let being in love become a way of defining myself. Alone, I didn't know who I was.

Mora came along just when I was beginning to spend so much time in Village bars that the bartenders knew my name, occupation, and marital status. One of them was an actor I had used as a model. He knew a woman who needed some pictures.

"She comes in here all the time. Lives just around the block. She's real intense."

"You don't understand. I take pictures of products, not egos. I don't do portfolio glossies and I don't want to meet any women."

It was noisy in the bar, right before dinner. Maybe he didn't hear me.

"She's a lot of fun. Just let me tell her you'll do it."

A few days later she showed up at my studio. I was fussing with lights around an ornate, old-fashioned bathtub with claw feet. Later in the day, the agency that had had it delivered to me would come to fill it with towels – I did catalogues, too.

I earn a living with a 35 millimetre camera because when I was a boy I picked up a Brownie for the first time and discovered my third eye. I have a gift for seeing with the camera lens what the naked eye misses, moments when formlessness becomes form. When Mora walked through the door, it was one of those moments.

I stared. She stared back. She was so small I could have fitted her in a large camera bag. The top of her head came to the middle of my chest. Her curly hair was short but not mannishly cut, a chestnut brown that smelled like oranges.

Her white skirt showed off her slender legs, and she had thrown a linen jacket over her thin shoulders. She wore a *figa* – a small, fist-shaped Brazilian good luck charm – on a gold chain around her throat, but no earrings, no bracelets: only a trace of lip gloss. Her tan was so deep, she looked like she'd just stepped off a plane from someplace south.

I looked away first, after seeing the mischief in her calm green eyes. "Ever modelled before?"

She shook her head. "Only for my boyfriend's Polaroid, but the pictures always came out blurry – you know how those things go. He found it hard to concentrate." She suppressed a smirk.

"You don't say."

We were grinning at each other. Hers was impish, provocative. "Have you acted before?"

"Never, if you don't count Gilbert and Sullivan in grade school. But I've tried everything else and all my friends are in theatre this year, so I thought, why not?"

Her self-confidence was dazzling. It came out in the standard portrait shots I did of her. Her dark features were wonderfully mobile, and she kept that glint in her eye. After the shooting, I cancelled my appointment with the bath towel people and took Mora to dinner.

And so we met. And we made love. She was just as bold in bed as she was before the camera, very passionate and open; her energy was astonishing. A month later, I left Brooklyn and moved into her second-floor apartment on Cornelia Street. Things happened fast around Mora.

We lived together for a year, more happily than I'd thought

possible. Business went so well in the studio, I hired a part-time assistant; Mora didn't have to work because her father owned a shopping mall and sent her a monthly allowance. When she decided she had no acting talent, she got into politics for a while, and then she just started spending all her time at home cooking exotic meals; she told her friends she was too happy to concentrate on anything more.

What happened was that we got cocky. All the traditional signals had gone off at the right times, and we started thinking we were different, that we could nail our feelings to the wall where they would never change. One thing led to another and, before we knew it, we were standing in City Hall, saying our vows. Afterwards, we threw a party for our friends, and then when the shock wore off and we realized what we'd done, we stayed drunk for two days and had a terrific fight so we could squeeze the last ounce of passion out of making up.

Why did we do it? Talk to anyone: marriage is like getting a diploma in living as an adult. The licence certifies a certain wilful madness for, as we found out, everyone lies about marriage, especially its kinkier aspects: the manacles of words at each wrist and ankle, the eager vows that become expectations. The endless expectations.

We were on our third round of drinks and Mora was snapping her foot back and forth restlessly and staring off into space. I looked around for a waiter so we could order dinner, when I saw Charles Venturi sit down at a table near us. He was the last person I expected to see. He'd been off in Europe for years – since the early seventies, when we had served time together on the same slick magazines. We were never close, but I had sought him out and spent time with him because he fascinated me.

Sitting across from him was a tall blonde woman in her late twenties who had lovely cheekbones, hollow cheeks, and long delicate wrists, the supple carriage of a dancer, the long neck and waist of a model. She was beautiful in the wiredrawn way that well-bred New England daughters who sing Bach on Sundays can be.

"Look over there," I said to Mora. "That's Charles Venturi."

"They're a handsome couple," she admitted. "They look interesting."

She followed me over to their table.

"Charles! How long have you been back?"

We shook hands and I introduced Mora. The woman with him was Vy Cameron. In the years I'd known Charles, I hadn't seen him with a woman who looked so capable of keeping up. I liked the determination I saw in her pale grey-blue eyes, and the demure way she shook my hand, fingers wrapped lightly around fingers. A lady, with an agenda.

The two of us exchanged the usual inane comments that pass for casual conversation in the Hamptons, but we kept our eyes on our mates. Mora and Charles were hitting it off. While he talked, she was giving him what I think of as the Treatment. The Treatment consists of her undivided attention, of long, smouldering looks, and sudden, surprising smiles that promise a lot more than understanding. It's flattering, and nearly always effective.

After a while, I interrupted them. I saw a chance to change the weather between Mora and I, the possibility of sun behind the clouds.

"Let's get together. Where are you staying?"

"With the man Vy lives with, Maurice."

I raised my eyebrows, and he looked unexpectedly sheepish for a minute.

"It's a long story. I'll save it for later." He winked.

He suggested that we meet on the beach next day. We talked about time and place – he knew a beach where it was possible to go without bathing suits – and returned to our table.

In bed later, Mora asked me to tell her more about him. I was suspicious of her interest and reluctant at first, but she cuddled up to me and I starting stroking her and talking. In the dark, her emerald eyes glowed like a cat's. A cat in heat.

## TWO

When it comes to women, Charles has a gift. He hears what they're saying between the lines. They find him inordinately seductive, although there isn't much about his appearance other than his provocative black eyes that would suggest such powers of attraction. But he's solid and dark and intense.

His restless energy is the source of his charisma. His hunger for the varieties of experience. He grew up fast on the Italian Catholic streets of East Harlem, where he learned to see the world as a stage, and his part in it as an infinitely adaptable player. He was attracted to both the smell of incense and the smell of sex, the sharp aroma of men and the secret fragrance of women. By the age of forty his résumé read like eight lives had been crammed into one. He'd been a translator, a student of Gurdjieffian teachings, a psychotherapist, a librarian, an editor of men's magazines – even a novice with shaved head in a Zen monastery. His appetite for biography was prodigious.

All this time, he was writing furiously; when he published the books that established his reputation, his radical ideas about sexuality were treated respectfully by slick national magazines, a few maverick critics, and even one incautious Nobel Laureate. It didn't hurt that he was called a pornographer by a few midwestern district attorneys who had no idea what he was talking about.

He became a cult figure in the sexual underground. When he stepped out of the shadows into the spotlight, he represented the forces of Eros to the media. There was applause. He titillated people. Amused them. Sometimes even succeeded in outraging them. Then, one week, he was on the cover of *Life* magazine wearing eye shadow and mascara and grinning about the confusion of sex roles he embodied. It seems improbable, but it was the sixties. The pot boiled, and he was there to take his turn stirring it, along with student radicals, Black Panthers, Yippies, Weather People, and self-destructive rock stars. The seventies were a let-down for him. I think he went off to Europe primarily because he was bored and he wanted to see if he'd been missing anything there.

When we met him on the beach, next day, the sky was cobalt blue, and the ocean was calm as bathwater. Mora smiled at the sun. She was happy again. We found Charles sitting cross-legged on an orange beach towel at the foot of a golden dune, brown arms on his knees, gazing out over the rippling water. A lone sailboat patrolled the line of the horizon. I was disappointed when I didn't see Vy.

"Thank God for the sun," I said.

"That's a big ocean. I'm glad to be on this side of it."

I unfurled our blue chintz beach spread and Mora helped me to anchor it with our sandals. We took off our jeans and sprawled next to Charles. Mora began rubbing lotion into her legs.

"Where's Vy?"

"She had to play hostess for a while."

"For Maurice?"

He nodded. "She won't be long."

"You share her with him?"

He shrugged. "That's how it is."

"How do you feel about that?"

"He loves her in his own way, I guess." A faint smile played on his lips as he studied Mora. Her tight smooth flesh overwhelmed the white terrycloth bikini she wore.

"You're so casual," she said. "Have you known her long?"

"I met her when I got back from Europe. Some friends threw a welcome home party, and she was there. As soon as I saw her, I knew I was in trouble."

"Trouble?"

"I was turned on, and I knew we wouldn't be any good for each other – but I had to have her. I met my match."

"I want to hear more. All about her," Mora said. Erotic style fascinated her, and any woman who could live with two men deserved a great deal of study.

"What does she do?"

"She's a dancer. But she has many talents."

"You can tell us more than that."

"Well, you can ask her yourself," Charles said, pointing to a tall, erect figure walking down the beach towards us. Vy wore a Japanese kimono and clogs, and her blonde hair was piled on top of her head. We could hear her singing in a high, lilting voice when she got closer, but the words were lost in the muffled slap of the surf on the beach.

Her first words were breathless, almost hoarse. "I'm so fucking dry I'm going to have to do a little deep throat to get my voice in the right register. I'm a tenor in the heat." She patted her chest. Her palpitating heart.

Mora and I looked at each other. What heat?

"It's my colouring," Vy said. "I'm more susceptible than most people. I don't like the sun. It causes cancer and it dries up the skin."

"I worship the sun," Mora said.

"Well, nothing could have seduced me down to this beach but the thought of you three doing something delicious without me." She was overwhelming, regal. In supplication I opened the bottle of cold Retsina we'd brought, filled four paper cups, and handed one to her. Charles lit a joint and passed it around.

She settled herself on our blue spread. Mora watched her with narrowed, admiring eyes. "Now tell me what I've missed. Have you been talking about me? I hope so – it would make me feel so good. All Maurice talks about any more is deals. Buy that, sell this. Sometimes when he refers to me it's in the same tone of voice, and I feel like a jewel he's tucked into his safety deposit box."

She leaned back on her elbows, her gaze fixed on my face, the slender joint stuck in the corner of her mouth.

"I don't own a safety deposit box," Charles said.

"I don't own a bathing suit," she purred in a cool, milky voice, removing her kimono with ladylike panache. Her plump, berry-tipped breasts, flat white belly and wide hips were exquisite. Her skin blushed that faint pinkish hue found in the centre of certain roses. In the cool salt breeze, she trembled almost imperceptibly, like a rabbit in a field of shotgun fire. I felt a sudden stabbing urge to take her in the crook of my arm and press my fingers gently in the wet hollows of her throat, her elbows, her knees; my groin was beating like a second heart.

Mora wasn't to be upstaged. She untied her bikini top with what was meant to be a casual gesture, but I knew that she was tense. Her normally puffy copper nipples were tight and hopeful.

Charles grinned happily at the women. "We are fortunate men, Richard." Then he told us a story that set the mood for what happened later as much as the hot sun or the empty beach.

"I was walking on the beach this morning. I didn't know where I was going, just walking and thinking and looking for driftwood. There were no people around, so I took off my trunks. It was about ten o'clock when I realized I was walking through a gay beach. I almost stepped on a man who was lying in the surf, masturbating. Something in his face made me stop – whether it was pleasure or invitation, I don't know. I went down on him, and for five minutes, maybe ten – it seemed like hours – we were as close as any two bodies can get. Such an absolute passion – and it happened with a total stranger! Afterwards we didn't say anything, but neither of us were looking for romance."

"I *love* it," Mora exclaimed excitedly, clapping her hands. Her cat eyes flashed. "Anonymous sex, no attachments. It's too bad heterosexuals can't be so honest. I see so many people I'm turned on to, yet I don't want to talk to them. I want to *take* them. Just make love. Between men, it's better. You both know what you want, without any illusions . . ." She was breathless.

Vy crossed her arms and cupped her hands over her breasts protectively, as if guarding her heart. She closed her eyes and sat quite straight and still. "All there is is romance. The rest is technique," she said, without opening her eyes. "I've had expert lovers who couldn't get me wet because they didn't know any of the magic words."

She opened her eyes and focused on Charles. He stretched out casually next to her, propped on his elbows, looking out to sea. Something seemed to draw him: he started crawling crablike on his belly out to the water, leaving a broad, wrinkled trail in the tawny sand.

We all stared after him. Mora sighed wistfully. "I should have been a man. You just don't know how much I fantasize about certain . . . situations."

"Well, my dear," Vy said coldly. "We all have to learn the hard way."

"I guess it's something I want to learn," Mora replied, unwilling to give Vy the last word. "Anyway, Charles says you're a part of the world I want to learn about."

The sharks might have envied Vy's smile. "I keep myself entertained."

The static between them made me decide to follow Charles into the surf. I crawled for a bit, felt silly, and walked the rest of the way. He was lying on his back, letting the sudsy foam wash over his body, decorating his hirsute chest and legs with green seaweed and fragments of sea shells. Looking at him lying there, I thought of the man in his story.

"Let the two of them work it out," he said. "We're just in the way."

"I'm grateful that Mora's found someone to talk to. She's been in a funk."

"Tell me about her."

"What you see is Mora. She hides nothing. She's an all-or-nothing type. Black or white, no greys."

"Get out of her way when she decides what she wants."

"Exactly. She wants my soul. She gets jealous if I talk with a bank clerk too long. I try to tell her that I'm not interested in anyone but her, but she sees what she wants to see. Marriage has done us in, I think."

He shook his head sympathetically. "But before you got married – how were things?"

"God was in his heaven and all was right with the world . . . You know what it's like."

"So why did you do it?"

"Get married? I guess I'd have to plead insanity. I knew better, and I did it anyway."

He snorted in recognition. "I'm sorry, but I think you're taking it all too seriously, Richard. Loosen up."

"How do I do that?"

"Stop arguing. Stop anticipating."

"Is that what you learned in Europe?"

He laughed this time. His eyes lit up with mirth. There was a patch of wet sand on his cheek. "What do you know about me, Richard?"

"Not much. But I always thought you knew about women."

"Then let me tell you something: Mora wants more than marriage can offer her right now. She wants to play, it's as simple as that."

"Simple?" I couldn't swallow that.

"Look, you're on vacation. Try something different."

He winked amiably, walked into the water to clean the sand off, and sprinted up the beach. I knew what he meant because the idea had been lurking in the back of my mind since we'd met at Peaches; but I knew that I didn't want anyone but me making love to Mora.

I knew she'd had lovers in the past, but they were shadows framed by shadows. Charles was sharp and immediate. Yet I had to admit to myself that the image of the four of us together on a bed heated my imagination – that perhaps my curiosity was stronger than my apprehension.

I wanted Vy, but I tried to shake my head clear of her as I walked back up the beach to our blue chintz island in the sand. Sleeping with other people when you're married leads to trouble, I told myself.

I should have listened, but of course I didn't.

Indelible image: Charles was standing in a half crouch, swimming briefs kicked aside, feet planted heavily in the sand, calves bulging, body glistening, while Vy's blonde head bobbed vigorously between his thighs. Mora was leaning back, breasts free, snapping pictures with my Pentax. In her hands it was almost a sexual instrument. I threw up my hands in surprise and she swung around to take my picture. Far down the empty beach, a boy was throwing rocks into the surf, but he was a speck in the distance.

*Snap.* There are glimpses, in a late afternoon sun, of the future. They come unbidden, and they enter the heart and lodge there. The dark fuzz on Charles's thighs; the shuddering in Vy's back as she pulled him into her; Mora's obvious arousal as she clicked the shutter. There was an excitement in the air – of people about to experiment with their lives – that wasn't to be dissipated by the salt breeze.

"It feels right," Mora said brightly when she handed me the camera.

"Does it?" I was doubtful. I had fists at the ends of my arms, fingers closed tightly into my palms. My tongue fluttered helplessly, like the tail of an animal I'd got stuck in my throat.

Vy leaned back from Charles, licked her lips delicately, and lighted a black Sobranie cigarette. She winked at me. Charles sat in the sand, looking seductive. I thought I could hear the wheels turning in his head.

"Why don't we have dinner together? We can whip up something easy at Maurice's, and let the evening take care of itself."

## THREE

Vy drove off in a blue Mercedes. She blew a kiss through the window and scrunched gravel as she left the beach parking lot. The gesture seemed to enlarge her: fingertips to her lips, the wide unexpected smile, the pressure of her foot on the gas pedal. We followed in Charles's Clunker Deluxe. "'The station car'," he joked. "That's what they call vintage Detroit iron out here. It's what I can afford. Maurice watches that Mercedes like a hawk. I think he has the soul of a chauffeur."

I shrugged. "Shoulders were made for burdens."

I sat on the outside and Mora was squeezed between us. We dripped sand on the floor of the car and the hot vinyl seats stuck to our thighs. Despite the heat, Mora's skin was cool and moist.

"You're a Scorpio sandwich," Charles said to her, reminding me that we shared our birthdays. Then he touched her.

We were heading down the Montauk Highway and had slowed on the outskirts of Amagansett, where a train had derailed. The road swarmed with police, gawkers, and dazed passengers. Charles lifted his hand from the steering wheel and pressed the back of it against Mora's breasts. Lightly. It was the simplest, most casual of gestures, so natural I felt like I was stealing something from them because I stared. I looked quickly out the window, feeling embarrassed – and angry at myself for feeling that way.

Mora giggled and clapped a hand over her mouth. She put her left hand on Charles's knee and her right hand on my thigh and stroked us both. Her face was red, even through her tan.

I don't know how to explain it, but I was as shocked as if Charles had stroked *my* nipples. Those weren't *his* breasts, they were mine. Mine. But I could tell by the way Mora was breathing that she didn't agree that marriage had made me a man of property.

We passed dunes tufted with islands of waving sword grass, rows of beach cottages, the potato fields of July, and then I saw the windmill in East Hampton. We drove through the town's sparkling centre. In the late afternoon light it was still, unreal, a postcard.

"An extraordinary afternoon," I said in the silence. There was more I wanted to say, but I couldn't find the words. Mora's fingers were having the desired effect on me.

I was confused by the male complicity I felt with Charles. When he touched Mora, she became a strange woman we'd picked up together. From then on, two plus one equalled more than three.

## FOUR

However shocking or perhaps just plain perverse it may seem, when I saw Mora naked with Charles and Vy it wasn't jealousy that I felt. It was lust that grew in my belly, like a sapling putting down roots. I knew the voyeur's stunned delight in achieving erotic perspective. Our nakedness created the illusion that we had entered another dimension, a counter world of the id, where our apprehensions were removed with our clothes and past and future ceased to exist.

Vy's bedroom was white, but by no means chaste. White walls, white sheepskin rugs on the parquet floor, huge antique mirrors, white vases filled with daisies, and a platform bed on which the three of them sat as if on a tongue sticking out of fluffy clouds, for the silk spread was white, but the sheets underneath were crimson. Satin.

I sauntered around the room, determined to be casual, sipping my brandy and looking at things, conscious of the cool night air on my bare skin. I studied four large framed photographs of Vy on one gleaming white wall, two of them by young fashion photographers I knew. In the portraits, she was elegant and stylish, with formidable cheekbones and a frosty gaze; I didn't see in them the woman I'd watched kneeling before Charles on the beach.

When I walked over to the bed, Mora and Vy were lying on each side of Charles like houris, watching him stroke himself. His tongue moistened his dry lips, and his strong hands moved slowly from his knees up his firm thighs to his rounded belly. His breath came in shallow gasps. His chest swelled and his nipples pointed. I shivered. We would play a game, a sexual Simon says.

We drew matches and Charles won. He asked that Vy and Mora stretch out between his thighs and handed me the Polaroid. I was happy to hide behind it because I felt flushed and my ears were ringing.

It was the first time I'd seen Mora hesitant about lovemaking; her touch was tentative at first and she followed Vy's lead. Charles's swollen flesh glowed wetly in the soft light of a bedside candle. From my new perspective as voyeur, I saw that what was exciting about oral sex was not the mechanics of one person satisfying another, but the selfless art of it, the submission of ego to pleasure. The women's tongues and fingers worked gently and assiduously; Charles groaned. The phrases that broke from his lips were the mutterings of gratified desire. I waited until they had forgotten the camera before I snapped a picture.

They all blinked and looked around dazedly when the flash went off. Once again; and then it was time to draw matches. Mora's turn. I was surprised when she moved towards Vy instead of Charles, but when she touched Vy's breasts, Vy turned her long body to the side.

"Not yet," she said huskily. "Let me warm up, first."

Mora smiled as if she'd expected the rebuff, and crawled to Charles, climbing atop him, swivelling her hips to claim his hardness. The two of them flowed into each other.

For a moment then, it hurt like hell. I remembered every time Mora and I had made love, the heat and wetness, our nerves rushing to release, our ragged romantic promises, the closeness of sex during times when we couldn't even speak to each other. I was drawn to her; I handed Vy the camera and kneeled beside them, kissing Mora and stroking her taut breasts, placing my fingertips on her pubic mound to feel the movement of Charles's flesh inside her, beneath the soft maidenhair.

The room melted, contracting so that only the bed existed. My hands moved over their bodies, urging them together, teaching Charles about Mora's responses, sculpting them. When the flashbulb went off, we blinked like animals in the dark.

It was Vy's turn. "*Whoo*, boy," she exclaimed. "This is most extraordinary. Hot, hot, hot."

"Tell us what you want, before things get out of hand."

"I want to take Richard into the next room."

"No pictures?"

"Just the two of us, no silly cameras."

I was more than a little frightened of Vy. Shyness, I suppose, and the fact that I was attracted to her. The room she took me to was obviously a guest room. Rattan furniture in the shadows, a colourful hand-sewn quilt on a large brass bed, moonlight making patterns on a faded Chinese rug.

We didn't make it to the bed. I reached for her but she slipped away, onto her knees, and took my flesh into her warm mouth. I thought my knees would fold, and my hands went to her shoulders for support while fire raced up and down my spine. It was over before I could take a deep breath, while my fingers were still caressing her silky hair and finding the secret places of her delicate skull.

I was shaking all over. "*Whew!*" I breathed after a moment spent looking for my head, which had shot like a rocket to the ceiling. "That was too fast."

She chuckled, licking her lips like a cat over a saucer of milk. She rose gracefully and shrugged her square shoulders into her caftan. "That calls for a drink," she said, going into the next room for the brandy.

I was aware of a steady, rhythmic thumping through the wall and wondered for a minute if she'd return. I lighted a hurricane lamp next to the bed and waited. She reappeared with the bottle and two glasses, looking younger and more vulnerable in the flickering light.

"So the doors of marriage creak open," she said.

"I think you oiled the hinges with that one."

"Well, I'm good at what I do. I enjoy the power of doing that. It wasn't until I saw men from that perspective – on my knees, in absolute control of them – that I realized they weren't omnipotent."

She was too glib; it had bothered me since our first conversation. She sensed my scepticism. Not about what she'd said, but about her sophistication in regard to swinging.

"I was born this way. No illusions. I look at things in black and white. It's like not having eyelids."

I wanted to hold her, to press my body against hers, to feel the length of her thighs on mine, but she sat away from me, smoking one of her cigarettes. Her sharp profile cut through the aromatic blue haze.

"I wish I didn't love Charles so much, that I could turn it on and off."

I lifted my glass. "Here's to marriage."

She sniffled. She was squinting and her eyes were wet, but that might have been the smoke.

"Marriage? That's for victims. I don't intend to be a victim ever again. That's why I stay with Maurice, even though I know it drives Charles crazy."

"What have you got against marriage?"

She pouted mock-dramatically.

"His name is James Lee Tait. My used-to-be. Three years of holy wedlock made a sorrowful woman of me. He promised everything – he had the gift of promise, you know? – but in the end it was the same old song and dance."

"So you divorced him."

"Not without a lot of turmoil. A woman gets attached to you creatures, and a divorce is like losing . . . your past, maybe your future."

I wanted to understand. "Do you hate him?"

"No, not really. Let's just say I envy his get-up-and-gall. I suffered over that. He's a singer, and I waited in the wings of his career and let mine slide; I had my own ambitions."

"You make marriage sound like a minefield."

"It's no picnic. It's the most dangerous relationship you can have. A contract made in hell."

"And Charles? How does he fit in?"

"He doesn't believe in marriage, and he lets me do what I want to do. We have a pact: no apologies. Jimmy was the kind of man who was always saying 'I'm sorry' while he was stepping on my feet – but I could have twisted his balls into a daisy chain. Charles, on the other hand, makes no bones about being exactly who he is, and he never apologizes. I don't expect anything from him, so I'm never disappointed."

I stretched out in the bed, thinking about marriage, and Mora and Charles in the next room.

"Sorry. I'm rattling on, and I know you're thinking about Mora. She's so restless."

I told her about my first wife, wishing that the scars were visible so I could show her. I tried to explain about Mora. "Sometimes I feel like she's only mine on loan, that nothing will ever satisfy her."

"She's vibrating like a spinning top. Nothing will slow her down; she's like a natural force. Take it from another woman."

"I love her. You love Charles. We're crazy."

"Charles says two plus two equals twelve."

"Charles is crazy."

"I know."

"But you'd rather be with him right now, wouldn't you?"

"Well? Wouldn't you rather be with Mora?"

"That's not what's happening."

"You're evading the question. I mean, what if Charles fucks her better than you ever did? He's very good."

Check. I couldn't bear any more conversation. I wanted to make love to Vy. It was the only answer I had.

"I can't," she protested when I touched her. I put my hand through the opening in her caftan onto her cool stomach. "I absolutely cannot, I'm sorry."

"I don't understand."

"Charles and I made love while you were off looking for Mora before dinner. He's big, and I'm sore. It's my background," she sighed theatrically. "Fair-skinned mothers. Delicate skin. Look here, I'll show you."

She opened the caftan and spread her white thighs. "You see the blood?"

The lips of her vulva were irritated and swollen, and there was a tiny drop of blood on her clitoris. Imagine the centre of a rose with a drop of blood on a petal . . .

I found cotton and peroxide in a bathroom medicine cabinet and brought them back without looking in on Charles and Mora. I heard them talking through the closed door and I wanted to eavesdrop, but I wanted to make love to Vy more.

"Your hands are so gentle," she told me when I wiped away the drop of blood and covered her soreness with Vaseline. The glistening petals of her sex opened beneath my fingers.

"I'll stop. I promise you. If it hurts, I'll stop."

She squirmed evasively when I penetrated her. I stopped, moving again only when she opened to receive me. She whispered hotly in my ear while she licked it with the point of her tongue. "I trust you. No reason, but I do. I know you'll stop – but *please* don't stop now."

I cupped the plump weight of her buttocks in my palms and let myself be swallowed by her. We got lost in the dialogue of bodies, questioning and answering, alone on a gently rolling sea in the blackest night.

She pulled a yellow popper out of the darkness and crushed it between her fingers, holding the amyl nitrate to my nose and then to her own. We both inhaled deeply and felt our hearts rush to where our genitals were, riding on the cloudy, pungent chemical high like surfers on a wave.

"*Oooo!*" she cried out, as if in a dream. I heard someone wailing, without realizing it was me. Each wave that took us was bigger than the last, and we were no longer rocking gently but struggling together to stay afloat.

I heard tapping on the floor and looked down to see my fingers doing a fast dance on the wide boards. I was half off the bed and sweat was pouring from me. Vy's body was arched, a dying swan. There was a roaring in my ears like the ocean at the same time I heard knocking on the door, and then I hit the last, biggest wave and was dragged head over heels into shore. Vy's whole body clenched and she followed me, digging her nails into the backs of my arms. A high thin noise came from her throat.

When I opened my eyes, Charles was standing over us, naked, grinning, scratching his chest. "Birds would give up a winter's feed to hit that note," he said, while Vy shuddered and I navigated the re-entry to consciousness.

"What time is it?"

"Half past four. You two make a lot of noise."

Mora moved from the shadows to stand beside him, her hand on his shoulder. Her hair was matted and wet and she was ragged around the edges. They looked like weasels who'd been in the chicken coop. There should have been feathers hanging from their swollen satisfied mouths.

"I won't be able to explain this away tomorrow morning," Charles said. "I won't believe it. It was so incredibly high at times. So intense."

"I guess we did it after all." Mora smiled tiredly, shaking her head in happy disbelief.

"I don't know what could be bad about this," I said.

Vy sat up and stretched, pulling Charles's hand to her breast. "It was divine, and I love you all, and I don't know what to say, except that we've been very wicked."

Charles yawned and rubbed his eyes sleepily. Mora came to sit next to me on the rumpled bed that smelled of sex and poppers and cigarettes. We kissed Charles and Vy goodnight with the gentle exhaustion of sated lovers, and Mora and I curled up spoon-fashion on the bed. She was mine again, for a few hours.

from his face with a handkerchief. Mora saw her chance. She squeezed my hand, whispered, "Be back in a minute," and walked up to him. I watched him lean forward to talk with her over the noise, look in my direction, nod a few times, and then she was back.

"That's a smirk on your face," I said.

"He turns me on. He says we should go to the locker room and get undressed."

"That's friendly of him. Which one is the woman he came with? The brunette?"

"He works here."

"Oh."

"He says once you've got your clothes off, you won't have any trouble picking someone up."

She didn't get it.

In the locker room, he was waiting for us, talking with a dumpy woman in a Plato's T-shirt who was in charge of towels and padlocks. We undressed and he introduced himself, blinking myopically. His hand was large and wet.

"Richard, my name is Stanley. Mora says this is your first time here."

"That's right."

"I could tell when you walked in."

"How's that?"

"You're not lookin' at the women like you're here for the same thing they're here for, if you know what I mean."

Mora was standing between us, adjusting her towel to cover her breasts. He took her arm, winked at me, and started to leave.

"How long will you be? I mean, where will we meet?"

"Don't wait around," Stanley advised over his shoulder. "Just say hello. Just be friendly."

I was stunned. The dumpy woman looked at me like she knew what I was thinking and handed me a towel to wrap around my waist. "He's smooth, isn't he?" she said. The son of a bitch.

I made my way slowly through the crowd back to the bar, feeling self-conscious about my nakedness, feet avoiding people with shoes on, my chest brushing against fabric, fingers hooked in the towel so it wouldn't come unknotted. I got another drink at the bar and sat down on a nearby couch.

I tried to remember what it was like to pick up a woman, how it was done in the movies and on television. I hadn't tried to pick up anyone since high school. As I remembered, it was no fun.

If Vy had walked in the room right then, I would have climbed all over her.

After a while, I found myself staring at a Puerto Rican woman in a clinging black dress who was sitting on the other end of the couch. She had a nice, shy smile and a diamond ring on her finger, and she was watching her husband – a muscular man with more cleavage showing than most of the women in the room – flirt with a blonde dancing in front of him. The blonde was attracting an audience of still-clothed men who stood around, whispering their admiration, but she was playing to the Puerto Rican hunk. She wore a black lace camisole and one thin strap kept falling off her shoulder, baring a small, firm round breast; as she whirled, she flipped up the front of her undergarment, revealing plump boyish buttocks and pale straw pubic hair shaved in the form of a heart.

Seeing her husband so transfixed, the Puerto Rican woman moved towards me on the couch. I smiled cautiously and looked into eyes as round and bright as new black buttons. Thinking that no one was looking, that her husband was preoccupied with the blonde, I put my hand on her knee. She looked pleased but nervous.

I was wrong about her husband. The next thing I knew, he was angrily knocking my hand away and hissing at me. Spitting words of warning. I'm sure I blushed. I muttered my apologies and turned my head back to the dance floor.

Mora had predicted that people would loosen up as it got later, and they did. Those who'd come to gawk were leaving, clothes were disappearing, and towels were slipping provocatively. I didn't see Mora anywhere. The Bee Gees' "Stayin' Alive" bounced around the room like a badminton ball on moving jets of water. The smoothness of disco music, its continuous, creamy beat, its plaintive voices echoing forever the rhythmic invitation to dance, pulled me to my feet.

Mora wasn't in the swing rooms, so I went to the steamy, wet room where three whirlpool baths churned in semi-darkness. Couples cavorted in the bubbly water. I saw Mora and started to join her. A man next to me came to life.

"Couples only," he growled, pointing to a sign above the door that the rising steam had obscured. I noted his thick biceps and stepped back, but a small boy inside me jumped up and down in protest.

"But I'm half of a couple. The other half is in there, and I want to say hello to her."

"Maybe she don't want to see you right now. Wait till she comes out. Be a gentleman."

I took a deep breath and nodded. There was nothing to do but wait for her at the bar. All that mattered was that one of us was having a good time, I told myself. The booze made the lie somewhat more palatable.

I tried to strike up conversations with various women at the bar, but they could smell my desperation, the way dogs smell fear. Mora emerged at last, wrapped in a white towel. She glowed. Her pupils were bright, and her damp skin was red from the heat of the whirlpool. Her small hands were water-wrinkled.

"*Whew*! I am wiped out, Richard."

She put her arms around my waist and nuzzled her damp forehead into my shoulder like a puppy.

"I saw you in there – you were very busy."

"I don't have the words to express it . . . You know how, when you're a kid, you don't think you belong anywhere?"

"I do, sure."

"Richard, I felt like I *belonged*, like there was a secret society of people like me . . ."

I was upset. "Like a stamp club?"

She stepped back. "Oh, shit, Richard. If you don't understand, I don't know who will."

"I've been feeling like an outcast from that secret society of yours."

"I'm really sorry I was gone so long. Why didn't you join us?"

I told her about the bouncer and she frowned.

"Come on, we'll go back in. We'll stay together."

Our bare feet squished on the wet carpeting of the whirlpool room. I blinked my eyes to adjust to the darkness. She dropped her towel and lowered herself into the swirling water slowly, until she was covered up to the neck. Hazy amber lights set into the side of the tub made her look silver, like a mermaid shimmering in the warm water. I settled next to her, my genitals floating free. We were alone, although small groups of people nearby were groaning and splashing about enthusiastically.

She beamed like a kid at Christmas and fondled me, her hand making waves in the water. We kissed long and slowly, and didn't come up for air until we heard splashing in the water near us.

"I think we've got company," Mora whispered in my ear, the point of her tongue playing warmly in its whorls.

When I looked up, I saw the blonde from the dance floor sitting between Stanley's legs. He grinned at me like a benevolent pasha and winked at Mora. I stared at the blonde's long slender legs and the heart-shaped pubic hair between them, and she smiled back at me with curiosity in her eyes.

"People are talking about you two," Stanley said.

"Who?" I was sceptical.

"The regulars. People in the scene."

"Maybe they're talking about Mora, but I've been batting zero."

"Shyness turns women on. Tracey noticed you."

Bullshit she'd noticed me, but I didn't care – for some reason, Stanley had brought her along, she was sitting not four feet away, and all I had to do was figure out some clever way of crossing the ocean between us.

She made it easy by speaking first, in a squeaky voice that managed to make Brooklyn sound sexy. "I saw your moustache, and I just adore moustaches, and Stanley said you were probably a really nice guy, so when he asked me to come in here with him for just a minute I decided to forget that it was two in the morning because I like nice people more than I like going home in a cab by myself – don't you think Plato's is really neat? I feel right at home . . ."

Mora and I looked at each other in disbelief, and then turned to study Tracey from top to bottom. It was true: she was indeed one of the most beautiful women either of us had seen outside of the pages of *Playboy*. The important details were all in place: her firm breasts and plump buttocks belonged in a centrefold, her skin was smooth and soft, and she was without wrinkles or scars. She even wrinkled her nose like a cheerleader.

I looked her straight in the eyes, all at once sure where I had hesitated before.

"Tracey," I said. "You are a goddess. I say that without a doubt in my mind."

She cooed. "I *knew* you were going to be a sweety! I can always pick them out – and nice equals sexy."

I felt buoyant. Maybe it was the water, but I think it was relief. I reached for her ankle and she let me hold it while Stanley floated through the water to Mora. Then she took my hand and placed it on her belly. "I want to feel you in my belly, filling me up."

I couldn't believe my luck. Like a kid about to raid the cookie jar, I looked around to see if anyone was watching. Mora was riding Stanley in the water, holding on to his shoulders with her fingertips and looking into his eyes. I touched Tracey's breasts and felt electricity course through my palm and wrist and up my arm. I thought I heard her purring when I kissed her inner thighs, and then she folded herself into me, hands braced against the edge of the tub, and we became deep sea divers, carrying on like oestrous dolphins.

It seemed like hours later that we surfaced, only to hear the announcement over the sound system that the club was about to close. Sex had stretched time like a rubber band.

Close? Tracey and I held on to each other like exhausted boxers against the ropes. Mora and Stanley were out of the water, drying themselves off. I hadn't had enough – I didn't care what time it was, I had only just discovered the delights of Plato's, and I wasn't ready to go home. Another ten minutes . . .

I was also water-logged; every cell squished. Tracey gave me a huge grin as she climbed out of the whirlpool, and I managed to plant a kiss on her firm left buttock.

"It's four o'clock in the morning, lover," she said. "Time to go home."

I stood up. "Here's a towel, Richard," Mora said.

I took it reluctantly, looking around like a man who's been rudely awakened from a glorious wet dream. I heard Stanley's laughter in the background.

Mora put her arm around me and whispered in my ear, "You see what it's like now. You see how you can get lost in it. Can you blame me for doing what I can?"

"Not any more. Not now." I was sure that I could promise her that understanding.

Out on the street, we blinked at the dawn light like sleepy moles and walked down Fifth Avenue with our arms around each other. The early morning city was like an open bedroom; we scrutinized the people we passed on the sidewalk as if they were hurrying naked through Plato's. The world was sexualized.

"I told you that you would meet someone," Mora said.

"If it hadn't been for you . . ."

"Stanley gave me his telephone number. He made a big deal of it."

"Do they live together?"

"I think so. Do you want to do it again?"

"It's not fair to ask me now," I told her. "It's Christmas morning."

She squeezed me. "You know what? I'm happy. I think we make a good team."

"Sweet Jesus, take pity on our lust."

## SIX

Mora was sitting up to her neck in a tub of hot water and I was scrubbing her back. Her skin was turning red from the water and my fingernails, and the rising steam was curling the yellow wallpaper. Her slippery soft body was light as cork under my hands, the delicate bones of her arms and legs like wires holding her in the water.

We were talking about Plato's. She said her mother had always told her that in marriage you can't have your cake and eat it too. She referred to her mother when she was uncertain; it helped her make up her mind, usually the other way.

"You can't have it both ways."

I wondered. Most of the people at Plato's were married, and I supposed they lived tolerable lives together, no different from ours except that they shared a recreational interest – they went to bed with strangers. Sex to them was an end in itself, its own perfect justification.

"Your mother also said marriage was for ever."

"Only bachelors, loose women and divorced people fucked around."

"But swingers don't have to get divorced – they divorce sex from love. The advantages are obvious."

She chuckled. "They don't have to say they're working late."

"Or rent motel rooms."

"And they can still file joint returns."

I lifted the damp hair from the back of her neck and kissed the hollow there – it always gave her goose pimples. "They don't have to tell lies, but they must get jealous sometimes, like everyone else," I whispered.

"That tickles!"

We messed around until everything got slippery. A little later, the phone rang in the bedroom. It was Stanley, inviting us to a private party at his place in New Jersey. Mora was tentative when she talked with him, but I knew she wanted to go. So did I.

Stanley lived in one of those high-rise towers on the bluffs in New Jersey, ten minutes by taxi on the other side of the Lincoln Tunnel. It was an evening in late November, and there was a promise of snow in the air. A uniformed doorman checked off our names against a typed guest list. He was businesslike, but his eyes lingered on Mora's breasts. *He* knew what we were up to.

Tracey opened the door and squealed happily at the sight of us.

Her black silk blouse gaped open and, when she kissed me on the cheek, my hand slipped inside of its own accord.

"Stanley, come see who's here," she called over her shoulder. "I'm really happy you decided to come. Stanley wasn't sure . . ."

He appeared behind Tracey and moved to kiss Mora. It was the first time I'd seen him dressed – patent leather loafers, loud green slacks, loose patterned shirt open four buttons. He looked better in a towel.

When he kissed Mora's neck, he looked up at me from under her ear, blowing her hair away, his stiff palms moving down her back to cup the soft weight of her ass.

"My queen for the evening." He smiled.

Tracey frowned at this and took my hand from her breast, leading me into the apartment.

She showed me where I could hang our coats, playing the hostess. "I bet he says that to all the girls," I said.

She smiled brightly and excused herself. There were more people at the door, and Stanley and Mora were holding up traffic. "I don't know where we're going to put them all. If people don't start moving into the bedrooms, this is going to turn into a cocktail party – you know what I mean?"

People were sitting on couches and chairs and on the carpeted floor, passing around joints and talking about lawn care, good gas mileage, swingers' clubs – and relationships.

Relationships. It might have been a party of middle-aged people anywhere in America, except they weren't talking about business because, for swingers, it's not status that's important – what you *do* – but what you look like, and what turns you on. They were talking about the arrangements men and women make in order to balance desire with duty. The structures of love. Marital balance sheets.

I listened because it was an opportunity to hear how serious swingers – the people who pursued this life week after week, year after year – dealt with the problems Mora and I had encountered since we stepped outside the closed circle of marriage.

As a group, they were no more nor less attractive than the crowd you'd find on a Saturday night in a disco in Fort Lee, New Jersey. No matter what shape their bodies were in, they dressed in tight, light clothing; they wore gold chains and digital watches, and the men tended to show more chest than their women showed cleavage. They smoked a lot of cigarettes but they didn't drink much.

At first, their faces were hard to distinguish, because the only light in the large living room came from recessed spots set behind greenery that grew on one wall, over a bubbling fountain constructed of plaster made to look like stone. Another wall was decorated with paintings of bull fights and crossed swords on wooden plaques, but the opposite two walls were glass, to take advantage of a magnificent view of the Manhattan skyline at night. I was sitting on the floor, in a line with the Empire State Building, and when I stood up I could see the twinkling lights of the city reflected in the inky blackness of the Hudson. Some people were looking through a telescope set on a tripod in the corner of the room.

You could tell the party hadn't really got underway by the lack of people in the bedrooms. We strolled in and out of four of them, and saw a few people having serious conversations or simply petting, before I noticed a brunette lying on a bed masturbating. Her skirt was thrown up around her waist and her ankles were locked together. She had both hands between her legs, her back was arched, and the sweat poured from her forehead. Her eyes were shut tight.

A man wearing a white turtleneck and blue blazer – a man in his mid-fifties with a grey toothbrush moustache – was kneeling on the bed next to her, with the intent expression of a man helping his wife give birth by breathing with her. He didn't notice us.

Both their faces were bright red and she was babbling when he put his hand on her thigh.

Her eyes snapped open and she brought her hands up to hold out to him. He clasped them and kissed her fingers, one by one.

"Can I get you a drink, darling?" he asked solicitously. He had an English accent.

"You're not getting me drunk tonight."

"No, of course not. That's not my intention. But I do want you to have a good time. I want you to mix with people and be gay."

He treated her like she might explode, like someone who's just been released from a mental hospital. I was fascinated. She jerked her skirt down when she noticed us standing there in the darkness.

"I wasn't putting on a show," she growled.

"Didn't mean to intrude, but it was getting crowded in the living room," I explained hastily.

"Oh, hello," the Englishman said, stepping around the bed and holding out his hand. "Peter's my name. This is Johanna."

He and Mora smiled at each other.

Johanna looked coldly at me. "You're a voyeur," she accused.

"Look, if you wanted to play with yourself in private, you could have stayed home and drawn the blinds."

I was glad she hadn't; she was ravishing, with long dark hair loose about her shoulders and breasts heaving beneath her sweater. She had delicate nostrils and a thin, painted mouth and her eyes burned with frustration.

"Wait a minute, darling," Peter said. "No reason to get upset. We'll go get some drinks and give you a chance to get yourself together." He pushed us out and closed the door.

"The first attractive woman besides you I've seen, and she's crazy," I whispered to Mora.

"She's off, tonight," Peter said. "But Johanna is as changeable as New England weather. You just have to be patient. When she's good she's very, very good, but when she's bad . . ." He sighed, and shook his head. Then he looked at me and brightened. "But maybe your meeting was fortuitous. I've known her to start out an evening hating someone, and then surprise me. She likes the unexpected move."

"It must be exhausting to deal with her," Mora said.

"I know she's much too young for me. She's on her own trip, as you say here. She says I can accompany her on it, if I want to, but I'm not allowed to complain."

We refilled our glasses and he went back to collect Johanna. While we'd been gone, the crowd in the living room had thinned out.

Then I heard a familiar voice. Stanley led Vy and Charles into the room, feathers of snow in their hair. They looked glamourous and happy and the talk in the room stopped for a minute to register their presence. Stanley made an attempt to introduce them, but Vy stopped him.

"Surely I haven't been gone that long, Stanley – that people have forgotten. This is like a family reunion. Hello, Peter. Is that Johanna in the corner, over there?"

"Hello, Vy," I said.

"I was hoping you'd be here. Baby, it's *so* good to see you! Did you know they'd be here, Charles?"

Our reunion was a four-way hug in the middle of the living room; for the moment we were a closed circle, oblivious of everyone around us.

"I hear you liked Plato's," Charles said. He smirked.

"You know we did," Mora told him.

Vy examined us both with a look of mock severity. "So while the cat's away, the mice played? You let the Devil tempt you – you couldn't wait for me?"

She exchanged greetings with the other people in the room –

apparently she knew them all – and sat down on the rug to pull off her tight velvet trousers. Like a restless hen on a nest, she squirmed provocatively until her long white legs were bare. The dark blonde tuft of hair at the bottom of her belly gleamed like wheat. She reached for her big leather bag and pulled out a long madras skirt to wrap around her waist.

"No more underwear, thank God. For some reason, Maurice insisted on lingerie in London. He said that his friends would be shocked if I didn't have any, but I think he had a kinkier motive."

She hadn't lost her ability to grab the centre of attention. Every eye in the room watched her get into her skirt. What was it that made me think she was changed – or had my perception of her altered? The circles under her eyes were darker, she'd braided her hair, her fingernails were bitten – but it wasn't the details that made me see her fresh; it was an aura, as if she'd learned something about herself in England and the knowledge was spreading in circles from the centre of her being.

Peter handed her a drink, and Stanley asked her about England. She was gracious, a queen with her court. Maybe that was what I noticed about her: a new authority that enabled her to hold the floor with ease.

"I met more submissives in England than I could shake a stick at," she chuckled drily. "And more lords this-and-that with beautiful soft eyes and eccentric tastes . . . They all have old names and large country places with butlers, and their great soft eyes get wickedly moist when you flick a riding crop. Leather is very popular, very chic with Maurice's friends." S&M was unexplored territory for us.

Mora and I looked quizzically at each other. We had only the vaguest notion of what she meant, but I could see that everyone else knew what Vy was talking about and that she was a star.

Charles walked into the kitchen to get himself a drink – I think he was probably feeling neglected – and I followed him, hoping that he could enlighten me.

"What is a 'submissive'?" I asked.

"Stop putting me on, Richard. You're being ingenuous."

I held up my hands. "I ask in all innocence. I really don't know what she's talking about. She's changed – hasn't she?"

He stared at me, his lower lip dropped in thought. "You really have some catching up to do . . ."

Peter had been pouring himself a straight vodka without ice at the counter next to where we were standing. He broke in. "Excuse me, I couldn't help overhearing what you said, Richard. About Vy, I mean. I've been a fan of hers since we met – I'd call it an encounter, because it was very dramatic, but she may have forgotten – at a party at the UN Plaza last winter. Do you remember how grand she was, Charles? Some of us were in awe."

"Tell him what a submissive is, Peter."

"I'd rather talk about Vy. She's much more fun to talk about than my Johanna. Vy is a queen, but Johanna has become a pumpkin. Vy understands what a terrible responsibility she has. There isn't enough of her to go around."

"You lost me," I admitted. "I thought I knew something about Vy, but I guess I don't."

"There's a lot people don't know about Vy. She shows everyone a slightly different angle – it's definitely one of her charms."

Having said this, he drifted off in search of Johanna.

"I'm still in the dark," I said to Charles.

"The English don't know how to get to the point. Vy says sex with them is like a Japanese tea ceremony."

"I have the feeling that I'm going to have to ask Vy to explain – you're being just as vague as Peter."

"And you're being dense. One trip to Plato's and you end up in the inner circle of the sex world on the East Coast, and yet you won't see what's right in front of your eyes. Vy is a dominatrix – that's why Maurice took her to England. Do you know what she carries in that big leather bag? Whips. Leather cuffs. Nipple clamps. Dildoes. Rush . . ."

I shook my head. "You could have told me."

"For Christ's sake, Richard. You fell in love with her, didn't you?"

The living room was almost empty. I wandered down the hall towards the bedrooms, wondering what scenes I'd find Mora and Vy and Charles in the middle of, hoping that Tracey would be sitting somewhere by herself.

The first bedroom I walked into was occupied by people I didn't know. I stood and watched them for a while, feeling curiously lustless. Mora was in the next room, on a couch with Charles and Stanley and Tracey. It was a four-way connection: Stanley kneeled behind Mora, who had Charles in her mouth while Tracey kneeled above Charles's lips. Stanley wore a bottle of Rush on a chain around his neck and I watched him lean over Mora's back to hold the bottle to her nostrils before bringing it back to his own nose. They looked like a team of acrobats, totally absorbed in a difficult manoeuvre they hadn't rehearsed for.

In the third bedroom, Vy was sitting in an easy chair, next to a queen-sized bed two couples were romping about on. Peter was kneeling before her, caressing and kissing her feet. She was idly untwisting her braids, looking bored.

"I'm glad you're back," I said, touching her hair.

"I thought about you over there, Richard. Maybe more than I thought about Charles – isn't that strange?"

"Charles just told me how naive I am."

"Naive?"

"About you. And what you carry in your bag."

She blushed. "I hope he told you good things."

"You're a star."

"I do what turns me on when I'm in the mood. Are you shocked?"

"Why should I be? It was just something I didn't know about. Now I know."

"Does it make any difference?"

"I don't think so."

She reached for my hand and pressed it to her check and we remained like that for a while, staring and not saying anything.

Peter stood up, realizing that he'd lost Vy's attention. "Have you seen Johanna, old man?"

"She's in the living room."

"Oh, God. I'd better go rescue her. She'll be getting drunk, and then she's impossible to deal with."

"Poor Peter. He can't handle that woman at any time. He's an old teddy bear."

"I want to make love to you."

"I would like that very much."

She stood up and I pulled her into my arms, pressing her long body into mine so that I could feel her knees and pelvic bones and breasts. She shuddered, and I felt it go down her body.

"If Charles and Mora saw us right now, I don't think they'd understand," she whispered in my ear.

I knew what she meant – that fucking was all right, but a long embrace was a sign that something serious was going on.

"Can't leave you two alone for a minute," Charles said, from behind us. Mora was with him and they were both naked. A streak of semen glistened on Mora's left thigh and her hair was matted. Her eyes looked like she'd been on a long trip.

"Enjoying yourself, lover?" Vy asked, stepping away from me.

"It's like a geriatrics convention here. Mora and I are ready to play, and everyone is sitting around talking about relationships and the etiquette of a good swing. Can you imagine?"

I kissed Mora and she snuggled into my chest.

"How are you doing?"

"I'm throbbing from my toes up. I could go on all night, but Charles is right – there's nobody left to party with."

"We could always go to Plato's."

Charles and Vy didn't like the idea. I wasn't crazy about it myself, but I wanted more time with Vy. I knew that Charles was getting restless and, if he went home, Vy would go with him.

"If you feel like being adventuresome," Vy suggested, "there's a new place called Night Moves we could try. Maurice told me about it."

"I'm game," Charles said, "as long as it's not the same *old* faces."

"It's on-premise, like Plato's. Very hip, Maurice said."

"How do we get there?" Mora asked. "It's too late for a bus."

"We'll grab a cab, or maybe we can find a ride," Vy said.

"Let's do it," I agreed.

"Who has a car?"

"I have an idea," Vy volunteered. "I'll talk to Peter."

We all groaned in unison. Not Peter.

"Have faith, children. Don't forget that I carry special powers in my bag. Let me deal with this."

Charles and Mora dressed while Vy went off to talk with Peter. Ten minutes later, she came to get the three of us and she had her coat on. Obviously she had conquered.

"Johanna is going to drive us in Peter's Cadillac. He'll get a ride with someone."

"How did you manage that?"

"He wants a private session with me. And Johanna wants to party. She's weird, and she's getting drunk, but I approve of her nuttiness."

"Just a bunch of old farts," Johanna said when we left, jingling the keys of the Cadillac in her hand. When Peter had tried to kiss her goodbye she'd turned her head so that he was presented with her ear.

Mora and I sat in the front seat with her. We had to hang on to each other when she took the corners, but she was a good driver. She steered the big beast with one hand, swinging wide around taxis and surprised pedestrains. She glided over the dark slick streets, wet with the melting snow, like a skate on ice.

## SEVEN

Night Moves was discreetly planted in the middle of a block of factory buildings and warehouses. Noisy with hand carts, trucks and honking traffic during the day, at midnight it was a closed drawer. The only signs of life on the empty street were the coloured lights of the firehouse across from the club. I could see firemen inside polishing a giant red engine.

The light snow had stopped and a thin layer of white slush covered the sidewalks. Vy strode regally in front, head back, heels tapping impatiently.

"Pinch me," Mora said when we stopped at the glass front of the club to wait for Johanna to park her car. The sign said NIGHT MOVES, but otherwise it looked like the wholesale soda and beer distributor next door, blank and black and anonymous.

I knew what Mora meant, so I kissed her instead.

"Yes, it's true. We're doing *this* again."

"Just like we know what the hell we're doing."

"Well, at least we all share the same fantasy. We have that in common." I was excited but apprehensive.

The five of us were a crowd in the pocket-sized reception area. There was a cigarette machine, a pay phone, a few hand-lettered posters too small to read in the dark (one announced a wet T-shirt contest), and – standing behind a counter next to the curtained entrance – a thin young black man with tack-sharp smartass eyes. He recognized Vy and made a small fuss over her while he checked our coats.

"And I thought this was going to be a slow night," he drawled, looking Mora and Johanna over.

Just as Charles and I were digging in our wallets for the twenty-dollar membership fee a sign on the counter asked for, a man who was obviously in charge stepped from behind the curtain and waved us in. Vy introduced him as Bob, the manager. He wore a thick moustache and a three-piece suit.

"I'm president of this lady's fan club," he told us proudly, taking her hand and pressing it to his heart.

Inside, we stood around chatting for a while, blinking in the darkness. Clever track lighting and plenty of candles illuminated an intimate stage set. To our right, a gleaming oak bar was tended by female bartenders in T-shirts and satin shorts. Across from it and on a higher level was a carpeted lounge that led to a small mirrored disco floor. A young, lively looking crowd filled the moulded plastic booths.

I saw two Lacoste shirts, I swear it. The men who wore them had long blow-dried blond hair and they glowed with sun and good health. Tourists. Sitting with them were two of the most luscious-looking college girls I'd ever had the pleasure of ogling from afar.

I nudged Charles, to point them out, but he was focused on Johanna. He couldn't take his eyes off the way she wiggled her behind on the bar stool, alternately flirting and scowling and sipping Scotch. Vy and Mora stood on the other side of her at the end of the bar, foreheads pressed together as they compared notes on the people they saw.

"She's a heartbreaker," he sighed.

"She's drunk, too. But look over there – it's the flesh God promised us. In our adolescent fantasies."

He studied them sceptically.

"I grant you that they are flowers of young American womanhood, but they're also tourists. They'll sit and watch and look decorative and, after they've got excited, they'll go home with the guys they came with. Mark my words – they won't even leave a trail of smoke behind them."

"I'm going to talk to them a little later."

"God bless. They'll write in their diaries about you."

We were in the way of incoming traffic. A dozen attractive couples passed the bar, conscious of being on display. There was a lot of eye contact and body movement, but I didn't see anybody as good-looking as the college girls. I sipped my drink and thought about them, trying out and discarding various introductory lines in my mind, telling myself to be bold, that I had nothing to lose and everything to gain by approaching one of them.

A man who was probably telling himself the same thing walked up to Vy and Mora and got brushed off, but he didn't even pause to acknowledge defeat before moving on to Johanna, who practically jumped into his arms. As he led her off towards the back room, she turned and winked at Charles.

"Perfidious bitch," Charles muttered after her.

"Let's go talk to Mora and Vy. We'll all go into the back room."

But they wanted to dance.

We moved onto the dance floor, and let a Rod Stewart song lead us around the polyurethaned oak floorboards beneath the silk parachute canopy. The floor-to-ceiling mirrors multiplied our images as we shook our bodies and whirled about.

Dancing loosened me up. When the music stopped, I sat on a carpeted step, aware that the college girls were right above me. I wasn't surprised when Mora danced Charles off the floor and through the curtains into the back room.

Vy joined me on the step, sitting with her elbows on her knees.

"I'm tired. Maybe it's just jet lag, but I can't boogie the way I used to."

"Dancing is a warm-up exercise for the real thing."

I put my arm around her shoulders and she looked down at my hand for a long moment before covering my fingers with hers.

"And how do you like Night Moves?"

"It's not a circus, like Plato's. It's just the right size."

"This is the first time I've dared to bring Charles here. He's been funny since I got back, anyway."

"Funny?"

"Different. He didn't want me to go to England – almost as if he's jealous and can't talk about it. I think he wants to punish me, but he doesn't know how to go about it."

I thought about her relationship with Maurice, her reputation as a dominatrix, and said something I immediately regretted.

"You could teach him about punishment, couldn't you?"

She was stung. "Don't be a son of a bitch, Richard."

"I can't help thinking about that bag of yours. And Maurice."

She pushed my arm from her shoulder and stood up. Her eyes were cold. "I thought . . . Well, never mind what I thought. I don't have to explain myself to anyone. Not even you, Richard."

Before I could say anything – and if I could have grabbed my words from her ears and crushed them underfoot, I would have – she squared her shoulders and strode across the dance floor, straight into the back room.

I sighed and stood up, just as one of the college girls passed me, trailed by the blandly smiling Lacoste shirts. The three of them started to jiggle and strut and I decided, what the hell, and approached the remaining college girl. I bent over to whisper in her pink, shell-like ear, blowing aside wisps of soft gold hair.

"I like the way you look. You are so special, it takes my breath away. I would love to . . ."

I have to give her credit for a classy brush-off. Without looking up, she shook her head slightly and said, "It's not me you're looking for."

I was surprised – and relieved – to find Charles back at the bar. His expression was cloudy. Disappointed.

"I didn't expect to find you here," I said, ordering another glass of wine.

"I'm surprised myself. Mora's hard to hold on to."

"So what happened?" As if I couldn't guess.

"The manager, Bob. He saw her and came over to collect on the entrance fee. She went off without a whimper."

"She's a woman with a strong sense of duty." We drank to her.

"I ran into Johanna – actually it was more of a tripping motion – and stopped to say hello."

"Had she changed her mind about you?"

"She hissed at me like a wet cat."

"Maybe she's serious."

"You know I'm persistent, Richard. I can't help myself for trying, but I go ahead and try. Know what I said to her? 'You look best on your knees, giving head.' "

"The direct approach. I see."

He looked around. "I don't see the college girls."

"It wasn't me they were looking for," I admitted.

"Lord, what makes women so contrary? So . . . ungrateful for our efforts, so closed of heart."

We might have sung the Chasing Male Blues right there, in the middle of a sexual game park, but Mora interrupted in time to remind us of our opportunities. She slid in between us.

"Why are you sitting out here?"

"Just taking a break, you know."

"Well, there are a lot of women in the back."

"What's Vy up to?" Charles asked. "It must be like old Home Week."

"Last time I saw her, she was talking to Johanna."

Charles did a quick double-take at the news. I watched his mind turning over the possibilities, like a hungry raccoon turning stones over in a creekbed. When his curiosity was tickled, he rumpled his hair from back to front, raising a crest above his forehead. His eyes turned heavenward for a sign.

"I wonder what *that's* all about . . ."

"Well, let's go find out," Mora said, taking our arms as if we were brothers out courting the same young maid, and pointing us to the back room.

Stepping into the back room at Night Moves was like walking into the Arabian Nights. The plush sprawling orgy room seemed fur-lined. We walked across mattresses and around huge pillows on which people lay in every position making love, inhaling the mixed odours of warm flesh, marijuana and tobacco smoke, amyl nitrate and perspiration, perfume and incense. Above the low, throbbing music rose the sounds of orgasm and of bodies moving together in the dark; the whispered, urgent imprecations of those close to the edge, and the quick, breath-snatching sobs of those who'd gone over it.

I remembered what Mora had said about a secret society of people who liked to make love as much as she did, and I wasn't surprised when a black hand reached out to circle her ankle. The kid with the smartass eyes who worked the door showed white teeth. Mora smiled, shrugged helplessly at us – *noblesse oblige* – and allowed herself to be pulled down into the darkness next to him.

We found Vy at the centre of a circle of naked onlookers. She was kneeling beside Johanna, who lay on her side, also naked, her wrists tied behind her with a black silk scarf. There were beads of perspiration on her upper lip and between her heaving breasts, and her pupils were dilated.

"I'm not going to . . ." she sputtered, but Vy put her hand over her mouth, and she stopped.

"There you are, dear. And Richard, too. Johanna has been asking for you. I warned her that you might be busy."

Johanna shot Charles the fierce look of a victim who is determined that the sacrifice will be conducted according to her own fantasies.

"What made her change her mind?"

"She didn't. You were always the object of her fancy."

"Of her hostility, you mean."

"The more of that, the better."

I saw then that he recognized what Johanna wanted, what Vy meant, and the wicked anticipation in his eyes made me feel sick with fear and disgust for a minute. I didn't understand; why wasn't making love enough?

Did the people watching understand? Or were they, too, just curious about a need greater than theirs?

"You don't like that, do you?" Vy asked me when we moved to a space of our own, between two massive pillows.

"I don't understand it. Why isn't fucking enough?"

I waited for an answer, but she was suddenly impatient with my earnest innocence. I saw pity and scorn mix in her eyes, and – just as suddenly as she'd entered it – she left my life. I was stunned. I expected the floor to open and swallow me. I knew her well enough to know it was a definitive exit.

Looking around at the moving shadows, I wondered wearily why I was there among them. I was overcome by a feeling of lostness. Vacancy. Sitting there in the middle of the orgy, I argued with myself: marriage and freedom. Life sexualized. The sweet power of lust. The evils of jealousy.

Let it be over, I thought. I just wanted to escape, to take Mora home and lock the door. I needed her – and she was my wife. My wife.

I found her with her legs over the black guy's shoulders, split open for him as he drove deep into her, spanking her ass with each powerful thrust. I kneeled beside them and whispered in her ear, "It's time to go home."

## EIGHT

I hit her, and she sneezed, but I hit her again, and her head bounced against the metal cyclone fence. It was just before dawn on Ninth Avenue. Bleak, so bleak. There was an excavation behind the fence and I wondered if I had the insane strength to pick her up and throw her into it – and if there was enough loose dirt to bury her with. I hated her with the white-hot intensity of a jealousy freed at last from civilized constraints.

"*You motherfucker-bastard-son-of-a-bitch*!" she screamed, wailing like an outraged child, rubbing her knuckles over her bruised cheek.

"You had to fuck so much, you couldn't come with me even at five in the morning?" I shouted, hitting her again.

"Just because you couldn't get laid in a whorehouse doesn't mean *I* have to stop!"

She grabbed my jaw in her strong small hands and twisted my head towards her. "*Look at me, Richard*! Just look at me! My nose is bleeding and there's snot . . ."

I pulled out my handkerchief to give to her – like a good husband – and she knocked it to the ground.

"Did you have to yell that I was crazy to the whole club, just because I wanted you to come home with me?" I was so hurt that I thought I would vomit right there at her feet. Self-disgust choked me.

"Fuck you! You bastard, to hit me, *fuck* you and your feelings! I don't *care* how you feel any more!"

She came at me with her fists and feet, pummelling me in the belly and on the chest, kicking my shins.

"All I wanted was for you to come home with me," I pleaded, holding up both hands to protect myself.

"I was coming, God damn it!"

My eyes filled with hot tears. "But what about us? You love me and I love you, and that should mean *something*."

"This is my life, and this is how I want to live it, Richard."

The morning sun struck her wet face. I couldn't hit her, and I couldn't hold her. She wasn't mine.

"Come home?"

"I can't stop now. I can't."

# Movements

Michael Hemmingson

## I. Suite for an End to a Marriage

The first time I saw my wife fucking another man, she was by our jacuzzi the night of The Party. I was fairly convinced it would be the last party we'd throw as husband and wife.

Actually, she was with two men. One was a fellow I didn't know and he was fucking her from behind – his large, hairy hands tightly grasping her hips in an attempt to control the backward thrust of her pelvis as if she were a wild animal. The other one (my best friend) had his dick in her mouth. She was taking this dick down her throat pretty deep, and he was no bigger than myself. She never did that for me. Maybe she never liked my dick; and this is something I could believe, given the recent sour circumstances of our marriage.

"I don't think I'm in love with you any more," she told me three months before. I was trying to have sex with her. Her pussy was dry like a dry cunt. Finally she pushed my hand away and said she didn't want to. We hadn't made love in quite a while.

"What do you mean?"

"Is it hard to understand?" she said. "How can I illustrate it any better? *I don't think I'm in love with you any more.*"

"I see," I said.

"No," she said, "you don't."

We tried the marriage counsellor routine, and that only proved to drive us further apart, snickering at all the flowery, New Age suggestions the counsellor was trying to sell us.

"What a fucking waste of money," my wife said.

Her name is Beryl, by the way.

* * *

I stood there, looking out the kitchen window, and watched Beryl fuck. The one who was my best friend, his name is Art.

I wasn't surprised. The night seemed to be heading for this. Beryl was on the warpath to have sex with someone – other than me.

"I'm feeling frisky tonight," she said when she pulled me aside during The Party.

She was drunk. I told her so.

"So I'm *drunk*," she said, "and I'm feeling *good*."

I wasn't feeling good. "Thanks for the information."

"I just want you to know," she said, "that I might do something *wild*, I might do something *sexy*, and I don't want you to get in the *way*."

"I won't," I said.

"I don't want you to get in the way of my being *happy*."

"I won't," I said.

It started, I suppose, with her dance – or striptease. She put on some electronic music, the kind that gives me a headache. I don't know where she got this music. She began to dance, and had an audience of men cheering as she lifted her skirt and flashed her panties; then she opened her blouse and exposed her tits. She had small, pointed, brown breasts. She was a tall, slender woman with long legs and tanned skin and straight blonde hair, a very appealing woman to many men.

"That's some wife of yours!" someone said to me, slapping me on the back.

"Yeah," I said.

Beryl had stripped down to her thong. Drunken hands groped for her. One pair of hands belonged to Art. Beryl giggled and ran out back and jumped into the jacuzzi.

Watching her fuck, I knew it was the hottest sight I'd ever viewed. It was better than watching a porno: this was real.

I wasn't the only person watching, either. Several men, some I knew, some I didn't, moved towards the threesome. I moved with them. We were all like mesmerized cattle.

Two months ago I was sitting in a bar with Art. We were on our fourth or fifth drinks.

"I think Beryl and I are getting a divorce," I said.

"You think?" Art said.

"Probably," I said. "She doesn't love me any more."

"*No.*"

"Yes."

"*No*."

"She said this."

"Do you still love her?" he asked.

"I'm not sure," I said. "I think I do."

"What went wrong? You two used to be the happy fun couple."

"I'm not sure," I said. "I think she might be having an affair."

"You *think*?"

"I wouldn't put it past her."

When Beryl was done with Art and the man I didn't know, she started having sex with two other men. The Party was becoming something else. Other people departed – old friends giving me strange looks. Someone said, "You didn't say this was going to turn into an *orgy*." It was past one in the morning anyway, the time for most parties to start winding down.

Art, with his clothes back on, passed me.

I grabbed his arm.

"Hey," he said softly.

I just looked at him.

"We should talk," he said.

"Yeah," I said.

The Party was over, people were gone. Four a.m. I lay in bed, listening to my wife taking a bath. The door was unlocked. I went in. She stared at me. She was sitting in the tub, water and soap all around her. She started to say something, I held up a finger to stop her. I unzipped my pants and showed her my hard prick.

"Do you plan to do something with that?" she said.

"I have some ideas," I said.

"You look all worked up."

"I am that," I said.

"I haven't seen your dick that bulging and red since . . . since we first met."

I approached her, my body shaking. "Did you like fucking those men tonight?"

Softly, "You know I did."

"I could tell. I haven't seen you fuck like that since . . . since we first met."

She said, "Did you like me fucking those men?"

I grabbed Beryl's head. I was fast and she was surprised. I pushed her face into my crotch. I bunched up her slick wet hair in my fists, like I was angry. I was more horny than angry, or on a fine line that crosses both conditions. She took my cock in her mouth. I wondered how many loads of come she'd swallowed this evening. Mine would be just another. Beryl pulled my pants down and grabbed at the flesh of my ass, yanking me forward, so that I was partially in the water with her, getting wet . . .

In bed, I asked her how long she'd been fucking Art. I knew that tonight wasn't the first time – the way they were with each other: that familiarity of the body. Beryl said, "For a while now."

## II. Sonata for a New Phase in Marriage

The three of us were in the jacuzzi. This was inevitable, this had to happen; I knew it, Beryl knew it, Art knew it.

We'd had dinner. It was a quiet dinner. I savoured every bite of the mushroom sauteed chicken Beryl had prepared, the potatoes that reminded me of being a child and eating Mother's well-cooked meals. It was a warm night. Beryl suggested we relax in the jacuzzi, drink wine. Art wanted beer. Beryl drank wine. We got naked, acting like excited, modest teenagers doing something daring and naughty and went into the water.

It was a clear night out, a lot of stars.

I was also drinking wine.

"That's Mars up there." Beryl pointed at the sky, to a bright star with a red tint.

"Think there's life up there?" Art said.

"Mars? Or elsewhere?"

"Mars."

"Sure," she said.

"What do you think?" Art asked me.

"As long as they don't invade us," I said, "I don't care."

"I'm glad you're not mad," he said.

"I'm not mad," I said. "I keep telling myself I should be. But I'm not."

"It's good that you're not," Beryl said. "It means you're growing. It means you're moving in the direction I am, and that makes me happy."

Art waded through the water in her direction. She giggled. He backed her against the Jacuzzi wall. They kissed. I sipped my glass of wine and watched him kiss her. I watched him lift her body up, sit her on the edge of the jacuzzi, spread her legs, and go down on her. Beryl liked this. She ran her fingers through his wet hair and made familiar sounds of pleasure. I knew those sounds like a distant cousin one has fond memories of. She leaned back, propping herself on her elbows, and let Art work his tongue between her legs, his hairy hands rubbing her stomach and breasts. She looked at me and said, "Come here and stick that dick in my mouth."

I got out of the water. The hair on my body was matted, I was dripping. I liked walking about like this, my cock pointing the way. I crouched before Beryl so she could take me in her mouth as Art continued to eat her pussy, grunting sounds coming from his throat.

We then moved away from the jacuzzi to a lounge chair, where she sucked on us both: Art and I standing close, almost touching, Beryl going from one cock to another. I could smell Art's body. I could smell the musk from his crotch, and I wondered if I was emitting any odours he could sense. Needless to say, the smell of sex permeated the immediate air around us.

We took turns fucking my wife. Art went first. I wanted to watch them; watching them made me want her all the more.

"Whore," I whispered in her ear when it was my turn.

"Yeah," she said, "talk dirty to me."

When we went to the bed, Beryl wanted us both inside her at the same time. "One in my kitty," she said with a seductive voice, touching herself, "and one in my booty."

"I have hope for us," she said later.

We were lying in bed alone. The sex had been good. I remembered a night, not a month ago, when we were in bed together and she had said, "We should just have wild sex right now, that'd solve all our problems," but neither of us could do it.

"That's good," I said.

"I really do." She kissed me.

I kissed her back.

"I feel so sexual, so alive again. I want to fuck more men. I want to fuck *a lot* of men. I love you. Will you help me do this?"

She could have done it by herself, or with Art, but she wanted me involved, and I wanted to be involved. And Art, of course, wished to be there too.

It started with the gang bang. Art made the arrangements for this, being the resourceful fellow that he is, getting the guys Beryl had fucked at The Party together for another go at it. There were nine of them in all, more than I had originally imagined. Had my wife really fucked nine men that night? I suppose so. Ten, including Art. Eleven, including me.

If I should ever think that what happened was just a wild fantasy, or a dream, I have the evidence on videotape. It was, yes, Art's idea to capture this night for posterity. When he suggested it to Beryl, she got this wild look in her eyes and said, "Yes." I was beginning to know that look better and better. I wanted her to say no. I wanted her to say no because I liked the idea myself.

(A number of times, alone, feeling lonely, thinking of the life I once had, I will put that tape into the VCR and watch. I will watch my wife fuck all those men in a single session, fucking in every combination possible.

Others have watched her. Hundreds, thousands, all over the world. This is really what this story is about.)

It was Art's idea – again – to create a website and place stills from the gang-bang video on it. He created the web page and allowed people to access it for free. In a matter of days, the site was getting thousands of hits. Art said this was a combination of posting stills to various news groups with sexual themes, and the help of a number of search engines.

After a month, he – or we – announced that the whole videotape could be purchased for $34.95.

In a matter of weeks, two thousand orders came in.

First we were just some people doing kinky things, and now we were in business.

We were, I guess you can say, pornographers.

## III. Solo in the Jacuzzi, with Memory

I was alone in the jacuzzi. It was another clear night. That red star was indeed Mars. I stared at it. I wanted to go there. I wondered what sex life was like on Mars.

In the bedroom, in the house, Art and Beryl were fucking. He had been fucking her in the ass when I had left, and came out here, turned on the jet streams, and sat in the warm bubbling water. I closed my eyes while looking up.

In the water, I thought about the two of them. I pictured his cock going in and out of her butt, the muscles of her sphincter contracting with each thrust. As I thought of this, I started to become aroused. The image in my head was far more enticing than returning to the bedroom and seeing and smelling it. In my mind, I was the director, I was in control, and I made my own movie of the act.

I also pictured scenes from the night of The Party.

I touched myself. I had my cock in my hand under the water, and I began to jack off.

I watched my semen clump in the water and float to the top, getting caught in a whirlwind of bubbles, spinning around, blending in with water and chlorine.

## Intermission

*How We Met*

I met Beryl at the recital of an experimental cellist; he was on tour for his new CD. In the first half of his performance, he presented classical pieces by Debussy and Mozart. I had difficulty listening – I kept glancing at the blonde woman who was sitting alone, across from me in the small concert hall. She was wearing black slacks and a white cotton blouse. She kept looking at me as well. We talked during the intermission. Small talk: *What do you think of the cellist? Oh, he's good.* We sat together for the second half, and the cellist presented his own iconoclastic work, hooking his instrument to microphones, adding special effects, or playing along with a tape full of strange sounds. towards the end, he did a manic solo and broke two strings. After, I asked the blonde woman – Beryl – if she'd like to go get some coffee. "No," she said, "but how about a beer?" Two months later, we were living together. Six months later, we were married.

## IV. Quartet

"We've been approached with a business deal," Art said on the phone. Beryl and I were on separate phones in different rooms, listening together.

"Go on," she said.

He said, "There's this couple – here in the city – who have a successful online business. They do the same as us: sell videos and pix of them fucking, or the wife fucking some guys. Then they started to make and distribute vids of other couples. Acting as distributors, growing their business. You know. They came across our website, and they want Beryl. I mean, they can sell five times the amount of videos we do. Or so they say."

"What does this mean?" I said.

"More money," Art said.

"More money," Beryl said, "sounds good to me."

This couple – Fred and Donna – invited the three of us for dinner to talk about the possibility of a business venture. Art drove in his own car and was late. Beryl and I were both nervous and we didn't know why.

They had a nice, modestly furnished suburban house, not the kind of place you'd think a big internet porn outfit would be located. Fred and Donna were also the kind of couple you might see at a PTA meeting – almost conservatively dressed, quiet, and friendly. They were in their late thirties, attractive and unassuming.

Over dinner, we talked about our lives, not sex.

I wondered why I was here. I was expecting drugs, hard booze, triple-X love acts.

Fred suggested we go to the water.

They also had a jacuzzi, but this one could fit ten people. It was very nice and spacious. Fred and Donna disrobed before us and got in. Donna was a bit on the chubby side, but had a magnificent tan and silicone-enhanced breasts. Fred, I was quick to notice, didn't have a hair on his well-muscled body, and his dick had to be ten inches long.

Art stripped and jumped in. Beryl and I took our clothes off slowly, still uncertain, and joined the party.

We were all drinking champagne, by the way. It always begins with some kind of party.

"You have a great body," Donna said to Beryl.

"Thank you," Beryl said.

"I'd love to fuck you," Donna said.

"I'm not bi," Beryl said.

"Too bad," Donna said. "But maybe Fred can fuck you. I like to watch him fuck other women."

"Sounds good to me." Beryl laughed.

"You got a look-see at his tool?" Donna said.

"Oh, yes," Beryl said. "I wonder if I could take it."

"It takes some getting used to," Donna said. "His cock is very nice."

"Yeah," Beryl said.

Art and I looked at each other.

"Let's talk business," Fred said.

"Let's," Art said.

"This past year," Fred said, "we've cleared three million in sales."

I almost choked on my champagne. Beryl did.

"You're shitting me," Art said.

"No," Fred said.

Donna smiled. "We'll make more each year."

"Porn is the backbone of e-commerce," Fred said, "and the amateur market is in a boom. A huge boom. There are dozens, hundreds of people like us making a living off pleasure. We have something many people out there want."

"Intimacy," Donna said, "and love."

"This business saved our marriage," Fred said. He drew Donna close to him. They held each other. They kissed. "We wouldn't be together now," he went on. "It added . . . excitement. It delivered us from an absolutely dull life, the same thing day after day. You know what I mean."

"I was ready to leave him," Donna said. "I wanted something more."

"We both did," Fred said.

"And we found it," Donna said.

Beryl and I looked at each other. I moved to kiss her. She kissed me. Art looked away.

"We like what you have," Donna said.

"We can get rich together," Fred said.

"I like the sound of that," Beryl said.

"Me too," I said.

Fred said, "So let's fuck and seal the deal."

We all laughed.

"Hey, buddy," Fred said to Art, "there's a camera in the house, and a light. Why don't you get it."

Art nodded and got out of the water. He looked lonely, walking away wet and naked. I can't say that I felt sorry for him.

Donna moved to me, and Beryl moved to Fred. I took Donna's large breasts in my hands and rubbed them. Her pink nipples were pointing at me. Beryl was stroking Fred's big dick and she said something like, "Oh, my." He sat on the edge of the spa, and Beryl did her best to take him in her mouth.

"You want me to suck your dick too?" Donna whispered. "What

do you want me to do? I'll do anything, anything." Art set up the camera.

Donna and I got out of the water to fuck. I had her on her back, her thick legs on my shoulders. She smelled strongly of perfume. She reached up and bit my nipple as I fucked her. Beryl was still sucking on Fred.

"Hey," Fred said, turning to me with a smile. "I think I'm about to come in your wife's mouth."

Art didn't join us. As he operated the video camera, he jerked off. He was now an observer. I could see it on his face: something was missing. He looked lonely and I didn't care.

## V. Epilogue

Our hair was still wet when we got in the car. We were electrified. The sex had been good, the idea of success even better.

I touched my wife's face.

"We don't need Art," she said.

"I was thinking the same thing."

"Our marriage will work, won't it?"

"I hope so."

"We can be as happy and wealthy as Donna and Fred."

I wanted to say that we *were* Donna and Fred. We'd just made love to our mirror images, and it was caught on tape.

I started the car.

"Turn on the heater," Beryl said. "I don't want to catch cold."

I did, and as we drove, the warmth started at our feet and moved up our bodies and to our faces. We were holding hands the whole way.

Home, our hair dry, we went into our own jacuzzi and fucked in the water and under the stars, and there was only us, and it was very nice again, for a while.

# Do What You Love

Susannah Indigo

Sitting up here on the kitchen counter with my blue plaid skirt up over my hips and my legs spread open, I watch him slice carrots for the soup. He likes me to sit here and tell him stories about my day in school. Especially about boys. When he walked in he lifted me up onto the counter without a word, pulled my panties off, spread my legs and propped my knees up. He watches my bare pussy and cooks while I talk. This may be the kinkiest Daddy I have ever had.

"Eddie Burke pulled my skirt up again after maths class, Daddy," I begin. I know he loves this, and it's a true story, just a very old one. "And then he said I was a slut because he looked at my panties and they were blue and not white. I hate him."

Daddy comes over and kisses me, stroking his fingers across my clit. This is part of what makes him so kinky, those damn fingers. I've never seen his cock in the daylight, but he drives me wild with his fingers.

"Those little boys who tease you in school don't even know what a clit is, do they, baby?" he says. His fingers are everywhere. It's his fingers and the spankings that get to me. This Daddy can spank me like nobody else can. I think it's because he makes me wait so long – always talking about what he's going to do, talking about how my ass looks when I'm over his knee, about how deep his finger is going to go up my ass if I don't hold still for him.

The only time I ever feel his cock is in the middle of the night, long after he's brushed my teeth and read me a bedtime story and dressed me in the soft pink ruffled nightgown he bought for me. Then when I'm sound asleep, I'll wake up on my belly with his weight on top of me and the nightgown raised to my waist and his lips against my ear whispering, "It's OK, baby, Daddy's here, it's OK, Daddy will make you feel better, just lift your bottom up in the air for Daddy, yes, baby," and his hard cock forces its way all at once up into my pussy and Daddy whispers and rocks his hips hard into me and I cry a little bit because I'm not ready and it hurts and that makes him fuck me harder and harder until I'm more than ready and Daddy comes hard and fast up inside of me and he falls back asleep with his full weight pressing me down into the bed, whispering, "You're such a good little girl, you're so good to your Daddy. You make your Daddy come so hard."

It really does hurt, in an intensely erotic kind of way. But he's not the Daddy that worries me.

A book got me started in this, one of the dozens of motivational ones I read back when I worked for a corporation and thought I needed it. *Do What You Love, the Money Will Follow* was the name of it and I liked that one because it told me what I wanted to hear: that you could make money having fun. I already knew what my kind of fun was – painting, feeling sexy and getting well fucked.

Money and energy underlie all our dreams, no matter what those dreams are. They said I was a good painter back in college but then real life and two babies – their father is long gone – took over my energy and priorities. I started my own graphic design business on a surge of energy, but it exhausted me trying to make ends meet.

Not long after I read that book, I found myself at a charity masquerade ball at the Black Palace Hotel. I wasn't planning on going, but my friend Cheryl dragged me there at the last minute. All I could find to wear was my high-school cheerleader outfit.

"Katie," Cheryl whispered to me over by the bar where I was spending most of my time. "See that man over there, the one with the silver hair and the black cape?" I did. "He's so toasted! You won't believe this. He pointed to you and said, 'I'd give anything to fuck that little cheerleader.' "

I turned and smiled at him. I smoothed my little green and white pleated skirt, which has the same effect on men that it had on boys in my senior year of high school.

"Tell him I have my price."

"What?"

"Ask him what it's worth." I could blame it on the wine if I had to, but I was really tired of being so straight and working so hard.

Cheryl had been drinking enough that she marched over to him without hesitation. She came back in a few minutes, laughing. "He says a thousand bucks, cash."

"You're kidding." I looked down at my tennis shoes and bobby socks. "Tell him he's on – to bring me the cash and a room key and he's in for a fantasy night."

Cheryl likes to be adventurous through other people – she works for the biggest bank in town and doesn't get around too much. "I'll check the room number, just in case I never see you again," she said.

When my pink-nightgown Daddy leaves in the morning he tucks the sheet up around my chin, kisses me chastely on the cheek, leaves the thousand dollars on my dresser and closes the door softly. That's all he wants – to tease me mercilessly all evening in my schoolgirl clothes and then fuck me hard and fast in the middle of the night. There are worse ways to earn a living.

I kept the name of my graphics business, Ariel Design, and still use the corporate identity just as though I was spending untold hours at my Mac producing work for clients to pick apart. I think of this as my Little Girl Slut business, delivering dreams to men with plenty of money and fantasies. I'm even thinking of writing one of those motivational books of my own – *The 7 Habits of Highly Effective Sluts*. I pay taxes on all of this, of course. I'm not an unethical person. I just happen to be illegal in this state.

That first night dressed as a cheerleader was wild. He treated me like a bimbo and I loved it. I was so tired of being smart all day long. He told me to keep my long dark-brown hair in the ponytail, stripped my letter-sweater off of me, and made me lay across the bed while he lifted my pleated skirt. "This," he said, "is for every girl who ever snubbed me in high school." He started to spank me with his bare hand. I had no idea how much I would like being spanked. He made me perform a cheer for him naked. The fucking afterwards was ordinary after the intensity of the spanking, but he did pay me the thousand dollars, cash.

I spent weeks afterwards sliding between feeling cheap and getting so hot I had to masturbate several times a day. I loved it, but I could never tell anyone except Cheryl about it.

I called the cheerleader-fuck man up at his office a month later and told him how much I enjoyed our evening. He told me if I really liked it he knew where I could get lots more.

My first real "trick" – such a cheap word – called me beforehand and explained what he wanted. I was nervous – I had Cheryl run a credit check on him, as though that would help. Now she does that for all my new Daddies. Running unauthorized credit checks was a walk on the wild side for her, so of course I started to kickback some of my tips her way.

"Katie," my first real Daddy said, "I want you to call me nothing but Daddy when I'm with you." That's what they all want. Daddy fantasies run deep and they're not so uncommon. My name is carefully passed around to certain men. "And I want you to wear is a little-girl dress – deep-green taffeta. Petticoats, white cotton panties, little white socks, patent leather shoes. Your hair pulled back in two white barrettes. No make-up, no nail polish. The suite's reserved – see you on Friday at seven."

It was hard to find just the right little-girl frilly dress for a size-ten woman, but I did, and as I dressed before the full-length mirror and slipped on the patent leather shoes and wiped the lipstick from my lips, I got a little scared – I actually felt like a little girl. I wanted to sit on the floor of that luxurious hotel suite and wait for my Daddy to come home and take care of me.

Which is exactly what I did. When he arrived, this man I now call my petticoat Daddy stood in front of me in his expensive suit and shining loafers and told me to stay where I was on the floor and to be a good girl and kiss his feet. Just those words made me wet. I bent over and kissed each foot slowly.

He took off his jacket and walked across the room near the full-length mirror on the wall. "Crawl to me, baby. Crawl to Daddy."

I stayed on my hands and knees and crawled to him, unable to take my eyes from his. He stood me up in front of the mirror, lifted my stiff petticoats and began to examine me. It took a long time. He pulled off my white cotton panties and told me he expected my pussy hair to be completely gone by the next time we met. He approved of the white plastic barrettes in my hair and said the size of my breasts was just perfect for little-girl clothes.

He explained that I could never wear a bra because little-girl nipples were meant to be seen at all times.

"Yes, Daddy," I said obediently.

He pushed me back down on my knees. "Unzip my pants, little girl. Daddy wants his cock down your throat."

I opened my mouth and he wrapped his fists in my hair and fucked my mouth like it had never been fucked before. I could see the image in the mirror – a little girl serving her Daddy. He stopped before he came and threw me down on my belly, lifted my petticoats, spread my legs and kneeled over me.

"Daddy wants your ass, little girl."

My first Daddy fucked me until I couldn't move that night. My mouth, my ass, my pussy, my breasts. I never got off the floor or even took the green taffeta dress off. It was covered with come when he left.

"Say 'Thank you, Daddy,' " he commanded before leaving. "And get that dress cleaned before next time."

I was torn between being glad he was leaving and begging him to stay to give me more. But I knew he'd left the thousand dollars on the table and that he was done with me for the moment.

"Thank you, Daddy," I whispered as I kissed his feet again before he walked out the door.

I looked at myself in the mirror after he left. I was a mess, but I loved what I saw. I was in business.

I had lunch with Cheryl at our usual table at the health club one day and noticed she was reading *What Colour is Your Parachute?*

"I'm pretty sure my parachute's black," I told her.

Cheryl laughed and put the book down. "How can you do it, Katie?" she asked.

"By specializing."

"No, I'm serious."

"How can I do which part?" It's a good question to ask of anyone who doubts the value of selling your body. "Which part bothers you? That it's illegal? That I'm making serious money?"

"I don't know," she admitted. "Maybe the little girl part. What if you make these guys want real little girls? You could make them perverts."

I laughed. "No, I'm pretty sure they come to me as full-blown perverts. You know what they say about the correct conjugation of the word 'kinky' – I am erotic, you are kinky, they are perverts. We're all adults, and we're certainly all consenting."

Cheryl sighed. "You can never do anything simple. Couldn't you just fuck them straight and skip the abnormal psych stuff?"

Of course not. The secret is that it turns me on as much as it does them. "I don't think my petticoat Daddy knows how to fuck straight, Cheryl. I can barely sit down after he leaves."

"Katie, I'm worried about you."

I told her not to worry. At least not about the sex I was having. But I carefully explained how she could make some extra money and help me if she wanted to – taking messages, clearing introductions. I promised not to call her my pimp on my business records – officially, she would be freelancing for me as a fact-checker.

Everything seems possible in this life. I can paint, I have time to bake cookies for my kids' classes. I can dream, I have time to hear myself think. I follow the natural rhythms of my body and stay up at night in my studio painting and sleep while my kids are at school. It takes time and space and focus to create dreams. But it's working – my paintings have started to sell, and I'm talking to the owner of a gallery about the possibility of my own show there in the spring. Henry Miller said it best – "Paint as you like and die happy." All I have to do to get the time I need is to live out my sexual fantasies.

"You know I screen some by email nowadays, Katie. Wait 'til you hear this one."

I always smile at the vision of Cheryl in her business suit and floppy bowtie sitting in front of her computer at her desk on the third floor of the bank pimping for me.

"It's a woman. I told her no, women weren't your thing, but she says she's a Daddy too."

"Really? A female Daddy?" My imagination had stretched so far since I redesigned my business that everything seemed possible.

"Yeah. And a kinky one too. Look what she sent for you."

Cheryl slid me the folder with the information. On top of the papers was a faxed photo of a Barbie doll. Except this Barbie doll was blindfolded, half-naked, and had her wrists and ankles tied together with bright pink ribbons.

"Oh my." Barbie was making me wet.

Cheryl looked at me in surprise and maybe a little bit of satisfaction. She seemed awfully interested in this woman.

"Well, you know," I finally said, wondering when my mind slid so far down between my legs, "maybe I can do it if she's a Daddy."

My Barbie doll Daddy rattled my brain from the first minute she arrived. She was tall, with black cropped hair, ruby-red lipstick and a wicked grin that said she was ready to play.

She brought me a Barbie doll. I was already wearing Barbie's pink leotard outfit per her instructions, and now here I sat with my plastic twin. "Play with the doll for me," she commanded.

I knew right away that this Daddy and I had the same kind of girlhood. While some girls were making cute little prom dresses for their Barbies, some of us were stripping her down, checking her out, making her the slut she was meant to be. Let's face it, Barbie is built to get fucked.

She tied me up with pink satin ribbons just like the doll. She stood over me and fucked with my mind and then let me go to work on her body.

"Suck Daddy's breasts," she ordered, leaning down close to my mouth. "Yes, sweetheart, yes, suck Daddy's nipples harder."

I learned something incredible that first night with my Barbie-doll Daddy. It didn't matter that I had had no experience with women. My kink has nothing to do with gender.

"Lick Daddy's pussy, baby," she said, and she was straddling me and riding my mouth and I was tasting her juices and she was hard and I was soft and she was completely in control of me and taking me down where all good Daddies take me. I was her little doll and I was serving her and she made me bring her to orgasm over and over until she finally wrapped the pink ribbons loosely around both of our bodies and we fell asleep breast to breast, her knee pressed up hard against my own untouched pussy.

The Barbie doll sits on my office shelf as a reminder. Cheryl begged me for every single detail afterwards. I gave her the high points the best I could remember. I swear she's going to ask me to videotape it all before I know it.

The only problem in my big business plan is my charm-bracelet Daddy. He came into my life six months ago. My charm-bracelet Daddy took me to the amusement park on our first night together. He held me tight on the roller coaster, ordered food for me and when we left he bought me a balloon and tied the string around my wrist. We went back to the hotel and spent the night together. There was no sex, and I just slept wrapped in his arms. It was intensely erotic. This Daddy not only rattles my brain, he rattles my heart. Nobody's been allowed to do that in so many years I'd forgotten how it could be.

In the morning he fastened the heavy silver charm bracelet around my wrist. There was just one charm – a silver ferris wheel. "I know you, Katie," he whispered softly. "You'll wear this bracelet for me, and only for me." I did.

This Daddy gets to my heart like no one ever has. His name is Jeffrey and he's a writer. I know all their names, of course, but he's the only one I think of by name, since I'm not supposed to call them anything but Daddy. He ties me to the bed and tells me stories.

Sometimes he unbuttons my blouse and ties my hands behind my back and reads to me and I close my eyes and enter the warm and loving childhood I never had. A few times he's even tied me up and talked about baseball. He says he likes the captive audience.

He tells me it's all about power. He takes my control away little by little until it's all real and it's all new and it all matters. The sex is spectacular when he gets me like that – it's like I enter another space, another realm, where only the sensual and the artistic sides of life can be seen. This Daddy knows some secrets about me that even I don't know and it scares me more every time I see him.

There are ten charms on the bracelet now. Some of them are reminders of the places we've gone to – the ferris wheel, a little sailboat, a roller skate, a Rockies baseball cap. One of the prettiest ones is a little silver and gold pair of ballet slippers, a reminder of the night he took me to the ballet and we went out dancing afterwards and he held his hands on my hips in just that way that only certain men know, making me beg him to take me home and fuck me.

The other three charms are a little more intense, from different kinds of nights when we never set foot out the door. There's a baby rattle, a miniature dildo and a baby bottle. I could never explain them to anyone. It's enough to say that I was definitely doing what I loved when he gave them to me.

He's on his way over now. He's the only Daddy I've ever let come to my house. The kids are at Cheryl's and my upstairs studio is locked up. I've put on the outfit he requested – red halter top, blue jean short shorts that show my ass if I bend over, bare feet. The charm bracelet weighs heavily on my wrist.

He brings dinner, a big bouquet of my favourite orange roses, a new Van Morrison CD and a small wrapped box. I sit on his lap to open it. His hand high and hard on my thigh makes me almost forget about presents.

I open it and it's a new charm, of course, signifying what we're going to do tonight, just as all the others have. I hold it up to the light. "It's beautiful, Daddy, thank you." A tiny silver paintbrush and palette. "It's very pretty. But I don't understand?"

Daddy kisses me like I'm his. "Take me upstairs, Katie, to your studio. It's time."

Nobody ever goes in there except close friends. "No."

Daddy finishes fastening the charm on my bracelet and wraps my legs around his waist. "Yes, baby, you're going to let me into your life tonight. From now on, no more secrets. You're mine."

Only for tonight, I feel like saying, and only for a price. This is just business.

He stands up and carries me like a child up the stairs, pausing to get the studio key. "I know what you need," he whispers.

I don't stop him. Maybe it's the weight of the charms or maybe it's just the way he's holding me with my face buried in his neck. Or maybe it's the love I forgot existed.

He carries me around my studio and looks at every single canvas, admiring them and commenting in detail. He even seems to know something about art, thank God. But not as much as I do. I like that. He stops for a long time at the painting I made of a headstone with my imaginary epitaph on it:

KATHERINE ELLIS

PAINTER
MOTHER
DANCER
LOVER

WHILE ALIVE
SHE LIVED

I don't think I can stand it – it's making me cry. I don't want this closeness, not here, not yet.

"Katie, it will all be OK. You can trust me." He lays me down on the hardwood floor and begins to make love to me softly, gently, with his tongue, with his hands, and the kisses, the kisses, the kisses that I know will never stop until they reach down into my soul and bring me all the way out for him. Daddy unties my shirt and starts in on my nipples, teasing, twisting, biting, staying there until he knows I will feel him hard on me tomorrow. I cry softly, so softly that it feels like joy and Daddy wipes my tears away with his cock. He straddles my face and caresses it with his cock, stroking my lips, my eyes, my cheeks, until I can't see anything but my Daddy.

"You belong under me, baby, always." Daddy rolls me over and lifts my skirt and enters me hard, laying his full weight flat out on top of me, pinning me to the floor, holding me down, keeping me still, giving me the force I need. When he begins to move into me, slowly at first and then harder, rolling his hips into mine, I give way to his power and I cry for my Daddy, I cry and I come and I pray that he will never stop, never release me, never let me be anywhere but here.

I fall asleep curled between his legs with his soft cock in my mouth and his hand wrapped in my hair. This Daddy knows how to hold me down, how to own me, and how to lift me back up and give me wings.

In the morning he stands before me. "I'm leaving, Katie. The money is on the dresser. But it's the last time."

Oh God, he's never coming back.

"I'll be here next Friday night, same time. I'm not anything to you any more but your Daddy. If you want to be with your Daddy, it has to be for love, not money." He pauses to give me a look that melts me back into the bed. "Do you want to keep the appointment? Do you want to move forward, Katie? I'm your Daddy. I'll take care of you."

This is not in the business plan. But taking risks is. I rise from the bed and kneel before him, nipples tingling and heart fully awake. Do what you love. Do what you love.

"Yes, Daddy, I do."

What will Cheryl think? Maybe she's ready to take over the business and find out what she loves.

# Only Connect

Lauren Henderson

It's a truism that men can only concentrate on one thing at a time. Isn't that the stereotype, that women can juggle twenty different tasks at once, running from one pole to the next, keeping the plates spinning with a few swift flicks of the wrist? Men are supposed to be the opposite: so single-minded that if they try to do more than one thing simultaneously they end up messing up both. It's a neat little theory but it completely fails to account for what Dan is doing to me right now. One hand on the wheel, the other between my legs, his eyes never leaving the road, his index and third fingers stroking me through my silky French knickers. A stereotypical man would be completely thrown by the speed bumps; but Dan, far from treating them as an obstacle, is actually using them as a choreographic motif, working his fingers round the edge of the material and into me a split-second before the front wheels hit the first bump, then remaining frustratingly still, allowing each subsequent bump to drive his fingers a little deeper into me, like a wedge, so that I find myself grinding my hips in anticipation as we reach the next one, barely able to wait. Dan starts rubbing the heel of his hand against me, his fingers still inside me. The seam of my knickers, caught between us, chafes against me so successfully that it might have been specially designed for the purpose. I am moaning. Dan is still looking straight ahead – it's pretty much a point of honour – but his lips are curved into the smuggest smile I have ever seen on a man.

I'm the one here who can't concentrate on anything else. It doesn't occur to me for a moment to reach over and stroke Dan through his jeans, slip my fingers between his waistband and belly, rub my thumb down the coarse hairy line of skin to the hot, smooth, slightly damp and swollen-to-bursting head below. I am totally selfish when I'm being fingered, incapable of doing anything but lying back and letting out a crescendo of what I hope are highly encouraging moans.

To be fair to me, I am just the same when I'm going down on someone; I don't want any interruptions, no matter how well meant. I like to give my full attention to the task in hand.

By the time we reach my flat I have come once and am looking almost as smug as Dan. Not quite, though. Dan's one of those strong silent types who loves nothing more – not even football – than seeing me go completely out of control. He gets excited too, of course, but only once he's already reduced me to a babbling, jelly-legged sex object with glazed eyes and rising damp.

Which is fine with me. Every relationship has its patterns and if Dan insists on making me come repeatedly before even so much as unzipping his trousers, who am I to complain? Early on, in the interests of balance as well as for my own enjoyment, I tried to buck this trend, but Dan just removed my hands, threw me over the sofa and slid his thumb into me as if he were testing me for ripeness, and I promptly forgot about everything else.

I manage to get out of the car without falling over, though my legs are so weak by now this is more of an achievement than it sounds. We walk decorously, which is to say without touching, up the steps to my front door and I am just pulling out my keys when Dan sits down on the stone wall that borders the flight of steps. He's just waiting for me to get the door open, but I look at him, his eyes meet mine, and I can't manage a moment longer without being in physical contact with him; dropping the keys back into my pocket I climb onto his lap, my bottom on his thighs, my feet on the wall for balance, and start kissing him. It's a dark night and as usual half of the street lights are out, or at best flickering spasmodically. And the steps are high off the street, at first-floor level. We're in the shadows, a couple of closely entwined shapes, no more. What we're actually doing would be visible only to someone with night-vision goggles and a good vantage point. I hope.

Because by now Dan has what feels like his entire hand up me and is fucking me with it in slow steady strokes, fucking me actually better than he does with his cock, which is a curiosity I've noticed before but never really have much time to dwell on because my brain is pretty much fully occupied with other things, foremost of which right now is doing my best not to scream. I have what feels like my entire fist crammed into my mouth and am biting down on the knuckles in pursuit of this good-neighbourly goal, an arrangement which is amusing Dan tremendously. His hand is almost hurting me, slamming into me like a pile-driver, but I couldn't bear him to stop.

I lean fully into his other hand, on my back, balancing me, supporting me so I can take the full force of what his other hand is doing to me without falling off the wall. God, this is good. There are so few moments in life of absolute transcendence. Or maybe that's an over-elevated way of putting it. I cannot think about anything else right now, anything at all; disconnected thoughts rush through my brain, gone almost before I've registered them, so fleeting that they come only to remind me that there is something outside this intense sensation, to stop me losing myself to it so completely that I can never find my way back.

Dan gives a particularly frenzied thrust into me which definitely emphasizes the pain aspect over the pleasure. He's losing control. We have to get inside my flat. We have to have sex. We are having sex, of course, but I mean something more specific by that. I grab Dan's wrist as he pulls back for another grind into me, though I'm whimpering with frustration at making him stop, even for a moment. With a near-heroic effort of will I drag out my keys and get the door open. We manoeuvre past the ground-floor neighbour's damned bicycles – why was I trying not to make any noise outside? I should have wailed like a siren and woken the bastards up, the amount of times I've ripped my tights on their bicycle spokes. Stumbling past the second one I reach the stairs and hold out a hand for Dan, who is momentarily snagged on a handlebar. He drags himself free, grabs my hand and trips over a pedal, all at once, landing on the steps with a stumble that could send us both off-balance.

In that moment our eyes meet. We could recover; I could grab the newel post and brace myself against Dan's fall; but I don't. We don't. I let myself tumble back onto the stairs – which are carpeted, I'm not that much of a masochist – and Dan's weight comes down on top of me like the one thing I've been craving all my life. As soon as he lands we are scrabbling at each other's clothes, grinding into each other, every bit of our bodies that can wrap around the other's doing so as if for dear life; feet, knees, hands all desperate for as much contact as we can possibly manage. It must look anatomically impossible. I have a flash of intense frustration that I'm not completely double-jointed.

My skirt's around my waist, my knickers are down, Dan's unzipping himself – ah, that sound, that wonderful anticipatory sound, like a trumpet fanfare before the entrance of the key player on the scene – and two seconds later he has jammed himself up into me and we're fucking on the stairs. The relief is almost unbearable. I mean, I love everything else, all the preliminaries and the flourishes and the fanfares; I come much more thoroughly and repeatedly before the actual act of fucking than I ever do during it; but by God there is absolutely nothing like it. My eyes roll back, my hips tilt up so that Dan can get his hands under them, my feet lock round the back of his calves, I am bracing my hands clumsily against the wall and the stair riser, and we're fucking, thank God, I thought I would die if we didn't manage to fuck at this precise moment, not a second later, I thought I would actually explode.

Dan never lasts that long, which is maybe why he dedicates so much time to all the other variations before the main theme. I can scarcely complain; he's already reduced me to a boneless sex-craving wreck, dripping with moisture – how unattractive that sounds, though it's exactly what I feel like – and now he's taking a much briefer pleasure than mine. His hip bones grind into my inner thighs, his fingers bite into my bottom and with an arch of his back and a split-second pause he sinks into me one last time, his lips curled back from his teeth in that sneer he always makes when he comes, his eyes almost closed, the slits of white glinting as eerily as if he were having a fit. He collapses on top of me. That's good too. I love the weight, and Dan isn't too big, not a great slab of meat trying to crush me out of existence. Besides, he's completely absorbed in his own sensations, overcome by them; even as I take the full weight of his body, his entire focus is on the spasms of his cock, me beneath him a collection of body parts, the woman he loves to fuck, nothing more. I hope. Otherwise I'd feel as suffocated as if he were twenty stone of loose rolls of fat.

His cock gives a couple of convulsive twitches inside me, last moments of past glory, and then everything subsides and suddenly we can hear our breathing, which is as frenzied as if we had just done a three-mile sprint. I'm always reluctant to move, even if right now the stair riser is biting into my back as painfully as if I just had sex up against an iron joist. I like to lie here, feeling the cock slowly shrink and curl up inside me before slipping out wistfully, stickily, a sad little aftermath of what was once such a proud trophy. No wonder it was a man who invented existentialism. Think of the mood swings: how important it must be to them to live in the moment. A limp, post-orgasmic cock always provokes great tenderness in me – well, if it's just done its job to my satisfaction – but one quickly learns not to use the words "sweet" or "cute" about a cock, even if you have just demonstrated how much you like getting fucked by it, tucks it away immediately, almost always insists on wearing briefs in bed. I gave up trying to understand men a long time ago. Now I just go with what seems to work. It's so much easier.

Dan braces himself against the stairs and lifts himself off me. As always, the removal of his weight is sad, but immediately makes me stretch my limbs, as if to test their new freedom of movement. He hauls me to my feet. One thought has been running through my mind for the last ten minutes, almost as soon as Dan's cock slid into me; I don't want him to stay the night. This is perfect just as it is. If he even comes into my flat it will be ruined. Tactics have been running through my brain. If I were really brazen I would just wish him goodnight firmly and continue upstairs, but I can't quite manage that.

"God, I'm exhausted," I say. "You've worn me out."

"Yeah?" He smirks, bless him.

"I'm just going to pass out. I'm shattered."

I try to look regretful, intimating that I would love to ask him in but have already been so overcome by his prowess as a lover that any further bout tonight would severely damage my immune-deficiency system. This is of course a total lie – it's Dan who couldn't manage another bout; once at night, once, if I'm lucky, in the morning is his limit. But it works perfectly.

"You'd better get some rest, then," he says, smugger than ever. "I'll see you round."

We kiss. He goes, climbing uncomfortably through the massed ranks of mountain bikes to the door. I sigh in relief and head upstairs. I don't even mind the fact that I live on the fifth floor. It's more distance between me and Dan.

My best friend David says that men adore being treated like sex objects and I should stop being concerned about this kind of thing with Dan. "Just pay him lots of compliments about the sex and he'll be fine," David assured me. I don't agree. I remember all too well the guy in college with whom I was supposed to be having a sex-only relationship who agreed eagerly the first night and then never wanted to have sex with me again. Moreover he became very bitter towards me, especially when I started going out with someone. I think this is a much truer reflection of the male psyche. Men think they want sex only, but they are only comfortable with this set-up when they're the ones after sex while the women want something more. As soon as you make it clear that you too just want to fuck their brains out on a regular basis but not have to talk to them about their families in the interim periods, they're off faster than a speeding bullet.

My body is exhausted, quite literally – temporarily worn out, used and satisfied – but my brain is buzzing. It's partly frustration; it didn't get used much this evening. Dan insists on us going out to dinner every so often. I much prefer a film, a drink, and a swift journey to my flat, as this limits the conversational necessities as much as possible. But despite the fact that we obviously have very little in common and any occasion in which we try to talk for more than ten minutes is full of laboured questions and terrible pauses, Dan still keeps suggesting dinner. God knows why. It's another reason I part company with David. Dan's constant wish to go out to dinner with me can only be explained as a need to enact what he sees as being the tableaux of a conventional relationship, the other things men and women do together apart from fucking on staircases, as if you have to have the one to be able to do the other. I plead my way out of the dinner dates as much as I can but sometimes he just won't take no for an answer. Tonight was as awful as ever. It never gets any better.

I look at my watch. Midnight. Perfect. Plenty of time for a long, hot soak in the bath. I wish now that I had made the appointment for 1.00, instead of 2.00: I thought it would be too early. But Dan and I have managed to satisfactorily conclude the evening's business in much less time than I had projected. How efficient we're getting. I have a long bath, make myself some coffee, pour myself a drink, and by 1.40 I'm wrapped in a big towel, wafting aromatic bath oil every time I move, logged on, in the chat room, waiting for my second date of the evening.

I know it's stupid, but there are butterflies in my stomach as I sit there waiting for him. I know it's stupid because he'll be there; he always is. And sure enough, at 1.56 it scrolls across the screen:

trollfan 1234>: Hi! So did you finish it?

and a lovely wave of relief and happiness floods through me and I type:

lola666>sure. Disappointed though.

trollfan1234>?

lola666>it's all just the same plot isn't it? Rich boy falls in love with poor girl/waits it out for a year or so to prove he means it/finally the family agrees. Only this time it turns out she's rich after all so it's OK. And there isn't even any tension, we know from the beginning that she's the only relative of the rich old man so when he finds that out he'll leave her all the money.

trollfan1234>OK, agreed, it's not his strongest book

lola666>Trollope should at least have made it more of a mystery, but we know that they'll get together ANYWAY so it still wouldn't have helped much.

trollfan1234> but isn't there satisfaction watching the pattern work itself out?

lola666>get more of that out of an Agatha Christle I've read 100 times.

trollfan1234>Hmmn.

lola666>he should have fallen for someone else while he was away all that time, create a hit of tension that way.

trollfan1234>Trollope does that sometimes.

lola666>but you know it'll never happen, like Phineas/Madame Goetz or John & Madeleine, the women they fall in love with in big cities are always adventuresses, then they come home to the nice girl without flashy looks, Trollope really cliched old-fashioned romantic author, why does he have an intellectual reputation I really don't have much to say about this book AT ALL sorry

trollfan1234>don't get started on the Joanna T v. Anthony T thing again

lola666>but it's true I really think J Trollope much more sophisticated in view of human nature, at least she sees it as protean, endlessly changeable, AT thinks everyone's personalities carved in stone

trollfan1234>do people really change that much?

lola666>oh yes I think so

trollfan1234>OK we may change opinions whatever but do our ACTIONS really change that much

lola666>Hmmn interesting maybe after lots of therapy.

trollfan1234>haha

lola666>Pallisers are better

trollfan1234>well OK devil's advocate: who really changes in the Pallisers?

lola666>Hmmn I like Maud not being able to make up her mind until too late

trollfan1234>yeah but it's the right thing she didn't really love him

lola666>but she'll never meet anyone else she's too old by their standards anyway! she would have been happy with Silverbridge.

trollfan1234>do you think so

lola666>or at least content, yeah, she'd have been a duchess and he was v attractive

trollfan1234>funny youre arguing the way a man's supposed to & Im more romantic (like a woman) don't think Maud would have been happy

lola666>what about Lily Dale

trollfan1234>John made big mistake, he was always there like a dog, should have tried to disappear/make her jealous

lola666>so she didn't see him like the perpetual little boy

trollfan1234>exactly, women hate men slobbering over their feet lola666>dyou speak from experience.

trollfan1234>never slobbered! teenage years had mad crushes on girls, made it too obvious, never got them, cooler now I hope

lola666>you're right about John/Lily he really needed to go away for a long time & come back as a man – you know what I mean by that, not being sexist (he should have been masterful, etc)

trollfan1234>no its fine we agreed that we completely understand each other male/female stuff dont worry about that OK?

lola666>great! forgot!

trollfan1234>interesting we always come back to discussing relationships in AT

lola666>well I was thinking about that (am I being stereotypical woman always talking about LOVE) but youre a man allegedly

trollfan1234>yes, am looking at proof of that right now

lola666>not literally I hope

trollfan1234>no, wearing boxers

lola666>anyway I worked that out. AT's political dilemmas not half as interesting as emotional ones/politics used really only to present moral choices (will X do right thing) as are emotional ones (will he marry nice girl at home)

trollfan1234>bit unfair, Maud has hard moral choice too.

lola666>OK, true, and Madame Goetz

trollfan 1234>God yeah, lots of them, and she gets rewarded in the end

lola666>nice idea the older/more sophisticated you get the more interesting the choices trollfan1234>obviously I'm not old/sophisticated enough yet

lola666>me neither mine are always brutally obvious

trollfan1234>??? example

lola666>no, no personal stuff we agreed

trollfan1234>?

lola666>

trollfan1234>after all, we're analysing other relationships all the time, we're not talking in traditional litcrit terms

lola666>relationships in BOOKS

trollfan1234>pretend it's a story

lola666>no.

trollfan1234>sigh

lola666>

trollfan1234>OK, enough of AT, pick another author?

lola666>I know we just finished Barchester but there must be others

trollfan1234>Minor, would annoy you even more

lola666>OK well let's do Dickens then

trollfan1234>

lola666>what?

trollfan1234>Dickens takes v long time to read, we wouldn't talk for weeks lola666>flattered

trollfan1234>well I like talking to you

lola666>me too

trollfan1234>pick short books!!!

lola666>we could do Dickens but split up the books/discuss them every 10th chapter?

trollfan1234>Great idea they're written as serials after all

lola666>shall we do it chronologically?

trollfan1234>no one's ever asked me that before!

lola666>funny

trollfan1234>let's start with David Copperfield I've always meant to read that

lola666>OK I'll go to the library

trollfan1234>lovely library books with hard plastic covers you can read in the bath

lola666>and that dirty, musty smell

trollfan1234>I thought you said no personal stuff

lola666>funny. Not.

trollfan1234>when's good for you next time?

lola666>Monday? 1.00?

trollfan1234>five days . . . do I have time . . .

lola666>thought you were the one complaining about not meeting for ages trollfan1234>OK you talked me into it. I may be a bit behind

lola666>do your best

trollfan1234>yes ma'am

lola666>see you on Monday

trollfan1234>I wish!

lola666>TALK to you Monday

trollfan1234>sigh

lola666>I'm very disappointing you know

trollfan1234> me too we could be disappointing together.

lola666>

trollfan1234>OK, I know, I know. Want me to talk about the weather?

lola666>will it be interesting?

trollfan1234>actually no, I never know what the weather's like, I have no idea what's happening outside right now. I'm on the 8th floor, I have double glazing and my windows aren't that clean because the landlord's lazy about getting that done, also they have these catches which slip and slam back down on your hands so I'm nervous about opening them . . . sometimes I don't even know if it's raining. I'll go out into the street and feel like an idiot.

lola666>happens to me too, most of my windows are stuck, the only one I can put my head out of is the bathroom and it looks onto an air shaft. And I have five floors/no lift, it's a nightmare working out *what coat to wear in the morning.*

trollfan1234>my offices are airconditioned, windows can't open, etc, even more insulated. Once I was working late &

there was a hurricane & I didn't even realize, got out onto the dark street and it was covered with broken glass and people with cardboard patching up their windows. Ours were fine, we're all triple-strength glass etc. More insulation. Shows how detached we are from the world.

lola666>my offices are like that too

trollfan1234>so we end up talking to each other through computers – down a modem line and bounced off a server to end up God knows where – insulation again.

lola666>that was a very neat connection

trollfan1234>thanks. I was quite impressed with it myself

lola666>have to go now

trollfan1234>OK, till Monday

lola666>bye

trollfan1234>bye

I turn off the computer and get into my pyjamas: flannel, huge, the kind of thing you can only wear when you sleep alone. A shot of whisky, to take to bed with me. And the nagging annoyance: why must he always push for more? Why does he keep asking to meet me? Can't he see that the whole point of this is this perfect, focused connection? Meeting would ruin everything. It's not that we might find each other unattractive; just the opposite. What if we did? It would ruin everything. I have everything in balance just the way I want it and I'm not going to mess with that. It's working. I'm happy. I take half a sleeping pill and wash it down with a gulp of whisky. Library tomorrow. Lovely. I'm happy. I really am.

# Bottomless on Bourbon

Maxim Jakubowski

He had often promised to take Kathryn to New Orleans.

But it had never happened. They had spectacularly fallen apart long before the opportunity arose. In fact, the travel they had managed to do in between feverish fucks had proven rather prosaic. So much for promises. They hadn't even visited Paris, Amsterdam or New York either.

So, whenever he could, he now took other women to the Crescent City.

For sex.

And fantasized about Kathryn's face, and eyes, and pale breasts, and cunt and more.

New Orleans was for him a city with two faces. Almost two different places, the aristocratic and slightly dishevelled languor of the Garden District on one hand and the hustle and bustle of the French Quarter on the other, contrasting like night and day. The touristic charms concealing darker, ever so venomous charms. The heavy placid flow of the Mississippi River zigzagging in serpentine manner through the opposing twin shores of Jackson Square and Algiers. The gently alcoholic haze of New Orleans days and the enticing, dangerous attraction of fragrant New Orleans nights. Nights that smelled and tasted of sex.

He loved to see the women sweat as he made love to them, enjoyed the feel of bodies sliding against each other in moist, clammy embraces as sheets tangled around them. He took unerring voyeuristic pleasure in watching them shower after, washing his seed away from their openings, cleaning away his bites, the saliva that still coated their nipples, neck or ear lobes which he had assaulted with military-like amorous precision.

Those were all memories he treasured. Stored away for all eternity in his mental bank vaults. The curve of a back, the soft blonde down slowly being submerged in a small pool of perspiration just inches away from her rump, highlighted by a solitary light bulb, as she kneeled on all fours on the bed and he breached the final defences of her sphincter and impaled himself in her bowels. The sound of a moan, of pleasure, of joy. Ohhh . . . AAAAHHH . . . Chriiiiiist . . . The tremor that coursed through the girl's taut body as he discharged inside her or she rode the ocean waves of her oncoming orgasm.

Yes, New Orelans, his city of sex.

Endless walks through the small streets between hotel room episodes. Invigorating breakfasts of beignets and coffee and ice-cold orange juice at the Café du Monde; oysters and thick, syrupy gumbo at The Pearl off Canal Street; loitering hand in hand in the markets full of the smell of spices and seafood, chewing on garlic-flavoured pistachio nuts; obscene mounds of boiled crawfish at Lemoyne's Landing; hunting for vintage paperbacks through the dusty shelves at Beckham's; po'boys at the Napoleon House; zydeco rhythms at the House of Blues; a routine he could live on for days on end. Until he would tire of the woman, because she bored him once past the mechanics of fornication, never said the right thing or talked too much or simply because she wasn't the woman he really wanted to be with in New Orleans.

There had been Lisa, the software executive, Clare, a lawyer who looked like Anne Frank had she ever grown up and liked to be handled roughly, Pamela Jane, the investment banker he had met at the hotel bar who wanted to be a writer and Helene the biology teacher from Montreal. He didn't feel he was being promiscuous: four women in six years since Kathryn. Some he had found here, others he had brought.

But somehow none had fitted in with this strange city and, even though the sex had been loose and fun, and the company never less than pleasant, there had been something lacking. Even at midnight, buckling under his thrusts on bed or floor or sucking him off under the water streams of the shower, he knew they were creatures of the day, anonymous, predictable; they had no touch of night, no share of darkness. And the darkness was what he sought. In women. In New Orleans. What he knew he had once detected under Kathryn's fulsome exterior.

He had high hopes for Susi.

She was Austrian, in her late twenties, and worked in a managerial capacity for a travel agency in Vienna, which made it easier (and cheaper) for her to jump on a plane for purposes of pleasure.

They had met in New York some months earlier. It was spring and the weather was appalling for the season. The rain poured down in buckets and all Manhattan was gridlocked like only New York can manage. He'd been in town promoting a book and negotiating the next contract with his publishers there (he never used an agent) and was booked on an evening flight back to London. He'd been staying, as usual, at a hotel down by the Village, off Washington Square. He had booked a car to JFK and it was already half an hour late. They had checked at reception and found out that the driver was still blocked in traffic near Central Square and Columbus Circle. He had promptly cancelled the car and rushed with his suitcase to the hotel's front steps to hail a yellow cab. They were few and far between, and he wasn't the only hotel guest heading for the airport. Both he and the tall, slim red-headed woman went for the same cab which declined the airport ride pretexting the conditions. They agreed to share the next cab to come along. She was even later than him, as her flight preceded his by twenty minutes.

"My name is Susanne, but my friends call me Susi with an i," she had introduced herself as the driver made his slow way towards the Midtown Tunnel.

Despite clever shortcuts through Queens, the journey took well over an hour and a quarter, so they had much opportunity to talk as they inched towards their planes. She had been in town for a week, visiting her parents who both worked as diplomats for one of the big international organizations.

She did miss her flight, while he caught his with a few minutes to spare. Email addresses were exchanged, and they had remained in touch since.

They had quickly become intimate. He'd sent her one of his books, and she had remarked on the sexual nature of many of his stories and confessed to some of her own sexual quirks. She was an exhibitionist. Would sometimes take the subway back in Vienna dressed in a particularly short skirt and without underwear and allow men to spy on her genitals. She was shaven, so they had a full view of her naked mound. She was also in the habit of masturbating in parks, where she could be seen by passers-by, actually encouraged voyeurs to do so and knew that, sometimes, men were jerking off watching her just a few metres away.

She would pretend her name was Lolita. He asked her why.

Because she had little in the way of breasts and her bare pubis evoked a child or a doll, she answered. She was submissive by nature, she told him.

She sent him a series of photographs taken by an ex-boyfriend she had broken up with shortly before the New York trip. He found them wonderfully provocative in a tender sort of way. In the first, her long, skinny frame stood in contrast to the sluttish, traditional black lingerie of embroidered knickers, suspender belt and stockings almost a size too big for her. Yes, she had no breasts, barely a hillock worth of elevation and no cleavage and, he imagined (the photographs were all black and white), pale-pink nipples like a gentle stain in the landscape of her flesh. Her hair was a bit longer than when she had been in New York, her eyes dead to the world. In the second photograph – he could guess the sequence they had been taken in, pruriently imagined what the boyfriend in question had made her do, perform, submit to, after the camera had been set aside – she was now squatting only clad in suspender belt and stockings, her cunt in sharp focus, lips ever so ready to open, her head thrown back so you could barely recognize her features. Photograph number three saw her spreadeagled over a Persian carpet and parquet floor, one arm in the air, both legs straight, holding herself up by one arm, like a gymnast, her face in profile, a most elegant and beautiful vision of nudity with no hint of obscenity at all, her body like a fine-tuned machine, a sculpture. In the fourth, she was standing and the photographer had shot away from crotch level and her body was deformed like in a hall of mirrors by the skewed perspective, the focus on her enlarged midriff. The one thing that struck him as he kept on examining the photos on his laptop screen was how her sex lips didn't part and how he wished to see inside her. The final photograph she had sent him (were there more? more explicit or extreme? she answered that others were just out of focus but his imagination as ever played wildly on) was both the sexiest and the most vulgar. She was on all fours, her arse raised towards the camera in a fuck-me pose, long legs bent, rear a bit bony, the line of her cunt lips straight as a ruler and continued by her arse crack and darker hole. Every time he looked at this one, he couldn't help getting hard. And he knew that she enjoyed knowing that.

He told her about the delights of New Orleans and invited her to join him there one day.

To explore possibilities, he said.

Initially, she only said maybe.

But he persisted, courting her with a modicum of elegance, and she agreed. It took a couple of months to find a week when both could free themselves from previous commitments (ah, the sheer logistics of lust!) and arrangements were made. Flights to New York were coordinated – her job came in useful – and they both arrived in Newark an hour or so apart.

Curiously enough, there are no direct flights between New York and New Orleans and their connection went via Raleigh-Durham.

As they emerged from the airport luggage area, Susi smelled the heat that now surrounded them like a blanket and turned towards him, kissed him gently on the cheek and said, "I just know I'm going to like it here . . . Thanks ever so much for bringing me."

By the time the taxi dropped them off at the small hotel he had booked on Burgundy it was already dark.

It was summer. Moist, no wind from the Gulf, the air heavy with the powers of the night, the remains of the day lingering in patchy clouds; they were both sweating, their bodies not yet acclimatized.

They dropped their bags, and he switched the air conditioning a notch higher and suggested a shower.

He undressed her. Now she was no longer black and white. The nipples were a darker pink, closer to red than he expected and darkened a shade further when he kissed them. Her pale body was like porcelain. Long, thin, exquisitely supple. Since Kathryn, none of the other women, here or elsewhere, had been anywhere as tall.

He escorted Susi to the shower cubicle and switched the water on. She looked at his cock, growing slowly at the sheer sight of her nudity. He soaped her with infinite delicacy and tenderness and explored her body under guise of washing, refreshing her from the transatlantic journey and its grime and tiredness. He fell to his knees and wiped the suds away from her crotch. Her gash red against the mottled pinkness of her pubic mound. She hadn't shaved there for a week or so; they had agreed she would let him shave her clean. A delight he had long fantasized about. He parted her thin lips, like opening a rare flower and darted his tongue inside to taste her. Susi shuddered.

The first time was good.

They were shy, affectionate, slow, tentative, testing pleasure points and limits with great delicacy.

She was extremely self-conscious of her lack of opulence breast-wise and he lavished particular care on her there, sucking, licking, nibbling, fingering her with casual precision until he caught the precise pulse of her pleasure behind the gentle swell of her darkening nipples.

They came closely together. Silently.

* * *

The later days filled quickly between wet embraces and ever-more feverish fucks as they grew used to each other's quirks and secret desires. She had always wanted to take a riverboat down the Mississippi and they spent a day doing so, passing the Civil War mansions and lawns and observing the rare crocodiles still lingering in the musty bayous. Just like tourists. Which they were. Sexual tourists with, so far, no taste for the local fare. Breezing down Magazine Street in mid-afternoon as the antique shops reopened for business. Taking a tram to the Garden District. Lingering, with verbose guides, in the atmospheric cemeteries, with their ornate crypts and walls of bones. Visiting the voodoo museum, trying to repress their unceremonious giggles. He covertly fingering signed first editions at the Faulkner House.

Susi never wore a bra – she had no need for one – and neither did she slip knickers on when they would go out walking. Long, flowing, thin skirts revealing the shape of her legs when she faced the sun, only he knowing how unfettered her cunt lips were beneath the fabric, sometimes even imagining he could smell her inner fragrance as they walked along hand in hand and conjuring up the thoughts of other, lubricious men passing by had they known of her naked vulnerability. It turned him on, this constant availability of hers, this exhibitionistic desire to provoke. Walking along Decatur, passing one of the horse-drawn carriages waiting there for tourists, a dog held in a leash by a small black child wagged a tail frenetically and brushed against Susi's leg. He smiled. She asked him why.

"He could smell your cunt," he said.

"Do you think so?" she remarked, her eyes all wide.

"Yes," he told her. "You smell of sex. Strongly."

Her face went all red, approximating the shade of her short bob, and he watched the flush spread to her chest and beneath the thin silk blouse.

"It turned him on," he said.

"Oh . . ."

"And me, knowing how naked you are under those thin, light clothes," he added.

She smiled.

Later, back in their hotel room, she insisted they keep the curtains open when they made love, knowing any passing maid or room-service staff might see them in the throws of sex as they walked past on the steps outside the window and, as he moved frantically inside her, he saw she kept her eyes open, was actually hoping they would be seen. The idea excited her.

The same night, a few blocks before Bourbon, she suddenly said, "I have to pee."

They'd only left the hotel a hundred yards or so ago, so she must have known the need would arise. He offered to go back to the room.

"No," she said. "The side street there. That will do."

It was dark, no one around, although the risk of passers-by emerging off Toulouse was likely.

Susi pulled her long skirt upwards and bunched it around her waist, her thin, unending legs bursting into pale view, the plumpness of her cunt in full display under the light from the illuminated wrought-iron balcony above them, and squatted down. He watched, hypnotized, as the hot stream of urine burst through her labia and splashed onto the New Orleans pavement. Her eyes darted towards the main street, begging for someone to come by. None did. Her bladder empty, she rose to her feet, the skirt still held above her waist in insolent provocation.

"It's a bit wet," she said to him. "Would you dry me?"

He got down on his knees, wiped her cunt lips clean with the back of his hand then impulsively licked her briefly. Her clit was hard, swollen. Susi was in heat.

"Fuck me here," she asked him. "I don't mind if people see us."

"I can't," he said. "We've only just got out of bed. I don't think I could get hard enough again so quickly."

Susi glanced at him with disapproval.

She dropped the folds of her dress.

They began talking.

"Does it turn you on?"

"Yes."

"What is it? A feeling of control over people, men, that they can see you but not touch?"

"I don't know," Susi remarked. "My body is nothing special, but I love to show myself. Gives me meaning. It's a bit confusing."

"Your body's great. You shouldn't underestimate yourself," he answered. "But you must be careful. On the nude beach outside Vienna, with your girlfriend along, there's an element of safety, but elsewhere it could be risky, you know."

"Yes."

"Some people could read other things in your need to exhibit yourself. You could get yourself raped."

"I know," Susi answered, with a slight sigh in her voice. "Sometimes, I even imagine what it would be like. Several men."

"Really?"

"Yes. Five of them. First they fuck my every hole, then I am made to kneel, still naked, at their feet and they all jerk off and come in my face and hair."

"A bit extreme . . ."

"I know . . ."

He tried to lighten the mood. Already anxious as the darkness neared. "The ultimate facial treatment. Better than soap!"

Susi laughed and led the way back towards Bourbon Street.

He described how Bourbon Street would be when Mardi Gras came. The noise, the coloured beads, the floats, the beer, the wonderfully hedonistic atmosphere that gripped the whole French Quarter, the fever that rose insidiously as the alcohol loosened inhibitions and the music from the bars of either side of the street grew in loudness, competing rhythms criss-crossing on every corner, clouding minds and bodies.

How the revellers on the balconies would bait the walkers below, sprinkling them with drink, offering beads for the flash of a nipple or a quickly bared backside to massive roars of approval from the wild crowds.

He could see Susi's eyes light up. Yes, she would enjoy Carnival here. No longer requiring an excuse to bare her parts to one and all and the more the merrier.

"And what happens behind doors?" she asked him.

He shuddered to think. He'd only ever stayed in New Orleans for the first night of Mardi Gras. Had heard mad rumours of uncontrollable excess, of sex in the streets. He'd once come across a range of video cassettes in a 7th Avenue porn joint in New York documenting the sexual side of Mardi Gras here year after year. But like with wine, he was unaware which were the good years or the bad years and had never sampled any of the cassettes in question.

His mind raced forward. To a clandestine video cassette in a white box and Polaroid cover shot of Susi's porcelain-white body, face covered with come, labelled SUSANNE "LOLITA" WIEN, MARDI GRAS 1999. A vintage performance, no doubt.

Bourbon Street night deepened as the beer flowed ever more freely, spilling into the gutters from plastic cups being carried up and down the street by the Saturday night revellers. The music surging from all around grew louder, the lights more aggressive and the crowds swayed uncertainly. Young kids tapped away for a few cents or break-danced outside the bars, the neon signs of the strip clubs entered battle, pitting male strippers against female ones, topless joints against bottomless ones. A row of mechanical legs danced a cancan from the top of a bar window, advertising further displays of flesh inside.

Susi was curious. "I've never been to a striptease place before. Can we?"

"Why not?" he acquiesced.

They entered the dark bar. A woman down to a shining lamé bikini was dancing around a metal pole at its centre. A few men sat by the stage desultorily sipping from half-empty glasses. They ordered their drinks from a sultry waitress and watched the stripper shed her bra with a brief flourish. The performance was uninspiring and the most exciting thing about the dancer for him was her gold navel ring which shimmied in the fluctuating light. His mind went walkabout as he tried to recognize the rock and roll tune she was, badly, dancing to.

Several shimmies and swirls later, and a liberal shake of silicon-enhanced mammaries exposed, the song (some country and western standard given an electric and gloom Americana twist) came to an end and the stripper quickly bowed, picking up a few stray dollar notes thrown onto the stage by the isolated punters on her way off.

"Is that all?" Susi turned to him asking.

"I think so," he said.

"But it's not even bottomless. She didn't even show her cunt!"

"Maybe because it's a bar. I don't know," he said, 'there must be some local by-laws or something. Don't know much about the rules in American strip clubs," he continued, surprised by Susi's interest.

Another stripper, black, stocky, took to the stage and a soul number burst out of the speakers. The previous performer was on the other side of the dance area, soliciting tips from some of the men. One whispered in her ear as she accosted him. She nodded. The man rose and he followed the woman, who now wore a dressing gown, to a darker corner at the far end of the bar. Susi nudged him and they both peered in that direction.

They could just about see the stripper throw back her gown and squat over the lap of the man who had now seated himself.

"A private dance," he said to Susi.

"Wow! Cool!" she said, one of the more irritating mannerisms he had picked up on when they chatted online back in Europe.

There wasn't much to see. The stripper moved in silence. The man appeared to keep his hands to himself, but the darkness engulfed the couple.

"I'm turned on," Susi said in his ear.

"Really?" he said, finding the atmosphere in the bar quite unerotic, the black stripper now strutting her square rump a few feet away from his face.

"Yes," Susi added. "I don't think I'd make a good stripper. No tits, as you well know. But I sure could lap or table dance. I'd like to do that for you . . ."

He grinned.

"Sure. Later in our hotel room, I'll look forward to your demonstration."

"No. Here," Susi said, a deep tone of excitement in her voice.

"Here?" he queried.

"Yes." He could see that her right hand was buried in the folds of her dress, that she was fingering herself through the material. "Can you arrange it? Please. See the guy at the bar, he appears to be in charge. Get him to agree. Please pretty please?"

He shrugged.

It cost him fifty bucks and some haggling.

He walked back towards the stage where Susi was downing the rest of her Jack Daniel's.

He nodded. "It's yes," he said.

She rose, a mischievous glint in her eye. She took him by the hand and led him to a chair, nowhere near the darkness that offered shelter further down the bar but in full view of all. She pointed a finger, indicating he should sit down, which he did. Sensing what was to happen now, the bar attendant stationed himself at the door to Bourbon Street to prevent further spectators and a possible loss of his licence. Susi camped herself facing the chair he now sat on and pulled her dress above her head. You could hear a pin drop as the barman and the few spectators dotted around the stage witnessed her naked form emerge from the cocoon of the fabric, whiter than white, shaven mound plump, and so bare, like a magnet for their disbelieving eyes. A couple of the attendant strippers peered out from the dressing room on the side of the bar counter.

The music began and he had no clue what it was, his mind in such turmoil.

Susi began writhing a few inches away from him, knowing all too well how much she was the centre of attraction.

She danced, wriggled, swerved, bent, squatted, obscenely, indecently, her hands moving across her bare flesh in a snakelike manner, her fingers grazing her, by now, erect nipples, descending across the flatness of her pale stomach and even, although he hoped he was the only one to notice, lingering in the region of her cunt and actually holding her lips open for a second or so.

He felt hot. Even though he by now knew every square inch of her skin, this was a new Susi, a creature he had only guessed at.

It was quickly over.

He held his breath.

A few people clapped in the background.

Susi's face was impassive but flushed.

She picked up her discarded dress and slipped into it. "That was good," she said. "Can we go, now?"

On their way to the door and the muted sounds of Bourbon Street, the barman handed Susi a card. "You're quite a gal," he said, as she brushed past him. "My name is Louis. If you're seeking more serious fun, just call me."

Susi slipped the card into her side pocket without even acknowledging him and emerged into the twilight. "I'm hungry," she said.

One of the nearby hotels had an oyster bar. They shared a plateful each of oysters and clams. She smothered them with a generous helping of tomato-flavoured horseradish as she gulped them down.

"One of your fantasies realized?" he asked her.

"You might say that," Susi answered. "But there are others."

"I have no doubt." He smirked, still uncertain of the path they had embarked upon.

"Don't look so glum." She smiled. "You did say we would come to New Orleans and explore possibilities, didn't you?"

"I suppose I did."

The rawness of their sex that night was compelling and savage. She sucked him with hungry determination and wouldn't allow him to withdraw from her mouth when he felt his excitement rise. Usually, he would hold back and penetrate her, which prolonged the pleasure. He came in her mouth. She let him go, and he watched her tasting his come before she finally swallowed it.

"You taste sweet and sour," Susi said.

The following day, she insisted they visit a place called the Orgy Room. On Bourbon, of course. As pornographic films were projected on the walls, a group of people pressed together like sardines in a can were force-fed into an exiguous room and allowed to jostle and play on pneumatic fun-fair carpets or were they water beds? Most were drunk. The constant contact was, he felt, somewhat unpleasant, and far from arousing. Soon, he was separated from Susi in the swaying crowd but could still see her at the other end of the room. She deliberately exaggerated her movements and rubbed herself against others, often pulling her short black leather miniskirt up her thighs so her genitals were fully visible to those closer to her. He observed as various men took note of her and soon congregated around her. He could see her face flush amongst the laughs, and the human wave of bodies soon directed her against the back wall where she stood motionless, her skirt now bunched at her midriff and a couple of men frantically fingering her as she pretended to ignore them. He watched from afar, not quite knowing what he now felt. Eventually, the siren rang and the crowds thinned and made for the exit. As Susi reached him, trailed by the puzzled men she had snared in her net, she took his hand in hers. The men observed this and interrupted their progress towards her. Sweat poured down her forehead, her thin red hair plastered down against her scalp. They walked out. He looked up at the sky. There was a storm brewing.

"I came," she remarked. "Jesus . . ."

"Susi . . ."

"Take me back to the hotel," she ordered. "Tonight, I want you to fuck my arse."

The next morning, she expressed a desire for breakfast in bed. They had woken up too late for the hotel room service. He volunteered to fetch food from a nearby twenty-four-hour deli. The night rain had swept away the heat momentarily and the cool air came as a welcome relief as he walked the few hundred metres to the shop and back.

When he returned to the room, Susi was speaking on the phone. She put the receiver down as he walked in.

Maybe he shouldn't have asked, but he did. Force of habit. He'd left the hotel number with a few friends back in London, in case of sudden business, magazine commissions.

"Was that for me?" he asked Susi.

"No," she replied. "It was Louis, from the bar."

"I see."

"I wanted to find out about the . . . secret places, the real New Orleans, so to speak . . ." She looked down as she spoke, the white sheet lowered down to the whirl of her navel. There were dark patches under her green eyes, from lack of sleep and the intensity of the sex. He'd never found her as attractive as now, he knew.

He set the bread, snacks and fruit juice bottles down on the bedside table. "And?"

"And he's given me a few addresses. Said it's his night off, offered to show us around."

"We barely know him. Do you think it would be safe?"

"You always told me that New Orleans was a city of sex. Not vampires or voodoo. That it was constantly in the air, you used to say, remember."

"I did."

"Well, it would be silly not to find out more, wouldn't it?"

"I suppose so."

"He's picking us up from the hotel lobby around nine tonight. He'll show us beyond Bourbon."

They walked through the market at midday. Beyond the food area full of cajun spice mixtures, chicory blends, pralines, nuts and colourful fruit and fish, there was a flea market of sorts, stalls selling souvenirs, bric-a-brac, clothing, counterfeit tapes of zydeco music, hand-made bracelets and all the flotsam that brings people to a tourist town. On a previous visit on their second day here, Susi had spotted a black felt table where a long-haired superannuated hippy was selling fake body jewellery, which could be worn without the need for piercings. She selected several pieces.

Late afternoon, back in the room, she retreated to the bathroom for a shower. She emerged half an hour later, splendidly naked and scrubbed clean, her dark-red hair still wet. "Do you like it?" she asked him.

He looked up from his magazine.

She took his breath away. How could her body be so damn pale and so heartbreakingly beautiful? She had rouged her nipples a darker shade of scarlet and accentuated the bloody gash of her sex lips with the same lipstick. A courtesan adorned for sexual use.

She had also strategically placed the small rings and clips she had purchased in the market across her body. A ring hung from her lower lip, stainless-steel clamps from her hardened nipples and a stud appeared to have been pierced into her clitoris from which a thin golden chain hung, which she had until now worn around her wrist.

"Like a creature from a dream," he said. "From a very dirty dream, may I add. You look great." He could feel his cock swell already inside his boxer shorts. "Come here," he suggested.

"No," she said. "I have to dry my hair. Anyway I also want you to conserve your energy. Your seed . . ." she concluded with a smile.

"As you wish," he said, unable to keep his eyes away from her jewelled cunt.

"This is my fantasy night," she said.

It felt like a stab to his chest. He already knew what she had arranged with Louis.

It was a very private club on Ramparts, at the other end of the Quarter. From outside, it looked like any other house, slightly run-down and seedy. But the moment you passed the door, you could almost smell the familiar fragrance of money and sin.

"You sure you still want to?" Louis asked her as they walked in to the lobby.

"Yes," Susi said.

Louis guided them into a large room full of framed Audubon prints and a fake fireplace and asked them to make themselves comfortable. And left through another door after showing them the drinks cabinet.

Alone with her, he said nothing at first. Then, seeing his unease, Susi said: "It's not quite the fantasy I told you about. Just the second part, really . . ."

"Oh . . ."

"And I want you to be one of the men . . ."

"I'm not sure I—"

"I'd feel more comfortable with you there," she interrupted him. "You'll enjoy it, you'll see. Anyway, you knew what I am, what I like, when you suggested we come here. You'll get a kick out of it. You like watching. I see it in you. Even when we fuck, your brain is like a machine, recording it all, storing every feeling, every tremor, every moan away. Memories that will last for ever."

Before he could answer her, the door opened and Louis came through with three other men. Two of them were black, tall, built like football players, the other white man was middle-aged, stocky, silver-haired.

"Here we are, Susanne," he said, without introducing the others. "You're in charge now . . ."

The thought occurred to him he had called her Susanne. "Friends call me Susi" she had said back all those months ago as they caught that New York cab. So Louis was not considered a friend!

Susi indicated the centre of the heavily carpeted room. "A circle around here." There was something more Germanic than usual in her voice as she ordered them to clear the heavy chairs away from the room's epicentre.

The circle soon emerged, as the furniture was set aside.

Susi stationed herself there and undressed. "You all stay dressed," she said to the five men. "Just cocks out, OK?"

She positioned herself and, as the men's eyes followed her every movement, she opened her legs and stuck a finger inside herself. She was visibly already very wet and there was an audible squishing sound as the finger penetrated her. Louis unzipped his jeans and pulled his cock out. The others followed his example. One of the black guys, he noticed, was enormous, at least ten inches and thick as hell. He discreetly examined the other cocks, and was reassured that his was still reasonably sized in comparison. Joint second biggest, he reckoned, not without a wry thought.

Susi now introduced a second finger into her cunt, secretions now flooding out and dripping down the gold chain.

There was both a sense of the ceremonial and a sense of the absurd about them all. Six human beings masturbating frantically. Five men with their cocks out, fingers clenching their shafts, rubbing their coronas, teasing their glans, heavy balls shuddering below as the woman in white at their centre teased her cunt in a parody of lovemaking.

"Not yet," she warned. Had one of them intimated he was close to come?

Time felt as if it had come to a standstill, swallowing all their halting sounds of lust.

She adjusted her stance, now kneeling, her hand buried deep inside her crotch, almost like praying, and indicated she was finally ready for her baptism of come.

The men came, one by one, spurting their thick, white seed into her face, as she leaned forward to receive them. He was the third to orgasm and noticed the arc of his ejaculate strain in the air separating him from her body and the final drips landing in the thin valley between her muted breasts. Soon, she was covered with the men's seed, like syrup dribbling across her thin eyebrows and down her cheeks. He didn't think she herself had actually come, although all five men had.

There was a long silence as they all stood there, the men with their cocks shrivelling already, the drenched woman in quiet repose.

Finally, Louis spoke: "Well, Susanne, just the way you wanted it?"

She nodded as the men began zipping up.

"Care to move on to your next fantasy?"

What next fantasy? he wondered. What else was she after?

"Yes," she said, rising to her feet and picking up the green towel Louis had previously left on a nearby chair and wiping her face clean.

"Good," Louis said. "There's quite a crowd out there waiting."

Still not bothering to put her clothes on again, Susi asked him: "Can you give us a few minutes alone, before, please?"

"Sure, Susanne," he said and the four men trooped out of the room.

"So," he asked her the moment after they had closed the door. "What else have you planned for the menu, Susi? It must be a fantasy I am unaware of. You're full of surprises."

"I know," she answered. "I should have told you before. I'm sorry. It'll only happen once and then I shall return to my boring life, you know. Maybe the time will come for me to settle down, marry some decent guy and even have kids. A nice *hausfrau*."

"What are you talking about, Susi?"

"I want to be fucked in public . . ."

"What?"

"Just one man, that's all. But I have to know what it feels like with people watching, you see. You said this was a city of sex, I'll never have the opportunity again. Just this once. We're miles away from home, no one knows us, we'll likely not come here again. Only you and I will know . . ."

"You mean with me?" he asked.

"Yes. If you wish to be the one."

"I . . ." He was at a loss for words.

"It's all arranged with Louis. We'll even get paid five hundred dollars."

"It's not the money . . ."

"I know . . . I understand if you don't want to. Arrangements have also been made for another man, if you decline. But I do want you to watch . . . really . . ."

His thoughts were in turmoil. This had all gone too far. He had played with fire and the flames were now reaching all the way through to his gut. As they always did. He never learned the lessons, did he? Long before Kathryn, he'd been going out with a woman who was avowedly bisexual and it had planted a bad seed in his mind. Not for him the common fantasy of watching two women together, no. The idea of bisexuality had preyed on his mind for months and one day, curious to know what it must feel like to suck a man's cock, from the woman's point of view (after all, they never minded sucking his, did they?), he had agreed to an encounter with another man. He distressingly discovered he enjoyed sucking cock and had been irregularly doing so for years now, in secret, whenever a woman was not available and the tides of lust submerged him. He had never told any woman about this. Feared they would misunderstand. Blamed his insatiable sexual curiosity. Even Susi wouldn't understand, he knew. Not that this was the time to tell her. He always went that step too far. And paid for it. Emotionally.

"I just can't, Susi. I can't."

"But will you . . ."

"Yes, I will watch."

There was a crowd in the other room of the house on Ramparts. They had been drinking liberally for an hour or so, it appeared. There was a heavy air of expectation about them.

Louis led Susi in. Like a ritual, holding the thin gold chain secured to her clitoris, her eyes covered by a piece of dark-blue cloth. This is how she had wanted it to happen. She didn't wish to see the audience. Just feel it and hear it around her as she was fucked.

They had cleared a low table in a corner of the room and Susi was taken to it, carefully installed across so that all the light was focused on her already gaping and wet red gash, and positioned on all fours, her fake jewellery taken from her body. She was helped to arch her back and raise her rump to the right level. The man who had won the quickly organized auction came forward. He looked quite ordinary, late twenties, an athlete's build, not very hairy. He had kept his shirt on but his cock already jutted forward as he approached Susi's receptive body. He was uncut and his foreskin bunched heavily below the mushroom cone of his glans. He was very big.

The man found his position at Susi's entrance and buckled forward and speared her. A few spectators applauded but most remained quite silent. From where he sat, he couldn't see Susi's face, only her white arse and the hypnotizing sight of the dark-purple cock moving in and out of her, faster and faster, every thrust echoed by a wave of movement on the periphery of her flesh, like a gentle wind caressing the surface of a sand dune.

It lasted an eternity, longer he knew than he would have ever managed. The guy was getting his money's worth. And the audience, many of whom were blatantly playing with themselves in response to the spectacle unfolding before them. She would be very sore at the end of this. Sweat coated Susi's body like a thin shroud as the man digged deeper and deeper into her and he watched her opening enlarge obscenely under the pressure of that monstrous cock.

Shamefully, he couldn't keep his eyes away from the immediate perimeter of penetration, noting every anatomical feature with minute precision, the vein bulging on the side of the invading cock as it moved in and out of sight, in and out of her, the very shade of crimson of her bruised labia as they were shoved aside by the thrusts, the thin stream of inner secretions pearling down her inner thigh, and neither could he help himself getting hard again watching the woman he knew he had fallen in love with getting fucked in public by a total stranger.

That night, she curled up against him in the slightly exiguous hotel room bed, drawing his warmth and tearing him apart.

They had packed and waited in the hotel's lobby for the airport shuttle they had booked earlier that morning. One suitcase each, a Samsonite and a Pierre Cardin. They hadn't discussed the previous night, acted as if nothing had happened. They had the same flight to Chicago where they would part. He on to London, she to Vienna. Now he knew he would want to see her again, in Europe. It would be easier. They had come through this crazy experience and he realized how much she had touched his heart.

The blue mini-coach finally arrived, ten minutes late, and he picked up the suitcases and carried them to the pavement. As he was about to give her case to the shuttle's driver, Susi put her hand on his arm.

"Yes?"

He had never realized how green her eyes were.

"I'm not coming," she calmly said. "There's nothing for me back home; I'm staying in New Orleans."

"But . . ."

She silenced him with a tender kiss to his cheek. When he tried to talk again, she just quietly put a finger to his lips indicating he should remain silent. "No," she said. "No explanations. It's better like this."

The driver urged him to get on board.

As the shuttle moved down Burgundy, he looked out of the window and saw Susi walking to a parked car with her suitcase. Louis stood next to it. The shuttle turned the corner and he lost them from sight.

The short drive to Moisan was the loneliest and the longest he had taken in his life.

He would, in the following years, continue to write many stories. That was his job after all. In many of them, women had red hair, green eyes and bodies of porcelain white. And terrible things happened to them: rape, multiple sex, prostitution, drug addiction, even unnatural forced sexual relationships with domestic animals. But they all accepted their fate with a quiet detachment.

He would continue to occasionally meet up with strange men and take uncommon pleasure in sucking them off. This he did with serene indifference, because in his mind it didn't count. It was just sex, meat, it was devoid of feelings.

He never visited New Orleans or saw or heard of Susi again.

# Paying My Friends for Sex

Matt Thorne

Not having money was hard. But sometimes having money seems harder. It's not as if I'm rich or anything, but having enough cash to get yourself in trouble, well, you'd be surprised how quickly that becomes a burden.

I've never been an avaricious individual. Ever since I was a kid, my cash has gone on three things, and three things only: CDs, books and the cinema. Most of my clothes were given to me; the rest come from second-hand shops. And although I spend more money on food than I used to, all this really means is these days I eat in expensive restaurants instead of McDonald's. I always eat out, and will do so until the day I die.

So when I unexpectedly started having more money, the only real evidence of my newfound wealth was in the increase of my book and CD collections. My cinema habits remained unchanged: there are, after all, only so many films you can see in a day. But although it was fun to fill out my literature and music libraries, after a while I realized there was little pleasure in buying music or books by bands or authors you didn't like. After that, I confined myself to only buying new books or CDs, or the back catalogues of bands I knew I loved. Even that got tiresome after a while (as much as I love Neil Young and Lou Reed, there's really no reason to own copies of *Landing on Water* or *Minstrel*). This meant I needed to find some new way of enjoying my money. At first I considered developing an interest in pornography. There seemed to be hundreds of adult videos, and it seemed likely that collecting these sorts of films would give me pleasure. But after I had ten or so, I realized I didn't really enjoy pornography, and was also embarrassed about having the tapes around the house.

The same morning I chucked the cassettes away, I got a letter from an ex-girlfriend. When we'd broken up I'd been quite stern with her, telling her not to try to get in contact with me. It was over two years since we'd last seen each other, and she was writing to ask whether I would now be prepared to meet her for dinner. She made no mention of her own romantic situation, although she did say in one line that she just knew I would have a girlfriend and if I wanted I could bring her along. I hadn't thought about this ex-girlfriend that much, mainly because I had been so upset when she'd broken up with me that I'd experienced a mini-breakdown that I didn't want anyone to know about. The main reason why I had told her not to get in contact with me was because I knew she had a habit of falling back in love with her boyfriends after she'd broken up with them and I thought it was probably safer to stay away from her until I'd made a fresh start. Once I'd got back on my feet, I'd always intended to contact her, but for one reason or another I didn't get round to it, and as I've never been one for nostalgia, not having her in my life didn't really worry me.

I wrote back to her a few hours later, telling her that I didn't have a girlfriend and hadn't been involved with anyone since we split up. As I wrote this I remembered reading somewhere about how when writing love letters you should always forget about yourself and concentrate only on arousing pleasure in the person you're addressing. I couldn't remember if the passage came from Freud or Barthes (it sounded like something from *A Lover's Discourse*, but when I checked my library this volume was missing) or someone else entirely, but I realized that this was what I was doing now, and wondered whether it was such a good idea for me to meet up with Tracey again. I had always composed my letters to please her, and felt wounded every time a reply arrived. Not because they were deliberately hurtful, but because they seemed written with no awareness of the emotions they would arouse in me, which was fine when we saw each other all the time, but more difficult during the year we spent a continent apart. The address on the top of her letter was from somewhere in Chalk Farm, so I suggested we go for dinner at the Lavender in Primrose Hill. Three days later, her reply arrived. She would be happy to meet me in the location I'd suggested.

The reason why I had been single for so long was because of a random act of kindness I had committed two years earlier. A friend of a friend had died of a heart attack at an unexpectedly early age. His girlfriend, Marianne, needed someone to look after her and, having the space and the time, I invited her to move in with me. I had expected her mourning period to last three or four months, but it showed no sign of coming to an end. Over the previous two years she had become increasingly dependent on me and, although there had been nothing sexual between us, I felt too guilty to indulge in anything other than the odd one-nightstand.

I arrived at the restaurant just before eight. Tracey was already waiting. She was wearing a short black dress. Smiling warmly as I entered the restaurant, she got up to embrace me.

"Tracey," I said as she hugged me, "it's so good to see you."

"You too." She looked down. "I wasn't sure if you'd come."

"So," I said, "tell me everything. Do you have a job?"

She laughed. "You're not going to believe what I do."

"Should I guess?"

"Not just yet. I have to give you some background details first."

"OK, start from the beginning. The last time I saw you, you were about to start drama school."

Tracey smiled with her head slightly tilted to one side and leaned back in her chair. It was more exciting to see her than I'd anticipated, and I was already trying to calculate how I would feel if we ended up going to bed together. The candlelight in the Lavender was doing an incredible job of bringing out all of my ex-girlfriend's most alluring features, from the small, springy, brown mole just above her soft upper lip to the exact colour of her curly brown hair. As always I was drawn in by her guilty-looking blue eyes, getting a sudden flashback of how her expression would harden when I trapped her into an argument.

"Drama school was great for the first term," she told me, "because there were so many new people and you can remember how lonely I was before we split up."

"Yeah," I replied, "I'm sorry about that."

"Sorry, why?" she asked, sounding as if her question was genuine.

"Gosh, I don't know if I'm ready to get into this."

"Get into what?"

"I had a breakdown just after you left me. And although initially when it happened I wasn't able to do anything or see anyone, eventually I managed to get myself together enough to start having therapy. And through the sessions I worked out why I treated you the way I did."

I noticed from the direction Tracey's eyes were pointing that a waitress had come across to our table. I felt glad of the interruption, amazed that I'd started talking about this stuff so quickly. Then I remembered how my therapist had spent our final session trying to convince me that I wouldn't feel properly healed until I'd seen Tracey again, and how adamant I'd been that that wasn't a good idea.

The waitress told us the specials and we looked up to the blackboard to decide what we wanted. I guessed from Tracey's small order that she was having money problems. While not wanting to embarrass her, I attempted to persuade her to have more than just a starter by letting her know that I'd pay.

"It's OK," she told me, "I'm really not that hungry. But if you order a nice bottle of wine I'd be happy to drink it."

I ordered the wine and my food, then said, "I feel terrible now, isolating you like that. But it wasn't jealousy. I always thought it was jealousy, but my therapist made me realize it wasn't that at all. I just needed to get something from you, something secret, something from inside, something you probably couldn't give. That's why I took us away from everyone else."

She nodded. "I do understand, and that's kind of why I wanted to see you. You see, like I said, drama school was great for the first term, but then I started missing you. And I looked back on our time together with a fondness you'd never believe. Every day I thanked God that we'd had those two whole years together so I had something from every season to remind me of you. Like, pick a day . . ."

"Hallowe'en."

"Scary badger."

"What?"

"You remember."

I thought about it and realized that I did. We'd gone to the cinema together and on the way back we'd seen two liberal-type parents trick-or-treating with a small child wearing a cardboard badger mask. And we'd joked with each other about how the parents would've convinced their child he didn't want to be anything as horrible as a hobgoblin or Freddy Krueger. "No, we imagined the two well-meaning parents saying to their child, 'what you want to be is a scary . . . badger.' "

I smiled. "I find it hard to remember stuff."

"I know. When we broke up you said you'd never think of me again."

"I didn't say that."

"You did."

"Well, it wasn't true. So, are you going to tell me what your job is?"

"Phone sex."

"Huh?"

"I knew you'd like that. Can I tell you about my audition?"

"For the job?"

"Yeah. Well, I'd been working for TicketMaster for a while and it just wasn't working out. The rest of the people in the office didn't like me because every now and again I'd have an audition for an advert and they'd all get really upset because I had a life outside work. So, anyway, there was one woman there who I became work friends with, and one day she told me she was leaving. She'd got a job working for a sex line and it was five times as much money for nowhere near as much work. I was a bit sceptical, but she told me that, although there were a few dodgy men at the company, the main people in charge were all women, and by that time the little pound signs were dancing in front of my eyes and I'd agreed to go in for an interview."

The waitress reappeared at my elbow with the wine and the squid salad I'd ordered for a starter. I asked her what had happened to Tracey's food and she said she'd thought it would be better to bring it at the same time as my main course. Tracey nodded and said that was fine. I still felt guilty about ordering so much food when she was having hardly anything and tried to make up for it by overfilling her glass with wine.

Tracey continued. "So I went in for my interview and found myself in this windowless room with two women and one man. Although the man did most of the talking, it was obvious from the outset that the women were in charge. Anyway, my audition consisted of three exercises. The first two exercises were pieces I had to read from a script. This is quite a long anecdote, but the punchline's in the middle instead of the end so get ready to laugh. The script I was reading from was supposed to be as if I was talking from the perspective of a woman who had been led into sexual ruin. I had to go through this catalogue of things that my boyfriend had made me do and the twist at the end was that I had to tell the caller that I was now completely cock crazy and even just knowing there was a man on the other end listening to my past exploits got me off. The script was kind of torturous and confused and I was trying to understand it as well as read it so I kept stumbling over my words, and I got to this bit where I said my boyfriend introduced me to swimming and just as I was thinking that was odd and waiting for some subaqua exploits, the man stood up and shouted at me, 'It's swinging, not swimming. My boyfriend introduced me to swinging.' "

It wasn't that great a line – she knew that – but the delivery was so perfectly Tracey that it made me laugh, identify with her and feel horny all at the same time. I knew one day lots of men would share this feeling, and it was this knowledge that made me certain that, in spite of Tracey's considerable fragility, she would one day achieve success as an actress.

She went on. "The second script was less interesting. Standard sexy housewife, naughty knickers stuff. But then the final exercise was an improvisation. It'd been a while since I'd been to a proper audition and you know how much I like that sort of thing anyway so I got all overexcited and started acting as if I was auditioning for a movie instead of a job on a sex line. You would have liked the scenario though. It was a bit close to home and I could tell they'd come up with this idea for an audition piece deliberately to make me feel uncomfortable so I decided to take it to a real extreme. I was supposed to be an actress who'd come for an audition for a part in a film and then when I'd arrived I'd found out it was actually a porno instead of a normal movie."

I popped a large piece of squid into my mouth and started chewing. Tracey brushed a strand of stray hair out of her face and carefully lifted her overfilled wine glass to her lips. As she did so, I noticed her lipstick was completely the wrong shade for her, making it look as if she'd been sucking gob-stoppers all day long.

"The weird thing about this last exercise was that they wanted me to do it over the phone. I suppose it wasn't that weird, given that I was meant to be proving I could do a sex-line job, but the way they handled it was odd. First off the women came across and hooked me up to a headset, then the guy went off into another room on his own.

"Like I said, from the moment I was told what the exercise was I felt really irritated and wanted to embarrass them, so I tried to make what I was saying as disturbing as possible, telling him that I was only taking this job to support my baby, and that I came from a really religious background, and had wanted to be an actress my whole life, grown up on the kids from *Fame*, stuff like that . . ."

"How did he respond?"

"Well, that was it, after I'd been talking a couple of minutes or so he stopped asking me questions and just kept saying, 'Go on, go on', and I could hear the clink of his belt and, y'know, I knew what he was doing."

"What did you do?"

"What could I do? I kept talking, but I tried to make it sound as unsexy as possible, just praying he would stop. But he kept going and I kept going until he came."

"Ugh."

"I know. And the worst thing was he didn't even try to hide it. I think I probably could've handled the situation if he was just some pervert doing this job as a sneaky way of getting his rocks off, but he came back into the main room with his fly undone, shirt tail still sticking out, and the two women looked at him and made another mark on their clipboards as if this was just another test I'd passed."

"Tracey," I said gently.

"Yes?"

"How long have you had this job?"

"Only a couple of months. It's all right once you get used to it. And I make it fun, playing little games with myself like working out which words will make them . . ." She looked at me. "Oh dear. When I imagined telling you about this I thought it would make me sound glamourous and sexy."

Not wanting her to worry, I smiled at Tracey and let my fork drop back on my plate.

We stayed in the restaurant until eleven. By that time we were both a little drunk and I was reluctant for the evening to end. I felt more aroused than I had in months and didn't want to go back to the sexless friendship waiting for me at home. So I persuaded Tracey to walk down to a nearby pub for one final drink. The front of the pub was crowded so we went through to the back bar, which was empty except for an old man and a fruit machine. I bought us both Stellas and sat opposite Tracey. Her legs were crossed at the ankles and I found myself staring at the line where the hem of her dress pulled tightly around her toned thighs. She was telling me about a friend's play but I had long stopped listening to her words. Taking a large gulp from my drink, I swooped in on her, sliding my hand up under her skirt. My fingers stopped as they reached the soft crotch of her knickers. My lips stopped as I realized they were pressing against a resistant mouth.

"I'm sorry," she said, with tears in her eyes, "I don't want to do this."

When I was sixteen I went on a school-organized trip to Keele University. The trip was designed to introduce potential students to college life and, given the excesses of this weekend away, I think the organizers managed an accurate distillation of most people's three-year experience. I was the only one my school expected to make it to university, so I went alone, although by the end of the coach journey up I had befriended a sizeable number of sixth-formers sent by other schools in the city. As my school was ridiculously suburban, a haven of bubble perms and teenage pregnancies, I had always been an outsider, so much so that the first-years started a rumour that I slept in a coffin. I didn't go into school that much, spending most of my time in my bedroom listening to the Pixies and those first three Ride EPs. This was considered so outré in my neighbourhood that I was amazed to find that my tastes were shared not only by the sixth-formers I'd befriended on the bus, but also the students who organized the last night's disco.

Those two days at Keele were, to that point, the best of my life. But as I returned to my isolation, I saw no likelihood of them ever being repeated. My parents were both intensely antisocial people, ashamed of their marriage and quick to discourage me from forming friendships with others. But my newfound comrades were reluctant to let me disappear back to my previous existence, bombarding me with calls until I agreed to come with them to a Primal Scream concert. I went with them and, over the next few weeks, found myself with my first ever social circle.

And after friendship came the inevitable romantic infatuation. Among my new gang was a beautiful redhead with goth tendencies and a tart sense of humour. The rest of my friends were dubious about some of her more extreme tastes, and I was the only one willing to accompany her to a Cranes concert at a local polytechnic. The show was terrible but the night was transcendental, and in the taxi home I tried to kiss her. She stiffened, pushed me away, and said she wasn't interested. As far as I could remember, I'd never told Tracey about this, but it was definitely a formative moment, making me overcautious in the opening stages of any subsequent relationship. If I got any sense that the woman I wanted didn't want me, I immediately backed off, even if their reluctance was only part of an elaborate flirtation. In some ways, I'd never really got over that first rejection, and now the same thing was happening to me again, I felt a fresh desperation. But that doesn't explain what I said next.

"Tracey?"

"Yes?"

"I'll give you five hundred pounds to fuck me."

During the taxi ride home, I wondered whether I regretted making my offer. There was no question that Tracey had been horrified, turning me down immediately and remaining upset until we said goodbye, but when I thought back to my sessions with my therapist, I realized the fact that Tracey would never want to see me again was probably a positive thing. My therapist had never accepted my excuse that I couldn't start another relationship because I was giving house-space to Marianne, trying to make me believe it was really because I held out hope that Tracey and I would get back together. Now that definitely wouldn't happen, I was free to get on with my new life.

Marianne was waiting for me when I got home, sitting in front of our television drinking a mug of mulled wine and watching a film featuring Veronica Lake. She moved her legs down so I could sit next to her. As usual, her eyes were rimmed with red and she'd dressed with the bare minimum of effort. I squeezed her hand and she flashed me a brief smile.

The following morning I went out with three female friends of mine. Hazel, Ivy and Elizabeth were all young, recently married mothers. I had met them through Marianne. Initially, they had been her friends, calling me up for news about how she was coping. But as she hadn't seen them in two years and they had stopped asking about her, I now considered them my friends, meeting with them once a week for a few hours of coffee and chat in a café in St John's Wood.

Every now and again, we were joined by the unofficial fifth member of our party. Her name was Anita and she was by far the most glamourous member of our quintet. Marianne would've been furious if she'd known Anita occasionally accompanied us, as Anita had supplied Marianne's boyfriend Donald with the drugs she believed had precipitated his premature heart attack. Anita had been having a low-key affair with Donald for several years, and Marianne blamed herself for being so understanding about his infidelity, knowing that if she'd been more possessive she might've saved his life. Donald was one of many men Anita had spent years seeing on the side, although she usually went for men of more considerable means. Between affairs, she was always short of money, lost without someone to pay for her.

Hazel, Ivy and Elizabeth were all fascinated by the fact that I had been single for so long. Ivy was the only one who flirted with me, although I knew this didn't count for anything, as she was as certain in her marriage as the others. But they couldn't understand why I didn't make a move on Anita. Every time the subject came up, I used the same excuse, "Marianne would kill me."

"But how would she know?" This was Elizabeth, the most persistent of my three friends.

"She'd know. She'd smell it on me."

"I don't see why you're worried about that," said Ivy, sucking her lip. "You've let Marianne live with you rent-free for two years. She's in no position to tell you who you can sleep with."

"There's too many demons."

"Between you and Anita?" Elizabeth asked. "Why? You hardly knew Donald. Besides, you two have an incredible chemistry. I bet the sex would be amazing."

"I don't think so."

"Why not?"

"I get the impression that Anita can keep people at a distance even when she's fucking them. I hate having sex with someone who's got their barriers up."

"You only say that because you've heard how she talks about her businessmen blokes. It'd be different for you. You'd be able to break her down." The other two chuckled darkly at this, encouraging Ivy to add, "If I had your body I could do it."

I sipped my coffee and took a bite from my Russian cake, feeling unsettled. I still wasn't really over last night and felt less comfortable bantering than I usually did. I knew myself well enough to know what I really needed was sexual reassurance and although, in a strange sort of way, that was what my friends were trying to offer me, thinking about Anita made me uneasy.

"Let's talk about something else."

That evening, I went to a party with my bank manager. She was one of the normal girls who'd made my life so difficult at school. We'd become friends by chance when I went into my hometown bank to open a third account. She'd been impressed by the amount of money I'd been depositing and asked me out on a date. We'd quickly discovered that there were the same differences between us now that there'd been at school, and we'd gone home separately. This had been a big blow to me as she'd been one of the most unobtainable girls in my school and, having spent a large part of my adolescence masturbating with her in my head, I was keen to see whether the real deal rivalled the fantasy.

After our unsuccessful date, we had concentrated on forming a workable business relationship. I needed more from my bank manager than most people, and was on the phone to her several times a week. And once long enough had elapsed for us not to be embarrassed in each other's company, we started going out together as friends. I became her walker, accompanying Vicki to social events once or twice a month. These events were not grand affairs, consisting mainly of nights in the pub or dinner parties organized by her friends. Tonight's party was in Jamie's Bar in Charlotte Street. One of Vicki's friends had just returned from two years in Australia and a gathering had been organized to welcome him back.

Vicki didn't seem that excited about the party, and unusually for her, wasn't even worried about changing for the evening, meeting me straight from work. Seeing her in a conservative suit reminded me of how great she used to look in her school uniform, and I wondered again about my impotent reaction to the women in my life. It was odd: I was excellent with strangers, no matter how attractive, able to go into a club or bar, find someone single, and persuade them to take me home with them. But as soon as it came to anyone with whom I had the slightest emotional connection, I became a complete drip. Feeling depressed, I drank too much and found myself telling Vicki what had happened with Tracey. I made a joke out of it, saying that it was probably not a good idea for me to tell my bank manager I'd been offering ex-girlfriends extravagant amounts of money for them to sleep with me.

She downed her glass, winked at me, and said, "I could do with some money."

We went to her place. In the taxi we bartered about the price: Vicki saying she wanted twice the amount I'd offered my ex-girlfriend; me saying for that much money I expected something special.

I wasn't that surprised by the way she reacted. Vicki had spent the whole of her adult life working with money, and no doubt saw this as a neat way of mocking its black magic. The idea of being paid for sex clearly appealed to her, as did taking a human transaction so lightly. I paid the driver and we went into her house.

"So," she asked, "how do you want me?"

I thought back to all those adolescent afternoons. My fantasy had always been that while I was masturbating about Vicki she was somewhere masturbating about me. I told her this, thinking that was maybe how we'd start.

She chuckled. "You know, I never did. Not about you. I must've done it about almost every boy in the class, but never about you."

I couldn't reply. She noticed my sadness and said hurriedly, "I would've done, though, you know, if I'd known you were doing it about me."

"You must've known."

"Why?"

"Every boy in the year used to masturbate about you. We used to compare experiences."

She looked at me. "Really? I honestly had no idea. Can I tell you about a fantasy of mine?"

"Of course."

"I used to fantasize about groups of boys in the class masturbating over me. You know, with all that AIDS talk in assemblies sperm was seen as such an evil substance. But it didn't seem that way to me. I wanted to be totally coated in it."

She must've noticed my horrified expression, as she immediately eased back from our sexual conversation and asked me instead if I wanted a coffee. I nodded and she went out into the kitchen to make me one. I took advantage of the spare moment to assess my surroundings. Houses always look strange when there's only one person living in them, but Vicki had done a good job of making her place look comfortable. Before Marianne moved in with me, there had always been something defiant about my decoration, as if I was trying to create a home that would be the envy of anyone who visited it. But nothing I could buy from a shop could add the warmth created by another person's belongings.

Vicki was clearly less troubled by being alone, and although she couldn't quite disguise the fact that she had too much space to herself, the lounge looked like somewhere she'd be equally happy entertaining friends or watching television alone. I liked the fact that she'd left stuff out (a hairdryer lying on its side next to a rectangular white extension plug; a box set of *Friends* episodes by the television; three cotton-wool balls dyed scarlet with nail varnish on a copy of the *Express* next to the electric fire), and began to relax as I settled down into her settee.

She returned with my cup of coffee. After her revelations about her childhood come-fantasies, I didn't feel like watching her masturbate any more, and anyway, that was far too passive. It was time for me to become masterful.

"Take your trousers off," I told her.

"Let's see the money first."

"What?"

"Cash up front. I don't want you changing your mind after you've had me and pretending the payment thing was just a joke."

"OK. How much did we agree on?"

"A thousand. Do you carry that kind of money with you?"

"No. Will you take a cheque? You know I'm good for it."

"Do you have your cheque book on you?"

"No, but come on, Vicki, you're my bank manager. You can easily debit my account whenever you want."

"Write me an IOU."

"I don't have a pen."

"There's one on the table."

"I got up and wrote out an IOU, wondering what was behind this banter. Although a thousand pounds wasn't bad for one night's work, I couldn't believe that Vicki was genuinely only doing this for the money. The way I looked at it, the play with potential prostitution was just spice to stoke up enough excitement to get us through a one-nightstand. If she was taking it seriously . . . well, fuck it, if she was taking it seriously, I'd just make sure I got my money's worth.

"Right. Now get those trousers off."

She stood up, walked across to the table and checked the IOU. Seemingly satisfied, Vicki came across to me and put one foot up between my legs.

"Unbuckle my shoes first."

I felt pleased she was bossing me back, thinking that this proved she was getting into what we were doing. I gripped her ankle before following her instruction, a motion that seemed to please her. Shoes removed, she turned her back to me. I sank down slightly so her bottom was directly in front of my face, then waited as she undid the buckle on her belt and slowly lowered her trousers over her buttocks. She was wearing a flimsy pair of white translucent knickers: the kind that pulled tight between her legs so that the material covering her bum formed a triangle. I gripped her hips. She let her trousers fall to the floor and stepped out of them.

"I bet you're a man who likes bottoms."

I giggled. "What?"

"Let's see, shall we? What happens when I do this?"

She slid her fingers under the elastic of her knickers and pulled them down. Using a foot to flip them onto a pile with her trousers, she leaned forwards and pushed her bum up in my face, using her fingers to pull open her cheeks. The light was good in Vicki's apartment and I had a full view of the soft creases of her anus. She was right: I did like this sight, although few of the girls I'd been out with had shown it to me so readily, and it was a hard thing to request of a one-nightstand. I could see why Vicki was so willing to reveal hers to me. I know this sounds strange, but it was absolutely beautiful, the skin moving so perfectly to the small hole in the centre with each tuck in exactly the right place. From this angle I could also see a rear view of her vagina, which was equally well defined, the flesh of her outer labia almost spookily symmetrical. Vicki seemed to revel in my slow appraisal and after my nice, long look I pushed my tongue onto her welcoming folds. I held Vicki's hips and managed to get deep into her, curious whether she liked having this done to her as much as I liked having it done to me. I licked for a while and then asked her, "Can you touch yourself while I do this to you?"

"Well, I can, but you'll have to hold me open."

"That's OK."

She released her buttocks and I took over, opening her even wider. The muscles in my tongue felt pleasurably strained as I buried my mouth into her bottom, wanting her to feel totally loose. She fingered herself slowly at first, but when I showed no sign of wearying she speeded up. I wondered if she would be prepared to come with me and felt scared about how much I wanted that to happen. But I also wanted to come too, and as her moans grew shallower I stopped sucking her asshole.

"What's wrong?" she asked.

"Nothing. I realize it's not very romantic to interrupt the sex like this but, seeing as I'm paying . . ."

"Yes?" she asked, impatient.

"What are you like with orgasms? Do you come? Can you come? Do you always need fingers, or can you come just from fucking? Can you come lots of times or is it one-time-only, lights out?"

"I'm weird. Back to front. When I masturbate it takes for ever, but I guarantee if you fuck me for more than three minutes that'll hit the spot."

"That's not back to front, that's perfect. And can you still fuck after you've come?"

"Yeah, but if we're gonna do that can we use lubricant? You don't have to wear a condom."

"Of course. Have you got some?"

"I'll fetch it."

She moved away from me and went out into the hallway. I watched her go, finding it sexy to see her bare legs beneath the jacket of the work suit she was still wearing. I waited while she went upstairs, rubbing my cock through the pocket of my trousers. When Vicki returned she could tell I was looking at her cunt and stopped beneath the main light, letting me see her. As I'd expected, she had a neat bikini line, an unnecessary precaution for one so fair, but nice to look at all the same. Although this was definitely an incredibly sexy moment for me, I couldn't help feeling slightly disappointed. Seeing Vicki Wade's cunt . . . this was a childhood dream come true, but how could it hold the same magic for me now that it had done back then? I remembered one time when a boy from our school had told us that he'd seen Vicki doing stretches in the gym, and her leotard had ridden up so high that, as he'd put it, "he even saw her pin". For months afterwards I'd dreamed about being in his place, even (if you'd caught me in a weak moment) prepared to give up my life to share the sight.

Maybe I should've offered her money back then. She probably wouldn't have accepted it, but who knows? Of course, in those days I couldn't even get near her, let alone start a conversation that would lead up to me offering her money to show me her cunt. It's odd, but even now, the thought of Vicki's adolescent vagina tucked inside that unfaithful leotard seemed sexier than the reality in front of me. I'm not a pervert, and have no interest in schoolgirls (even women my age dressed up in school uniform), but the power of that missed moment was so strong that the fantasy almost managed to obliterate what was happening now.

Vicki seemed to notice my distraction and brushed her fingers down over herself. She pretended that she too was distracted, but then quickly looked back at me and smiled when she saw me grip myself through my trousers again.

"What do you want me to do?"

"I want to come inside you."

"I've already said that's fine."

"I know, but I need to be sucked first."

"Oh, OK." She walked back to me, kneeled down and unzipped my fly. Pulling open my trousers, she slid my cock out through the slit in my boxer shorts and took it into her mouth. I don't really need to describe the experience other than to tell you she was good at it, although to be honest I've never been with a woman who wasn't. Remembering her promise of how little sex she needed to orgasm, I let her suck me longer than I normally would, eventually stopping her with a gentle pat on both shoulders.

She looked up at me, and her expression seemed so open that I snapped out of porno mode and stroked the side of her face. She bent down, unlaced my shoes, and stripped me from the waist downwards. Picking up her blue tube of lubricant, she squeezed a blob onto her palm, spread it over my cock then rubbed the rest inside her. Pulling my cock forwards, she slid herself gently on top of me. I kissed her, realizing as I did so that it was the first time our lips had touched. It's embarrassing and inappropriate, but the first time I fuck someone I always want to tell them I love them. Thankfully, tonight I conquered that urge and mouthed it softly to myself instead. Our fucking was surprisingly (for me, anyway) forceful: a proper, deep, heterosexual shag that carried us both to orgasm and left us woozily clinging to each other.

We stayed like that until Vicki climbed off of me and asked, "Did you get your money's worth?"

Marianne was asleep in front of the television when I got back. She often nodded out in the lounge, waking up again about three or four and going to bed. Feeling bolder than usual, I decided to carry her upstairs. When we reached the landing she awoke and, after taking a few seconds to adjust to the situation, sniffed my neck.

"You smell of sex."

I didn't say anything. She smiled, and let me carry her to her room and drop her on the bed. As I turned out her light she said, "Someone called for you. There's a message on the machine."

I went downstairs and played the message. It was Tracey, apologizing for the other night and saying she wanted to see me again. Tomorrow. Although it was after one, I called her straight back. She reminded me of her address and told me to come over at seven o'clock. I replaced the receiver and went to bed.

The following morning Marianne and I both awoke earlier than usual and decided to have breakfast together. This was quite an unusual occurrence for both of us and, as we lacked even the most basic supplies, I headed off to the deli. When I came back Marianne had made me a coffee and was sitting at the end of the table sipping hers, wrapped in a dark-blue silk dressing gown.

'So," she said, as I hunted for a grapefruit knife, "who was the lucky girl?"

"On the phone?"

"No . . . last night."

"Oh. My bank manager."

"Really?" She laughed. "I thought you were too rich to have to sleep with someone for a raised overdraft."

"I was. Until someone started eating me out of house and home."

She looked at me, clearly shocked. I'd never referred to money before, and she'd stopped bringing it up after her third straight week of thanking me for my generosity.

"I do feel ready to start looking for a job," she said in a small voice, "although if it's all right with you I'd rather stay here and pay you rent than move out. I'm just so comfortable here."

I didn't answer, preparing her grapefruit in silence and placing it in a bowl in front of her.

I arrived at Tracey's house an hour and a half late. This was a deliberate tactic, my childish way of getting revenge for her knocking me back after our previous date. She pretended she wasn't aware of the time, greeting me with a hug. Feeling optimistic, I'd stopped off at an ATM on the way and taken cash out of each of my three main accounts, now having nearly a thousand pounds on me. It was good to feel my ex-girlfriend's body against mine and I clung on to her until she broke away.

"Would you like a drink?" she asked. "I have beer. Or whisky."

"Beer, please."

She fetched a bottle from the kitchen and handed it to me. Tracey had already strategically placed an opener on the coffee table and I used it to uncap the drink.

"Aren't you having anything?"

"I will in a minute. I already had a little too much this afternoon."

I could tell she was nervous. Tracey was not a casual drinker, and when we'd been going out together she had only drunk at home at moments of extreme emotion.

"Are you OK, Tracey?"

"I'm fine," she replied, sitting on her sofa.

She was wearing a cream cardigan, a white halter-neck and a short grey skirt. Tracey had always had a thing for flesh-coloured stockings, and was wearing a pair this evening, with no shoes. I sipped my beer, waiting to hear why she had summoned me here.

"The offer you made the other night."

"Yes?"

"Does it still stand?"

"Of course."

"What if I don't want to have sex with you?"

I wasn't in the mood for this sort of game playing, and wasn't about to beg. I put down my beer and stood up. "Then I don't think you should."

"No," she said, looking up at me, "I don't mean that. Oh, God . . ." She rubbed her forehead. "What if I want to do other things?"

I sat back down. "What sort of other things?"

"Safer things."

"I can wear a condom."

"I don't mean that sort of safe. I mean, emotionally safe."

"I'm not sure I follow."

"Well," she said, "would you want to see me?"

I smiled. "Of course. But let's not make this so clinical. Why don't you come over here with me?"

"But how will we work out the money?"

"The money doesn't matter to me. How about if I give you five hundred pounds anyway, and then you can decide how far you want to go?"

"And you won't get angry with me?"

"Of course not. Don't be stupid."

"Or tell anyone? Or hold it against me?"

"I don't know anyone you know. And it's my idea. How can I hold it against you?"

She still didn't seem satisfied. I was beginning to wonder if this was such a good idea, but was feeling too turned on to leave.

"And you accept that this will be a one-off? You won't force me to do it again later because I agreed to it now?"

I couldn't understand why she was being like this. Throughout our relationship I had almost always been the submissive one, never forcing her to do anything. I might have been a little more forthcoming than her about my desires, but that'd only been because she rarely talked about what she wanted, preferring to go unhappy than verbalize her discontent.

"Tracey, I'm not about to cast judgement on you. I offered you money the other night because I was desperate to sleep with you and couldn't cope with being rejected. I can understand why you were offended . . ."

"I wasn't offended, just scared. I'm frightened by you wanting me."

"Why? You work on a sex line. You have men wanting you all the time."

I realized the moment I said this that it was a mistake. Suddenly, everything became clear to me and I saw my way out of this. But first I had to listen to her response.

"Jesse, this is why I got so upset the other night. I told you about the sex line because I thought you'd find it sexy and funny, but I didn't think it would change the way you thought about me. After I said it I remembered how afraid I was about telling you about my sexuality. This is something I've been wanting to tell you for ages, in fact, that's the whole reason why I got in touch with you again. But then at dinner you told me you'd had a breakdown and I couldn't tell you the truth . . . well, I mean, I told you part of the truth, about how I missed you and was glad we had all that time together, but I couldn't get to the heart of it. I couldn't tell you . . . Look, you know what you said about your therapist telling you that what you were feeling with me, when you isolated us, wasn't jealousy but you wanting something from me, something I couldn't give?"

"Of course."

"Well, you and your therapist got it completely round the wrong way. What you wanted was to know the truth about me, but because you were so jealous you didn't want to hear it."

What she was saying made sense. I thought back to my bank manager telling me about her come-fantasy and how that hadn't turned me on at all. I had often told Tracey I wanted to know what she masturbated about – and in my head I thought I did – but the truth was, if she wasn't doing it about me I didn't want to know.

"The truth is, the reason I freaked out the other night was because it felt like you were making the offer out of anger. And it reminded me of how you always used to view sex as something you had to take from me, as if I was deliberately withholding it. That 'something I couldn't give' was an honest sexual response, because I always felt you were judging me.

"But the thing is, I do want to do something with you. Something that'll get rid of all the hurt and make you think well of me. And, although it sounds strange, and it did upset me at first, I think you paying me for sex is a good idea. Only you have to be doing it for pure motives. You have to do it because you want me."

"I do want you."

"Good." She came across and sat next to me. Taking control, she straddled me and pushed me back on the sofa. She'd washed her hair recently and I could smell her shampoo as her long brunette curls fell over her face. As she started kissing me, I considered how this evening's experience was already so different from my previous night with Vicki. I had completely forgotten how Tracey kissed, the soft pulling that felt so reassuring after her resistance in the bar after the restaurant and, as I let her take charge, I found myself thinking back to when I first got my money and was trying to develop an interest in pornography. Although it had quickly stopped working for me, it was only now that I realized why. It was my lack of imagination, and my inability to bring details from my own life into my appreciation of the films. My one-nightstands were few and far between and, to be honest, they weren't fantasy-occasions, instead usually arising from desperation and mutual need. And although I've always had lots of women in my life, it's been hard to eroticize them, as I've known them as friends rather than sex objects (I realize the two are by no means mutually exclusive, but until last night with Vicki, it'd always seemed that way to me). So when I watched pornography, I found it hard to enjoy the variety, which I guess is the whole point in the first place. It was difficult to identify with the well-built men, and unless the women looked like Tracey, or other ex-girlfriends, they didn't seem sexy either. I'm not a natural voyeur, and watching other people having sex always makes me feel like I'm the one being exploited, not them, as if I'm stuck in someone's house and still having to be the polite guest even when my hosts start going down on each other.

Now that I was having sex with Tracey so soon after I'd had sex with Vicki, and was rediscovering myself as a sexual person (albeit in quite an unconventional way), I felt like I might like to watch pornography again, using the woman on screen as a point of connection between Tracey and Vicki and whomever I ended up having sex with next.

I was amazed at how much the money was adding an extra energy. When I'd been going out with Tracey, our intercourse had always been extremely fraught, a cycle of tears, excitement, pain, pleasure and tears. The first few times had been terrifying, a form of lovemaking I was completely unused to, having previously only been with women who saw sex as a friendly adult kinship. Now I was paying Tracey she seemed to be trying to fit her need around working out how to make me happy. The way she was kissing me showed she wanted me, which is something I've always needed to know in order to enjoy sex with anyone. These last two statements sounds antithetical. Let me explain. What I mean is, nothing is as big a turn-off for me as a woman saying, "I want to make you happy." But a woman who wants me (even if she's only pretending) is all I need for the sex to work. This is why I always aimed low when picking people up, and why paying my friends for sex was turning out to be so successful. I'm not vain enough to imagine I could sexually excite a professional prostitute, but I also knew that it would be impossible for a friend (or an ex) to have sex with me without feeling something. And with Tracey I thought it went much further than that, as I saw now that she'd always needed this sort of excuse to really enjoy sex, and may even previously have had this sort of fantasy herself.

She stopped kissing me and pushed herself up. "How much would you pay to pull down my top?"

"I told you. I'll give you five hundred pounds whatever we end up doing."

She shook her head. "No," she said, "I want to negotiate."

"OK." I smiled. "I guess that could be fun. Are you wearing a bra?"

Tracey got up and pulled her curtains. Then she turned on a table lamp and switched off the main light. Before taking her position on top of me, she pulled off her cardigan and hung it over the back of a chair.

"Yes, I'm wearing a bra."

"So you're only talking about me seeing your bra, not your breasts?"

"For the moment, yes."

"And, let me get this straight, am I paying you to pull down your top yourself or for me to do it?"

"Either."

"So there's no price difference between those two options?"

"No. Come on, how much?"

"Well, it seems quite minor, so let's say ten pounds."

"Twenty. I take it you have the money with you?"

I felt surprised that Tracey was being as serious about the money as Vicki had been yesterday, especially as I'd assumed I'd have to persuade her to take the cash. But I enjoyed my role in the fantasy, taking a twenty-pound note from my inside pocket and laying it out on the table.

"OK," she said, fingers going to the thin cord around her neck.

I reached up and stopped her, saying, "No, I want to do it."

I untied her and pulled the top down over her breasts. She was wearing a white strapless bra and her nipples were visible through the material. I attempted to stroke them.

"No, no," she told me, "you haven't paid for that yet. How much to see my knickers?"

"What type are you wearing?"

"Does that affect the price?"

"No, I'm just curious."

"Mmm," she said, "you just reminded me of something."

"Dinner in the oven?"

"No. A memory. From when we were together."

"Dangerous territory."

"Doesn't have to be. Anyway, this is a nice memory. It was about the third or fourth time we slept together, and we met unexpectedly, or maybe I hadn't been planning to go to bed with you but it ended up happening anyway, and you were surprised because I wasn't wearing matching underwear and I felt really weird because I didn't even have that many matching sets and you'd already seen most of them."

"So you're not wearing matching underwear today?"

"I am, actually, although I didn't think about that this morning. Well, kind of matching, they're white string-knickers, with a small red design in one corner."

"Let me see."

"How much?"

"Forty."

"Cash on the table."

I unfolded another two notes. "Are you sure you don't want me to give you the whole five hundred right now?"

"And spoil the fun? I'm enjoying myself, aren't you?"

"Of course."

"Good." She smiled at me and pulled her skirt up. She tried to make the material stay as high up her thighs as possible so I could get a proper look at her knickers. Shortly after we'd started going out, I'd discovered Tracey's diary. Just before we met she'd had a lonely night with some unsatisfactory ex-partner and come home and detailed all the things she liked and didn't like. Eventually I was forced to admit my betrayal of her trust, but prior to my confession it provided a useful shorthand on how to please her. She liked having her breasts caressed rather than kissed, preferred having her knickers gently slipped down her thighs rather than taking them off herself, sometimes enjoyed being fingered to orgasm with her knickers still on, although that was never quite as nice as being eaten out. She liked sucking cock; sometimes more than being fucked. Her favourite fantasy was imaginary incest (something only ever exciting to those who hadn't suffered the irritation of real-life siblings) and except for very, very rare occasions, hated being on top.

She laughed. "I bet you're just dying to touch me, aren't you?"

Tracey never used to be this confident. I knew it had something to do with the money, but I also thought it was probably connected to her new job. I'd always known Tracey had the perfect voice for sex-line work, but felt surprised that she'd actually gone through with it. I wanted to ask her more about what the job was like, but after her previous outburst, felt scared about spoiling the mood.

"Can I touch your cunt and breasts at the same time?"

"If you're prepared to pay for it."

"I'll give you fifty pounds. But you also have to rub my cock."

"For fifty, I'll only do it through your trousers."

"That's all I want, for the minute." I counted out the cash and put it on the table. "Although let me touch you for a bit first."

"OK. Can I lie back more?"

"Of course. It'll make things easier."

She shuffled backwards, reclining against the arm of the sofa. I moved round between her legs, leaning in to kiss her as I began to gently stroke and squeeze her breasts. Her kisses were more open now, her mouth more relaxed. I quickly embraced her and then began to rub the heel of my hand over her cunt. I touched her breasts at the same time, kissing her again. After a few minutes, she pushed me back up and began stroking the tight crotch of my trousers. She stroked her hand around my shape, the heel of her hand rubbing my cock while her fingers softly dug against the underside of my balls. I let her do this for a short while, then pushed her back.

"Another fifty to see your tits."

She laughed. "Shall I undo it?"

"No, let me."

I put a fifty-pound note on the table, and Tracey leaned forward to let me unhook her bra. I was amazed at how unfamiliar her breasts looked, and wondered how I could've forgotten something so important. Why are visual memories the hardest to preserve? Especially sexual memories. I couldn't believe that in my fantasy world I had robbed Tracey of her real body and replaced it with an anonymous alternative. I had forgotten how easily she flushed; that her shoulders were lightly freckled. Her breasts had become bigger in my memory, her nipples smaller, and the real-life combination was much sexier. But strangest of all, I had forgotten how Tracey looked at me differently when I started to undress her.

She kissed me. "Knickers too?"

"Let me do it. You know what you said earlier about not wanting to have sex with me, do you still feel like that?"

"I don't want to have penetrative sex. But everything else is OK."

I considered this. "All right then, I'll give you a hundred and fifty pounds to pull your knickers off and go down on you."

"OK."

Placing the cash on the table, I gently lifted Tracey from the sofa and brought her down onto the floor. She raised her knees and I slipped my fingers under the waistband of her knickers and gently tugged them down. Her cunt was already wet and slightly open, the pink bright beneath the spring of her light-brown pubic hair. I pulled her legs slightly more open and gave her cunt a first kiss. She murmured something and I moved up to hear what she said.

"What was that?"

"I said I've fantasized so much about you doing this. Especially since the other night."

Remembering Vicki, I asked, "What did you do when you fantasized?"

"Touched myself, of course," she said, sounding surprised.

I couldn't stop myself asking, "When was the last time?"

She sounded slightly irritated as she replied, "In the shower at the gym this morning," and, not wanting to push my luck, I went back down on her.

It was incredible to be between Tracey's legs again, and I felt disappointed when she came quickly. I wanted to carry on and see if I could bring her to a second orgasm, but she stopped me and made me come up alongside her for a hug.

We lay like that for a while and then I asked her, "Would you like to see my cock?"

"Do I have to pay you?"

"No." I laughed. "It's a freebie."

I pulled open my fly. She looked at me, surprised.

"You wear underwear now?"

"Since Michael Hutchence died."

"Show me then."

I pulled out my cock. She stared at it for a minute and then looked up at me.

"I remember it."

"Do you?" I asked, surprised. "Exactly?"

"Exactly."

I looked at her, wondering if women's memories worked differently to men's, or whether the fault lay solely with me.

"So," I said, "two hundred quid for a blow job."

"It's extra to come in my mouth."

"Two-fifty, then."

I counted out the cash and she went down on me.

Marianne was already in bed when I got home. I knew she was probably still upset about what I'd said that morning, but found I didn't really regret it. Since I'd started paying people for sex, my generosity to her had started to seem unfathomable, and I couldn't understand why I'd been kind to her for so long. No one else seemed interested in her (in the whole time she'd lived with me she'd never mentioned her parents once) and she hardly contributed anything around the home. Besides, if it wasn't for her living here I could have my sexual adventures without venturing outside the front door. I wasn't quite ready to kick her out, but from now on I felt she should start doing something to justify her board.

I didn't have much to do the next day. I arose late, masturbated, then went out for lunch alone. When I got back Marianne was sitting in the garden, reading a book. I went through to my study and called Vicki.

"Hi, Jesse, how are you?"

"Good."

There was a moment of silence. I hadn't imagined that it'd be hard to talk to her, assuming that we'd quickly fall back into a friendly intimacy, maybe with a pleasant new sexual undercurrent to our conversation. But suddenly I was experiencing the same sort of shyness I usually only felt when I was talking to someone I really fancied.

"Is this a money conversation?"

"Kind of," I laughed.

"Oh," she said, "I'm glad you've brought that up. The thing is, Jesse, the other night and everything I did enjoy it, but I don't think it should happen again."

"Really?" I replied, wondering if she was serious, or just wanted to be persuaded.

"Yeah," she said, "I'm sorry. I can't really explain. It's not you, or the money. It's just that I'm not very good at the stage between casual sex and a proper relationship, and I know you're not looking for that right now . . ."

"Well . . ."

"I mean, I'm not either, and I want you to carry on being my walker, and well, if I'm going to be absolutely honest, the next day I was a bit freaked out by the fact that I'd taken money from you and if you'll let me I'd like to give it back."

"No, Vicki, don't be silly, it was worth it."

"I don't have to give you the actual money. If you want I can just credit your account."

"No," I said, "I'm glad I paid you. But I understand why you don't want to do it again, and don't worry, this won't damage our friendship."

"Oh, good," she replied, "thanks, Jesse."

I finished the call, found my address book and flipped through until I found Anita's number. I dialled, and got her answerphone. So I tried her mobile.

"Hello?" she said, the background noise of a lively pub behind her voice.

"Hi, Anita, it's Jesse."

"Hi, Jesse, how are you?"

"Good. Where are you?"

"In Soho. Why?"

"Are you alone?"

"Yeah. Why?"

"I wondered whether I could meet up with you."

"Now?"

"Is that OK?"

"Of course. I'm in Waxy's Little Sister. Do you know where that is?"

"No."

"Opposite the Metro."

"The cinema?"

"Yeah. How long are you going to be?"

"About forty-five minutes."

"OK. I'll see you then."

I told Marianne I was going out and took a taxi into Soho. Part of me wanted to reveal that I was meeting Anita, just to see how she'd react. But I worried that giving Marianne clues as to what I had planned might inhibit me, so I kept quiet.

During the drive, I thought about Anita and wondered whether she would go for my suggestion. The fact that she was drinking alone in the afternoon seemed a good sign, as she only lapsed back into alcoholism between affairs, focusing more heavily on drugs when she was involved with someone.

I remembered talking about Anita with Hazel, Ivy and Elizabeth, and how they were convinced I'd be able to seduce her. It was almost worth not using the money as a motivation, but I realized when I thought about having sex with Anita the financial transaction was the part I was looking forward to most. It was knowing that I was going to offer Anita money that stopped me feeling intimidated by her, as it seemed more adult, honest and decadent than her booze, coke and affairs.

Waxy's Little Sister was a ghastly Irish theme pub, and I couldn't understand what Anita was doing there. She was sitting alone with a pint and a small glass of whisky. I walked across and joined her.

"Hi, Jesse. So what's wrong? Is this to do with Marianne?"

"No, nothing like that. I was just at a loose end and wanting someone to have a drink with. You were the first person who came to mind. Well, second, after my bank manager."

She chuckled. "Isn't he working?"

"She. And yes, she is. But I thought I could persuade her to knock off early. Anyway, I'm glad you were free. Are you all right for drinks?"

She nodded. I got myself a pint and pulled up a chair beside her. Even when she was getting wasted alone Anita looked incredible. She looked posh and innocent, a fatal combination even without the added spice of her exciting private life. I'd always wanted her, but had been held back by fear. Her red hair (always a warning sign to me, since that first experience of adolescent rejection) made her look a little like Nicole Kidman at her most elegant, although with a slightly more inviting, open face.

"How are you then?" I asked, still nervous.

"All right. Starting to get a little bit wobbly. How about you?"

"OK . . . a little drained."

"Ennui?" She smiled.

"Something like that. Too much money and too much free time."

"I wish I had that worry."

I sipped my beer, sensing an opening. "You're all right for money, aren't you?"

"Are you kidding? I'm broke. I've never had this little money in my life."

"Really?" I said, and after enough large swallows, began my pitch.

The following evening I was feeling lonely again. I couldn't get hold of Anita, or Tracey, and knew it would be undignified to have another go at persuading Vicki to change her mind. Frustrated, I went downstairs to the lounge.

Marianne was lying on the floor, watching television. She was wearing a short skirt and a black top and when I sat on the sofa behind her I could see her knickers. She paid no attention to me, concentrating on the television. I stayed there for fifteen minutes, but finally couldn't take it any longer and asked, "How much money would you want to suck my cock?"

Marianne moved out the following morning. I would've been happy if she'd left the night before, but she clearly wanted to drag out her departure. I wasn't sad to see her go and, although I had said some seriously mean things to her in our argument the night before, none of my comments had been unfair. Two years of frustration had come out too fast, that's all. I wasn't a bad person.

"I think it's good that you kicked Marianne out," Elizabeth told me. "She's been sponging off of you for far too long."

"What was the argument about?" asked Hazel.

"Never mind that," Ivy interrupted, "what I want to know is, what is Anita like in bed?"

I answered both their questions, at length, by telling them the story of my past week. This time I definitely wasn't trying to reel anyone in, knowing that all three of my friends were happily married mothers who weren't short of money and liked to think of themselves as decent, moral individuals. Ivy was the first to start turning the conversation. Her approach was obvious, getting me to repeat the concept over and over again ("So, let me get this straight. You've been paying your friends for sex?" "Yes, Ivy, that's right, I've been paying my friends for sex.") until it no longer sounded outrageous and they'd all accepted it as an acceptable thing to do.

But Hazel was the one who made it personal.

"Would you pay me for sex?" she asked.

"Would you like to have sex with me?"

"Maybe. How much money are we talking about?"

"Well, I paid Vicki a thousand, Tracey somewhere around five hundred and Anita two-fifty."

"You paid Anita the least amount of money?" Ivy exclaimed, shocked.

I smiled, amused by her indignation. "I asked all three of them to name their price. Anita wanted two-fifty."

"That's terrible," said Elizabeth. "She must have such low self-esteem."

"How much would you want to sleep with Jesse?" Ivy asked Elizabeth.

"Definitely a thousand," she said, "at the very least."

It was fun checking into a hotel with three women. We went to the Tenderloin, a tacky rock-themed hotel that Ivy claimed was the only place for an afternoon assignation. I was shocked by her knowledge and wondered whether I'd been right to think of these women as being so innocent after all. We took the lift up to the third floor and found our room. I could tell the three women were enjoying themselves, although I thought it probably had less to do with the sex than the fact that we were all doing something secretive together. They always got like this whenever we left the café, even on the most innocent of missions. I think it was because we were moving outside the expected limits of our friendship, and none of us had the emotional maturity to cope with that.

Ivy took off her shoes and jumped backwards onto the bed. She was the shortest of my prospective partners, although none of them was tall.

"So how are we going to do this?" asked Hazel. "Are you up to having sex with all three of us?"

"Not in a straight way."

Elizabeth looked worried. "I'm not doing any lesbian stuff."

I laughed.

"I mean, not that I don't like you both and everything," she said to Ivy and Hazel, "I just don't think I could bear it."

"I'm not sure about the masturbation part either," Ivy admitted. "I don't even do that in front of my husband."

"What is it that embarrasses you?" I asked. "Doing it in front of me or doing it in front of each other?"

"Each other," they agreed.

" 'Cause I could call down to reception for three blindfolds. They do do that sort of thing here, don't they?"

"They do," Ivy admitted. "There's an S&M bag they give to favoured customers."

"What do you think?" I asked them.

"I'd still be embarrassed," said Elizabeth, "even with only you watching."

"I don't mind doing it," Hazel told me, "as long as you do get the blindfolds."

"Ivy?"

"Oh, God, honestly, Jesse, I don't think I'd even enjoy it. Can't you just fuck me?"

"Well, I will, but I wanted us all to do something together."

"OK, how about if I strip down to my underwear and watch you having sex with Elizabeth while Hazel masturbates?"

"But Hazel doesn't want you to see her masturbating."

"And I don't want you to watch Jesse having sex with me," added Elizabeth.

Sighing, I decided to cut my losses. Ivy would wait in the bathroom, Hazel would masturbate, I would fuck Elizabeth. The women would all wear blindfolds. I worried that this would turn the afternoon into a slapstick comedy, but they were adamant. We moved everything they might bump into and called reception, who sent up a boy with three blindfolds on a silver tray.

I asked if anyone wanted to undress before I blindfolded them, but they all wanted to stay fully clothed to begin with. Their anxieties had made me feel uncomfortable and I began to wonder whether this was such a good idea. But even if we stopped now our friendship would still be changed for ever, and in spite of everything, this was still a sexual experience I wanted to have.

"You are going to wear a condom, aren't you?" asked Ivy.

"And not the same one," Hazel added. "A different one for each of us."

"I don't have any," I said.

We called reception and they sent the boy back with a packet of extra-safe Mates. Ivy went out into the bathroom and closed the door. Hazel took off her shoes. Elizabeth lay on the bed. She whispered to me that she wanted me to undress her, so I took her shoes off and unbuttoned her jeans. I felt most worried about having sex with Elizabeth and was trying to make sure the experience didn't feel inappropriately intimate. I pulled off her jeans. She was wearing simple pale-cream knickers. I removed them quickly and looked up at her face, watching her breathing as I went down on her, again trying to make the sex feel as straightforward and competent as possible.

I was paying so much attention to Elizabeth that I hadn't even had a chance to look at Hazel, who was probably the one of the three I was most excited about going to bed with. I gently nuzzled and kissed Elizabeth's clit, reaching up under her jumper and pulling the cups of her bra down from her large breasts. Behind me I had heard Hazel getting out of her dress, but she was managing to masturbate almost without making any sound at all.

I continued sucking Elizabeth, realizing my only real opportunity to look back at Hazel without Elizabeth sensing it was during the few moments it would take me to move from licking her cunt to fucking her. After that I could probably get another couple of glimpses but would have to really strain my neck. I would've sucked Elizabeth for longer, but I was so eager to see Hazel that the moment I thought Elizabeth was wet enough to fuck, I stopped and turned round. Hazel was wearing a long stripy top that, together with her hand, almost entirely obscured my view of her cunt, but her facial expression and the quick movement of her finger suggested that she had got over her embarrassment of masturbating in front of me.

I turned back from her, fixed my condom and slid my hard cock into Elizabeth's cunt. She was wet, but it did take a couple of thrusts before I was moving smoothly inside her. Seeing Hazel like that made me excited again, and I worried I wouldn't be able to last long enough to satisfy all three women. Elizabeth had been avoiding kissing me, so I didn't force it, gratified when I felt her hands holding my hips. I didn't want to get Elizabeth too close and then stop, as I knew that would prove frustrating to her. I also didn't know where she was going to go when I swapped over to Hazel. In the bathroom with Ivy, I guess. I slowed down, and Elizabeth nodded, seemingly happy for me to stop. I pulled out of her, and helped her get dressed and go into the bathroom. The moment the bathroom door closed, I walked over and snogged Hazel. She seemed perfectly happy to kiss me, wrapping her arms around me and reaching for my cock.

"Hang on," I said, "I've just got to get rid of the condom."

"Forget the condom. Just get rid of it and fuck me."

She reached up and untied the blindfold. I snapped off the condom and lifted her off the chair, pushing my cock into her as I pressed her against the wall. She grabbed my hair and we started fucking furiously, finding a satisfactory position somewhere between standing and a crouch. We continued like that until I said, "I'm sorry, I'm getting close. And I've got to stay hard for Ivy."

"Can't you come twice?"

"Not usually."

"OK. Go down on me then. I'm pretty close too."

She lay back on the bed and I gave her head until she came. Afterwards, she squirmed and reached for my hand. I kissed her and we stayed on the bed until Hazel called out to Ivy, "He's all yours."

"Come in here then," she called back.

"No, don't worry, I'm going down to the bar."

Hazel dressed and left the room. Ivy walked in, still blindfolded. I let her come towards me. She gave a short, dirty laugh as her fingers reached my chest.

"Come on, then, what have you got left for me?"

I felt vaguely irritated at Ivy for stopping me from properly satisfying Hazel, and for the way she had always previously been so flirtatious with me, but then joined in with Elizabeth's squeamishness when it actually came down to us all getting together. So I went down on her until her fingers were digging into my head, then fingered her as I fucked her from behind, making her come just before I emptied myself into her.

That was the last I saw of Elizabeth, Hazel and Ivy. They never contacted me again, and didn't return my calls or emails. Anita and I met once more for sex, but then she got involved with someone else and said she couldn't see me any more. Tracey, too, seemed to have decided against further meetings with me, and although Vicki was happy to talk to me about money, there was no chance of anything sexual happening between us. At first I was glad to be free of Marianne, happy to have the house to myself, but it didn't take me long to become lonely. And with no friends left, there was no possibility of pursuing my previous path. I lasted two weeks before I started buying pornographic videos again, watching them with a hunger I had never had previously. And when they stopped working I found myself in a phone box, intending to try Tracey again, but after getting halfway through her number, stopping and dialling the digits on a small colour card in front of me, finally ready to begin the next stage of my existence.

# Gators

Vicki Hendricks

It was a goddamned one-armed alligator put me over the line. After that I was looking for trouble. Carl and me had been married for two years, second marriage for both, and the situation was drastic – hateful most times – but I could tell he didn't realize there was anything better in the world. It made me feel bad that he never learned how to love – grew up with nothing but cruelty. I kept trying way too long to show him there was something else.

I was on my last straw when I suggested a road trip for Labor Day weekend – stupidly thinking that I could amuse him and wouldn't have to listen to his bitching about me and the vile universe on all my days off work. I figured at a motel he'd get that vacation feeling, lighten up, and stick me good, and I could get by for the few waking hours I had to see him the rest of the week.

We headed out to the Everglades for our little trip. Being recent transplants from Texas, we hadn't seen the natural wonders in Florida. Carl started griping by mid-afternoon about how I told him there were so many alligators and we couldn't find a fucking one. I didn't dare say that there would've been plenty if he hadn't taken two hours to read the paper and sit on the john. We could've made it before the usual thunderstorms and had time to take a tour. As it was, he didn't want to pay the bucks to ride the tram in the rain – even though the cars were covered. We were pretty much stuck with what we could see driving, billboards for Seminole gambling and airboats, and lots of soggy grassland under heavy black and blue-layered skies. True, it had a bleak, haunting kind of beauty.

Carl refused to put on the air conditioner because he said it sapped the power of the engine, so all day we suffocated. We could only crack the truck windows because of the rain. By late afternoon my back was soaked with sweat and I could smell my armpits. And, get this – he was smoking cigarettes. Like I said, I was plain stupid coming up with the idea – or maybe blinded by the fact that he had a nice piece of well-working equipment that seemed worth saving.

At that point, I started to wonder if I could make us swerve into a canal and end the suffering. I was studying the landscape, looking ahead for deep water, when I spotted a couple vehicles pulled off the road.

"Carl, look. I bet you they see gators."

"Fuckin' A," he bellowed.

He was driving twenty over the limit, as always – in a hurry to get to hell – but he nailed the brakes and managed to turn onto a gravel road that ran a few hundred yards off the side of a small lake. One car pulled out past us, but a couple and a little girl were still standing near the edge of the water.

It was only drizzling by then, and Carl pulled next to their pickup and shut off the ignition. My side of the truck was over a puddle about four inches deep. I opened the door and plodded through in my sandals, while Carl stood grimacing at the horizon, rubbing his dark unshaved chin.

We walked towards the people. The woman was brown-haired, wearing a loose print dress – the kind my grandma would've called a house-dress – and I felt how sweet and old-fashioned she was next to me in short shorts and halter top, with my white-blonde hair and black roots haystack style. The man was a wiry, muscular type in tight jeans and a white T-shirt – tattoos on both biceps, like Carl, but arms half the size. He was bending down by some rocks a little further along. The little girl, maybe four years old, and her mother were holding hands by the edge.

Carl boomed out, "Hey, there," in his usual megaphone, overly friendly voice, and the mother and child glanced up with a kind of mousy suspiciousness I sometimes felt in my own face. It was almost like they had him pegged instantly.

We stopped near them. The guy came walking over. He had his hands cupped together in front of him and motioned with his arms towards the water. I looked into the short water weeds and sticks and saw two small eyes and nose holes rising above the ripples a few yards out. It was a baby gator, maybe four feet long, judging by the closeness of his parts.

"There he is!" Carl yelled.

"Just you watch this," the guy said. He tossed something into the water in front of the nose and I caught the scrambling of tiny lizard legs just before the gator lurched and snapped him up. "They just love them lizards," the man said.

Carl started laughing, "Ho, ho, ho," like it was the funniest thing he'd ever seen, and the guy joined in because he'd made such a big hit.

Us women looked at each other and kind of smiled with our lips tight. The mother had her arm around the little girl's shoulder holding her against her hip. The girl squirmed away. "Daddy, can I help you catch another one?"

"Sure, darlin', come right over here." He led her towards the rocks and I saw the mother cast him a look as he went by. He laughed and took his daughter's hand.

The whole thing was plenty creepy, but Carl was still chuckling. It seemed like maybe he was having a good time for a change.

"Cannibals. Reptiles eating reptiles," he said. "Yup." He did that eh-eh-eh laugh in the back of his throat. It made me wince. He took my hand and leered towards my face. "It's a scrawny one, Virginia – not like a Texas gator – but I guess I have to say you weren't lying. Florida has one." He put his arm across my shoulder and leaned on me, still laughing at his own sense of humour. I widened my legs, to keep from falling over, and chuckled so he wouldn't demand to know what was the matter, then insist I spoiled the day by telling him.

We stood there watching the gator float in place hoping for another snack, and in a few minutes, the squeals of the little girl told us that it wouldn't be long. They came shuffling over slowly, the father bent, cupping his hands over the girl's.

"This is the last one now, OK, sweetheart?" the mother said as they stopped beside her. She was talking to the little girl. "We need to get home in time to make supper." From her voice it sounded like they'd been sacrificing lizards for a while.

The two flung the prey into the water. It fell short, but there was no place for the lizard to go. It floundered in the direction it was pointed, the only high ground, the gator's waiting snout. He snapped it up. This time he'd pushed further out of the water and I saw that he was missing one of his limbs.

"Look, Carl, the gator only has one arm. I wonder what got him?"

"Probably a Texas gator," he said. "It figures, the one gator you find me is a cripple."

Carl had an answer for everything. "No," I said. "Why would one gator tear off another one's arm?"

"Leg. One big chomp without thinkin'. Probably got his leg in between his mother and some tasty tidbit – a small dog or kid. Life is cruel, babycakes – survival of the fittest." He stopped talking to light a cigarette. He waved it near my face to make his point. "You gotta protect yourself – be cruel first. That's why you got me – to do it for you." He gave me one of his grins with all the teeth showing.

"Oh, is *that* why?" I laughed, like it was a joke. Yeah, Carl would take care of his own all right – it was like having a mad dog at my side, never knowing when he might tum. He wouldn't hesitate to rip anybody's arm off, mine included, if it got in his way.

The mother called to her husband, "Can we get going, honey? I have fish to clean."

The guy didn't look up. "Good job," he said to his daughter. He reached down and gave her a pat on the butt. "Let's get another one."

It started to rain a little harder, thank God, and Carl motioned with his head towards the car and started walking. I looked at the woman still standing there. "Bye," I called.

She nodded at me, her face empty of life. "Goodbye, sweetie." It was then she turned enough for me to see that the sleeve on the far side of the dress was empty, pinned up – her arm was gone. Jesus. I felt my eyes bulge. She couldn't have missed what I said. I burned through ten shades of red in a split second. I turned and sprinted to catch up with Carl.

He glanced at me. "What's your hurry, sugar? You ain't gonna melt. Think I'd leave without you?"

"Nope," I said. I swallowed and tried to lighten up. I didn't want to share what I saw with him.

He looked at me odd and I knew he wasn't fooled. "What's with you?"

"Hungry," I said.

"I told you, you should've had a ham sandwich before we left. You never listen to me. I won't be ready to eat for a couple more hours."

"I have to pee too. We passed a restaurant a quarter-mile back."

He pointed across the road. "There's the bushes. I'm not stopping anywhere else till the motel."

We crossed the state and got a cheap room outside of Naples for the night. Carl ordered a pepperoni pizza from Domino's, no mushrooms like he wanted. The room was clean and the air and remote worked, but it was miles from the beach. We sat in bed and ate the pizza. I was trying to stick with the plan for having fun and I suggested we could get up early and drive to the beach to find shells.

"Fucking seashells? Forget it."

His volume warned me. I decided to drop it. I gave him all my pepperonis and finished up my piece. I had a murder book to curl up with. He found a football game on TV.

I was in the midst of the murder scene when Carl started working his hands under the covers. It was half-time. He found my thigh and stroked inward. I read fast to get to the end of the chapter. He grabbed the book and flung it across the room onto the other bed.

"I'm trying to make love to you, and you have your nose stuck in a book. What's the problem? You gettin' it somewhere else and don't need it from me? Huh?"

I shook my head violently. His tone and volume had me scared. "No, for Christsakes." His face was an inch from mine. Rather than say anything else, I took his shoulders and pulled myself to him for a kiss. He was stiff, so I started sucking his lower lip and moving my tongue around. His body relaxed.

Pretty soon he yanked down the covers, pulled up my nighty and climbed on top. I couldn't feel him inside me – I was numb. Nothing new. I smelled his breath.

I moaned like he expected, and after a few long minutes of pumping and grabbing at my tits, he got that strained look on his face. "I love you to death," he rasped. "Love you to death." I felt him get rigid inside me, and a chill ran all the way from his cock to my head. He groaned deep and let himself down on my chest. "It's supernatural what you do to me, doll face, supernatural."

"Mmm."

He lit up a cigarette and puffed a few breaths in my face. "I couldn't live without you. Know that? You know that, don't you? You ever left me, I'd have to kill myself."

"No. Don't say that."

"Why? You thinking of leaving? *I would* kill myself. I would. And, knowing me, I'd take you along." He rolled on his side laughing "eh-eh-eh" to himself. My arm was pinned, and for a second I panicked. I yanked it out from under him. He shifted and in seconds started snoring. Son of a bitch. He had me afraid to speak.

The woman and the gator came into my head, and I knew her life without having to live it, casual cruelty and then the injury that changed her whole future. I could land in her place easy, trapped with a kid, no job, and a bastard of a husband that thought he was God. Carl said he was God at least three times a week, trying to convince himself. I shuddered. More like the devil. He might take an arm first, or go straight for my soul, just a matter of time. He'd rather see me dead than gone.

* * *

There was no thought of a road trip the next weekend, so we both slept late that Saturday. By then, the fear and hatred in my heart had taken over my brain. I was frying eggs, the bathroom door was open, and Carl was on the toilet – his place of serious thinking – when he used the words that struck me with the juicy, seedy, sweet fantasy of getting rid of him.

"I ought to kill my brother-in-law," he yelled. The words were followed by grunts of pleasure and plunking noises I could hear from the kitchen.

"Uh, huh," I said to myself. Neon was flashing in my head, but I pretended to be half hearing – as if that were possible – and splashed the eggs with bacon grease like he wanted them. I didn't say anything. He could build up rage on the sound of his own voice alone.

"The fuck went out on Labor Day and left Penny and the kids home. She didn't say anything about him drinkin', but I could hear it in her voice when I called last night. I can't keep ignoring this. I oughta get a flight over there and take ol' Raymond out."

"How's he doing after his knife wound?"

"Son of a bitch is finally back at work. I should just take him out. Penny and the kids would be fine with the insurance she'd get from GM."

"Oh?"

"Those slimy titty bars he hangs out in – like Babydoe's – I could just fly into Dallas, do him and fly back. Nobody would think a thing unusual."

I heard the flush and then his continued pulling of toilet paper. He always flushed before he wiped. I knew if I went in there after him I would see streaky wads of paper still floating. He came striding into the kitchen with a towel wrapped around him, his gut hanging over. He seemed to rock back as he walked to keep from falling forward. He turned and poured his eighth cup of coffee, added milk, held it over the sink and stirred wildly. Half of it slopped over the sides of the cup. His face was mottled with red and he growled to himself.

I looked away. I remembered that at seventeen he had thrown his father out of the house – for beating his mother. He found out later they snuck around for years to see each other behind his back – they were that scared of him.

I knew going opposite whatever he said would push him. I pointed to the phone. "Calm down and call your sister. Her and the kids might want to keep Ray around."

"Yeah? Uh, uh. She's too nice. She'll give that son of a bitch chance after chance while he spends all their money on ass and booze. If anybody's gonna take advantage of somebody, it's gonna be me."

I handed him his plate of eggs and turned away to take my shower and let him spew. He picked up the paper again and started with how all the "assholes in the news" should be killed.

Before this, it didn't occur to me as an asset that he was always a hair's breath from violence. I'd tried for peace. I didn't want to know details about the trouble he'd been in before we met. I knew he'd been plunked in jail for violating a restraining order. He'd broken down a door too – I had that from his sister because she thought I should know. I figured he deserved another chance in life. He had a lousy childhood with the drunk old man and all. But now I realized how foolish I was to think that if I treated him nice enough – turned the other cheek – he would be nice back. Thought that was human nature. Wrong. Slap after slap to my dignity, until there was none of it left. I was a goddamned angelic saviour for over a year and not a speck of it rubbed off. He took me for a sucker to use and abuse. It was a lesson I'd never forget, learned too late.

Something about the alligator incident made me know Carl's true capabilities, and I was fucking scared. That gator told me that a flight for Carl to Dallas was my only ticket out. It was a harsh thought, but Penny's husband wasn't God's gift either, and if Carl didn't get him, it was just a matter of time till some other motherfucker did.

At first I felt scared of the wicked thoughts in my heart. But after a few days, each time Carl hawked up a big gob and spit it out the car window or screamed at me because the elevator at the apartment complex was too slow, the idea became less sinful. He was always saying how he used to break guys' legs for a living, collecting, and he might decide to find some employment of that kind in Florida since the pay was so lousy for construction. Besides that, there was his drunk driving. If I could get him behind bars, it would be an asset to the whole state.

One morning he woke up and bit my nipple hard before I was even awake. "Ouch," I yelled. It drew blood and made my eyes fill up.

"The world's a hard place," he told me.

"You make it that way."

He laughed. "You lived your little pussy life long enough. It's time you find out what it's all about." He covered my mouth with his booze and cigarette breath, and I knew that was the day I'd make a call to his sister. He wasn't going to go away on his own.

Penny did mail-outs at home in the morning, so I called her from work. I could hear her stuffing envelopes while we talked. I asked about the kids and the dog. "So how's your husband?" I added. "Carl said he went back to work."

"Yeah. We're getting along much better. He's cut back on the drinking and brings home his paycheck. Doesn't go to the bar half as much."

"He's still going to that bar where he got hurt?"

"Oh, no, a new one, Cactus Jack's – no nude dancers, and it's only a couple miles from here, so he takes a cab home if he needs to. He promised he wouldn't go back over to Babydoe's."

Done. Smooth. I didn't even have to ask any suspicious questions. "Yeah," I said. "He gets to the job in the morning. That's important."

"He only goes out Fridays and maybe one or two other days. I can handle that. I'm not complaining."

She was a sweetheart. I felt tears well in my eyes. "You're a saint, honey. I have to get back to work now – the truckers are coming in for their checks. Carl would like to hear from you one night soon. He worries."

I had all I needed to know – likely she'd wanted to tell somebody, anybody, and didn't care to stir Carl up and listen to all his godly orders. She wasn't complaining – goddamn. It was amazing that her and my husband were of the same blood. And, yeah, she was being taken advantage of – I could hear it. Now I had to tell Carl when and where to go without him realizing it was my plan.

That night I started to move him along. "I talked to your sister Penny this morning," I told him at the dinner table.

"Oh, yeah?" He was shovelling in chicken-fried steak, mashed potatoes with sawmill gravy, and corn, one of his favourite meals.

I realized I was eating with one arm behind my back, keeping it out of reach from any quick snaps. "She's a trooper," I said. "Wow."

"Huh?"

"I never heard of anybody with such a big heart. You told me she adopted Ray's son, right?

"Yeah. Unbelievable." He chewed a mouthful. "Him and Penny already had one kid, and he was fuckin' around on her. I'd've killed the motherfucker, if I'd known at the time. I was in Alaska – working on the pipeline. Penny kept it all from me till after the adoption." He shook his head and wiped the last gravy from his plate with a roll. "Lumps in the mashed potatoes, hon."

"She works hard too – all those jobs – and doesn't say a thing about him having a boys' night out at some new bar whenever he wants. I couldn't handle it." I paused and took a drink of my beer to let the thought sink in. "He's a damn good-looking guy. Bet he has no trouble screwing around on her."

Carl looked up and wiped his mouth on his hand. "You mean now? Where'd you get that idea?"

I shrugged. "Just her tone. Shit. If anybody's going to heaven, she will."

"You think he's hot, don't you? I'll kill the son of a bitch. What new bar?"

"Cactus Jack's. I bet you he's doing it. She'd be the last to say anything. Why else would he stay out half the night?"

Carl threw his silverware on the plate. "I'll kill the bastard."

"I don't like to hear that stuff."

"It's the real world, and he's a fuckin' asshole. He needs to be fucked."

"I hate to hear a woman being beat down, thinking she's doing the right thing for the kids. 'Course, you never know what's the glue between two people."

"My sister's done the right thing all her life, and it's never got her anywhere." He was seething.

"She's one of a kind, a saint really." I tucked my hand under my leg – feeling protective of my arm – took a bite of fried steak, and chewed.

Carl rocked back on the legs of the chair. His eyes were focused up near the ceiling. "Hmm," he said. "Hmm."

"Don't think about getting involved. We have enough problems."

"You don't have a thing to do with this. It's family."

I gathered up the dishes and went to the sink feeling smug, even though I was a little freaked by the feeling that the plan might work. I was wiping the stove when the phone rang.

"Got it," Carl yelled.

It was Penny. She'd followed my suggestion to call. I could hear him trying to draw her out. He went on and on, and it didn't sound like he made any progress. By the time he slammed down the receiver, he had himself more angry at her than he was at her husband. He went raging into the bathroom and slammed the door shut. I was surprised the mirror didn't fall off.

I finished up in the kitchen and was watching *Wheel of Fortune* by the time he came out.

He sat down on the couch next to me and put his hand on my

thigh, squeezed it. "You got some room on your Visa, don't you? How 'bout making me a reservation to Dallas? I'll pay you back. I need to talk to that asshole Raymond face to face."

I stared at the TV, trying to control my breathing. "He's not going to listen to you. He thinks you're a moron."

"A moron, huh? I think not. Make a reservation for me—"

I was shaking my head. "You can't go out there. What about work?"

"Do it – get me a flight out on Friday, back home Saturday."

"Not much of a visit."

He squinted and ran his tongue from cheek to cheek inside his mouth. "I'm just gonna talk to the motherfucker."

I'd never seen murder in anybody's eyes, but it was hard to miss. I took a deep, rattling breath. It was too goddamned easy – blood-curdling easy. I reminded myself it was for my own survival. I needed both goddamned arms.

That night I called for a reservation. I had to book two weeks in advance to get a decent fare. I'd saved up some Christmas money, so that way I didn't have to put the ticket on my charge. I could only hope nobody ripped Raymond before Carl got his chance. The guy that stuck Ray the first time was out on probation. It would be just my luck.

The days dragged. The hope that I would soon be free made Carl's behaviour unbearable. I got myself a half-dozen detective novels and kept my nose stuck inside one when I could. I cooked the rest of the time, lots of his favourite foods, and pie, trying to keep his mouth full so I wouldn't have to listen to it. I also hoped to throw him off if he was the least bit suspicious of what I had in mind. It was tough to put on the act in bed, but he was in a hurry most of the time, and his ego made him blind, thinking that I could possibly still love him – and that he was smarter than everybody else.

Thursday morning, the day before Carl was supposed to leave, he walked into the bedroom before work. I smelled his coffee breath and kept my eyes shut. A tap came on my shoulder. "I don't know where that new bar is," he said. "What was it? Cactus Bob's? Near their place?"

"Jack's. Cactus Jack's. No problem. I'll get directions at work, online."

"Get the shortest route from the airport to Babydoe's and from there to the Cactus place. He's probably lying to Penny, still going back to Doe's for the tits and ass."

I printed out the route during lunch. It was a little complicated.

When I came in the door that evening, I handed Carl three pages of directions and maps. He flipped through them. "Write these on one sheet. I can't be shuffling this shit in the dark while I'm driving a rental around Arlington."

"Sure," I said. A pain in the ass to the end, I thought. I reminded myself it was almost over. I copied the directions on a legal sheet and added, "Love ya, Your babycakes." Between his ego and my eagerness to please, I was sure he didn't suspect a thing. I couldn't wait to show him the real world when I gave him my ultimatum.

I got up in the morning and packed him a few clothes and set the bag by the door. I called to him in the bathroom. "Your ticket receipt is in the side pocket. Don't forget to give Penny my love." I knew he really hadn't told her about the visit.

He came out and took a hard look down my body. His eyes glinted and I could see satisfaction in the upturn of his lips, despite their being pressed together hard. There was some macho thing mixed in with the caretaking for his sister. In a twisted way, he was doing this for me too, proving how he could protect a poor, weak woman from men like himself.

I thought he was going to kiss me, so I brought on a coughing fit and waved him away. He thumped me on the back a few times, gave up, and went on out. He paused a second at the bottom of the steps, turned back, and grinned, showing all those white teeth. For a second, I thought he was reading my mind. Instead he said softly, "You're my right arm, doll face." He went on.

I shivered. I watched his car all the way down the street. I was scared even though I was sure he had every intention of doing the deed, and I was betting on success. He was smarter and stronger than Ray, and had surprise on his side. Then I would hold the cards – with his record, a simple tip to the cops could put his ass in a sling.

I was tense all day at the office, wondering what he was thinking with that grin. I wondered if he'd packed his knife. When I got home, I went straight to his bureau. The boot knife was gone from the sock drawer. I pictured him splashed with blood, standing over Ray's body in a dark alley. I felt relieved. He was set up good.

I went to the grocery and got myself a six-pack, a bag of mesquite-grilled potato chips, and a pint of fudge royale ice cream. I rented three videos so I wouldn't have to think. On the way back, I cracked up laughing in the car, my emotions stretched between joy and hysteria. I couldn't stop worrying, but the thought of peace to come was delicious.

Carl was due home around noon on Saturday, and I realized I didn't want to be there. I got a few hours' sleep and woke up early. I did his dirty laundry and packed all his clothes and personal stuff into garbage bags and set them just inside the door. I put his bicycle and tools there. I wrote a note on the legal pad and propped it against one of the bags, telling him to leave Fort Lauderdale and never come back – if he did, I'd turn him in. I said that I didn't care if we ever got a divorce, and he could take the stereo and TV – everything. I just wanted to be left alone.

I packed a bathing suit, a book and my overnight stuff and drove down to Key Largo. The further away I was when Carl read that note, the safer I'd feel.

I stayed at a little motel and read and swam most of Saturday, got a pizza with mushrooms, like Carl hated. On Sunday morning I went out by the pool and caught a few more rays before heading home. I stopped for a grouper sandwich on the drive back, to congratulate myself on how well I was doing. I could barely eat it. Jesus, was I nervous. I got home around four, pulled into the parking lot and saw Carl's empty space. I sighed with relief. I looked up at the apartment window. I'd move out for good, as soon as I saved up enough. I unlocked the door and stepped inside. The clothes and tools were gone. I shut the door behind me, locked it, and set down my bag.

The toilet flushed. "Eh-eh-eh-eh."

I jumped. My chest turned to water.

The toilet paper rolled. Carl came swaggering out of the bathroom. "Eh-eh-eh-eh," he laughed. The sound was deafening.

"Where's your car?" I asked him. "What are you doing here?"

"Car's around back. I wanted to surprise my babycakes."

I looked around wildly. "Didn't you get my note? You're supposed to be gone – I'm calling—" I moved towards the phone.

He stepped in front of me. "I'm not going anywhere. I love you. We're a team. Two of a kind."

"You didn't do it." I spat the words in his face. "You chickened out."

He came closer. I could smell the cloud of alcohol seeping from his skin and breath, a sick, fermented odour. "Oh, I did it, babe, right behind Doe's. Stuck that seven-inch blade below his ribcage and gave it a mighty twist. I left that bastard in a puddle of blood the size Texas could be proud of." He winked. "I let ol' Ray know why he was gettin it too."

He took my hair and yanked me close against him. He stuck his tongue in my mouth. I gagged but he kept forcing it down my throat. Finally, he drew back and stared into my eyes. "I did some thinkin on the flight over," he said. "Penny'll remember telling you about the bars. Also, the directions are in your handwriting, hon. I rubbed off the prints against my stomach, balled up the sheet, and dropped it right between his legs. Cool, huh?" He licked his lower lip from one side to the other. "Oh, yeah, I found one of your hairs in my suitcase, so I put that in for extra measure."

My skin went to ice and I froze clear through.

"I was figuring it as insurance on our marriage – a nice little threat if I needed it to keep you around. A tip to the cops would be all it takes. Guess I saved myself a lot of trouble. Where I go, you go, baby girl. Eh-eh-eh-eh. Together for ever, sweetheart."

He grabbed my T-shirt and twisted it tight around my chest. All the air wheezed out of my lungs, and he rubbed his palm across my nipples till they burned. He lifted my hand to his mouth, kissed it, and grinned with all his teeth showing. He slobbered kisses along my arm, while I stood limp. "Eh-eh."

Like the snap of a bone, his laugh shot chills up my spine and the sorry truth to my brain. I was the same as Carl, only he'd been desperate all his life. My damned arm would be second to go. I'd already handed Satan my soul.

# The Colour of Lust

M. Christian

POOL, the sign said, and BILLIARDS, in typography that somehow managed to be early forties without any of that period's style.

Below TEVIS'S POOL & BILLIARDS was a tobacconist's, a dark little corner store with displays of musty boxes lined with greasy old cigars. Next to it a door stood open, showing a heavy green runner on a narrow flight of stairs. The banister was polished to a dark mahogany glow from endless palms.

A row of narrow smoke-stained windows, once gold-trimmed, ran around the second storey. Islands of threadbare rugs and strips of matted oil-stained carpeting were cast adrift the ancient parquet floor. A cage stood against the far wall containing an old black man in a crisp white cotton shirt and simple black dress tie. His eyes were too sharp and clear for him to need protection. Daisy imagined him as a dapper tiger, kept locked away for the safety of the hall, and not as a precaution against the half-dozen sharks circling lazily around the tables.

Standing next to her, Eddy's hard, narrow face slipped into a wry grin. Tevis's was a heavy place, burdened by architecture, sagging from decade after decade of a meticulous game played by tough, desperate people. It was a place that didn't know joy or ecstasy, only winning or losing in a game played with sticks and little round balls. Eddy was there, Eddy was on, Eddy was in her place and pool was her game.

Daisy also knew what her role was supposed to be. "Eddy," she said with an exasperated little sigh, "there's not even a fucking bar."

"We can get a drink later, doll," Eddy said, walking away, towards the dapper man behind the bars, the narrow leather case swinging gently in her long, thin hand. "I promise."

"Yeah, right," Daisy said, catching up to Eddy with a quick dash. Her own thin hand clutched at his sleeve. "Come on, Eddy, let's go get something to eat, OK?"

Eddy turned to her, looked straight in her pale-blue eyes. Daisy was small, like a model. Sometimes, when Eddy kissed her, when she held her in her arms, a bitter surge of guilt swept up from deep inside her. She was small, like a child. But the feeling rarely lasted more than one or two heartbeats. Eddy had been around, had kissed – and more than kissed – a lot of girls. None of them, even the ones with the leather and the rock-solid attitudes, had been as much of a hurricane in bed. Yes, she was small, but "concentrated" would be a better word. "I've got to do this, doll," Eddy said.

"No, Eddy, you don't." Daisy aimed fiery eyes up at the taller woman. "You don't have to do anything but go back to the hotel room with me." In her little blue and white cotton dress with her long blonde hair hanging straight down, Daisy looked every inch like Dorothy or Alice, stepped right out of their native pages. But the heat in her eyes revealed the edge that hid under her candy and silk.

"Baby, you know I gotta," Eddy said with firmness, certainty. "You know this is something I have to do."

"No, Eddy you don't. You have to eat, you have to drink, you have to fucking breathe, but you don't have to play pool. You don't have to."

Eddy stood and looked down at her, the narrow leather satchel still in her long-fingered hand. Daisy's eyes flicked, and Eddy knew she was right. It was a game played with a stick and a few coloured balls. It wasn't life, it wasn't love. It was just a game. Life was many small hotel rooms, a Gideon in a drawer, a blue plate special for dinner, and Daisy.

Daisy standing naked in a beam of merciless sunlight, her little body graceful and fine. Her nipples were red kernels on breasts as luscious as her thighs; her thighs were as soft and tender as her breasts. The gentle swell of her belly, the tight blonde curls just below, the shocking pinkness of her cunt, the sweet taste of her juice. The way her tongue danced with Eddy's as they kissed, mingling hot breaths; and the way her tongue danced between Eddy's thighs, always with the right tempo, the right steps. Other lovers had stepped on her clit's toes – too much, too little, not enough – but Daisy knew ballet, she knew just the right steps. She was light and strong, and had a perfect sense of rhythm.

It was a good life. But there was something missing; it all seemed too simple. They were dancing in an empty hall to a predictable tune. There was lust, but it was a lazy, easy lust. Eddy absently stroked the handle of the case with her thumb, feeling the worn smoothness of it and the way the leather warmed under her touch. There was something thundering and powerful in the game: skill, risk, reward . . . a reward not as spectacular as when Daisy danced her tongue between her thighs, but sweeter because Eddy won with her own talent.

Eddy was possessed by two different kinds of lust. Lust for the green felt, the cue, and the coloured balls, fighting roughly in the back of her mind with that other lust: lust for Daisy in a cheap hotel room, her skin a patina of hot sweat, her small breasts tented, tipped with tight, hard nipples, her legs spread gently apart, her lips pink like Georgia O'Keefe's flowery labia.

A solid click, the hollow sound of a ball falling home in a pocket. Eddy shook her head, clearing her eyes and mind. "I have to do this, Daisy," she said, turned back to the man in the cage. "I just have to."

Daisy just glowered, the fire in her blue eyes only burning brighter.

"I hear you've got quite a pool player here," Eddy said to the man behind the bars.

The little man gazed at Eddy for a long time. When he was done sizing her up, he drawled: "So who's looking?"

"Just someone interested in a game of pool, that's all. Just someone looking for a game," Eddy said with a sly grin. Out of the corner of her eye, she caught Daisy heading towards a chair at the edge of the hall. Her little ass moved like poetry when she walked.

The man in the cage smiled, showing two porcelain teeth and many more of tarnished gold; then in a shockingly loud voice, he yelled, "Hey, Fats, some guy named Eddy wants to shoot some pool."

The place had four walls. Two of them had narrow windows, two were banked with chairs. Eight tables. The cage. The stairs. From somewhere Eddy hadn't looked, Fats appeared.

It was as if a smudge of night stepped out into the cool twilight of the pool hall. Big and round, she walked – she didn't lurch, she didn't struggle, she didn't roll. Fats had a grace that froze Eddy in her tracks and made her incapable of doing anything but watch as Fats materialized from her hidden corner of Tevis's Pool & Billiards. She moved as if on oiled bearings, as if she'd discovered the pure beauty of what walking could be, and was now demonstrating it to Eddy.

She was middle-aged, her dark face a play of round cheeks and dark, hooded eyes. Her hair was the purest black, cut so short that the shape of her perfectly round skull was showing. Fats wore an immaculate white cotton shirt, perfectly pressed and buttoned up tight to her dark throat. No tie, but instead a tiny cross hanging from a thin gold chain. At her wrists she sported gold and onyx cufflinks. Her pants were black, almost invisible in the shadows of the hall. She wore black and white men's shoes that looked brand new. The room was warm and getting warmer in the growing day, but Fats looked elegant, refined, immaculate and cool. "Yes, Winthrop?" she said in a deep, drum-roll voice, naming the black man in the cage.

"Girl here is interested in a game of pool," Winthrop said, with a tilt of his head to Eddy.

"Is that true?" Fats said, turning her dark face to towards Eddy. Suddenly she smiled, showing a row of perfect white teeth.

Before Winthrop could answer, and before the allure of Daisy and another soft hotel bed could change her mind, Eddy said: "I heard you're one of the best, Fats. I heard it in Oakland, I heard it in Chicago, I heard it just the other day on the train. I just want to see if it's true."

Fats slowly measured her, looking Eddy up and down as if sizing up a lobster in a tank. Under her dark-eyed gaze Eddy felt a surge of heat in her face and chest. She felt herself shrink under her scrutiny.

Someone put a small, very strong hand on Eddy's shoulder. "Come on, Eddy. Come on back to the room with me," Daisy said, her voice edged with tired anger. "It's just a game, Eddy. Come on, it's just a game."

Eddy felt the anger thrill up her spine, tension bloom in her long arms: "Come on, fat girl. You wanna play or not?"

The smile returned to Fat's face – but it was worse, much worse than her cool scrutiny. "Let's play pool, Eddy."

Eddy put her case on the table and carefully popped the tiny latches. "What we shooting for, Fats? Hundred a game?"

Fats nodded, a long, slow motion as if she had all the time in the world. "Let's see your roll first, girl."

Eddy smiled, showing sparkling, perfect teeth. From a deep pocket she pulled a fat roll, tossed it down onto the velvet. "Ten grand, Fats. Count it if you want to."

Fats picked up the roll, weighing it in her chubby, dark hands, her face suddenly cool and earnest. Then she smiled, tossed it neatly back to Eddy. "Looks good, girl."

They rolled to break; despite her humming nerves, Eddy got the opening. In her hand the cue was steady, a part of her body. Languishing before the virgin balls, she cocked and slid the pale pine along her fingers, driving the cue in a perfect strike – just enough, and no more, to snap the eight and four balls away to bounce gently against the cushions and return to the pack. No quarter taken, none given.

"Deal with that, fat girl," Eddy said with a note of bravery she barely felt.

Fats smiled, showing the sparkle of a gold tooth. There is a mastery that disguises itself as bored, casual actions. Without looking, with a careless stroke, she smashed the pack, sending the right two balls into side and right corner pockets with hollow sounds of perfection.

Eddy could do nothing but watch her clear the table.

As the next to the last ball fell neatly into a side pocket, a hand suddenly rested on Eddy's shoulder, and firm but soft voice whispered in her ear: "Come on, Eddy, let's go back to the room."

Eddy wanted to shrug off Daisy's pity, her simple answer of a soft bed and a hot cunt, but she didn't. The first burn of failure was too hot. Instead, she patted Daisy's hand and said, "Maybe, but not yet."

During their words, the last two balls had sunk neatly into pockets. Winthrop had emerged from his cage, swimming lazily through the murky depths of the hall, and had quietly racked them up.

"You're good, fat girl," Eddy said, stepping away from the wiry energy of her lover to peel off some bills from her fat roll, slap five of them down on the table. "You're damned good. But you're not the best."

"Are you going to talk, or shoot pool, Eddy?" Fats said, her coal-dark face calm and inscrutable.

"I'm going to do what I came here to do, Fats; I'm going to show you the best damned pool player there is."

With that, leaning into the shot, pine slick and fast between her fingers, Eddy made the first break – sinking the right two balls, neat and clean.

"I already own a mirror, Eddy," Fats said with a frighteningly cruel smile as she signalled Winthrop for a cold beer.

Despite the deep sting, Eddy cleared the table and won the game. Then the next, and the one after that. She was on, she was there; right there, in that hall and in that game. Every ball obeyed her will, every shot was sweet perfection. It wasn't the body scream of orgasm, or the thrill of Daisy's nipple in her mouth, but it was the climbing glory of winning.

A hand, again on her shoulder. "I want you, Eddy," the sultry voice said, low and deep, whispered in her ear. "I want you, back in our room. Your fingers deep inside me, your lips on mine, my nipples hard, yours as well."

"Not yet, not yet," Eddy said, chalking the tip of her cue and smiling slyly at Fats.

"Eddy, you've won. Please, Eddy, come back to the room with me. Lick me, fuck me, suck me, put those sweet fingers in my cunt, my ass. I want you to come with me; I want to come with you. Don't bathe, don't shower, just spread your legs for me – I love the smell, the taste of your sweat, the perfume of your cunt. I want it all. I want it now."

Eddy hesitated in the game to look down into Daisy's burning, hungry eyes. There was so much hot and steamy stuff. But then she looked at the table, saw the balls still in play. "Not yet. Maybe later."

Eddy won the next game – making it ten to six – but her edge slipped away in the middle of the one after that and Fats ran the table clean. Then the big black woman won the next, and the next after that. Eddy felt the world slip away, felt it vanish like chalk between her fingertips, like one of Fats's balls falling into a deep, dark, bottomless pocket.

"Come back to the room with me," Daisy said, whispering again in her ear. "Make my clit hard, make my juices flow. Make me scream and cry. I want to lay in bed half asleep and watch you, naked, walk to the bathroom for a drink – I love to watch your ass jiggle, your neat little tits jiggle when you walk. You're so beautiful."

She did OK with the next game. But as the seven ball sped towards the cushion Eddy felt the edge fade again; the ball bounced just short of the pocket and lazily rolled away, giving Fats the perfect opportunity to run the table.

"Come with me, Eddy," Daisy said, arm wrapped around her, holding Eddy close. "I want you, warm and soft in my arms. I want you in me, on me, I want to hear the way your voice changes when you come, the way you breathe quicker and quicker till it just bursts out of you in a great, wonderful sigh of release. I want to feel your cunt grab my fingers, your muscles holding on tight as the come surges up and out through you. Come on, Eddy, this is only a game."

Eddy stared at the table, hypnotized by the way Winthrop racked up the balls, nestling them together in momentary perfect geometry, waiting to be shattered apart and scattered across the table.

A game . . . only a game? Absently, Eddy chalked her cue as she walked over to the table. She could just put the cue down, shake Fats's hand and walk out into the fresh night. Maybe a cup of coffee, a cheeseburger in some diner, then back to their cheap room. A kiss, Eddy's hand cupping Daisy's small, firm breast; Daisy reaching down, pulling her cotton dress up and off, standing in the cool night air of the room in bra and panties. White cotton below and yellowed nylon above, holding Daisy's perky little breasts like deep secrets. With a sly smile, she'd reach behind her back, unsnap and reveal herself – two neat puddings, pale and silky, yet firm and upswept. Nipples burning pink, like they'd been lipstick-painted.

Then, reaching down, she'd step out of her simple cotton, revealing the uncommon beauty of her golden-coloured curls. Then she'd stand, naked in the dim light, a lithe nymph, a Kansas goddess, a strong little wheat and plains sprite.

They'd kiss, they'd suck nipples, they'd lick clits, they'd come. Eddy was the easiest, the quickest to scream, shout, with Daisy sometime thereafter. It would be wonderful; and then they'd do it the next morning, the next afternoon, the next night.

The table was green felt, a deep verdant green – like the Amazon must look from high above. An impenetrable green. Just a game?

"Come on, Eddy," Daisy said with firm exhaustion, determined tones in her voice. "Come on."

But this wasn't about winning and losing. It was Eddy's way, her real passion; the green of the felt was the colour of her special lust. Her lust to be the best, to be better than anyone. "Go back to the room, Daisy. I have a game to play." Then, not waiting to see if her lover had left, she turned to Fats and added in level tones: "Let's play some pool."

Eddy lost the next game, and the one after that, but the pain of losing wasn't there. Instead she was building up speed, accelerating to where Fats was steadily cruising. She wasn't there, not yet, but she could feel the groove, and knew that catching it was just a matter of time.

She won the next game, but like the loss, the win wasn't hot. Eddy wasn't there yet, not yet.

After she won the next game and the last ball sank home in its pocket, she knew she had the edge. She could taste it, she could hear the prolonged low note in her ears, there was a new clarity to everything. She almost put her cue away, almost shook Fats's hand and walked out. She knew she had it, and she knew she'd win every game. The edge was there.

But she didn't leave. Just knowing she had it wasn't enough. She won the next three games; with each sinking ball her game grew clearer and more perfect until the cue was more than just an extension of her body, it was an extension of her will, a part of her mind. It was fifteen to twelve.

The sun had set a long time ago, and would rise soon. Time had become nothing but a way to measure the game. That she'd played through the whole night, that she hadn't slept or eaten in over twelve hours, meant nothing. Only the game mattered.

It was good. It was very, very good.

Suddenly Fats's voice broke loudly through the edge to reach Eddy: "That's it, Eddy. You've won, you've beaten me."

Eddy blinked away the glamour, saw Fats for what seemed like the first time. The gleam was gone from her gold tooth; her hands were bilious green from the velvet and the chalk, her skin was gleaming with sweat, and her shirt was sticking to her stomach and tits.

Eddy smiled, wide and true, and shook her damp hand. "Thanks for the game," she said.

"Thank you, Eddy," Fats said. "You play a damned good game of pool."

Which Eddy knew meant she was the best. The best there was.

Daisy didn't know the girl's name and didn't care. All she did care about was that the girl was there in the bed.

She was fresh, maybe too young, but eager and willing. They'd started flirting earlier in the night, just an hour after Daisy left the pool hall. She was behind the counter in a place called, simply, Eats. Young, plump – soft skin billowy and yielding under Daisy's fingers – but best of all willing. It just wouldn't do, to have such a perfect opportunity and have no one who wanted to play with her.

The girl had actually blushed when Daisy had taken her coat, hanging it behind the hotel room door: "You're so gorgeous. I wanted to kiss you the instant I set eyes on you."

Then Daisy did, and the girl's blush deepened even more. "T-thank you," she'd stammered gently when the kiss ended. Was it for the compliment or the touch of her lips? Daisy didn't know what the girl was thanking her for.

It didn't take long. Her dress buttoned up the back, easy pickings. As they sat on the too-soft hotel bed, kissing meekly and then with growing passion, Daisy's knowledgeable fingers neatly popped one, two, three, then all of the girl's buttons.

Weakly protesting, she'd tried to hold the dress together, only giving Daisy an excuse to tickle and nibble her mercilessly. When the tears had stopped and the laughter had died down the girl was in her bra and panties. Daisy looked at her for a long moment, savouring her plumpness: the way her breasts pushed up and around the confining bra, the twin little mounds of her nipples, the scratchy hairs peering around the elastic of her everyday panties, her gentle little swell of belly. "Tasty," she'd mumbled as she took the nameless girl in her arms, and kissed her long and deep as her fingers explored the seams of those panties.

Wet – a marvellously pure wetness greeted her hunting fingers. A wetness of legend, a hungry virgin's kind of wetness. Looking the girl in the eyes, she withdrew her hand to taste and murmur delighted sounds at the girl's savoury cunt. Then she pushed her back onto the bed, kneeled between her legs, gently pulled aside her so-wet panties and kissed, then licked her into a quick, shuddering orgasm – one of many.

The girl was young, juicy, and naive. When it was time for her to return the favour her tongue slipped and missed, her fingers gripped Daisy's thighs too tight, and her thumb and forefinger were too meek with Daisy's nipples. When Daisy did come, it was more from her own quick fingers showing the way than from the girl's timid explorations of Daisy's body. Still, it was a good come. But simply coming wasn't what made Daisy smile like a kitten that feasted on cream.

"I should be going," she said as Daisy let her hands roam over her luscious body. When Daisy found a plump nipple and gently teased it into rubber hardness she whistled softly in excitement. "Don't you have a girlfriend?"

"Yes," Daisy said, dropping her mouth to the nipple, sucking and nibbling it into even further firmness. "I do."

"What if she comes back?" the girl said with sudden fear.

"Maybe she will, maybe she won't – not for a while yet anyway. Not if I played it well, that is."

"I should still go," the girl said, but Daisy pushed her back on the bed, resting a firm hand on her still wet cunt.

"Stay. I want to come again, and I want to make you come again, too." Daisy bent down to part her fat labia and lick – once, very fast – making the girl whistle with a quick intake of breath. "I think I played it perfectly well; just the right amount of tantrum, the right amount of ego stroke. No, she won't be back till dawn, at least. She won't be back till she sweeps the table. We've got hours."

"I don't . . . understand," the girl tried to say as Daisy licked her harder, longer, circling the throbbing bead of her clit.

"My Eddy has her game, and I have mine. And mine is to keep her busy while I fuck you at least five more times. Eddy's good," Daisy said with a wicked smile as she absently rubbed the girl's hard clit, "but I'm the best there is."

# The End of Daphne Greenwood's Travel Career

Tara Alton

It started with the pen. I wouldn't call it a stupendously fancy pen, but rather a clumsy, space-aged-like missile from a hotel vendor visit, where sales people fob off cheap little gifts so you'll book them. If you click the pen, different chain names spin around in a tiny display on the barrel. It belonged to my team leader, Pam. She loved that pen. Pam also loved to think she was hot shit because she had a degree in travel from a university, while the rest of us have travel school certificates under our belts. I would say she's not a team leader because of this. She's a team leader because she doesn't mind sticking her head up our boss's ass.

What have I done with this pen? I've moved it a few times so she had to look for it, stuck it in my mouth, licked it, doodled penises with it and took it into the bathroom. Why? Let's just say I had sexual relations with it. I know it wasn't consensual, but who is the pen going to tell? Besides the little bugger was so uptight. I didn't even come. Still, I got some satisfaction planting it back on Pam's desk, watching her face when she realized it was sticky and trying to figure out what it was before she wiped it with one of those antibacterial wipes for anal retentives.

Pam left me a chastising note on my desk about someone whom I like to call Passenger Thirteen. Why Thirteen? I like to think that this row of seats on an airplane is the travel agent's row of hell. If a passenger pisses me off, I put him in that row. Well, this guy really yanked me around over a trip to Des Moines, so every time since I've tried to deposit him there. Apparently, he wasn't too happy about being in a middle seat again either, but it wasn't my fault since the rest of the seats were under airport control. Well, they weren't, but we won't tell, will we?

I crumpled up Pam's note, tossed it in the trash and picked up my book. Between calls, management doesn't care what we do as long as we are ready to take a call. Some girls knit. Some read fashion magazines. Some write bills or clip coupons. I read porn. Not outright crotch-shot magazines, but rather anthologies of porn pretending to be erotica, but there are still a lot of muffs and cocks bouncing around, only in a more civilized manner.

Reading about a girl who was having an erotic thrill ride on a cable car in San Francisco, I started to get all squirmy. I thought I might have to go to the bathroom to relieve myself in that special way, when Passenger Thirteen rings in. On and on he went about being in the middle seat again. It's uncomfortable, blah blah blah. *Well you shouldn't have been such an ass to me about Des Moines,* I wanted to tell him. My gaze swept back to the open page of my book. He was doing what to her? Could I slip a finger under my skirt?

Looking up, I realized Pam had on her headset and her eyes were on me. She was monitoring me, the bitch.

"I'll definitely try for the aisle seat next time," I said to him. "I'll do that. I will."

The operative word there was *try*.

The moment I hung up, Pam put down her headset and wrote something down. That night, I threw her pen away.

The next day, I watched her look for her pen, and I felt the thrill of a job well done. I had wrapped it in several layers of toilet paper and stuffed it in the sanitary disposal bin in the bathroom. It was long gone.

Actually, I was feeling quite good over all because I forgot to wear underwear, and the seam of my tights was riding up into my crotch.

Suddenly, Miranda, Pam's boss, strode over to me. I thought she was going to say something about the pen, and I quickly concocted several stories about where I saw Pam with it last, but instead she hauled me into her office and chastised me about my clothing.

Apparently I'd forgotten it was a client walk through today, and I'd worn a short corduroy skirt, a slightly ratty, white cotton blouse and my regulation black tights, instead of business attire, which meant a suit. After giving me a long lecture on the difference between business and business-casual, she released me to my desk.

Feeling like my neck had been whiplashed from nodding to convince her I was listening when I really wasn't, I tossed myself down on my seat. Oh great. Now my keyboard tray was stuck. I couldn't pull it out to do my travel agent duties. I called the maintenance man, Ayad. A lot of girls thought he was thick because of the language barrier, but I thought he was adorable.

Moments later, he was under my desk, fiddling with my tray. I kept checking him out. Was it warm in here?

"Do you want to know why I wear dark tights all the time?" I asked him.

He looked up at me. I tried not to imagine him giving me that look between my legs in the bedroom.

"Tattoos. I have tattoos of flowers on my legs," I said.

He paused, a blank look on his face. Did he even know what a tattoo was? How could I explain it?

"Do you want to see what I'm reading?" I asked him instead and showed him my book. He flipped through the pages. Now, I got a reaction out of him. He raised an eyebrow.

"You read this at work?" he asked.

I nodded, happily. He shook his head, handed me back the book and checked the batteries on his cordless drill. Surely what I had to say was more interesting than that piece of cheap plastic crap.

"I'll let you in on a secret," I said in a low voice. "I'm not wearing panties."

Slowly, I opened my legs. He looked.

"You're still wearing something over your legs," he said.

"But nothing underneath. Use your imagination."

He shrugged and peered in closer. Just when I thought I had him, Miranda approached us. I clapped shut my legs.

"The clients are walking through," she said. "You can either put this on or you can go wait in ticketing."

She held up the cast-off sweater from the closet. No one knew who it belonged to. It had been in there for ever, and for good reason with its light blue knit and ruffled collar.

I wasn't wearing that sweater, so I chose ticketing, a cave of a room where underpaid employees who got bad grades in travel school shuffled ticket stock together. Pam breezed by with a smirk at me.

That bitch. I had to do something else to get her back. Plus, Miranda was on my shit list as well because she told ticketing I could help them for a half-hour if I showed up. I wasn't about to stamp parking coupons with our logo as instructed by a timid girl with a set of chin whiskers, so I set out to find a suitable box for my next project.

An empty staple box became my voodoo box. I drew hex signs all over it with a black magic marker, and by the end of the day, I had acquired an earring of Miranda's and a miniature green frog eraser off Pam's desk. I loved the way they rattled inside it, sort of like little bones.

The next day, I decided to add someone else to my voodoo box. Crystal. She had been sexually harassing me for the longest time, and I was finally fed up. You wouldn't believe the things she said to me, like: I love it when you wear purple. I like it when your hair is all wild like that.

Women don't say things like that to one another. They say "cute skirt" or "nice blouse". Also, she's always brushing up against me or stroking my arm. I've tried to put her off by talking about how much I like men whenever I'm near her, but it's not working. The last time, I told her how much bone I had in me that weekend, but she said all I needed to do was to make love to a woman.

I was in the lunch room, chewing on a hangnail in front of the vending machine as I contemplated what I should steal from her desk for my voodoo box, when she made an appearance. Ayad came in as well to stuff his lunch in the fridge.

Crystal leered at the candy bars.

"You wouldn't believe how much I like eating boxes of goodies," she said. "Especially a mound."

I rolled my eyes and let out a deep breath.

"Listen, I like guys," I said. "I like a good, hard cock, and you don't have one. Stop hitting on me, or I'll report you for sexual harassment."

With that said, I bought a package of old-fashioned caramel creams, shot Ayad a look, who had his eyebrow raised at me once more and flounced back to my desk.

She must have told her little group of friends what I said because for the rest of the day they all kept giving me dirty looks. Give me a break. I saw them waiting for me in the hallway after work, like they were in Junior High, waiting to beat me up. Little did they know I had a secret weapon. The fish eye. Yeah, I got some crazy genes in my gene pool. My mom, for example, was truly nuts.

I whipped it out, glared at them, and strode past them like shit wouldn't even stink on me. They didn't say a word.

The next morning, no one was waiting for me in the hallway, but my water cup looked odd. It was one of those plastic tumblers you get at the dollar store, but the water inside it had a yellowish tint. I smelled it and took it straight to Miranda.

"Someone pissed in my cup," I said.

She smelled it.

"Probably the cleaning people," she said, handing it back.

I looked at her, waiting for her to say something else, show some indignation at this appalling act, but she acted like the matter was already closed.

Disgusted, I went to the sink to pour it out when Ayad came by.

"How are you?" he asked.

"I'm being sexually harassed by Crystal, and someone pissed in my water cup," I said.

I tossed the cup in the trash.

"I'm pretty sure she did it," I said.

I realized he wasn't making eye contact. Rather, he was looking down at my tights.

"How is your drawer?" he asked.

"It's still sticking," I said. "You never did finish fixing it."

He followed me back to my desk. It was like he had never left. As he adjusted the screws, I kicked off my shoes and rubbed my foot slowly up his leg. I dug my toes in his crotch and wiggled them around. Then I pushed the ball of my foot up his chest where he took my foot in his hands and bit my big toe. He ripped the seam, his tongue touching flesh. I nearly fell off my chair.

Miranda stopped by my desk. Thank God she could only see his legs and tool box.

"There are calls on hold," she said. "Can this wait?"

Once more abandoned to a sticky drawer and a throbbing mound, I watched him gather up his tools and leave. Reluctantly, I put on my headset, feeling buzzed from the flirting. Across the office, I realized Crystal was watching me. Her hunger for me simmered in her eyes. Why shouldn't she want me? I was hot stuff.

I should make love to a woman.

I always felt bad about the austerity of my desk when everyone else had their trophy photos all over the place because of this innate need to prove to the world they are loved. Finally, I had a photograph to bring in to work. Last night, I visited my childhood friend who happens to be a stripper. One of her friends gave me a lap dance and we took a picture.

I showed it to Crystal, who at first looked so pleased I had walked over to her and then so sheet-white at what she saw. I don't know why. Everything was covered. My hands were on my pretend girlfriend's thighs, her tits in my face, but that was it. Like a proud mother of a freakish sense of justice, I displayed the photo on my desk.

Word of it zipped around the office like a plague. It took no time at all for Miranda to stomp over.

"Take it down," she ordered.

I wrested up an expression of mock indignation.

"Everyone defends Crystal," I said. "So I took her up on her advice. She told me to make love to a woman so I did. This is my girlfriend. I'm allowed to have pictures of my loved ones on my desk."

Miranda snatched it down and opened my drawer to toss it in. Her gaze locked on my voodoo box.

"What is that?" she asked.

I did the only thing I could. I acted like I had never seen it in my life.

Acting as if it was covered in rat shit, she picked it up and opened it. Her earring and the frog came tumbling out. I'd never seen her speechless before. Mostly it involved her turning quite red and acting like she couldn't swallow.

Of course, she felt compelled to go through the rest of my desk.

The sanctity of my travel agent's rights being violated, I stormed off, spotting Crystal's cigarettes and lighter left on the water cooler. As quick as a bee, I snatched them off and headed for a smoke in the storeroom to calm my nerves.

I spotted Ayad, bending over as he looked at a wall socket. He did have a fine ass. I thought about my toe poking through the hole in my tights, his tongue on my skin. Suddenly, my legs felt unsteady. I sauntered over to him.

"Does your mouth taste like toe cheese?" I asked.

He looked up at me, a hint of a smile on his mouth. I gave him a come hither look. He stood up. I shrugged in the direction of the conference room. Like someone with their pants on fire, which they were, I scooted inside and held my breath. Would he follow? Would he be up for it? For a moment, the suspense was stupendous. He appeared in the doorway. I shut the door behind us, letting out my breath, a little more than dizzy now.

Jumping on the conference table, I kicked off my shoe. My big toe poked out.

"I think I need to file a lawsuit. Someone ripped my tights," I said.

It was sort of romantic, the way he looked at me with lust in his eyes, his package standing out and how he got down on one knee.

The moment he put my big toe all the way in his mouth, I nearly passed out. A giggle escaped me that shook my ribcage. He ripped open my tights further, working his tongue between my toes. It was the best foot massage ever. All these knots in my shoulders relaxed, and I felt my body melting into the table.

He pulled my foot out of his mouth and stood up.

"Now I have toe cheese on my breath," he said.

"Yes. You do," I replied smiling.

I waited for him to do something else to me. Anything. Really. For a second, I thought he might turn around and leave, that maybe he was just a foot guy, but he ripped my tights a little more.

"I think these need to come off," he said.

I couldn't get out of them fast enough. They got caught twisted down my legs. He helped, yanking them down. Thank God, I hadn't worn my old cotton panties, but my blue sparkly ones instead. He didn't even bother pulling those down. He unzipped his pants, pushed aside the thin fabric and entered me. God, he felt big. I was either tighter than I thought, or he had a really big dick.

I tried to hang on to him, but he was fucking me too hard. So I flopped back on the table, let him pull my hips to him and went along for the ride. I was just about ready to start pinching my nipples when I heard the conference room door open.

To my horror, I saw Miranda standing there with the nicest looking man I ever saw, tall, dark, brooding, oozing masculinity and mystique. He was New York and Ayad was a suburb outside Detroit. I couldn't believe I was checking him out with another man's dick in me.

"Oh my goodness," Miranda cried out.

Like I was suddenly made of battery acid, Ayad zipped up and jumped away from me. Sheepishly, I pushed down my skirt with an oops I accidentally fell on the table, devil may care attitude.

Miranda didn't buy it.

"Ayad, I would have thought better of you. Getting caught up in her shenanigans. This has to be the most appalling thing I've ever seen here. You're treading on thin ice, mister."

Ayad shot by her through the doorway, deserting me. Suddenly I wasn't so impressed by him, big dick or not. I picked up my tights and my shoes, very aware that the slickness of our love was beginning to trail down my thigh.

"And as for you . . ." she started to say to me.

"Yeah. I know," I said. "Daphne Greenwood is a screw-up."

"Exactly. See me in my office in fifteen minutes."

They were still in the doorway. I had no choice but to squeeze by them. Good-looking man was looking highly amused. Glad I could make your day, I wanted to say to him. Instead, I got a whiff of him. Damn. He smelled good.

"I'm so sorry, Mr Andrews," Miranda said. "This will never happen again. The girl is plain crazy."

I shot a glance back. That was Mr Andrews. Passenger Thirteen!

I still had Crystal's cigarettes and lighter. Why not have a smoke before I faced the firing squad? Now I needed it more than ever. I was so pissed off at Ayad for abandoning me, and I was terrified Miranda was going to have a Daphne Greenwood ass buffet when she got a hold of me. She had plenty of chafing dishes filled with my misadventures – a picture of me with a stripper, a voodoo box with one of her earrings in it and me screwing the maintenance man on the conference room table.

Behind me, I locked the storeroom door and stood by the vent, where I lit up. A cigarette never tasted so good. In the corner stood an old gumball vending machine. It must have come from the lunchroom at some point. That was soon going to be me – empty, forgotten.

Cigarette still in hand, I adjusted my panties. My tights were useless. Everyone was going to see my tattoos. Another thing for Miranda to yell about. Great, why not just parade around naked. I try to fit in. I do. And look what happens.

I could talk my way out of this. I could tell her that the stress of being sexually harassed by Crystal had made me doubt my heterosexuality, so I took up with a stripper, had a breakdown and I had to screw Ayad to find myself again. It wasn't my fault. It was Crystal's.

I was using the fabric of my tights to sort of clean between my thighs when the cigarette fell from my hand and landed in an open box of file folders.

At first, I thought nothing happened. The stupid thing disappeared. Maybe the fall had snuffed it out. I poked around in the box. Nothing. Maybe I should just dump the whole thing out, but the box was huge. Pulling out some of the folders occurred to me, but then I saw it. A wisp of smoke. The box was smoking my cigarette. All that angst from travel agents and travellers was inhaling. I wasn't sticking my hand in there.

How on earth was I going to put it out? There wasn't a fire extinguisher in here. What did fire need? Fuel? Air? The door looked pretty airtight. Being the good citizen I was, I fled the room and shut the door.

Please go out. Please go out. I glanced at the crack at the bottom of the door. Blast it. Smoke. Then there was this sound like a whoosh and an intense crackling. Orange light joined the smoke at the crack.

What do I do? I wasn't about to leave the building without my purse. As calmly as I could, I walked back to my desk. I didn't see Miranda. She must still be in the meeting with Thirteen. Just as I sat and opened my drawer to get my purse, I heard the fire alarm go off. Everyone leaped up.

"This isn't a drill. We have a situation on the third floor, please leave the building."

Anyone who was on the phone got to say there was an emergency and hang up on the client. The one time we get to do that, and I missed it.

Down the three flights of stairs I traipsed with the others. You could smell the smoke now. Once we were outside we were supposed to meet in a designated spot in the parking lot, far from the building, in case it blew up or something.

You would have thought it was a national emergency or something with all the fire trucks that pulled up, even the kind with the long ladders.

I stood away from the others, including Pam, Crystal and Crystal's friends. Not on purpose or anything. It just happened that no one else stood with me, not even Ayad, who was shooting me dirty looks from beside a tree. *It takes two to tango, buddy*, I wanted to call to him. You're the one who had my toe in your mouth. I couldn't believe his dick had just been inside me and now this. He was the owner of a seriously defective character.

Miranda finally came out, wearing a fire marshall red vest. She must have stayed behind to make sure everyone was out. How very brave. She shot me a look that could have burned Lycra off a hooker.

I managed a wan smile in return. Not in a million years was she going to believe my sexual harassment breakdown story. Not after today. Especially if they found out who started the fire. I'd never get out of my crappy trailer or get a better life. I didn't belong here. It was so obvious with us standing out in the open. No one else was standing apart. What had I been doing at this place? Torturing myself trying to fit in. Who was I kidding anyway? I wasn't an office girl, a travel agent. I never traveled because I couldn't afford the hotels or the food even with a free airline pass.

Someone cleared their throat behind me. I turned. It was him, devastatingly handsome him.

"Passenger Thirteen," I said.

"Thirteen?"

"That's what I like to call you. A nickname of sorts."

He looked mystified.

"Haven't you noticed you frequently end up in row thirteen?" I asked.

"Oh, that. Actually I probably deserve it. I can be quite abrasive sometimes."

How had I ever been shitty to such a fine man?

"You probably shouldn't be speaking to me," I said. "I'm a doomed woman."

He smiled, obviously not heeding my warning.

"That was some meeting you were having in the conference room," he said.

"You liked that?"

He nodded. "You could probably do better with your choice in colleagues though," he said.

I glanced at Ayad.

"You can see someone's true colours when the chips are down," he continued.

"Or when the skirts are up." I blushed. I was so blatantly flirting with him. Hysterical flirting.

"I probably won't be booking your travel any longer," I said. "I think I'm all through here."

I was debating going back inside to get my things when the fire was out, but it was all crap wasn't it. I realized Thirteen was looking at my legs.

"Nice tattoos," he said.

"Do you want to see a picture of my pretend girlfriend?" I asked.

He looked at it. For a moment, I thought shock was registering, but then I saw that same bemused look I saw in the conference room.

"This is a very interesting photograph," he said. "I think we should get together sometime."

"You do?" I asked. "Even if I'm working as a waitress at a strip club? Because that's what I'm going to be doing next."

He nodded. I heard Miranda shriek. The fire was out. With a fireman in tow, she headed over to Crystal. I saw something glint in his hand. I knew what that was. I'd left it in the storeroom. The lighter!

Thirteen got out a scrap of paper and a pen to write down my phone number.

"Nice pen," I said. "I know a lot of uses."

The sexual tension between us was crackling. I never wanted to fuck someone so bad in my life. All that conflict on the phone between us had been like some sort of intense foreplay. I knew he was feeling it. I could see it in his eyes.

He raised an eyebrow at me.

"I have a lot more pens in my car," he said.

And just like that, I trotted off after him towards his car, like a dog in heat. Miranda caught sight of us.

"Where do you think you're going, missy?" she called out. I waved her off and caught up with him.

"This could cause you problems," I said.

"No. It won't. I wasn't going to use your travel agency any longer anyway. That's why I came in for a meeting."

His expensive car was parked in two-hour parking. The moment I got inside with him, I forgot all about the pens. He was as horny as I was. Over the console, he pulled me into his lap so I straddled him. Pushing my panties aside much like Ayad, he was inside me lightning fast. I was really tight today, or he was big as well. Very big.

"Don't you think it's perverted you met me with another guy's dick in me and now you're screwing me?" I asked.

"Yes."

"And you don't care about sloppy seconds."

"No."

I shoved my tongue down his throat, licked his tonsils, and bumped his uglies with a passion I never knew. The moment I came up for air, I realized the entire office was watching us with open mouths, Miranda, Pam, Ayad and Crystal. And there it was. The end of my travel career.

Hitting the window button with my elbow, I leaned out my head as Thirteen was grabbing my hips and ramming me into him. He was quite the fucker.

"See, Crystal. I do like a lot of bone," I called out.

# Eye of the Beholder

Mark Timlin

I'd been sitting on the floor inside the walk-in closet for over an hour before I heard the key in the door of the hotel suite. I'd slid in like a ghost using a duplicate when I knew she'd left to meet him, and before I went to my hiding place I wandered around for a few minutes picking up things here and there: a used glass, an item of soiled underwear that I'd put to my face to smell her musk. I wondered what the hell I was putting myself through again. She'd left her portable CD player on repeat, playing an old Joni Mitchell album that I'd always liked, and I nodded my head in time to the music.

Inside the closet her clothes hung close to me and I could smell old perfume, old make-up and just the hint of sweat. But that might have been from me. It was hot in there and I had only cracked the sliding, mirrored doors an inch or so, just enough to see the king-size bed lit softly by the bedside lamps that she'd left burning.

The two of them had been drinking and were noisy as they came in, straight to the bedroom, where I was waiting. No messing with niceties like a schooner of sherry or an after-dinner mint. I appreciated that. The closet was getting warmer and warmer by the minute, and as they entered the room I squinted through the gap to see them both, and what they were going to do to each other.

The woman was tall and blonde in a leather coat with her hair piled up on top, and they'd obviously been having such a good time in the bar that some of it had come loose and strands hung around her face. Even so, she looked great, and even better when she did something to it at the back and it fell to her shoulders. Her hair had always been beautiful: shiny, lustrous, the colour of butter melting in the sun.

Lucky bloke, I thought as they stood by the door and kissed. She had the face of a Hollywood star on a movie poster and blue eyes that said, "Come to bed, and I mean right now."

He was taller, older, florid, ugly, as it goes, and I felt my spine contract at the sight of his face. He was big, but not fat, in a pinstripe suit cut to make him look slimmer, a blue shirt, striped tie and black slip-on shoes. When they broke away from each other he slammed the bedroom door behind them, as she slipped off her coat to reveal the inevitable little black dress. She tossed her coat over a chair and he threw his jacket down and grabbed her again. She didn't object when he kissed her once more, and neither did she object when he spun her round and pulled the zip of her dress down to her waist and peeled it off her shoulders so that it fell to her feet like a pool of ink before she stepped out of it.

Underneath she was wearing tart's gear, whore's kit. But by Christ she did look good in it. Black fuck-me shoes with five-inch heels, black nylons that gleamed in the light with thick bands of double black at their tops, then pure white thighs, the colour of fresh milk, slashed by the black bondage of suspenders, lace briefs just see-through enough to give a hint of the goodies underneath, and a black lace bra that her breasts hardly needed for support but to flaunt their beauty. To tease. Her tummy was flat as a billiard table, her waist was tiny then flared into rounded hips and when she turned round she shook the twin peaches of an arse to die for.

I could see he appreciated the sight as the front of his pinstripe trousers tented, and when she turned back she reached for his cock straight away. She seemed to be pleased with what she found and she kneeled down and unzipped him, reached in and pulled out his prick. It was long and thick, gorged with blood, and she spat on her fingers and rolled back the foreskin before taking it in her mouth, both of them groaning with pleasure.

It was getting hotter in the closet as I watched, and I felt myself harden too and I hated myself for it.

"Wait," he said, and she stopped for a moment, releasing his prick. He kicked off his shoes, undid the button on his trousers, and pushed them and his boxer shorts off, looking comical in shirt-tails and socks. No one ever knows how silly they look having sex.

As he tugged off his tie and pulled at the buttons on his shirt, almost popping them off the material in his haste, his cock hardened even more as she took it inside her soft mouth again and she put her fingers in the bush of his pubic hair and gathered his balls into her hand. Bitch, I thought, as she sucked on his dick like a baby at a tit. Bitch. Just you wait. It didn't help that my cock was now unbearably hard and all caught up in my underwear, and in the position I was in I couldn't adjust the damn thing to get it comfortable.

Anyway, after she'd feasted on his prick for a few minutes she let it slip out of her mouth and it was all shiny with spit and they went over to the bed and really got down to it after he'd pulled off those stupid socks. First, off comes her bra and by God she's got a pair of tits. He held them in his big hands and started sucking on each nipple until they were as pink and hard as pencil erasers, and she started wanking his cock in her hand and I was worried he was going to come all over her and I'd be stuck in that damned closet until he could get it up again. But she knew just how to get him to the peak of orgasm before she let him slip back.

He was loving all that, squeezing her breasts and rolling her nipples between his fingers, making her cry out half in pain, half in pleasure. After a minute or two he went for the main event, running his hand down her belly and inside her knickers and he obviously liked what he found as I could see his fingers were slippery with cunt juice, and he took a big lick and then kissed her again, a long, lingering snog, and at the same time pulled her pants over her hips and down those long legs and let her kick them off. She opened her legs wide and I could see that her cunt was shaven close to the skin which somehow made her look even more naked, like a young girl, even though she was still wearing the suspender belt, nylons and those shiny black shoes. So now was the time for them to start fucking. The man lay on his back and she climbed on top, her favourite position, and she guided his prick up inside her and slid down hard.

Come on, I thought, get on with it. We haven't got all day. But she took her time, riding him like a jockey, her head thrown back, eyes closed, her hands clenched tightly in the hairs on his barrel chest, until she froze solid, gripping him tighter inside, and came with a whoop. They stayed like that, a human tableau, for a moment that seemed to go on for ever before she rolled off onto her side, her cunt opened to my eyes, all red and wet and raw inside before she leaned up on one elbow and looked directly at the closet door. I imagined she was looking straight into my eyes but she gave no sign that she could see me or anything else after her climax. Maybe she was admiring herself in the mirror, or may be she just didn't give a damn.

But the man wasn't going to allow her a rest. His fat, red cock was still erect. Still ready to shoot his spunk up into her belly. Good job, I thought, as he grabbed her again and stuck his face between her legs, slurping like a pig at the trough, then with dripping lips, covered her face with her own juice and threw her down onto the bed. I waited until he climbed on top and pushed his cock deep inside and started to move. As he rose and fell I could see her cunt bulge from the girth of his knob and his huge balls banging against the crack of her arse, and I swear I could smell the stink of their sex clear across the room.

They both began to moan as they approached climax, she for the second time, he for the first. Hers a slight whimper from the back of the throat and his harsher, louder, just as I had expected, and was waiting for. There was no chance they could hear as I gently slid the closet door open, its runners carefully greased earlier. I stood up slowly, the surgical gloves on my hands hot and damp inside, much like her vagina, I thought, but dismissed the thought immediately. On rubber soles I crossed the carpet silently, and just as he was beginning on the short strokes I tapped him on his big, bare, suntanned shoulder with the silencer on the end of the .22 automatic I held tightly, but not too tightly, in my right hand.

He stopped in mid-thrust and turned his head with a look of astonishment on his heavy features.

"Hi. How's it going?" I asked, "Having a good time?"

"What . . . ?" was the only word I let him say before I stuck the barrel of the pistol in his ear and fired once. The report was no louder than a virgin's sigh, but I could imagine the small, powerful bullet ripping around inside his skull, scrambling his brains into a bloody mush, as his eyes almost popped from their sockets from the pressure within his head. He collapsed onto the woman's body.

She screamed a small scream then, not as loud as the one she'd made when she'd orgasmed a few minutes before, and tried to heave his dead weight off herself. I put the smoking barrel of the gun to her forehead and smiled a smile I was glad I couldn't see, and she flinched as I knew she would when my finger tightened on the trigger again.

We stayed like that for a brief moment before I said, "Come on," in a voice I hardly recognized as my own, as I eased off the pressure and removed the gun from her face. "We've done what we were paid for, let's get this place cleaned up and get out of here."

"You didn't even let the poor bastard come," she said as she pushed at his torso and I helped her roll him over, his almost flaccid cock popping out of her cunt like a cork from a bottle. "You could've at least let him do that."

"Fuck him," I said, "No one comes into my wife but me."

# American Holidays

Mike Kimera

*Memorial Day*

"So what was your best?"

"Best what?"

"Best erotic experience."

Mark is a sex bore. He talks about it so much it's a wonder he gets time to do it.

"Mine was with two Swedish twins in a sauna," he says, leaning towards me conspiratorially. "I'd added a day to a Swiss business trip to get some skiing in and these two and I were first back to the hotel from the piste. Well, you know how the Europeans are with saunas, everyone together and no clothes allowed. Just one of these girls would have been amazing – snow-white hair, all-over tan and sleek body – but twins! I thought I'd died and gone to pussy heaven."

I hate men who say "pussy" like that. Like a woman starts and ends at her cunt. But I've known Mark since grade school, so I give him some latitude. Turning slightly away from him, I look towards the lake where my wife, Helen, and Barbara are sunning themselves. They are the best of friends, and they tell each other everything. I want to sit quietly beside them and listen to their talk. Instead I am standing next to Mark at the barbecue pit, burning burgers.

"So anyway, the shock came when the first one took me inside her. In the heat of the sauna her pussy felt cool. No shit. Cool pussy from an ice maiden in a sauna. How sexy is that! Then, when her sister joined in . . ."

I think Mark is making this up. Maybe the twins were real. Maybe he even saw them in the sauna. But I want to believe that he doesn't cheat on Barbara on his business trips.

I am a little in love with Barbara. Helen pointed it out to me one night as we drove back from dinner at their house. She said that she'd noticed that Barbara is always the last person I look at in a room, and that I avoid being alone with her, both sure signs of my attraction. Denial would have been pointless; Helen knows me too well.

After a few seconds of guilt-ridden silence, Helen pulled the car over to the side of the road, and right there, on a tree-lined suburban street, where nice neighbours repaint their picket fences every spring, she fucked me. She didn't say a word. Mouth on mine, she freed my cock, pushed aside her panties and rode me. I came like a boy. She grinned at me, held my face in her hands and said, "If you ever call me Barbara while we fuck, I'll cut your dick off." Then she drove us home.

Only when Mark says, "Your turn," do I realize I've missed his sauna-sex story, and he is now waiting for mine.

"Come on, Pete", he says, "even a terminally married man like you must have had some erotic adventures. Fess up"

An image of Helen blossoms in my mind. She is nineteen and has just let me fuck her for the first time. She'd insisted that we use her parents' bed. "It will make up for all the times I've had to listen to them screwing," she'd said as she led me into the master bedroom. I am lying on my back, wrists still tied to the headboard, sated and happy, watching her between half-closed eyes, pretending to be asleep. She is sitting at her mother's dressing table, brushing her long black hair. The sun streaming through the window behind her seems to me to be a kind of halo. She leans her head to one side so that she can push the comb through the full length of her thick glossy hair. This causes one small upturned breast to push off the silk robe that Helen has "borrowed" from her mother, and to stretch triumphantly up towards the sun.

I am hypnotized by the play of light on her hair; the smooth movement of her arm as she wields the brush and the slight but attention-grabbing movement of her silhouetted breast. She puts the brush back on the dressing table, looks at me and smiles. Many times since, I have returned to that moment of still happiness, crowned with the love in her smile.

"Well?" Mark says.

"Sorry, Mark," I say, "nobody seems to want erotic adventures with me."

I mean it as a playful way of changing the subject. Mark takes me literally.

"I don't know," he says, "you're not bad-looking. I know Barbara thinks you're sexy. You just need to read the signs."

"I think the food is ready now," I say, gathering the half-burned/half-frozen products of Mark's culinary skill onto plates.

"You must have been tempted. At least once," Mark says.

"I'm happily married, Mark. Temptation is easy enough to overcome."

"Ah yes," Mark says, "I'd forgotten about the 'Peter Brader, man-of-steel' act."

I start to walk back towards the lake, hoping to bring an end to the conversation before we get into a fight. Mark has always taken my abstinence from casual sex as a personal affront. Briefly I wonder if he thinks it's all an act and I'm just refusing to share the details with him.

"Barbara really does think you're sexy, you know."

I stop and look at him. He laughs.

"No need to look so horrified. She's not going to rape you or anything. But she told me that she admires your serenity. Isn't that a great phrase? Admires your serenity."

I try for a wry smile but Mark is already striding ahead of me, so it is lost on him.

"OK, girls, the hunters have returned with freshly charred dead animals for their women to feast upon," he shouts.

Sometimes I think Mark is locked in a parallel dimension. The "girls", both in their late-twenties, exchange pained glances at Mark's return, but he either doesn't notice or doesn't care.

This meal is a tradition amongst us going back eight years, to when we were both newly married couples. Every Memorial Day we drive out to the lake and have a barbecue on the public beach. Back then we slept in our trucks and drank beer with our burgers. Now we rent a large cabin and sip Pinot Noir. Sometimes I think the burgers are the last talisman of the days when we had more hope than history.

I have my head in Helen's lap. She smells of sunshine and cotton. I relax, content to listen to her telling Barbara stories about the people in her office. I have never visited Helen's office. I am reluctant to have reality superimposed on the vivid images I have of her colleagues. Barbara and Helen used to work together, and Helen introduced Barbara to Mark.

When Barbara laughs at the punchline of Helen's story, it is a raucous laugh that seems to escape from her. I turn my head slightly, knowing that Barbara will have one hand in front of her face. Helen feels me move, recognizes the reason and, unseen by the others, pinches my ear lobe as she pulls me back to my original position. I look up at her. She mouths the word "later" and I shiver at the thought.

Despite Helen's admonition, I find myself wondering about Barbara's laugh. It reminds me of Miss Honeychurch in *Room With a View*, whose passionate nature is discernible only by the way in which she plays piano. With a stab of guilt, accompanied by a sudden erection, I have a flash of Barbara coming as raucously as she laughs.

On our second year out here, we almost got into a group thing. We'd stopped talking and started kissing, still in couples but with each couple acutely aware of the presence of the other. I left the decision to Helen, who in turn looked to Barbara. Mark was thinking with his cock and pushed up Barbara's T-shirt to take her nipple into his mouth. The discomfort on Barbara's face was obvious.

Helen grabbed me by the belt and said, more loudly than she needed to, "Come on, Peter, I need a bed to tie you to."

I was happy to leave. Barbara smiled her gratitude while trying to keep Mark's fingers out of her shorts. Civilized man that I am, I still could not erase the sight of Barbara's stiff nipple topping a small neat breast that just demanded to be taken into my mouth. Helen knew what I was thinking. When she rode me she held my nipples between her fingernails and used them like a bridle. I was sore for a week but my cock was made of ivory that night.

The scene was never repeated. Barbara confided in Helen her embarrassment at how Mark fucks her. I was puzzled when Helen passed on the remark. She just laughed and said, "Well, you've seen him dance, haven't you?" Mark thinks he dances like John Travolta, but he looks more like Fred Flintstone. He dances vigorously, with his eyes closed, paying little attention to either his partner or the rhythm of the music. The magnitude of the criticism made my balls retract.

I am constantly amazed at what women tell each other. Men brag, women tell the truth. It's a frightening thought.

A tinny rendition of the James Bond theme fractures the silence. Mark has brought his cell phone, even on Memorial Day. Barbara glares at him, but he turns his back on her and takes the call. Mark uses an earpiece on his phone. He says he doesn't want to fry the brain cells that survived the drugs. He looks demented as he paces in a circle, apparently talking to himself.

We overhear enough of the conversation to know that he has been summoned back to the city by some European emergency that he must respond to at once. I wonder at that – it's 9 p.m. in Berlin right now. It occurs to me that I have just seen a piece of performance art. Maybe Mark doesn't make his adventures up. Perhaps there is someone waiting for him even now in a city centre hotel room.

To my surprise, Barbara lets Mark go without complaint – she just sits and watches as he takes the car, leaving her behind like luggage that we will forward to him later.

"I'm going to lie down in the cabin for a while," Barbara says once the car is out of sight.

"Are you OK?" I say. Dumb question. Helen digs her fingers into my side to tell me to shut up.

"No, Peter, I'm not OK, but I'm trying to get used to it. Not everyone has a marriage like yours. I live with a man who never touches me, but who tries to fuck anything female that can move without a Zimmer frame. He doesn't even have the tact not to embarrass me in front of my friends. So I'm trying to preserve my dignity by not letting myself cry until I get back to my room."

Barbara's eyes are wet, but she is standing straight and her voice is strong and clear. She holds my gaze until I look away, then she picks up a bottle of wine and heads back to the cabin. Helen follows her. They talk quietly but passionately. I can't hear what is said. Then they hug in that way that women do, halfway between a caress and a handshake.

Helen waits, head on one side, hands on her hips, for my questions. I don't ask any. She looks at me for the longest time. I seldom know what she is thinking. She moves to stand in front of me, tilts my head down towards hers and says, "I love you, Peter Brader."

We give Barbara an hour before we return to the cabin. I head into the kitchen to clear away the debris of our meal. Helen goes to check on Barbara. I have just loaded the dishwasher when I hear Helen say, "Come here, Peter."

I know from her tone that we have started to play. I am surprised, but out of long habit I go to her and wait, eyes downcast, for her instructions. I love surrendering to her like this. My cock is already thickening and my heartbeat is elevated. It is so exciting not to know what will happen next. Even so, I am concerned. Surely she's not going to take me here, in the main room. The thought worries and thrills me at the same time.

"Strip, Peter."

Helen has never done this before. On our Memorial Day weekends she has always used the bedroom for our fucking.

I don't look at her or speak as I strip. I feel exposed standing there, my cock sending semaphore signals of desire to my mistress.

"Put your hands behind your back," Helen says.

The steel cuffs Helen produces from her bag are cold against my wrists. They make me feel pleasantly helpless.

"Peter, I want you to stay hard as long as you can. Let me help you." She ties a soft leather strap around my balls. My cock trembles at her touch. She grins and plants a chaste little kiss just underneath the head.

I wait for her to undress. She doesn't. Instead she reaches into her bag and pulls out a scarf. Standing behind me she blindfolds me with the scarf. I feel her breath on my neck. Her teeth sink into my ear lobe as her fist closes around my cock. I groan.

"You wanted Barbara today, didn't you," she says.

I nod.

"Say it. Tell me what you were thinking"

"I wanted to know how she sounds when she comes," I say.

She lets go of my cock. A cool finger probes my anus. "So you prefer her to me?"

"No. I love you. I need you."

"But . . ?"

"But I like Barbara."

"Would you like her to fuck you?"

"Yes," I say. I think I know where Helen is going with this but I can't believe she really means it.

Helen kisses me; a deep, slow kiss, exploring my mouth with hers. Except it is not Helen. Helen is still behind me.

The kissing stops. Before I can speak Helen presses against my back and whispers, "It will be OK, Peter. Trust me." I nod my head slightly and she whispers, "Thank you."

I understand the blindfold. It gives us the option to pretend that none of this has happened.

No one is touching me now. I wait. I assume the women are undressing. I wonder if they are touching. Suddenly it occurs to me that over the years they may have done more than just touch. My mind doubts that this is true, Helen would have told me, but my cock goes with the image and twitches ludicrously.

A hand, strong and purposeful, pushes on my shoulder, signalling for me to kneel. The floor is hard on my knees. I won't be able to do this for long. I recognize the smell of Helen's sex, seconds before it is pressed against my face. She holds my head and rubs herself against me. My tongue presents itself for use. She presses her labia against my mouth until my head is forced backwards. She rubs me in a figure of eight against her sex, then she is gone.

Seconds later another sex is pressed against my mouth. To my surprise it smells and tastes just like the first. Maybe I can't tell the difference between Helen and Barbara. Maybe Helen is returning to confuse me. The message is clear enough: stop trying to analyse, go with the flow, be the moment, let the sex flow through you. That message is at the heart of my sexuality, and I recognize it as their gift to me.

Hands guide me to lie first on my side and then on my back. Cushions are placed under my head and my butt. Care is taken to ensure that I am never touched by both women at the same time. I could let myself imagine that there is only Helen or only Barbara, but now is the time for feeling, not imagining.

A mouth suckles my nipple. The sound of it is loud against the eerie silence that possesses us like a spell. The tongue moves down my belly slowly, skilfully, until it reaches my pubic hair, then it goes away. A hand, warm, strong, grips my cock around the shaft. The palm of a second hand rubs my pre-come over the head of my cock, making me wriggle and moan. It takes effort not to come, but I control myself.

Attention shifts from my cock to my mouth. Swift butterfly kisses that make me smile. Then tickling. Tickling that goes on until I am giggling helplessly with tears wetting my blindfold.

I am allowed to get my breath back, then I am mounted. My cock slides into ripe wetness that grabs at me eagerly. Hands on my chest. Thighs around my legs. Deep forceful strokes, followed, after the shortest of times, by a tremor of passion that passes through to my bones. She falls forward onto me, sweat-slick breasts sliding over me, teeth nipping at my neck.

Then she rolls off me, leaving my cock straining for relief, my body demanding stimulus. Both are granted by the mouth that envelops my cock and the swollen labia that descend upon my face. I lick eagerly at first, then become distracted by the play of teeth and tongue and lips upon my cock.

I break the spell of silence, begging to be allowed to come. The mouth releases me as she slides down my body and impales herself on my cock. She does not move, but she squeezes me with her cunt, milking me irresistibly. She is moaning now, but quietly, as if she were gagged. Her hands are on my ankles; her cunt is pressed hard against my pubis. When I start to come, her grip on my ankles tightens and I hear a groan that starts in the back of her throat and becomes an explosive "Fuck!" She stays on me until my cock softens, then she lets it slide out.

I am exhausted. Cool fingers undo the leather around my balls. My cock is patted gently, like a Labrador being rewarded for performing a favourite trick. I find it hard to focus. My awareness always ebbs after I come.

I am being helped up and led somewhere. A bed. Fresh clean linen. The bed feels so comforting after the hardness of the floor. My hands are uncuffed. My arms are massaged vigorously and asexually. Scarves are used to tie my wrists to the headboard.

I am ready to give way to sleep when I hear that unmistakable buzz followed by the smell of lubricated latex. My asshole clenches in anticipation.

"Spread, Peter," Helen's voice. A calm command she knows will be obeyed.

The vibrator is slim and has a slight curve. It is perfect for stimulating the prostate. I relax and let it slide in, wondering who is holding it. My tired cock starts to rally. I think I hear a giggle from beside the bed, but I am distracted by having my balls sucked one after the other.

My brain is fuzzy. I want to sleep. I want to fuck for ever. I turn down the noise in my mind and focus on the cunt that is now raising and lowering itself on my cock. I have no control over the pace. I am a flesh dildo. I am happy.

With the vibrator in place, I manage to stay hard until after she comes. I am rewarded with a skilful handjob that drains my balls and takes the last of my energy.

I hear Helen say, "You can sleep now, Peter," and I know the game is over. As sleep washes over me, I think I hear a different voice say, very quietly, "Thank you."

I sleep late. When I awake my hands are free, the blindfold is gone, my ass is sore and my memory is confused. Before I can get out of bed, Helen and Barbara, both fully dressed and looking refreshed and relaxed, bring me breakfast on a tray.

"Good morning, sleepyhead," Helen says. "We've brought you something to build up your strength."

"Do I need building up?" I ask.

Helen ignores the question and hands me a glass of cold OJ. Barbara is standing at the foot of the bed. She is smiling, not broadly, but persistently. I doubt she is aware of it.

"Barbara is going to come and stay with us for a while," Helen says.

I look at both of them. Helen posed it as a statement, but we all know it was a question. The silence continues while I think about it.

"It's only until I decide what to do about Mark," Barbara says, "Helen thought I could stay in the guest room for a while."

I think about how long I have known Mark and yet how little I really like him. I consider how comfortable Helen and Barbara are together. I remember the carefully anonymous passion we shared last night. I know that if I say yes, it will change things for ever in ways that I can't yet predict.

"I'm sorry about you and Mark," I say to Barbara, "but I'm glad you're coming to stay. I'm sure we'll work something out."

The look on Helen's face tells me I've done the right thing. I don't know if last night will be repeated. I trust Helen to work that out. I do know that I am still naked under the bedclothes and that I desperately need to use the bathroom.

"If you ladies will excuse me," I say, "I have some urgent business to attend to, privately."

Helen grins and leads Barbara by the elbow, saying, "A man's gotta do what a man's gotta do," in a terrible John Wayne accent.

Barbara picks up the theme and says, "Yep, and there are some things a man must do alone." They are both laughing as they leave the room.

I'm still not sure what I've just agreed to, but however it turns out, it won't be dull. I head off to the bathroom, whistling happily.

*Independence Day*

"So how often do you fuck my soon-to-be ex-wife, Peter?"

Peter looks the way he always looks, calm to the point of not being there. I wonder if he even sees me.

"Is she good? Does she moan for you? Or does the frigid bitch freeze your dick off?"

I don't want to be saying this. I don't plan it. It just comes.

"Or maybe it's your bulldyke wife that she has between her legs?" I hear myself say.

My mouth fills with blood, my jaw is on fire and the floor of the bar is much closer than it was. The bastard hit me.

By the time I make it to my feet he's gone. People are trying not to look at me. No one offers to help.

Who would have thought Peter would know how to punch? I knew he was the silent type, but I didn't think he was the violent silent type. Shit, this is a man who lets his wife tie him to the bed before they fuck – not exactly Mr Macho. I haven't seen him hit anyone since grade school. And then he just walks away like he's John Wayne and I'm a bit-part player from central casting.

So much for trying to arrange a meeting with Barbara for tomorrow. Just once I wish I could keep my smart mouth shut. My wife's been living at Peter and Helen's since she left me on Memorial Day. Great sense of timing she has. We've all been friends for years, Peter, Helen, Barbara and I. At least I thought we had. Now I wonder when I became the odd one out; an unfortunate addition that arrived whenever they invited Barbara anywhere.

I'm sure there's nothing going on; Barbara is just staying with them while she sorts herself out. At least she hasn't tried to throw me out of our house. I should be grateful, but you know how it is in the dark hours of the night. I keep imagining them in a continuous three-way. If Peter wasn't so terminally monogamous and Helen wasn't such a control freak, I could almost believe it.

All I'd wanted out of the meeting today was to arrange to see Barbara face to face. She won't talk to me on the phone, but Peter agreed to meet me here. We used to do a lot of drinking here once. Well I did. I don't think I've ever seen Peter really shit-faced. So I get him here and insult him badly enough that Peter the placid actually hits me. Good job!

I decide to stop being the barroom floor show and go to the restroom to clean myself up. The man in the mirror looks older than me, he hasn't had enough sleep, and his bottom lip is split just below the left incisor. My shirt is history, blood all over the collar. I'm meeting Kirsten for lunch in an hour. "Welcome to the fucked-up life of Mark Grady," I say. Even my reflection in the mirror doesn't smile.

My cell phone goes off and the *Mission Impossible* theme tune, my latest choice of ringtone, bounces around the restroom. This strikes me as absurdly appropriate. "Your mission, Mr Grady, should you decide to accept it, is to get a life." I start to laugh, way too loudly. I'm still laughing when I answer the call.

"Well, you sound like you're having a good time," Kirsten says, "did you start to party without me?"

"Not exactly."

"Listen, Mark, I know it's a bummer but I'm going have to blow you off for lunch today."

"Why?" I say, sounding petulant even to my own ears. I hate the but-mom-you-promised whine in my voice.

"I've got to work, Mark. To get things done before the holiday tomorrow."

I hear a male voice I almost recognize calling out impatiently, "Come on, Kirsten, or we'll lose our table."

I pretend I didn't hear that, and put a leer into my voice to say, "I'd rather you were blowing me than just blowing me off."

"So would I," Kirsten said, "in fact, didn't I do that this morning?" I don't know if she's being humourous or genuinely can't remember.

We always have sex in the mornings. In seven years of marriage with Barbara she never once woke up wanting to fuck. Kirsten does it like it's part of her morning exercise routine; a warm-up before she goes jogging.

The first time we spent the whole night together I was delighted to wake with my cock already in Kirsten's mouth. She likes to be on top. She does what she calls "the jockey". She tells me it's very good for her pelvic floor. She squats over me so that only the palms of her hands and the inside of her cunt are touching me. Then she rides me. She squeezes me like she's making orange juice with my cock. She looks wonderful up there: fit, young, tanned, little tits that don't move when she fucks, topped by nipples so hard you could hang your coat on one. I was in heaven that first morning.

But here's the thing: she does it every morning. Great, right? Wrong. Some mornings I want to sleep or just hold her. But Kirsten has a schedule and she's never late. Last week I timed her by the bedside clock. The fuck takes eight minutes. Every day. Exactly. If I'm slow to rise, she grows impatient. I think that if I couldn't get it up one day, she'd just use her vibrator and then go jogging. But listen to me, I'm fucking an ambitious intern who does sexercises on my cock each morning and I'm feeling sorry for myself? Loser!

"Mark, you there? You've gone all quiet. Listen, I have to go. I'll be late this evening but we can spend all day tomorrow together, OK?" She hangs up before I can reply.

I put my phone away, look at my bruised and bleeding face in the mirror once more, and wonder how the hell I let all this happen. "I couldda been a contenda," I mumble at the bum in the mirror. Not funny. Not funny at all.

Outside the bar I have difficulty getting a cab to stop. Too much blood on my shirt. So I indulge myself. I'm good at that. I walk three blocks in the noon heat to my favourite hotel and I rent a room for the afternoon. I love luxury hotels. All life should work the way they do. From the comfort of my room I order a fresh shirt from the hotel store, some Tylenol for my aching head, and a good room-service meal with a decent bottle of wine.

I pour myself four fingers of J&B and relish that first-taste-of-the-day moment. Ah, that's better. So Peter hit me. I can cope with that.

Maybe even use it to get some sympathy from Barbara. The day is definitely getting better, until my phone goes off and it's Anthea the Hun, my boss, looking for me. I made a pass at Anthea once, before she was my boss. Bad mistake.

Anthea comes from that mix of Norwegian and German stock that produces blonde Amazons that can work in the fields all day long and then drink you under the table at night. We'd been working late together on an important project. We got along very well. We had had some Chinese delivered to the office so we could work even later. The meal felt relaxed and fun. It also felt sexy. Something about watching Anthea's powerful jaw suck down those noodles made my flesh tingle.

We were in the little kitchen area, the only people on the entire floor. We'd been laughing at something. Anthea bent over to dump her cartons in the trash and I couldn't resist it, I ran my hand up the inside of her leg. She was wearing stockings. Who would have thought it? I love stockings. I love that transition from the rougher surface of the silk to the smooth warm flesh of the upper thigh. It gives me a hard-on every time. Then I got a bit carried away and let my fingers rush upwards and push into her.

The effect was dramatic and unexpected; she clamped her thighs around my hand and then turned rapidly on her heels. I was pulled off balance and ended up on the floor. Anthea stood on my wrist and pressed hard enough to hurt. I was pinned to the floor, wondering how I got there, and trying hard not to look up her skirt. She looked wonderful from that angle. If it hadn't been for the pain I might have enjoyed myself.

The idea of fun ended the moment I heard her speak. "They told me you were a hopeless letch," she said, "but I thought they were wrong. You're bright. You have a nice wife. You don't need to screw around."

She sounded very angry and I found myself wondering if she was stronger than me.

"I'm sorry," I said, "I just . . ."

"You just thought you'd shove your fingers up my cunt. Did you think I'd like that? Or that I'd be a good sport and put up with it anyway? Or do you just see me as a cunt on legs, a slot to be filled?"

I didn't know what to say. I hadn't meant any harm. I mean, things had gone too far too fast, but it's not like I raped her or anything. But I'd really pissed her off and she looked scary. She took her foot off my wrist and I went to get up.

"Don't move," she said.

I lay still.

"I hate shits like you, Mark. I could have you fired, you know that, don't you? But then I'd be the ball-breaking bitch who her co-workers can't work late with in case she accuses them of rape."

"Anthea, look, I . . ."

"I'm talking now. You're listening. I'm going to teach you a lesson, Mark. And then you're going to leave. Show me your cock."

Nothing she said could have surprised me more.

"Come on, Mark, get it out. Show me what you were thinking with."

"I don't want . . ."

"Or should I get it out for you? Maybe I should just unzip you and find out what you're made of."

She bent towards me and I found myself shuffling backwards on the floor.

"Just a quick feel," she said. "A compliment really. What's the matter, Mark? Be a good sport."

She reached for me again. I was frightened. She looked like she could kill me. I bumped into the cupboard behind me. Instinctively, I covered my cock with my hands, unable even to speak.

Then she stood up straight and looked down at me. "I want you to remember this, Mark. I want you to remember just how it feels. Tomorrow, you're going to phone in sick. You'll stay sick for a week and I'll finish this project alone. Do you understand?"

I nodded. She left. I did phone in sick. She got a promotion for completing that project. We worked together from time to time after that, but always in a bigger group. She never mentioned it again, but there was always some hostility there.

When she was made head of my section, I knew she'd fire me. She called me into her new office. Before I could speak she said, "I'm not going to fire you, Grady—" she never calls me Mark any more "—because you are going to work your balls off for me aren't you? And I will make sure you get the bonuses that go with that. OK? Good. You can go." And that was it.

I've worked for her for six months now, and every week I wish I had the courage to tell her to stuff her job. One moment of weakness and she crucifies me.

So, as I answer Anthea's call on my cell phone, all enjoyment of the hotel fades. Jesus, even my balls retract slightly. I hate her for making me feel like this.

"Why aren't you here, Grady? Did you quit and forget to send me an email? Just let me know where you want the stuff from your desk sent and I'll have it couriered over."

Bitch, I think to myself, but I put a smile in my voice and say, "Hi, Anthea. I was just about to call in. I'm not feeling too good. I think I'm coming down with something. Good thing tomorrow's a holiday."

"You poor thing," she says, "Which is it, the booze getting to you, or the intern wearing you out?"

"Look, I came in above target last month, didn't I? I always make my numbers. I can afford the time."

"So far, Grady. You've always made your numbers so far. But try looking in the mirror some time. You look like a man who's losing it. I don't have losers on my team. Are you hearing me?"

I really want to come up with some smart remark; to tell her how wrong she is, but a small voice in my head is whispering to me, "Loser, loser, loser." I empty my glass of J&B in one swallow to try and make the voice go away.

"Yes, Anthea, I hear you," I say. I sound resigned and a bit pathetic.

"One more thing, Grady." She makes me wait three seconds, wondering what the sting will be. "Happy fourth of July," she says. Then she hangs up.

Shit. Not good. Not good at all.

I strip and head for the shower, wondering when the damn painkillers will kick in. I love showers. It makes me feel I can start everything again from the beginning. Clean, wrapped in a bathrobe so thick and soft it cuddles me, I pour another three fingers of J&B into my glass and I feel better.

I start thinking about tomorrow, Independence Day. I always have a barbecue at my house. Barbara does the cooking, so the guests survive OK. I get to go round making sure everyone has enough to drink. Barbara's parents moved down to St Pete's in Florida two years back and mine are both dead now, so it's a friends and neighbours deal mostly. No one stays long, but lots of people drop by. I think having the game on the projection TV on the patio helps. I call it Al Fresco's Sports Bar. When I told Kirsten that, she asked who Al was.

It's not that Kirsten is stupid, in fact she's very bright, but she's into numbers and the markets and good health and doesn't have time for a lot else. The first thing she said to me was, "I really admire your portfolio."

It was late on a Friday. Kirsten had been on staff for a week. I'd noticed her. She'd noticed me noticing and hadn't seemed to mind.

So, Friday she comes into my office just as I'm going out and hits me with the portfolio line. I don't know what to make of it, but she's young and pretty and standing very close, so I decide to smile and wait.

She steps slightly close, too close for normal conversation but not close enough to touch. "I've been told you have the biggest one in the office." No doubting the tone there. She looks me up and down, slowly. Then she says, "Maybe we could stay late one night and you could show it to me?"

"How about Monday," I say.

"I'll look forward to it," she says. She stepped back and then turned to walk away. I enjoyed watching her walk. When she got to the elevators she looked back over her shoulder. "I hope you and your wife have a great weekend." To me it seemed like she'd just offered a no-strings-attached fuck. I couldn't believe my luck.

That night I took Barbara to bed early and fucked her hard. She was delighted that, for once, I did the asking. That made me feel bad. We don't fuck much and I felt like a shit when I saw how pleased she was. But I was a shit with a hard-on and, hell, if I could win points and get off at the same time, why not? Well, because it's the wrong thing to do and I'd feel bad about it later is why not. But with me, now always wins out over later, so I fucked her anyway.

She was a little dry at first, but once we got going, she lubed up just fine. We did it doggy style, my favourite. When I was in the rhythm, slamming into her and making those flesh-slapping noises that are sort of nasty and exciting at the same time, I closed my eyes and imagined Kirsten in her place. I dug my fingers into Barbara's buttocks and wondered how Kirsten's smaller, rounder ass would feel. I came hard, deep inside Barbara. It was good. At least for me. I knew Barbara hadn't come yet. I knew I should've done something about that. What I actually did was pretend to fall asleep. I do that real well. I wish I had really slept, then I wouldn't have had to lie there listening to Barbara trying to cry silently.

Shit, I hate it when I make myself think about stuff like this. It's like part of me just wants to keep rubbing my nose in it and say "bad boy". Well, fuck that. We all do stuff we shouldn't. It's part of being human.

I'm glad when room service interrupts my thoughts by bringing me my meal. They know how to do this here: real linen tablecloths, heavy cutlery and crystal glasses. For an hour I manage to lose myself in tastes and smells and textures. The wine is full-bodied and mellow. I probably shouldn't have drunk the whole bottle, but I enjoyed every sip.

Food is a passion of mine. I don't cook but I love to eat. Barbara is a great cook. I sometimes think food is the closest we ever came to satisfying each other's desires.

Now I'm back on Barbara again. That keeps happening to me. It won't do me any good. Deep down I know she's right to divorce me. The thing is that my mother-in-law was right: she is too good for me.

I lay back on the bed, wine glass resting comfortably on my belly, and pull out the mental picture album labelled BARBARA AND MARK: THE EARLY YEARS.

The couple in the album is young and inexperienced. Young Mark has learned how to make the quiet and mysterious Barbara laugh. Her laugh is a wonderful thing. It knows no inhibitions. It fills him with warmth, close to lust, that he thinks for a while is love. He will do anything, no matter how absurd, to provoke that laugh.

In the early pictures, Barbara is always laughing, one hand in front of her face, as if trying to cover up accidental nakedness.

In the wedding photos, Barbara has a faraway look, as if she cannot quite believe that she has gone through with the wedding, Young Mark looks as though he has just won the lottery.

I know I am going through these memories because I am drunk. For all my practice, I have never learned to be a happy drunk. Alcohol makes me too honest with myself.

I go to the bathroom and splash my face, hoping to drive away the ghosts of my marriage. They refuse to leave. I know what they want. They want a confession. I look in the mirror above the sink and say the words that will lay the ghosts.

"I am a lousy fuck and I'm sorry."

This is what I'd always wanted to say to Barbara and never could.

Barbara, in those early years, was a good lover. She wanted to fuck the way she laughed. She was uninhibited and enthusiastic. And she intimidated the hell out of me.

I'd mainly done one-nightstands and orgy fucks before. I'd never had to try to fuck the same woman night after night. It's not that she was a bad lay, the opposite in fact. But when we had sex I had this image of her as a powerful car that I never got out of first gear. She was patient. She got into foreplay. She read me erotica. She dressed up in sexy lingerie. She shared her fantasies. And every single thing she did made me shrivel up a little more.

Eventually, in the third year of our marriage, she stopped all the fancy stuff and settled for my clumsy, short-lived fucks. She even faked orgasms. And, dumb fuck that I am, I didn't notice. I thought

I'd cracked it. I was walking around thinking, First I learned to make her laugh, then I learned to make her come.

The bubble burst when I came home early one afternoon. I heard her as soon as I came through the door. She was moaning. A deep, low, continuous moan that I could not mistake.

So this is what she really sounds like when she comes, I thought.

I was angry. Some bastard was fucking my wife in our bed and making her come better than I could. I moved up the stairs quietly, looking forward to my dramatic entrance.

The moans were subsiding as I reached the bedroom door. I went in via the bathroom, which has doors to the hall and the bedroom. Barbara was on her belly. Her face was buried in one of my sweatshirts. She was alone. The room smelled of sweat and sex. Her fingers were still trapped beneath her cunt.

When I realized what I was seeing, I left at once. I didn't want her to know that I knew she preferred her own fingers to me.

My drinking increased after that, and I started to chase women. I hoped that one of them would prove to me that I was a good fuck after all. None of them have. Oh, most of them enjoy themselves, but they aren't looking for the same thing as Barbara. They fuck me because they like fucking, and I'm safe and generous and no worse than average. Barbara fucked me in the hope that we would fly together. She is the swan who married the penguin because he made her laugh.

OK, so now I'm getting maudlin. Penguin! Jesus wept, where do I get this stuff?

I should get dressed now and go home and wait for Kirsten. But what I want is to talk to Barbara. I want to tell her that I miss her and that I don't deserve her and I want her back. With the certainty of the very drunk, I know this is the right thing to do.

I dial Peter's number. The gods are on my side; Barbara answers.

"B," I say, "It's me. Mark."

"What did you do to Peter?"

"What? Nothing. Listen. I have something to say."

"I saw his hand. Did you hit him?"

"Yeah, real hard. With my chin." I'm laughing and I want to stop but I can't.

"You're drunk aren't you?" She sounds sad, not angry. "Is she there with you, listening?"

"Who?"

"Who? Can't you remember her name now?"

"Oh, Kirsten. No she's coming later. Listen. I wanted to tell you . . ."

"I don't want to hear it, Mark. I'm not listening to you any more. It hurts too much."

"But . . ."

"Tomorrow is Independence Day, Mark. Take it as a sign. From tomorrow we are completely independent."

She is almost crying now. I can hear it at the edge of her voice.

"Please, B, I just want . . ."

"Goodbye, Mark." She hangs up.

I feel a hundred years old. The phone stays in my hand because I can't think what to do with it. I listen to the drone of the dial tone and it seems to be singing the song of my life.

Anger helps. Anger is good. I throw the phone away.

Bitch, I think.

I say it out loud, "Bitch."

Then, "Heartless, man-eating BITCH."

That's better; much better.

The hotel arranges a taxi for me. Soon I will be home. Maybe Kirsten will want to fuck when she gets in. Or maybe it can wait until I get my eight minutes tomorrow morning.

*Labor Day*

"You OK?"

The concern in Peter's voice makes me smile.

"Yeah, I'm fine. Just taking a moment, you know?"

His stillness in the doorway calms me.

I stand, check my hair in the mirror and say, "I'll be out in a minute and I'll be the life and soul of the party, honest. After all, it's a holiday, right?"

He says, "You've done the right thing, Barbara," like it's not a non sequitur. Then he leaves.

I hope I've done the right thing. I hope it with all my heart.

There has been so much change in my life, in such a short time, that I feel giddy. I sit back down, composing myself, staring at the woman in the mirror, looking for signs that she has changed.

When I was a child I used to love to play blindman's bluff; to be blindfolded and turned round and round and round until all sense of direction was lost and the only way left was forward, into the arms of whomever I could catch. These past months I've been playing that game with my life. Now it's time to take off the blindfold and seize what I have found.

God, I sound like some New-Ager peddling rebirthing seminars. How Mark would laugh at that. I can imagine the "commercial break" voice in which he would say, "Tired of the old you? Give birth to a new and improved one after only five days at our woodland retreat!"

I've always sneered at the idea of such fundamental change. You are who you are. You don't suddenly become someone else. But maybe, sometimes, we settle for not being all of who we are. We shut down the parts that don't fit. We grow, but we grow stunted, like plants raised in a too-small pot. At the beginning of the summer it came to me that my life had become pot-bound. So I smashed the pot.

God knows, Mark had already put a few cracks in it, with his serial seductions of silly girls. But in the end it was me, not him, who shattered our marriage beyond hope of repair.

When he abandoned me, in the middle of a Memorial Day barbecue with our best friends, so that he could go and fuck his latest Barbie, everything suddenly changed. I didn't get angry. I got cold and still and then I cracked, like an iceberg snapping off from a glacier and sliding into the sea. One moment Mark and I were connected, the next we were separated by an unbridgeable stretch of despair and disappointment.

I think I might have frozen for ever on that day. Gone into shock and never come out. But Helen and Peter rescued me, right there and then. They took me into their hearts and, for a while, into their bed. I know that sounds bizarre and weird, but it didn't feel that way. I've known them both for ever and I love them in my way. Helen, so brave and fierce and full of energy. Peter, her rock, her keel, always there for her, always calm and true. Being with them felt like coming home. Like rejoining my family. Except, of course, I don't fuck my family.

But now it's time to leave. The summer, that started so badly, is coming to an end. It's Labor Day today. Helen and Peter are having a little party to wish me well in my new job in big bad Chicago. All my friends are waiting out there and yet I can't bring myself to leave this room which has been my refuge from having to deal with the reality of divorcing Mark and learning to live on my own.

I know I should despise Mark. Everybody else does. But I can't. He's weak, not wicked. I know all about being weak. I was weak for years. In a way, my whole married life was a result of weakness.

I let Mark marry me because he wanted it so much. He was the first man in a long time to see past the cloak of invisibility I had wrapped myself in. The dowdy clothes, the shyness, the lack of make-up, didn't put him off. He wanted me and he wanted to please me. That was flattering. He found ways to make me laugh. That was endearing. And he was always there, like a faithful hound waiting to be taken for a walk. All I had to do was look at him for his tail to start to wag. That, in the end, turned out to be irresistible.

It's not that I didn't love Mark, I did. I still do. But the thought of him never made me wet. When we kissed it was nice rather than good. When we fucked it was urgent rather than potent. I told myself that things would get better; that we would learn how to please each other; that we had plenty of time. But that isn't how it worked out. Things got worse, not better. We never talked about it, but it was always with us; an absence of the passion that should have made our marriage grow.

In the end, that absence became the centre of our marriage. We walked around the hole it left in our lives every day, until it became our habit to circumnavigate sex, at least with each other. Mark found solace in sport-fucking shallow, undemanding women. I let my fingers release what I couldn't suppress.

I wonder sometimes if things would have been different if I'd been a virgin when I married Mark. But I wasn't. Not by a long shot. Todd had seen to that.

"You thinking of Mark?" Helen says. "You look upset."

I didn't hear her come in. I knew she would want to see me alone before I left. I have, I realize, been avoiding it. Now she is here, looking at me in the mirror, and I can't read the expression on her face. She can do that sometimes; just switch her face to neutral. It's disturbing because she is normally so expressive. Mark christened her "Helen, the face that launched a thousand quips".

"Actually, I was thinking of Todd," I say.

"Todd the Impaler? What brought him to mind?" Helen moves closer to me. Her face has softened a bit. She knows Todd is a difficult subject for me.

"I was wondering if being with him screwed up my marriage."

My voice sounds like I'm on the edge of crying. I didn't expect that. I hate that I cry so easily.

Helen is smaller than me. When she hugs me, I have to bend slightly to put my head on her shoulder. She leads me to the bed and we sit for a moment, next to one another. She holds both my hands within hers and, suddenly, I see her as she was when we were both in our first year in college.

She was my first adult female friend. She told me everything about herself. No embarrassment. No restraints. It was infectious. And one night, when we were sitting on her bed in her room, I started to tell her about Todd. I hadn't told anyone about Todd. She let me talk. For hours. I think that Helen performed an exorcism that night.

When I had finished she said to me, "You are a good person." It felt like a blessing.

If I had been prettier earlier, I would never have gone with Todd. Up to my senior year in high school, I was the invisible girl. The one everyone wrote, "I hope you have a great summer" to when they signed my yearbook, trying to remember who the hell I was.

The summer before my senior year I had a growth spurt. I grew three inches, lost some weight, and acquired a waist and hips. Suddenly I had long legs and a good ass. Barbara the boring became Babs the beautiful overnight.

My mother was so pleased that she bought me outfit after outfit. "I've been waiting to take you shopping for such a long time," she said. In the store I became the centre of attention. My legs were applauded and I was encouraged to buy skirts that would display them. I went back to school feeling wonderful.

It didn't last long. I'd broken one of the prime rules of high school: I'd tried to move out of the slot that my peers had allocated to me. My best friend, Alice, felt slighted by my new look. My study mate, Carl, suddenly became tongue-tied and uncomfortable. But the toughest reaction came from the wannabe prom queens. They started to call me Babs the Booty. They said I looked like a slut. But I wouldn't give in. I wouldn't sacrifice the look of pride on my mother's face just to fit in in high school.

So now I looked good but no one talked to me. Then the boys found me. They weren't bad boys. They were polite and nice and muscular and I ached for them. I hadn't dated much so I wasn't really sure what to do. I knew enough not to fuck on the first date. But the second seemed reasonable. And the boys wanted it so badly. And they were so nice to me. And besides, the sex was good. Sometimes very good.

I was Barbara the Queen Bee, surrounded by a group of adoring drone-boys. We went everywhere together. We had fun. And at the end of the evening one of them would take me home and on the way we would park and I would find out one more time just how good it felt to ride a fresh strong cock.

Looking back now, I think I went a little crazy for a while. The thinking me was switched off. I stopped being shy and introverted and tried hard to live in the now. The now where I was beautiful and the boys were eager. I was aware that they didn't love me. I knew I didn't love them. But it felt so damned good.

I'd been Queen Bee for about a month when Todd Rawlins showed up. Todd was two years older than me and had been the star of our football team in his senior year. If it hadn't been for a knee injury, Todd would have made it to college on a sports scholarship. Instead he was working at his daddy's Chrysler dealership.

Every girl in school knew three things about Todd: he drove a brand-new LeBaron Convertible, he partied hard and he had the biggest dick in town. One Friday night the drones and I were coming out of the bowling alley and I was teasing them about who would get to drive me home, when Todd pulled up next to us in his killer car. No "hello"s. No "baby, you look good"s. He just said, "Get in," and I did.

Once we were away from the boys, Todd was nicer to me. He told me how he'd heard that I'd become hot and said he'd decided he had to take a look for himself. I asked him if he liked what he saw. He told me that he hadn't seen it all yet and that he'd let me know later.

In a way I was still a virgin until Todd fucked me. I mean, I'd had sex, lots of it, but I'd never been possessed by it. Never had it take over my whole mind until I was just a set of nerve endings surfing on wave after wave of orgasm.

That first time, he took me to the woods and we parked. He led me out of the car and made me sit on the hood.

"I got something for you, baby and you're gonna like it a lot," he said.

I nearly laughed at that, but realized in time that no joke was intended.

Then Todd unzipped and took out his dick. It wasn't fully hard yet but it was already bigger than most of the cocks I'd had inside me. My cunt contracted and my mouth went dry. I wanted to see it stand and I wanted to feel it stretch me. That dick of his brought out desires that I didn't even know I had.

"Told you you'd like it," he said, "they all do."

I wasn't listening. I was spreading my legs and pushing my panties aside and staring at his dick and wondering if it would tear me. There may have been a small voice saying, "Why are you fucking this dick?" but even if I had heard it, my only answer would have been, "Because it's there! Now shut up bitch and let me fuck."

The first fuck, he just grabbed me by the back of the knees, spread me so wide that it hurt and rammed it home. Nothing had ever made me feel so full. It hurt but it hurt good. He pounded away at me so hard I thought we'd dent the car. I was breathless and stunned. Not ready to orgasm yet; still amazed at how full I felt; almost afraid to move in case I hurt something.

Then he came and I thought, Shit no, not yet!

I must have said some of that aloud because Todd grinned at me and said, "We ain't done yet, baby. You feel anything getting smaller down there? All we've done is get you nice and lubed."

It was true. He'd come, but he was still hard. I pushed against him gratefully, eager to chase my orgasm. But he pulled out.

"Time to say hello properly, baby," he said.

I didn't know what he meant.

He stepped back from the car and said, "On your knees, baby. Come and show Mr Pecker here your deep appreciation."

I wish I had laughed then. I wish I had told him and Mr Pecker to fuck off. But I didn't. I got on my knees and I took him in my mouth. It was bitter tasting and unpleasant but sort of compelling at the same time. There was just so damned much of it.

I didn't have a lot of experience with giving head. The drones and I had skipped that part and gone straight for the main course. It must have showed.

Todd said, "Jesus, girl, mind those teeth," and took Mr Pecker away from me.

I thought it was all over then, but Todd wasn't done. He bent me over his car and took me doggy style. You wouldn't believe how deep he could get like that. And he was slow now. No hurry at all. It went on and on. He made me come the first time just from the way his cock moved. The second time he got me there by working on my clit while still going with that slow deep stretching in and out movement. My third orgasm was triggered when he spurted inside me.

My legs were shaking when he pulled out. I couldn't move off the hood of his car, even though I could feel his come running down my thigh. I'd never come three times one after another like that. My mind had gone away completely, a bit like the way you lose your hearing after a gun goes off. I wanted to sleep right there.

Todd guided me back into the car. We drove to my house in silence. I don't think I could have talked even if I'd wanted to. When we reached my house, Todd just waited for me to get out.

I struggled onto the curb and he said, "You have a great cunt, baby, but you've really gotta learn to give head. See you tomorrow."

Then he drove off.

I lay on my bed thinking about what had happened. It was shameful. I knew that. Todd was using me and I was letting him. My cunt was sore. My legs ached. My pride wanted to say, "Screw you, Todd Rawlins." I fell asleep still undecided about whether to see him again.

I was late for school the next day. By the time I got there, everyone seemed to know I was one of Todd's girls. Not Todd's girl. Just one of them. The drone-boys all found reasons not to be available that night. My ex-best friend told me I should be ashamed of myself.

After school, Todd was there with his shiny car and his big smile. We did it all again. The only difference was that I nearly threw up on him when he tried to push Mr Pecker down my throat.

At the time it seemed to me I was out of options. I couldn't go back and I didn't know how to go forward so I just let Todd go on fucking me. It lasted a whole month.

My cunt was sore by then. My mind was working loose from the corner I'd tied her up in and was shouting, "Stop this nonsense right now, young lady." I gagged her because I didn't want to hear it.

It ended when Todd called me and asked me to come over to his house. He said his parents were away and he wanted to show me something special.

I went because I couldn't figure out how to say no.

When I got there the door was open so I went into the family room. Todd was on the big sofa watching a porno movie. Amy Shanks, universally known at school as Amy Skanks, was on her knees sucking his dick. I must have just stood there looking stunned.

Todd said, "Hi, baby. This is what I wanted to show you." Then he turned to Amy and said, "Do it, baby."

Amy looked at me. She held eye contact while she lowered her mouth onto Todd's dick. She swallowed it. All of it. It made her throat bulge but it she swallowed it all. Todd placed his hand on the back of her head and started to move her up and down on his dick.

"Amazing, isn't it?" Todd said. "And Amy here is gonna show you how it's done. Come on over, baby and get a better look."

My mind finally broke free of her bonds and all I heard was her shouting, "Run, Barbara, and don't stop until you're home in bed."

I don't remember getting home. I don't remember anything until I woke up the next day. Then it all hit me. I was a slut. I had been a slut for months. Everybody but me knew that. And my grades. My grades had seemed so unimportant while I was slutting around but now I knew that they were dropping enough to put college at risk. I stayed in bed all day. And the next day.

Finally, I told my mom that there was a problem at school but I didn't want to talk about it. I think maybe some of the neighbours had already been talking about it, because Mom quickly sorted things out without any questions. She arranged private tuition to rescue my grades. I worked hard. I made it to college.

But I still had a secret. The secret was that I had wanted to be fucked like that. I'd enjoyed it. I wanted more of it.

My mind was firmly back in control now and she tried hard to banish Miss Libido. She made me dress in baggy clothes and to stop even talking to boys. I became invisible again. But at night, before I fell asleep, my fingers would find my cunt and I would think of Todd and wonder if I would ever find anyone who could make me come like that ever again.

Helen is waiting for me to tell her what's on my mind.

I manage a smile. "Remember when we talked about Todd that night? You were wonderful. And then you introduced me to Mark," I say.

"Yeah, sorry about that," Helen says. "He seemed like a nice guy at the time."

"He was a nice guy at the time."

We are both smiling now and I can finally say to Helen the thing that needs to be said. "Helen, about Peter . . ."

Helen's smile goes. I feel her stiffen.

"I'm so sorry," I say.

"It's over now," Helen says. She removes her hands from mine but manages a smile that almost reaches her eyes. "No harm done," she says, moving towards the door. "Now stop moping and come and join the party."

No harm done. I hope that's true.

The day Mark left me, the day when I could have shrivelled up and nursed my sense of worthlessness, Helen rescued me. She knew that I was attracted to Peter. She'd told me that he was a little in love with me. We'd laughed about that. Imagine quiet Peter harbouring a passion for Barbara. That was back when Helen and I would trade stories about our husbands. When I still felt married. Before the lack of passion in my life made me feel dried up and useless and unlovable.

By the time I reached that Memorial Day barbecue it was painful for me to watch Helen and Peter together. I was like a starving beggar pressing my face against the window of a restaurant, tormented by the sight of food but unable to look away.

When Mark left the barbecue with some insultingly see-through excuse, I headed back to the cabin to cry and to feel sorry for myself.

Helen stopped me. She spoke softly. What she said surprised me. "We love you, Barbara. You deserve better. Let us care for you. Let me share Peter with you. Be with us for a while."

I could tell that she was sincere and that what she was saying wasn't springing spontaneously into her head. I knew what "share Peter" meant. Something in the way that Helen said it left no doubt.

Above all else, this felt like an act of friendship. I accepted it, my numb distress starting to be replaced by a sense of dislocation from reality.

The sex was fun.

Helen likes to tie Peter. I'd known that for a long time. Mark was always going on about how odd that was and how Helen "had Peter's pecker in her pocket". I couldn't quite imagine it.

That night, Helen tied and blindfolded Peter and then we both . . . played with him. My memory of it is so clear. Time slowed down. I tried not to look at Helen. I was at such a high level of awareness that reality was too vivid to be anything but a dream. Peter surrendered himself to us. We took him in turns, never speaking, always preserving the convention that it could have been just the two of them in the room. But we all knew. And we all wanted it.

My orgasm was like a return to sanity. It sounds an extravagant claim, but it healed me. I felt, for the first time in a very long time, happy.

I moved in with Helen and Peter after that. I had my own room. There was no more sharing. But there was love and support and a space to learn to be me again.

Things might have been fine if the walls had been thicker, or if Helen had been less noisy when she came, or if Peter had not been just a little in love with me. I lay there at night and listened to them having sex. I could tell they were trying to be quiet, but there would always be that last moment in which Helen lost control. I would close my eyes and try to remember Peter being inside me. I would try to come when Helen came.

After a while we all started to become less comfortable with each other in the mornings. We took care to dress before coming down for breakfast. I tried not to watch Peter's every move. I tried not to yearn for him. I failed.

Later Peter told me that he couldn't get me out of his head. He said the blindfold had meant that he was never sure when it was me and when it was Helen he was with. He felt like he should have been able to tell. He felt like he wanted to experience the difference.

One evening, Helen went to fix us some drinks. While she was out of the room Peter and I accidentally looked into each other's eyes. We'd each been trying to sneak a quick look at the other. We were still looking at each other when Helen came back. We broke contact guiltily. Helen just stood there. No one spoke.

I wanted to leave or to apologize. I felt as if she had walked in on us fucking.

Helen handed us both a drink. Then she said, "It's OK. Really. I'll sleep in the other room tonight."

Peter started to rise from his chair to protest. Helen stopped him with a glance that I couldn't read but which brought him to a complete halt. Then she was gone. She took my room.

I was standing too now, staring at the closed door between Helen and us.

Peter and I turned towards each other. I was uncertain. I wanted Peter. Really wanted him. He was so close and so alive that I thought sparks might jump the small gap between us.

I reached up and stroked the side of his face. He was very still. I kissed him.

It was as I had imagined it. Soft lips. Warm. Accepting. Except that it felt wrong. It felt like betrayal.

Peter didn't kiss me back but he didn't resist. I know that if I had continued he would have let me. To please me. To please Helen. But I stopped.

Still we didn't speak. I took Peter by the hand and led him, quietly, into my room. Helen was curled up in a ball facing the wall. She didn't hear us come in. I said her name. She turned and looked at both of us. There were tears in her eyes. I held Peter's hand out to her. She jumped up off the bed and hugged him. When I left, they were kissing fiercely, as if they were sucking in oxygen after almost drowning. I went for a drive. They were in their room when I came back and everything was quiet.

The next morning I declared my intent to look for a job. Here I am, five weeks later, ready to move to one.

"B. Are you in there, B? Come out, come out, wherever you are." It is Mark's voice calling from the garden. He sounds drunk. I rush out. The last time he and Peter met there was trouble. I expect to see

Peter dragging Mark away, but it is Helen, little Helen, who is blocking Mark's path.

"B. Please, B."

I put my hand on Helen's shoulder and she lets me step in front of her. She continues to glare at Mark.

"B, I'm drunk. I'm sorry I'm drunk but I've got something important to say to you."

Mark looks ill. His clothes are dirty and his complexion is pale. I wonder how long he has been drunk this time.

He staggers towards me, reaching for me. I stay still and he stops short.

"I know you're going away. The lawyer told me. I want to tell you . . . to say . . . to let you know that I love you, B. I've always loved you."

He is crying now. He looks lost. I assume his nympho intern has left him. He looks like he wants me to take him in my arms as I have so many times before.

Everybody at the party is looking at us. I step forward so that I can speak directly into Mark's ear. His arms fold about me as I say, "I know you love me, Mark. I love you. But it will never be enough, will it?"

His face turns towards me. He seems suddenly sober. I wait for the tantrum or the insult. Instead he says quietly, "Good luck in your new job, B," and walks, a little too precisely, towards his car. Helen sends Peter after him to drive him home.

The party doesn't last long. Mark has taken the edge off it. By the time Peter gets back people are already leaving. It's getting dark earlier already. Summer is over and fall, "Season of mists and mellow fruitfulness", is here.

The last of the guests leaves just before sunset. I stand and watch the slow ignition of the sky. Peter and Helen come and stand on either side of me. I take their hands.

I don't know who Barbara will become in Chicago. I hope Barbara the Bold, ready to make her own future. But right here and right now, she feels like Barbara the Blessed.

*Halloween*

"You can't do this to me, Anthea."

Mark is more pathetic than fierce. The smell of alcohol preceded him into my office. He looks slightly jaundiced. His cheeks and chin sport small islands of stubble that managed to evade his razor this morning. I'm surprised he can keep his hand steady enough to shave.

"I'm not doing it to you, Mark," I say. "You're doing it to yourself. You've lost it. Look at yourself. How long can you last between drinks now, Mark? An hour? Two, if you really try? I'm giving you a simple choice: either dry out or ship out."

For a moment I think he's going to tell me to fuck off. I almost wish he would.

When we first met, before his long-suffering wife finally left him, he was a maverick. He always had a comeback ready. I liked him. He reminded me of Davey, my younger brother. Or at least how Davey would have been if he hadn't wrapped himself around a tree riding that motorcycle of his.

I've never found it easy to talk to men. Somehow it always turned into a conflict: the strong ones saw me as a challenge, someone to put down either by bedding or ridiculing; the weak ones were afraid of me and their fear made me despise them and despise myself for feeling that way. I built a shell around myself. I out-manned them; being tougher than the strong and ruthlessly removing the weak.

I thought Mark was the exception, that for once I could drop the macho crap and make a friend. I liked the way he smiled and he was easy to talk to. Then, one evening, when we were working late, Mark pushed his fingers between my legs. I wanted to kill him. I felt betrayed. Stupid really, he wasn't to know that he reminded me of my dead brother.

Mark works for me now. I should probably have fired him, but I always hoped that he'd pull himself together and be the guy I wanted him to be. Now he's sitting on the other side of my desk with nothing to say. Oh shit. He's crying. Not big sobs. More like his eyes are leaking.

Part of me wants to hug him and help him, but most of me just wants to slap him. How could he fuck up his life like this?

Of course, I can't do either of these things. I'm the boss, Anthea the Hun they call me: strong, logical, unemotional.

I look at my watch. Mark is my last chore before I head home. It's Halloween tonight and I have things to prepare. I let my eyes rest on the picture of Drazen and his daughter that I keep on my desk. The picture is supposed to remind me of home, give me a smile in the middle of the day; increasingly it just reminds me that I spend too many hours at work and most of them are wasted on cleaning up the messes other people make. Time to clear up my last mess of the day.

"I'm going to leave these details with you, Mark. If you want to keep your job then I will get a phone call from the clinic on Monday saying that you've checked in. If you want to continue to drown yourself in booze, then just clear your desk and don't come back. This is your last chance, Mark. Choose wisely."

Why do I always sound so pompous when I'm doing something unpleasant?

Even though it's my office, I get up to leave. I want to be home. I want to be somewhere where I don't have to be in charge and where I can let people love me. Mark starts to cry properly as I leave. I pretend not to hear him and keep moving.

The express elevator, a perk of my executive status, is softly lit and lined with mirrors, presumably so that executives can maintain a positive image. I stand in the centre of the elevator and stare at the infinite number of Antheas that head off in each direction. I don't recognize them. I don't want these uptight, asexual women to be me.

Perhaps it is the shock of seeing the wreck Mark has become, or perhaps it is the news I want to give to Drazen tonight, but I feel a strong need to change the images in the mirror. I reach up and release my hair, letting it fall around my shoulders. My hair is thick and soft; I love the feel of it against my face, the taste of it in my mouth. My hair is my freedom, my sexuality. Which is why I bind it so tightly at work, but why I refuse to have it cut.

I bend forward at the waist, letting my hair fall forward over my head. It is almost long enough to touch the floor. Then I flick myself upright, casting my hair behind me like a mane. The images in the mirror, with their legs apart, shoulders back, hair shining in the massaged light, seem more recognizable now. I wave to myself just as the deferential tone sounds to let me know that I have reached the ground.

I opt for a limo rather than taking the train. I tell myself that it's because I'm late and I need to hurry home, but I know that what I want is the privacy.

In the car I settle back against the leather seat and slip off my shoes. I will be home in less than an hour, but I need Drazen right now. The wireless earpiece of my cell phone (Anthea the Hun always has all the latest boys' toys) is hidden beneath my hair. I say, "Drazen," and the speed dial starts.

"Anthea." A statement, not a question. Drazen's voice, soft and calm, slides into my ear and makes me shiver. In his mouth my name is "Ann-Tea-Ah" and immediately "the Hun" is left behind. I remain silent, waiting.

"So . . ." he says, "you can be overheard, but you want to play. Soon, I hope, you will be home, but then there will be other things before . . . I understand."

I can hear him walking through the house. He will go to his studio. Soundproofed and secure. I recognize the noise the door lock makes as it snaps shut.

When he speaks again he is more relaxed. His voice is still soft but it has energy to it suggesting the confident strength and controlled arousal of a predator stalking his prey.

"You are in a car. No, it is quiet enough to be a limo. I can hear your breathing, Anthea. Press your shoulders back against the leather seat. Keep your thighs together. Tight together. Squeeze. Close your eyes and remember how it feels when your thighs close against my beard, when my tongue dips into you. Remember the smell of your arousal, the soft drizzle of your juices onto my chin. Remember how hard it is for you to stay still, how much you want to move, to grind, to rock, to press, to drive yourself down upon my tongue until it impales you. Remember all of that but keep a calm expression on your face."

I look forward at the rear-view mirror. The driver's eyes are on the road, but if he looks up he will see me.

It feels as though Drazen is behind me, breathing into my ear, as if it is him I am pressing into. I want to open my legs, just a little, slide a finger along my thigh, draw small circles on my mound.

"No touching, Anthea. Keep your legs closed and your mind open."

I smile. I know he will be imagining me smiling.

"Stretch your legs. Feel the muscles at the back of your thighs tense. Keep them tense. Can you smell yourself yet? Do you think your driver can smell you? Not yet perhaps, but soon."

My face flushes at the thought. I check the rear-view again. The driver looks up, then looks away.

"You will feign sleep, Anthea. Let your beautiful head rest against the leather. Hold some of your hair across your mouth. Keep it in place. Remember how my thumb feels, pressing against your lower lip, my fingers resting on your cheek, how good it feels to dip your head forward and feel the thumb press into the roof of your mouth."

I bite down on my hair as the first little contraction hits. Memory flares. The first time that he fucked me in a public place it started like that, a small dip of my head on his thumb, my face scarlet with embarrassment, my sex damp with need. It ended with me bent over the back of a park bench, Drazen behind me, pushing slowly and calmly into my ass, as if anal sex was a normal pursuit on a Sunday morning stroll in the park.

"Good girl, Anthea. Good girl."

His voice is stroking me. Soothing me. I hear him unzip his fly and a small moan escapes from me.

"Shh, Anthea is sleeping. She cannot see how hard I am at the thought of her, cannot smell the musk of that arousal."

I love the smell of him. The taste of him. The fascination of playing with his foreskin. The strong scent that rises when I roll back that soft skin.

"In her sleep Anthea will reach beneath her respectable executive jacket, open one button of her pressed and spotless white blouse, push aside the cup of the plain white cotton bra and let her breast rest in the palm of her hand."

Slowly, shifting to one side as if in sleep, I let my hand slide onto my breast.

My nipples are so sensitive that I can hardly bare to have them touched. Before Drazen, my lovers had always been too rough: pinching and biting when they should have been caressing. I had begun to think that I was a freak with hair-trigger nipples that would be constantly off limits. Drazen, with his pianist's hands, showed me how wrong I was. He would stand behind me, his mouth on my neck, my breasts cupped gently in his hands, just the underside of them resting against his skin, lifted slightly but with no pressure. Then his thumbs, light as butterflies, would graze the tip of the nipples, coaxing them, letting them rise, working them until they throbbed, finally pushing them back firmly into my breasts and biting down on my neck until I was wriggling with pleasure.

"Anthea is dreaming. In her dream my cock slides, slick and stiff, out of her mouth. She guides it to her breasts. Uses it to draw a wet circle around her nipple. Laughs when I flinch with the extremity of the sensation. Rubs the underside of the gland over the stubby arousal of her nipple, then squeezes the head of my cock until the slit opens. She looks up at me, her eyes on mine as she pushes her nipple into the slit, fucking me and fucking me."

Drazen's voice has a ragged edge now. He will be touching himself. His eyes will be closed as he remembers how I took him that night. The first time I really took the initiative.

"Stroke the nipple, Anthea. Slow strokes. Persistent strokes. Suck on the hair in your mouth. Squeeze your thighs. Sweat for me inside your executive suit in your oversized limo. Come for me. Come hard. Come silently. Come for me, Anthea."

And I do. Not at once. Not on command. It takes maybe a minute of silent struggle. I can hear him breathing hard into my ear, listening to me, sniffing at me through the phone line. The come is a sunburst of warmth spreading up from my stomach, exorcising the tension of the day.

"Good girl, Anthea. Very good girl. Now come home to me."

The line goes dead in my ear.

I open my eyes and sit up straight. The driver's eyes flick away a little too quickly when I look into the rear-view. I realize that I am smiling. "Ann-Tea-Ah" smiles a lot.

I open the window, even though the day is cold. I don't want my smell to stay in the car.

I am nearly home now. We've left the freeway behind and are driving slowly through tree-lined streets. I can see jack-o'-lanterns on porches. They are all grinning at me. I grin back.

Drazen was my New Year's resolution. It was part of project APTGAL (Anthea's Plan To Get A Life) that I dreamed up when I found myself alone in my house on New Year's Eve. If I'd been sober when I put the plan together, I'm fairly sure that step one would not have read "Take piano lessons". Nothing might have come of it except for the card I saw the next day on the noticeboard at the convenience store. It read DRAZEN BEBIC: PIANO TEACHER.

For some reason, "Piano Teacher" had summoned up an image of a kindly old man wearing spectacles and an old brown cardigan and speaking with a Professor Von Duck accent. Drazen was nothing like that. First there was his hair: thick, jet black, and brushed straight back so that it seemed to cascade to his shoulders. Then there was his beard: short, precise, somehow emphasizing the sensual softness of his lips. But most of all there were his eyes, dark but filled with light, and hard to look away from.

He was at least fifteen years older than me and I'd only just laid eyes on him but, by the time he stepped forward and shook my hand, my palm was already damp. When he touched me, my nipples hardened. No one had ever had that effect on me before. Then he said my name, "Ann-Tea-Ah," and I understood what gives cats the urge to purr.

He sat me down in front of the huge piano that dominated his tiny apartment. I felt like Jane Eyre, asked to play for Mr Rochester, and knowing that every note would diminish her in his eyes. Yet I'd been good at the piano once, back before work spread itself across my life like a gorse bush, leaving room for nothing else, so when, standing so close behind me that I could smell his cologne, he said, "I would like to hear you, Anthea," I started to play.

He listened and watched. There was nothing flirtatious, but I had his complete attention. I played quite well once I got started. Enough to demonstrate some technique at least. He didn't tell me to stop, so I played every piece I knew. When I finished I wondered why I'd ever given up playing. I was good and this was fun.

"I would like to know what it is that you want, Anthea," Drazen said.

I had turned to face him, waiting for praise or at least coaching, wanting to look into his eyes again. His question surprised me.

"I want to play the piano."

"Ah, I had hoped that perhaps you wanted me to teach you."

"What?"

"You already play the piano. But you play with these . . ." He reached out and picked up my hand, holding it gently by the tips of the fingers. My skin prickled where it touched him. "When you could be playing with this."

He held me by the wrist and placed the palm of my hand against my chest, between my breasts. The contact wasn't overtly sexual but I felt naked in front of him. The surprising thing was that my body was clearly happy about that. My mind was offended.

I shook his hand off my wrist and stood up. "I'm leaving now," I said.

Drazen bowed his head. I'd never seen anyone do that in real life before. His eyes stayed on me during the bow. I couldn't read them but I didn't want to look away from them. I had to remind myself that he had been rude to me and that I wasn't going to stand for it.

"Are you always so—" I realized that "rude" was the wrong word. He'd been polite but . . . "—personal with your students?"

"What is life if it is not personal, Anthea?"

That was pretty much the question I'd been asking myself on New Year's Eve.

"I'm going now."

He stepped back and to one side so that I had a clear route to the door.

I didn't leave. It was Anthea the Hun who wanted to leave. The rest of me wanted to stay. I sat down. "I'm sorry," I said. "You caught me by surprise. I'd like to stay."

He didn't look surprised, but he did smile. "Then I'm glad that I 'caught' you at all," he said.

And he had caught me. We became lovers within the week. But even in bed he was my teacher. He taught me to listen to the now, to surrender to the needs of my body in order to feed my soul. Another man talking like that would sound ridiculous, Drazen just sounds truthful.

Months afterwards, lying in his arms after sex, I asked him about the day we met. I wanted to know what he thought of me then.

He lifted my chin off his chest to make me look at him and said, "I thought then, what I think now. That I want you. That, if you will let me, I will take you. That sometimes life is worth living." I knew then that he loved me.

"We're here ma'am," the driver says.

There are no lascivious looks, no innuendo. I smile at him and tip him more generously than usual.

Anja is waiting for me when I get home. She has the same grave face as her father, one that is transformed when she smiles.

Anja is doing her best to find a place for herself in America, but she has a solemnity about her that is not normal for an eleven-year-old American girl, but she is strong, a survivor. She has survived the war in Bosnia, the death of her mother, her exile in America. Seeing her standing there on the porch, her face lit by the huge jack-o'-lantern that I helped her carve last night, I want to rid her of her ghosts. I want to see her filled with joy.

"Hello, Morticia," she says, holding out her hand in a formal invitation, "come and meet Gomez."

Tonight we are, at Anja's insistence, the Addams family. She will, of course, be Wednesday.

Drazen is already in the double-breasted pinstriped suit that is his concession to costume. I wonder if he was wearing it when I called.

"Gomez, *mon cher*, *mon amour*," I say in a voice I hope is like Anjelica Houston's.

"Ah, Tish, you spoke French," he says on cue, taking my outstretched arm and kissing his way from the back of my hand up my arm to my neck. I glance sideways at Anja/Wednesday wondering if she approves, fearing that moments like this summon the spirit of her mother. The edges of her mouth are slightly upturned. I take that as warm approbation.

When Drazen's head is at my neck I twist sideways, plant a quick kiss on his cheek and say, "Thank you. That was delicious." Then I send him away so that Anja and I can change.

Anja has prepared everything, the clothes are laid out on the bed, the wigs are on the dressing table. It is all I can do to slip away and shower before she sets about her work.

There is an intimacy in dressing each other that is like nothing else. It is recognition of trust and an offer to reveal and to transform. The costumes emphasize this. I never wear black at home, yet now I am wrapped in it like a shroud.

"How do I look?" I ask as the wig goes on.

"Believable," Anja says.

Not quite the comment I expected. I wonder how I normally look to her. There is a short silence during which I grow nervous in front of this child.

Then she hands me the make-up bag and says, "Make me look sad, but scary."

It doesn't take long.

"Gomez" declines to walk the streets with us. Waving a thick cigar, which I know he will not smoke, he says, "My dears, the two of you are frightful enough, three of us could prove fatal."

By the standards of the day, our costumes are sedate, yet at every door Anja makes a killing. She never once steps out of character, extorting treats because, from her, the threat of tricks seems so real.

I let her walk ahead of me, keeping to the shadows, arms folded across my breasts, whenever we reach a house. Watching Anja, I see her father, his stillness, his confidence. I wonder which of her gestures belong to her mother, Sanja.

I realize that I am jealous of Sanja, for having Drazen before me. Crazy to be jealous of a dead woman, and yet tonight I feel as though, at any moment, I might meet her.

When Anja's sack is full we return home. She is so serious that I am uncertain whether she has enjoyed herself or whether this has all been a bizarre experiment in which she has tested the sanity of those around her and found them wanting. Yet when she sees Drazen on the porch, she runs to him.

"Dada," she says, holding up her sack, "look how much they gave me."

"You must have made them tremble, little one."

"No, it was Anthea, standing in the shadows like a threat. She was perfect."

Drazen looks over Anja's head at me and smiles. I feel as though I have won a medal. I wait for Anja to turn and thank me, but she grabs her sack and runs into the house.

"Happiness still catches her by surprise," Drazen says. "She wants to go and hug it to herself in private." He takes my hand in his, rubs his thumb against my palm and says, "You understand that, I'm sure."

I almost tell him then, but I don't want to do it in my costume so I wait. Dinner comes and goes without me finding the right moment. Anja gets permission to sleep in her Wednesday outfit because, as she explained very seriously, "It is still Halloween until morning," and then Drazen and I are alone.

I go into the bedroom to change out of my Morticia costume. Drazen follows me. Leaning against the door frame, he looks at me, waiting for something.

I want to tell him. But not yet. I need to think some more, I tell myself. Coward, I reply.

"Come to bed," Drazen says.

"I have to do some work first. I'll be back later."

I can see he doesn't believe me, but he makes no comment when I go back downstairs.

I sit at my laptop, pretending to work, trying to find my courage. I make some coffee and go out onto the back porch.

The moon is full tonight. It sits in the sky, large and round and proud. It occurs to me that the moon and I are both pregnant, except that I don't show yet.

This is what I need to tell Drazen. So what's stopping me? We aren't married. We've never really talked about the future. A man with a past like Drazen's can be forgiven for living in the present. I don't want to drive him away and I don't want to force him to commit. And I don't know how I feel about being pregnant.

I know exactly when this baby was conceived. It was on the anniversary of Sanja's death. Drazen had never talked to me about how his wife died, but then I'd never found him crying before. I held him and let him cry.

"They hurt her, Anthea, before they killed her; they spent a day hurting her. And I couldn't stop them. I didn't even know what was happening until they dumped her body at my door."

I rocked him, holding his head to my breast.

"She was my life, Anthea. And they killed her."

There was nothing to say, so I stayed silent.

After a while, he looked up. His eyes had no strength in them, only sorrow. I kissed them one at a time. Then I kissed his mouth, again and again, small healing kisses.

I put his hand between my legs. I don't know why I did it. Words seemed so inadequate. I gave him what I had. The sex started slowly. I sat astride him and pulled him into me. Then I carried on kissing him. He stopped crying. He held me so tightly that it left bruises. Then he started to fuck me, fiercely, passionately, as if fucking me was the only thing that kept him alive. He clung to me even after he had come. I still hadn't spoken to him, but now it was me who was crying.

I think he was saying goodbye to his wife that night. I know he was choosing me, choosing life. It turns out that we were also creating one.

I shiver in the cold and realize I have been outside a long time. Drazen is asleep when I reach the bedroom. The moon is washing his face with silver. He looks older, more vulnerable. I want him so badly it frightens me.

Time to choose: trick or treat?

I stroke his face, following the moon, then I sit astride him. He doesn't wake until I kiss him. I place his hands on my breasts and rock gently on his cock, which is lying flat against his belly. I lift my hips and he slides into me. So good to have him there. So good to have him.

"There is something I need to tell you," I say.

Drazen puts his finger across my lips pulls my head down to him. He pushes upwards, slowly, without urgency, until he is all the way in. "What shall we call the child?" he says.

*Thanksgiving*

"You want me to sleep here?"

"Well, this is where you slept when you lived here, Helen. Why should it change now? I thought you'd be pleased to have your old room back."

I try to read my mother's face. She must being doing this deliberately. And she must know that I can see what she is doing. But she still has that innocent, not-quite-connected-to-planet-earth look that she uses to avoid any minor questions about her decisions that my father might be rash enough to voice.

I stare in disbelief at the single bed that I slept in as a child. It's a very narrow single bed.

"I know that you prefer to ignore the fact that Peter and I are married, Mother, but he is my husband and I expect to have him in my bed. We can't sleep here."

"Really, Helen, I have no idea where you get these impressions from. I have no opinion about Peter. As I said at the time, who you chose to marry was up to you."

What she'd said at the time was, "Are you sure you want to marry Paul, dear? He's such a bland man. I can see the advantage of having someone manageable but marriage needs a little spice if it's to last. I've always preferred to wake up to Huevos Rancheros. The problem with Paul is that he's just so . . . oatmeal."

I'd stood there, with my hands balled into fists and my jaw clenched, trying to quell the desire to hit her. "His name is Peter, Mother," I'd spat out.

"You see, dear, not even his name is memorable. Ah well. It is your decision, of course."

Now, seven years later, I find myself having to bite back my anger one more time. My mother is talking. I'm trying not to strangle her.

"I didn't think that you and Peter would mind being separated for one night. I've given him the fold-down bed in your father's den. He'll be perfectly comfortable. I had to give the guest bedroom to Troy and Dianna; after all, they have the baby to think of."

The baby. Of course, we should be thinking about the baby. My younger brother (what kind of mother calls their kids Helen and Troy?) produced a grandchild right off the bat. I, of course, committed the sin of putting my career ahead of my duty to deliver grandchildren, although even that became Peter's fault in my mother's mind. "If Peter has a problem dear, I can recommend an excellent clinic." My mother had left that helpful tip on our answerphone in the second year of my marriage. Peter played it back to me when I got home from work.

I don't resent the fact that Troy and Dianna got the big bed. I resent the implication that Peter is so bland that I won't even notice his absence.

"I want him here with me, Mother."

Even I can hear how petulant I sound.

"Well, if it's that important to you, dear, I'll ask your father to move the fold-down bed in here. I'm sure he won't mind. Although, of course, he has only just set everything up in the den. But then your father always makes sure that his little Helen gets what she wants, doesn't he?"

I don't believe it. She is still jealous of the fact that Dad will do things for me.

"There won't be a lot of room in here. You'll have to fold up the bed before you can open the door. But, if that's what you want . . ."

Oh God. It is always like this. A constant trickle of words that erode my will. I either have to get angry or shut down and give in. Giving in is easier. If I push her now, the topic will come up at dinner. And again in the morning. And the next time we come to the house. If there is a next time.

"Never mind, Mother. Peter can stay where he is. Let's just concentrate on getting dinner ready."

"Well, if you're sure, dear."

How did this woman live so long?

"You look tense, Helen. Why don't you take a moment to freshen up? Dianna is changing the baby in the bathroom but you can use the en suite in the master bedroom. I'll be in the kitchen when you're ready."

And then she is gone. The relief is physical, like when your ears pop at altitude.

I don't really need to freshen up but it gives me a reason to delay going downstairs. Nothing has changed in my parents' bedroom. The huge wrought-iron bed with the chintz canopy over it is still there. I used that bed the first time that I fucked Peter. I used it because I liked the headboard, because I wanted revenge on my mother for all the times I'd had to listen to her thrashing in this bed in the middle of the night, and because I wanted to see if good, nice, sensible Peter Brader would do what I wanted him to do.

I sit on the stool by the dressing table and summon up the memory of a nineteen-year-old Peter, lying on this bed with his wrists tied to the headboard; so calm and trusting that, except for the impressive erection he was saluting me with, he might almost have been ready to sleep.

Other boys I'd known had only pretended to submit. They'd made comments as I tied them to establish that it was all a game and, as soon as they'd come, they'd started to fret at their bonds, demanding to be let free. Peter didn't do any of that. He just waited for me to use him. But his serenity wasn't passive. Somehow it managed to amplify everything I did. The harder I fucked him, the harder I wanted to fuck him. His cock was my lightning rod, calling me forth, daring me to spend myself on him, taking everything that I could give and leaving me discharged and sated.

Afterwards I'd left him tied to the bed while I sat and brushed my hair. A beam of sunlight was shining down on him, highlighting the sweat on his muscles and the small scratches and bites I'd visited on him. He looked happy, even grateful. I'd shown him my wildest side.

I'd sworn and fucked and bitten and scratched and shouted my come with my head thrown back and he hadn't pulled away, he hadn't been threatened. He was waiting for more. He was waiting for me. For the first time in my adult life I felt as if I'd found a home.

Peter wasn't my first fuck, but he was my first lover. Actually, he is my only lover. To me that is a statement of how rich my life is rather than how narrow my experience has been.

"Helen dear, if you've finished up there, you can help your father lay the table."

The sound of my mother's voice makes me feel guilty and furtive and childish. I get off the stool quickly and smooth the cover of the bed, as if I had just used it. Why does coming home always turn me back into a little girl? And why do I hate that so much?

There are six of us at dinner but there is food for at least a dozen. The conversation is stilted at first. Troy and Peter have the mandatory road-number-filled review of the drive to my parents' house, even though I actually did the driving. I ask Dianna about the baby, revealing my ignorance of modern child-rearing with each question that I ask. Mother fusses over Dad, ensuring that he gets the best slices of meat, touching his hand when she passes him things, keeping his glass full. She always makes sure that he knows he is the centre of her attention. Dad catches me watching them and gives me an unapologetic grin. This is how the world is, that grin says, and it's too late now to change it.

As the wine flows, words become easier for everybody but me. I feel as though an invisible barrier has settled between me and everyone else. I watch but I don't speak.

Peter fits in so well. He is a good listener. People relax when they talk with him. When they talk with me it is as if they are always just a little on their guard. Dianna is talking to him now. Peter isn't talking to her about the baby. Somehow he has learned that she paints and within a few moments the woman I could barely exchange a word with is sharing her passion for abstract art.

As the courses go by, I drink and eat more than I should. I want to speak to Troy. I want to sit and exchange deep truths with him, except that those truths remain just out of reach of my tongue so I remain silent. By the time we reach dessert I am quite drunk. It seems to me that Peter has abandoned me. Everyone has abandoned me.

"I think you might want to have little lie down, dear." My mother is leading me back to my little virgin bed. I'd protest except that I can't find the words. And I'm tired. Very, very tired.

I wake with a fierce thirst and a vicious headache. It's dark. I've slept through the afternoon. I groan in self-pity. I've made such a fool of myself. I know that mother will be secretly pleased.

I want Peter. Except Peter isn't here, my mother saw to that.

Sitting up is not pleasant so I lie down again.

The room has not changed since I left it seven years ago. I've changed so much since then that it seems incongruous for me to be occupying the same space that I did then. Peter is responsible for most of those changes. Living up to how he sees me, using the quiet space he provides for me to seek refuge in, has changed who I am.

Who would I have been without Peter?

Back before Peter, I'd never really been that comfortable with boys. It wasn't that I was shy; it was more that I saw them too clearly and I didn't like what I saw. For them, girls were trophies to show off to other boys. I used to imagine them at swap meets, talking to each other about girls like they were baseball cards: "Had her. Had her. Had her. Want her. I'll swap you two Heathers for an Alicia." But the worse thing was that, when it came to sex, they all seemed to want to be in charge although very few of them seemed to know what to do.

I knew enough about my own body to know what I wanted: where and how I wanted to be touched and for how long. I also knew the kind of body I wanted to do the touching: tall, lean, strong. Unfortunately, most of those bodies seemed to come with the supersized ego option as standard.

I tried a few anyway. It wasn't hard to get their attention – I was attractive enough in a petite, androgynous sort of way – the challenge was to stay in control. The first couple of attempts were an education.

"Tall 'n' Lean #1" put his hands everywhere but he didn't know what to do with them. And he got irritated when I moved around. I was supposed to be his bendyfucktoy, something he could pose for his convenience. His dick was nice, smooth and hard, but he wasn't interested in me touching it for long, he wanted to "slide it home". I moved to climb up on his lap but he wanted me on my back. He wasn't in me for long before he came. Then he asked me if I wanted to go get a burger. I realized I'd just had the sexual equivalent of a drive-thru meal: smells good, is over too quickly and lies like a lump on your stomach afterwards.

"Tall 'n' Lean #2" wasn't interested in entering anything other than my mouth. He wanted me on my knees, looking up into his eyes. I had no objection to the idea in principle. It was corny but it had a sense of theatre to it. What turned me off was him placing his hand on the back of my head and using my mouth like an extension of his hand. I've seen drains unblocked with more finesse. I had to grab his balls to make him stop. I thought he'd be angry with me, maybe even try to hit me, but he actually whined like a little boy, "What did you do that for?" It was the question I was beginning to ask about sex as a whole.

I decided to do some research before seeking out "Tall 'n' Lean #3". I went to Barnes and Noble to see what kind of books I could find on sex. I'd done the "Insert Part A into Part B" manuals and the *Joy of Sex* hippy-type manuals but they didn't give me what I wanted. They were too much like cookery lessons and not enough like good food. I moved on to the erotica section and found *The Story of O* and *The Taking of Sleeping Beauty*. They definitely got my attention. Hours of it. The thing was, I didn't want to be O or Beauty, I wanted to be the person doing things to them. Well, not them in particular. I wanted to be doing things to "Tall 'n' Leans". I'd lie in my narrow little bed, exhausted from my reading or listening to my parents having sex in the room next door, and I'd think about what it would be like to have that kind of control. Then I got to thinking about how I might make it happen. As it turned out, it wasn't that difficult but it wasn't that much fun either.

I found "Tall 'n' Lean #3" in a karate class. I'd signed up because I wanted to be able to protect myself and because I figured the boys there would be more disciplined. He was beautiful, his sweat smelled good, he was a black belt and he was older than me. I waited for him in the parking lot after class. I had decided to be direct.

"Would you like me to fuck you?"

He didn't look stunned, offended or even pleased, just curious. "Are you sure you mean it that way around? Most girls want me to fuck them."

"I'm very sure."

He eyes licked slowly over my body. Then he smiled. "OK," he said, like he was agreeing to grab a pizza, "but I have a question."

"Yes?"

"What's your name?"

I blushed at that. It hadn't occurred to me that while I'd been noticing the muscles in his forearm and the tight curve of his butt, all he'd been paying attention to was his karate technique.

My parents were away on one of their pagan weekends. Sex was the bedrock of their marriage; you only had to look at the two of them together to see that. The pagan weekends gave them the opportunity to concentrate on fucking each other's brains out without worrying about making a noise.

I'd decided to have a mini pagan weekend of my own. I brought Tall 'n' Lean #3" back to my house. I was more than a little nervous. He didn't touch me or hassle me but there was a confidence behind his eyes that was unsettling. I took him into my dad's den and gave him the speech I'd rehearsed.

"OK, here are the rules. I want to fuck you. I want you to do what I tell you while I fuck you. If you don't do what I tell you, the fucking will stop. Do you understand?"

It was supposed to be my first step to establishing mastery over him. He sat on the edge of my dad's desk, like he had a right to be there, and said, "That speech would work better if you said, 'I am going to fuck you. You will do what I want.' You have to sound like you mean it."

He slipped off the desk and onto his knees in front of me without breaking eye contact. "Tell me how to serve you, Mistress."

In theory this was just what I wanted. But he was laughing at me. It was gentle laughter, but laughter all the same.

"Shit," I said.

For a second he looked surprised. He thought I was giving an instruction.

"I so wanted to tie you to my dad's chair and tease you and fuck you. But it's not going to work, is it?"

He stood up, lifting me like I weighed nothing at all and placed me on Dad's desk. I felt a little bit of panic and a lot of excitement.

"Your dad's chair? How old are you, Helen? No. Don't answer that. You're a pretty girl, Helen, and a brave one. You know what you want but you don't yet know how to recognize who can give it to you."

I'd known he was a little older than me but I hadn't expected him to talk to me like I was a child. Who did he think he was, my camp counsellor?

"Well, why did you come here, then?" My eyes were hot with embarrassment.

"You sounded convincing in the parking lot. And I don't mind switching from time to time."

"Switching?"

"I'm a dom, Helen. I normally do the tying up."

"You think I'm stupid, don't you?"

"No. But I think you need to learn to recognize a sub when you meet one."

Then he kissed me. It was a slow kiss, passionate but friendly. It made me wonder what it would be like to be tied up by him. To let him do whatever he wanted. Then he wasn't kissing me any more. "Gotta go, Helen. My name is Jon, by the way. I'll see you at karate next week."

I picked up a book from the desk and threw it, but it only hit the door closing behind him. I was mad at Jon for the rest of the day. Then I started to think about how things might have gone wrong: about the risks that I'd taken; about how gentle he'd been. Gentle and strong. I could see why women would let him tie them.

Jon and I became friends but not lovers. He gave me things to read and told me about his life. I left the "Tall 'n' Leans" alone for a while and concentrated on getting to college. I'd got through two more "Tall 'n' Leans" in college before I met Peter, both of them one-nightstands, both of them left me feeling hungry and somehow cheated.

My head is feeling better so I check my watch. Somehow it has reached 10 p.m. I've missed Thanksgiving and they've all forgotten about me. I hug my sense of hurt to me tightly. It serves me right that I've been abandoned. You see, I made a mistake. Such a big mistake. I gave Peter away to my best friend. I was so sure of him you see. So certain that I was what he wanted. I thought I could lend him out. Share him with a friend.

It started out OK. Barbara was sad and needed comfort so I tied Peter and blindfolded him and then I shared him with her. It was fun. It felt human and loving. I was so proud of all of us. But the thing is, I get jealous. Just the way my mother does. I hate myself for it but I can't help it.

I'd invited Barbara to stay with us, to join the Peter and Helen household. I knew they liked each other but I was too vain to think it through. And then I saw how Peter looked at her. How he wanted her. It was my doing, not his. Peter followed my lead, trusting me to do the right thing, and I gave him away.

Except Barbara gave him back. Barbara gave him back. I don't know if he'd have come back on his own.

I must still be a little drunk. I've spent months carefully not thinking about this and now I'm crying into my pillow afraid that Peter hasn't really come back to me.

You see, I know that I'm not worthy of Peter. I'm not really the person he deserves. For weeks now I've been watching him, wondering if I'm living in a charade; whether Peter would rather be with Barbara but is just too nice to leave me. Maybe my mother was right to put him on the other side of the house.

"Helen?"

Peter is standing over me. I didn't even hear him come in. I sit up on the bed, conscious of how red my eyes must be and how strongly I must smell of drink. I want to get up and hug him but I can't make myself move.

Peter has brought the toy bag with him. I didn't even know he'd packed it. Shit, he's brought the toy bag to my parents' house.

He places the toy bag on the bed beside me. Normally I choose the toys, but this time it is Peter who opens the bag. He takes out the strap-on. It's a complicated affair. The strap that goes between my legs will push a dildo and a butt plug into me and leave a long thin curved black latex cock jutting out from my belly.

"I'd like you to use this. I want us to make some noise."

Peter wants me to fuck him and he wants everyone to know it's happening. Joy spreads through me like liquid sunlight. Peter wants me.

He's been watching me figure it out. When he sees my smile start, he kisses me. I am Sleeping Beauty being brought back to life. Except I'm going to reward my prince by reaming his ass as hard as I can.

I take the strap-on from him. "Strip, Peter," I say.

He sheds his clothes calmly but quickly. He is already hard. I make him wait while I shrug out of my clothes, then I stand with one leg on the bed and tell him to tool me up. I mean to sound stern but I can't keep the joy out of my voice.

Then it starts for real. Peter lubes me slowly and thoroughly and straps me tight. With both holes full and a strong black cock thrusting in front of me, I feel powerful and as randy as hell.

"Get on your back on the bed, Peter, and hold on to your ankles."

I love the sound of that. Love the calm excitement with which he obeys. He doesn't ask why he's on his back when he should be bent over. He does what I tell him.

I spread lube over my mock-cock, place my finger and thumb around the base of Peter's erection and push the strap-on hard into his anus.

"Keep your hands around your ankles, Peter." Then I make the noise he's been waiting for: in my best rodeo tones I shout, "YEEHAW," and we're off.

I ride him hard enough to make him buck on the bed. I keep his cock in my hand like a joystick or perhaps a saddle horn, squeezing it as I pound his ass. The harder I push into him, the deeper the dildo rises into me. When I'm close, I slap his hands away from his ankles, lift his feet up over my shoulders and fuck for depth. The bed is bouncing now.

"Jack off, Peter. Jack off hard."

His hand moves eagerly on his cock. I am so close that I'm groaning as I grind into him. The heat of his sperm splashing onto my belly pushes me over and I growl my come at him.

I pull out of Peter's poor abused asshole and collapse on top of him. I feel strong and whole and loved.

Peter holds me gently and whispers, "Welcome back, Helen."

It turns out that the bed is not too narrow if we lie like spoons. As I fall asleep, I remember that I'm still wearing the strap-on but I'm too tired to move.

We are both sore the next morning but that doesn't stop us grinning at one another.

"Do you think they heard us?"

"Your parents' bedroom is still next door, isn't it, Helen?"

We both laugh.

At breakfast I wait for my mother to say something. She discusses the weather and asks if we really have to leave straight after breakfast but makes no mention of our exploits. As we say our goodbyes, Mother hugs Peter and says something to him. I miss the exchange because I have a crying baby in my arms at the time.

When I've driven as far as the freeway, I ask Peter what my mother said.

"She told me you were lucky to have me."

"What did you say?"

"I said that you would always have me and that I would always give thanks for that."

I try to imagine the expression on my mother's face when she heard that. I decide that it would probably be one of approval. Thank God for Peter, I think to myself. Then I start to look for the next rest stop. I want a quiet place where we can do a bit more thanksgiving.

# Screen Play

A. F. Waddell

In a dimly lit room I stood at the bottom of a winding staircase; the sound of wind chimes played from an upstairs porch on a hot night. I wore a white blouse, tight red skirt and spiked high heels. I watched the man walk towards my front pane-glass double doors. His brown hair was slicked back; his cheekbones were prominent; his long thin nose slightly flared over his moustache. He jiggled my door handle; the door was locked. As I watched him he searched the ground for something. Picking up a large stone, he used it to break my glass door pane; he reached inside and turned the lock. He threw open the door and approached me, holding and kissing me and unbuttoning my blouse. His hand rubbed my cunt through my silk skirt and panties.

"Maybe . . ." I whispered.

He lowered me to the floor. He pushed up my skirt and pulled down my white panties, slipping them over my thighs, knees and calves, and over my strapped, spiked heels. I breathlessly shook.

I awoke moaning in bed from another orgasmic dream; I'd mentally recreated a scene from the film *Body Heat.* I was Matty Walker: my perfect, fit-in-a-champagne-glass breasts throbbing in my perfect white blouse, my hungry cunt throbbing in my perfect red skirt. I recalled the first time I'd seen the film in the early eighties. In a cold, empty house I'd sat huddled under a blanket. I was emotionally and physically transported to the lush, warm, wet environs of South Florida – was it my imagination or did steam visibly rise from grass and earth, from Matty and Ned, as they fucked in the boathouse? I thought of my vibrator nestled in the nightstand drawer. I deferred. It was getting late. I got up, dressed in a robe, and went to the kitchen for coffee. I took a cup of Colombian into my office and checked my schedule for the day. I'd get off easy today, only one appointment, later in the day.

* * *

Driving southwest through the hills in my Jeep was relaxing, a perk before hitting the freeway. To the sound of Santana's "Samba Pa Ti" I floated through green-hilled space. Highway 120 was winding. With my tendency to speed I had to be careful, lest I totally lose it on a curve. The hitchhiker stood on the west side of the highway. He wore a blue flannel shirt and jeans. His long dark hair was tied in a ponytail. What would he be like? I wondered. A snake-hipped stud with knowledge of the *Kama Sutra* and tantric sex? A masseur and sex magician? A lover who'd spend hours discovering and lingering on a woman's sensitive spots? Did he smell of recently showered male and exotic fragrance, his hair of coconut shampoo? I imagined the male bouquet drifting from his skin and through my nostrils, into the limbic system of my brain. *Get a grip, girl. He's probably a serial killer.*

Dr Wellman's office was located on Citrus Avenue between Back, Neck and Shoulder Pain, and the Anti-Aging Clinic. I walked the maze between offices and entered the lobby at 3.50 p.m. The receptionist, Melanie, was pretty, perky and tan.

"Hi! Have a seat, Ms Waites. He'll be right with you."

I sat on a cream-coloured leather sofa. The decor reminded me of a Woody Allen film set, with its calming vibes of neutral shades: white, off-white, eggshell, oatmeal, beige, mushroom and sand. At 3.59 I walked into the office and took a seat opposite Barry. We sat in comfortable overstuffed chairs.

"How've you been, Anna?"

"Busy."

"Anna, are you taking care of yourself? Exercising? Eating right? Socially interacting?"

"Yes, yes. Who are you, my mother?"

Barry smiled. "How's work going?"

"I'm adapting my novel into a screenplay, remember?"

"That's right. That's wonderful, your novel about the female independent filmmaker?"

"Yes, that's right! But I wonder if people will pay to see yet another inside-the-industry satire. No action figures or computer games will result. Industry accountants will likely be unenthusiastic."

"Do the work, Anna. You must complete the work in order to get to the next work."

"Yes."

"Sleeping well? Dreaming?"

"I dreamed of Matty again. That I was Matty."

"Why do you suppose you dream of being a femme fatale?"

"I suppose I'm attracted to the power. The sexuality."

"Yes?" Barry rested his chin on his intertwined hands and leaned slightly forward; the furrow between his brows deepened.

"Dr Wellman, do you realize that Matty's character is bad, and isn't punished for it? Quite unusual for a story, for a film. Oh. And don't forget Bridget in *The Last Seduction*. Another exception to the rule."

"Anna . . . we don't use the 'b' word in this office."

I smiled. "Sorry! And this morning I fantasized about picking up a hitchhiker."

"Yes . . . ?"

"Spontaneous sex with a complete stranger would be hot."

"Well, yes, but a distinction must be made between fantasy and reality. Many fantasies are meant to remain unrealized. Violating prohibition is however a strong basis for eroticism."

I had images of forbidden fruit. Dates. Smooth and rich on the tongue. High carb. Sugary. Dangerous.

I took Citrus Ave to I-5. As I drove north through green foothills, the air quality improved; dusk gave fantastical quality to the hills and lights. Pockets of housing development imposed their squares and rectangles backing out, pushing between the natural curves of the foothills, boxes juxtaposing green jutting breasts. Driving east towards Shadow Valley, I looked forward to getting home, putting on a robe and puttering around the house. I wondered when my muse might visit and send me scurrying to my notebook or word processor.

At home I reclined on the sofa and thumbed a magazine. *Goddess* targeted a female professional demographic. I skimmed the food section and made a mental note on the salmon and spinach diet. I skimmed the health section and noted the latest miracle supplement. I skipped ahead to Indulgences. Blurbed were spas, vacation getaways, and specialty services: *Retreat caters to your special needs. Nestled in the natural environment of the Golden Haze foothills, our facility offers the utmost in comfort, privacy and natural beauty. Our select, discreet staff is here to indulge you. For more, visit our web presence at retreat.com.* I went into my office, signed online and accessed the site. The design was simple, understated, clean. Shades of light blue, cream and black were accented by soft-focus photos of foothills, cabins, interior design and bodies under the hands of masseur and masseuse. I accessed the reservations page.

A link provided a request form. *Let us assist you in designing your experience*. Interesting, I thought.

I bookmarked the website, got ready for bed, climbed between the sheets and randomly took a book from the nightstand. *The Mind of Eros* by Frederick Borman PhD could be a deeply psychological read, but also included sexual fantasies and experiences. I liked to skip around. I first hungrily, then sleepily, read.

The dark-haired woman sat in the centre of the small movie theatre; she seemed to be the only woman there. Men watched the screen with a focused yet wild energy. In giant close-up, a pink quivering cunt and cock devoured and attacked the other. Reminiscent of some fifties American sci-fi/horror film, sans the cheesy costumes with visible zippers in the back, slimy odd-shaped creatures wrought havoc and spewed mysterious, dangerous fluids. A large prick pumped a perfect, hairless, tanned, pink-edged wet cunt. The Maw-Creature appeared impossibly small to accommodate the Prick-Monster which inched inside it, stretching and spreading its edges.

A pink, belled tip and shaft vigorously slid through slick fingers and thumb, fingers and thumb, fingers and thumb. From its slitted tip spurted whiteness into brunette hair it ran; onto a soft tan face over heavily blushed cheeks; over cotton-candy pink lip gloss; over a delicately dimpled chin. The dark-haired female viewer looked at the screen. Recognizing her own face, her jaw slackened as the cinematic action reflected in her eyes.

I awoke and touched my face. Lying on my back in bed, I stared at the ceiling and replayed my unusual dream.

Under a skylight I crawled on the hardwood floor and arranged three-by-five cards. Breaking down a novel into key film scenes could be torture. How to effectively condense, yet retain meaning? I agonized. Many screen treatments in any case eventually suffered drastic rewrites; the further into the process one got, the less original meaning likely remained, until a work could appear unrecognizable. Casting-wise, Cate Blanchett and Jeremy Irons might devolve into . . . who knew? I thought the first scene would be of protagonist Claire giving direction on a film set. Scene two would begin a series of flashbacks of Claire in the early years, as continuity person and script supervisor on various low-budget location films, including the comic relief of behind-the-scenes on horror films. Relationships would be broken into love scenes, interspersed with her industry climb and disappointments, climaxing in her Cannes win for *Sighs and Whispers*. I gathered my three-by-five cards, mixed them up, and threw them into the air. I spun and chanted as the cards fluttered to the floor. Not bad! I thought of their reordering.

I drove west on Mountain View. It had been a while since I'd seen him – since he'd closely stood, caressed my shoulders and neck, and run his fingers through my hair. Rick was a good listener, sensitive and had a sense of humour. I'd date him, I thought, but then we'd have sex and break up, and I'd lose a damned good hairstylist.

"What are we doing today, Anna?"

"A trim and a blow-dry, please, Rick."

Draped in plastic at the shampoo sink, I leaned back, closed my eyes and relaxed into the experience. Wet. Lather. Rick's hands vigorously massaged my scalp, moving in circles, moving skin over bone, messaging nerves and limbs. Rinse. Condition. Rinse. Back at his work station, I sat as he precisely combed and trimmed my hair. He continuously repositioned my head, as if I were a fidgety child. At the next station a female stylist did a man's hair. It was funny, I thought, most men came into a hair salon with a maximum of two or three inches of hair, yet the stylist could take for ever to trim a quarter-inch. She did a hair-styling dance of sorts, delicately fluttering around the man, smiling and chatting and flirting.

"Let's blow this dry, Anna, I want to double-check the line."

"I want volume and tousle. Every hair needn't be in place."

"Sure! Lean forward and flip your hair, please." Through the fringe of my hair I noticed the intersection of his thighs and groin; his well-tailored navy cotton slacks; the tucked black cotton shirt; the thin black leather belt with the silver buckle. Stylist and patron seemed often body parts to one another, varying with the point of view.

"How is it? You like?"

I looked at my hair. It was full and wavy and not too short.

"It's good. Thanks, Rick." We smiled.

I drove east on Eucalyptus. Towne & Country Centre boasted an upscale grocery market. I aimed my Jeep towards the parking lot and put it in a space between a Mercedes and a BMW. Dear God, I thought, Christmas decorations were up. Red, green and gold frou-frou contrasted the clean lines of the beige stucco building. The upscale neighbourhood seemed sometimes surreal, perhaps too quiet, too clean, too calm, with lurking noise and dirt and chaos threatening sudden explosion. Inside, market patrons had a weird social energy, sugary perkiness covering vitriol. Perfect suburban dolls shopped in tennis dresses, smiles drawn back over teeth that would love to bite. Suntanned champagne blondes filled their carts. Clothing fashion changed little throughout the year in Southern California; the temperature changed little, and might allow halter tops, cut-offs and platform sandals in December.

The produce department boasted obscene abundance; it seemed the vegetables had been inflated with a bicycle pump, or were futuristic monsters. The produce area smelled wonderful, I thought, as I touched Japanese eggplant, English cucumber and Italian squash. To my right a man shopped and watched me. Was it my imagination, or was he slightly smiling and smirking as I handled the green and purple vegetable shafts?

An instrumental version of "Let It Snow" played as I wandered the store aisles. At the bakery, red and green packaging contained myriad sweets. The world shimmered with candy. The muzak was seeping into my brain. I had to get out! I focused on filling my small basket. Mixed baby greens. Zucchini. Chicken breasts. Merlot. Chocolate ice cream.

At the express lane, Aileen rang up my stuff.

"Paper or plastic?" asked Kyle.

"Paper, please."

In the kitchen I unpacked groceries and poured a glass of Merlot; it tasted fruity, plummy, spicy, low herbal. I stood and looked out my kitchen window, sipped, gulped and poured another glass. On the counter I preheated my grill. I heavily spiced a boneless chicken breast, put it on the grill and put down the lid. I mixed baby greens with extra virgin olive oil. Wine chewed at my empty gut; I drank more. My brain clicked, warmed and sweetened. I stood at the counter and wolfed down my chicken breast and salad.

I went into the living room and put a DVD into the player. I sat on the sofa. Energetic acoustic guitar began the film soundtrack.

"Garbage!" began the dialogue.

The beautiful young Southern woman discussed imagery with her therapist. Garbage. What if garbage cans were actually producing more garbage? she wondered. The doctor smiled. They'd soon be discussing masturbation, the woman blushing and stammering, denying her need. Fast-forward. The woman sat on a plaid sofa in a hot, sparsely furnished room. She wore a gold blazer, black T-shirt, black miniskirt and black leather cowboy boots. A man in T-shirt and jeans sat on the hardwood floor in front of her, looking up at her. His camera rolled. "Do you remember the first time that you saw a penis?" he began. She narrowed her eyes, parted her lips, cocked her head to the side and began to talk. As she shed her blazer and rearranged herself on the sofa, her leather boots rubbed together, making soft squeaking sounds. Fast-forward. In a bedroom, a man and woman shouted at one another. "Did you have to masturbate in front of him?" he demanded of her. "No. I wanted to. So there!"

*Sex, Lies, and a Video Cam* was another favourite film of mine, transporting me to yet another humid Southern clime. I'd felt voyeuristic viewing its seeming raw intimacy and dialogue; I'd thought its editing amazing; it had inspired my purchase of black leather cowboy boots. I soon slept on the sofa, in blue screen light.

I opened my eyes to filtered sun. I got up, made coffee and went to my desk. I checked my schedule: no appointments for the day. I sipped my coffee and tiredly made notes on my writing projects. A drive to the coast might be inspirational, I thought. I took a shower, dressed in a pullover scoop-neck sweater, skirt and leather sandals.

Highway 120 wound through velvet hills and grassy flats on its way to the sea. The two-lane road could be lonely, with little traffic. The dark-skinned hitchhiker stood on the north side of the road. He wore a Henley shirt and jeans. His dark hair was tied into a ponytail. I passed him, checked the rear-view, braked and pulled onto the shoulder. He smiled as he loped towards the Jeep. I unlocked the passenger door. He hoisted himself into the leather bucket seat, threw his bag to the floorboard, closed the door, and fastened his seat belt.

"Hello. Thank you very much for stopping. *Gracias*." He warmly smiled, his dark-brown eyes making direct contact with mine.

"Hi. Call me Anna."

"I'm Manuel. Manny."

"Where are you headed?"

"Caida Del Cielo. Heaven's Fall. The beach."

"Where's that?"

"Near Fuego Que Sopla. Blowing Fire."

"It's on my way."

Darkness was beautiful; I thought of the deep reds of roses and blood and wine; the tan brown of bread and chocolate and exotic skins; the dark liquid of brown, drowning-pool eyes pulling one in.

Contrast could be interesting. I thought of sophistication and innocence; vanilla cream swirling with caramel tan.

"Where are you coming from, Manny?"

"Palmville."

"Do you hitch much?"

"Do you pick up much?"

We smiled.

"Would you like a beer? There's a cooler in the back seat."

"Thank you."

Over a hill, the road turned and opened to the Pacific Coast. Heaven's Fall seemed deserted. I saw no parking area. I wondered where to park.

"Don't park too close to water. The sand is wet and deep," Manny cautioned.

"Thanks. Do you have time for another beer? Or do you need to meet someone?" I glanced at the pier and the vast, empty shoreline.

"I'm meeting no one."

I parked a distance from the shore, near a small dune. I scavenged a blanket from the back and spread it on the sand.

We wordlessly sat on the blanket next to the Jeep, drinking amber lager, getting stoned on nature and negative ionization and brew. I wasn't sure whether minutes or hours had passed.

"Let me touch you . . . ?" he asked.

"Where?" I smiled.

"Here . . . here . . ." His hands brushed my cheeks; he lightly ran his hands down my neck to my breasts. "Soft *pechos* . . . sweet *pechos* . . ." He gently pulled a bare breast from my sweater. His thickly sensual lips took my nipple; his mouth pulled. He stood and pulled me up and kissed me. "Wait," he said, opening the rear passenger-side Jeep door. He lifted me onto the edge of the high bucket seat. He pulled down my scoop-neck sweater; my breasts lightly hung over the purple velvety material. He pushed my stretch skirt up around my waist. I sat, legs askew on the leather seat, grains of sand sticking to my skin, the sea wind blowing against me. He kneeled and placed his hands on my lower inner thighs, slowly moving up. I leaned back and more widely spread my legs. His head moved towards my centre; I held it and felt the texture of his hair, removing the tie that held it. It softly fell and draped my thighs. His finger centered the outer lips of my cunt, moving into the inner.

"Ahhh . . . *ostra rosada* . . . pink oyster," he murmured.

Licking and entering me with his tongue then fingers, he moaned and intermittently gave soft voice. "*Mar salado* . . . salty sea." The Spanish language would never be the same, I thought. It now seemed even more beautiful, if that was possible. I clenched and came around his fingers.

"Wait." He pulled away, his erection straining against his jeans. He unzipped his fly and lowered his jeans, releasing his prick. He fumbled in his small travel sack, pulling a small square brightly coloured packet from it. *Gallo* read the lettering; the art was of a red rooster. He removed the white condom, held the tip, and rolled it onto his brown erection, vanilla white engulfing caramel tan. The wind grabbed and whipped the empty condom wrapper down the beach. I dripped onto the leather seat. He held my hips and slowly slid his cock into me. He moved deeply into and out of me, gliding clitoris and G-spot, clitoris and G-spot. Orgasm rolled from my wet centre, sensation becoming sound, escaping through my O-shaped mouth. I envisioned my orgasm having come from the sea and returning to it; my cries metamorphosing into ocean roar.

"*Caliente caliente* . . . hot . . . *mojado*! Anna!"

In front of my television, I drank Shiraz and ate take-out crab and shrimp enchiladas and squash with red peppers. I clicked my DVD play button. *Sexo En El Camino* was subtitled. Miquel entered his girlfriend's bedroom, and her, in rapid succession, with no foreplay. The girl had long dark hair, perky breasts, a thin build. In a fascinating, non-American quality she had lots of thick, dark pubic hair. The film's logic seemed to imply that women were in a perpetually pre-moistened state. It worked. The sex was quick and intense and hot, with penises and vaginas artistically filmed in shadow. Fast-forward. In a dilapidated motel room in Oaxaco, the young naked Sergio stood with an erection. "Drop the towel," commanded Gabriella, from the edge of the bed. He stood in front of her and kneeled. "I'm wet for you. Eat me . . ." she said. He lowered his mouth to her and began to lick. "Wait! Let me take off my panties!" She laughed. He very soon fucked her, in another quick, intense scene. Miquel watched his friend from a doorway, a hurt look in his eyes. Fast-forward. The two young male friends and the older woman drove through mountainous jungles and small villages towards an allegedly mythical beach, laughing and telling stories, stopping in run-down cantinas for beer and food. At the beach the three fucked. The men fought and drove away together. She stayed at Heaven's Mouth for the rest of her short life. Fade to black. I sighed and thought of a spontaneous, passionate man who made love in soft whispers, intense cries and beautiful words; who could have been manifesting Tourette's or channeling spirits as he thrust and came.

I drove 120, and I-5 to the Citrus exit. The generica of strip malls seemed somehow obscene. I pulled into the medical plaza and parked. I walked the maze between offices and entered the lobby at 3.50 p.m.

I took a seat on the sofa in Dr Wellman's lobby.

"Hi, Anna! He'll be right with you."

# Secretly Wishing for Rain

Claude Lalumière

My palm pressed between Tamara's small breasts, I feel her heartbeat. The raindrops pounding on the skylight reflect the city lights, provide our only illumination. Tamara's fingers are entwined in my chest hair; my perception of the rhythm of my heart is intensified by the warm, steady pressure of her hand.

This mutual pressing of hands against chests is our nightly ritual. Our faces almost touching, we silently stare at each other in the gloom. This is how it is for me (and how I believe it must also be for her): I abandon myself to the dim reflection of light in her eyes, the rhythms of our hearts, the softness of her skin, the pressure of her hand; I let go of all conscious thought or intent. We whisper meaningless absurdities to each other. One of us says: "There are fishes so beautiful that cinnamon nectar spouts from their eyeballs"; the other replies: "Your mouth is infinite space and contains all the marvels of gravity." Most nights we explore each other's flesh, revelling in each other's smells and touches. Deliriously abandoned in each other's embrace, we reach orgasm, remembering the loss that binds us. Some nights, as tonight, we simply fall asleep, snugly intertwined.

The cliché would be that I was jealous of Andrei's mischievous charm, his tall-dark-and-handsome good looks, his quick wit, his svelte elegance, his easy way with women . . . but no. His omnipotent charm defused the pissing-contest resentment that heterosexual pretty boys usually provoke in the rest of the straight male population. Everyone – men, women, straights, gays – was helpless before his androgynous beauty, his complicit grin and his playful brashness. Perhaps I was even more helpless than most.

Andrei avoided being in the company of more than one person at a time. Whoever he was with enjoyed the full intensity of his meticulous attention. I never felt so alive as when I basked in his gaze.

Andrei may have been desired by many, but few had their lust satisfied. Men weren't even a blip on his sexual radar. Most women also fell short of his unvoiced standards – the existence of which he would always deny. The women who could boast of the privilege of walking down the street arm in arm with Andrei were tall and slim with graceful long legs, hair down to at least their shoulder blades, subtle make-up and cover-girl faces. And, most importantly, they had to be sharp dressers. Age was not an issue. I'd first met him when we were both nineteen, and during the seven years of our friendship, I'd seen him hook up with girls as young as thirteen and women as old as fifty-five. All that mattered was that they have the look. Actually, that wasn't all. Andrei possessed a probing intelligence. He read voraciously, and he expected his assembly-line lovers to be able to discuss at length the minutiae of his favourite books. Invariably, he grew bored with his women, or contemptuous if they read one of the books in his pantheon and proceeded to display the depth of their incomprehension. Rarely would he declare to the injured party that their short-lived romance was over. Instead, at the end of an affair, he'd simply vanish for several weeks without a word. Even I – his closest friend – never found out where he vanished to.

Ten years ago, Tamara had been one of those women. The last of those women.

At nineteen, I moved to Montreal from Deep River, Ontario. I wanted to learn French, to live in a cosmopolitan environment. See foreign films on the big screen. Go to operas. Museums. Concerts. Art galleries. Listen to street musicians. Hear people converse in languages I couldn't understand.

I never did learn French. I'm often embarrassed about that. Montreal isn't nearly as French as most outsiders think, and it's all too easy to live exclusively in its English-language demi-monde.

I'd taken a year off after high school, intending to travel, but I never did. I never had enough money, and I languished resentfully in Deep River. I applied to McGill University for the following year, was accepted, chose philosophy as my major.

In early September, less than a week after classes started, I attended a midnight screening of Haynes's *Bestial Acts* at the Rialto. I'd heard so much about that film, but, of course, it had never come to Deep River, even on video. There were only two of us in the theatre. The other cinephile was a stunningly handsome guy I guessed was about my age. He was already there when I walked in, his face buried in a book, despite the dim lighting. I sat two rows ahead of him.

After the credits stopped rolling, the lights went on, and I felt a tap on my shoulder. When I turned, the handsome guy – Andrei, I would soon learn – said, "I feel like walking. Let's go." I had no choice but to obey; I didn't want to have a choice. So I followed him, already ensorcelled.

We walked all over the city, and he brought me to secret places where its night-time beauty was startlingly delicate. The water fountain in the concrete park next to the Ville-Marie Expressway. The roof of a Plateau apartment building – its access always left unlocked in violation of safety regulations. We snuck into a lush private courtyard covered in ancient-looking leafy vines; the windows reflected and re-reflected the moonlight to create a subtly complex tapestry of light. All the while, we talked about *Bestial Acts*, trying to understand it all, to pierce the veil of its mysteries.

As dawn neared, he said, "You've never read the book it's based on, have you?" There was disappointment in his voice.

I felt like this was a test. I looked him straight in the eye. "No. Before seeing the 'adapted from' credit on the screen tonight, I didn't even know about it."

His face changed, and he laughed. He'd decided to forgive my ignorance. He dug out a paperback from the inside of his jacket. "Here. Read this. Let's have lunch on Sunday, and we can talk some more."

The book's spine was creased from countless rereadings, the corners furled and frayed. It was a small book called *The Door to Lost Pages*, and the film was named after the title of the first chapter. The back-cover blurb said that the author lived here in Montreal. Andrei saw my eyes grow wide; he told me, "No. I didn't write that book. That's not a pseudonym. I don't even know the guy."

So we had lunch that Sunday, and then became nearly inseparable. As for all those women of his – well, yes, I admired their beauty, but they were unattainable, too glamourous and self-confident for me to even fantasize about. Was I jealous of them? Of the love he spent on them? No; it was abundantly clear that I was permanent, that spending time with me took precedence over his dalliances. And they were only ephemeral mirrors into which he'd gaze to see his own beauty reflected.

As I do every morning, I wake up at six. The rain is still splattering on the skylight window. Although it's summer and sunlight should be flooding the bedroom by now, under this thick blanket of dark clouds it's still as dark as midnight.

I turn around and spoon Tamara. My nose rests lightly on her shoulder; I breathe in her unwashed aromas. She is intoxicating. Her soft back is luxuriant against my chest. My semi-erect cock jerks lightly, probing the smoothness of her buttocks.

She moans, but she's still hours from waking up. She rarely wakes before noon. Then, eventually, she heads out; without a word, without a goodbye kiss. Brunch with friends? Museums? The gym? Does she even have friends? I can only speculate. She always returns past eleven in the evening, and we go to bed together around midnight.

I get up. Normally, I would go jogging, but I'm too fed up with the rain.

Andrei never worked. But money never seemed to be a problem. I was curious, but I knew better than to enquire. Whatever he wanted to share, he would tell me.

Actually, it's not fair to say that he never worked.

He wrote. He wrote for hours every day, the words pouring out of him with the relentless flow of a waterfall. He never tried to publish. He disdained the very idea of publication; nevertheless, he was supportive of my futile efforts at getting my own work into print.

He wrote poetry, fiction, philosophical ramblings and other prose that segued from genre to genre. All of it was brilliant. Yes, I envied his way with women, but what inspired my jealousy was his prodigious literary talent. It often took me months to finish a short story, while he would write several of them a week, in addition to countless other pieces. And he worked on a number of long Proustian novels simultaneously, each of them accumulating wordage but never seeming to reach any kind of conclusion.

We'd spend sleepless nights poring over each other's work with a harsh and unforgiving love. We questioned every word, every comma, every idea. We revised and reread and rearranged. He was unfailingly generous with his talent and editorial acumen. His input imbued my feeble scribblings with a depth of allusion and empathy I could never have achieved on my own.

If he was aware of my jealousy, he never showed any sign of it. He considered me his only friend and let no one but me read his work. And so my jealousy was tempered by exclusivity. Although I urged him time and again to seek publication, I secretly thrilled like a teenage girl who, magically, knew that she – and no one else – had the privilege of sucking the cock of her favourite rock star.

Tamara and I rarely talk, rarely spend any time together, save for the night-time in bed. Our lives are separate, save for that nightly communion. We are strangers.

Occasionally, she walks in on me, whether I'm in my study or in the living room or taking a nap, and asks, "Read to me."

What she means is, "Read me something of Andrei's." And I always do. Sometimes I grab a book, sometimes an unpublished manuscript. Andrei left so much behind. She nestles into my lap and chest, and I enfold her as best I can, breathing in the heady blend of sweat, perfume, shampoo and lotions, wishing for the weight of her body to leave permanent impressions in my flesh.

When I stop reading, we neck like teenagers, fondle each other tenderly, hungrily, with unfeigned clumsiness.

Before, she used to read voraciously. Now, all she desires of the world of literature is to hear me read Andrei's words.

During most of my years-long friendship with Andrei, I never had a lover, never seriously pursued anyone. Andrei had awakened the writer in me, and that was all that mattered. I'd quit school. I supported myself with a string of meaningless jobs, and devoted all my spare energies to, inseparably, my writing and my friendship with Andrei.

I met Tamara one late afternoon coming home from work. I had noticed her further down the line at the bus stop: dark wavy hair to below her shoulders; complex features that managed to be both softly round and strongly aquiline; a large mouth; full lips; a brownish-olive tint to her skin; tall and svelte, yet with a pronounced curve at the waist. I thought, she's Andrei's type. Gorgeous. Glamourous.

The bus was crowded. She sat down next to me. My throat dried up. I was suddenly overwhelmed with desire for this woman. I knew that Andrei would have no problem initiating contact with this beautiful stranger, but I lacked his grace and confidence.

As the bus took off, each of us dug a book out of our bags.

We were reading the same book, *Bestial Acts*. Probably buoyed by the film's cult celebrity, the author had written a sequel to *The Door to Lost Pages*, expanding on the events and characters emphasized in the film, but this new volume wasn't very good.

We looked up at each other, and we both laughed. I don't remember who started talking to whom, but we fell into an easy, friendly conversation and ended up eating veggie burgers and gourmet fries on St-Laurent, and then walked down to a cocktail bar in the Gay Village that played postmodern lounge music in a colourful high-kitsch decor.

We laughed easily with each other, and she frequently touched me, letting her hands linger just long enough for me to know she meant it.

It was nearly two in the morning when I walked her home. She gave me a firm hug; I felt her breasts press against my chest, and she surely felt my erection. She grinned as she disengaged, and, while holding both my hands, she kissed my cheek – the contact with her lips made me shiver.

I watched her climb the stairs to her second-storey apartment. I stood there for a couple of minutes after she closed the door behind her.

I don't remember walking home, so lost was I in my reveries of seeing her again.

Next thing I knew, I was lying naked in bed, prudishly fighting the impulse to masturbate while replaying moments of my evening with Tamara.

And then I remembered that I had promised to meet Andrei that evening.

Ten years after Andrei's death, I still have no other friends. I have no lovers but Tamara.

My days are always the same.

I wake up at six. I work until noon. Often that consists of editing Andrei's large inventory of unpublished manuscripts. Sometimes, I work on my own writing.

I go out for lunch. There's a wonderful pressed-sandwich shop on St-Denis. If it's too crowded, I go for noodles. These days, there's a noodle shop on almost every corner.

In the afternoon, I catch a matinee movie, then I go shopping – books, CDs, DVDs, clothes, food – hoping that something, anything, will bring me pleasure or elicit any kind of reaction. Nothing ever does.

I drop my purchases at home. I check for messages. Then I go out for dinner. Usually Indian. Sometimes Thai. Or something new I read about in the newspaper.

I come back home around eight in the evening, put on some

music, make some tea. I read until I hear Tamara come home. Then I get ready for bed.

If the weather's bad, I just stay in all day.

It's the middle of the afternoon, and it's still raining. It's as dark as dusk. It's been like this for five days straight, and it's been having a languorous effect on me. I've noticed that Tamara, usually less sensitive than I to the weather and light, has been somewhat morose of late. I do not pry. We never pry into each other's affairs or emotions.

But today I'm feeling a bit better. I'm just off the phone with my agent. She had good news for me. Dardick Press had made a six-figure offer for my new novel. Not that I really need the money, but they want the book. My book.

To the outside world, I'm the author of a wildly successful thematic trilogy of Proustian ambitions; of an allegorical fantasy novel the *Washington Post* welcomed by trumpeting: "Finally, an English-language writer whose depths of empathy and imagination surpass Márquez"; of an immense thousand-page short-story collection praised for its cross-genre audacity, the precision and beauty of its language, and its parade of heartbreaking characters; of a poetry collection that stayed for more than a year on the bestseller lists; and of a blockbuster philosophical novel – adapted once as a film and once as a television mini-series.

Although all of these appeared under my byline, none of them are mine (well, I snuck two of my own short stories into the collection; I still feel guilty about that). I did edit the manuscripts into their final format – I was certainly familiar enough with much of the material from my years with Andrei – but they were his works, not mine.

Despite Andrei's immense posthumous success under my byline, my own work has been consistently rejected by publishers: "Let's not oversaturate the market"; "We're not sure how to categorize this one"; a litany of insulting excuses . . . until today, that is.

I feel like celebrating, but I can't think of anything appropriate. Take Tamara out for lunch? I fantasize further: maybe we could even go on vacation. Spend a few weeks in Venice. I've always wanted to see Venice. We can certainly afford it.

But we never travel. We never do anything together. We stay here, slaves to our habits and our grief.

Besides, I would never dare upset the fragile equilibrium of our tacit agreement with even anything as mundane as a lunch invitation.

Just then, Tamara walks into my study. She's dishevelled, clearly having just woken. She's wearing black panties and a white camisole that contrasts vividly with her skin. I'm still visited by images of our fantasy holiday; seeing her – so beautiful, so subtly out of my reach, the constant pain that haunts her imbuing her with an aura of delicate fragility that I find, despite myself, overwhelmingly arousing – I catch my breath in admiration.

She doesn't notice, or she ignores me. Does it really matter which?

Nevertheless, for a second, I even half convince myself – both fearing it and desiring it – that she'll propose an outing or even converse with me. But no. The inevitable words, full of mournful loss and despairing love, come out of her mouth: "Read to me." Not even waiting for a response, she heads towards the living room.

I rise from my desk, my hand resting for a moment on the third volume of Andrei's Proustian trilogy, but then, emboldened by my agent's good news, I mischievously and pridefully grab a copy of my novel manuscript instead. Tamara won't know the difference.

I join Tamara on the couch, and she snuggles up to me. She smells delicious. I nibble on her bare shoulder, and she moans, grabbing my hand and rubbing it against her breasts. She nuzzles my neck and whispers, "Read."

Momentarily, I feel guilty for deceiving her. But I start to read my novel, and I quickly get seduced by the allure of my own words, my own characters.

I'm only a few pages into the manuscript when Tamara suddenly gets up.

She mumbles, "I'm tired . . ." – heading back to the bedroom, not even glancing at me, shutting the door.

For the next five days – after I stood him up for Tamara – Andrei didn't answer my calls. Was my friendship ultimately as meaningless to him as his dalliances with his glamourous girlfriends? Had I finally suffered his inevitable rejection?

Tamara called me, and we saw each other once. We went for a walk on Mount Royal. She held my hand. She sensed my dark mood and did not push.

Her goodbye hug conveyed less promise than her first; she asked me to call her soon. Translation: if you want me, show it.

I mumbled that I would, knowing that I'd made a mess of what should have been a great evening. I had been much too distracted by my anxiety about Andrei.

Finally, I showed up at his apartment without calling. He hated it when people did that.

When I got there, there was a girl with him. She was stunning: the kind of face that stared back at you from magazine covers; long, shapely legs; delicate toes; toenails painted bright orange peeking out from elegant high-heeled sandals. She was crying.

I ignored her. I didn't say anything. I stood firm and did my best to stare Andrei down. I needed to prove to him that I aspired to be his equal.

He surprised me. He smiled at me, turned towards the girl, and said, "Get out. Can't you see that my friend is here now?"

She opened her mouth to say something, but then closed it sharply, visibly trying to hold on to some degree of dignity.

She didn't even glance at Andrei, but she shot me a disdainful sneer as she hurried past.

The rain never lets up. I stay in all day. Tamara never leaves the bedroom. I hear her use the adjoining bathroom a few times.

Finally, at midnight, I open the bedroom door. I get undressed and slip into bed.

Tamara is feigning sleep. I know her body language and the rhythms of her breathing too intimately to be fooled.

We do not press hands against each other's chest tonight. We do not whisper absurdities to each other. We do not touch. We do not have sex.

We've never skipped our ritual before; in sickness and in health.

A despairing loneliness chews on my innards, chasing sleep away.

Tamara gets up in the middle of the night. I hear her bustle in the kitchen. When she's done eating, she climbs back into bed, carefully not touching me, and falls asleep immediately.

I stay awake until dawn.

I realize that the rain has finally stopped, the clouds finally gone. Sunlight hits Tamara's bare shoulder. I yearn to kiss it, to taste her. But I dare not.

I didn't know whether or not to believe Andrei, but I didn't question him, didn't push my luck. I was too relieved, thrilled, exhilarated that our friendship was still intact. He claimed not to care that I had stood him up. He hadn't been in touch because he'd spent the last few days with the woman he'd just thrown out of his apartment. He had known it would only last a few days.

Suddenly, it seemed so egocentric to think that Andrei would have been affected by my absence the other night. I chastised myself for my arrogance and self-importance.

Nevertheless, I told him all about Tamara. Was it him or me who suggested that we all three get together for a meal? I did, I think, but was it only because he wanted me to?

I called her from his apartment; we would meet there on the weekend, and he would cook for both of us. Already, my mouth watered. Andrei was a fabulous cook.

We spent the rest of the night as usual: we pored over his latest writings until sunup.

I am running. The morning sun spurs me on. I am exhausted from my sleepless night. My muscles are complaining because of the days of inactivity I imposed on them during the recent rains.

But I run, nevertheless. I don't even notice where. I just run and sweat.

I come back home. I look at the clock. It's nine fifteen. I've been out running for three hours. I walk through the bedroom to get to the shower although I don't have to. I could use one of the other bathrooms. But I want to gaze at Tamara.

She's not in bed.

I call out her name, look through every room.

She's not here. She's never awake this early.

I go out again.

I run.

I run until the pain and exhaustion is all that I can feel. I just run; and sweat – so much that it's impossible to distinguish the tears from the sweat.

I knew, of course, that whatever spark I ignited in Tamara's imagination would be dimmed by the greater conflagration that Andrei would provoke. I was not wrong.

They were beautiful together, but I also knew that Andrei would soon tire of her.

Pathetically, I fantasized about consoling her after Andrei inevitably broke her heart. Fearfully, I never spoke to Tamara – about my feelings, about Andrei who discarded lovers like flakes of dead skin. Boldly, I imagined telling Andrei he had no right to use Tamara like a disposable mirror, when I could love her more truly than he ever would. Stupidly, I confronted Andrei in such a way.

It would be inaccurate to say that we had a fight. I said my piece, and he just laughed at me. I got angrier, and he just laughed harder.

"You're my friend," he said, between guffaws. "But go home now. When you get over your anger, come back, and we'll work on one of your stories." He was still laughing.

I left his apartment, melodramatically slamming the door, feeling self-conscious for doing so, but unable to express myself any other way in the face of Andrei's dismissal.

There are messages from my agent. Details to work out. Contracts to sign.

So what? It's not like I need the money.

Am I betraying Andrei's legacy by publishing my own work under my name? Should I use a pseudonym? Or maybe scrap the whole idea. I'll never be the writer he was.

I lie on the couch all day. The phone rings. Again. And again. I let it ring. Tamara wouldn't call, and there's no one else I want to talk to, even if, as I fear might now happen because of my transgression, we never see each other again.

When Tamara wakes me by caressing my cheek, I realize that I had fallen asleep.

Andrei's relationship with Tamara lasted a full year, months longer than any of his previous affairs. I had barely seen either of them since I'd stormed out of Andrei's apartment like a bad actor. After a few weeks, I visited Andrei twice, but my resentment was too overpowering, and the encounters were forced and awkward. I was physically unable to be around Tamara without feeling nauseous. So I stopped calling them, and I never heard from either of them. Occasionally, I'd spot them downtown, but I always managed to creep away unseen.

Then one day I found a handwritten invitation in my mailbox. I recognized Andrei's precise, feminine script. There were no details, save for a time and the name and address of a restaurant. I dreaded some sort of wedding announcement. Or that he'd finally shooed Tamara out of his life like all the others before her. I didn't know which of the two I feared more.

Of course, I went. I was lonely, bored and miserable, and I missed my friend.

I'd never heard of the restaurant, so I was unprepared. I'd dressed casually, and this turned out to be an intimidatingly swanky establishment. I was sure they weren't going to let me in. True to my expectations, the maître d' sneered at me when I stepped through the door, but when I said Andrei's name he repeated it almost reverentially and instructed a waiter to escort me to Andrei's table.

Andrei's table turned out to be a private room, lushly decorated with museum-quality reproductions and fresh flowers. I recognized Debussy's String Quartet – a favourite of Andrei's – playing at just the right volume. The table was set for two; there was an empty chair waiting for me. Tamara sat in the other chair.

Tamara asked, "What are you doing here? I mean, where's Andrei?"

I shrugged. "Andrei sent me an invitation. I didn't know you'd be here."

"But it's our anniversary. Where—?"

I knew, then, that Andrei had left her. And indeed he had, but that wasn't the whole truth. That came later.

Before either of us could say anything more, the waiter brought in the hors d'oeuvres.

Tamara said, "But we haven't ordered anything."

We learned that Andrei had arranged our evening's menu in advance. We ate in silence, but not even that tense awkwardness could mask the heavenly taste of the food.

We finally spoke to each other when it came time to argue over who would get the bill, but we were informed that Andrei had already paid for everything, and that not even a gratuity would be accepted from either of us.

Befuddled, we walked out together. We glanced at each other, and we both laughed at ourselves. Still chuckling, Tamara took my arm, and we walked together through downtown, all the while talking like dear old friends. We didn't utter a word about Andrei.

When we parted, she gave me a chaste kiss on the cheek, but there was genuine warmth in her smile. Silently, I cursed Andrei for what I believed he was doing to her.

The next day, I received a couriered letter, requesting my presence at the law office of Laurent Tavernier the following Monday at nine in the morning. Not a little alarmed, I called to know what this was all about. The attorney's secretary told me: "We can say nothing of this matter until the appointed time."

Tamara called me every day. She was worried about Andrei's disappearance. More than once, she cried over the phone. As much as I wanted to, I couldn't bring myself to tell her that I thought Andrei had deserted her. I grunted non-committal responses and sidestepped any suggestion that we should meet. I refused to follow Andrei's transparent script, no matter how much it matched my own desires.

The following Monday, I was startled to see Tamara sitting in the attorney's waiting room. A few minutes later, we were both ushered into Tavernier's office, wondering to each other what Andrei had planned for us this time.

This is what we learned: Andrei was dead, had poisoned himself on the day he'd set us up to meet at the restaurant; Andrei was wealthy, worth millions of dollars, all of which was now ours . . . in a joint account, no strings attached. Tavernier needed our signatures to make this official.

In addition, Andrei bequeathed all of his writings to me, with instructions that I seek to publish them under my own name only and that, with his blessing, I should edit his works as I saw fit.

There was a letter addressed to both of us; the attorney read it. It was terse.

*I had nothing more to write*, it said.

But that wasn't true. In death, Andrei was writing the script of my and Tamara's lives, and we followed every stage direction like fawning understudies.

I almost speak, but Tamara shushes me. I can't decipher her expression.

She's sitting on the floor, next to the couch. She looks away from me and into her lap. I hear the rustle of paper.

I look down and see that she's holding my manuscript. My novel.

She starts to read. I cry.

I cry because I see her mouth form the words that I've written, because I hear the tenderness in her voice when she speaks my words.

She reads a few chapters. She takes her time. She forms the words carefully, imbues their articulation with a slow sensuality.

Finally, she pauses. She looks at me, and she's crying too.

She says, "I like it."

When I come back from my morning run, Tamara is still asleep. Her feet are sticking out from under the sheets. This is one of my favourite sights: tenderly domestic and deliciously sensual. I fantasize about straying from our scripted lives, about indulging in spontaneous intimacies outside the confines of our rituals, and . . .

Fuck Andrei.

I look at Tamara's sleeping body and let the sight of her overwhelm me.

I stoop down and kiss her toes. I slip my tongue between them, slide it around each one. I nibble on them.

She moans, still asleep, and throws off the sheets.

The sun hits her skin, from her nipples to just below her luxuriant pubes. The prospect of transgression makes my blood rush, but I rein in my impatience and move with slow but focused intensity.

Cupping her heels, I raise her legs in the air. Below, I catch a glimpse of her moist vulva, framed by her butt cheeks and by the backs of her thighs. I bend down and breathe on her wetness. She gasps, still asleep.

I smell her and close my eyes. Her pubes tickle my nose, and I can't help laughing.

That wakes her up.

I fear her reaction to this unscheduled intimacy, but she opens her arms in invitation.

I let go of her legs and fold myself into her sleepy embrace.

"You're sweaty," she mumbles. I'm still wearing my jogging clothes. "I love your smell." Have we broken free? Can we write our own lives? Together. Finally, truly, together.

She disentangles herself and sits up. She hugs me, drowsily rubbing her face against my chest.

She pulls off my T-shirt, and she runs her tongue from my belly button to my armpit.

She squeezes my stiff cock through my shorts, and we both laugh. She smiles coyly, letting go of me, then runs her hand in circles around my crotch, never quite touching it. She gently bites my nipples. She moves as if to squeeze me again, but then she pulls away and slips behind me.

She hugs me from behind, bites my shoulders hard enough to hurt, sinuously licks my nape. I feel her breasts squish against my back, and I get even harder. Her hands start to slip into my shorts, brushing against my pubes, but, again, she pulls away, laughing.

I grab for her. I lock her wrists in my hands and push her down on the bed. I bite her nipples – alternating from one to the other – and she gasps and squirms. I pull her up and place her fingers on the elastic waist of my shorts. She pulls down my shorts, takes my dripping cock into her mouth.

She delicately scratches my chest while her mouth goes up and down the length of my penis. I could come right now. But I pull out of her mouth. I stick my thigh between her legs and rub her moistness against my skin while I play with her breasts.

After a while, I turn her around and push her down on the bed. I run my wet, hard cock on her skin, from her butt crack, along her spine, to the side of her neck. Her tongue slips out and licks me.

Leaving my cock next to her mouth, I reach down and grab her ass. I fondle it, kiss it, bite into it. I dip a finger into her moist cleft, and I tease her anus. She squirms and coos. I plunge deep into her asshole with my wet finger, and she screams in pleasure. I wriggle my finger inside her, slide it in and out tenderly. I look at her writhe with delight, and my heart swells up.

Eventually, she pulls her butt away and flips over.

She again takes my cock into her mouth. She pushes her crotch up against my mouth, and I slip my tongue inside her vagina. I pull back slightly and gently kiss her labia. I tease her by running my tongue on either side of her clit, never quite touching it.

Meanwhile, her mouth slides up and down my cock; her fingers play with my balls. Then, she lets my cock slip out of her mouth, and works on me with her hands.

I can barely keep from bursting. I struggle to hold on just a little longer.

I cover her vagina with my mouth and work on her clit with my tongue. Her breathing changes, and I can tell she's going to come soon.

In a sudden, almost violent, move, I pull away. She whimpers.

I grab her feet and run my teeth against her soles. Her whimpers turn to moans. I spread her legs, my tongue licking her inner thighs. Her moans become sharp cries. I kiss her belly. My hands find her breasts, my fingers squeeze her nipples. My lips find her mouth. My cock finds the wet opening between her legs.

I plunge deep into her; and she screams, comes, and then whispers the syllables I desperately want to hear, the inevitable name: "Andrei . . ."

And then I come inside of her, and the jism spurts out of me in neverending waves. In my mind's eye, I see the beautiful face of my dead friend.

# What Happened to That Girl

Marie Lyn Bernard

Christy, my fourth and final foster sister, disappeared from our home on the morning of her eighteenth birthday, three weeks before both Jason and I left for college in Santa Barbara. Now apparently Christy's a porn star. Jason called me this morning at 9 a.m. to break the news.

We're grown-ups now, the kind that don't talk about things like Christy or things like porn. We have grown-up lives – I'm working on my masters in biology, Jay's a computer programmer. I still masturbate to those eighties videos we'd buy at the smut shop out by the airport; I still salivate for the women in legwarmers, their bangs as fluffy as whipped cream. But when we talk about sex now, it's a lot like talking about football.

I remember the afternoon of Christy's departure vividly, even though Jason and I never speak of it. She shared a room with our other foster sister, Rochelle, but Rochelle was at tap class that afternoon and so we were free to lie in Christy's bed and bask in the air she left behind: the lingering scent of drugstore Vanilla Musk and weed. We held her abandoned panties to our faces and inhaled. We closed our eyes and remembered her, mutually avoiding the fact of one another's hard-ons, those nasty flags in our track pants.

I often reminded myself: Jason wasn't my real brother and Christy wasn't my real sister. Our family played host to a number of foster kids over the years and our house felt, at times, like some sort of privatized orphanage. My mother liked it that way. Perhaps she felt the guilt of the newly and unfortunately wealthy – my father was killed in a car accident while I was still a baby – or perhaps she was just restless without her husband. My mother has a heart like the Tupperware she hawked at neighbourhood barbecues: sturdy, durable, long-lasting. She has a fierce ability to endure heartbreak. I, her only biological son, do not.

Jason, the son of a Dominican teenager, was the closest thing I had to a permanent sibling. He moved in when I was eight and stayed. He was the kind of guy that never looked back, and I'm the guy who misses things even before they go, who clings to worthless relationships, dead-end jobs. Even when Jason reminded me that Christy would surely flee upon becoming legal, I imagined she'd change her mind, that our lives of varsity athletics and chicken dinners would quell her thirst for fast cars and drugs and the dark corners of the human psyche that enabled her to live so easily without love, and without family.

That afternoon was a mess of taboo. Resigned to unrequited lust in Christy's bed, we pumped our hands around our own shafts, simultaneously, the air dense with the potential of our love. I worked my clean-cut dick and saw that it was smaller than Jason's, which was uncircumcised and thick, the kind of dick I imagined girls wanted inside them, the dick that still makes me tentative to unveil my own.

A strange kind of dance, that mutual masturbation: our synchronized movements, my fingers rubbing the rim of the head, our exhalations swimming in a fog of long-deferred desire.

I still think of Christy every day, of how she was then: a year older than us with the reading skills of a grade-schooler and the coy wit of someone who didn't need something so trivial as reading skills. She streaked her short black hair with skunk-lines of red and white, wore pigtails and stocking caps and bandanas during all the wrong seasons. I remember her slight body; her handful-sized breasts, her skinny pale limbs, her irresistibly full mouth lined with shoplifted glamazon lipstick. She hung out in punk bars, and hung out on my favourite couch, legs sprawled everywhere, playing Chutes and Ladders with Rochelle and yelling at the adulterers on television talk shows. When I dream of her, it's those legs, wrapping around my back like some kind of giant, earth-shattering hug.

"Seth, you aren't gonna believe this," Jason tells me on the phone. "You're gonna bust a nut. I was like – I don't even know. All I know is, you gotta see this. You gotta see it, like, now."

"Bring it over," I say. "I was gonna study, but I mean, this is like, a special occasion or some shit—"

"Dude, I'll be there in twenty minutes." I feel my chest. Hot. My forehead. Hot.

"All right, man, I'll see ya."

Hot. Hot.

* * *

By the time Christy moved in we were grown. Mom was always out – taking yoga, flitting around with her social circle of estranged housewives – so she didn't care, really, that Christy pranced around the house in men's wifebeaters, her nipples visible beneath the flimsy fabric, or that Christy sometimes didn't sleep at home, or that Christy had become Rochelle's mentor, or that Christy played loud music at inappropriate times. Christy went to school – diligently, dressed in my father's old college hoodies – and she was always on time for dinner, so it didn't matter.

And my mother didn't know that Christy liked to bound through the bathroom door when I was washing up, announce, "Shower time!" and strip bare, naked all of a sudden and setting my veins on fire with her callousness, to jump into the shower, pulling the curtain tight just before my erection reached full-mast.

The first time, she peeked out only moments later, her smooth skin covered in droplets of water: "I'm sorry – does that bother you? I'm so used to like, well, living with a bunch of girls." Christy had been in a home. Or rehab. These were the things we didn't know about her, because she never talked about anything but the immediate present.

"Um . . . no," I said, maybe too enthusiastically, and she grinned.

"I didn't think you minded."

But that was the closest I got to sex. Instead, I fumbled around with the breasts of my bright girlfriends, trying to get someone into bed before graduation. Even in the thrust of high-school love, I thought of Christy.

It occurred to me once – maybe she got naked for Jason, too? But I could've thought about that until it split me open, so I chose not to.

An hour later, Jason's here, in sweatpants, grinning.

"Get ready for the best hour of your fucking life, dude," he says, pushing past me to the living room.

"Can I see the cover?" I ask. "Is she on the cover?"

Jason hands it to me as he clears a spot on the couch, fiddling with the remote.

She is on the cover. Christy. Christy-of-the-shower, Christy-of-the-white-tank-top, Christy-of-my-wettest-wet-dreams. *Honour Roll Cocksuckers*. Christy, clad in a plaid skirt and saddle shoes with suspenders tight across her new boobs. Her face is covered in come and her hand is down her skirt.

"Hot, right?" Jason asks. "I always wondered what happened to that girl."

All the time, I want to say, I wonder about her all the time. "Yeah, me too. Kinda makes sense, y'know?"

"Yeah, especially if she's still into drugs."

I brush off his accusation. "You've already seen the whole thing?"

"Nah," he says. "I watched like, the first five minutes. I thought – uh – I should save the rest to see with you."

A silence. We're men now, I think, but weren't we men then? In college, a buddy and I bought blow jobs from the same hooker, and I waited in the room during his and then he saw me get mine, and wasn't this like that, except less so? And why should I feel unsettled anyhow, with the object of our desire so clearly a woman? But I prefer him being here. I'm drawn to that nakedness, that vulnerability that feels like family.

"Cool, cool," I nod.

*Honour Roll Cocksuckers* is the opposite of seeing a movie star on the street. Christy, in pigtails and a skirt with breasts straining against her selectively buttoned shirt, is "taught a lesson" by the principal and then the janitor, and then both at once. The film unfolds at a pace that's like your train charging past when it's supposed to stop, like watching a game that you wish would go into a third overtime just to see if he can score like that again – over, and over, and over.

Bend her over, I yell silently. Bend her over and fuck her everywhere. I wanna see that round white ass, the same ass that lazed around the house on Sunday afternoons in boxer shorts, the ass connected to those legs laid absently across my lap as we watched TV.

The janitor bends her over the desk and yanks her panties off. She yelps. He smacks her ass and she yelps again.

A close-up: beneath the thicket of black hair that once coated her pussy lies a shaven, beautiful hole, lips like a canoe around the slippery line of her clit, better than I imagined. The janitor rubs his dick against her and slips in. She yelps again, and he smacks again. Then he fucks her madly, pounding her – it cuts to her face, her intense eyes and her skin still white as soap.

The principal approaches the front of the desk, fitting his body between her arms and shoving his dick into her mouth. She moans and tightens her glossy lips around him.

I look at Jason but he won't look at me. Maybe this is too much, I think, maybe this isn't right, Jason with a dick like the Hispanic janitor's, and me skinny and white like the principal, me at her front and him at her back, me fucking Christy's throat and him, now, pulling his dick from her cunt to tickle the rim of her asshole, which flexes, eager for penetration.

When he breaks into that tiny hole, cupped by her perfect cheeks, I can't take it any more. I slowly unbutton my pants and extract my dick . . . and rub. I have no inhibitions now; just a kind of drunkenness.

Out of the corner of my eye I see Jason doing the same.

The janitor lies on the floor and Christy mounts him. The principal takes her from behind while her ass bounces over the janitor's dick.

"Double penetration," Jason says. I smile too, and feel better everywhere.

The moment I pop is bright white, like Christy's spotless ass.

I look at Jason smiling at me, his hand unapologetically smeared. He goes to the bathroom, and I'm limp, rendered half conscious by the power of porn. By Christy and the Honour Roll Cocksuckers.

The movie moves on to other girls, other scenes, as Jason and I navigate the tender terrain of our situation. He brings washcloths and we clean up. He sneaks me another smile and I feel okay, a safe distance from our frightening adolescent desires.

When Jason speaks it's like the end of a football game: "Some good shit, man, right? She did good."

"Hell, yeah, she did."

Jason nods solemnly. I zip my pants.

"But dude – I didn't even tell you the best part."

"I don't think I can handle anything else," I say, laughing. I'm in a dark room surrounded by ghosts, and naked girls are fucking on television.

"OK. I'll call you tomorrow," Jason says. "Get some work done, schoolboy."

Jason takes the movie with him, and I'm back in my apartment feeling like I've just had the best sex of my life. I dream of smacking Christy's ass, of punishing her with her skirt over her head. I wake up wet and alone.

Jason picks me up after the exam. "We're going on a road trip, my man."

"A road trip?" I'm groggy, half awake. "Where?"

Jason grins. "You'll see."

The rocks in my head knock around wearily, too worn out to imagine anything. I fall asleep.

I wake up as we pull up to a nondescript office building. Jason calls someone as we lumber out of the car, and I fix my hair in the window's reflection.

"Where the fuck are we, dude?" I ask. It's painfully sunny. I'm thinking of Christy, of all the bodies that came in and out of our house, no one ever sticking. I feel the emptiness that pounds when I think of her, of Jason, of my mother, of the difference between knowing where you've come from and knowing you've come from nowhere.

My mind is still murky as we ride the elevator up to "Untitled Scream Productions". Jason's grinning like a kid on his birthday.

I rub my eyes. Is this real? Will I see her, knowing now what it's like inside that quivering pussy? Will I slide my hand along her taut stomach, tickle the Playboy bunny in her bellybutton?

There's an empty desk and Jason buzzes in. We're greeted by the principal. He and Jason are – apparently – friends. I'm dizzy, everything in slow motion like an acid trip. It's one of those moments where life slows down and opens itself up like an orgasm and everything in you turns into so much air.

I am following Jason, feeling like I'm in a children's book, the kind where you feel three times smaller and follow imaginary friends into strange rooms.

This sparse room, with black leather couches and a view of the Hollywood Hills, is strange. Because Christy is in it.

Right there. There she is. She's wearing grey sweatpants and a white tank top, her full breasts peeking out of the sides. I liked her real tits better, but I don't care; being near her is more than I can bear. I don't know if I'm going to get a hard-on or throw up.

"Blast from the past," she says, but it sounds like a come-on. What has Jason set up? "It's my brothers."

She hugs us, and squeezes me as she hugs. I'm already hard.

"Things haven't changed, I see," she whispers in my ear, tapping the head of my dick.

She's still so skinny, but she's a woman now; why is she still so skinny? Still so pale, living in the Valley and still so pale?

But I don't care. I want to bend her over the table, fuck her with the wrath of all my mornings of blue balls, all the times she riled me up and left me dry.

I want to fuck her for not leaving a note. I'd said that to Jason, too, then, that she didn't leave a note and he'd scowled and said, *It's not like she killed herself, and besides, look, she left all her panties.*

"Sit down, boys," she says, and we sit on either side of her.

She makes small talk, asks us what we're doing, how Mom is, tells us she dropped out of art school, that she's been doing porn for a year now and she really likes it, that it's her calling, that she lives with Matt, who co-owns the company with Jeff, who's a friend of Jason's from college, and that she was surprised, really, when Jeff told her that we'd called. She thought about us, she said, from time to time, not all the time but sometimes, and felt a little bad about leaving without saying anything, but she was just a kid, not that she was all together now, but that she knew things, some things, like why people leave notes when they leave for ever, and why people tell other people where they are going and why they don't.

Then she has her hand on Jason's inner thigh, tickling near his dick. He leans back and closes his eyes.

"I wanted to do this then," she says, getting on her knees in front of Jason. She breathes hot between his legs.

There's something sad lingering in her face, something that makes me angry and mixed up but then she's pulling Jason's huge cock out of his pants and scratching his balls, wrapping her lips around his dick. Did Jason pay for this? I wonder. Is this why we're here? Or is she just doing this because she wants to – because she wants us?

Is she so good at performing on cue?

She undresses and I'm wide-eyed at her new breasts. I want to watch all her other movies, over and over again for hours and hours, for as long as I live.

She sucks Jason's dick like a porn star, all the moaning and the moisture, all the upward glances for approval. She doesn't resist when he places his hand on the back of her head, pulling her closer and shoving himself deeper. I watch her lips move up and down the length of his cock and mine hardens like concrete. Her breasts nudge his knees.

"Seth," she says, popping Jason out of her mouth. "Why don't you fuck me while I suck Jason off?"

I look around like there's another Seth in the room.

"You want me to, uh – fuck – to fuck you?"

"You want to, don't you?"

"Uh – um – of course."

She stands up, walks to the desk and bends over it.

"Jason, wanna break me in first?"

Jason, glee in his eyes, erection in hand, goes over to the table and rubs himself against her ass, like in *Honour Roll*. He gives me a look: *Isn't this a good movie?*

She reaches back and guides him south into the sticky wetness of her hole. She grabs his balls, rolling them in her palm. Then he begins to nail her, and my mouth falls open. He makes sounds I've never heard from him before. He fucks her like a hellhound, like he's drilling into something thick and thorny and that he's got to get through to the other side.

Then he whips it out, jerking, and the foam from his dick slides over her ass like soapsuds.

"You ready, Seth?" she says, still bent over. Ready? I want to fuck her up the ass. I want to fuck her in the mouth. I want to come in her ass, on her tits, I want her to take my cock in her mouth and swallow my come until she gags. Fuck, I want to be a porn star too. Fuck fuck fuck fuck.

But I don't.

"Let's, uh—" I'm nervous. "Go to the couch?"

Jason's on the other couch, cleaning himself with paper napkins. I try to pretend he isn't there as Christy leaps across the room, obediently, and bends over. I edge closer to her, my dick in my hand, but my stomach flips, and flips again, and I can't.

"No – no—" I say. "Lie on it."

She does, looking confused.

"On your back," I say, watching her pert ass roll over.

I get on top of her, our eyes locked, and I ease myself in like I'm the first one, breaking her open, setting that thing loose in her that got her here in the first place. She gasps but doesn't moan and I shift, in and out, gently. I look into her eyes and I grab her hair in fists.

I make love. To her. Inside her it feels pure, a million miles away from cameras and lights. It feels utterly private.

We kiss, we suck and pull, our tongues courting and wedding and dancing.

I lie on top of her. I kiss her ear. I want to whisper so many things but instead I just tickle her ear lobe with my tongue. I kiss her nose, which is red at the rims and sad. I look at her eyes, and she looks back at mine, and it's almost like I could cry.

She reaches out and grabs my ass with her hands, her finger softly rimming the outside of my asshole, but she doesn't enter it. We roll over and she's on top of me.

The muscles of her cunt tighten around my cock – she's a pro – and she rides me. Her breasts bounce like tennis balls, her soft hands grip my biceps. She rubs back and forth, her clit grazing the hair above my dick.

"This feels so goood, baby."

"Yeah, it does," I say. There are dirty words we could exchange like endearment, but we don't.

She smiles, clenches her muscles hard around my cock. "Ah – yeah!"

She lowers to me. "Let's go back the other way. I wanna feel you over me, is that OK?"

So we roll back over. We are careful, athletic, on the limited space of the couch.

Jason might still be in the room, and he might not be. But as I continue, thrusting deeply, feeling her clench around me at just the right moments and grind her ass up and down with finesse, I see that she's going to come, and I know that I can too, and so we do, together, and I come inside her even though I know I shouldn't.

I rest my head between her breasts, which are supple though clearly fake. I feel her breathe. Jason is no longer in the room; I can hear him laughing outside, him and another man laughing.

I feel naked but not empty any more. Not for just that second, the second that I lie inside her, silent.

"That was nice," she says finally.

"It was," I respond, giving a smile that looks like an apology. "Thank you."

She smiles. "Thank you, Seth."

"For what?"

She shrugs as I slip out of her and stand up. She sits up, thinking. She's naked. With me.

"For loving me, I guess. Even if it's just for—" She looks at the clock. "For twenty minutes."

I shake my head and laugh. "Twenty years. At least twenty years."

I watch as she dresses, her eyes still huge and empty. I realize that I've never known someone who needed love as badly as this girl – more than my mother, more than the twelve other kids shuffled in and out of our house like supporting actors, more than Jason when he first arrived on our doorstep, tattered and broken and hardened to the bone. Maybe even more than I do.

"Maybe I'll see you guys again?" she asks.

"Maybe." I smile. "I hope so." Even though I don't know if that's true or not.

That's the last thing I say, because then Jason comes in, triumphant and sportsmanlike. "Dude, you ready to bust?"

I nod. In that same dreamlike state I entered with, I leave the office and we get in the car. We pull onto the highway and drive until the building fades into the millions of office buildings around us, recedes under the ominous landscape of the hills.

Jason recites his play-by-play, eager, and then says, "Hey man, what happened after I left?"

I shrug. "Same thing, more or less."

He nods. He keeps talking. The radio plays, the car moves, and we move on, together, in his car, in our strange, beautiful brotherhood, the kind that stands naked in front of itself, unashamed.

# Blinded

## Donna George Storey

I kneel down and he ties the blindfold over my eyes.

Strictly speaking, it isn't a blindfold, it's a silk scarf. My brother and his wife gave it to me for Christmas, a pretty thing with a floral design in crimson, deep blue and gold. But when I opened the gift, I was thinking: *When will I ever wear* this?

But I gave it a try. When we got home, I spent a good fifteen minutes in front of the mirror attempting to knot it into an appealing fashion accessory. He sat on the edge of the bed and watched smugly – my brother had got *him* some Charlie Parker CDs.

Then I got the idea to wear the scarf as a headband, to keep my bangs off my face. Another failure.

"I can't do anything with this thing. I'm sure it was expensive, too. Do you think they'd get mad if I took it back?"

He walked over to me. "How about this way?" He pulled the bottom edge of the scarf down over my eyes.

I could still see him hazily through the single layer of loose silk. He looked at me for a moment, his head tilted to one side as if he were deciding what to do. Then he kissed me. Hard.

When we finally came up for air, my lips felt tender, a little swollen.

I said, "Now tie it on so I can't see."

That was the beginning. I've lost count of how many times we've done it since then, but it's got us through this long winter. Sometimes he blindfolds me. Sometimes I blindfold him. It all depends on who comes up with a new idea. It's never the same. That's our unspoken rule.

Not that it's entirely unpredictable. He seems to prefer that I wear some sort of clothing: one of his shirts or a teddy, something he can eventually slip off. After more than a year together, it still excites him to uncover my breasts, weigh them in his hands as if he is touching them for the first time. That's one of the things I like about him.

I prefer him to be completely naked. The first time I blindfolded him, I was the one who was trembling. Although it was my idea that he kneel on the bed wearing nothing but the blindfold, when he actually began to undress with a cool smile, I almost told him to stop. I wasn't sure I really wanted to see his big body so exposed, a band of flowered silk over his eyes with the long, loose ends falling softly down his back. I thought it might somehow diminish him.

But I was wrong. I'd never realized how beautiful his body was. Not that I hadn't appreciated it before, but I'd always focused my gaze on his eyes, his expressions. The rest of him I knew better by touch. But now, with his eyes hidden, I could see him with a new clarity: the rich, taut curves of his arms and chest, the hint of soft flesh at his waist that I found oddly pleasing. I noticed that the hair on his belly fanned out more luxuriantly to the left, and, by contrast, his right thigh was slightly more muscular, a legacy of his college fencing days. It didn't take long for him to get hard – it never did when we used the blindfold – and I got to watch that, the delicate jerking movements of his penis as it rose and thickened, drawn upward by invisible puppet strings which, I imagined, led straight to my hands.

I felt like a thief.

I felt my own desire grow within me in a completely new way. This time the familiar ache seemed to originate from behind my eyes, from the very sight of him unseeing. Then it seeped downward, bringing a warm flush to my cheeks and neck, making my nipples grow erect. It finally reached my belly, pooling there as a sharp, shimmering hunger.

I bent closer to feast, on the smell of him first, the cuminy scent of crotch, sharply male, yet intimate, intoxicating. I'd never studied a cock so carefully, the web of tiny veins embedded in the skin like red lace, the puckered ridge below the head, as if the flesh had been pinched when it was still fresh and soft. With no eyes glowing down at me, urging me to lick and suck and swallow, I could gaze into that other eye, slit vertically like a cat's, or maybe it was more like a tiny, hairless cunt, what they'd have on Barbie if she were anatomically correct. I pressed my tongue against it, lightly, tasting bitterness and salt, the tang of soap, then took the whole smooth helmet of the head into my mouth.

He moaned.

At last I had the sound of him.

Music.

When he decides the game, he often feeds me things. A dish of rice pudding in baby-sized bites from a spoon. Morsels of praline truffle he pushes through my lips with his tongue. And most often, his cock. I don't know why, but his semen tastes sweeter when I am wearing the blindfold.

One time he slipped a tiny wedge of soft paper between my lips, struck a match, and instructed me to inhale. It was a joint. *Where did you get this?* I wanted to ask, but I knew I wasn't supposed to talk – he had a way of letting me know such things – so I just lay quietly next to him on the bed and took long drags whenever he held it to my mouth. It must have been good stuff, because soon I was tingling all over just this side of numbness, floating off the bed into the past. It had been years since I'd smoked a joint. I never bought drugs myself. They were always presented to me as an offering from a boy in exchange for what I could offer him in return. So many things had changed since then, but it took me back to a time when I was so dumb about men, I might as well have been wearing a scarf over my eyes.

It's been a difficult winter for both of us. I know things aren't going well for him at work, but I didn't realize how upset he was until that day when I came home to find him practising with his saber.

Once, when we first started going out, he gave me a demonstration of fencing moves. I liked the way he looked in that white jacket, the single leather glove on his right hand, but I wasn't so sure about the wire-mesh mask. I thought it made him look like a huge insect. Or an executioner.

"Forget *The Three Musketeers*," he told me, "what you want to do is keep the blade within an imaginary frame around your body, to move as little as possible and still protect yourself. The most important part, though, is reading your opponent. It's like a game of chess, move and countermove," he said. "And when you get it just right, it's the best feeling in the world."

But as I watched him, so graceful on his feet as he advanced then retreated, I thought it seemed less like a game than a strange and beautiful dance.

This second time, it was different. He wore no mask and his T-shirt was stained with sweat. There was a fierceness in his concentration, his brow furrowed, his lips pale. I don't even think he saw me at first. Again and again he lunged at his imaginary opponent: a feint to the chest, then the quick and fatal strike to the head. I could see the metal meet flesh, then the cold satisfaction in his eyes as he watched the body crumple to the floor. Whoever it was died several times over.

Finally he turned to me. He was too far away to touch me with the blade, but he extended his wrist towards me as if he were pointing me out to some unseen stranger.

I frowned. "Hey, watch out, you could hurt someone with that."

His mouth curved into a slight smile. "That's the idea," he said, tilting the saber back in salute.

I've been having troubles of my own. My father was in the hospital with another heart attack, and there was talk of surgery. The first time I went to visit, he came with me. As we walked through the corridors, the pallid fluorescent light and muted antiseptic smell began to make me feel ill, so I reached for his hand, the only warm, real thing in the whole place.

He waited in the hall while I went into the room. My father was sleeping. He looked so old, his body sprouting tubes and wires, his face all creases and shadows. My mother was sitting by the bed staring down at the book on her lap. I glanced back at him, leaning against the wall across from the doorway, arms crossed, gazing straight ahead. His expression was patient, blank. I knew he didn't see me then. I wanted to be where he was – far, far away – but my mother pulled me back with her cool lips on my cheek, her anxious reassurances.

When she saw him, she stiffened, but, ever courteous, walked out to greet him. I watched them come together in a brief, guarded embrace, watched his lips move as he said something to her, watched her nod without really looking at him.

I'd known from the beginning that she didn't really approve of him. *Does he love you?* she asked me once, quietly, almost under her breath. I shrugged because that was the only answer I could give.

I wonder if she could have understood the attraction better if I had told her about the blindfold?

Strangely enough, one of my best ideas came from my mother. She was going through her sewing scrap box, when she pulled out a square of deep-red velvet and said, "Remember this? It's from that dress I made you for Christmas when you were – how old – eight or nine?" The fabric was soft with age and I instinctively rubbed it over my hand, up over my wrist. It felt especially nice when I ran a velvet-covered finger along the inside of my arm. I was so lost in my sweet memories of that dress, how grown-up and glamourous I felt when I wore it to church on Christmas morning then over to my aunt's house for dinner, that I didn't realize for several moments that I held in my hand the perfect surprise for our next game.

It was a good one. After I blindfolded him, I had him lie face down on the bed and guess what I was rubbing over his skin: the tip of my nose along his spine, the loose end of blindfold across his shoulders, my finger in the valley of his ass, my breasts across the back of his knees. I saved the velvet until last and stroked the length of him with it like I was polishing a precious, breakable object. He usually didn't make much noise when we made love, but by the time I was done with the back of him, he was almost mewing. And more than ready to turn over.

I dusted his chest and the discs of his nipples, then forced myself to linger at his belly, soothing the skin in small circles, ignoring his cock that reared up and twitched with each new caress. At last I wrapped the velvet around it and began to burnish it like a newel post, with careful attention to the glossy knob. It was then I told him about the dress, about how I wore it with white tights and patent leather shoes and had a bow with holly on it in my hair, and about how thrilled I was when all of the adults told me I looked so pretty.

"I'll bet you were cute," he said with a smile, as I lowered myself onto him and started my slow ride.

So cute, I told him, that even my oldest cousin – the one I had a crush on, the one who lives in Texas now – gallantly offered me a turn with his train set. Before I'd always had to beg and whine. But that day, I felt like a princess. And in trying to figure out what was different about it, I had my first inkling that the way to get something from boys is to look pretty. Then they'll do anything for you. Isn't that true? I asked him.

"Uh-huh," he replied, arching back into the pillow.

Not long after that he asked me to kneel when he put on the blindfold. Then he went on to position my body with his hands, telling me to keep my back straight, my shoulders down, my chin up. He told me not to move, not even to smile. He proceeded to caress me, starting at my cheeks just below the edge of the blindfold. He traced my lips with one fingertip, drew ovals on my chin, brushed my neck and collarbone with feathery strokes. I managed to hold myself still until his hands moved to my breasts. That's when he had to remind me of the rules and rearrange my body in the proper position. He even reprimanded me for breathing too quickly. "Slow, baby, nice and slow," he whispered, smoothing the tension from my lips and jaw until I was quiet.

But then he started up again, rolling my nipples between his fingers like he was fine-tuning a radio, rubbing one breast then the other with a spit-moistened palm. He knew my body. I had my proof then, if there was any doubt before. And all I could do was squeeze my eyes shut tighter and tighter under the blindfold as my cheeks began to burn and a fine sweat rose like lubricant on the skin beneath his hands. Soon my chest was throbbing so violently, my ribs ached. By then he'd moved down to my belly, drawing strange shapes that sometimes – just sometimes – extended further down. Then he'd come back to tease my belly button with a wet finger, stroking, circling, slipping softly inside.

All the while my clit was growing heavy and hot. I imagined he could see it, poking out between my lips, flushed scarlet and shameless in its need. When he finally did touch it, I shuddered, earning me another scolding.

"Now, now. Don't you remember? Good girls keep still and quiet while their wet, swollen clits are being rubbed."

By then there was nothing I could do to stop myself from whimpering, *Please, oh, please, I think I'm gonna come*, but I guess the rules suddenly changed, because he pushed me back on the bed and entered me with an urgency that surprised me, that tiny part of me that was still capable of coherent thought. How could just touching me – a statue – excite him so much? But his breath was coming as fast as his thrusts, and I was not far behind.

The experience of orgasm in general is something I can easily conjure in my mind, but specific ones elude me. Even when I remember the circumstances of the lovemaking, the things we said and did, the climax blurs into a vague sensation of bliss. An ending. But that orgasm is one I still remember in my body, a searing rush of pleasure as my desire finally burst free, my skull blasted open to the rush of night wind, the chilled fire of the stars. And I remember marvelling afterwards that we had done it: we had found a way to make each time better than the last.

Of course it couldn't go on for ever.

* * *

Earlier tonight I convinced him to watch an episode of an English TV series about a king with too many wives, because it was one of my favourite shows as a child. I had fond memories of sitting before the television with a notebook, sketching the Tudor gowns. But as I watched it again, I realized there was a lot I didn't remember. The growing sense of doom, the ugly marital quarrels, the political intrigue, the scene where the queen's musician was blinded under torture with a knotted rope. It was altogether too gloomy and talky, so I didn't complain when he started reading something halfway through. I decided to be satisfied he was there with me, idly rubbing my toes with one hand, holding the magazine with the other.

I noticed, however, that he started paying attention again when the queen was imprisoned on trumped-up charges of adultery. When it got to the execution scene, he put down the magazine. And so we both watched, transfixed, as the queen glided over to the scaffold, made her poignant farewell speech, kneeled down before the block. The lady-in-waiting tied a narrow, snow-white blindfold over the kneeling woman's eyes. In that one moment, before the sword, the actress looked more beautiful than ever, at least those parts of her set off by the blindfold above and the low-cut dress below: her pouting crimson lips, her fragile neck and the swelling of her breasts that rose and fell with each breath. I remembered something else from long ago, my brother and cousins in the back of the station wagon on a hot summer day, talking about that same television show. The only part of interest to them was when the queen "got her head chopped off". At the time, I didn't understand the edge of excitement in their voices.

But now I did.

We turn to each other with the same crooked, tight-lipped smiles.

"So, that was your favourite show?"

"Mmm," I reply. "I'd forgotten about that part."

We sit in silence.

Then I say to him, "What do you think goes through someone's mind at a time like that?"

He thinks, brow furrowed, then shakes his head.

More silence.

"So what do you want to do now?" I ask.

He shakes his head again. "I don't know. I'm in a weird mood."

I'm well aware that interesting things happen when he is in a weird mood.

I give him a sidelong glance. "Do you want to blindfold me?" I can't remember the last time we'd made love without it.

He looks at me curiously. "Now that would be too weird."

"But I want you to. I guess I'm in a weird mood, too. How about it?" I poke him.

"No," he replies sharply.

"How about 'yes'?" I say, taking up the challenge. I'll overcome his reluctance, make him want to do it. Before we had always glided into the game together, willingly, but I discover that this new element of conflict excites me.

He seems uneasy. "What's with you tonight?"

"What's with me? Who started this blindfold business anyway?"

"You didn't take much convincing, if I remember correctly."

This goes on for a while, until finally I ask, "Come on, what are you afraid of?"

That's when I know I've won, even before he stalks off to the bedroom and returns with the blindfold balled up in his fist.

"Should I get undressed?" I ask with a coy smile. I am still expecting him to smile back, still waiting for that flicker of desire in his eyes. It's always the last thing I see before the blindfold goes on.

But he just stares at me coldly. I'd never seen him quite like this before.

I sit up. "Well, what should I do?"

"Just get down on your fucking knees."

He doesn't seem to be pretending. I know I'm not pretending when I jump, when my jaw falls open in surprise. I really am afraid of him. Afraid to meet his eyes. Afraid to breathe.

I stand up and look around the living room for a place to kneel. The coffee table takes up most of the well-worn oval rug, but there is plenty of scarred hardwood floor.

"Can I get a pillow or something?" I attempt another smile.

"Shut up and kneel," he says.

So, I kneel down and he ties the blindfold over my eyes.

The floor is hard and cold. I hear the tip-tap of his shoes as he leaves the room. I am alone. At first my mind is racing as I wonder what he could be doing. But then, as I wait in the stillness, with the blindfold on, I begin to feel safe. This darkness is familiar, with its memory and promise of pleasure, of yielding myself to him. The very air seems to press against me, heavy and faintly moist, the boundaries of my body softening with each breath.

Suddenly I hear footsteps behind me, a faint metallic clink. My shoulders tense, the air grows thin. Something very cool and smooth settles on the right side of my neck. In the next instant I realize it is his hand. In a glove. A leather glove. It rests there for a moment, the fingers gripping my throat. The leather grows warm, sucking up the heat of my skin. Then it begins to move, stroking my neck, brushing my cheek. I sigh.

"Do you like this?" His voice sounds far away.

I hesitate, afraid to get the answer wrong. "Yes."

"Then enjoy it while you can. Because after tonight I'll never touch you again."

"What? What do you mean?"

"I mean, this is the last time." His hand slips away.

"I don't understand. You're leaving me?"

"Don't worry, when it's all over, you won't care."

"What are you going to do?"

"Come on now." His voice is low, mocking as he turns my own words against me. "What are you afraid of?"

I swallow hard.

It is fear, this tightness in my chest, the tingling where my neck curves into my shoulder, the very place a blade would strike.

But he wouldn't really go that far, would he?

Maybe he just enjoys watching me like this, the way my breasts quiver with each gasp and my lips part in an "o" as if I'm about to come. It would be more like him to tease me with the saber, ease the cool metal up between my thighs so I'm forced to ride it, avoiding the edges with exquisite care. He might even hold it to my neck as he pushes his cock into me and whispers, *The last time, the last time*, the words alone awakening hot tendrils of pleasure deep inside my cunt. And the ending would be sweet: no slow, grey withering, but a flash of silver behind my eyelids, a crimson flush rolling across my skin, a princess suspended in the prime of her beauty.

"This is part of the game, right?" My voice is pleading, hopeful.

At first he doesn't reply. I hear the floorboards creak, another clink of metal. Footsteps circle around to my left and stop somewhere in front of me. Then he snorts, a soft hiss of air. "Don't you see I'm tired of playing your sick games?"

*My* games?

For a moment I am aware of nothing but a coldness spreading up through my chest, down my arms, settling in my fingers as a dull, distant ache.

But suddenly I do see it, hovering against the blindfold: the image of myself as he really sees me now, as he must have seen me all along. A body – exposed and vulnerable – but not beautiful, not beloved.

"Why are you doing this to me?" I cry out, half choking on the words as I collapse to the floor, chest sagging onto my knees. I don't want to cry, not in front of him, not now, so I press my palms over my eyes, but the tears come anyway, stinging as they rise, spilling over into the silk.

Hands grasp my shoulders. I twist away instinctively, but they hold me fast, and I begin to feel, through the cloth of my shirt, the warmth of skin, a gentleness in his fingers. Then he pulls me up, murmuring something I can't hear through my own sobs. I struggle to my feet and bury my face in his shoulder. He strokes my back, swaying.

As I cling to him, I say less in accusation than wonder, "You were torturing me. Do you see that?"

"Isn't it what you wanted?" he whispers.

"No. I don't think so. I don't know," I say. In truth, I don't think I'd ever really been aware of what I was asking him to do.

"Believe me, I didn't mean to hurt you. I never want to hurt you." His arms tighten around me, squeezing me with a force just short of actual pain.

It is the blindfold that suddenly seems unbearably tight.

"Take it off now. Please?" I could pull it off myself – it has always been a voluntary bondage – but I want him to do it. I want him to break the spell.

His hands fumble at the knot. Then he pulls the scarf free and lets it fall to the floor.

I look up and see that his eyes are wet, too, like wounds. I lean towards him. He closes his eyes, and so do I, an unthinking act that all lovers do. In that simple darkness we find each other's lips. I want at this moment nothing more than the exquisitely ordinary comfort of his lips against mine.

It is enough.

# The Penis of My Beloved

Ian Watson and Roberto Quaglia

During my Beloved's lifetime his penis was of great importance to me – how could it be otherwise? Of course, there was much more to my Beloved than his penis. For instance, there was his tongue. I don't merely refer to his skill at licking, but also to all the words he said to me (except obviously whilst licking). Words are so important to a woman during love, just as they are in the everyday aspects of life. Also, there were his dark eyes, which spoke volumes of silent poetry. Also, there were his arms which held me. I need not enumerate more – there was all of Oliver.

When my Beloved suddenly died of a heart attack, how desperately I craved to have him back again, alive.

This was possible due to advances in rapid cloning. However, a whole body cost a small fortune. Oliver and I had never given much thought to the morrow. Even by availing myself of a special offer from the Bodies'r'Us Clinic, and by paying on the instalment plan, the most I could afford was the cloning of a small part of Oliver.

Which part should it be? His right hand, sustained by an artificial blood supply and activated to a limited extent by a nerve impulse box with control buttons? Even a whole hand was out of my financial reach!

Should it be his tongue, likewise sustained by a costly blood supply?

Minus mouth and throat and vocal cords, a tongue could never say anything even if it wanted to, although it ought to be able to lick, for such is the nature of tongues. Body parts are aware of the role they play in the entirety of the body, consequently this memory lingers on even when they're amputated or dissected, or in this case cloned. Oh yes, his tongue ought to be able to lick, although the sensation might seem to me more like a warm slug than his robust tongue of yore.

How about one of his eyes, which spoke volumes? The eye could rest upon an egg cup and form an image of me. Before going to bed I could perform a striptease for his eye. Yet to be perfectly frank, what could his eye *do* for me? Also, although I had no intention of ever being unfaithful to my Beloved, a naked eyeball might seem like a spy camera keeping watch. This wasn't the kind of continuing intimacy I craved.

Really, my choice could only be the penis, especially as the cost was based upon the "normal" size when flaccid rather than erect. In this instance, the money I would be paying in any event for the blood supply, so as to keep the part alive, would provide a special bonus benefit, namely erection when the penis was caressed. You couldn't say about any other cloned body part that your investment could grow ten-fold, as it were!

"You mightn't realize," the cloning salesman said to me, "that a penis becomes stiff not because of blood pumped actively into it by an excited body, but because certain penile muscles *relax*, which allows the blood to flow in and fill it. Normally the muscles are tense and inhibit the volume of blood – otherwise men would have permanent erections."

"So if you feel nervous and tense, you never get an erection?"

The salesman flushed, as though I had touched on a sore point. He was a young man with ginger hair and many freckles. The wallpaper of the consultation room was Klimt, so we were surrounded by hybrids of slender women and flowers.

"Madam, it's simply that you might be expecting too much. We can't absolutely guarantee erection, for that would be to alter the biology of the penis. In effect we would be providing you with a bio-dildo rather than with a genuine cloned organ – and we don't supply such things. Prostho-porn isn't our profession." This was spoken a shade tartly. The salesman may have been upset by my previous remark, supposing that it reflected upon his own virility.

I was sure that my Beloved's cloned penis would remember my own particular touch and wouldn't feel inhibited.

I made like a wide-eyed innocent. "Is 'prostho-porn' *anyone's* profession?"

"I've heard that in China . . ." The salesman lowered his voice. "Multiple cloned cunts of pop stars in pleasure parlours . . ." Now he seemed mollified and was all smiles again. "This won't be the case here! Your commission will be unique to you."

"I should hope so!"

* * *

It goes without saying that I'd arranged for sample cells from all of Oliver's important organs and limbs to be frozen in liquid nitrogen – which wasn't too expensive – before the majority of his dear chilled body finally entered the furnace at the crematorium. I'd read that in another few years it might be possible to coax a finger or a penis, say, to diversify and regenerate from itself an entire body, but apparently this was a speculative line of research pursued by only a handful of maverick scientists. Small wonder: it's much more common for a body to lose a penis than for a penis to lose a body! So I was sceptical of this possibility. In the meantime my dream of recreating the entirety of Oliver, to rejoin his penis, would remain a dream because of the cost.

"So that's the famous penis!" exclaimed my neighbour Andorra, who was short and who spoke her mind. Andorra and I were best friends even before the sudden death of my Beloved, about which she was very consoling. Currently Andorra was working for the Blood Donor service.

Her parents chose the name Andorra to suggest that she would be adorable. Naming her after the tiniest independent state in Europe did prove prophetic as regards her stature and personality – she was short and assertive. Yet as regards adorability in the eyes of the opposite sex, the ploy failed. Andorra had only had one boyfriend, and he was a disaster. No one else tried to get into bed with her, or courted her. I think Andorra trained as a nurse due to reading too many doctor–nurse romance novels, many of which still littered her apartment next door to mine.

Next door to *our* apartment, I should say. Oliver's and mine; mine and that of his penis.

Andorra's dog Coochie sometimes chewed her romance novels or carried them around her apartment while awaiting her return from work, and a walk, and an emptying. Coochie was a yellowish Labrador.

"Famous?" I replied. "There's nothing famous about it except in my own eyes." And in my hand, of course.

"It's a bit small . . ." But then she quickly added, "At the moment." She eyed the apparatus to which the penis was attached by two long connecting tubes. "Will you pump some more blood into it?"

So that she could behold an actual erect penis in the flesh at last?

"That isn't why a penis stiffens. Don't you know anatomy? What's important is the receptive mood of the penis."

"Well, it would be more impressive . . ." She tailed off.

Did she hope that I would stimulate the penis of my Beloved for her benefit? I almost succumbed to her implied entreaty, if only to demonstrate Oliver's penis in full gory, I mean glory, but this was an intimate matter.

"I'm perfectly satisfied," I told her. Only as I spoke did I realize how this might imply smugly that Andorra herself remained unsatisfied. She had mentioned dissatisfaction with dildos. I might seem to be cock-crowing, lording it over my friend.

Andorra looked thoughtful.

Due to the length of the blood-tubes it was easy to take the penis to bed with me so as to stroke it in just the way my Beloved had liked, then pleasure myself after it stiffened. It remembered me. Because only Oliver's penis was cloned, not his prostate and other attachments, inevitably there was no ejaculation, yet this was no disadvantage – on the contrary! I would hold the rubber grip-mount, shaped like a small plant pot, in which his penis (as it were) grew, and much prolonged joy was mine. I was blissful. Sometimes after an orgasm I would take the penis out of me and talk to it, or use my mouth for a different purpose. I felt like a little girl: the penis of my Beloved, my lollipop.

But then came a problem with the blood supply – I don't mean the tubes and pump, but rather my finances. Bodies'r'Us strongly recommended renewing the blood each month to prevent degeneration of the penis. As part of the initial cost, I'd received five vouchers for replacement blood. Now I'd used those vouchers, and I discovered that in the meantime the cost of blood had risen by 25 per cent.

Bodies'r'Us was a significant user and retailer of blood, needing to buy blood, good blood, too, from healthy sellers. Nobody would donate blood charitably so that some rich woman could maintain a clone of her dead poodle, or me a cloned penis. Andorra had complained to me that the Donor Service, which supplied hospitals, was suffering a bit of a blood drain because former donors were choosing to sell rather than donate, but luckily altruism and generosity still prevailed in society, not to mention donations by way of the vampire churches as part of their safe sex campaign.

At this point I consulted Andorra and she made me an offer . . .

. . . to smuggle blood from the Donor Service – providing that I let her use the penis of my Beloved privately one evening each week, say every Friday.

I was astonished and disconcerted.

"I'm your best friend," she pointed out.

"It won't respond to you," I said.

She pouted at me, full-lipped. "I'll find a way."

I should have refused. Yet if I refused, I might embitter Andorra. It must have cost her dear to make this request, this admission of craving for the real thing – or at least for the cloned and partial thing. Refusal might seem like a slap in the face. But also, of a sudden, I was curious as to whether my Beloved *would* respond to the touch of a stranger!

According to Andorra, the penis did react to her, and very satisfyingly too. She might be fibbing so as to salve her pride, and I could hardly ask to be present while Andorra writhed on her bed. Besides, I wouldn't have wished to behold this personally. Consequently, every Friday evening Andorra would carefully carry the pump and the penis along to her apartment and bring them back to me a couple of hours later. During this interval I would watch TV and try not to think about what might be happening. Once the penis was mine again, I would wash it, irrespective of whether Andorra had already done so. Washing excited the penis as much as caresses, since the actions were very similar. The penis seemed to be wishing to make up to me for what had occurred, even though it was I who owed the penis an apology.

I would kiss it. "Forgive me, my Beloved. You earned your blood, that's the main thing."

After some weeks I made a terrible discovery. When Andorra brought the penis back, Coochie was with her, pawing at her thigh and sniffing.

"Stay!" ordered Andorra, but Coochie pushed his way into my apartment. The dog's gaze was fixed on the now floppy penis. He seemed to want it – not for a snack, which was my first fear, soon dispelled by a much worse realization: Coochie wanted the penis as a *penis*.

When I stared accusingly at Andorra, she broke down in tears of remorse.

"He's become addicted," she confessed.

"Do you mean . . . do you mean . . . you've been giving your dog *bestiality* treats with the penis of my Beloved?"

"He's an unusual dog! I love Coochie, and Coochie loves me, but I knew he was gay!"

"Gay? How did you know that?"

Andorra remained silent.

"Did Coochie bugger some other male dog while out walkies with you?"

More silence. My best friend couldn't tell me an outright lie. Suddenly I realized that if Andorra's discovery had *not* occurred during walkies then only one possibility remained . . .

"You used to try to get Coochie to fuck you! But no matter how you went about it, Coochie couldn't get it up because—"

"—because Coochie's gay. It's the only explanation."

I felt sorry for Andorra. Yet I also had a persistent image in my mind . . . of Coochie, who was gallumphing around, his anus frequently visible. How degrading for the penis of my Beloved!

While performing that canine service, Oliver's penis must have been stiff! Was the penis utterly undiscriminating?

"Look," I told Andorra, "you must promise me, don't do it with Coochie again. That's unhygienic."

"I always did me *after* I did Coochie."

That would have cleaned the penis?

Resulting in Andorra's vagina smelling of male dog? In due course Coochie might learn to associate . . . Andorra had not given up hope.

"I'd be well within my rights to refuse you the penis ever again."

"And I to refuse you blood," she murmured.

She had a point. Consequently we didn't quarrel.

With some difficulty she hauled Coochie away. Alone once again, I eyed the wilted penis. "Beloved, how could you do it with a dog?"

I tried to come to terms with what had happened by being objective and logical. The episode with Coochie was not my Beloved's fault.

The next week Andorra remarked, "Maybe the penis has erections in a Pavlovian way regardless of with whom or with what. Poor Oliver loves you, but he can't resist. You really ought to have more of him cloned."

How would I pay for that?

Oh but she had the answer!

At the hospital where Andorra worked previously, she knew a junior anaesthetist who moonlighted as a stud in porn movies. Mark's rugged good looks and intelligence made him a desirable actor. As for his prowess, before each performance Mark would sniff a stimulant gas to keep himself stiff irrespective of ejaculation. Unfortunately, Mark had recently been sacked for stealing gas from the hospital. Now he needed to rely full-time on porn to earn his living just at the time when he'd lost access to what boosted him.

What, suggested Andorra, if I were to offer the penis of my Beloved as a stand-in for Mark's penis while limp? With clever editing, viewers mightn't notice the temporary substitution, the tubes, the little plant pot clutched by Mark, or by whichever woman.

My Beloved's penis would be earning some money with which to recover more of himself for me.

"How is Coochie coping?" I asked.

"I lock him in the bathroom with a lot of cold turkey. He loves that. It takes his mind off the penis."

Andorra made arrangements. A couple of weeks later I watched a copy of the video in order to see with what sort of woman the penis was unfaithful.

The poor editing hid little. It was obvious that part of the time a detached, hand-held penis was in use. Not a dildo, oh no, but a living penis which happened to lack a man attached to it.

What a dream for a woman, you may well say! And you would be right. Thanks to chat on the internet, word spread rapidly. The video became a wow among women. Few men bought it, maybe because of castration fears, but the producer was jubilant. Here at last was a porn video uniquely suited to females. Therefore, we must make another video quickly – starring the detached living penis itself. Mark would play the role of a sex counsellor administering the penis as therapy to a patient.

Not long after this second video was released, requests began arriving from dozens of sophisticated high-society women requesting "private performances", and offering to pay well.

Thus it was that at a private orgy, held in a woodland clearing on the outskirts of the city, the penis of my Beloved was mounted on the bonnet of a Jaguar car in place of the usual little model of a leaping jaguar. Several naked women wearing Venetian carnival masks took turns ascending the front of the car while friends cheered. This gave a new meaning to auto-eroticism.

Because of those private performances I was accumulating money fast. A down-payment on cloning all the rest of my Beloved looked possible, not least because the wife of one of the directors of

Bodies'r'Us was one of those who had privately enjoyed the penis of my Beloved. She regarded my quest for the entirety of my Beloved as so romantic.

This woman, Natalie, made short art films as a hobby. She was convinced that a film made by her about my eventual reunion with my Beloved might win her a prestigious award given for short art movies featuring sexual themes, the Shiny Palm. This trophy took the form of a polished feminine metal hand grasping an erect penis made of purple glass.

On account of the porn movie about the autonomous penis, Bodies'r'Us had gained new customers. Wives who had seen that movie, and whose husbands failed to satisfy them sufficiently, urged their spouses to have their penises cloned so as to support the men's performance in bed. An identical understudy, or penis double, would increase the women's pleasure and offer extra possibilities.

Excellent publicity for Bodies'r'Us! In Natalie's opinion an artistic movie would add true chic to the cloning of small body parts.

Not necessarily always penises, either! A lovely nose might be cloned and mounted on a plaque, like a small hunting trophy, the blood supply out of sight in a hidden compartment. A hand might be cloned. Or a finger. Due to lack of auxiliary muscles, one couldn't expect the hand to flex its fingers dramatically, or the finger to bend much. A finger is not a penis. Probably penises would be most popular.

"Rivalry might even arise among men who have cloned penises," Natalie declared to me on the phone one day. "Those can be displayed on the wall as a talking point at a dinner party. You know how men boast – but it would be most unsuitable for a man actually to pull his own trousers down during a fashionable dinner party! Besides, he mightn't rise to the occasion on account of too much alcohol or shyness. A cloned penis, which wouldn't imbibe, can represent him at his best. Wives will take pride in demonstrating the penis to their guests."

She speculated further: "Failure to mount your cloned penis on the wall might even give rise to suspicions as to the quality of the original penis. Too small? Too thin? Whatever! Maybe deficient men will buy more magnificent penises not cloned from themselves – provided by third-world companies without the scruples of Bodies'r'Us. On the other hand, the display of a less than splendid penis on the dining room wall might be a form of inverted boastfulness: 'It may not look much, but if only you knew what I can do with it, and for how long!' You do want your Beloved back, don't you, dear? If you let me make a film about your quest, I'm sure Bodies'r'Us will be very easy on the terms for a full Beloved. My film wouldn't be intrusive, just a few remote-control mini-cameras concealed in your apartment."

I was so excited I would have agreed to almost anything.

Bodies'r'Us must have exploited some of that research by those maverick scientists I mentioned. Instead of cloning 100 per cent new body complete with brand new penis, they *integrated* – as they put it – the already cloned penis into the ensemble of all the rest of Oliver's cloned anatomy. The cloned penis which I already knew was precious to me – it stood for continuity. I could hardly discard it, but it would be downright silly to maintain that autonomous penis unused, expensively keeping a blood pump working at the same time as the full Oliver maintained a blood supply to another cloned penis by natural means. It was only sensible that the original cloned penis should be coupled to the rest of the clone.

And so my Beloved came back to me.

Along with some cameras and microphones for my apartment.

In years gone by, scientists predicted that a duplicated brain shouldn't retain any of the memories of the brain that it was cloned from. According to past scientific wisdom, the new brain should only exhibit the same capacities and personality traits and tendencies as the original brain – for instance, the tendency to fall in love with somebody looking much like me, or the ability to learn languages easily.

*Now* we know that a cloned brain actually inherits many of the typical *dreams* of its source brain. This is because dreams are deeply archetypal. The original brain and the cloned brain are genetically identical, so by morphic resonance the cloned brain acquires much of the dream experience of the original from out of the collective storehouse from which dreams emerge, and into which they return.

Thus my cloned Beloved couldn't remember any actual incidents of our waking life together, but he knew who I was in a dreamy way. And because dreams contain speech, he could speak, although in rather a dreamlike manner.

"You are an almond tree," he told me, shortly after Bodies'r'Us delivered him to the apartment. Was that because of the colour of my eyes? If so, this must be an endearment.

Yet to my horror I very quickly found that my Beloved was

impotent with me! No matter what I did, or how I displayed myself, his penis remained limp – that very penis which had previously responded so enthusiastically! This shocked and chagrined me – and I regretted the cameras and microphones Natalie had installed.

We have all heard how the arm of the executed German mass-murderer, Sigmund Hammerfest, was grafted on to an amputee, Rolf Heinz, who'd lost his arm in a car crash, and how the murderer's arm subsequently made Herr Heinz homicidal. While Herr Heinz was making love to his wife one night, the arm broke Frau Heinz's neck. The organs and limbs of the body possess a kind of memory, as I've said.

Could it be that, rejoined to its body, the penis conveyed memories of its multiple infidelities to my Beloved's body? And the body, now powering the penis, developed *guilt*, which disabled the penis? Thus the memory of the penis was contaminating the true wishes of its owner.

Yet what really *were* the true wishes of my Beloved? Could it be that the penis had truly loved me, but that Oliver himself as a complete person hadn't been quite so devoted? Could it be that formerly the penis had been ordering my Beloved to love me and nobody else? That it was the desire of the penis, rather than true love, which had made Oliver want to fuck me? Yet I had permitted the penis to respond to anybody; in a sense I had trained it to do so. Consequently, now I was no longer a unique focus of desire. My Beloved might call me an almond tree like some medieval Arabian poet, but those were just pretty words! This was very confusing.

Why, oh why, had I cloned all of Oliver at such cost when the penis had been my real lover all along! I had prostituted the penis, the only part of him that truly loved me. Now Oliver was inhibiting the penis from performing, and I might be discovering all too late that my Beloved's flowery sentiments were hypocritical!

I accused my Beloved.

His replies were hard to understand – unlike the formerly clear, if non-verbal, responses of the stiff penis to me.

"You didn't truly love me," I cried.

"Balloons bring roses," said Oliver. "Scent escapes from bursting balloons." Did this mean that love dies?

"It was your penis that loved me, not you!"

"The rubies of your nipples are so hard they could cut glass." Was he complaining about my nipples? In the old days of our passion, had they hurt his chest?

I was shouting at him in angry disappointment when a knock came at the door.

Andorra stood outside, Coochie on a leash.

The blood froze in my veins. Here was the moment I had been fearing.

"May we come in?" Andorra asked with a big, insincere smile. The dog wagged his tail, excited, probably foreseeing who knows what kind of filthy development.

*No, no, no!* I thought with all the power of my mind. However, I heard my voice answer politely: "Yes, of course, feel at home." Oh the hypocrisy of etiquette. I could have bitten off my tongue. But there was no escaping from destiny.

Oliver remained expressionless as he met the gaze of Andorra, then of the dog. Andorra was observing Oliver inquisitively, as if to perceive a penis improbably hidden between his eyes. The gay dog was salivating, detecting the smell of a friendly penis that it knew . . . in the biblical sense. Coochie pushed close to Oliver and insolently sniffed his genitals through the trousers. Was the trace of an erection swelling in there? Oliver's forehead was knit. Did Coochie awake in him those dreams that I feared? Under no circumstances should I leave Oliver, and above all *my* penis, alone together with these two sexual jackals. As yet we were only in my hallway, which was quite large.

The doorbell rang and I turned to open the door once more. Etiquette!

Outside stood two mature women.

"We're from the Church for the Protection of Genital Organs," announced one of the ladies. "We'd like to interview you for our religious magazine."

This church had sprung up recently. Advances in plastic surgery were making it possible to have one's genitals exotically customized. Surely this insulted the sexual organs God designed for Adam and Eve and for all of us! Biblical believers had long since abandoned defending the sanctity of marriage as a lost cause, consequently they poured their piety into defending the sanctity of copulation as God intended, using the exact organs He provided, not pudenda reshaped into orchids or trumpets, or giant clitorises or bifurcated dicks.

As I later discovered, Bodies'r'Us – who approved of exact copies, not baroque variations – had given some money to the Church of PGO and encouraged them to interview me to make an interesting scene in the movie. Drawing the attention of the Church of PGO was a big mistake, as subsequent events proved. But meanwhile I got rid of the two women as quickly as possible, although not fast enough. When I turned back to my guests, they were not there any more. Andorra and Coochie had vanished along with my Beloved and his/my penis!

Obviously they had gone into the lounge, but why then had they closed the door? Worry clutched at me. I gripped the door handle to follow them only to discover that the door was locked! With a shiver I imagined the spectators of the movie seeing my face turn pale at this point as the most horrible of scenes formed in my mind, of my beloved Oliver buggering the Labrador, who in turn was buggering Andorra who, between moans, was sipping champagne from one of the crystal glasses my grandmother had left me in her will.

Was the artistic, romantic movie of reunion with the Oliver of my penis destined to turn into the usual bestiality porn reality show, the commonplace of television? I banged loudly on the door, but the only response was what sounded like a suffocated whine. Nobody came to let me into my own lounge.

"Oliver!" I shouted. "Andorra!" For answer, just another whine.

This was too much. I fainted.

When I recovered, I was lying on the couch in the lounge. Andorra and Oliver were watching me with worried expressions. Coochie was sitting looking sleepy.

"How long have I been unconscious?"

"A few minutes," replied Andorra, whether this was true or not. "We heard a thump and found you behind the door. You ought to have the handle seen to. I don't think it works properly."

Was she sincere?

"Why did you close the door at all?"

"To be discreet. You had visitors." Oh, etiquette again. If I believed her.

I turned to Oliver. "What happened in here before you found me passed out?"

"What is passed or past is the turd of the fall, come springtime."

In other words, *No use crying over spilt milk?* By which he might mean spilled semen. Did *turd* allude to a dog's anus? To my mind those two items are always closely linked. Oliver was no help at all. I'd been getting along better with his, or rather *my* penis.

Ignoring the gaze of my Beloved, I looked lower, so as to distinguish within his pants my more beloved penis, probably the only part of

Oliver which ever really loved me. That wasn't difficult – an evident protuberance seemed likely to perforate his pants at any moment. Obviously Oliver's penis was completely erect, the way I remembered it, the way I had long loved it. Hidden as it was by trousers I couldn't actually see it, and this seemed unjust. Forgetting about the presence of Andorra and the hidden cameras, instinctively I reached out a hand sweetly to caress my beloved penis, which I hadn't seen – nor felt – in its full, majestic, generous erection for far too long. In the very moment when my hand grazed it, the penis imploded like the Hindenburg airship, deflating at once and evading my contact. Suddenly everything became atrociously clear beyond any doubt!

The penis itself could not know so quickly that it was me who touched it, because the trousers were a barrier to its sensitive nerve endings. Therefore, the order to deflate must have come directly from the brain of Oliver. I became furious and shouted: "You treacherous fuckface prickhead, get out of my home! Get out, but leave my penis here!"

Seizing Oliver, I propelled him with all my strength out of the lounge, through the hall, to the front door. He didn't resist but let himself be thrown out, although of course he took my/his penis with him. Those two damn churchwomen were still loitering outside, index fingers scribbling on smartscreens nestling in their palms. Were they inventing a non-existent interview? Aurora and Coochie hurried past me without a word or a woof, and I slammed the door behind them. Then I allowed myself the wisest feminine recourse in emergency circumstances: I began to cry.

Oliver took up residence in Andorra's flat. Some days later a man with the face of a mummified pig presented himself at my door.

"I'm the lawyer of the penis," he introduced himself.

I discovered that the Church for the Protection of Genital Organs had arrogated to itself the right to represent the interests of Oliver's penis. From Pigface I heard talk about the rights of genital organs to self-determination and about some Treaty of Independence from the Bearer of the Organ. Oh the mysteries of jurisprudence! The ways that lawyers get rich!

Pigface explained to me that Oliver's penis had gained the status of an individual by virtue of having lived independently for a sufficient time before finding itself again attached to a human bearer. The Church for the Protection of Genital Organs was entitled to represent the penis because it was the first to claim that right, without the penis raising any objection.

"But the penis wouldn't be able to understand any of this!"

"Exactly. So it needed legal representation."

Later I learned how the judge at the court in question had become obsessed with making controversial landmark judgments in the hope of being retired soon with a knighthood or some other honour. The Church of PGO had been well aware of this.

In Andorra's flat there were no hidden cameras. Andorra had refused the TV company permission to install any cameras in her home – probably so as not to expose to the world her affair with the dog. For the TV company and for Bodies'r'Us this was unacceptable. On the other hand, the impotence Oliver's penis displayed towards me when it was attached to Oliver hardly made his return to my own home a very exciting prospect for Natalie and the other people involved in the production of the movie. The public doesn't much care for erotic dramas with impotent characters. Therefore, the lawyers for Natalie and Bodies'r'Us were petitioning to have Oliver and his penis separated again, so that the penis could go back to performing in the role that had made it so famous, the penis without a man.

The penis without its Oliver had already become a star. A poll revealed that as an anonymous part of a normal person it wouldn't be so interesting to people.

The Church for the Protection of Genital Organs likewise wanted the penis to be separated from Oliver, yet not so that it could perform in porn movies or couple with me again, which they viewed as unnatural. Instead, they wanted it to retire to a zen monastery. Oh, the moral obsessions of churches!

Thus there was conflict between the movie producers, with whom I had signed an agreement on behalf of the cloned Oliver, and the lawyers for the penis and the Church of PGO.

"We won't allow you to go on sexually exploiting that poor penis," Pigface told me at a deposition hearing.

"It's a sexual organ. It was born to be sexually exploited," I retorted.

"He's an individual with full rights, including the right of freely choosing the modality of his sexuality."

"It's a penis. If it becomes hard that means it wants to fuck."

"Not at all! Diseases exist, such as priapism. Erection can be the symptom of a pathology."

I decided to change my strategy. "It's a piece of meat without a brain. It's not compos mentis."

"Another reason to protect his dignity. We will never allow that poor penis to be forced into any more intercourse for which he didn't give written consent."

"How can a penis write anything?"

"If held properly, it can produce a DNA signature."

"Without a prostate it can't ejaculate, so where's the ink?"

"We can prepare all necessary documents *before* the separation."

Suits and countersuits were heard, and the lawyers were all very happy until at last no legal problems prohibited the penis being separated from Oliver. Final judgment was that since the penis was cloned *before* the body, *it* was the one who owned the other, and not the contrary. The penis owned the man, namely the cloned Oliver; Oliver did not own the penis. If it's legitimate for a man to cut off his own penis, provided that he isn't attempting suicide, logically the penis could decide to cut off its own man. The lawyer for the penis, as his legal representative, had full power to act in this regard – and to *steal* the penis of my Beloved, I was thinking in anger and frustration.

The judge duly retired and became a lord.

However, we live in a strange and unpredictable world.

Under its various Patriot Acts, the USA had permitted itself to intervene in any part of the world in defence of its homeland security and its supplies of oil and cheap obesity fast food, full of oil and sugar and additives. To signal to the world its rise as a rival superpower, China enacted the Salvation of Culture Law, by which the Chinese gave themselves the right to intervene anywhere to protect the interests of art. This was something that the American government found hard to understand, so they did not threaten the Chinese with thermonuclear war.

If the USA was the Global Cop, China would be the Global Curator. A popular US slogan was "Kick Ass America!" So Beijing declared "Save Art China!" And why not, China being the oldest civilization on Earth? When Venice began to sink rapidly, swift intervention by Chinese technology had rescued the Italian city, preserving it in a dome to the applause of most nations. From then on, China could take great liberties in the defence of art.

Art included performance art, and one of the many ways of

preserving art was Gor-Gon, a polymerizing nanotechnology inspired by Gunther Von Hagen's corpse plastination factory in the north-eastern Chinese port city of Dalian. In just a few seconds, a jab of Gor-Gon administered by injection or by a dart fired from a gun could transform any living being into plastinated artwork, petrifying for ever (though by no means as stiffly as stone) the target animal or person at that moment.

The penis had been quite a performer, and the legal case was by now notorious worldwide, as was the prospect of cloned penis and cloned person parting company. So Chinese art agents targeted Oliver. Already Chinese art agents had overenthusiastically targeted several famous opera singers and actors for a Hall of Fame. Since the salvation of Venice, the Chinese could do pretty much as they pleased, but plastinating artists suddenly while they were on stage caused demands for ticket refunds, arguments about civil rights, and also poorer performances by many divas and stars who didn't wish to be plastinated, which was all very regrettable and counter-productive. So this was made illegal. But according to Chinese law, plastinating a clone was just as acceptable as plastinating a criminal for export to medical schools . . .

I'm so lucky. At the moment of petrification, the penis of my former Beloved was fully erect – he had to be slid out of Andorra by the Chinese agents who invaded her flat. So now I live in China, inside a big transparent cube. I couple with the penis attached to Oliver whenever I want. Plastination keeps the penis stiff, yet soft and comfortable to use. Of course, plastinated Oliver never says a thing, nor moves, although I arrange him artistically just as I please.

Outside the cube every day, crowds of visiting art lovers and connoisseurs admire us and shoot holographic movies, so that we never feel alone. Inside the cube, the air is always fresh and rich in happy-making hormones. The Chinese takeaway meals supplied to me free are so varied and delicious. Life is beautiful! Or maybe life is simply too complex to understand.

# Nothing But This

Kristina Lloyd

I call him the Boy although he isn't. He's skinny enough, it's true – as skinny as the kids who do backflips in the square – and there's not a single hair on his flat brown chest. But his age is in his eyes, eyes as green as a cat's, and when I look right at him, though we're meant to be ignoring him, I see eyes that might be a thousand years old.

He's been following us for half an hour, weaving among the crowds, his flip-flops slap-slapping in the dust of the souk. "Hey, mister! Hey, lady!" he keeps calling. "You wanna buy carpet? Teapot? Saffron? You wanna buy incense? Come, come! Come to meet my uncle."

His urge to "come, come" sounds grubby and erotic and the refrain pulses in my head like some dark drumbeat, weird enough for me to wonder if it's going to bring on one of my migraines.

"Lady, you wanna buy handbag? Real leather! The best! Hey, mister, nice wallet for you! Look this way! You are my guest. Come!" The Boy averts his eyes, head down and spinning, and the whole song and dance routine seems a pastiche of the real hustlers, an empty act he can turn off at will. No wonder he can't look at us: we'd see right through him.

"I feel like David bloody Niven," mutters Tom.

Tom's posh as fuck, so self-assured and confident you don't even notice it. He's relaxed and ironic. A bit on the prim side, it has to be said, but I adore every hot salty inch of him. I like to draw him, standing, sitting, lying, sprawling, my futile bid to capture him in charcoal and pencils. In evening class, I learned to draw not just the object but the space around it. I learned to see absence. "What's not there is as important as what is," said our tutor, although personally

I'd contest that with Tom. I'm quite a fan of what's there. Naked, he's pale and softly muscled with strong swimmer's shoulders and thighs like hams. Sometimes I sketch his cock, big and randy or just lolling on his thigh, framed in dark curls, and when I show him the end

result he'll invariably wince. "Oh God," he drawls, looking away and sounding slightly camp. "You're so *vulgar*." But he can't help smiling and I know deep down he likes it.

"*Pssst!*"

It's the Boy. I can't see him, only hear him. The medina is crammed with noise, its maze of tiny streets choked with the scents of paraffin, leather, spit-roast meats, sour sweat, baked earth and strong rough tobacco. Here and there, the souk opens out, exposing its squinting stallholders to a livid blue sky. But for now we're in the thick of it, two clueless pink-skins in an ancient labyrinth, lost among beggars, hawkers, shoppers, mopeds, donkey carts and big wire cages squawking with heaps of angry hens. The Boy's hiss slices through the chaos, clean as a whistle, but I can't spot him anywhere.

I'm disappointed. I'm supposed to be relieved because the official line is, he's been annoying us from the off, prancing around like some mad imp of consumerism, urging us to buy this, buy that, buy the other. The thing is, we do want to buy a carpet, a nice Berber runner for the hallway, but he's probably on commission and, besides, we'd rather do it in peace.

My disappointment tempers the arousal I'm half ashamed to acknowledge. At first, I couldn't be sure it was sexual although I suspected it was. Heck, it usually is with me. And then I knew damn well it was when my groin flickered its need and I grew aware of my inner thighs, filmy with sweat, sliding wetly as I walked, my sarong flapping around my ankles. But it's a weird kind of sexual. It's not as if I fancy him, this slip of a lad with the calm, creepy eyes, but I'm drawn to him in a way I can't identify. He keeps dropping back from us to sidle among the crowd or prowl at a distance, elegant and stealthy, stalking us like prey. My money's in a belt. I must have checked it a dozen times. I don't think he's a thief though.

I don't know what he is. All I know is he's sparked off in me some intrigue, some furtive hunger that makes me not quite trust myself. We keep walking, Tom and I, and within the humid fabric of my knickers, I'm as sticky and swollen as a Barbary fig.

"*Pssst!*"

His call sounds so close I actually look over my shoulder, expecting him right there, but no sign. It's as if he's invisible, some mythical djinni up to no good or a golem from the old Jewish quarter, laughing to himself as I pat my money belt once again.

"Seem to have shaken him off, the little shit," Tom says mildly as he unscrews his water bottle.

I realize Tom's not hearing what I hear, making me question my senses. The heat in this place stupefies me and I haven't been sleeping well either. At night, after an evening of jugglers, magicians, fire-eaters and snake-charmers, the bedsheets tangle themselves around my legs, cobras for the pipe-player, and my mind whirls with madness and enchantments. To soothe me, I think of the stillness beyond the town: snow-capped mountains, endless deserts and a black velvet night sprayed with silver stars. But I sleep fitfully, slipping in and out of dreamscapes, grotesque and lewd, and I wake each morning sloppy with desire. When I sink onto Tom's cock, drowsy and heavy, I feel fucked already, post-coitally limp, as if I've been possessed by an incubus, a gleeful demon who screwed me senseless as I slept. My limbs seem to liquefy as I ride Tom, awash with vagueness, remembering feral creatures, how they pawed at my flesh, and priapic monsters with gas-mask faces, rutting in steamy swamps.

I don't imagine we'll buy a carpet today. I'm not really in the mood. Feeling a tad psychotic, to tell the truth. But I hide it well. I'm probably just premenstrual.

A few minutes later and the Boy's with us again. I don't see him but I smell him, a pungent sexual whiff as we pass stalls selling metalware, shards of sunlight glancing off pewter, copper and brass. Then, in the shadows behind, I see two green beads peering out from the gloom, points of luminescence, freakishly bright. My heart pumps faster. Among so many brown-eyed folk, those eyes are hauntingly strange, non-human almost. He doesn't belong to these people, I think. An outsider, perhaps; a man who leaps across gullies high in the Atlas mountains, surviving on thin air.

"Oh, God, there's that smell again," complains Tom.

A few yards ahead, the Boy darts beneath a tatty awning. He's wearing filthy, calf-length shorts and his legs, I notice, are dark with hair. He's a youth, I think, and then some. Old enough, I'm quite sure, to go snuffling under my sarong.

"It's foul," says Tom. "Really fucking rank."

I think he's talking about the Boy. I think he's smelled his appetite and is repulsed. Then it dawns on me he's talking about the tannery. When we were last here, I was about ready to retch with the stink of it but now the tannery's just a backnote and it's the Boy's odour I'm getting. It's as if my senses are tuning in to him, to the sound, smell and sight of him, and everything else recedes. The whole thing's starting to make me nervous.

Tom offers me the water before taking a swig himself. He has beautiful manners, partly because he's from Surrey but stemming too from a naturally submissive streak he doesn't fully acknowledge. He's no pushover, believe me, but his gentle manner combined with a curious intellect, makes him tend to the deferential or at least a fascinated passivity. Give him a good book and he's lost for hours. Give him a good woman – or better still a bad one – and he's lost for months. I took him away from someone else. Well, he left her for me at any rate. Two years down the line and we're still in love, half daft and quite besotted.

But I'm no fool. I know damn well if some other woman caught his heart he'd be gone in a flash, leaving me spitting with rage. I like Tom a lot. I want to hang on to him. I want to keep him mine. But all I can do is hope for the best. And meanwhile, I try to catch him as I can, all those impossible charcoals and pencils, all that seductive permanent ink.

My favourite sketches are the ones I do in bed at night, Tom lying there with his mouth agape, dreaming eyeballs quivering beneath his lids. I love him so much when he's fast asleep, when he doesn't even know he exists. Tom doesn't realize I do this. I keep the sketches well hidden, my treasured possessions, proof of all the hours I stole from him while I watched him sleep. I have bouts of insomnia, you see. It's not only out here.

"Half a mo'. Batteries," says Tom. He edges past slow, swathed people, and I wait for him by a spice stall. Black strips of tamarind and threaded figs hang like jungle vegetation over sacks heaped with nuts, dried fruit, tea leaves and herbs. SNORING CURE – NEVER FAIL! says a sign and APHRODISIAC FOR THE KING! proclaims another. The air is powder dry and colours catch in my throat: scarlet, copper, ochre and rust, an earthy rainbow of seasonings that makes me cough like a hag. "I have medicine! Never fail!" cries a djellaba-hooded man, and I protest my health, realizing there's some seriously dodgy shit for sale here: a turtle strapped to the canopy's scaffold, bunches of goats' feet, dried hedgehogs, chameleons, snake skins and live lizards flicking around in giant-sized jars.

"*Pssst! Lady!*"

His voice goes straight to my cunt. The sensation's so strong he might have tongued me there. My senses reel and I turn, catching a glimpse of sharp brown shoulder blades before he's swallowed up by the crowd. Across the way, Tom's holding a pack of batteries, appealing to a stallholder who looks out with a half-blind gaze, his eyes veiled with cataracts. A woman with a wispy beard jostles me.

Instinctively, I check my money belt and I see the Boy just feet away, throwing a backwards glance, an invitation to follow. I cannot refuse him. I don't even question my options. I just go.

As I move, Tom turns. He catches my eyes, nodding acknowledgement of my direction. It's fine, he's cool. He rarely makes a fuss. And, should we lose each other, we've both got our phones. An image comes to me of my mobile trilling away, whiskery rats nosing the screen where the words "*Tom calling . . .*" glow for no one. I push the image away. It's not important. But the Boy is.

Anxious not to lose him, I squirm through the crowds, keeping his shorn head in my sights. A man with a monkey distracts me briefly and for a terrible moment I think I've lost him. Frantic, I whirl around, a vortex of faces blurring past me, colours racing. He's gone, he's gone. But seconds later, I have him again. I watch as he vanishes into an archway so narrow that at first I think he's ghost-walked through a wall. Panicking, I hurry, elbowing people aside. Somebody curses me but I don't care. I'm high with fear. I don't know why I'm following him. I only know I can't stop. Dark eyes flash around me, and my cunt's pumping nearly as hard as my heart. I'm in the grip of something scary, my juices are hot, and I try to remember if I've eaten something funny. Maybe I stood too close to those desiccated hedgehogs. God knows what they were for. God knows what I'm doing.

In the alley, I pause to catch my breath. I've got the Boy in view again. The alley's cool and whitewashed, not much wider than a person, and a few feet in, the racket of the souk goes dead. There's no one around but us. Suddenly, it is so still. So silent. My own breath surrounds me, a whispering rush like a seashell to my ear. I walk on and yet I don't think I move. I just pant. The sun doesn't fall here, but the alley seems to shine with its own light, the white walls reflecting each other in a numinous glow, and I wonder if this is it. I wonder if I'm dying on an operating table, my soul sailing up to enter the kingdom of heaven, or to at least try tapping on its door. I want to look back to see where I've come from but my head's far too heavy. I can't turn.

There is nothing but this: me, my breath and the Boy. It's as if I've slipped into a chink in the world.

Several yards ahead, half crouched, he creeps along with cautious grace. His slender torso is sweet and supple, the rack of his ribs visible beneath grimy, fudge-brown skin. The scent of him drifts in his wake, pheromonal and ripe. Civet, perhaps, or musk. How pliant his body must be, I think. How smooth his skin, how eager his hands, how tireless those beautiful, plum-coloured lips.

I follow, both of us keeping a steady pace, then the Boy stops, poised low. His arched spine protrudes in a knobbly ridge and the stubble of his hair prickles with light. I freeze, feeling I ought to, and realize I'm barely breathing. Then, slowly, the Boy swivels his head around to face me. And that's when I nearly keel over. Because the eyes that look into mine belong to no man on earth. For several stunned seconds, I stare back. They are cat's eyes: green as gooseberries with black, slit pupils.

Fear thumps me in the gut but I cannot scream. I cannot move either. I can't do anything. I just gawp, rooted to the spot.

He smirks and turns away. I think I must be in one of my dreams. Soon, I tell myself, I'll wake at the hotel and I'll straddle Tom's cock in a trance of remembering. I'll rock back and forth, head swimming with a post-human dystopia, a stinking medieval market peopled with DNA freaks or inter-species offspring. Look around and they all seem perfectly normal till you spot their webbed feet, forked tongues, folded wings or dog-fang teeth. And I'll climax and so will Tom. Then we'll get up, have breakfast, take a bus to a town with tiled palaces, koi carp and orange trees, and we'll buy something lovely in Spanish leather or cedar wood and everything will be all right.

The Boy creeps forward. I'm so scared and I'm so wet. But wet is winning. I follow, turning a corner then another until he ducks into a small archway in the wall. Moments later, I'm there too, head down and heart hammering as I descend three worn white steps.

In front of me, a cool cavernous chamber opens out. Hung with tapestries and oil lamps, its edges are banked with stacks of carpets, and in a far corner stands a cluster of earthenware jugs alongside sacks of grain. Sunbeams, soft and fuzzed with dust, slant down from high plasterwork arches, a tranquil light for prayer. It smells of straw and mice.

I catch a glimpse of the Boy as he flits from one stone pillar to another then stays there, hiding. Sitting cross-legged on a tall pile of carpets is a bald, muscular man with dark skin and heavy brows, his jawline shadowed with bristles. He's bare-chested, whorls of black hair clouding his pecs and making a seam over his neatly rounded paunch. He looks like a cross between the Buddha and a thug. It's not a look I'm familiar with but I do like it. He has a small, neat smile, and he's observing me steadily, chin propped on his fist. I get the feeling he's been expecting me.

"Hi," I say, trying to sound brave.

I walk deeper into the chamber, across the flagstone floor,

shoulders back. I know this man is going to fuck me and, frankly, I'm ready for it.

No one replies. The man keeps watching me, smiling. Though I'm still scared, I have an inkling of a new confidence. I'm starting to feel powerful and ageless, like some whore of the Old Testament. The Boy emerges from behind his pillar to lean against it, arms folded and smirking. His attitude's changed. He has the jaded, haughty air of a rent boy, hard faced and sleazy. It's attractive in a sick kind of way. His eyes are normal too. Well, relatively speaking. They are the most astonishing sea green – *National Geographic* eyes – but they are normal in that they are human. I must have been seeing things earlier, a trick of the light, nothing more.

They both watch me as I sashay forward. I feel deliciously easy. I'm a harlot, houri, concubine, slave. I could dance like Salome, seduce them with a strip show, except I don't have seven veils, just sarong, vest and Birkenstocks.

Besides, my guess is, these guys really don't need seducing.

"You chose well," says the man, addressing the Boy.

Now hang on, I think. Didn't I just walk here myself of my own free will? Then I correct myself. Who am I trying to kid? I've been picked up, haven't I?

"My uncle." The Boy grins and nods at the man.

Uncle tips up his chin in a curt greeting. "Show her to me," he says to the Boy.

Barefoot, the Boy saunters forward. He parts my sarong, exposing my legs, and presses his hand between my thigh. All the weight of my body is suddenly in my cunt, resting in that skinny hand. My gusset is damp and he paddles his fingers there, grinning at me before latching onto my clit. He rubs through the fabric, judging my expression. I want to appear impassive but the smell and touch of him make me dizzy with longing. Truly, I can't remember ever feeling so horny. I guess I don't manage to pull off the cool, composed look because the Boy chuckles softly. In a whisper, he says, "Ah, you like that, don't you? Hot little bitch."

Well, you got me there, I think.

"She's OK, Uncle," announces the Boy. "Nice and wet." He tucks the gusset aside then pushes two fingers up inside me. My knees nearly buckle. "Really wet," he adds, stirring his two fingers around. In the silence, I hear my juices clicking.

"Excellent," says Uncle in a thick, languid voice. "We have a willing woman."

"A willing slut," says the Boy, "who wants to get fucked." He seems to be relishing the words, testing their strangeness like an adolescent keen to rid himself of innocence.

I'm relishing them too. I like being objectified. It takes the heat off having to be yourself.

The Boy, still working me with his fingers, slips his other hand up my top. He strokes me through my bra before pushing up the cups to squeeze and massage. My nipples are crinkled tight and he flicks and rocks them, bringing my nerve endings to seething life. Then, just as I start to feel I'm losing myself, falling open to ecstasy, the Boy pulls away and crosses the floor to Uncle.

It's a cruel, desolate moment. I'm about to protest but, before I can utter a word, the Boy has sprung up onto the carpets, leaping from a standstill like a mighty ballet dancer. On his haunches, he straddles Uncle who reclines, mouth parted, to suck on the Boy's fingers, offered like dangling grapes. The Boy cups the man's shiny head, supporting it, and Uncle goes slack with surrender, eyes closed in bliss, as he slurps and snuffles on a sample of my snatch.

Now, I'm not averse to a spot of guy-on-guy action but I've only just arrived and I'm feeling a touch neglected. So I walk towards them because, dammit, I want to play too. As I near, they stop their weird feeding and, holding the pose, look down at me with benign curiosity, blinking heavily. It's as if they've never seen me before. Jesus, it's creepy. Without smiling, they continue to stare and blink for what seems like an age. A pair of green eyes and a pair of bright brown ones.

Then Uncle perks up, his expression changing to a villainous leer. He looks seriously gorgeous, like he ought to be behind bars. Sneering, he sits straight, swinging his legs over the edge of the carpet pile, and delves into the crotch of his baggy pants. His pants are slate-blue silk, and a materialistic impulse asserts itself because that's just the shade I want in the hallway. I consider asking for a thread so I can choose a carpet with a matching weave but the moment passes. I have a different object of desire, other needs to gratify.

"Suck my dick for me," says the man, grinning. He releases a big fat erection, wanking it gently, the muscles of his beefy arm flexing under dark skin. It's a beautiful brute of a cock, arrogant and obscenely large.

"Dirty bitch," adds the Boy. He still sounds like a kid trying out rude words. "Suck the man's dick."

I'm happy to oblige. The stack of carpets are almost shoulder height and all I need do is lower my head to engulf him. His pubes tickle my nose and, butting deep within my mouth, he's superbly stout and powerful. My head bobs between his thighs and I'm getting weaker and wetter as I dream how it'll be when this beast slides into me. The Boy drops to the floor and I feel him at my feet, nuzzling my ankles then crawling under my sarong. I spread my legs for him and feel him rising, the heat of him on my skin, his shorn, silky head, his tongue trailing a path up my inner thighs. He pulls down my knickers and I feel him between my legs, his hot breath on my cunt before his tongue, so delicate and perfect, dances over my clit and squirms into my folds.

Oh, my. That tongue has truly been places. Like his eyes, it could be a thousand years old, a tongue that's pleasured Geisha girls, ladyboys and Babylonian whores. Fingers fill my cunt, a thumb rubs my arsehole and moments later I'm coming hard, gasping around Uncle's cock, Uncle clutching my head, keeping me steady for fear I neglect his pleasure in favour of my own.

"She's a slippery little bitch, isn't she, huh?"

Uncle's voice is loud enough to carry across the chamber. He's talking to someone else; not to the Boy, and certainly not to me. I pull back and turn, wiping saliva from my mouth.

Tom, of course. Hell's teeth, I'd forgotten him. He's standing within the white stone archway, looking somewhat dazed. Really, I'd completely forgotten him, forgotten the man I love. Well, I guess fresh meat can do that to a girl.

Tom stares, mouth sagging dumbly. I worry for a moment, fearing my blue-eyed boy is going to be appalled, but I can see he's interested, absorbing the scene. It's that fascinated passivity again. "My God," I can almost hear him say. "You're so *vulgar*."

"Come, come," cries Uncle, jumping down from the carpets. "Welcome, my brother!" He pumps Tom's hand and claps him on the shoulder as if they're the best of mates. "You want her to suck your dick too, huh?" Pleased with himself, Uncle laughs over-loudly.

I think Tom's had a hit of whatever I've had, the scent of dried hedgehog or something. He smiles. I know exactly what he's going to say. He's going to say, "*I* don't mind," in that sing-song way he does when I say, "Shall we have coffee here or there? Rice for dinner or pasta?" It can get a bit annoying, to tell the truth. He looks at me; his smile's ironic. "*I* don't mind," he says, and I realize he knew that I knew he was going to say that, and his tongue's in his cheek because he knows all that knowing will amuse me. Long-term relationships can be so nice.

The Boy, on his hands and knees, peeps out from under my sarong to edge a cautious pace forward. Then he's motionless, watching as Uncle leads Tom to a low bank of carpets, stacked at three levels like a shallow flight of steps. A hazy shaft of sunlight falls across them, revealing tiny squalls of dust as the men clamber and sprawl across this wool-woven stage. Uncle sits on the higher level, legs akimbo, and Tom lolls within his silk-clad thighs, head resting there as he yields to an off-centre shoulder massage. Uncle bows forward, murmurs in Tom's ear, and Tom smiles gently, stretching his spine in a discreet arch, his pleasure private and contained, as the man kneads with big oafish hands.

I stand there, entranced, hardly able to believe what I'm seeing. The Boy edges closer, moving gingerly as if wary of disturbing them. Sitting back on his heels, he watches intently as Tom relaxes deeper into the massage, occasionally grunting.

When Tom and I fuck, a glazed expression sometimes settles on his face. His eyes close, his mouth drops open, and he looks completely gone, blanked out with bliss as I move on top. He's got that slightly dead quality about him now, and when Uncle reaches forward to remove his T-shirt, Tom acquiesces, raising his arms, as docile and obliging as a sleepy child. He doesn't even protest when the Boy pads forward to nuzzle his pale chest. All he does is smile fondly and, like a basking chimp, he stretches his arms back, exposing their white undersides, tendons taut, his dark patches of armpit hair attracting the Boy who tentatively sniffs, a hand sweeping broad caresses over Tom's flexing body. Tom is clearly loving it.

Well, you sly old tart, I think.

I can't take my eyes off him. I wonder if they've drugged him. And then I'm clearly not thinking straight myself because soon I'm wondering whether it actually *is* Tom. Perhaps someone – or something – has got inside his body because I've never seen him like this before. Tom likes to size up situations, to tread carefully, to fret unnecessarily; and he's never shown even the slightest interest in men. And now look at him, pushing the boundaries of his experience as if it were a walk in the park. I start to fear I may never get him back.

But then I notice his smile fading and he moistens his lips, a small moment of nervous desire. It's exquisite, so tender and Tom-like, and I feel I know who he is again. I see his Adam's apple bob in his throat and, in his neck, a hint of tension, as he tests the air for a kiss. The Boy bends over him, their lips meet, and lust flares in my groin. I watch a knot of muscle shifting in the Boy's jaw, movement in

Tom's neck, and I'm all eyes as, without breaking the kiss, the Boy reaches down to unzip Tom's fly. Tom's erection springs out, weighty and lascivious.

I don't know what I want to do most: watch or join in.

Then Uncle grins at me, rummaging around in his silky blue crotch. He exposes his cock and moves it against Tom's face, tipping it back and forth like a windscreen wiper. "Come here," Uncle says to me. "Bring us titties."

He's dead right: I want to join in. So I cross to them, whipping off my top half as I do so. Greedy and urgent, I scramble up onto the carpets and Uncle welcomes me by holding out a brawny arm. He opens his mouth and I fill it immediately with soft, pink breast, pressing a hand to his crisp chest hair, my body pushing against the bulk of his belly. His tongue lashes my nipple and he delves under my sarong, searching eagerly for my hole. With a force that makes me gasp, he plugs my wetness with thick, crude fingers. Grinning up at me, he holds my nipple between his teeth and gently pulls on it, stretching my flesh. I hold his gaze, daring him to keep right on going.

For the first time, I notice how stunning his eyes are. They're a hard amber brown, sparkling up at me like topaz. But this is no time to be romanticizing because the guy's moving us into position, my sarong and belt are off, and I'm utterly naked, poised above that prodigious cock, buttocks split in his big, rough hands, cunt wide open. With heavy luxury, I sink down on him, groaning all the way until I'm stretched and stuffed to capacity.

Truly, it's a beautiful moment, made more beautiful by the fact that beside me is Tom, being sucked off by the Boy. They're both naked too, Tom with his knees apart, the Boy's shorn head bobbing in his crotch, his pert little butt stuck up in the air. Sprawled against the carpets, Tom has an arm flung wide, eyes closed, mouth open. I've never seen him looking quite so dead. I wonder if his expression's the same when I go down on him. My guess is not. All the same, I try to commit that face to memory, thinking maybe I can reproduce it some time in charcoal and pencil.

Tom must sense me looking because, as I start to slide on Uncle's cock, he reaches out with a blind hand to stroke my arse. In that tiny affectionate gesture, I feel such a connection with him, such warmth. And I feel free to fuck like there's no tomorrow, knowing Tom and I are united, mutual support in mutual depravity; for richer, for poorer; for better, for worse.

Uncle clasps my hips, bouncing me up and down, and I'm as light as a doll in his hands. This man can do what he wants with me, I think. And I don't mind if he does. It's a while since I've been overpowered. The two of us mash and grind, silk hissing beneath me, sweat forming on my back where sunlight heats my skin.

"Hey, brother," calls Uncle, addressing Tom. "Does she like it in her ass? Huh? A big prick in her tiny little asshole?"

Tom's too zonked to reply immediately. He just sprawls there, half dead, before his head rolls sideways, eyes still closed. When he finally speaks, it sounds as if it's costing him an enormous effort. "Probably," he croaks.

The Boy pulls away from him. Tom groans in despair.

"Dirty little slut," says the Boy excitedly. His cock is ramrod stiff, its ruddy tip gleaming, and against his scrawny frame it looks grotesquely large. He springs off the carpets, takes a small copper can from near an Aladdin's lamp, and pours thick clear liquid into the palm of his hand. "Uncle," he says. "You in her pussy, me in her ass. Bam, bam, bam. We fuck her hard, yes?"

Uncle laughs lightly.

"No," I whisper. Then louder: "Yes. God, yes."

The Boy leaps back onto the carpets, lubricating his cock with lamp oil. Tom groans again. I reach out, feeling sorry for him, and Uncle, gent that he is, shuffles us closer. I lean over to kiss Tom and he responds eagerly, our tongues lashing awkwardly as Uncle pounds into me. Sweat dribbles down my back into the crack of my buttocks and I feel the Boy's greasy fingers press against my arsehole. He wriggles a finger past my entrance and I'm groaning into Tom's mouth as the Boy opens me out, forcing the ring of my muscles wider, making me slick and ready.

"Keep her still," urges the Boy, and Uncle obliges, his cock lodged high.

"Lean forward," orders the Boy and I obey. His knob nudges my arsehole and pushes into my resistance. I think I'm going to be too small for him, my other hole too full, and that it's all going to hurt like hell. I make a feeble cry of protest.

"Don't pretend," snaps the Boy. He grasps my hips then there's a flash of pain and, with a sudden slippery rush, he's fully inside me, and I'm swamped by dark, fierce pleasure. Uncle calls out triumphantly. I feel I'm on the brink of collapse, the intensity of having both holes packed so solidly taking me to a place I didn't know existed. I gasp into Tom's mouth, quite beyond kisses now, as the two men start to drive into me. Bam, bam, bam, as the Boy said. I have to pull away from Tom. I need air. I need to groan and wail.

Beneath me, Uncle's face is flushed with exertion. He spots me looking at him and he grins, meeting my eye with a deliberate gaze. There's the weirdest kind of friction going on inside me, the two men jostling my body as they fuck. And then I know I've lost it. I know pleasure has reduced me to lunacy because I see something wild in Uncle's eyes. His pupils contract and, for a moment, they are like the Boy's: bright with black, slit pupils.

It's the light, I tell myself, the light, the light. And I can't bear to look. I flop forward onto Tom, seeking a kiss, wanting the reassurance of his mouth, his nose, his face. I'm close to coming and so is Tom because the Boy, gorgeous greedy creature, is sucking him off again. As the two cocks shove fast and hard inside me, I nudge my clit and then gasp into Tom's mouth, our lips so hot, so wet and loose: "I'm coming, I'm coming." That sets him off and he groans and pants, his body twitching as he peaks. My orgasm rolls on and on, and Tom is still gasping into my mouth, still coming. It feels sublime, orgasm-without-end. Our lips slide and smear, and nothing else can touch us. It's as if we're melting into each other at every breath. And I am him and he is me, and we are all ecstasy, all delirium, all gone.

Sex, I think, will never be the same again.

We didn't buy a carpet for the hallway that holiday. But sometimes it's like that. You go out hoping to buy one thing and come home with something totally different. I've stopped drawing Tom in the middle of the night as well. I don't feel the need any more. I don't have that yearning to capture him. Because I have my Tom, I have him entirely, from now until the end of time. And if I ever start to doubt it, I just need to picture his face, glazed with rapture at the point of climax. He doesn't know what he looks like. I don't know what I look like either. People don't, generally speaking, do they?

All I know is that he'll never look at another woman like that; he'll never be able to. Because when he comes, something shifts in his eyes. He rides the wave, annihilated with bliss, the two of us breathing so hard and so deep. And when he looks at me, his beautiful blue eyes have black, slit pupils. And I am him and he is me. And I know we are possessed.

# Don't Look Back

Alison Tyler

I Google him. Sometimes occasionally, if I've got a minute to kill while the printer is churning out my latest project. Sometimes obsessively, staring at the computer screen until my eyes water, drinking straight vodka as the minutes blur. Sometimes recklessly – not bothering to delete my history afterwards. "Deleting history" seems like too much of a cheat. It would be dangerously easy to strike out all the pages I've visited on my endless, circular search. You can't do that in real life.

I know he isn't the doctor in Minneapolis who specializes in exotic-sounding diseases, or the professor on sabbatical in the Orient who beams his latest pictures up to his website every two or three days – lovely lush landscapes that I've grown fond of viewing. Sure, people change, but not *that* much. I'm absolutely certain he's not one of a pair of Bluegrass-loving brothers who live in Utah. They hit local bars every few weeks, playing warm-up for bands I've never heard of.

I've done the online White Pages searches, as well, turning up addresses from fifteen years ago, six or seven places in a row, apartments I remember visiting when I cut class to fuck him. I actually think about calling the numbers – one might be current – but I can't make myself. There was no caller ID back then. Now, I might get caught. And what would happen to my well-ordered life if he Star-69-ned me and my sweet boyfriend answered?

So I resort to Googling.

Googling takes the place of those late-night drive-bys, looking to see if his Harley was in the spot out front of his building. My muscles tighten up the same way now as they did back then. Maybe I'll see him. Maybe I won't. So why do I even bother? Because I fantasize that one day when I type in his name, up will come all the information that I crave. What he's been doing for the past decade and a half. What he's doing now. Who he's with. How he's aged.

Truthfully, I don't know all that much about him. If I were to tally up all the facts, they wouldn't fill an index card. Or a matchbook cover. He was older than me, but by exactly how much, I don't know. Twenty-seven to my eighteen. That's what I remember, but he lied all the time. He could have been lying about that. In my online search, I found a man with his name who graduated high school in 1978 somewhere in Southern California. Is that him? His middle initial was D, but he never told me what it stood for. Donald? David? Daniel? Dean? None of those seem right, yet I've found men with those middle names on the internet. Might he be one of them?

There's a fellow in the midwest who runs marathons. I can't imagine Mark breaking a sweat unless he were running from a cop. But he had a sleek runner's physique way back when. Could he have transformed himself to an athlete? Has he given up pot in favour of healthier substances? Has he hit the pavement to kill his demons?

Googling takes my mind off my modern-day problems. Googling makes me forget about deadlines and pressures and what we're going to have for dinner. Delivery pizza, again? Sounds good. Far easier to answer that mundane query than the other nagging questions pulling on me until my stomach aches: should I pay the $29.95 and do a search of prison records? Because that's where I'll find him. I'm sure of it.

I don't enter my credit card. I don't think I actually want to know.

After spending hours on the computer, I dream about him. My eyes hurt and my head spins. I hit the pillow and recreate his image from the puzzle pieces that I remember: the black-ink Zig-Zag man tattoo on his upper arm. The way his blue eyes could turn grey or green depending on what he was wearing. Depending, even, on his mood. His paint-splattered jeans. His grey shirt. His body.

Oh, God, his body.

I remember our first date, if you can call it a date. A walk from the beauty supply store where I worked after school back to my home – with a lengthy sojourn in a deserted alley behind the beauty supply. And I remember our first kiss – moments into our first date. What was I doing out in the rapidly darkening twilight with him? Who was looking out for me? He was.

He pushed me up against a wall and kissed me so ferociously that there are days I swear I can still feel his lips on mine. When I run my tongue over my bottom lip I feel where he bit me. Can you feel a kiss fifteen years later? You bet you can.

His large, warm hands gripped my wrists over my head while his powerful body held mine in place. He pressed against me, and I could tell how hard he was, and I could understand – finally – what all those whispers about sex were about. I hadn't got it before. Look, I wasn't an idiot. Just naive. I knew where babies came from. I'd watched enough old movies to understand the steaminess of the looks between hero and heroine. But there'd been no appeal to me in the high-school fumblings at dances. In the background make-out sessions at parties. I'd been an outsider, an alien, gazing in wistfully from a distance and knowing for certain that nothing present was right for me.

With Mark, everything was different.

In that back alley behind the cosmetic store where I was a shop girl, he slid a hand up under my shirt and ran his fingers over my pale-pink satin bra. In a flash, I wished that the bra was made of black lace instead. He touched my breasts firmly, as if he owned them, as if he owned me. He took my clothes off, unbuttoning my jeans himself, pulling my shirt up over my head, exposing me for what I really was.

"A slut," he said, "You're my little slut—"

I shivered, but stayed silent. I knew who the sluts were at school. I knew that I wasn't one.

"Aren't you? Tell the truth." His hands were everywhere. His mouth on my neck, his fingers pulling down my panties and parting my lips to see how wet I was.

"Come on, Carla. Tell the truth—"

I Google him. Endlessly. Dangerously. Desperately.

Because he knew me. I was just out, taking that first shy step out into the world . . . and he knew me.

I understand why I do it. So why the hell do I find it so odd that he Googles me, too? That I get an email, short but not sweet, asking if I'm the one he remembers.

Yeah, I am. Sure, I am. Of course, I am.

I think I am.

Mark waits for me in our spot, leaning against a grey concrete wall, looking almost exactly the same despite a fifteen-year absence. Do I look the same, too? I'm not. Not a teenager any more, not trembling with desire, not – dare I say it? – young.

But I was young. Back then, I was new.

We were inseparable for months, me, a high-school kid, and this twenty-seven-year-old hoodlum. This handsome, so handsome, man with the cold blue eyes out of a Who song and the iron jawline. A man who seemed to know everything about me. What was I doing? What was I thinking? Christ, what am I thinking now, fifteen years later? He's in his forties, but still effortlessly lean and tough with only the slightest lines around his eyes and the same tall, hard body I remember. I have on jeans and a black sleeveless T-shirt that says, "I break things" on the front, something I dug out of a box filled with memories in the attic. I can pass for twenty-three rather than thirty-three if I have to. My dark hair is long to my shoulders, my glossy bangs in my eyes, as always.

He doesn't say a word. He just looks at me. I close my eyes tight and remember – the loss of him when he disappeared, the way no boy could replace him after he was gone. I spent years trying to recreate the exact connection that we'd had. I slutted myself out with a variety of losers, all of whom possessed at least one rebellious quality of Mark's, but none who owned the whole package. Some spanked me. Some fucked me in public places. None made me feel anything other than disillusioned. Ultimately, I gave up hope. Now, even though I am with someone else, I've come running at Mark's call.

What the *fuck* am I doing here?

"Carla," he says, hands in my thick hair, lips on mine, and it is suddenly summertime again, and I'm missing him.

"Carla," he says, and I open my eyes and I look at him, and see him, the man, the danger, the reason I'm who I am today. If I hadn't met him in high school, who would I have become? Some other girl. Some smart chick. Not a person who would leave a loving relationship in order to track down that fleeting emotion of lust from a decade and a half ago. Not a moron who could still go weak-kneed at the first sight of her long-time crush.

"What do you need, baby?" he asks, and I find myself cradled in his strong arms, as always, my legs shaky, my heart pounding at triple-speed so that I can feel the timpani-throb in my chest and hear the clatter in my ears. "Can you say it, now? Can you tell Daddy what you need?"

My throat grows tight. There's a man at home, waiting for me. A simple man with a true soul who does not know where I am, but who trusts me to always return nonetheless. Yet suddenly the very concept of trust seems immensely overrated. What's trust to lust? Which emotion would win every time?

"Carla," Mark says. Just that word. Just my name, and I am lost all over again, head spinning, heart dying.

"Let's go."

He has no power over me. I'm not a kid any more. You can't impress me with a stolen Harley. You can't turn me into a puddle with a single kiss. I'm only here on a crazy dare. I'm only here because of Google. I can leave him. I can run. I have a safe home furnished with faux antiques from Pottery Barn and appliances purchased only after careful consideration of the advice of *Consumers' Choice*. I have a place to be. Mark doesn't own me, not any part of me.

"Come on, baby."

I suppose I've hidden it well, the desires that burn in me. I chose normal over interesting. I chose safety over adventure.

"You know you want to."

Back then, I'd never have been so fucking lame. Back then, I'd always take the risks when offered. Jesus, I invented the risks when there were none available. Slipping out my bedroom window to meet him. Cutting class to ride to his apartment on the back of his pilfered Harley. Letting him handcuff me to his bedframe so that he could do anything he wanted to me. Anything at all.

Can I change? Is it too late?

My hand is trapped in his, held so tightly. The heat between us is palpable. Some people never find that heat. That summertime heat that melts over your body and leaves you breathless. Some people search their whole miserable fucking lives for some semblance of a sizzling kiss, and they die believing that "true love always" is just a bitter myth. But I found that heat as a teenage kid and I knew for real that it existed. Even if I'd never found it again, I'd had it once.

How many places have I looked? How many other dark alleys have I gone down with nameless, faceless men, trying to find that old summertime magic from years ago?

Mark bends to kiss my neck and I remember in a flash, in one of those blinding jolts, that he'd covered me in suntan oil one sultry afternoon. I'd spent the whole day at the beach, the first truly hot spring day, and he'd come to my house afterwards and dumped out my red-striped canvas tote bag onto my floor and found that bottle of oil. My group of friends had no fear of wrinkles yet, no worry about sun damage, not like the ladies in my circle now, the ones who Google StriVectin with the passion that I've Googled this man. We used the oil back then, for "the San Tropez tan". Mark coated his strong hands while he told me to strip, and I'd watched his hands for a moment, dripping with the oil, knowing what he was going to do.

I remember being shy, so nervous, still unaccustomed to being naked in front of a man. I could strip at the gym, in front of my peers, but taking off my clothes while he watched was something entirely different. Mark liked me like that. Not just naked, but nervous. He liked to put me off centre, to make me feel as if I were always on a teeter-totter, the ground rushing up to meet me when I fell. He watched through half-shut eyes that told me of his appreciation as I slowly took off my pink halter top, my cut-off jeans, my candy-coloured bikini top and bottoms.

And then he covered me with the scented liquid, until I gleamed, shiny and gold, the smell of papayas and coconut swirling around us. He rubbed the oil into my breasts, and over my flat belly, and down my hips. He coated me with the shimmering liquid, and then he fucked me like that, slippery and glistening, staining my sheets, ruining his pants.

Nobody had fucked me like that before.

Nobody's fucked me like that since.

"Come on, Carla," he says now, leading me from the nondescript alley to the parking lot in back. There is a pickup truck waiting. I know it's his. He always drove motorcycles or pickups. They suited him. I look behind us, take one last look like Lot's doomed wife. I could go back, wander through the alley, hit the shelves in the nearby Borders, buy the latest issue of *Allure* magazine, get an iced coffee in the café. I could go back to beige and safety and predictability. To reviews in *Consumers'*. To my Mr Coffee machine – a six-time winner.

"What do you need, Carla? Tell Daddy what you need."

Back in high school, I'd needed to be spanked, and he'd taken care of that need with the most exquisite care. He hadn't laughed at me. He hadn't refused my desires or been disgusted by them. He'd simply assumed the role, once I confessed. Once I'd finally got the nerve and spelled it out:

I'd needed him to bend me over his lap and lower my jeans. I'd needed his firm hand on my naked ass, punishing me. Or his belt, whispering seductively in the air before it connected with my pale skin. Then I'd needed him to cuff me to his bed and fuck me, to flip me over and fuck my ass until I cried. Until I screamed. Is that what he'd seen on the day we met? A yearning in my eyes that told him I was in need? How had he found me? How had he known?

Most importantly, I'd needed him to show me that I wasn't a freak for having the cravings that I did, the white-hot yearnings that kept me up late at night, kept me away from the high-school boys and the safety of what I was supposed to do and who I was supposed to be, and he'd given me everything I needed.

Don Henley says: *You can never look back.*

"What do you need, now?" Mark murmurs, lips to my ear. I know suddenly what I don't need. I don't need to erase my history with a keystroke, when history is all that I've got.

My fingertips grip the handle of his vintage blue Ford. I slide the door open and climb inside.

You know, I never liked Don Henley much anyway.

# The Erotica Writer's Husband

Jennifer D. Munro

The erotica writer's husband bangs open the front door and stomps outside. Barefoot, with his fly half open, he'd interrupted his current activity when he heard barks and feline screeches.

His wife's cat, puffed up to dramatic size, hisses from the safety of the yellow window box. Marigolds splash against bristling black fur. Fastening the buttons of his 501s, the sex author's spouse scans the yard for the offending dog, but the husband's eyes meet the neighbor's, instead.

"Sorry!" The neighbor snaps a leash onto the collar of his now slash-nosed and cowering mutt. He notes the open-flied jeans of the erotica writer's husband. "Oh *hoh*, your wife must be home. I bet you spend a lot of time with your pants down, being married to a porn writer and all. Doing *research*."

"Uh-huh. Well. Gotta get back. She's waiting."

"Don't let me keep you!"

The sex author's spouse waves and carries the angry cat inside. The cat rakes his wrist in one final protest and leaps free. But instead of returning to the slick and sprawled wife his neighbor imagines, pen tucked behind her ear to take notes as she commands him to enact tawdry scenarios, he returns to the john to finish his interrupted piss.

His buddies and neighbours, jealous of a man married to a scribbler of lewd tales, imagine his rampant and orgiastic sex life. His wife is obsessed with sex manuals and adult websites, they think, not home decor catalogues like theirs.

In fact, as husband to a smutty authoress, he suspects that he's getting less than they are. He doesn't know whether to dissuade them from their faulty beliefs in order to gain their sympathy or to continue to bask in the glow of their misplaced admiration. After all, they think he'd been stud muffin enough to capture a lusty wench in matrimony, whereas they had landed frumpy *fraus* more interested in dozing than dildos. There were worse things a guy's friends could assume. They'd given him unsolicited and unearned respect, rarely seen by a monogamous, suburban man with no aptitude for sports. How empty would their lives be if they no longer had his prowess to worship? Who was he to disappoint them by correcting their misapprehension?

As he contemplates the remote control or a nap, the erotica writer herself cracks open her study door. Her laser printer huffs in the background, expending more energy over sex than husband and wife have in the past month. "Everything OK?" she asks.

"Just Dufus Rufus chasing Frizbeehead again. She scratched me." He holds out his clawed arm.

"Better sterilize that. Antiseptic's in the bathroom cabinet. Oh, mind doing the dishes? I've got this deadline."

"Sure, hon. Listen, can we talk, I—"

"Damn, now I've forgotten that perfect word. Shit, I spent the last half hour with a Thesaurus and now . . . stupid dog. Somebody needs to put him out of our misery." She scoops the cat up and closes the door.

He wishes she would spend a half-hour with her finger in something other than a book.

That evening he suggests that they might spend some time together, since it's the weekend, but she encourages him to go watch the game with his pals. "Go out and have some fun. Becky's giving me her feedback on that story I've been working on."

"The slaves in the ice castle one? In Greenland?"

"Not Greenland. A hidden fjord in Svalbard. No, I couldn't figure out how the characters could stay warm enough to be turned on. I got cold just thinking about it. Now they're on a boat. Only the Master goes ashore, but that gives the favourite slave time to secretly practise his violin. But of course someone hears him playing the *Paganini Caprice No. 24* and finds him, and then he has to decide whether he wants to stay willingly."

"Still working the gay market? I thought you'd had it with all that spunk." He knows better than anyone that both the dentist and doctor have documented her strong gag reflex, which precludes certain bedroom activities.

"Pays better, and you said yourself the truck transmission's about to go. Anyway, the slave's going to have a *guiche*, so I need to do some research before Becky gets here."

"I know how to make quiche."

"A *guiche*. Not quiche. A piercing *down there*."

"Ouch."

"Then I'm hitting the hay early so I can get up to do my edits. Mind sleeping on the couch when you get home so you don't wake me up?"

"How about we roll in the hay instead of hitting it?"

"Funny man. I married you for your sense of humour."

He receives an ovation when he arrives at the bar. His friends clear a stool for him.

"Have a beer!" Dean cries. "You must be exhausted!"

"Drink up!" Doug says. "Replenish those fluids!"

"Do a shot, man," Dave advises. "You can't spare the time for a pint! Gotta get back to the little wife!"

They check their watches. "How long you need to regenerate, man? We'll let you know when time's up."

His cell phone rings. "It's my wife. I better pick up."

"Time for dessert!" they all jeer. "Second helpings!"

"Mind picking up some buttermilk on your way home?" his wife asks. "I'm making bread tomorrow."

"Sure, hon." He wishes she would knead something other than flour. The only thing rising in his house is dough. They could milk his meat instead. Beat his eggs. Eat her jelly roll. Toss his nuts. Warm her bread basket. Hot cross his buns. Maybe make baby batter and put a bun in the oven.

"So, what'd she want? Come on, you can tell us."

"Lovin' in her oven."

They whoop and slap him on the back. His Hefeweizen splashes his shirt.

"Come on, spill the beans, man. You never tell us anything."

He swipes at his soggy shirt, imagining:

*He bangs the front door open and stomps inside, adjusting his wide load. His wife pauses with her lipstick-stained teacup halfway to her lips. "You're home early, honey," she says tremulously from her jasmine steam cloud.*

*"Jig's up," he growls. "Be my whore, or I'll divulge your pen name to the neighbours."*

*Her hand goes up to the red-rimmed "O" of her lips. She sets down the cup in its saucer with a small clink and drops to her knees. "Of course, whatever you want, honey." She lifts her Save the Manatees sweatshirt to reveal a red lace teddy with nipple cutouts.*

"Hello?" Dean snaps in his ear. "Yo, dick brain?"

"Earth to Stud Man," Doug says. "You gonna give us some dirt, or what?"

"Yeah, your mind's definitely in the gutter." Dave orders another round. "Should've seen the look on your face."

"Well, you know, it's private. Husband and wife."

"Yeah, and the thirty thousand people who read her stories!"

He can't blame his wife for his current status as a begrudging icon of virility. She would have kept her kinky stories a secret, but he blurted out the news to the world when the *Penthouse* check arrived. He hadn't considered the ramifications. Well, maybe he had, just a little. He was not without pride at his own magnanimity in allowing her to be who she was. That he didn't hold his wife's rampant public perversions in check, but allowed them to march unfettered across magazine racks far and wide, was a testament to his part in Steinem's new race of unthreatened Man. What other husband would be so secure in his manhood that he would be permissive – nay, *encouraging* – of his wife's transgressive acts, particularly when they did not involve his own penis? Involved a whole parade of phantom penises, in point of fact.

Ironically, from what he's heard, his neighbourhood has an above average *times-per-week* compared to most suburban outposts, owing to the fervour of imagination the erotica writer and her husband inspire.

Does he want them to know the truth, or does he want to continue to stand tall among them as the man who is getting the most nookie? The rare beast who has to keep up with his wife's ravenous appetite? The stallion who snagged a nymphomaniac? The man who has the pleasure of acting out every filthy scenario she devises? He has more sexual intrigue than the guys on covers of romance novels. He's not mowing the lawn like the rest of these poor schmucks; he's munching her bush.

"It's fiction," he finally ventures to his bar mates in response. "You don't have to commit murder to write a mystery."

They snort and pump their hips suggestively. A woman down the bar looks at them in disgust and carries her Pinot Grigio to a distant table.

Dean notes his scratched wrists. "Whoa! She got a little carried away, huh?"

"So what *is* the little lady up to tonight?" Doug asks.

"She's got a friend coming over."

"You dog!" Dave wipes his beer moustache. "A threesome!"

*He bangs the front door open and stomps inside. His wife and her friend pause with their lipstick-stained teacups halfway to their lips. "Jig's up," he growls. "Be my sluts, or I'll delete your* American Idols *off the TiVo."*

*Her hand goes up to the red-rimmed "O" of her lips. She sets down the cup in its saucer with a small clink and drops to her knees. "Of course, whatever you want, honey. You, too, right, Becky?" His wife lifts her orange knit poncho to reveal a black leather teddy with nipple cutouts. But Becky, being small, quick, and lithe, has already crawled halfway across the floor, on a mission to get his cock into her mouth before his wife can. Her breasts fall out of her cardigan as she makes like a Slinky towards him. "I've been hungry for you to ask me! All of my sinful stories are just flimsy cover-ups for the real fantasies I'm having about you! Come to Mama, my divine sausage, and gimme the works."*

"It's a dirty job, but somebody's gotta do it."

When he leaves a while later, whistles and catcalls follow him out the door into the rainy night.

He pulls into the driveway of 613 Cedar Lane and surveys the dark house. He takes his shoes off on the front porch and carries them inside, careful in his socked feet to make no noise on the wood floor. She's a light sleeper, and the smallest creak that jars her from REM will disrupt her circadian rhythm for weeks.

He hears a small voice calling to him, and he cracks open the bedroom door. His wife sits propped up in the bed, in a dim circle of light from her bed lamp, sudoku book and pencil in hand. A teacup and saucer perch on the comforter beside her.

"Glad you're home." She yawns. "You saved me from myself. I was about to cheat. How pathetic."

"What're you doing still up? Thought you had to get back to work at the crack of dawn."

"Couldn't sleep. Missed you." She pats the bed beside her.

"Hold on a sec." He holds up the buttermilk. "Lemme put this away first."

"Nuke this for me while you're up?" She holds out the teacup.

He punches in twenty-two seconds on the microwave. There's not a lot he feels he can do for her, other than the occasional oil change or too-tight jar lid. But if she's comfy on the couch and in the middle of a book, she can, without a word, hold out her half-finished tea to him on his way past. He's got it down to a science and punches in numbers on the timer depending on how empty the cup is. She likes her tea hot, but not too hot.

He hands her the warmed cup and stretches out beside her. She wrinkles her nose while she sips.

"Too hot?" Impossible.

"No. It's just that it's chamomile."

"I thought you hated chamomile."

"I do. It's so horsy-smelling. I feel like I'm chewing cud. In a barn. In Kentucky. But it's supposed to be good for you. Helps with dewy skin or better eyesight or memory or something. I'm old and fat. I need all the help I can get. Can't hurt. Think I should cover my grey?"

Uh-oh, bad writing day, he can tell. "What grey?"

"I don't believe you, but thanks, hon. What'd you and the boys talk about tonight?"

"That crabbing show. They filmed the last episode at the same bar we were at."

"That *Deadliest Crabs* one?"

"No, I had those once, and it's nothing you'd care to film."

She laughs. "What else?"

"Just the game and stuff."

She rolls her eyes. "You boys have no imagination."

*He bangs the front door open and stomps inside. Naked, his wife sits backwards on his favourite armchair, her breasts pressed to the chair back. Her legs are spread side, and the crack of her ass holds communion with the seat. Tattoos of naked women cover her back. "Oh, honey," she looks at him over her shoulder. "Look what I got done today. I was out shopping for pumps, you know with the arch support like I need? Which reminds me, I need to take my glucosamine later. Anyway, I just felt like something a little more fun, y'know? Some good ole retail therapy. The grind's really getting to me lately. I started with stilettos, and wound up with ink, and a nipple and a* guiche *piercing, too. I just figured, why not go the whole nine yards? Come see." She swivels around and slouches low in the chair, hooking her legs up over the arms to give him a full display. "Slather some ointment on me, and then fuck me up the ass, hard as you can, OK? And tomorrow we'll get you something fun, too. Maybe a cock ring. Although," she muses, "it might be tough to find one big enough for you. Maybe special order?"*

* * *

"You don't think so, huh?"

She snaps the book shut. "Try me."

"What've you got on under that nightie?" Tonight it's the daisy-print flannel. The nursing one she bought by mistake, with lots of convenient buttons that she starts to undo.

"Guess, Mr. Cocky Brainstorm."

"Nothing."

"Bingo."

"My favourite."

"What'd you boys *really* talk about? Were they at it again? All with anal sex on their mind but too afraid to ask about it? Like it makes them pansies or something?"

She still wants to talk. He's in no hurry. It's one of those things all those sex movies fail to mention: the small talk. He shifts closer towards her. He knows what this is, these superficial questions of hers. To someone else it might seem like idle chit-chat, meaningless dithering going nowhere. But he recognizes it for what it is: foreplay. Getting reacquainted again after the daily separations of a humdrum life. A casual reconnection before the more intimate one that he knows is around the next bend. Step on the gas and try to cut a corner and it's all over before it started. She'll cut the engine.

"They think I'm having a threesome."

She looks around the room. "There's always the cat."

"That's not the pussy I had in mind."

"No?"

His hand creeps up under her nightie, finds her inner thigh, and he lets it rest there, just shy of his ultimate target. Her hand simultaneously finds his fly, and she starts undoing the buttons with one hand. All that typing has at least helped keep her fingers strong.

"I was thinking," he says, his hands just brushing the tips of her pubic hair. "Maybe I'll write a story."

"Oh, sure, everyone thinks it's easy. But try coming up with new ideas all the time."

"Yeah," he says, his finger finding the bull's-eye, "that must be tough."